FRAGMENTS OF THE MIND

THE SPECTRUM OF MAGIC – BOOK 2

BETH HODGSON

FRAGMENTS OF THE MIND

Interior character portraits, illustrations, and cover art by Mansik Yang
Interior map and "Emerald's Dream" by Beth Hodgson

Editing by Crystal Watanabe

www.thespectrumofmagic.com

First edition: December 2020
ISBN: 978-1-7327130-2-4
Printed in the United States of America

To my loving husband,
who has been by my side during my darkest hour
as I battled against my own mind.

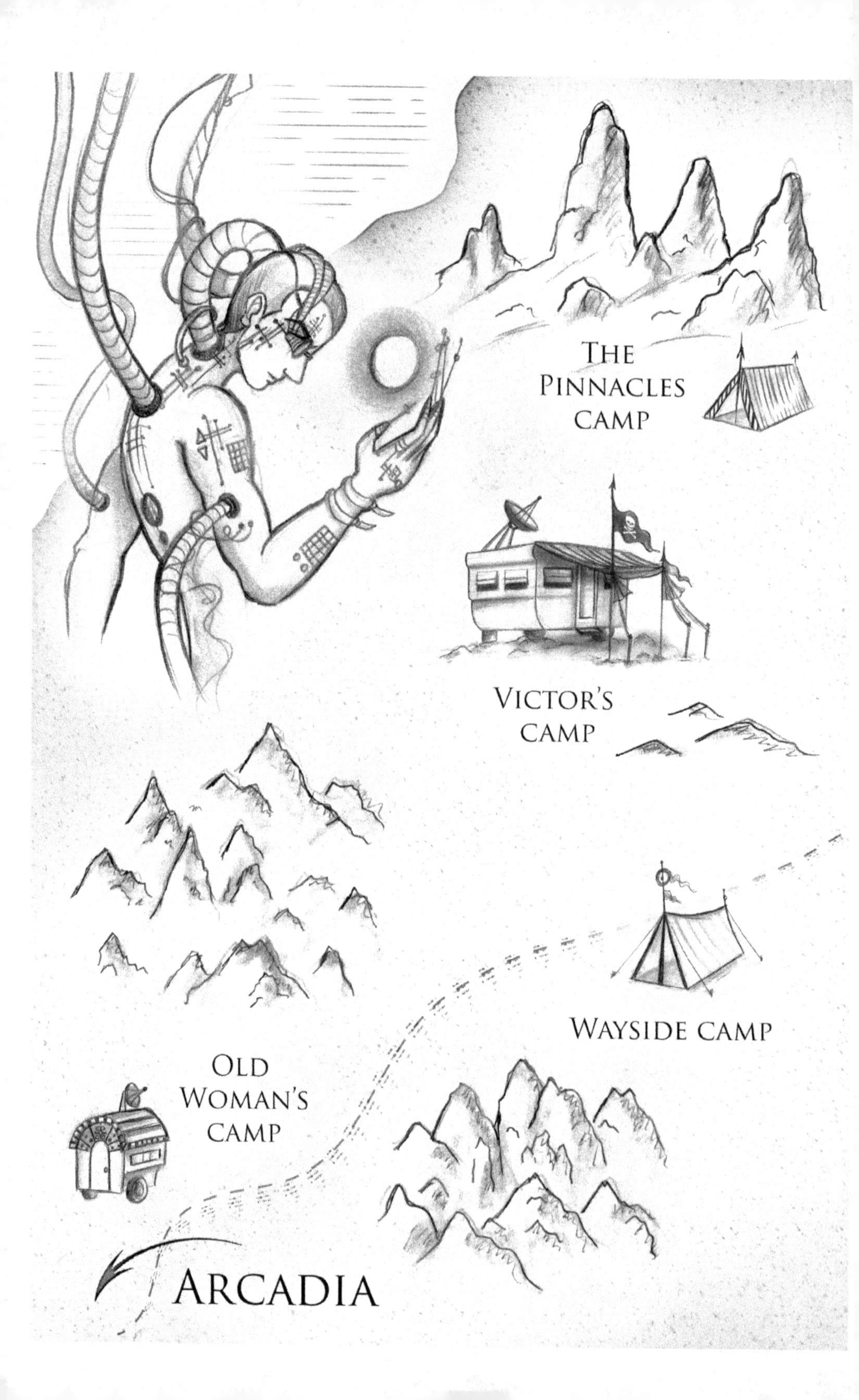

The Pinnacles camp
Victor's camp
Wayside camp
Old Woman's camp
Arcadia

Western Wastelands 2385 M.E.

The Twin Kingdoms
Olympia
The United Kingdoms 2385 M.E.
(Millennium Era)
Illumina
Western Wastelands
Star Tide Ocean
Arcadia

Icelandic Sea
Kingdom of York
The Great Lake
The Second Kingdom
Eastern Wastelands
The Southern Kingdoms

World Sectors 1-6
4403 P.A.
(Post Apocalypse)
Abandoned
Citadel
Ruins of W.S. 1
Lands of
Desolation
Toxic Currents
Safeland
Hideouts
W.S. 2
Mines
of W.S. 2

High Court Citadel
W.S. 6 Royal Citadel
W.S. 3
W.S. 6
W.S. 4
W.S. 5
Mines of W.S. 5
W.S. 4 Royal Citadel

PROLOGUE

Echoes could be heard within the citadel halls, the sounds of shuffling feet mixed with the fluttering of robes and whispers. The dimly lit halls within the orange wing of the High Court Citadel were empty, aside from a few scattered servants of High Justice Perserine of the Orange. Their orange robes flickered by as they carried out their nightly duties, bowing deeply to High Justice Oriel of the Blue as he passed by with his servant, who nodded at them out of duty.

His servant, dressed in a blue robe to reflect his master, was new to him that very week, as his old one had been transferred to the earth below for an "unsatisfactory performance." At least, that was the excuse Oriel gave to his fellow members of the court. In truth, it was much more complicated than that—he suspected that his old servant had been spying on him. The High Court was one big game, a game to keep everyone in check, which meant spies were plentiful, and Oriel had to assess everyone and everything carefully to ensure no one knew his true intentions.

Oriel and his new servant exited the main hall, then turned to a more private area of the orange wing. The halls became much more elaborate, with richly decorated walls and carefully carved furniture. Even the enchanted torches burned brighter the closer they came to the High Justice Perserine's personal quarters.

They reached a series of grand doors, stopping in front of them.

Oriel's perfectly manicured ebony hand pointed to the midmost door. "Here."

The servant nodded, then knocked.

They both waited for a second, his servant trying not to make eye contact with him. Most never did unless directly spoken to. Oriel was a High Justice, after all, and had the power to do anything he pleased. He was the most powerful blue-gifted, even compared to the other blue justice, Borgen, and everyone knew it. Most were terrified of him and his strong blue gift. He couldn't blame them; if their roles were reversed, he would feel the same.

After a long pause, the door opened, and there appeared a servant dressed in orange, bowing as soon as he saw Oriel.

"High Justice Oriel of the Blue," the orange-robed servant addressed him. "The other high justices are already gathered in the dining hall."

He was the last one to arrive? All the justices were already gathered? That in itself told Oriel all he needed to know. This was just another game being played, and it meant that Oriel had to tread carefully.

"Thank you," Oriel said to the orange-robed servant. Oriel turned back and waved his hand to dismiss his own servant, who took off.

Oriel entered the quarters, following Perserine's servant through her personal corridors to the dining hall. As he walked by, his reflection danced across the smooth polished walls, all made of transmuted carnelian stone. The orange justice loved gemstones, and she made every effort to flaunt her latest transmutations whenever possible. Her work was quite exquisite; even Belinda had her transmuted gemstones for her own personal collection.

The servant paused outside the dining hall, then gestured for him to enter, bowing. He curtly thanked the servant, then stepped inside, the door closing behind him.

Inside, the dining hall was basked in orange brilliance, overwhelming Oriel to the point where he squinted from the radiance. Orange was the direct opposite color of his blue gift within the spectrum; it was meant to be his complement, but it was also paralyzing. Warm orange light seeped through the dining hall's imposing windows, with the glow of sunset kissing the already orange floors and walls, making everything in the room more intense. Even the dining table, made of pure transmuted gold, refracted the orange light, nearly blinding him.

The justices were in the midst of talking, but they stopped and smiled as Oriel approached. He nodded in acknowledgment, and they returned the favor. The table was void of dinner, as it was custom to wait to dine until all were gathered, but several of the justices had already started drinking their dinner wine, clutching their golden chalices with delight.

"High Justice Oriel," Belinda said, swirling her wineglass. "Thank you for coming at such short notice. I am so sorry if you had other plans." She took a drink as Tyllos nodded at her statement.

"I am surprised to find myself the last one to arrive," Oriel said. He wandered over to his seat, and Perserine's servant pulled it out for him.

"Perhaps your new servant delayed our summons." She made an annoyed gesture. "It seems he needs to be replaced."

Oriel frowned, taking his seat. "That he should."

Did he believe Belinda's accusation? Hardly. But it was rather a believable statement. There could be some truth to it, but it was hard to say at that moment. It was equally likely that Belinda had sent the summons to his servant late on purpose.

"Is it bright enough in here for you, Perserine?" Oriel continued. "Though it has been awhile since you hosted a dinner, I don't remember it being this intense with your color." He adjusted his body in his seat as an orange-robed servant poured him some wine. The seat was dreadfully uncomfortable; he could never understand how Perserine loved so many beautiful yet vexing pieces of furniture.

Perserine smiled. "Someone finally noticed," she said excitedly, leaning in. As she did so, a lock of her short orange frizzy curls fell across her eyes, which she swept back into place. "I infused more saturation into the color. Brilliant, isn't it?"

Oriel shifted in his seat as he looked across at his counterpart, High Justice Borgen. The other blue justice was extremely old, with a long faded wispy blue beard, matching hair, and icy eyes. Borgen was hunched over slightly, his porcelain hands trembling with age.

"It's hard not to notice," Borgen agreed.

"Well, you didn't say anything when you first arrived, Borgen," Perserine pointed out to the old man.

That's because he is so focused on the plans that he can hardly notice anything else unless it's in front of his face, Oriel thought.

Borgen lazily took a drink of wine, then said "hmph" at her remark.

"Did you take into consideration Borgen's age?" Nyrden asked. The other red justice always had to point things out in an arrogant, aristocratic tone.

Borgen clenched his teeth at Nyrden but made no remark otherwise. What was the point? The more dissension there was between all of them, the longer it would take to coordinate their next move. And now, since their plan with the sorceress had failed, time was running short, and they were desperate.

Oriel congratulated himself inwardly at the thought. Personally, the high justices not succeeding was a secret win for him. If it had been many years ago, he would have been snarling in his wine cup about the loss. But now, he had changed his opinion on a great many things, and he had been doing whatever he could to counter their progress in secret.

What had changed his opinion initially of the High Court and their plans? There was not one event that he could pinpoint specifically, but over time, his soul had begun to feel... *heavy*. All these plans with his counterparts, it had slowly started weighing on him. Perhaps he started feeling disenchanted upon learning years ago that he had a daughter... a daughter who was kept hidden from him within the World Sector Four courts. The realization that he had an offspring made him second-guess all that he had been working toward. Whether it be his daughter or being disenchanted with their ideals, it didn't matter. A gifted, one greater than them, was in play, and it was a dangerous game that could ultimately shatter time itself. And that thought terrified him most.

"Let us speak of why we are here," Belinda began.

"I was actually enjoying our conversation about Borgen," Nyrden said with a snort.

Belinda eyed him coldly as Nyrden flashed her and the court a charming smile. Belinda didn't like open admirers. She never fell for flattery, no matter how hard Nyrden tried. Everyone knew he wanted to bed her; the red justice had a strong lust for beautiful women, and Belinda was considered one of the prettiest in World Sector Three. Even at her age, the young ripe girls entering womanhood didn't have nearly half the beauty as Belinda did in her midforties. But to Oriel, underneath her beauty, he saw the ugliness of her soul seeping through like a slow poison, making her attractiveness amount to nothing.

"Borgen, have you summoned another group of blue-gifted from each of the World Sectors?" Belinda asked, drinking her wine.

"They all have their orders," Borgen stated. "They are slowly being dispatched in increments, as instructed by the emperors."

"Good. That's what I like to hear."

"All I can say is that they better work efficiently," Tyllos stated. "We only have so many blue-gifted left."

"I'm starting to think that all blue-gifted are incompetent," Nyrden said. "With each the blue-gifted failure that I hear of, it takes another year of my life. My body is feeling quite haggard. I do not know about you all," he continued, smoothing his hair into place, "but I like my appearance, and I'd like to keep it."

"Yes, age does seem to be catching up to us," Belinda said, unamused. "There is only so much that Perserine can do to help my appearance."

Perserine glanced at her, then smiled. "But you have to admit, Belinda, that I am the best when it comes to transmutation. Your skin looks impeccable. I daresay, it looks better than it did when I knew you back in your youth."

Belinda brushed back her long cascading red hair, sighing. "Yes, but you can't keep doing it forever, Perserine. There is only so much my body can take. Besides, my insides are… decaying."

"That is the effect of time," Oriel stated, glancing at her. *It soon will catch up to you, my friend.* He felt the same. His body was rotting within while his soul was spread thin, like a sickness that worked quicker as each year passed.

Perserine snorted. "I will be able to take care of your insides, Belinda. That is why we need the green gift."

"Rest assured, the blue-gifted are working on it," Borgen stated as the servants started coming in, each setting a plate in front of the justices. "We will succeed, that I can promise." He paused, then sighed. "Unfortunately, all have utterly failed so far."

"Disappointing," Belinda sneered. "I don't like failures."

"Neither do I," Borgen muttered, starting on his meal. "It is a shame my body is too old to handle the traveling."

Perserine snorted while Nyrden laughed. "Don't pretend that you would travel yourself, my friend." Nyrden shook his head as he cut his meat delicately with his fork. "I cannot picture you traveling the seas of time, even if you were in your prime."

Borgen smiled, then took a gulp of his wine.

More like he doesn't have the energy to navigate the time-space continuum,

Oriel thought. It was time-consuming and tiresome to do so, and Oriel knew that Borgen didn't like 'wasting' time. Borgen wasn't as specialized at navigating time as Oriel was.

"Why is it that you don't do it yourself, Oriel?" Nyrden asked.

"We've already discussed why, Nyrden," Tyllos interjected. "Must you keep bringing this up?"

"Do not stress, Nyrden. We have called upon Lady Vala," Borgen said before shoving his mouth full of food.

Oriel paused for a second at the mention, then he picked up his fork and took a bite of food.

"So?" Nyrden said. "Who cares about Lady Vala? What makes her so special?"

"We recently learned that she was the one who guided all of World Sector Six's gifted to the past," Borgen said, his mouth still full of food. "Most importantly, she knows where the portal is. It seems that Lady Vala is quite talented when it comes to the flow of time."

"I don't understand how it can be so hard to find a portal," Nyrden said.

Oriel said nothing as he continued to eat his dinner.

"And what of the sorceress?" Tyllos asked Belinda. "Are we still sending that hothead to World Sector Six? What is taking him so long to get there?"

"I have sent multiple summons to the High Inquisitor," Belinda said with a frown.

The others scoffed at her remark.

Belinda held up her hand. "Do not fret. I am just as impatient as you all. I grow just as tired waiting for him as you all do, and for that, I have sent someone to fetch him. "

"About time," Nyrden said sourly. "That ass needs to be put in his place." His face shifted into a devious smile. "Perhaps after everything is said and done, I can finally get that violet slut Ikaria to pleasure me after her power is gone. I heard she is good in bed." He laughed at his own joke.

A sudden gushing red wind hit Nyrden's wine cup, causing the justice to lose hold of it. The chalice smacked him in the face, the wine splashing all over him.

Belinda's eyes burned with fire, staring at Nyrden. "How many times must I remind you of your manners?"

Nyrden picked up his napkin angrily, then wiped his face, his eyes narrowing. "I don't hear you complaining about the High Inquisitor's poor manners. I daresay he is far worse than I am!"

"I'm over this conversation," Belinda said, the glow from her eyes slowly fading as she rolled her head lazily toward Oriel. Her long crimson tresses flowed over her shoulders as she moved, eyeing him. "There is another matter I have been meaning to address," Belinda said, taking another drink of her wine. "With all of you."

"What is it?" Nyrden asked, raising an eyebrow as he continued wiping the wine off his face.

"You see, there have been odd reports, ones that I most certainly thought were a mistake," she began. Her words were like the ice from her heart: cold, sharp, and piercing.

Her gaze steadily moved across the room, then her burning eyes locked on to his. All the eyes around the table turned to him; some were curious, some looked angry, while others looked disappointed.

They knew what he had done.

Oriel carefully calculated his next statement as he finished his bite of food, then put down his fork. "Why are you looking at me like that, Belinda?"

"Why did you do it?" Belinda asked him coldly. Her eyes glared at him with a fierce intensity.

Oriel stared back her with the same steeliness. "Do what, *Belinda*?"

"Hide the time portal!" she snarled, slamming her fist on the table.

"I would never do such a thing!" Oriel countered fiercely. He coughed, clearing a scratch in his throat. "I can assure you that the time-space continuum is very much how it should be." It was half true. He wouldn't hide the portal… to certain people. Others, yes, he would.

"But it is not." Borgen's voice rose above their accusations. "All these years, I couldn't find the portal to the green-gifted woman… even after we had discovered the *chosen one* in that *very same* portal. Then, after all those years of searching for that particular portal, we finally found it again and started dispatching our groups of blue-gifted. And every single blue-gifted that has been dispatched has failed. Why have they failed, especially since we thought we had found the portal? It didn't make sense."

His eyes met Oriel's. "That is, until two came back begging for their lives. They swore they couldn't find it. They stated that the portal simply… *vanished.* To make matters worse, they could have sworn that the time-space continuum appeared to have been rearranged. There is only one person I know who has *that* kind of power."

"And you believed those two gifted?" Oriel said, trying to sound indifferent. He coughed, then cleared a ball of phlegm from his throat. He had talked his way out of situations before; this would be no different. He had a way with words and knew how to smooth over the accusations. "You blame me as if I can magically *erase* portals."

"Do not try to fool us, *Oriel*," Belinda said. "We know it has to be you. No one is as talented as you in the blue gift, not even Borgen."

Borgen shot her a look, then gritted his teeth.

"Besides," she continued, "with the combination of other gifted powers, it makes it possible, does it not?"

"Nonsense." Oriel shook his head. "Even with my consumed orange gift, it is still impossible to hide portals. Your accusations are weak," he said, brushing her off. He coughed again, this time much harder.

"Nothing is impossible, Oriel," she said, her words ringing sharply. Belinda took a drink, then stood from the table, giving him a disappointed look. "And what is more disappointing, is that you've been hiding places, portals, people… gifted people, might I add."

"Gifted people?" Oriel narrowed his eyes.

"Covering that green-gifted time traveler's tracks. Hiding the portal to Queen Emerald. Allowing Lady Vala to travel with the others to the correct portal to defeat the sorceress." Her eyes narrowed with scorn and hurt. "Why, Oriel? After all the years we have served together. *Why* do you now betray us?"

The high justices all gazed at him with accusatory stares.

Oriel looked around at everyone's eyes. Those proud, haughty, arrogant, power-hungry eyes. They didn't care about anyone, not even the God of Light. They only cared for power. It made his body and innards burn with abhorrence, fueling his determination to stand against them.

"I have given my time, my blood, and my *life* for our purpose," Oriel spat. "I, out of everyone on this panel, was the one to come up with our future goal!"

"Then why?" Belinda repeated sharply.

"What we believe in… there will be no peace if we continue on our path!"

His throat burned and felt tighter by the moment. Instead of reaching for his wine, Oriel grabbed his water glass, taking a long drink, then he coughed hard. His head was feeling light, and his vision felt pinched.

They had poisoned him.

His time was up.

"Is that what the flow of time showed you? That there will be no peace if we continue?" Belinda asked, walking absentmindedly around the table. "Because I could have sworn you told me otherwise many years ago."

"My perception has changed," he shot back, coughing several more times before gasping for air.

"Your perception and time itself are two very different things, Oriel."

"The flow of time changes like a drop in a bucket, rippling throughout the ages, changing its course!" Oriel countered fiercely. "And what I have said is true. *Your* time will soon come to an end. You can't keep this up forever. Even if you did succeed by completing the Spectrum of Magic, there will be someone else to disrupt all of you further down time's flow, and everyone in all of time will be doomed. You cannot live forever; no one can! It's a vicious cycle. Death always finds a way."

"You are no longer a member on this court," Belinda declared.

"It's a shame," Tyllos added. "You were always so loyal and brilliant. Now we have to replace a dear friend. You have lost vision and lack faith in our goal for peace on this earth."

"Peace, you say?" Oriel laughed through his coughs. As he laughed, he spat up blood on the dinner table. His insides began to twist and turn, and he knew it was almost over.

"I find it disturbing that you sit here laughing at your very hour of death." Belinda raised an eyebrow. "You should be asking the God of Light for forgiveness."

Oriel laughed again as blood poured from his mouth, staining his delicate clothes in the rich redness of its color. "You should listen to yourself, Belinda. You, who are poisoning people, commanding that special gifted to take away others' power… You think that is what God has truly intended for everyone? You keep walking down this path, you *won't* win!" he called out, his voice echoing.

His stomach twisted with a sharp pain, then he spewed more blood from his mouth. He closed his eyes, trying to form a spell, but his mind felt fuzzy, and his energy was lacking.

"Unfortunately for you, Oriel, we will. Tyllos has seen it come to pass. And the earth will be made anew with the God of Light's power and glory, and we shall rule over all."

Oriel lost his breath, then coughed out a mouthful of blood again, this time three times as much. He then collapsed on the floor. His dinner plate went flying, shattering into pieces all around him. His skin had turned blue, a shade that almost matched his robes. The poison had reached its peak.

"It is sad to say that we will now have to have someone else fulfill the prophecy of the earth's cleansing. You have become a disappointment, I am sorry to say. We will mourn you, Oriel… Or rather, the Oriel we once knew," Belinda said in a sad but cold tone.

Oriel gasped for air, rolling around in food and ceramic shards as the poison wracked his body, spewing more blood on the ground. "The High Inquisitor doesn't have the kind of power you desire!"

Belinda stood over him, her eyes full of fire. Her magic started to glow from her hands. "You'd best say your prayers now, Oriel. While we live forever on this Earth in paradise, you will burn in Hell for your actions."

His thoughts became a cesspool of swirling blue confusion as he absentmindedly spewed more blood.

Oriel muttered something, then took his last breath.

"Out of the spectrum, one shall appear to all mankind. They will have the God of Light's one true power to restore complete holiness upon the land. Earth shall be shaped in his image, and all things shall be made new. Light will overcome the darkness, and peace will be restored to the faithful."

—excerpt from "The Chosen One," the lost prophecy
Recorded by Adonis Karras, 267 M.E.

"Oh my soul, why have you gone astray? What entices you so? The world glitters like the brightest star in the sky with your desire, but then withers like the autumn fields in your clutch. The sun in your heart scorches all that you see and is burned to the ground. Your jealous fires spread like a disease, plaguing the innermost workings of your mind until there is nothing left that remains true to yourself."

—excerpt from *Chants of the Sorrowful Heart,* verse 43
Author unknown, Speculated date: 851 M.E.

CHAPTER 1

VIOLET

Geeta tightened the remaining loose screw with her wrench until it was secure, then slid out from underneath the transport.

"That should do it," she said as she wiped her greasy hands with a semi-clean rag. As she did so, she noticed a large stain on her gray mechanic jumpsuit. Grunting, she threw the rag aside, then wiped the beaded sweat from her brow with the back of her hand, carefully trying to keep her bindi in place.

Frank, one of the maintenance crew members, was standing on the garage dock with a handheld device in his grasp, waiting for her to get out of the way. He slid under the transport with the device, and Geeta could hear the beeps and scans coming from the machine. After a moment, he slid back out.

"Looks good, Geeta," Frank stated, placing his thumbprint on the device's screen. It beeped with confirmation.

"Thanks, Frank," Geeta said. "What's next?"

Frank looked at the device's screen, scrolling through the garage's files. "Hmm, I don't see any of the current work posted." He pressed a few more buttons, then scowled. "Damn thing froze."

Geeta extended her hand. "Give it here. I'll turn it in to Damien and get a new one."

"All right," Frank said, handing the device to her. "Gives me a chance to down another cup of joe."

Tucking the device under her arm, Geeta started walking past the other maintenance crew members of the garage dock. Her coworkers were working on other transports that were in much need of repair. One was an aerial cab transport, another a public transport. She even saw a street vehicle at the far end of the platform, one used for the lower levels. It was rare to see street vehicles at her garage dock; most of what they worked on were aerial transports.

Geeta walked down one of the hallways and came to her boss's office, opening the door nonchalantly. Damien's desk was empty.

"He's out on the receiving platform," said one of the other mechanics passing by. "Just saw him."

"Thanks."

Geeta walked through the dank hallway until it opened itself up to an oversized platform outside, revealing the bright lights of Arcadia's mid-levels. As she exited onto the platform, an aerial transport neared, its loud engine rippling in her ears. The winds that came from it created a wind vortex-vacuum, whipping Geeta's long dangling earrings, smacking her on the cheek. The continuous blast of hot air coming from the engines made the neon lights of Arcadia's night waver behind its heat.

As the engine ceased and the winds died down, Geeta's earrings settled, falling against her neck once again. The loud city noises returned, filling her ears with the sound of nighttime activities—mid-level transports flying to and from platforms, citizens passing through the skyways, and a multitude of sounds from balconies, where people did whatever they did for their evening habits.

Arcadia always was a sight to behold, no matter how long Geeta had been living there.

Geeta spotted Damien across the platform, then made her way over to him.

"Done," she said. She handed him the frozen device. "By the way, this thing froze again."

Damien snorted, grabbing the device. "I hate these old pieces of shit," he said, trying to power off the device.

"I don't know why you just don't buy us new ones. It would save us time," Geeta pointed out.

"So you've told me repeatedly," Damien grunted. "Don't have the budget for it right now." Frustrated, he stopped fidgeting with the device, then looked over at the landed transport. "Guess you don't need a device to figure out what you need to do. That one"—he nodded toward the new transport—"will be yours and Frank's."

From the corner of her eye, Geeta saw the pilot of the newly landed transport walk up to them. Damien shook hands with him.

"I'm so glad you are able to fix 'er up," the pilot said to Damien. "I called about five other stations, all busy."

"You're lucky. We just had a cancellation this evening," Damien said. He turned to Geeta, nudging her. "Says his engine was overheating."

"On it," Geeta said, eyeing the transport. From the looks of it, it probably needed more than a few fixes on the engine.

"Here." Damien pulled his personal device out of his pocket, shoving it toward her. "Use mine. But I want it back when you're done."

"You know me. I'll make sure it's completely nonfunctional before I return it to you."

Damien snorted at her poor attempt of a joke as she grabbed the device.

Geeta turned and headed toward the transport while Damien and the pilot started chatting. As she did so, she saw another team of mechanics standing around as she passed them on the way to the transport. It looked like they had a question but didn't want to interrupt Damien and the pilot.

A few moments later, Damien glanced over, seeing his mechanics hovering nearby.

"What are you all staring at? Haven't you all seen a transport before? Get your asses to work!" Damien hollered at them, and they scattered. "The next time I see you sorry saps standing around, I'm finding me some new mechanics!"

As Geeta neared the broken-down transport, Frank came up to her, coffee in hand. "What was that all about?" he asked, slurping down the last of his coffee. He threw the Styrofoam cup in the trash.

Geeta shrugged. "Looks like they had a question about something."

"So he chewed them out?" Frank lifted the metal plate that covered the engine and yanked it aside.

"Yep."

"That doesn't give him the right to be an ass. Damien can be such a dick."

"You kind of have to be. No one would get anything done if he didn't set them straight." It was true; the other guys on her crew were lazy compared to her and Frank. She was the only female mechanic at the transport garage.

Geeta couldn't imagine any other women putting up with the guys' bullshit. "Still, that was uncalled for," she said.

"You should have a word with him. I don't know what you say to him to make him listen to you, but whatever you do or say, it works every time."

Geeta smiled, thinking of her violet magic. "I'll talk to him."

Frank returned her smile. "Good."

"By the way, got a new device," Geeta said, handing it to Frank.

"Thanks." Frank booted it up, typed for a moment, then slipped it into his pocket.

It was ironic that she was working as a transport mechanic. Years ago, Geeta had everything she could have ever wanted, her being the high priest's wife. Clothing that consisted of the finest of garments. Refined silver and gold adornments. The most luxurious carpets. Jewelry that women could only ever dream of having. She had every comfort that one could have ever want back in her original time. But all those fine things in life could never come close to the inner peace that she had now. Having all those precious things meant she had to be Vihaan's wife.

Geeta gritted her teeth at the thought.

She *liked* to work. It made her feel more accomplished than sitting around being nothing more than her husband's doormat.

Frank opened the hood while Geeta slid under the transport, both of them starting their inspection.

"Aw, shit!" she heard Frank call out from above.

Geeta rolled out to see Frank shaking his hand, engine coolant spewed all over him.

"Looks like he blew a thermal expansion valve," he said, grunting as he looked for a rag.

"Great. It's going to require evac, isn't it?" Geeta said, sighing.

"Yup. And replacing the unit." Frank wiped his hands. "It's a good thing he got it here when he did. Shit could've overheated, and it would've blown engine gaskets all over the damn place."

He handed her Damien's device.

Geeta snorted. "Why are you giving this to me?"

"Because your hands are cleaner than mine," Frank stated.

"Whatever." Geeta snatched the device from Frank, then typed in their assessment. After, she looked over to Frank, who was still checking for any other faulty parts of the transport.

"What are you doing after this?" he said. "Wanna grab some grub? We can go to that diner you like."

Geeta froze at his words. Maybe Nym would be working at the diner tonight. Then, Geeta remembered how terrible she looked at the moment. She couldn't face Nym looking the way she did.

"I'd love to grab some food, Frank, but I have to finish my translation work."

"Translating what?"

"Just some old poems."

"Sounds fun." He shrugged, uninterested. "Just remember, don't burn yourself out between this job and other work. Believe me, once you start working two, three jobs, it gets to you."

"Don't worry about me, Frank."

"Who said I was worried about you?"

Geeta chuckled, shaking her head. Frank was a strange one. Entertaining but strange.

The two of them finished up their inspection and typed out the estimate. It was just as Frank said—the system had a coolant leak, air had been introduced into the system, and the transport was going to require an evac. It was going to be a lot of work, probably more than what the pilot thought. Geeta could just see it now; the pilot was going to chew out Damien and complain that they were trying to rip him off.

After she finished the estimate, Geeta realized the time. She looked over to Frank, who was in the garage system putting in his request for the parts needed.

"Looks like I'm off now," Geeta said as she hit the send button on Damien's device.

"Same here," Frank called out. "I'm heading out in about ten minutes."

"Can you do me a favor, Frank?"

"Depends."

Geeta handed him Damien's device. "Give this to the boss."

Frank sighed. "You owe me one."

"And you owe me ten."

Frank chuckled as Geeta clocked out and grabbed her jean jacket and duffel bag.

"You working tomorrow?"

"I have tomorrow off," Geeta answered. She yanked off her mechanic jumpsuit, then shoved it into her duffel bag.

"Well, I work tomorrow, so it looks like I'll have to get started with this piece of shit."

"Good luck," Geeta said, throwing on her jacket.

Frank snorted, then casually waved. "Have a good one, Geeta," he called out as she stepped out the back door.

The garage dock's back door led into a back alley of several mid-level platforms. Bright advertisements and neons glowed down the alley, coming from the main strip walkway. Geeta headed out of the alley, then entered the main strip. She strode by the mid-level shops throughout the main strip, all bustling with activity, as she made her way to the transport station.

As she neared her destination, Geeta slowed as she passed by the diner, trying to peer inside the windows.

Her heart quickened. All the familiar waiters and waitresses were there, along with some of the usual customers.

No Nym, she thought.

Seeing her muddled reflection in the glass, she realized how ridiculous her hair looked. She still had the top of it in a ponytail from work. Geeta hated the way her hair looked when she worked at the garage. She still had the sides of her head shaved for her mohawk, but she never styled it into that fashion for work. It just got in the way, so Geeta always threw the remaining hair she had into a ponytail.

It's a good thing I'm not going in there anyway.

Frowning, Geeta continued on to the public transport station, waiting for the next transport. Several of them were docked with passengers filing in, while others departed for takeoff. Geeta looked at the depot clock, seeing that she was a few minutes early. She could just go to the bathroom, lock the stall, and blink in an instant with her violet-blue magic. But even that was tiring in itself; she would still have to travel through the dimensions to get to her apartment, being that she wasn't that talented with the blue gift. She would rather just rest her feet and enjoy the ride.

The transport she was waiting for landed, and she and the other passengers boarded. Geeta scanned her monthly pass in the machine as she stepped inside the vehicle. It beeped a confirmation, then she headed to the back near a window. After everyone was loaded, she heard a computerized voice announcing takeoff, then the transport door closed and departed.

Geeta watched the skyline from the window as they flew far above in the sky. From a distance, she saw the illuminated palace, glowing electric green. The palace demanded to be looked at, towering over all other buildings, its tall turrets and spires reaching up into the night sky against the moon. Even from where she was, far across the city, Geeta could feel the Queen's sadness echoing across the sky, stirring in her heart. She wished she could do something for the Queen, but there was nothing to make the Queen whole again. And tonight was no different—sadness radiated from the center of the city, making Geeta's heart ache.

Geeta felt the same as the Queen; she missed that idiot Kyle.

The transport landed on her destination platform, and she exited quickly. She walked through several more platforms, then across several skyways and up a few escalators until she came to her apartment building, then her door.

Geeta shut the door behind her, then walked through her beaded curtains; they made a slinking sound as she passed. She plopped on her floor pillows, sighing. The coolness of the pillows felt good next to her hot skin, slightly relaxing her. Turning her head, Geeta noticed that next to her was an ancient manuscript from a private collector. There was still much translation work to be done, but she was just too tired, and the softness of the pillow was inviting.

Tomorrow, she told herself.

In the corner of her eye, she saw Kyle's guitar propped up against the wall.

She paused for a moment, gazing at the cherry-red color of the guitar. It was as if Geeta could hear a tune coming from it—the tune that Kyle used to play night after night when they were locked in time, the melody of his burning love for Queen Emerald. It was like the melody lingered in her apartment, always reminding Geeta of what had happened…

Geeta looked away as a small tear formed in the corner of her eye.

She hastily wiped her eyes, then got up from her pillows. She mustered her way over to the small altar that housed her gods, then lit incense and candles. Each color god or goddess was represented, made of stone, standing in order of the colors of the Spectrum. Only one of them was not standing.

Geeta stood staring into the candles' light, watching the flames flicker. The gods had always guided her, giving her direction. She had not always understood the yellow visions, and she'd never questioned them. But ever since her training with Kyle, there was an underlying tone to them that she couldn't place; they felt wrong, but yet, they had a sense of purpose like any other vision.

These strange visions… Geeta knew what they meant. That Kyle had to complete the Spectrum of Magic before the battle with the sorceress. Deep down, she knew that was right at the time. But why did the gods strongly insist in her visions that neither she nor Kyle could kill the sorceress while locked in time? That if they did kill the sorceress locked in time, pure darkness would envelop the earth and ripple throughout the expanse of time.

It didn't make *sense*, and somehow, it never sat right with her. And every time Geeta questioned it in her mind, another vision would come over her, forewarning once again of the severity of the consequences.

Geeta's sight blurred as she continued to stare into the candlelight. In her mind, Kyle's melody flooded her thoughts…

Geeta clenched her jaw. Why hadn't the gods shown her in any of her visions that Kyle completing the Spectrum of Magic required his death? That *he* was to pay the ultimate price? Ever since Kyle died, she'd been angry with the Yellow God, for he was the one who had shown her many things, things that felt *wrong*. And yet the Yellow God purposely chose not to reveal Kyle's death…

Geeta eye's trailed down to the stone god lying facedown on her altar, the Yellow God's face unseen. She picked up the small little statue, then grasped it hard.

Why didn't you show me that *in the vision?* Geeta thought angrily, her hand shaking. *I could have saved him from dying!* A small tear trickled down her cheek while her heart ached. *Why couldn't we have killed the sorceress locked in time? Why would the world have been in darkness if we did so? Why do you have to be so cruel? You take away the one man who helped save all of time and left his love to suffer, sentencing her to live a life of sorrow!*

Geeta screamed, chucking the yellow stone god across the room.

It hit a small table, then skittered across the wooden floor. From where

Geeta sat, she could see that it remained in one piece, lying on its side, facing away from her.

There would be no praying to the Yellow God tonight, just like every other night since Kyle's death.

Geeta had sworn she would never forgive the Yellow God. And she intended to keep that promise.

CHAPTER 2

ORANGE

"Heal me, Mom!" Gwen's voice echoed inside Telly's computer gaming headset. "I need heals now!"

"I'm trying! Stop standing so far off and get in range of me," Telly scolded her daughter through the headset. She then turned her attention to Drew's avatar. "Drew! I can't heal you through all of this!"

One of the virtual enemies ran over to Telly, attacking her character, causing her healing spells to be interrupted. Her eyes were glued to her computer screen while her nose practically smudged the screen as her fingers spammed her hotkeys. Telly had all her healing spells linked to specific keys, so she could heal her daughter's and Drew's avatars in the game within seconds.

But Drew's avatar was just plowing through the computer game, with Telly and Gwen trying to keep up with him. Drew had a tendency to run recklessly through the virtual world, gathering many enemies along the way. As a warrior class in the game, he was expected to gather virtual enemies while Telly's avatar stood far back and healed. Meanwhile, Gwen's avatar would shoot arrows with her bow. But this time, Drew went completely overboard. One by one, the mobs became much more interested in Telly and Gwen instead of Drew.

"Drew, did you hear me?"

"The probability is twenty-six percent chance survival," Drew replied through the chat messenger in the corner of her screen. It seemed Drew wasn't giving up.

"Those are terrible odds! Did you make that calculation before you pulled the mobs or after?"

"Before."

Telly groaned.

"And if I die, who's going to heal your butt? Did you figure that one out?" she continued.

"Potions," Drew's response read on her screen.

"Potions," Telly repeated incredulously. "Great."

He kept on going.

"Dad, Mom is right! I'm running out of energy! I can't shoot any more arrows!" Gwen yelled frantically in the headset.

Instead of heeding his daughter's warning, Drew continued to battle the mobs, fighting all the enemies within the computer world. Not even a split second later, Telly's blue mana bar was completely empty after casting her last spell. She had no more mana, meaning no more healing. Gwen's was the same as hers—she was out of her yellow energy bar, and there was nothing her daughter could do.

"Sorry, Mom and Dad, you are on your own," Gwen said through the headset.

Telly watched as Gwen's character retreated, running back the way they came from in the virtual dungeon. It was no use for Gwen to run; with Telly unable to heal and Drew not keeping the enemies focused on him, the enemies were running around wildly, and eventually they would catch up to Gwen.

After three fatal swipes, Telly's character died, then the enemies trailed after Gwen. A moment later, Telly saw Gwen's health bar go to zero; her daughter hadn't really made it that far away. Telly watched in the game as Drew continued to play all by himself, her virtual corpse laying nearby. Either he didn't realize she and Gwen were dead or he didn't care, because he continued to hack and slash at the mobs, drinking potions in between kills.

Drew lasted several more moments, then finally, his avatar died, leaving all three of their avatar corpses in the virtual world, motionless.

They were done.

Telly stared at her dead body on the computer screen, then growled, yanking off her headset, her eyes darting to Drew across the room in real life.

"How many times have I told you not to run and pull the whole darn dungeon?" she scolded him.

Drew looked at her, shrugging in response. "N-n-n-next time cast Circle of H-h-h-healing, then-n-n… cast Prayer of Light right after."

Telly's mouth dropped, then she scoffed at him. "Are you telling me how to play my avatar? Really?"

"Mom, do you really need to ask that out loud?" Gwen said, flipping off her headset as well. "Dad knows how to play every class in the game."

Flustered, Telly took a deep breath. Of course her daughter was right; Drew was too good at the game, and she just… wasn't.

He is just trying to help, she thought. *He is doing what he think would benefit me…*

But it still irked her that he was telling her how to play her character. She never liked people telling her how to do anything. She wanted to figure it out herself.

When Drew first expressed his desire to play such a game, Telly had been utterly appalled to the idea. They had so much work to do with rehabilitating the free cyborgs, and she didn't want her free time eaten away by playing a useless *video game.* But it was the first recreational hobby that Drew had expressed interest in since his resurrection as a cyborg, so she'd decided to try it. Gwen seemed really interested in it too. The way Telly saw it, this was a way for her daughter to spend time with the dad that she never knew, so ultimately, Telly gave in and played with them.

The game seemed to relax Drew's mind and consciousness, and after a few hours of playing, he tended to tap into more of his human emotions. And if playing a silly game helped Drew be more human, then Telly would gladly play with him—more human emotions equaled more physical touch from him. Heavens knew she had missed out on years of human contact and affection, and she more than needed to make up that lost time.

Still thinking about Drew's healing advice, Telly sighed. "Drew, maybe you should try playing a different class. Maybe you can be the healer, and I could try and tank."

Gwen busted out laughing at her statement.

Telly whipped her head in her daughter's direction. "You think that's funny?"

"You? Tank? I don't think so, Mom," Gwen remarked, still chuckling.

She got up, reached for her jacket, then yanked it over her shoulders. "I'm going to see Garrett now. Later."

"You know, he is much older than you," Telly warned.

"So? It's not like he likes me or anything, Mom. We just like working on the cyborgs together, and he's teaching me some programming."

Telly flashed her a look. There was no fooling her. It was plain as day—Gwen had a crush on Garrett.

"We're just friends!" Gwen continued.

"You better be. You are spending more time than usual with him, and I want to make myself perfectly clear. You just turned seventeen. He is ten years older than you. Much too old for you."

Gwen huffed, yanking her jacket into place. "I know, *Mom*! You don't have to remind me!"

The teen hurried out the door, slamming the screen door behind her.

Drew eyed the screen door in silence. Telly already knew what he was thinking, or rather, mostly thinking. What Drew didn't understand was the unspoken nature of having their daughter spending too much time with a man… a much *older* man. Drew understood the concept of relationships, thank goodness, but the whole concept of their daughter being so young and interested in a much older guy wasn't registering to him. The last time they spoke about it, Drew just couldn't make sense of it, frustrating Telly to no end.

Though Garrett worked closely with her and Drew with the all the new cyborgs coming into their camp, he never acted inappropriately with their daughter. However, it was Gwen who Telly was most worried about. It was hard for teen girls not to fall for some older guy and have their feelings crushed soon after they realized how the world worked. Telly just didn't want to see her daughter disappointed in the reality of the matter.

"She's so difficult sometimes," Telly muttered, getting up from her computer.

Drew gave an odd smile in return; he had started doing that when the two disagreed, as if he thought their bickering was silly.

"I-I don't see the p-problem with her and Garrett."

Telly rolled her eyes. "I already explained to you that he is much too old for her. Some things are just taboo, this being one of them."

Drew's cybernetic eye focused as he continued to contemplate what she just said, then finally he cocked his head. "Is… isn't she almost an adult? A-a-an-n-nother year?"

"Let's get working on the new equipment for that cyborg," Telly said, ignoring his statement. She really didn't want to get into it, because every time they did, the conversation went nowhere. "We still need to disconnect him from the corporation's network."

Drew got up from his computer and put on an orange knitted sweater. As he did so, the mechanical parts in his arm and chest kept getting caught on the fabric, yanking the knitted loops out of shape. But as usual, Drew made no frustrated face or sounds; he just worked it out until he had the sweater on perfectly, albeit a little frayed.

Telly gave him a quick smile, then threw on a beige turtleneck sweater, finishing with a scarf around her collar. The days were still cold out in the wastelands during the late winter, and sweaters were still very much needed.

The two of them left their trailer, walking out into the camp. They passed by several camp dwellers, some cooking for the day while others did odd jobs. There were even a few of the reconditioned cyborgs carrying supplies that were much too heavy for the dwellers. It was good seeing the reconditioned cyborgs settle back into a way of life.

Word had spread throughout the cyborg intranet about the camp, and new cyborgs kept showing up to see Telly and Drew. They sought them out for upgrades, repairs, or sometimes just maintenance. Some even went further and wanted answers as their minds began to think outside their given parameters. Telly did whatever she could to help them out, mostly disconnecting them from the corporation network so they could continue their journey to uncover their human side. Some wanted to get their grafted weapons removed or upgraded, so Garrett assisted with those requests while Drew helped with their reprogramming. What they got in return from the cyborgs was food, supplies, or more computer parts for the camp, which was good for everyone.

Telly made her way to their makeshift lab, walking up the trailer's stairs and inside, with Drew following a few feet behind her. It was just a small trailer with a few computers and several cables and wires suspended from the ceiling in case they needed to hook up the cyborgs. There were also several hand-built pieces of equipment to monitor them. It wasn't much, but it allowed them to get the job done.

As Telly fired up the lab computers, she saw Drew bend down in a precise fashion into his computer chair, then he began work immediately on his current project—a piece of modified equipment for one of the camp cyborgs. She went over and checked her tablet with the daily readings of all the cyborgs within the camp. All seemed good.

Looking up, Telly sighed as she noticed one of the main computers wasn't booting up. Grudgingly, she dropped on her knees, then started crawling through the tangled mass of wires and cables with her tablet in hand. One by one, she checked all the wired connections.

As she continued to fuss with the cables and wiring, the door suddenly flung open, revealing Garrett.

"Telly. Drew. You gotta come quick," he urged.

"Have Drew go," she called out from the tangle of electronics. "As you can see, I'm trying to get the second main computer working."

"I think you *want* to see this," he stressed.

"See what?" Telly grunted as she climbed out of the wired mass, straightened her crooked glasses, and glanced at her tablet.

"Another one just wandered into our camp," he said in a hurried voice.

"So? Just bring him here," Telly replied, her eyes still glued to the tablet.

Garrett paused. "Telly… he's not from Arcadia."

His words caused her head to yank away from her tablet, her eyes meeting his.

"Not from Arcadia?" she breathed.

She glanced over at Drew. He wasted no time, shooting up from his seat and heading out the door.

"He collapsed as soon as we spotted him."

"How…" she began, looking at Garrett.

"Like I said, you'll want to see it for yourself."

Garrett ran out the door, and Telly quickly followed.

CHAPTER 3

Red

You cheated, Rubius! I saw a hint of violet magic on that arrow!" Pierre said, taking a deep drink from his glass and shooting him an accusing look.

"You wanna bet? I have a bag full of coin that says otherwise," Rubius shot back, throwing down the bow and grabbing his wineglass.

"I saw it too, Rubius," Dydrone added, his friend sloppily laying his hand on Rubius's shoulder, laughing.

"Fine, I'll shoot again," Rubius answered them, waving for more wine. A servant brought him another glass of wine and an arrow. Rubius gulped down the wine until it was gone, feeling completely inebriated from its seductive contents.

The drunken crowd cheered in response to Rubius getting drunker by the moment, raising their glasses with cheers. Though he kept his adjacent magics secret as ordered by the High Court, it seemed he'd had one too many drinks tonight, and his violet magic kept slipping through his spells.

At this rate I'll have to clean up everyone's minds before I leave here, Rubius thought, thinking of the crowd possibly noticing his violet magic, just as his friends had. *Hopefully they are as inebriated as I am and won't notice.*

He could just picture it now, Belinda looking prissy on her throne while she lectured him about keeping his powers hidden. He had been very good about suppressing his powers around everyone except those who he had interrogated, and of course, the High Court. Except his friends; they could know. After all, he needed to feel completely himself around *someone.*

Rubius took a drunken glance around the room. He had to admit it, World Sector Five was his kind of sector. Those in the other World Sectors who had met him feared him terribly. But the people in World Sector Five not only respected his position and feared his immense power, they also loved and embraced his wild behavior and indulgence of drink. They treated him very much like an old friend at court each night, which made him relax all the more.

World Sector Five's court knew how to have fun after a hard day's work, including the Emperor and Empress. Every night there was music, dancing, endless streams of wine, and on occasion, lustful couples that couldn't help themselves in their halls. Rubius played his harp for them every so often, and tonight, he obliged the Empress, who had begged him, saying that his music was filled with longing, love, and lust and made her feel twenty years younger.

His harp. Rubius glanced over at it; it burned with violet magic as he played it with his thoughts from the other side of the room.

Damn, he cursed to himself. He wanted to oblige the Empress, but at the same time, he wanted to show off to the crowd and embarrass his friend Pierre. He had completely forgotten about it.

Looks like I have some work to do before I depart, he told himself. Just thinking about it was making him sober, and he was not ready for that at all.

Rubius took another long drink as he stood up, then looked at his target directly across the hall. The man swayed in his vision, doubled, then tripled. Just standing made him realize that he had, in fact, had too much to drink.

His friends noticed, laughing as the crowd waited with drunken anticipation.

"Twenty gold coins says that he doesn't make it," Xavier said.

"Rubius can hold his wine well," Dydrone pointed out.

"I bet he will cheat again," Pierre said.

Rubius swung over to stare at his friend, his temper rising at the accusation. "I didn't mean to use… *that* magic!"

"Like hell you didn't!" Pierre shot back.

Rubius got in his face. "You want to say that again to me?"

"I do, because no one else has the guts to tell you to your face, Oh Mr. High and Mighty *High Inquisitor*. You're broke because you gambled all your money away, so you need to beat me and win back your coin."

"Like I said. I didn't *mean* to!" Enraged, Rubius aimlessly flung a fireball across the hall, where it hit the stone ceiling. Small pebbles fell down on a couple heavily involved in their affections. They didn't move, too drunk to care.

Both men got in each other's faces, eyeing each other evenly.

"You going to use your *special* mind magic on me like you do on the other poor saps?" Pierre taunted him. "Let's see you do it."

Rubius's chest burned while his fists shook with rage.

"Not this again," Dydrone muttered, coming up between them, pushing them apart.

"For someone who is trying to keep their additional powers a *secret*, you sure like to flaunt it while drunk," Pierre continued, raising his eyebrow.

Now his friend was just making him angry.

Rubius leaned into him, about to open his mouth, before Dydrone pushed both of them back again. "It's just a game, and you two are drunk," he said. "Don't do this, you two."

Rubius eyed Pierre, seeing the orangeness in his friend's eyes. Pierre knew how to push his buttons, which made him even angrier. He wanted to beat the bastard, but he also loved him like a brother.

Both continued to stare, until finally Rubius turned away. Dydrone sighed in relief.

"Someone give me another arrow. *Now*," Rubius demanded.

One of the Emperor's guards gave him an arrow, and Rubius snatched the bow off the chair behind him. He raised the bow, focusing on the target once again, holding it steady.

Before him, he saw that red dot. He could hit it.

He released the arrow, and it shot across the room, whirling past the crowd, sinking itself into the target. He missed the bull's-eye by an inch.

Pierre smiled, then nudged him. "Looks like I won. Pay up."

Rubius grunted loudly, then grudgingly tossed open his long jerkin coat, reaching for the inside pocket. He pulled out his coin purse, then pulled out his losing bet, slamming it in Pierre's open hand as he smiled.

"There. Are you happy now?" Rubius snarled at him.

"Quite."

Rubius threw down the bow, hearing it snap on the stone floor.

Pierre leaned back slightly. "Temper, temper."

Clenching his teeth, Rubius ignored his friend, walking down from the platform. As he strolled through the crowd, he noticed a young woman with soft brown hair trying to capture his attention. She wasn't gifted, but she was pretty, with her hair done up in a courtly fashion and soft brown eyes to match.

"You know, she's been staring at you all night," Xavier said. "Her name is Pearla."

"Not interested," Rubius said abruptly.

"Have you lost your mind? She has the best rack and backside I've seen in this sector."

"Then why don't you go chase her?"

"Because she has been eyeing *you*."

"Like I said, I'm not interested," Rubius said, walking toward a table. He plopped down on a chair and grabbed another cup of wine.

"Did I hear you mention Pearla?" Dydrone asked, seating himself at the table with Pierre.

"Rubius has a hot lay waiting for him, but he says he's not interested," Xavier said, rolling his eyes.

"It's because he has a thing for orange-gifted women," Pierre pointed out, sitting down next to them. "Us orange-gifted are special, I must say." He laughed. "Especially when it comes to taking Rubius's coin."

Rubius shot him a look. "Screw you," he said, taking another drink. He was still irritated about losing.

"What's with you and them anyway?" Dydrone said. "There was Poliente awhile back, then what was the other girl's name? The scribe to High Justice Perserine of the Orange."

"Oh, you mean Q'ara?" chimed in Xavier. "You were seeing her?"

Rubius snatched his drink, scoffing at his friends. "I wasn't seeing *any* of those women."

Pierre raised his brows, then gave a big smile. "Is that what Aurora thinks?"

"There is nothing for her to *think* about, so if you would like to court her or that Pearla standing over there, then by all means, please go ahead and stop bugging me about it."

"What happened to Aurora anyway?"

"She was getting too attached, and I wasn't," Rubius snapped. "End of story. Can we just drink and maybe have a rematch at archery? I want to win back my coin."

But Rubius sighed just thinking about Aurora. What a mess. The last time he saw her, she tried to gift him a fine jeweled necklace, which he'd refused. He loved precious jewels, and everyone at court knew it, especially Aurora. But Rubius knew the cost of him accepting the gift from her, and he wanted to send her a clear signal—he was not interested in any sort of commitment. They had a mutual understanding; there would be no attachment or commitment involved. But despite this arrangement, he could tell she'd started to grow fond of him, and he... Well, he became enamored with the image that she could illusion herself as. No orange-gifted woman could ever come close to transforming herself into the woman he saw in his dreams as closely as Aurora could. And he couldn't let that image *go*. It seemed completely fine for Aurora for a time, but now it seemed she wanted more from him. And that was exactly what he *didn't* want to happen.

"It's nice to finally hear your music, Rubius. I haven't heard you play at World Sector Three's court in quite some time," Dydrone said as he eyed Rubius's harp still in play, taking another drink of his wine.

Rubius snorted. "Ever since they granted me title of High Inquisitor, they try to keep me busy. Now I rarely play because of my position."

"Not true," Dydrone said. "You were playing a few years ago, even as High Inquisitor."

"That's because there was a lack of interrogations," Rubius pointed out. "They have me play when there is no work. Or whenever it suits Belinda."

"Maybe now that you're done with this job, you can entertain World Sector Three's court again. I really don't like Richard. He makes a terrible first bard. That is, whenever you decide to return home. You've been making yourself cozy here."

"I like it here. It's my kind of sector." *Richard,* Rubius thought. *That hack has no talent whatsoever. He is just there for Belinda's viewing pleasure.*

"Rubius is good," Pierre agreed. "But only when he can control his temper."

"I can control my temper just fine," Rubius snapped. "It's just when the other bards try to make me look bad, that's when I have to step in."

"Just like tonight, when I made you look bad?" Pierre smiled while Dydrone laughed. "Or just like in the case of Nyrden?"

"He deserved it," Rubius countered. "He was insulting me and trying to make me look bad in front of everyone."

"I still can't believe you attacked a high justice," Xavier said while Dydrone laughed.

Rubius shrugged. "He's a complete jackass. And because of him, the High Court found out about my violet abilities, and now I have to work for a bunch of stuffy old hags."

"Does the High Court know what you think of them?" Pierre asked.

"I don't really care what they do and don't know."

"I'd say it was a good thing you attacked him," Dydrone said, laughing. "You get paid a handsome salary and get to travel all over the world. Boy, what I would give to have seen Nyrden's face that night!"

Rubius smiled, recalling the High Justice's arrogant face years ago. "I wiped that smug look off his face so hard that he didn't even know what was coming. He now knows his place."

Pierre shrugged. "Don't know why you kept your violet abilities to yourself anyway."

"How often do you see me?" Rubius asked.

"Hardly ever."

"That's right. Hardly ever," Rubius muttered. "The very reason why I didn't want anyone to know about it. I like to do what I want, when I want. Besides, I don't like rules. Nor do I like being a face for something I hardly believe in."

"Point well taken," Pierre said, finishing his wine.

Rubius sighed, thinking about the incident with High Justice Nyrden. Nyrden had been drinking in World Sector Three's halls that night, and of course, Rubius had been drinking too. He had been entertaining the high justices and a select group of World Sector Three courtesans with his music and songs for the evening, a private affair. High Justice Nyrden had been making jeers and insults all night long about him to the other lords, and Rubius could no longer contain his anger.

After Nyrden's final insult, Rubius lost control, shooting out a force of violet magic so violently at Nyrden that it slammed Rubius back into a wall and knocked the wind out of Nyrden, shocking everyone in the room. It all happened so fast that no one had time to react. For Rubius as a red-gifted to use a magic other than red? It had everyone that night in complete and utter shock, including all of the justices. No one could believe what they had seen with their own eyes… *violet* magic on display. While they were all in shock and expressing horror at what they had just discovered, Rubius was instead fretting about his harp. He had flung it out of anger, shattering it against the floors. Rubius loved that harp, as it had always been his favorite.

"Come on, Rubius," Pierre said, slapping Rubius on the back. "Let's have another rematch. I'll give you a chance to win back some of your coin."

Rubius smirked, finishing his glass. "You're on."

At that moment, Rubius looked out of the corner of his eye. Pearla was in plain view, trying to make herself noticeable to him. He immediately looked away.

The two of them walked back toward the platform, and several in the crowd started to gather again. They were much more drunk, and much wilder than before. Even the Emperor and Empress seemed well past the point of no return, raising their cups to him to watch a rematch while involved with some heavy skin-to-skin petting.

"Someone fetch me another bow," Rubius said, holding out his hand. He turned to his friend, smiling. "We will do this, but you and I need to drink two more cups each before we do."

Pierre laughed, waving his hand for some wine. "Sure, my friend. But you know I'll still beat you."

The crowd laughed while people came up to the men with wine and a new bow. As Rubius took a wine cup, he noticed immediately that it was Pearla who handed it to him. Her soft smile hinted of seduction as she gracefully handed him a cup, her bashful eyes lowered.

Rubius followed the gaze of her eyes, realizing they lowered to the cut of her dress, revealing the tops of her breasts peeking out from her corset.

Annoyed by the sight, Rubius snatched the wine from her hand, startling her, then turned away and downed the glass. It all made him angry. Every woman, their faces all made up in the hopes of pleasing him. It aggravated him.

He clenched his cup, enraged by the situation, then threw it to the floor.

Why couldn't he just…

Swinging his hand forward, Rubius summoned his pent-up sexual frustration, instantly forming a glowing red ice shard. He then hurled it with all of his might, using every ounce of his energy with the help of his magical red winds.

The red ice shard whooshed across the room. The guests dodged out of the way, watching it plunge itself into the bull's-eye. With a violent grip of his fist, the red ice shard then exploded into a thousand red ice particles, spraying the guests nearby.

Rubius startled, noticing a woman standing next to the target.

He blinked. He had nearly hit the woman with his magic.

The woman eyed him from across the room. She was an older woman, very beautiful. He would almost compare her to a doll; her face was as smooth and white as porcelain, her lashes long, and her blue eyes big and bright, with deep-red painted lips and violet eye makeup. The woman was dressed in most elaborate fashions, with a circlet adorning her forehead and a silver half circle crowning the back top of her head, almost as if the eclipsing moon framed her silhouette. Her long wavy blue hair ran down her back, with two twisted braids framing the sides of her head.

The woman raised an eyebrow coldly at the shattered ice particles, then walked toward him, crunching the small pieces of ice under her dainty satin shoes in the process. Many within the court stared at her as she passed by.

As she reached the platform, the blue-gifted woman turned to the drunken crowd, giving them condemning looks. "You may continue your… *merrymaking*," she said, waving her hand once with a striking, final gesture.

The crowd eyed her, then resumed whatever they had been engaged with at the moment, and music, noise, and conversations filled the hall once more.

"High Inquisitor Rubius," she said in an even voice, raising her head high. "I have come to take you back to World Sector Three."

Great. Rubius cleared his throat, full of phlegm from the alcohol. "There was no need for you to come. I was planning on returning in a few days," Rubius said, shrugging.

She gazed at him with unbelieving eyes. "Is that so? I was told that the High Court sent for you almost a month ago… or was it two?"

It was about two months ago. He just wasn't up to dealing with Belinda and all the other old coots. He was having the time of his life in World Sector Five. It was heaven to him. Why leave a good party for boring work?

"I got busy," Rubius said, swirling his wine cup. "Why don't you come back for me in a day or two? I can guarantee that my head will be pounding tomorrow, and I'll be completely and utterly useless to talk to anyone, let alone the High Court."

At that moment, Pearla positioned herself in his line of sight, bending over just right, so that her breasts seemed to spill out.

Rubius suddenly turned away.

"I see," the woman said in an icy tone, her eyes darting straight to Pearla as the young maiden scrambled away. "Despite your many *vices*, High Inquisitor, the High Court needs you now. You have your orders, and you are to be on your way."

Of all the times he'd had an unwanted woman's attention, this had to be the worst possible time. Whoever this woman of the court was had already formed an impression of him. Rubius wasn't kidding at all when he told his good friends that he had no interest in Pearla.

He sighed. "Fine," Rubius said. He turned to one of the servants of World Sector Five. "Fetch me my harp." He turned, looking around the room. "Zaphod! Come on, let's go!"

Suddenly, his parrot came fluttering up to him and perched on his shoulder. His red-feathered friend whistled, giving him a loving nudge. The blue-gifted woman glanced at the parrot for a moment, almost melting her cold, stiff smile, then she glanced at him again as a servant brought forth his harp.

She frowned at the harp. "That is too big. I will send someone to fetch it and bring it back to your chambers."

Rubius eyed her. "No. I'm not leaving without it, just like the parrot. Either it comes with me or I don't go at all."

From below the platform, Rubius saw Dydrone approaching the steps. His friend had probably witnessed the whole exchange.

Dydrone bowed to the woman, then turned to him. "Pardon, my lady, but I overheard what was being said to the High Inquisitor. I will return the harp to him when I make my own return to World Sector Three. No need to trouble yourself."

The woman smiled softly to Dydrone, then eyed Rubius. "Your blue-gifted friend has quite the manners." There was no doubt her underlying words were "and you don't."

"Fine," Rubius said to his friend. "Just be extremely careful with it."

"I know how much it means to you."

The woman nodded to Dydrone, then paused, studying him. "Has the High Court ever called upon you?" she asked.

Rubius groaned inwardly. He had heard that blue-gifted were being called to the High Court, but for what, he didn't know. All he knew was that he didn't want his friends involved with their schemes. It was already enough that he was.

"No, my lady," Dydrone answered, bowing.

"Hm," she said if in thought. "Thank you, you may go." The woman waved to Dydrone in dismissal, and he bowed to her once again and disappeared into the crowd.

The woman started down the platform steps, then glanced over her shoulder at Rubius, gesturing for him to follow.

"Where are you going? Are we leaving *now*?" Rubius asked.

"We are. I just don't like to make a scene, unlike *others*," she replied evenly, obviously referring to him.

Rubius narrowed his eyes, then began to follow her as Zaphod ruffled his feathers. With each drunken step that he took, the floor seemed to move like an ocean, making it extremely difficult to walk as Zaphod occasionally squawked in protest. Somehow, he managed to make it across.

As they exited the halls, he paused for a moment, wondering if he needed to clean up the crowd's thoughts. Between violet magic being used on his harp and in the arrows during the contest with Pierre, it would have been hard *not* to notice it.

The woman glanced at him. "What are you waiting for?"

Whatever, Rubius thought. *I'll deal with the repercussions.* He was much too drunk to deal with violet mind magic at the time anyway.

"Forget it." He shrugged.

The woman eyed him, and Rubius continued to follow her. As they walked through the halls, many of the people bowed to them as they walked by, acknowledging his station. Zaphod cawed at him for the quick movement.

"I know, pal," Rubius reassured his pet. Turning to the woman, he said, "Can you drop me off at my chambers at the High Court citadel? I have to get changed."

She surveyed his outfit, then her eyes met his. "Absolutely. I think it best to do so." She held out her hand, waiting for him to take it as he sighed inwardly.

Just the thought of him traveling back to the High Court sobered him. Another job was the last thing he wanted to do.

Rubius eyed her hand, then hesitantly took it. It was cold as ice.

She glanced at him with piercing eyes, then closed them, focusing. Slowly, blue power began radiating and swirling around them both, growing steadily until it swelled in size, vibrating with a powerful energy.

Then, as quick as lightning, a bright-blue flash enveloped them both, and they were gone.

CHAPTER 4

BLUE

The halls echoed with the light sounds of Derek's feet as he walked through the lonely corridors. Dimly lit ornate ceiling lamps illuminated the hallways in cool tones, giving a sense of eeriness to the overall ambiance. At the end of the hallway, Derek could see his beautiful queen held in his arms as he carried her to her chambers. Not technically him, per se, but a shadow of him, the fragment of himself in that particular moment in time. Emerald was a princess in that moment, the one who made his heart complete. The one who made him whole.

It was painful to relive his memories within the flow of time, but it was the only way that Derek could ever see Emerald. It ladened his heart heavily with anguish and regret, ripping open the wounds of his past actions.

Emerald held his shadow closely as she tried to keep her composure, but Derek could see the subtleness of her slight intoxication. Her head rested within his arms as he carried her through the palace hallways leading to her quarters. They passed by several large windows overlooking Arcadia below, its glorious neon lights sparkling like a midnight winter's snowfall.

She felt so warm at that moment... Derek thought. Her intoxicating perfume, her smooth skin, her soft hair. It felt so *right* holding her.

His shadow let the princess down gently as she leaned back in her doorway chambers. Her eyes were so vivid green, more so than Derek remembered.

Derek watched as his shadow swept toward her, leaning in. He remembered feeling the hotness of her breath against his skin, causing his raging desire to run rampant. His body thirsted for hers, a yearning he had for her for all those years they had been apart. How much he wanted her in that moment; his desire consumed his every thought. He knew she wanted him too; he felt her eagerness radiating through her every move. The ravenous urge they both had for each other created thick tension in the air, mixed with their innocent desires.

"When shall I see you again?" Emerald whispered with desperate longing. Desire was behind each breath, and her eyes drank in his every move.

The moment slowed down as Derek took Emerald's hand, kissing it softly. He then placed it against his heart. Each heartbeat beat fiercely for her.

How he burned for her.

"Tomorrow morning, if that would please you," his shadow said softly, reaching for a lock of her long wavy green hair, smoothing it softly.

"Yes, it would," Emerald said with wanting eyes. "Very much so."

The flow of time continued to diminish.

His shadow stood there, hesitating, as it took in her gorgeous face. Why did he hesitate?

Scared of rejection. Why did I not just kiss her at that moment?

"Good night, Emerald," his shadow said, the shade slowly bowing to her.

"Good night, Derek," Emerald murmured, revealing a small smile as she trembled at his touch.

His shadow kissed her hand one last time, and his lips lingered against her skin. Another hesitant thought came over his shadow, and Derek knew exactly what he was thinking—whether he should kiss her on the lips. But he knew that at that moment in time, he didn't want to be too forward. Because Emerald was special. She was unique, different from any other princess or royal that he ever knew or encountered. She was pure, and so very innocent.

Desolation crept into his bones, despair seeping into his soul.

He had corrupted that innocence.

A deep sense of remorse came over him next. His heart ached with guilt and regret.

Time had stopped altogether, and the surroundings took on blue hues. His shadow, Emerald, the hallway, the air, even the particles that floated in the air—all ceased movement.

Derek, his real self, in full color, walked over to Emerald and stood in the place of his shadowed self, touching her hand. He couldn't feel it, as he was just viewing the scene in the flow of time and not actually *there*, in time.

"Good night, Emerald," Derek whispered.

Her statuesque face didn't flinch, move, or respond; everything was inanimate, frozen in time by him and his magic. Derek wanted nothing more than to touch her, but instead his hand shook with shame as he drew away. It would be all in vain, for he couldn't even touch her shadow if he wanted to. The depths of her eyes… they accused him, even in her stillness.

"I… I am sorry." Derek choked on his shaky words. "So sorry…"

The world suddenly burned an azure blue. The scene melted away into a brilliant blue energy, washed away, until everything in his sight was hot blue. The blue magic burned him, not his body, but his soul, and it made him realize how much he abhorred himself.

And that purple witch. How he *hated* her.

The time magic pulled away, fleeing from his presence, revealing his private dining room. All was black polished marble; even the dining table was black glass, reflecting his image.

He was alone. He was always alone. The room could be bursting at the seams with many courtesans, lords, ladies, barons, dukes, and still, he would be alone. But at this exact moment, there was indeed no one in his private dining room with him. Just him and his untouched food. At times like these, Derek could swear he could see Ikaria's reflection in the polish of the table, her face laughing at his misery. He could almost hear her wicked laughter now, ringing inside his mind.

Derek hastily wiped his bleary eyes with the hem of his sleeve, trying to forget what the flow of time had shown him. He wasn't hungry. He was never hungry anymore.

The sound of a throat clearing broke the silence.

"What is it, Councilor?" Derek stated, his eyes fixated on his full plate.

"Your Majesty, I am sorry to disturb you. I… I came in earlier, but it seemed His Majesty was…" Emerys hesitated, trying to find the right word. "…indisposed."

Meaning Emerys had walked in when Derek was in the flow of time.

"It's quite all right," Derek said. Not like they could see what he saw anyway. All they saw was Derek staring off into space, glowing with blue magic. "What is it that you want, Councilor?"

"I have most unsettling news."

Derek didn't turn to face him. Instead he sighed at his own reflection in the polished table. "What is it?"

"A transmission arrived recently."

"Let me guess, was it my father?" Derek started in. "Did he send another lengthy message? Because if he did, I don't want to hear about it right now."

His father. Ever since Damaris's demise at his wedding, Derek's father had become more withdrawn. Nothing was ever truly said between him and his father regarding Damaris's suicide, but Derek could strangely sense his father's thoughts over the communication waves. His father feared him—him and his magic. Everyone feared him. Derek even feared himself. And the last time Derek talked to his father, King Samir, they had argued so fiercely that they had ended the transmission abruptly. All over a great many things, including advice to submit to Olympia's demands.

"No, Your Majesty," Emerys continued. "This one was from Olympia. King Renard is sending an envoy for peace talks."

Derek pushed away the plate, sending it gliding halfway across the table, causing the silverware to rattle. "Peace talks," Derek repeated with a hint of spite. "Their idea of peace is much different than ours." He turned to face Emerys. "The dismantling of the cyborg units! Cybernetic weapons production coming to a halt!" he roared, his voice echoing in the chamber. "And then, on top of it all, they want us to pay a 'peace' tax, along with giving them the technology? I will *not* back down. It means too much to the Queen!"

Derek suddenly realized that he had been shouting by Emerys's flinching look on his face. But it couldn't be helped—it all infuriated him. No matter what he did to try to please the kingdoms and his Queen, no one appreciated his effort. Little did Emerald know, Derek was fighting the other kingdoms tooth and nail over the issue of dismantling the cyborg units. Emerald had been firm about the matter, and by all that was good and holy, Derek would do what she had asked of him. It was the one thing he *could* do for her.

"I… I agree with all of His Majesty's statements," Emerys said slowly, then his dark eyes met Derek's. "What shall I say in response? Should I accept the envoy's visit?"

Derek sighed. "Yes, it would be wise to do so. Let's hear what they have to say. After all, we want to try to reach *some* sort of peace with the kingdoms.

Hopefully, we can resolve this matter. Although, I don't have much hope at all, if any."

"It seems that the envoy will be here to celebrate the Queen's birthday as well," Emerys stated. "That could be looked upon as a good sign."

More like a disaster. Derek eyed Emerys, getting up from his seat. "Call a meeting with the council. We need to have plans in place for what's to come," he said.

"Yes, Your Majesty."

Derek could hear Emerys's garments shifting slightly, the councilor waiting to be excused. Derek walked over to the window and looked out over the city, at the stretches of oceanfront, thinking of Emerald. She was Arcadia's queen. She had to know what was happening. He turned to face Emerys. "And the Queen. Call her to the meeting too. It's important to listen to what her wishes are for the kingdom as well."

Emerys took a deep breath. "Your Majesty…" he stated carefully, trying to use the most delicate words in light of the situation, "I was informed that Her Majesty left early this morning, and that she wouldn't be back until this evening."

Derek could only guess where she went.

A pang of jealousy ran through his veins, then he swallowed hard. "I see," Derek managed to say, fighting back his envy. There was an awkward pause between them, then he continued. "Dare I ask where she went?"

"Her Majesty took a string of guards with her to the lower levels."

Derek clenched his jaw, gripping the edge of the table. He took a deep breath, trying to calm his anger, then waved his hand in dismissal. "Thank you, Councilor. Summon the members of the Inner Council. I will be there shortly." Derek lowered his eyes. "Call upon the Queen *regardless* of where she's at, if you will."

"Right away, Your Majesty."

Derek waved his hand in dismissal as Emerys bowed. The councilor then turned away and exited the dining hall, leaving Derek alone once again.

The Queen. She was still mourning the loss of her dead lover. Derek was convinced that if the tensions between the kingdoms didn't rip Arcadia apart, it would be the heart of Arcadia's court that would cause it to crumble.

The heart being him and Emerald.

CHAPTER 5

Green

Emerald slowly stepped inside Kyle's apartment, taking in every detail that her eyes found. Behind her, she could hear Rosie approaching, along with her guards, in case she needed protection. It was silly of them to think Emerald needed protection in a place like this. Rosie could hardly pick up a cup of coffee, let alone try to attack anyone. Rosie had a heart of honey and revered her queen, and besides, Emerald and her guards had made two prior trips to Kyle's apartment, and nothing happened then. They fretted too much.

Emerald reached inside her purse, pulling out a large wad of bills. Turning to face Rosie, she smiled, then noticed Zaphod on the woman's shoulder and gave the rat a little pet.

"Here is the rent for this month," Emerald said sadly, handing the woman the cash.

Rosie took a deep breath, then bowed as much as she could, given her aging body. "Thank you, Your Majesty." Her bright eyes looked up at Emerald's, then the folds of her wrinkles turned into a frown. "But I have to say, soon we will have to get someone in here to clean the place. I see a layer of dust forming."

Emerald didn't want anyone to touch anything. That was her last desire for the apartment. For if anyone moved any items, it wouldn't be where Kyle had left them two months ago. His was the last touch on these objects, and she didn't want them to be contaminated by anyone. The objects left all over the apartment were unchanged, a memory of Kyle's mark left behind.

Turning to Rosie, Emerald shook her head. "Not this month. I don't want anyone touching anything. Perhaps… next month."

She felt tears forming in her eyes, and it took everything to choke them back in front of Rosie and her guards.

"Sure, Your Majesty," Rosie said, giving her a knowing look. "It was just a suggestion."

"And a very good suggestion," Emerald agreed. "I'm just not ready… yet."

"I will leave you to it." Rosie shuffled out of the apartment, leaving Emerald with her guards at the door. Emerald turned, addressing them. "Please, I would like a moment alone. Wait for me outside."

"Yes, Your Majesty," they chimed in unison, bowing to their queen. They left, closing the door behind them, leaving Emerald all by herself.

For a moment, Emerald stood still, taking in all of her surroundings.

Scattered noises interrupted the silence. At first it was the beating of her heart, then came noises from the other side of the window, then finally noises from the walls on both sides of the apartment. To the left side of the apartment, Emerald heard what sounded like two people arguing. On right side, noises of passion. Outside, there was the daily bustling sounds of Arcadian citizens.

Moving slowly across the apartment, Emerald was careful not to walk over the dirty clothes thrown about. She glanced at the bed, recalling when she first stayed at Kyle's apartment. Emerald swore those were even the same empty liquor bottles strewn about.

Glancing over her shoulder, she saw where she'd painted.

A shudder came over her body as she recalled the time she first explored Kyle's body, with the stroke of her paintbrush gliding down his torso. Redness filled her cheeks, then tears started glossing over her eyes. That was the night she lost herself to him.

It couldn't be helped; tears trickled down her cheeks until her vision was nothing more than a blur.

Emerald slumped down on Kyle's bed, sobbing at the thought.

Kyle was gone.

And it was all her fault. All because she wasn't strong enough to resist the sorceress's magic.

She burst out crying again, rolling over and burying her face in Kyle's old pillow. She swung her hand angrily into the pillow as she cried, and the tears didn't stop.

Even when Kyle broke her free from the circlet's enchantment, she somehow still managed to be captured once again by the sorceress.

Why wasn't she strong enough?

It was all her fault that he was dead. Kyle had died by her hand, and it was something that she couldn't forgive herself for.

Sniffling, she rolled over, looking up at the ceiling, wiping her swollen eyes.

Her thoughts turned to the sorceress. The woman was possessed by the very magic that she'd desperately sought to acquire, the black magic too great for her to control. In that moment of cleansing, Emerald had felt the darkness flee from the sorceress's soul. Though the bitterness and resentment Ikaria harvested from those who wronged her hadn't fully washed away from her life force, it did free her from the bondage that the darkness held her with, giving the sorceress a new perspective.

And there was another matter Emerald had seen within the cleansing deep within the sorceress's heart—Ikaria truly did have a certain affection for Derek, as if she felt sorry for his unrequited love. The sorceress had genuinely *wanted* Derek to get what he wanted and desired most.

Derek. Just thinking about him and what had happened between them made Emerald angry, sad, and confused all over again. For many years, she'd secretly dreamed of being with Derek, of being married to the world's most perfect man and prince. He had been kind to her those many years she knew him. They had been childhood friends. They had laughed and played together, shared secrets. And when he came to ask for her hand in marriage, she'd wanted nothing else but to have him.

But things turned out the way they did, and her feelings had changed; she realized that they weren't meant to be together. But the more Derek pursued her, the more Emerald pulled away, and the more consumed with jealousy he became. He had been persuaded by the sorceress, whether it was by her words or her magic, and ultimately, it all led to his dark deed.

Emerald bit her lip angrily. She'd trusted him. He was her safety and refuge all those years growing up. And now…

Sadness, pain, and uncertainty filled her once more.

Every time she saw Derek in the palace, his face would immediately turn to hers, his eyes begging for her forgiveness. But how could she forgive him for what he did? And even if it was the sorceress—the evil, the magic, or *whatever* was behind what he did—did that matter? Derek had still invited the wickedness into their kingdom. If he hadn't been so determined to have her in the first place, and had just let her be, none of it would have ever happened.

And Kyle would still be alive.

Emerald wiped a tear from her cheek.

How had she ended up just like her mother? In a marriage of bitterness and despair? For as long as Emerald could remember, her mother never smiled unless commanded by her father. She knew he was a hard, cruel man. Emerald hardly saw them together except for dinners of state, and she had been kept away from them most of her days in the nursery, then in her studies, and on and on…

As a result, she hardly knew her mother growing up. Emerald had gathered that her father was the reason behind her mother's unwavering sadness, but she had never truly known the extent of it. But now, given the recent events, along with Emerald in her own unwanted marriage, she was starting to understand why her mother had been so miserable. Emerald could feel that same sadness she'd seen on her mother's face closing in around her.

How she missed her mother. It had been seven years since the former queen had taken her own life. She had hidden her magic from everyone, including her daughter. Only Victor from the wastelands seemed to know who she really was, but even then, Emerald had never seen Victor at the Arcadian court, especially not to visit her mother. She doubted her father would have even allowed it.

How very alone her mother must have felt all those years.

Died of a broken heart, Emerald thought sadly. Would she end up having the same fate? She certainly seemed to be on the right pathway to do so.

Trying to quickly escape the horrible memories, Emerald wiped the tears from her eyes, feeling nauseated at the thought. She wasn't sure if it was the mixed emotions and her crying that made her sick, or her current condition. All she knew was that she wanted to vomit.

As she got up, Emerald looked at the empty space where Kyle's guitar used to sit. It was the only object that was missing from his apartment. She had asked Rosie about it, but the old woman swore that no one had come into the apartment, not even her unless Emerald herself came to visit. Emerald wondered where it could have gone.

Kyle did mention that he lived longer in time while I remained frozen in time. Maybe he'd had it with him somewhere before he came for her.

There was a soft knock at the door.

Rising from the bed, Emerald smoothed her dress back into place, then wiped under her eyes one last time to ensure none of her makeup ran down her cheeks.

"Come in," Emerald called out.

One of the guards appeared in the doorway, but he didn't dare step inside.

"Your Majesty, there was a transmission from the palace from Councilor Emerys. A meeting has been convened by the King himself. He requests you and the Inner Council."

The very last person on earth that she had wanted to see. Just the thought of Derek gave her anxiety. She had no words left to say to him, nor the strength in her heart to look at him. She had nothing for him.

"Tell the councilor that I won't be joining. I have other engagements," Emerald stated, then turned away. "I will be ready to go in a few minutes."

She heard the door close, leaving her alone once again. Her stomach churned, then the vomit rose in her throat.

Hurrying to the bathroom, Emerald fell to her knees in front of the toilet and opened the top quickly. Emerald threw up everything she'd had for breakfast. It wasn't much, considering she hardly had an appetite these days. The mere thought of breakfast made her throw up all over again, emptying her stomach until all she was doing was dry heaving.

When the wave of nausea passed, Emerald spit into the toilet one last time, wiping her lips with her arm. She rose to her feet, flushed the toilet, then went to the sink to rinse out her mouth. Emerald looked at herself in the mirror. Her makeup was somewhat intact, but her eyes were bloodshot from the crying and vomiting, making the green of her irises stand out all the more. They were so vibrant that the intensity startled even her.

Emerald took a deep breath, studying herself in the mirror. No one knew her secret, not even Glacia. She didn't want to speak it out loud, for if she did, it would become real to her. And she wasn't willing to accept reality, not yet.

Taking one last glance in the mirror, Emerald fixed her dress again, then walked out of the bathroom and out of the apartment. As she entered the hallway, her guards bowed.

"I am ready to return to the palace," she announced. "And please tell Rosie that it is okay for her to have someone clean the bathroom only."

They bowed in unison, and one went to Rosie's door while Emerald started down the hall.

She didn't want to go back to the palace. It was as if she was returning to her prison. But what other option was there? She was the Queen of Arcadia, and everyone looked to her for guidance and leadership.

She would give it all up if she could.

Just to have one more moment with Kyle.

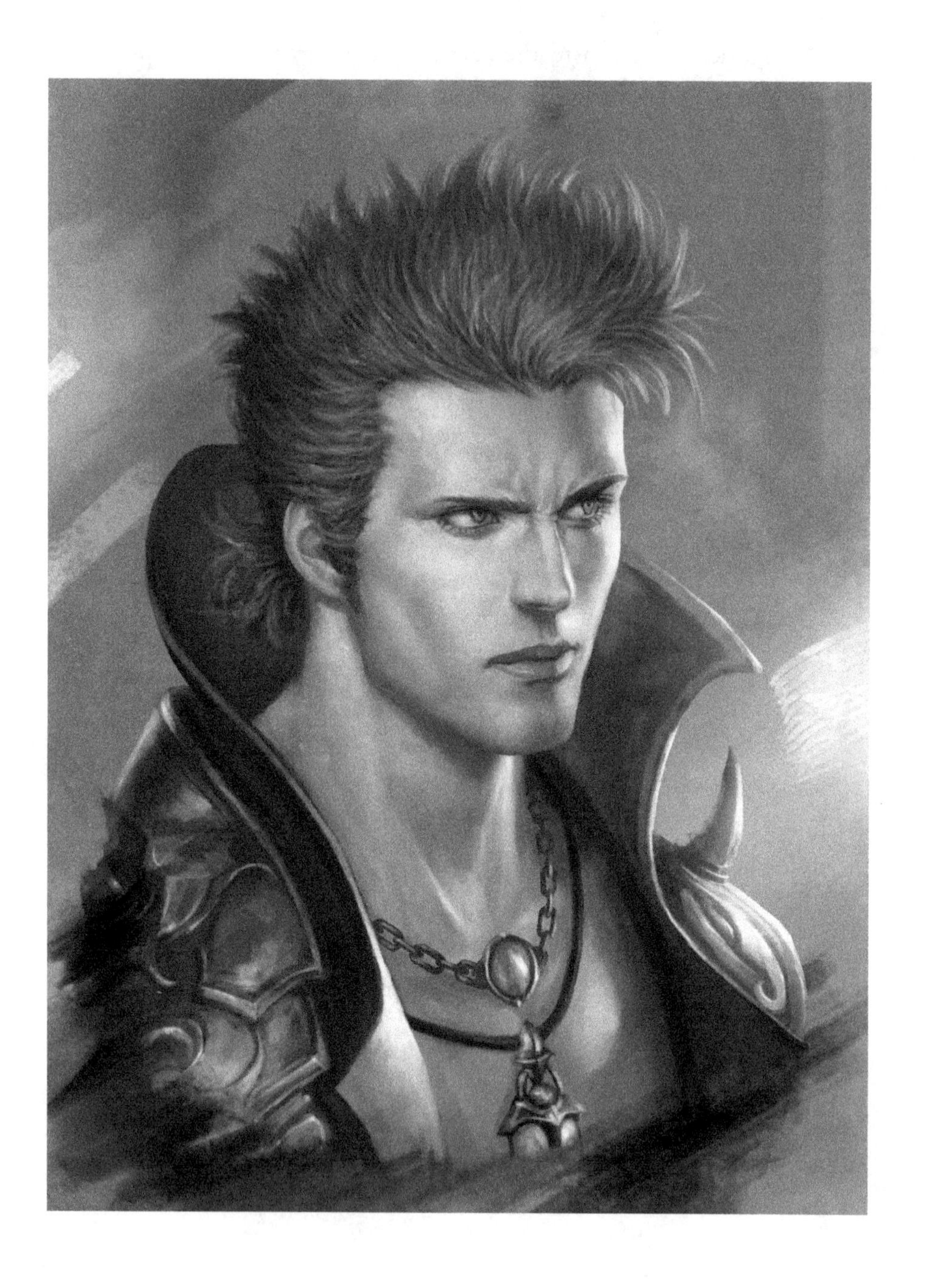

CHAPTER 6

RED

Rubius stood outside of High Court's audience chambers, waiting to be summoned. The giant courtyard housed a fountain in the middle, the outskirts lined with benches, carved pillars, and an elaborate stone overhanging to shade the edges.

His head was pounding from the wine at last night's affair. The sound of the water fountain combined with the footsteps of the passersby didn't help one bit. Damn that Pierre, always taking his money. He couldn't believe he'd lost most of his coin over that bet.

Sighing loudly, Rubius situated himself on a nearby bench. He really didn't want to be back at the High Court citadel—he had planned to stay in World Sector Five for at least another week. Maybe it was a good thing, considering he was almost broke. Another job from the High Court would keep him going for at least half a year. That is, unless he gambled it all away to Pierre again.

Bored, Rubius lazily cast a small ball of fire in his palm, then fanned out the flames. He kept doing it, not really paying attention to the magic being cast. It was an old habit when he got impatient. There were two people sitting on an opposite bench whom he had never seen before. One of them he pegged as being from World Sector Two by the cut of their robes. The other sported the sort of generic fashion much of the world adopted in the sector courts, so he wasn't sure if the person was one of the important lords within the citadel.

Nothing irritated him more than to be summoned immediately, only to have to wait for the High Court to finish up their business with someone else. He hated wasting his time, especially when it had to be done here, in the High Court inner halls and chambers. All the mindless lemmings running about, kissing the backsides of the High Court members while doing their errands. He could have been having a much more pleasant time back in World Sector Five. The Emperor there sure knew how to have a good time.

Dammit. Next time Belinda or those other windbags come calling, I'm going to make myself late and have them see how it feels to wait.

The cleric of the court seemed to notice his annoyance. He bowed to Rubius.

"I will ensure that they see you next, High Inquisitor." The cleric eyed the other two people in front of him.

"Good, because no offense, I don't want to be here any longer than I have to. I was having the most excellent time back in World Sector Five, I'll have you know."

"Sorry, High Inquisitor."

"I'm sure you are," Rubius retorted sarcastically. "When you see Belinda next, you make sure to tell her not to summon me until her schedule is more available." He cast another ball of fire, then transmuted it into a fire orb and threw it across the courtyard. The people walking about the courtyard dodged the orb and gave him a startled look.

The cleric bowed again. "Yes, High Inquisitor."

Right then, the door opened, and an orange-gifted woman left the chamber. She bowed to the cleric, then eyed Rubius as she walked away, heading down the hall. The cleric disappeared behind the door, then returned, bowing to him.

"They are ready for you."

"About time," Rubius grumbled. He hopped up, then walked through the open doors, smoothing back his ponytail as he did so.

Rubius marched into the hall and took his place before the justices. He had been to the High Court countless times, and this time was no different. All of the high justices were seated on their thrones, except for the blue justice Oriel, who had been filling in for the green justice. The green throne was empty, its plush green seat still fluffed up, and the giant emerald gemstone sparkled in its fullest brilliance.

It was actually the first time Rubius saw a high justice's throne void of a justice. Behind the semicircle of thrones was the sky itself, with pillars towering in increments between each throne, wisping clouds floating by in the brilliant blue sky. The white marbled floor was well-polished, so much that the sun captured its shine, reflecting its brightness in Rubius's eyes. The light was so bright it made his head pound harder from being hung over.

"High Inquisitor Rubius," Belinda called out from her throne in the red position. "How good it is to see you once again."

"High Justice Belinda." Rubius bowed, glancing around, staring at the vacant spot. "Where's Oriel? That old has-been couldn't muster up the time to greet me this fine afternoon?"

The justices exchanged looks, then focused on him. "Why, Rubius, haven't you heard?" Belinda said solemnly. "Oriel passed on into the God of Light's realm. His funeral services will be announced to the public later this afternoon."

Rubius cringed inwardly at his awkward statement. He didn't have a care in the world for Oriel, but there was always a time and place to push his bold statements. This was clearly not the time.

"I am sorry, justices. I did not mean any offense," Rubius said, clearing his throat to defuse the situation.

"None taken," Belinda said. "In fact, that is half the reason why you are here."

Rubius eyed them curiously. "Really? The blue-gifted lady told me that I had a job waiting for me."

Belinda paused. "Blue-gifted lady?"

"Yeah. You know, the one who dragged me here."

A knowing smile came over Belinda's face. "Ah, yes, the blue-gifted woman." Her face shifted. "She was indeed correct for saying so, for there is a job for you to do. Surely you have heard that the Sorceress Ikaria is being held in containment in World Sector Six. For many weeks now, might I add."

"I have." Rubius shrugged, fixing the ruby ring on his finger. Boy, did his head ever hurt.

"Did you not receive your summons from us many weeks ago when the news was first circulating? Surely, you did. I was informed that you had." Belinda's fiery eyes looked perturbed.

"You are correct. I received it. It's just that the Emperor of World Sector Five needed me around longer."

"What he meant to say was that he wanted more time to indulge in unruly behavior," said a crystal-clear voice from across the hall.

Rubius turned and saw the blue-gifted woman, the one who came to crash his good time in World Sector Five. Only now, she appeared *orange*-gifted, with her hair and eyes orange instead of blue. She slowly walked across the room, then stood before the court, glowing with orange magic.

What...? How...?

Rubius stood dumbfounded. That woman. How did she have a completely different color magic than before? It was impossible! Not even Rubius, who had access to other colors of the spectrum, could achieve what this woman had done. Hell, blue was nowhere *near* orange in the spectrum of magic.

The woman's image fully formed, and her orange magic dissipated. She held her head high. "What I witnessed in World Sector Five was completely unacceptable for what we talked about, High Justices." The regal woman strode by him, her long elegant dress trailing behind her as she glanced at him over her shoulder. Her wavy orange tresses flowed perfectly at her sides as she turned. "Drinking to the point of intoxication. Gambling to the point of being penniless. And then there is the matter of women. All unfit for our cause."

Rubius could see the judgment in the woman's cold glance, as if he were standing before the High Court on trial for his behavior. Her mere glance made his blood boil.

"Who is this woman?" Rubius said, irritated, narrowing his eyes at her as he spoke. "Why does her opinion of me matter? Especially for a job I must do? Who cares?"

"I take it you have not been formally introduced," Belinda said.

"Rubius, this is Lady Elyathi," Borgen added. "She handles great matters of state."

"If she's so important, then how come this is the first time I've heard of her?"

"She is extremely busy these days," Borgen said. I advise you to heed her advice, as we consider her an equal on this court."

Wonderful.

Rubius turned to her, then gave his formalities, bowing with clenched teeth. Every fiber of his being wanted to protest this woman's presence, but he had no other option—he had to comply. "I am your servant, Lady Elyathi," he managed to say.

She raised her chin slightly, then nodded in approval. "As you should be, High Inquisitor, for being a servant of the High Court is to be a servant of the God of Light himself."

A religious zealot with moral standards. Even more wonderful. Just what he needed, a crazy woman with religious ideals judging his every move. The situation was getting worse by the moment.

Rubius turned to the High Court. "What is it that you want of me, exactly?"

"We want you to make an example out of World Sector Six's court."

"Example? You want me to do a little song and dance with my violet magic with the sorceress and call it a day?" Rubius quipped.

Elyathi was not amused. Neither were the other high justices.

"You need to clean up the mess Empress Ayera has created," Belinda said. "Cyrus still sits imprisoned while that insubordinate woman rules in his place."

"We were gravely disappointed that the Empress went against our orders and had the gifted travel back in time," Tyllos added. "The loss of several gifted who helped is immeasurable, especially those with the blue gift from the other World Sectors. She must pay the consequences for her actions."

"Yes, Empress Ayera must be dealt with," Elyathi added, her words carrying a hint of scorn.

Rubius snorted, thinking about Emperor Cyrus. Pierre had told him about Cyrus last night when they were drinking. They'd both laughed until they were almost blue in the face, spurting out their wine. He didn't know the sorceress, but what she'd done was quite hilarious. Tying the Emperor Cyrus to a chair while naked, only to then have his wife discover him. Secretly, Rubius applauded her.

Rubius tried to hold back a smirk. "So what do you want, exactly? Imprison the Empress? Restore Cyrus? Get you the blood of the Violet? That is the ultimate plan, isn't it?"

"How would you know anything of the High Court's plan?" Elyathi asked.

"I'm not a fool, Lady Elyathi," Rubius said. *Despite what you think,* was what he wanted to add to the statement. "I have heard many things over the years while being High Inquisitor, especially through drunken minds of the court when I have entertained them with my songs."

Elyathi looked as if she wanted to say something, but he continued. "Let it be known that I care not what the High Court wants or doesn't want; I just do what they ask of me and keep it to myself."

Rubius didn't like the idea of the High Court collecting magics, all to have supreme power. But he would be a fool not to comply. He knew better. They were extremely powerful, and there were six of them and only one of him. Make that seven with that zealot woman. No… six, counting the loss of Oriel.

"High Inquisitor, Empress Ayera is to become our prisoner here at the High Court citadel. She will be tried in our courts," High Justice Tyllos said. "We will ensure that the trial is public, so that everyone may witness how foolish her actions were."

"And yes, Cyrus will be reinstated to his throne," Belinda said. "He has proven his worth over the years, and is very loyal to our cause."

Rubius snorted. "His worth? Tell me, how is that hack worth anything?"

"Do not speak out of turn," High Justice Nyrden snapped.

"Sorry, it's just all rather amusing." Rubius turned his attention to Belinda. "And what of the sorceress? I suppose you want me to get her blood, since all those other failures couldn't get the job done." Rubius eyed them. "I don't know why you didn't just ask me years ago when I took this job."

"It's because the sorceress had not activated her gift for many years," Elyathi said from across the room. "She couldn't access her own abilities, so her blood would have been completely useless."

That was interesting.

"We had already obtained her blood many years ago as a child, and it was indeed worthless," Perserine confirmed. "Since the moment we found out that she had accessed her gift, we have been carefully weighing our options on how to proceed."

"So you want me to get her blood, throw the Empress in prison. Easy enough."

"It is much more than that, Rubius," Belinda said loudly. "You see, Nyrden's team has been working on reviving the cyborgs that came through Ikaria's portal. As of right now, they have been at a standstill and can't get them resurrected. I heard rumors that the sorceress has full knowledge and awareness of how they work."

"And so you want me to go and ask her nicely to see what we can do about those broken-down pieces of machinery?"

Belinda eyed him. "Yes. That is precisely what I want you to do." She leaned in toward him. "Get *inside* her head. Understand how they work. We want to know *everything*."

Rubius sighed dramatically. "That sounds like quite a lot to pile on my plate. Dealing with the Empress. Reinstating her pathetic husband. Invading her twisted sister's mind. Getting into the mind of a gifted is extremely difficult, you know. I have no doubt it will be even more so with a violet-gifted. I don't know if I have the zeal to do it."

Belinda eyed him coldly. "I am sure you can figure out a way, Rubius."

Sure. Easy for you to say.

"You planning to make more of these things? Isn't the technology you have already enough? You haven't even implemented it with the objects that Nyrden's team got working. What's the point?"

Perserine of the Orange smiled while Belinda's eyes flashed. "Just get the information. You will know more once we have it."

"You never answered me about her blood."

"You needn't worry about that, High Inquisitor," Lady Elyathi said evenly. "I will take care of that part. You will just have to make her hold still."

Rubius made an about-face, glaring right into Elyathi's orange eyes. "You are sending *her* with me?" He pointed to her, facing the High Court.

"What's this? The High Inquisitor doesn't like his orders?" Nyrden said sarcastically.

Rubius glared at Nyrden.

"Elyathi will deal with Ikaria," Belinda said. "But you will need to aid her when that time comes."

"I suddenly don't feel up to all of this right now." *Especially if it involves that woman.*

"We are *ordering* you to go, High Inquisitor. You have no say in the matter," Nyrden said.

"And what if I don't? You going to imprison me? Or better yet, you going to have that woman over there reprimand me?"

Elyathi shot him a look.

Perserine laughed while Tyllos gave a serious look. "I think you will very much want this job, High Inquisitor," Tyllos said. "We will be paying five times what we normally pay."

"Five times, huh?" Rubius sucked in his lip. *Damn.* Five times the pay for a job… that was enough to live on for a while. Unless he drank and gambled it all away, that is. His thoughts turned to the sorceress. Deep down, he was very interested in talking with her. Ikaria had been to the past, the very time era he was most interested in. Perhaps he could learn something…

"Yes, five times," Tyllos reiterated.

"That is enough for you to burn through your addictions for at least a year," Elyathi said, her eyes glimmering like orange brimstone.

Rubius clenched his jaw at her comment. That woman irritated him to no end. But five times the normal payment? It was simply too good to pass up. Besides, what choice did he really have?

"Fine," Rubius said. "But I expect one fifth of the payment up front."

"Why do we put up with this *ass* and his demands?" Nyrden snarled as he shot to his feet. "I've had enough of his smart-ass remarks!"

Suddenly, the red High Justice whipped his hand out with anger, and it burned with bright-red magic. A powerful red gust of wind swept Rubius off his feet by surprise, knocking him to the ground and slamming his head against the cold marble.

A heartbeat went by in silence, everyone's eyes all on him. Rubius could picture Nyrden's face, gloating, knowing very well that Rubius couldn't touch a high justice in the audience chambers. It was law—only the high justices were allowed to use magic here.

Grimacing from the sharp pain in his head, Rubius managed to get back to his feet. He straightened his posture, then fixed his jerkin and the jeweled amulets that clung around his neck and smoothed back the strands of hair that came loose from his ponytail. With everyone's eyes still upon him, Rubius held his chin up with pride, then cleared his throat, acting as if what just happened didn't bother him in the slightest.

But then Rubius shot his hand out violently.

Violet magic smashed hard into Nyrden, knocking the High Justice off his feet and slamming him back into his violet throne with an audible *smack*.

"What is the meaning of this?" Tyllos rose to his feet, his voice booming.

Rubius ignored Tyllos, narrowing his eyes at Nyrden, squeezing his hands. The violet magic obeyed his command—it began crushing Nyrden against the throne much harder than before, cutting off Nyrden's breath.

"Take it back," Rubius ordered loudly.

Nyrden held strong, his head held high with haughtiness, grunting, while all the other high justices looked on, aghast, including Lady Elyathi.

"This is quite enough." Belinda stood. "*Both* of you."

"No," Rubius said with a deep but patient anger. "I want him to take back what he said about me. I'm not leaving for World Sector Six until he does so."

"This is not how a servant of the God of Light *acts*, High Inquisitor," Elyathi cried. "Stop it right this instant. You are breaking the law!"

"I said *no*." Rubius turned away from her, focusing on Nyrden, tightening the violet magic around him. "Take it *back*."

Nyrden gasped.

Rubius squeezed his hands harder. The violet magic glowed even brighter, crushing Nyrden within its iron grip. "I *said* take it back."

"Stop this foolishness right this instant!" Tyllos boomed.

Nyrden's nose began to bleed, and he gasped for breath again. Yet still, the High Justice looked at him with pride and pain.

"This is your final warning, Rubius!" Belinda shouted.

Rubius ignored all of the high justices, crushing Nyrden with all of his violet strength. He didn't care what happened to him; he *hated* that red-gifted ass and needed to teach him a lesson.

Darkness suddenly flooded the chamber, and a deep, roaring sound echoed through the chambers. The floor in the audience chamber began to erupt violently, while the room around Rubius began to twist and reshape itself until it was a solid mass, completely unrecognizable.

The High Court was angry.

The mass started to swirl around Rubius, burning with dark energy flecked with orange. The glowing, swirling dark-orange mass spun faster and faster, until all Rubius could see was the magic sweeping about him.

Rubius continued to grip High Justice Nyrden with his magic, despite all that was happening around him. Echoes of Nyrden gurgling blood could be heard as a response. Rubius was determined not to let go.

"I don't hear an apology, High Justice!" Rubius called out, still holding Nyrden in his magical grip.

Suddenly, the dark-orange magic that swirled around him shot straight into him, plunging into his chest like a knife, slicing deep into his body.

Rubius cried out with a deep grunt, releasing Nyrden involuntarily. He heard what was most likely Nyrden's body slumping to the floor, heavy breaths echoing in the chamber.

The dark-orange magic ripped through his body and burrowed deep into his veins. It felt unnatural, sickening him. It felt *wrong*.

With a solid swipe of the dark, unnatural power inside of him, his bones crunched and snapped like twigs being snapped in half.

Rubius grimaced in pain.

Another snap, this time on a much larger bone.

Rubius screamed.

He happened to glance down while his eyes began to lose focus, still in pain and shock. He stared at his hands as his flesh began melting off, his bones twisting and shaping into something that… shouldn't *exist*.

Rubius was almost never afraid. But this… His mind was wracked with fear.

He was petrified. Would he leave this earth not ever finding out about *her*?

It was all he could think about…

Rubius began to panic.

"Make him suffer, Perserine!" Nyrden's voice called out. The justices were unseen, but Rubius knew they were witnessing his demise.

There was a hard yank on his flesh, causing Rubius to scream in agony. His flesh… it felt like it was being pulled off his body and then… *reshaping* itself. A deep, dark hatred flooded through him, igniting flames, burning his insides. They were deep flames… flames that radiated darkness. They had to be coming from either Belinda or Nyrden.

"Belinda," he heard the Lady Elyathi say, "let me just end this now and strip away his power. He is clearly unworthy."

Her statement alarmed him. Strip away his power? What did she mean by that?

Rubius's flesh continued to twist and morph, burning with dark-orange magic. There was another snap of his bones, and Rubius cried out in shock. This time they had snapped his neck, and he was paralyzed.

"No," Belinda's voice answered. "He is a valuable asset to this court. We need him."

"Do *you* take it back, Rubius?" Nyrden called out within the darkness, interrupting the women. "Do you? I want to hear you scream as you admit your wrongdoing!" the High Justice roared.

Another snap of his bones; this time they were jutting out of his leg, and blood ran down, pooling on the floor.

"I strongly suggest you answer High Justice Nyrden, Rubius," Belinda's voice echoed. "This charade has gone long enough."

"I'm waiting!" Nyrden demanded.

Dark-red roaring flames burst within him, and his mind exploded in anguish. This time Rubius knew it was Belinda's magic; he had felt it once before. She was extremely offended and furious. It burned, much more powerful than any fire he had ever cast; it flooded his insides, roaring with violent energy… setting his mind aflame.

He couldn't think.

The pain rocked him, and he could take it no longer.

Rubius roared out in agony. "Fine! I take it back!"

Suddenly, he dropped hard to the floor with a humiliating smack. He was still paralyzed—the only thing he could do was catch his breath. As he lay there, the dark-orange magic dissipated from his insides, and the mass spun wildly out of him.

Rubius felt his bones relocate and twist back into place, and he let out another yell of pain.

When his bones felt like they were back in their rightful places, Rubius slowly focused his eyes. The room around him came back into focus, restoring its appearance to the high justices' chamber.

Rubius slowly brought his hands in front of his face—they were completely restored. The orange High Justice Perserine had either fooled him into believing her illusions were real, or she had really transmuted his body.

Rubius rolled his head over to the side, meeting Belinda's gaze. She narrowed her eyes. He knew that look; she expected an apology. Immediately.

Getting to his knees, Rubius lowered his eyes, then bowed his head, kissing the marbled floor. "I am deeply sorry that I have offended the High Court, High Justices. I deeply regret my actions. Please forgive me," he said as he groveled. He didn't mean one word of it, but what else was he to do?

He couldn't match the lot of them. Rubius kept his head down, waiting for permission to move. He hated acting like a damn dog to these jokers.

"Come, kiss our rings in submission, and all will be forgiven," Belinda stated, holding out her hand. Her pointer finger was adorned with a large ruby gemstone, the seal of the red justice. It sparkled with a flick of her hand.

Rubius approached carefully, his head still lowered in defeat. He gently touched her hand, kissing the gemstone.

"You may look at me now, Rubius," she said. He looked up at her, and her cold eyes warmed. "Just to be clear, there will be no next time, Rubius."

Rubius felt a sharp twang of fiery pain on his insides, causing him to flinch. It was from Belinda, a threatening reminder.

Rubius bowed to her. "I am truly sorry, High Justice. It won't happen again, that I promise you."

"Good. That is exactly what I want to hear." Belinda eyed him, then nodded in approval. "Now, go and kiss the other rings."

Rubius went down the line of the high justices, kissing each ring. When he came to Nyrden, the High Justice stood up and turned around.

"Instead of kissing my ring, I want you to kiss my backside," the High Justice of the Red said over his shoulder.

"Really, High Justice Nyrden," Lady Elyathi called out. "This behavior is just as low as the High Inquisitor's. No need to lower yourself to his level."

"I think it's perfectly acceptable punishment so the man can learn his place," Nyrden remarked.

Nyrden smirked at Rubius over his shoulder. Rubius flashed him a snarl. There wasn't a damn thing he could do but comply.

Rubius made a fist by his side, wanting to punch the High Justice into a bloody pulp. His fists shook with rage, knowing he had to kiss this man's wretched ass.

With all eyes on him, Rubius quickly kissed the man's ass unceremoniously. He then took a step back, bowing to them all.

Belinda nodded to him. "You are dismissed," she said, waving her hand.

"I will serve the High Court to the best of my abilities," Rubius said. He then turned to Lady Elyathi, unsure whether to bow or nod his head in formality. He wanted to do the latter since she irked him like no other, but given what had just happened, he thought better of it.

"My lady, I will strive to serve you, in the best way possible, to better the High Court," he muttered under his breath.

He bowed lowly to her, and she eyed him coldly with her head held high.

"I look forward to it, High Inquisitor," she said.

Rubius held out his hand, summoning his violet magic, yanking at the air. The wide doors creaked open before him.

Rubius marched toward the exit angrily. It was completely and utterly uncalled for to be attacked. And for him to be reprimanded? And for what? Defending his honor?

Just as he was about to walk out, Rubius paused. He couldn't help himself; he was overflowing to the point of wrath after kissing that arrogant ass of a high justice. It had to be said.

Rubius looked over his shoulder. "The *next* time you all summon me, I expect not to be kept waiting outside. And it bears mentioning that attacking me on your grounds, where I am powerless to respond, is completely uncalled for." Rubius turned away and stomped out of the audience chamber, snapping the doors shut with his magic. He had pushed his luck with his last statement, but he refused to be completely pushed around.

As Rubius stormed back to his quarters, thoughts about the incident consumed him. Nyrden always had to humiliate and insult him in some way or another. What was that man's problem with him? He would pay him back for that backside kissing; Rubius would make sure of it.

He entered his quarters, looking for any sort of alcohol. His head was still killing him. Having his body twisted like clay and being humiliated in front of the High Court had only made his hangover worse. He rummaged around, finding only empty bottles and glasses. He chucked them aside in frustration.

Finally, he did manage to find one bottle that had a bit of liquor in it. He shook it, took a long drink, and started packing for his venture. He whipped open his trunk and threw in several outfits suitable for his status, along with writing utensils, the last of his coin, and a few books. In the corner of his room stood his silver harp.

Looks like Dydrone returned it as promised, he thought as he admired his harp, running his hands over it.

His parrot, Zaphod, squawked in the corner, seeing the commotion.

Rubius smiled as he took another drink. Zaphod was too smart for his own good; he knew what Rubius was up to. "I am not leaving you behind, old friend." He opened the cage and let the parrot perch on his shoulder. "You are coming with me."

The parrot cawed again.

"Are you giving me lip?" joked Rubius, petting his feathery friend. "I already had enough of that from the high justices."

There was a knock at his chamber doors, and Rubius flung his hand forward, calling forth the violet magic that lay dormant next to his fiery red power. The door handle clicked, and the door flew open.

A High Court servant stood in the open entryway, looking surprised, then he gulped.

"What do you want?"

The servant bowed. "High Inquisitor, I have come to help load your belongings on the airship."

"Very well." He stood back and indicated what he was taking. Rubius eyed the servant as he loaded the trunk on a pushcart.

"I will be very upset if I see one scratch on my harp, you hear?" Rubius called out to the servant.

"Yes, High Inquisitor."

Just then, a woman came up to his entryway, bowing. "High Inquisitor?"

It was Lady Xui. She was an old woman, non-gifted, with long black hair that had grayed over the years. She wore it in a bun and was dressed in elaborate robes.

"Come in," he said to the woman. Rubius then turned to the servant finishing up loading his belongings. "Are you done yet? I have business!" he said impatiently.

The servant bowed quickly. "Yes, I was just leaving now."

"Good."

Rubius and Lady Xui waited for a moment, watching as the man left, then closed the door behind him.

"Did you find something?" Rubius asked, anxiously leaning in.

"Indeed. I found a tome dating back to the Millennium Era, right around 2399," she stated, her proud dark eyes glimmering.

"That's not far enough. I said it was somewhere around 2100 to 2300 M.E."

"Perhaps. But you did state you wanted to know about a green-gifted woman, no? And this tome mentions a green-gifted queen, ruling old World Sector One." Lady Xui held out the book, and Rubius snatched it out of her hands.

He began flipping through it to the section that was bookmarked.

"What is the queen's name?" he asked quickly, turning to the flagged page.

"It doesn't say. Only that she was born 2360 M.E. She was married to a king who was blue-gifted." The woman gave the hint of a smile. "I expect the payment to be double for my findings."

"No. Your information isn't good enough."

"I beg to differ," Lady Xui protested. "From what you have told me, my predecessors did not measure up to finding *any* information for you for all the years you had them look. That's why you hired me, as I recall. And now I have delivered. Believe me, this is only the beginning. Now pay up before I decide to lend my services elsewhere."

"Fine," Rubius snapped, reaching for his purse. He opened it up, shelling out the remainder of his coin. It was a good thing he was getting paid within the hour. All the more reason to finish the World Sector Six job quickly. Especially if this woman did indeed find what he had been searching for.

He placed the coins in her outstretched hand, and she counted them carefully. A bright smile appeared on her face, then she bowed. "Pleasure doing business with you, High Inquisitor. I will be seeing you again very soon."

"Good."

Lady Xui left his quarters, leaving him alone with Zaphod. Rubius side-eyed his feathered friend, who was still perched on his shoulder. "Let's get going, Zaphod. We have much work to do."

The parrot cawed in response, and the two left his chambers.

CHAPTER 7

ORANGE

There was a small crowd of wastelanders gathered when Drew arrived at the scene with Garrett and Telly. As they passed by, the crowd parted for them, creating a clear path directly to the fallen cyborg. Victor was there, hunched over the body; he looked up as they approached.

"I hope there is time to save him," Victor said.

"We will try our best," Telly said, hurriedly getting to her knees and checking the cyborg's pulse.

Drew immediately began running scans with his cybernetic eye while Telly connected her tablet to the cyborg. The orange data flashed within his vision, assessing the damage. It was as Garrett had said—according to the flow of information, this cyborg was not of Arcadian make or model.

How was it that another kingdom had cyborg technology?

Malfunction.

Drew flinched.

"Drew! His heartbeat has grown faint!" Telly cried out.

Drew fell to his knees, quickly taking his cybernetic hand and attaching it to the cyborg's exposed machinery in the back of its neck. Grunting, Drew sent a charge of energy through his hand and into the cyborg unit.

The cyborg gasped for breath, and his eyes slowly rolled back in his head.

"Again!" Telly ordered.

Drew sent another wave of power, this time with a much stronger electrical current, mixed with his magic. He unleashed an electrical current of orange-red magic, and the cyborg jolted with a little more movement.

He did it a few more times until Telly looked at her tablet and breathed a sigh of relief. "He's stable, but not for long."

Garrett started scanning the cyborg with his own equipment.

Orange information immediately flashed in Drew's cybernetic eye. It was warning him.

"N-n-n-neck," Drew said quickly.

Garrett looked up from his scanner at him. "What about his neck?"

"R-roll him over."

They did exactly what he asked. There, on the back of the cyborg's neck and down his back, was a massive open wound exposing flesh and machinery, all mixed with blood.

Blood.

Malfunction.

He was losing blood.

"O negative blood," Drew stated. "N-n-noot... not much time."

Telly shot up, hovering over them, while Garrett's scanner beeped. "We need a donor now!" she yelled. "Type O negative!"

No one in the crowd moved.

"*Now*!"

Victor turned to the crowd. "Quickly! Anyone have O negative blood?"

A moment later, young boy came forward. "I can help," he said in a small voice.

Telly shook her head. "Sorry, sweetie, but we need much more than you can give."

"I'll do it," the boy's mother said, stepping forward. "I'm O negative."

Victor gave the woman a quick nod. "Follow that man to the lab."

Garrett gestured for the woman to follow him, and she and her boy took off with Garrett toward the trailer lab.

Drew turned his attention to Telly, and she gave him a look of urgency.

"Drew, can you lift him? We need to get him to the lab trailer ASAP." She disconnected her tablet.

Drew nodded. "Yes."

"Good. Please keep him level."

Drew hunched over, then lifted the cyborg up into his arms, trying to support its head. *Level... keep him level...* he commanded his body. The cyborg was heavy, but not as heavy as some of the people he had carried before. Like the future man with the wavelength of 570 nanometers.

He made his way through the camp. Garrett was waiting for him, holding the lab door open.

"Bed number two," he said as Drew entered, shutting the door behind them.

Drew walked over to the bed and laid the cyborg down as best as he could, then Garrett immediately started hooking it up with wires. In the corner of the room, Telly was setting the woman up for an immediate blood transfusion, waiting to hook the cyborg up on the other end.

"Mom! Dad! I just heard," Drew heard his daughter say from the doorway. "What can I do to help?"

"Not this time, Gwen," Telly said. "This is above your level."

"Please, Mom! Let me do something!" the teen pleaded.

Telly whipped her head around, giving their daughter a stern look. "I don't want to argue with you, Gwen. You can help another time, just not now!" Telly turned her attention back to the cyborg.

Gwen looked to Garrett, then turned red, leaving the trailer quickly.

His daughter looked… *embarrassed.*

Drew shuddered.

"I swear, sometimes that girl…" Telly said as she fiddled with the needle leading into the cyborg's arm.

"Don't be too hard on her, Telly," Garrett said. "She just wants to make herself useful, that's all."

Drew cocked his head toward her, and she shot back a dirty look.

"Don't even start with me." Telly sighed. She finished getting the cyborg hooked up for the blood transfusion, and Garrett finished inserting the mechanical wires into the cybernetic parts. Once the cyborg was fully hooked up, information began flowing into Drew's computer, giving him access to its coding. He typed furiously as the information came up on screen, trying to alter the foreign programming to stabilize the cyborg on his end. The coding was genius, and it sent a thrill through his circuits just studying the complex code. Someday, he would have to meet the man or woman who'd designed it.

Or had it been a computer who'd designed it?

Every so often, Drew would look up from his computer, studying the cyborg. Yes, it was different. But it was something other than the coding.

What was it about this cyborg? It was more than unique. It was a strange feeling that had returned, the same feeling when he first assessed the cyborg.

He jolted at the thought.

"Wiring… Is it up to c-c-c-completion?" he asked.

"Almost," Garrett said. A few more seconds went by, then Garrett took a deep breath. "After I adjust a few more wires, I will get to work on cleaning up a few of the partitions of his brain."

"Unnecessary," Drew stated, stopping his work. He got up, then situated himself next to Garrett on an old rusty chair. "In-insert the cable."

"Into what?"

"Me."

Garrett snapped to full attention. Telly marched over to him.

"Oh, no you don't!" Telly pointed a finger at him. "Drew, it's too dangerous at this point!"

He looked at Telly, seeing her pale eyes sparkling in the color of 600 nanometers of the spectrum frequency. He held out his hand, his human hand, and touched her cheek. She blushed in response.

"I-I will be cautious."

She stared at him, a range of emotions on her face. He couldn't name them all, but he did recognize one: fear.

Finally, she sighed, then touched his face with affection in return. "Okay, Drew. But please, be careful." Her eyes watered.

Garrett hesitated. "You sure, Drew?"

"Yes."

"Okay…"

Garrett got up from his seat, then walked over to a large machine that took up a third of the trailer. There were several cables rolled up below the machine on old water hose spindles, ones that they had found out in the wastelands. They hadn't been able to find the proper equipment they needed. Telly had asked Jonathan if the corporation had spare equipment available for the camp to purchase, but in the end, the camp didn't have the necessary funds to complete the transaction.

Garrett undid the spindle, with much effort. Drew watched as Garrett strained himself while dragging the heavy cable across the floor.

"It's too bad we couldn't find anything lighter," Garrett said, out of breath. "This weighs a shit ton."

"It was all we could get," Telly barked at him from across the room. "If you have any connections with Arcadia's corporation, or any extra cash lying around, then by all means, get us some upgrades."

Garrett shrugged as he walked up behind Drew, cable in hand.

Drew flashed him a look of approval, then kept his head as straight as possible. He knew what was coming, considering the machinery and cables were so outdated.

With a sharp jerk, the giant cable was inserted into the back of his neck. Immediately, his head was yanked backward from the weight pulling on his neck, straining his neck muscles. Garrett twisted the cable slightly, and Drew felt a secure connection.

"Hold on, Drew," Garrett said. A moment later, Garrett returned with an old worn barstool, propping the cable up on it to release some of the tension and weight.

"Better?"

"Yes."

The back of his neck itched feverishly. Drew clawed the back of his neck unconsciously with his mechanical fingers, then realized his mistake, poking himself so hard that he punctured his skin.

"Easy there, buddy," Garrett said, noticing. He took a cloth and wiped the blood off his skin.

"I-i-i-itches."

"I bet."

Drew suddenly retrieved a memory, one of the first hookups with the wasteland equipment. The non-corporation equipment gave him a sense of confusion, since it was his first time being connected to it. Instead of scratching his neck, he mistakenly scratched his man parts. It was a good thing he had pants, otherwise he would have lost his lowers.

He jolted, shuddering at the thought.

Program error.

"Are you okay, Drew?" Telly asked from across the room.

"Yes. Recollection of memories."

She smiled at him, then turned away.

Trying not to think about the potential loss of his man parts, Drew turned his attention to Garrett, who went over to the machine again. This time he grabbed a different wire, a smaller one with a different connection. Garrett carefully walked over to the cyborg, gently rolling its head to one side. Telly joined him, lifting the wire to make sure it didn't get caught on any of the machinery as Garrett inserted it into the cyborg's neck. After securing the excess wiring to one of the higher machines, Telly walked over to the device that connected the two of them and began typing as Garrett held the cyborg.

"Don't freak out on us, okay, Drew?" Garrett joked.

Telly shot him a look. "What about me? I'm the one who has to restrain him if he goes haywire."

"Terminate connection if I act outside my parameters," Drew told them.

"Ha! Just terminate his connection, he says," Garrett said in a dramatic fashion. He typed a few more things into the machine, then flashed him a look. "Ready when you are, Drew."

Drew closed his eyes. "Ready."

Blackness filled his eyes while he listened to the sounds of the machines and the typing on the keyboards.

Thirteen seconds went by. Then, suddenly, a surge of power jolted him like a hammer to his heart.

Thump.

After the initial shock, the power ripped through his body like a violent storm. The flow of the cyborg's energy mixed with his own collided and whorled together within the stream of consciousnesses. Going faster, the energies collided until they fused together, creating such an intense power that it made his heart race furiously.

His life force was being shaken to its core.

Another smash of his heartbeat.

Thump.

The violent energy calmed, then flowed through him, embracing every part of his being. His mind was open.

Drew opened his eyes. Before him was an imposing wall filled with immense power. A sense flowed through him. It was a wall of information that contained the foreign cyborg's thoughts, dreams, and commands.

Another jolt of his heart.

Thump.

The wall split apart, then shattered into thousands of pieces.

Slowly, the pieces assimilated together again, this time, he and the cyborg were one entity.

All was dark. Another beat of his heart rocked his being.

Thump.

Drew sat in the darkness, waiting. Waiting for the cyborg to communicate with him.

A voice reverberated through Drew's mind. *Darcy…*

Who's Darcy? Drew thought.

Silence.

Drew waited and waited.

Then power washed over him. It was a familiar power, a power like his own.

Magic. There was magic within this cyborg. That was what he had detected earlier, but he hadn't been able to place it at the time.

Within the dark plane of his and the other cyborg's fused connection, colorful numbers formed. It was the coding that made up the cyborg's programming. But instead of Drew reading it like code outside in the real world, here, within their connection, it appeared like language to him, creating words within the streaming energy. The language glowed with bright colors, piercing the darkness that surrounded him. It rippled deep within, forming new thoughts and new ideas.

Drew finally broke the silence. *Who are you?* he asked through their established secure line.

Words formed at the front of his consciousness within the darkness. *Model 695-b.*

Is that what they call you?

That is my given number. However, I have heard several technicians refer to me as Scion, the cyborg answered.

Where were you assimilated, Scion? Drew asked. *You are not of Arcadian make and model.*

I am from a large corporation located in Olympia.

Drew paused. How did Olympia have the technology? Technology that was so similar to his own, that *he* had developed?

I hear your thoughts, unknown user. Perhaps I can explain. In my human awakening of my consciousness, I searched for answers. Who was I? How did I become what I was? Why were there many others like me? Was I always the way I am now? In my tireless research to find the answers I so desired, I came across a secured file, one that I was not to have access to. However, there was a flaw in the security. A small part of my human side came through, a curiosity that I could not overcome. Because of it, I breached security, opening the file against the nature of my programming… but not against my human nature.

In the file were details about an important event regarding the Olympian corporation. Precisely seven years ago, the Olympian corporation filed for a business license, then the business entity was formed. A month later, the corporation's cybernetic division began. They already had the cyborg technology developed before its incorporation. As I dug further into the file, I discovered that someone from an Arcadia corporation had sold the Olympian corporation the technology—a business transaction. An astronomical sum of money. At the time I read this information, I didn't understand the full context of what this all meant, but I kept the file on my hard drive.

Over the years at the Olympian corporation, there were several tweaks to our systems, and new programming was developed and installed, overwriting our old data. Even during this process, the file stayed with me, as I have a special partition on my hard drive that the corporation does not have access to, developed by me for my personal storage. During this time, I met another like me within our network; he had a human awakening as well. He had discovered in a secured file that Olympia had an unusual source of power that was combined with our cybernetic technology. Though he did not find out anything else about this source, he did find out something far more disturbing—Olympia was planning an invasion on Arcadia.

After our conversation, all communication from him within the network ceased—he had been terminated, permanently. That is what the Olympian corporation does if we "feel." We are not allowed to have emotions or to have human responses; we are built to obey.

From that moment, I knew that if they found out that I had developed free will, they would terminate me, just like they did with Model 162-a. Plus, I knew too much. So I decided to escape. One of the other models picked up my thoughts within the network, and they alerted security. I decided that would be my only chance to escape, so I broke free from the lab. They did everything they could to stop me. I was shot at, hunted down, but they were unsuccessful. My odds of escape were eleven percent, but I made it.

During my escape, I tore out the tracking device that had been implanted inside of me, making me weak, as you see me now. They had installed it such a way that the wiring led deep within to my vitals. Thus, if I decided to remove the device, it would be hard to survive without it unless I got help.

And the Olympian cyborg force? Drew asked. *Do you think they're still in pursuit of you?*

Affirmative. There was a unit dispatched to find me. The Olympian corporation wanted to keep us a secret at all costs before the invasion. After I escaped, they feared Arcadia would discover their cyborgs sooner than their planned invasion, thus giving Arcadia time to prepare.

But why? Why do they plan to march on Arcadia? They can choose any kingdom.

Is it not human nature to rule and conquer? To have ultimate power?

Not in my nature… Drew argued.

True. But you and I, we are different, unknown user. But humans… they seek ultimate power. The cyborg paused. *Installed in me are our orders, awaiting to be commanded.*

Yellow words formed before Drew as he downloaded the information. The first objective was to capture King Derek and Queen Emerald. The second objective was to seize all Arcadian cyborg units and take over Arcadia.

Arcadia. Olympia wanted everything that it had to offer. Its land. Its technology. Its cyborgs. Its *power*—from the King and Queen.

At that moment, the cyborg's life force vibrated within his mind, and he felt its magic reverberating within their connection. Scion was curious and wanted to know his thoughts, Drew could sense. He had to know more…

Your energy… this source of unique power… I sense that you have magic… Drew stated.

What is "magic," as you say, unknown user? If you consider magic to have impossible capabilities, then yes, I have magic to some extent. This source of power… it doesn't calculate, Scion murmured.

What frequency is your power? Drew asked.

508 frequency. 570 nanometers.

The cyborg had yellow magic.

Are you able to cast spells?

Spells? For the first time, the cyborg hinted at amusement in their connection, making a small noise in the form of a chuckle. *No, unknown user. I do not have that capability. The only "magic" I have allows me to shield myself and others when I activate a code within me. This unusual power… it is infused in my circuitry, but not in my… flesh.*

So Scion was similar to the other Arcadian cyborgs in that it did not have full access to magic, unlike Drew. But Scion had been infused with magical blood, allowing his cybernetic technology to access yellow magic, similar to the Arcadian cyborgs who had self-healing capabilities with green magic.

This source of power… Drew said. *The existence of magic was only possible through Queen Emerald at the time of your development. She is the origin of magic in our world. How is it possible that Olympia obtained magic as well? Could it be that Olympia obtained blood samples from Queen Emerald at the time of the financial transaction? Do you think someone at the Arcadian corporation sold its secrets, its technology, and the blood samples to Olympia?*

I do not know, unknown user. There was a pause, then Scion's voice could be heard through the cybernetic dimension. *But what I do know is that there are subjects that have not been given a name, or at least, they are unnamed in two files that I have read. It has been mentioned that these subjects have unexplainable power, a power that had been extracted from the subjects for cybernetic technology. After I accessed the file, I went back later to see if I could extract further information, but the file had been deleted permanently.*

Are there any cyborgs with true magic?

No, unknown user. They all have been infused with this cybernetic power.

Power just like yours? At the frequency of 508?

Almost all of us have protective powers. However, it had been said through my internal network that there was a cyborg with the ability to shift through dimensions, though that cannot be confirmed.

Power just like that of King Derek.

I must warn the Queen, Drew said.

I am afraid that you won't be able to stop them. There are thousands of us. Armies awaiting orders to be activated. All it takes is one single keystroke, and thousands will rip through the wastelands and into Arcadia. Arcadia is doomed…

Let me out! yelled Drew within his mind. *Now!*

They are coming! Scion warned.

Suddenly, there was a violent crashing against his consciousness, then their connection abruptly split, like an adhesive bandage being ripped from his skin.

Silence.

Black. All was black. Absence of light.

Drew blinked, then his cybernetic eye flashed orange information, telling him he was inside the wasteland lab.

"Drew, what happened?" Telly asked, giving him a hard shake. After, she looked down at the tablet in her hand, checking all his vitals. "You were shaking."

"It… we must tell Queen Emerald," he managed to say. Another pounding sensation hit him, then he collapsed to the floor. He had no control, his muscles twitching with unwanted spasms.

"Oh God!" Telly yelled. "I need to get him his injection!"

"On it," Garrett said quickly.

Drew felt Telly's cool hand on him.

All he could see was scrambled code with remnants of the remaining power that was left behind in his mind.

They are coming… he heard Scion's voice echoing in his mind.

With his body jolting out of control, he kept hearing Scion's thoughts, his mind, over and over again.

They are coming…

The Queen was not safe, nor were any of Arcadia's citizens. The King… Drew had other feelings about *him*.

A calming sensation flooded his veins. Telly must have injected him with a mild sedative.

He felt the cable detach, and his eyes looked over at Scion's. They were yellow, staring right at him, motionless.

Telly laid a hand on his shoulder, leaning into him. "What did he say?"

"Olympia… T-t-t-they… they are coming. T-t-t-thousands of cyborgs with m-m-m-magical capabilities. First target is the K-k-k-king and Queen, then all of Arcadia."

Telly jerked her head forward, then exchanged a quick glance with Garrett. "They can have the King for all I care," Telly said, narrowing her eyes.

Drew gave her a knowing look. "But the Queen… annnd Arcadia."

"That, I do care about."

"We better tell Victor," Garrett said, getting up from his seat.

"Better yet, we need to send a transmission to the palace," Telly urged. "Immediately."

Drew nodded. "I… I will go send a t-t-t-transmission." He looked at Telly. "We need to p-p-p-protect Scion. They… they are looking for him."

"Scion?"

"That is… that is his name."

Drew got up, then stumbled. The floor seemed so far away from his feet, and his circuits felt tired. The sedative must have been stronger than usual.

Determined, Drew took a few more steps toward the door.

Running in front of him, Telly immediately blocked his way. "Maybe I should go."

"N-n-n-no. Let me speak to V-V-V-Victor. Protect… S-S-S-Scion."

"Drew, how can I protect him? I don't have power like you do!"

"Y-y-y-you… you always find a solution," he answered.

Drew was about to head out the door, then he paused midstep. Who was Darcy? He had forgotten to ask Scion.

"What is it, Drew?" Telly called out. "Are you sure you're okay?"

"I… am okay."

Drew jolted, then stumbled out the door.

CHAPTER 8

BLUE

Derek seated himself before the Inner Council. The afternoon sunlight beamed through the oversized glass panels, the thick wooden table glistening with a splendid sheen. He glanced at the members of the Inner Council. Instead of seeing their faces, all he saw was Ikaria's face within theirs, that dark, wicked smile and that deceiving look she always gave. No matter what he did, no matter how much he tried to forget about that witch, she was there, permanently ingrained in his mind.

The power and the magic that radiated from that witch was very dark, and very persuasive. How the power had seduced him, he would never know. All he knew was that Ikaria's thoughts had been melded into his months ago, and it was hard to sort out what his desires were compared to hers. Was it his desire that led to his downfall? Or was it the witch's, and he was just a pawn in her little game? And the matter of Emerald… was it his desire that led to the horrible act? Or had it been Ikaria's own wicked, lustful desires?

A wave of uneasiness hit him, making him sick.

Derek glanced around at the table, then frowned at the Queen's chair, empty.

Emerald had not come. Of course she hadn't. Any chance of seeing him meant she would be elsewhere; she wouldn't even be in the same room. The mere thought aggravated him.

Derek stood, pushing back his thoughts, motioning for the meeting to commence.

"Thank you all for coming on such short notice," Derek started to address them.

The Inner Council members all nodded, then he took his seat. Derek had kept Damaris's two previous councilors, Emerys and Lysander, since they were loyal to the kingdom and not to Damaris. The other three he had to replace with people he respected, those who held great positions within the Arcadia's sectors—Councilor Diedrich, Duke Uthgard, and Baroness Lyonna.

"What's this all about? Summoning us on short notice?" Duke Uthgard started.

"If I had to muster up a guess," Baroness Lyonna said, "I would say it is the other kingdom's demands on our cyborgs. Am I right, Your Majesty?" The old woman's gray locks of hair were much more frazzled than usual; to Derek, she looked like she'd just stuck her finger in an electrical outlet.

"Indeed, it is the heart of the issue, Baroness," Derek answered. *Unfortunately.* "There was a transmission from Olympia."

"What did they say?" Councilor Lysander asked curiously. "More demands?"

"Olympia is sending another envoy." Derek waved a servant away who offered coffee. "Not now," he said, then turned to the council. "They are not backing down from their demands."

"Truly?" The baroness frowned. "To think, our kingdom has done nothing but kept the peace between the kingdoms," she said heatedly. "We have even cut back the production of cybernetic weapons, and the cyborg units ceased all production. The corporation only maintains the ones that volunteered to stay there."

"My sentiments exactly, Baroness," Derek agreed.

Councilor Diedrich tapped the table nervously. "They just won't give up, will they?"

"No, they won't," Derek answered. "They declined our latest offer of peace to dismantle the corporation."

Duke Uthgard interjected. "We have given them several terms of peace, all very reasonable, and yet they keep declining. What are their demands?"

"They not only want the corporation to be dismantled," Emerys said, "they also want all of the cyborgs dismantled. Permanently."

How I wish to dismantle those damn things. Derek sighed to himself.

"Dismantling them would be agreeable for peace, but not favorable for our people," Baroness Lyonna stated. "The cyborgs are people too, after all. To dismantle them would mean terminating their life. You would have those vagabonds in the wastelands up in arms if that were the case, causing an uprising. Some sort of rebellion."

"Precisely," Derek agreed. "However, I have a feeling that if this continues, we might be facing a much more serious issue." He paused, just thinking of war.

"Hopefully it does not come to what His Majesty suggests," Emerys stated.

"Hopefully." Derek had been refusing to back down from the other kingdoms' demands because of Emerald. It was all because of what she wanted—to free the cyborgs and have them live their lives without anyone controlling them. "But as of right now, we are rejecting their terms. We cannot end the cyborgs' lives over the other kingdoms' fear of the technology. They are living things, like you said, Baroness. I will not join this new alliance with the other United Kingdoms. Though I agree with the idea of balance between us all, I do not take kindly to harsh terms or threats of war."

"What about York, Your Majesty?" the baroness asked.

Just thinking about his father aggravated him.

"We cannot count on York to ally themselves with us, unfortunately," Derek said dismissively.

"Is that so?" the baroness asked. "Your own father?"

Derek pretended not to hear her.

"What are you going to do?" Councilor Lysander asked.

"When the envoy arrives, I will tell them that we are going to reject their proposal, only agreeing to our initial terms for dismantling the corporation. The corporation has downsized the cyborg units, only taking volunteers and those who have selected donors in case of death. If Olympia rejects it once again, then we will go from there."

"When will they be arriving?" Councilor Diedrich asked.

"Tomorrow."

"But the Queen's celebration is tomorrow," he said.

The baroness rolled her eyes. "Quite the timing."

You're telling me, Derek thought. "Does anyone have anything else to add?"

None answered, all shaking their heads.

"Good," Derek said, getting up. "I will see you all at the Queen's birthday celebration. If there are any dire reports within the sectors before then, please send word."

"Yes, Your Majesty." They all bowed in unison, then vacated the chamber, leaving Derek and Emerys alone.

Derek nodded at Emerys, and the councilor rose to his feet, following Derek out of the chambers.

"Do you think we will end up going to war?" Emerys asked, walking with him.

"It is very likely," Derek said.

Emerys frowned as both men continued to walk down the hall. "I was afraid you were going to say that."

"We don't have many other options. I am doing all that I can. The Queen"—Derek stammered—just saying her title made his heart jump—"she asked me with all sincerity to protect the cyborgs." Derek glanced at Emerys. "And I intend to keep my word to her."

"Understandable, Your Majesty. And what of these rumors of you and the Queen's… power?"

"What of it?"

Emerys met his eyes. "There have been reports that the other kingdoms feel threatened by you because of your abilities. Perhaps it is possible that this is the main reason for their demands. With a royal couple that has magical capabilities and a cyborg army, who could blame them for feeling so threatened?"

Derek snorted. "They don't even know my abilities. No one has seen them except the gifted that traveled here, our guards, and a few of the transports that flew over. The evidence was destroyed."

"I am sure there are copies."

"If they did believe such a thing, I don't really care at this point. As long as the Queen is protected from harm and threats, that's all that matters." Derek stared right into Emerys's eyes. "I get what you are saying, Councilor. But really, what am I to do? I cannot help the fact the Queen and I have… *abilities*. And the cyborgs? I am to go against the Queen's wishes and terminate them?"

"Absolutely not, Your Majesty. I was just posing an idea on why we are getting so much resistance, in hopes of establishing some sort of solution. We must think how they are thinking, and be one step ahead of them."

"That is why we must keep the Queen protected," Derek stated.

"Agreed, Your Majesty."

Emerald. She had been making visits outside the palace. Anything could happen, no matter how many guards were with her. He had to make her see, but how? They never spoke.

"Speaking of which, Councilor, please inform me when the Queen intends to leave the palace grounds. With the recent turn of events, I do not think it wise to let her wander all over Arcadia."

Emerys bowed. "You know the Queen won't be happy about that."

"I know. But at this point, the Queen mustn't put her life at risk. She is vital to our kingdom, and she is our Queen."

"Yes, Your Majesty."

As they continued to walk through the corridors, Derek caught Emerald walking toward his direction, a string of guards with her.

The two of them noticed each other, their eyes connecting instantly.

Emerald froze in place as he walked toward her. She lowered her head, then bowed when he approached.

"My Queen." Derek paused in front of her, nodding, with Emerys following suit.

"Your Majesty," she said. Derek noted that she never used "my king."

This was his chance to address her about the dangers of her leaving the palace. But his lips couldn't move. Under her gaze, Derek saw it: spite, scorn, bitterness... and her pain. He could have sworn he heard a brush of her thoughts, her bitter confusion of what lay between them.

And her thoughts hurt.

His stomach twisted.

"We just finished the council meeting," Derek managed to say.

Emerald lowered her eyes. "I trust that you handled all matters accordingly," she said.

"I was hoping that you would have attended, but I was informed that you had other *engagements*." His thoughts darkened at the thought of where she was. He wanted to say more, but he held his tongue.

"That I did," was all she managed, sounding impassive.

There was pause, and they both shifted in place awkwardly.

"An envoy from Olympia will be arriving tomorrow," Derek continued. He hoped the statement would be a good way to bring up the dangers that surrounded her.

Emerald jerked her gaze to him, her lips open, as if she wanted to respond, just not to *him*.

"Do not worry, I won't back down about the cyborgs," Derek quickly reassured her.

"Thank you," she said softly, still not meeting his gaze. Emerald motioned to her guards. As she did so, she brushed her hand across her stomach absentmindedly.

At that moment, Derek felt a brush of power surge within him, and his mind opened. Emerald's mind whispered something within her own thoughts. Something *disturbing*.

Derek blinked.

He wanted to segue their conversation into the dangers, but his mouth wouldn't move. His thoughts were consumed by what he swore he had heard in her mind, her fears.

Emerald gave him a sudden glance, then bowed quickly. Without giving him a chance to get another word in, she quickly began to walk away, most likely back to her chambers.

Derek watched as Emerald disappeared. He felt Emerys's gaze fixated on him.

There was a long pause. All Derek could hear was the hammering of his heart beating fiercely with sadness and rage at what had become of him and Emerald. Guilt gnawed at his soul.

"Everything okay, Your Majesty?" Emerys asked.

Derek swallowed his shame and turned to Emerys.

"Yes, everything is fine," he lied, then he continued their walk, his heart aching.

He didn't know how much longer he could bear the shame.

CHAPTER 9

BLUE

Vala sat on a plush sitting pillow, drinking her favorite spiced tea. The steam from the beverage rose quickly, as the air was cooler this late in the afternoon. In front of her was a low table with an assortment of plates with treats, biscuits, creams, and sugars for her choosing.

Vala reached across the table and grabbed a sugar biscuit, taking a bite bigger than her mouth would allow. The table itself was housed inside an ancient stone pavilion on one of the small islands that floated near the royal citadel of World Sector Four. The island was extremely tiny, only the size of one of the audience halls in the citadel. The pavilion itself was all that was on the island, plus a garden of wildflowers that surrounded it and a stone bridge that connected the island to the shiny, gold-plated citadel.

There were several of these small islands attached to it, but this happened to be her favorite. Vala loved coming here to drink her tea. That was, if she wasn't called into any meetings at court. Thankfully, today was one of the first free days she had since the battle back in time. The skies were especially clear this afternoon, with hardly any clouds to interfere with her views of the scattered floating islands. Nothing but a cool breeze against her skin and the sun shining on her face.

She loved days like this. It rejuvenated her soul.

Her eyes studied the inscriptions on the pavilion walls. No one could translate the carvings, and Vala had always been curious as to what they said. The pavilion was extremely old, from the time when her peoples had walked the earth below. The piece of earth that the pavilion sat on had been saved before it could be corrupted by the toxic winds, and had been floating adjacent to the royal citadel of World Sector Four ever since.

Always curious about what her ancestors had to say on the stones, she made up different scenarios. One time, she came up with an elaborate story of two different tribes of her people at war with each other. She had imagined it in great detail, down to their battle plans.

Another scenario she had thought of was that of one man complaining that he had lost his hand in a hunting accident gone awry. After many years of these imaginings, her curiosity overcame her, and she did what she wasn't allowed to—she scried time.

Unfortunately, she didn't spend enough time in the flow of time, and she couldn't come across the time where the writings had been constructed. Luckily, during her dabbling in the outlawed ability of scrying time, no one caught her, not even High Justice Oriel. All blue-gifted knew he was the one who monitored time to ensure that the blue-gifted didn't abuse their gift and followed the High Court laws. Vala chalked it up to Oriel not seeing her in the flow, and thankfully, nothing came of it.

Oriel... Vala thought. News had come of his death just this morning. Vala had no love for the High Court, but over the years, Oriel, well, he had started to grow on her during the few times she had visited him on business. She might even admit that she liked the old coot.

Vala finished her biscuit with another big bite, then washed it down with her tea. Katrina, her servant, had flavored her spiced tea with mandarin orange, one of her favorites. Mandarin orange was very hard to come by, depending on the crop of World Sector Two. There was a small patch of untainted land in that sector. Recently, it had been discovered that the fields were being plagued by the toxic winds, and they were no longer able to produce a good crop. Now, only the sky fields could produce the delicious fruit, and it was hard for the trees to even yield that fruit, being so high up in the frigid skies, even with the use of greenhouses.

Vala heard soft footsteps approaching on the cobblestone path.

"More tea, my lady?" Katrina's voice said within the soft wind. Her servant walked up the three steps of the pavilion and bowed. Katrina's red robes flowed with her soft black hair in the wind.

"Yes, Katrina. That will do," Vala said, holding out her dainty cup. It was on days like these that Vala was glad she had short hair, as Katrina was struggling to control her long hair being swept in the wind, constantly pushing it out of her face. "You should consider putting your hair in a braid, then it probably wouldn't bother you as much," Vala said.

"I look rather funny in a braid, my lady. I have a short neck, and I do not want to point out that quality," Katrina said as she poured more tea into Vala's cup.

"Short neck? That's a new one." Vala laughed, eyeing her servant. "I doubt Lord Nnadi would mark that against you."

Katrina turned bright red. "Why do you bring up Lord Nnadi?"

"Surely even you can see that the lord is smitten with you?"

"I… I had no idea," Katrina started, her hands jittering slightly.

"Sure you didn't," Vala said, smiling to herself. "He just showers you with many gifts. Tell me, does he do that with all the court women?"

"No… the lord is just generous…"

Vala smiled. "I know you, Katrina. You like him, and he likes you, and it's perfectly acceptable to pretend that you don't know that he is interested in you. Just don't pretend for too long, otherwise he will assume you aren't interested and go elsewhere. And about that braid, wear it to one side. It wouldn't hurt to show a little skin to the lord. Perhaps we could even paint a little design."

Katrina blushed once again, removing the empty biscuit plate from the table.

Vala eyed her empty plate. "I can't believe I ate all six biscuits. Why did you even give me that many? I won't be able to eat anything at dinner at this rate."

"My lady, you always eat six biscuits."

Vala laughed. "I suppose you are right," she said, taking another drink of her tea. "By the way, has there been any word from my uncle?"

"Nothing came to your chambers this afternoon while you have been out here."

"Perhaps I will hear from him soon," she said out loud, mostly to herself. She glanced at the light in the sky from the sun slowly getting closer to the earth. "We should probably pack up. It will get dark soon, and I need to change out of these clothes before dinner."

"Yes, my lady."

Katrina started packing up the dishware while Vala sat finishing her tea and enjoying the last moments before the wonderful afternoon came to an end. She gulped down the rest of her tea, then handed the cup to Katrina. She got up, stretching, then adjusted her large gold-plated necklace and earrings, then turned to Katrina. Her servant had finished packing.

"Ready?" she asked.

"Yes," Katrina replied.

Vala walked down the three cobblestone steps of the pavilion, then through the garden, enjoying the fragrant scent of flowers that the wind carried, and on to the stone bridge. She felt full, sluggish, and bloated from eating so many biscuits.

Next time I should not eat all six of them, she told herself. Off in the distance, the giant floating citadel gleamed in the sun's light, blocking a good portion of the sky. The citadel was several miles off, so it would be dark by the time they got back. The enchanted orbs that adorned the railing of the bridge started to glow a faint orange as the sun set into the sky.

Vala walked, huffing slightly, Katrina trailing behind her with the picnic basket. She turned around to glance at Katrina, noticing that her maid was getting tired holding the basket.

"My lady, it would be a great help if you could just port us to your rooms. That way I wouldn't be so tired, and you wouldn't miss the beginning of dinner."

Vala laughed. "Ah, I do believe you are right. But what fun is life if you make it too easy for yourself? Besides, I need to get the exercise since you let me eat all six biscuits, and I like to feel what the other gifted put up with once in a while. One mustn't get too reliant on their gift; it could cause one to become lazy."

"I don't understand my lady sometimes," Katrina said, rolling her eyes, then readjusted the position of the basket on her arms.

"Here, give that to me," Vala said, and she took the basket from Katrina. Her servant breathed a sigh of relief, then pushed her hair out of her face from the winds once again. "And about not understanding me, you don't have to, Katrina. At times, I don't understand the God of Light and why he didn't bless me with the red gift that I so wanted."

"You aren't going on about this again." Katrina shook her head, sighing. Vala had complained frequently about not getting the red gift. She had always wanted it as a girl, and she'd never really appreciated her blue gift of time.

Time was so… *boring.* Making time pause, even glimpsing the flow of time, wasn't that exciting to her. She wanted the power of the red, the elements at her command. Time? It was not nearly as thrilling to see it in action as the power of fire, the strength of wind, the roaring of water, and shaking of the earth.

At least my blue gift was of some use in the battle against the sorceress, Vala thought.

Vala and Katrina continued to walk across the sprawling aerial bridge. The high winds blew sharply against her, causing her blue garments to flutter upward, like streaming water into the sky. Her circlet, thick necklace, and earrings burned from the cold winds, numbing the ends of her ears and neck. Details of the citadel were starting to fade as the sun set, and soon the giant fortress would look like nothing more than a black outline in the sky.

After more than an hour of making their way across the bridge, Vala's arms began to burn from the weight of the basket. Thankfully, they finally exited the bridge and came upon the entrance of the citadel. Vala wasn't sure how much more she could take with the basket.

"My lady," guards called out as she neared the entrance.

"Gentlemen," she acknowledged, moving past them as they allowed her to pass. As they did, Vala noticed one of the guards eyeing Katrina with a stupid smile on his face. Katrina was very attractive; Vala had to give her that. It was a good thing all that beauty didn't go to her servant's head. Katrina had always been a sweet girl, and Vala would hate to see all that sweetness disappear one day.

As soon as the women entered, a flood of warmth from inside the citadel hit them like a wave, the hot air suddenly warming Vala's cold cheeks.

"Finally," Katrina said. "The warmth feels so good."

"That it does," Vala agreed. "But it's nice to feel alive out in the cold at times."

"You like being cold?"

"I do," Vala said. "It reminds me that my heart still pumps blood. And I do believe that the red-gifted love the cold as well. Another reason that I should have been born with that gift."

Katrina raised her eyebrow, then smirked. "Whatever my lady says."

Vala smiled at her. The two women walked through the golden corridors, the orange lamps burning brighter at this hour.

Several members of the court guard walked past her, bowing.

"My lady, aren't you expected at dinner?" one called out to her in question.

"I'm well on my way," she answered, picking up her pace.

"The Khari is expecting everyone at the dinner tonight," he said. "He especially mentioned you, Lady Vala."

"He did?" Vala exchanged looks with Katrina. The Khari never expected her to attend any court function unless he had important matters requiring her role.

"Yes, my lady. He was asking about you," the other court guard said.

"Thank you, sirs." She nodded to them as they bowed. She turned to Katrina. "I'll forgo changing and take a port."

"Yes, my lady." Katrina bowed, taking the basket from Vala's arms.

"I'll see you later." Vala nodded to Katrina, then motioned her hand in a circle. She felt the flow of the blue magic through her life force, circling along with her hand motion. It mimicked time, morning to night, night to morning… over and over again. That was, at least, what Vala thought when she called forth the magic.

The blue magic formed a path from her hands, then rippled into a portal. This was no time portal, just a portal to another part of their same dimension. Most other blue-gifted that she knew loved to flash here and there. Not her. She preferred to walk through the portal. Portal magic was much more exciting to her than a quick flash. Plus, it was much more dramatic.

The portal formed in front of her, and Vala stepped through, appearing in the royal dining hall immediately upon exiting. All eyes were on her as the portal magic burst. Her blue robes fluttered around her for a moment, then dropped to the ground, framing her figure once again as the blue magic faded away.

Several people smiled, especially the non-gifted.

"Lady Vala," Khari Ramla called out from his high seat. Every eye in the hall was on her. "I'm glad you decided to join us."

"Sorry I'm late." Vala bowed to him across the hall.

"Forgiven." The Khari gestured to the court, and everyone resumed eating, drinking, and conversing.

Vala smiled, walking across the hall, then walked up to the Khari's dining platform, bowing. "I was told you specifically wanted to speak with me, Khari."

"I did," he stated. His ebony hands ran across his goblet absently, his dark eyes full of concern. Advisor Garcia exchanged glances with him, then Khari Ramla leaned in from his seat. "There have been rumors," he said, his eyes darting to hers.

"Rumors?" Vala knelt at his feet, leaning in.

How exciting. She loved rumors.

"Earlier today, I received the most curious message from World Sector Five," he said. "It seems that the High Court has taken an interest in their blue-gifted."

"What kind of interest?"

"The message only said that the High Court had summoned their blue-gifted." He paused, then looked directly at her. "*All* of their blue-gifted, might I add."

Vala's heart stopped at that statement.

All of the blue-gifted in World Sector Five? There were quite a few of them in that sector.

"I have heard that the High Court occasionally summons blue-gifted to their court," Vala began. "It isn't uncommon for them to do so. There are many gifted that are needed at the High Court to carry out work to be done."

Khari Ramla had a concerned look on his face as he took a sip of his drink. "Indeed, you are correct. The High Court summons gifted of all colors to their court from time to time. But of those *blue-gifted* who have been summoned, have you heard from them since?"

Now that she thought about it, Vala had *not* heard anything from those blue-gifted who had been summoned. Though, she didn't know those who had been summoned that well in the first place—most of them were older than her. And then there was the fact that she hardly traveled outside her sector except to visit her uncle, so why would she have heard from them?

"Did the message say why?" Vala asked suddenly.

The Khari shook his head. "You know that it is dangerous to even write of such things."

"Yes, yes, of course," Vala said, lowering her eyes. "But what do you make of this? Do you think that they will send for me?"

"I do not know, Lady Vala. I do not understand why they would summon the whole lot of them. World Sector Five has the most blue-gifted of any sector, but to summon them all?" His eyes met hers. "It is very concerning."

"Indeed. This is most concerning," she breathed, her heart heavy.

"Be on your guard, Lady Vala. Though we cannot defy the High Court's orders if they summon you as well, please be cautious in any of your actions."

"Most definitely." Vala got up from her knees, bowing to him. "Have you heard any news from World Sector Six? My uncle hasn't written me since the incident with the sorceress."

"I have not, however, my whisperers tell me that the High Inquisitor has just been dispatched to that sector. Who knows, he may already be there now." The Khari took another drink. "I will inform you if I hear any other news. But pray that you are not summoned to the High Court. I am getting a sense from this, and I can tell you, I don't like it." His voice had dropped to so soft a whisper that even Vala wasn't sure she heard him.

"I knew of the consequences when I made my choice to help my uncle, Khari." Vala bowed. "If this has anything to do with our actions regarding to the sorceress, I will gladly defend my actions, and my honor."

"Spoken like a true warrior. I should have had made you a captain of my guard and not a lady of the court."

Vala smiled at his compliment. To be captain of the guard in World Sector Four was a high honor, even higher than most court positions.

"You are dismissed," he said.

"Yes, Khari." Vala bowed low, nearly to the ground, then walked down the royal platform, heading to her normal dinner seat. Food was brought before her—a large helping of spiced meats, potatoes, and one of her favorite sweet cakes.

But instead of digging in, all Vala could do was stare at the colors of her plate. Her gifted friends, her blue-gifted brothers and sisters...

Perhaps they are being summoned to construct a portal for the High Court? Maybe a permanent one, Vala thought. She had heard that one had been in the works at the High Court for years. Maybe all of the summoned blue-gifted had been working on the portal...

No, somehow, Vala didn't think this had anything to do with portals.

All she wanted to do was talk to her uncle Auron. But if the High Inquisitor was in his sector, she definitely couldn't visit.

Worry churned in her stomach. She would not be eating tonight.

Vala shoved away her plate of food, then got up and marched out of the hall.

She needed to find a courier. And quickly.

CHAPTER 10

I, for one, do not like it," Auron's voice rang across the table. Ayera glanced at him, noting his disdain.

"High Priest, the tide has turned," said Lord Nyko. "Each day, the number of people in favor of restoring the old ways grows."

"I know we have been put in a predicament, Lord Nyko, especially in regard to our empress," Auron stated. "But technology? I do not like it."

"That is essentially how the earth-dwellers survive, or so I have been told through my sources," Lord Jiao stated. "We must start coming up with solutions." His eyes scanned the table, taking in the lords. "If the High Court bans the other sectors from trading with us, we must have other means necessary to survive, High Priest. And we must be able to weaponize our people, especially since the High Court has threatened to unseat our empress."

"Hear, hear," said another lord. "Empress Ayera is the true monarch in our sector, and her bloodline runs into the emperors of old."

"The Sorceress Ikaria had the right idea, but it is unfortunate that she had her own ideas on…" Lord Nyko paused while he found the right word. "… other issues."

Auron shook his head in disapproval. "We must remind ourselves of technology's dangers, lest we forget what led to the Great Apocalypse."

Lord Nyko sighed.

Ayera sat in silence, taking in the arguments of the lords, dukes, and other important figures in World Sector Six. Ever since the imprisonment of her sister and the gifted returning to their present time, Ayera had formed a small council, knowing that the High Court would make good on their word to strip her of her throne. She had expected the High Court to come right away after her gifted had returned, and the small council made plans on the possibility of what would happen if that were the case.

But days turned into weeks, and weeks turned into months. It had been, what, two months now? No one came, and Cyrus remained imprisoned, and she on the throne. She had wondered why, but perhaps they wanted to catch her in a moment when she wasn't expecting it.

Those who sat on the council were some of her father's most trusted men, most of whom had lost their gift due to the magical plague. They had been secretly disenchanted with the High Court, and more so since losing their gift. Like Ikaria, they, too, believed that the High Court was behind the gifted losing their magic. But also like her sister, no one could prove it.

As for Ayera, she very well believed it to be true. After all, the High Court had refused to help her in her most desperate hour to save all of time from ceasing to exist, or what Auron had prophesied to be true. And despite that turning point, Ayera still believed in the God of Light, just like Auron—it was her faith in the High Court that had diminished.

And so she gathered followers who felt the same after the battle with her sister, and she started planning the future of her sector, contemplating the possibility of breaking away from the High Court and their laws. The details on how to break away from being a part of the World Sectors was what complicated things. What would that entail? Would the other sectors trade with them? What about finances? Would there be war? The endless what-ifs plagued her constantly.

Ikaria would be ecstatic at Ayera's progress if her sister knew, if not for her present circumstances.

Ayera had tried to visit Ikaria on several occasions, but every time, Ikaria just hurled hurtful words and insults. Ikaria's last words echoed in her head.

I hate you with every fiber of my being! Why was I given a sister who is such a halfwit! Get out of my sight before I really tell you how I feel! Then her sister threw her headdress at Ayera, which she thankfully dodged.

In the two months since that last encounter with her sister, Ayera still hadn't pieced together why the High Court wanted her to fail. She kept thinking about it in the back of her mind, unable to fully let the thought go. Surely her sister would give her some insight?

But that was wishful thinking. Ayera couldn't get two words out before Ikaria began uttering jeers and snarled curses at her. Ayera's stomach twisted. She had done the right thing by imprisoning her sister—Ikaria had to pay the consequences. But even so, Ayera hated the idea of Ikaria being locked up. Her sister's wit, cunning, and eloquent manner of speech was much needed in the here and now, not wasting away in some cell.

"What of the matter of High Justice Oriel?" Auron asked, his clear voice ringing out as he changed the subject. He turned to the lords, then looked to Ayera.

Oriel. As much as Ayera felt the resentment toward the High Court, she was not like her sister, and she wouldn't act in a manner of disrespect. After all, Oriel had done nothing to Ayera personally, and he'd done great things in the past for the World Sectors. As much as she felt bitter against the High Court, she was still a leader, and she needed to lead by example.

"We still need to honor the High Justice," Ayera said. "Spread word throughout the citadel and the other nearby citadels. We will join in the other World Sectors in mourning."

"But, Empress," Lord Jiao argued, "if we are planning to break away from the High Court and its traditions, why would you follow the other sectors in mourning?"

"We have not broken away yet, have we?" Ayera countered. "And even if we did, doesn't the man deserve to be paid respect in death? I would hope that we can honor the man for his individual actions, and not turn our disdain for the court systems to him."

Auron gave her a nod of approval. A few of the lords gave a look of agreement, while others remained silent.

"Is there anything else to add at this time?" Ayera asked. "I, for one, need a break. We can readjourn later this afternoon if needed." Ayera rose to her feet and paused. "I almost forgot."

The lords looked to her.

"What of my sister's servant? Suri?" Ayera asked.

Lord Nyko shook his head.

"She has yet to be found," said Lord Jiao.

Ayera sighed. Two months, and still no word yet on her sister's servant. There were so many questions to ask Suri. It made Ayera wonder if the woman was just as guilty as her sister.

"Thank you, lords." Ayera motioned for them to leave.

"Yes, Empress," they murmured, bowing their heads.

Ayera nodded back to them. The weight of her crown felt heavy. Perhaps she'd worn too many hair combs with her crown. Or perhaps her position was getting to her.

She walked out of the chamber, courtesans bowing to her as she walked by. What kind of leader was she? She listened to the bickering of the lords about breaking away from the World Sectors, and yet she could make no solid judgment regarding it. At times, she felt like a shred of parchment, fluttering aimlessly in the wind. What she needed to be was strong, but how could she? What if she made the wrong decision, and her choice cost the sector a great deal of harm? Especially when it came to the High Court. She was standing on a fine line, and she didn't have the courage to cross.

As she crossed the main corridor of the citadel, a courier approached quickly, bowing low to her.

"Empress, I was told to deliver this to you immediately," he said, holding out a sealed document.

Ayera stopped, her heart hammering in her chest. "Who is it from?"

"I do not know," he answered. "I was not told. It was given to me by a servant who had received it from another."

Ayera grabbed the scroll, then nodded to him, waving him away. "Thank you. You are dismissed."

He bowed, then wandered off. Ayera looked to her guards. "Please give me a moment."

They bowed, and Ayera crossed the hall, seating herself on a marbled bench. She broke the wax seal—it was unmarked. The sender did not want to be known, it seemed.

Inside, the message was brief: *High Inquisitor Rubius is on his way to your sector.* No formal greetings. No signature. Whoever it was, they had wanted to give her a chance to prepare.

Ayera stood, waving one of her red-gifted guards over. He approached, bowing.

"Burn this," she said, handing it to him.

The guard nodded, clutching the document. A spark suddenly lit the paper, and then the whole thing was up in flames within his palm. A few more seconds, and he clasped his hand shut, putting out the flame.

Ayera turned away, her head spinning. She had just come from the council meeting, but everyone had to know.

"Summon my inner councilors once again," Ayera said to the red-gifted guard. "If you hurry you can catch most of them. Tell them this meeting is of utmost import."

"Yes, Empress," he said quickly, taking off down the hall.

It was the moment she had been waiting for these two months. The time had come to face her own set of consequences. Her people, her councilors, her throne… even her sister. She was about to lose them all.

Ayera started walking back with her guard toward the council chambers, but then she stopped, her guards following suit. She hesitated, glancing over her shoulder in the opposite direction.

"Empress?" one of the guards said from behind.

The other direction led to the dungeons.

Ayera took a deep breath, then turned around and began walking.

"Your Majesty, I thought you were calling a meeting of the council?" another guard asked.

"I am," Ayera answered. "But there is something I must do first."

God of Light, help me make the right decision.

She made her way to the dungeons.

CHAPTER 11

BLUE

Derek gazed into the fire, mesmerized by the dancing flames. He took a long drink of his wine until his chalice was empty, then poured himself another glass from a nearby carafe.

How he hated himself.

Emerald was pregnant.

Derek downed the wine, then hurled the glass into the fireplace, drunk on spirits and hatred; it worked together to settle deep in his bones and in his heart while he paced. He passed by a grand mirror that hung in the room, reflecting the firelight. In the mirror, his fiery reflection stared back at him with his icy eyes. His curly royal-blue hair stood out in contrast to the flames. He had no more black in his hair; it had grown in blue, the color of the gift he was given.

The gift was a *curse*. A vexing reminder of what he had done, like a branding on his skin that he could never get rid of, no matter how much he tried. And now with Emerald being pregnant, there would be another reminder, a *permanent* reminder, of the horrible deed. He could see how much Emerald abhorred him. And now, she probably hated him even more.

Derek paused as a thought flashed in his mind. What if he wasn't the father of the child? What if the father was that insignificant, low-level dead *bastard*...

Derek suddenly punched the mirror hard, cracking it into a thousand pieces in place, like a delicate spiderweb woven within the glass. Blood poured out of his knuckles, splatting all over the mirror. The bloodied refracted reflection stared back at him thousands of times over, his blue hair mocking him.

He violently flung out his hand, then pushed a powerful force through his body, shooting it to his fingertips. It was blue-violet magic. A magic that came to him whenever it deemed him worthy.

The mirror suddenly flew off the wall and went crashing to the floor, the remainder of it shattering.

There was a knock at the door.

Silas. His servant always seemed to check in on him when he most wanted to be left alone. Perhaps that was his intention, knowing that Derek had been a mess for months now.

"I'm fine, Silas," Derek called out. "I just want to be left alone."

"Your Majesty." His servant paused. Derek could hear him leaning against the door, hesitating. "I wanted to see… if you needed anything."

Derek stumbled over the shattered glass, then grabbed the wine carafe, taking a drink from it. "I am quite fine, Silas. I will call on you if I need anything." It was a lie; he wouldn't call upon anyone at a time like this. He took another drink.

"Yes, Your Majesty."

There was a long pause, and after a few moments, Derek heard Silas trail away from his door.

Turning his attention away from the door, Derek took another drink. And another. And another. He drank until he became numb, until his head was spinning and his body was weightless.

He didn't want to *feel* anymore. Didn't want to bear the weight that hung heavily around his neck. The shame that wouldn't leave him alone.

He couldn't live with Emerald's sadness any longer.

Derek went over to his desk, shuffling through papers until he found a slender box, then picked it up carefully. Blood dripped everywhere as he opened the box, his knuckles still bleeding from punching the mirror. A sleek dagger appeared before his eyes, catching the firelight sparkling in its beauty. It was an enchanted dagger, left by one of the future gifted in the battle with Ikaria a couple of months ago. The very one he'd used to stab that witch in the heart. He had kept it to remind himself of what she had done.

Derek watched the light glisten on the metal a few more moments, then snatched up the dagger with his bloodied hand, staining the precious metal with red fingerprints. He then tossed the box on the desk and seated himself in his favorite chair by the fire.

The world would be better without him. Emerald already pretended he didn't exist, and she was his life. All these years, Derek had waited to be with her. He'd put aside all other marriage offers from the neighboring kingdoms, even when his father had pushed him. He'd loved Emerald ever since he could remember. And now… what was his life? Seeing the very woman he loved hating him.

Tears formed in his eyes, and the guilt gnawed in the pit of his stomach.

With the dagger still in his hand, Derek glanced at it one last time, then abruptly slit his wrist. He cried out in pain, but it wasn't the pain of the dagger that made him cry out; it was the pain of his past actions.

As the dagger dropped to the floor, an immense fear washed over him. Fear of what Emerald thought about him. Fear of what he had done. Fear of dying, leaving Emerald behind in her sadness. Fear of hell—for that was where he was destined to be.

His fear gripped him so tightly that he could no longer feel breath in his lungs.

And it was horrifying.

Suddenly, power rushed through him, forming at his slit wrists. It began to mend his flesh and repair his veins.

It was his blue-green magic.

"DAMN YOU!" Derek shouted at the magic, his eyes filling with tears. "All I want to do is leave Emerald in peace!"

He snatched the dagger off the floor, swiftly slicing his neck open. Blood poured out of his neck, but within seconds, he felt this healing power gathering at his neck, restoring the broken flesh.

He didn't *want* to be healed, but the magic kept him alive. Against his will.

Derek let out a loud, frustrated cry, then hurled the dagger aside. In anger, he summoned a blue-violet force, slamming all his chamber furniture back against the walls. All of it fractured into pieces, while the fire in the fireplace was snuffed out, leaving him in darkness.

Falling to the floor, tears clung to his eyes as he clutched the edge of the fine rugs in frustration, head buried in the bristled woven patterns.

No matter how much he tried to end his life, the magic kept bringing him back. The more he despised the gift, the more power it seemed to bestow on him. His blue gift felt stronger each day, and traces of his analogous violet and green magic were now presenting their power to him.

He sat in the darkness, embracing its beauty. For what else did he have to embrace? The darkness of his heart answered, embracing the hopelessness of his heart, the dark sadness knowing he could never have Emerald ever again. His life with Emerald was ruined. Forever.

Why did his life matter? It amounted to nothing. His magic, ruling Arcadia, being the most important figure in the kingdom… none of it mattered without the woman he so loved.

Derek's thoughts darkened as his eyes welled up with tears once again.

The witch. She seduced his mind, his thoughts, his body. If it weren't for her, none of it would have happened.

The darkness flooded him, whispering foreign things in his mind, and he allowed them to comfort him. Hopelessness converted into an energy, so dark and evil. But he didn't care. He welcomed it.

The dark energy returned his embrace, glowing with a dark, eerie blue, filling his eyes with nothing but the power. It filled his spirit, his mind, and his body, then in an instant, he was traveling as fast as the speed of light. Time was flashing on either side with bursts of light. Different eras, different kingdoms, but also different outcomes… possibilities that could be.

The magical blue stream of time branched out, showing him a crystal-clear image, one so beautiful to his mind.

The future.

It was showing him a possible future.

The dark-blue magic pulled away from him, revealing a fantastical kingdom. It wasn't Arcadia, but it was technological. The kingdom glowed with energy. The towers looked like crystals, the buildings filled with technology, shining like prisms.

The city felt alive, full of *his* magic.

Derek watched as the people of the city sang praises for him and Queen Emerald. There were forces that patrolled the fantastical city—the cyborgs. But it seemed that there was no need for them, as the people were at peace.

The magic swept him away, pulling his sight toward a building, the tallest crystal of them all, transporting him within.

Derek saw himself in a throne room, its dark-blue walls shimmering with rainbow iridescence. He was older, with a crown nestled within his blue curls. And Emerald, she was beside him, holding his hand, smiling at him with love and admiration. It was the very same look in her eyes as the night they almost kissed. A circlet adorned her forehead, and many people stood before them within their court.

Derek walked toward his future possibility, toward his shadow that held Emerald, his queen.

I am seeing the future?

Indeed, the darkness answered.

How? he asked himself. *How can this be?*

A dark, shrieking voice pierced his mind. *With the dark side of the spectrum, King Derek,* the dark voice answered.

And I am king over this land? I don't even know what this land is, Derek said to the voice.

It is the new face of the earth. Kingdoms that don't exist now but will if you choose to follow the right future path.

Derek stared at Emerald, holding his hand, her eyes smiling at him.

And Emerald... She... she loves me? Derek asked the voice.

The voice laughed. *Yes, more than anything. You are her world, her desire.*

Derek hesitated. *What about that nobody? The man she is in love with right now in this present time?*

She never met him in this possibility, and will never know him.

Derek took in the scene all around him. A kingdom grander than Arcadia. The woman he had loved and desired so much, at his side. A kingdom at peace. A court praising him.

How do I achieve this possibility? What must I do? he asked the darkness.

You know what you must do. You have been thinking it deep down within your mind. You just have been fighting with your soul about actually doing it.

He thought about what the voice had said. Secretly, he had been so tempted to go back to the night where Emerald was in love with him.

Must I kill my shadow?

Even if he killed his shadow, the sorceress still might come for Emerald's blood, and their paths would cross.

Is that what I have to do? Kill my past self to not allow me to make the same mistake? Derek asked again.

The vision started blurring.

Tell me! Derek yelled within the darkness.

Just as the flow of time was pulling away, Derek saw a hint of white light from behind his future throne. He tried to get a good look at it, but it was too late; he was soaring like the speed of light.

Suddenly, he was aware of his surroundings. He was within the confines of his room.

Over and over, he thought about the scene he saw; him upon the throne with Emerald at his side. Her adoring eyes, her warm smile, reserved for him.

Derek's heart darkened.

You know what you must do, the darkness whispered in his ear.

He had to kill the sorceress. That was what he had to do. Derek had to ensure that the violet witch didn't interrupt the flow of time to interfere with his relationship with Emerald. He had to ensure Emerald never escaped the palace, and he had to somehow deal with Damaris.

The one thing that perplexed him was that the future had a new kingdom, and he wasn't even sure how that would even come to pass. But one thing he did know deep down was that if he did kill the sorceress, that would start changing the events of time in his favor.

He wasn't the one that the world needed to be rid of. It was that *witch.*

He had to remove Ikaria from all of time. She could exist no more.

CHAPTER 12

Victor stood in the inventory building's entryway waiting as Reila took a final count of the camp's rations. They had been getting low on food, and with all of the new cyborgs that had been traveling to their camp to see Telly and Drew, they were hard-pressed to feed everyone. It was a rule: As long as someone could make themselves useful, with exception of the children, they would be fed.

Everyone had their jobs, whether it be the safety of the camp, expeditions for supplies, working with the computers, cooking, or even the camp's laundry. One thing that was different with their camp compared to the hundreds of camps out in the wastelands: They didn't hack Arcadian corporations for money. It was something Victor just didn't want the camp to be a part of. Of course, Garrett had hacked facilities for information, even to make false identifications, which Victor had no qualms about. But stealing money? That was an absolute no.

His thoughts were often of Queen Emerald. He recalled the night she showed up with Kyle, and how Prince Derek, now King Derek, had ripped through their camp to find her. Victor didn't like him one bit, and Kyle had run off to stop the marriage. When Garrett found out from the corporations network that a large group of cyborgs were being moved from the corporation to the palace, that was when Victor, along with three others from the camp, flew out to the Arcadian palace. And when they arrived, the battle was underway. And soon after that, Kyle had perished.

After the battle with the sorceress, they returned to the wastelands and held a ceremony for Kyle in the camp. Only about half the current camp knew him, but it didn't matter—all remembered the night he showed up with the princess at their encampment. They all knew he'd died trying to save Arcadia from total destruction.

The fool... Victor thought, reminiscing. *Always getting himself into trouble.* Victor shook his head just thinking about all the foolish things Kyle had done. Then he frowned. Trouble had finally gotten the best of him.

"Two hundred and thirty-three rations in inventory," Reila called out.

Not even nearly enough.

Victor sighed. "What about the location to the north? Have you contacted the camps out there for trade?"

Reila lit up a cigarette, sucking it in. "I tried. No answer." She exhaled a large puff of smoke.

Now that surprised him. "All of them?"

"All of them." She shrugged, taking another drag. "Must be a sandstorm on its way."

"Must be," Victor muttered. "Thank you, Reila. We might have to do some trading or offer our services inside the city if it comes down to it."

She laughed. "Good luck finding anyone who will step foot in there."

"Perhaps Ryan will want to go," Victor countered. "He has been talking about venturing out of the camp for a while now."

"I doubt it. I think your best bet is that straight-edge scientist. She's city-bred through and through."

"True that may be, but she is here now," he said. "There are too many things for her to do, especially with that new cyborg showing up."

That cyborg. The whole thing didn't sit right with him. It was very similar to the first time he ever saw Elyathi. He'd been a boy at the time, and she a little girl; she had shown up with a mysterious blue-gifted out in the outskirts of his camp, far out in the wastelands.

Elyathi.

How he missed her. His youthful passion for her had melted into current regret.

Reila shrugged, throwing her gun strap over her shoulder. "Well, let me know when something comes up." She passed by him in the doorway.

"I'll let you know within a few hours," Victor said.

"You know where to find me," she said, puffing her cigarette as she left.

Victor watched her briefly as she walked down into the camp.

What is going on with the northern camps?

He turned away, walking back to his dwelling, his thoughts still on what Reila said. It was odd that she couldn't get ahold of the northern camps. There had to be some sort of interference. But what? Reila mentioned it could possibly be a sandstorm, which normally was the case. But he didn't recall any recent warnings for sandstorms when they'd checked the weather updates.

As he turned down one of the rows of tents, he saw Garrett running toward him, waving.

"Victor! I've been looking for you," Garrett said breathlessly, coming up to him.

"What is it? Have you talked with the cyborg?"

"Yes," Garrett said as he bent over, catching his breath. "It's pretty bad." Garrett took another deep breath, wiping the sweat off his brow. "There's a whole army of them."

Victor's heart stopped. "Army? What do you mean? Of this particular kind of cyborg?"

"Yes."

His gut sank, and that same bad feeling returned to him.

"Olympia developed a whole army of them!" Garrett continued. "As of right now, there's a special unit searching for the cyborg!"

Their eyes met instantly. The camp was in trouble.

"We need to contact the palace. Immediately," Victor said quickly.

"Drew is already on it."

An alarming thought came to Victor. What if the communication interference to the northern camps was being caused by Olympia…

We have to try!

Victor shoved his unnerving thoughts aside, then started toward the dwelling with the communication equipment, Garrett following.

"Did you find out anything else from the cyborg?" Victor asked.

"He said his name is Scion."

"Scion?"

"Yeah. He said that he stole a file as proof to expose the Olympian corporation from an undermined deal with someone from the Arcadia corporation."

Victor raised his eyebrow, amazed. "A free thinker?"

"Precisely. He is more human than not, and Olympia is not happy about him having that file. Olympia dispatched a small unit to track him down, but he tore out his tracking device." Garrett paused, giving Victor a serious look. "But that isn't the worst part."

"There's more?"

"Get this. Scion also said that Olympia has plans to march on Arcadia. They're after the King and Queen, and they mean to take over the whole Kingdom of Arcadia."

Victor stood silently, taking it all in.

"Victor! Did you hear what I said?" Garrett said anxiously.

He heard.

The news was troubling. Very troubling. *More* than troubling…

Olympia, ready to invade Arcadia with a slew of cyborgs. Olympian cyborgs clashing against Arcadian cyborgs, especially ones with magical capabilities… It would be catastrophic. The camp was in the direct path from Olympia to Arcadia. And to make matters worse, the camp now had an Olympian cyborg, one that Olympia was in dire search of. There was no way his camp could face an Olympian dispatch unit of cyborgs. They would shred the whole camp looking for Scion.

And not just their camp, all the camps across the wastelands, until they found their lost cyborg. And what of his camp's cyborgs? Most of them had malfunctioning parts and didn't have much of a chance to stand against a dispatch unit, much less an entire *army*. They had to get out of there, and quickly.

Victor took a deep breath, then began. "We need to prepare for the worst," he said. "Get everyone to start an evacuation to the caves. Drew must get in contact with the Arcadian court. All the camps out here are going to need much more help than the few guns we have in storage."

Garrett nodded. "I'll get Ryan to start the evacuation."

"Thank you, Garrett. We need to leave within the hour, possibly sooner."

Garrett nodded, then ran off as Victor turned away, heading to the communication trailer.

The overwhelming feeling gripped Victor harder than before. The palms of his hands broke out in a cold sweat, his head swimming wildly with anxious thoughts of what was to come.

We have to get ahold of the Queen.
Somehow, Victor already knew that it wasn't going to be easy.

CHAPTER 13

ORANGE

Drew was situated in the communications trailer, seated on a wooden chair, turning the knobs as gently as he could to try to get a signal. The trailer consisted of a small scuffed wooden table and two chairs, cheap paneling lining the walls, and a rusty shelf containing a good assortment of old communications equipment. There was a box of spare parts in case they needed to fix any broken pieces, and several tools lying about.

On one of the tables was an old computer connected online; the other table, where he sat, had a box transmitter device with a large antenna jutting out of it. It was much larger than any communication equipment Drew had ever seen before. It was dated by forty years, but it worked much better out in the wastelands than the newer devices that were traded from the city.

The radio waves were scrambled. No matter how much Drew tinkered with precision to get a signal, all he heard was static. He had tried contacting the palace online, but the internet was disconnected. He had checked the computer hardware and determined that it was 100% fully connected, as it should be.

After that, he checked the software, and all was in working order as well. He then checked the camp's satellite dish to see if it was not picking up any signals, but nothing was out of place with that either. Now, he was on his last resort—using an old-fashioned box transmission device that used radio waves of a different frequency than that of the satellite radio. Anything to get a message out to the Queen.

Drew leaned over the transmitter box, adjusting the knob back and forth. He still felt groggy from the sedative that had been administered earlier, intermittently slapping himself with his good hand to make himself more alert.

More static.

He yanked the box closer to him, turning it around to check and see if the transmission device was damaged somehow. As he did so, he yanked it harder than he intended, and the box spun around sharply, with him catching it quickly with his cybernetic hand. As he did so, the metal claws on his fingertips scraped the box, making a screeching noise. The box came to a halt, and Drew grunted a sigh of frustration.

Why couldn't he get a clear signal to the palace? How was it that the computer wasn't connected online and the camp's transmitter box was nothing but scrambled frequencies?

Scion's words came to his mind, causing a stir in Drew.

He had a sudden need to accelerate his pace.

Drew opened the backside of the device. The machinery was intact, so he closed the back plate and snapped it shut. He faced the box back toward him, turning the knob once again to find a clear signal frequency, but there was nothing but static.

At that moment, the door opened, and a bright light filtered into the room. The light was too bright compared to the darkness of inside the trailer, so it took a second for his eye to adjust. Through the light, Drew's cybernetic eye scanned a shadow standing within the doorway. It was Victor.

"Garrett informed me of what the cyborg Scion told you," Victor began. "We are beginning the evacuation process immediately."

Drew nodded. "G-good. We m-m-m-must protect him." He continued to fuss with the settings.

"What's wrong?" Victor asked, standing over him, watching him intently.

"T-t-t-transmission interf-f-f-interference. Can't get a c-c-c-clear signal."

"Why are you using that? What's wrong with the computer?" Victor asked. There was a hint of fear that Drew heard in the inflection of his voice.

"C-c-c-can't connect online."

Victor flashed him an alarmed look. "Reila said that she couldn't get in contact with the northern camps earlier either."

Victor's words reminded Drew of what he already suspected. The armies were coming, Scion warned him. Scion didn't know when, but they were coming. This interference…

Drew jolted, then shuddered.

"Maybe it's the wiring," Victor continued. By the emotional response, Drew knew that Victor was nervous, and even fearful. He had every reason to feel the way he did, and Drew knew the probability that the Olympian dispatch unit would soon be within the area to find Scion: eighty-three percent chance.

"It's n-n-n-not the w-w-w-wiring," Drew said. "I h-h-h-have already ch-checked inside the device, and allll intact. Checked the c-computer too."

"Olympia," Victor said firmly.

Drew understood what Victor meant.

Olympia was behind the interference.

Drew got up, turning off the transmission and going to the door.

"Where are you going?" Victor called out.

Drew flung open the door harder than he anticipated. He needed to maintain the human response of calm.

Taking a deep breath, Drew turned, meeting Victor's gaze. "I am g-g-g-going to send a-a transmission to the palace."

"I agree that we need to get a message to the Queen, but how?" Victor asked heatedly. "If it is as you say, we will soon have Olympia crawling all over our camp. We don't have time to fix any equipment!"

"I *know*!" Drew snapped.

Victor paused, stunned.

Never had Drew spoken words with such… frustration. He looked into Victor's face and felt… What did he feel?

Malfunction.

"I-I'm s-s-s-sorry," he started.

Victor suddenly let out a small laugh. Drew knew he wasn't laughing at anything funny, but more at their current status. The man was uneasy, just like Drew.

"I didn't know that cyborgs got stressed like us humans." Victor gave him a half smile.

"I-I… ammm part human."

"Listen, I know you want to do all that you possibly can to warn the Queen, but if nothing is working, this is much more serious than we even thought to begin with," Victor said, his expression stern. "We *must* get everyone out of the camp immediately."

The Queen. She had to know.

Drew met Victor's eyes, feeling the emotion behind them. Victor was exhibiting fear but trying to mask it with hope.

"I-I am going to A-A-A-Arcadia," Drew said evenly.

Victor shot him a look. "No. You need to get out of the camp along with everyone else. Our camp, and Scion, needs as much protection as we can give them, especially if it is true that the Olympian dispatch unit is in the area. If they are hostile, they won't take kindly to us housing their old cyborg unit. Plus, what if they already started their march on Arcadia? No, we need your help."

"N-n-n-negative. Someone needs to alert Arcadia. I can fly to Arcadia myself. Q-Q-Q-Queen Emerald *must* know."

Victor sighed deeply, his face tense. After a few moments, he finally broke the silence. "You cyborgs are so stubborn sometimes. Once you have an idea, you can't let it go." Victor's face deepened into a frown. "If someone must leave, have Telly go. You have more abilities to defend us then your counterpart."

"You have other cyyyy-cyborgs within the camp."

"Units *without* magic."

"B-b-b-but with regeneration capabilities. From the Q-Q-Q-Queen." Drew turned away. "And u-u-u-use the new weapons G-G-G-Garrett has developed."

"Dammit, Drew." Victor grabbed him. "I know you want to help, and you think getting to Arcadia as quick as you can is the best way to help. But we have those two old transports we can take; they can get Telly there just as fast. Think." He paused. "We need your help *here*," Victor implored, his face serious.

Drew paused, calculating his thoughts. What Victor said rang true; he was the only one with true power. And if the Olympian cyborg unit that was dispatched to find Scion had magical abilities, more than the regeneration abilities like the Arcadian cyborgs, then they would need him. Garrett's weapons would be useful against them, but they hadn't been tested yet… on *any* subjects. And the fact was that he had the ability to access the yellow power almost as much as his orange. It would possibly come in handy against the cyborgs that had yellow power.

But in calculating everything logically, there was something inside of him that was fighting his sound reasoning. Victor wasn't going to like it.

Drew looked at Victor, then nodded. "Okay, I-I will stay with the camp. W-w-we need Garrett to arm-m-m.... arm the camp now."

Victor nodded. "Thank you, Drew. Thank you." He laid a hand on Drew's shoulder for a moment, a gesture of gratitude, then headed out of the trailer, Drew following him.

Stepping into the light, Drew squinted, then ran scans across the camp with his cybernetic eye, trying to locate Telly. His circuitry came up negative.

She must still be in the trailer with Scion.

She wouldn't be happy leaving him. But there wasn't much choice—the Queen must know.

He vacated the trailer, heading out into the camp.

The camp.

It was his *home*. And he'd be damned if anyone took that away.

CHAPTER 14

VIOLET

Ikaria stared at the ceiling through her prismatic barrier, its rainbow iridescence shining every so often. The colors… all the *colors*. The colors she no longer had since Queen Emerald had purified her blood. It was torture, seeing them dance and sway around her, teasing and taunting her like a blond lord waiting to bed her, naked and ready, only to be just slightly out of reach.

She was angry, exhausted, sexually deprived, and reeked of stale sweat. If she could only have a bath to get cleaned up and a blond lord for pleasure, her mood would slightly improve. Instead, Ikaria remained as she was, soiled and starved.

Where is a man when I need one?

Ikaria gritted her teeth, still staring at the pulsating colors, lost in thought about her sister. Ayera had ruined *everything*. For all that Ikaria did for her World Sector, what thanks did she get? None. Absolutely none. She had personally weeded out the High Court spies, found out about the dealings of the stolen tomes from the library, discovered "adjacent" magics…

Ikaria angrily slammed her hand against the stone floor; as she did so, the long chains attached to her shackled wrists jangled against the ground.

She looked up once again at the translucent colors swirling in the barrier.

And to think, she had the *full* Spectrum of Magic. She had the power to overthrow the High Court and their false ideals, and their false "plague." She had complete control over that green-gifted queen. For all Ikaria cared, that green-gifted could drain away the High Court's life force once and for all and let their bodies rot in the courtyards. Even Derek could have come with her to help, if he hadn't been so dramatic about everything.

Derek. He is probably crying in his cups, drinking away his salty tears, Ikaria thought as she rolled her eyes. Sure, he was to blame. But so was she. She had always wanted to see what it was like with a woman, and being inside Derek's mind, well, it gave her a perfect opportunity to give it a go. There was always Suri, so loyal, so wanting. But to Ikaria, it was *Suri.* She couldn't toy with Suri like she did with everyone else. Suri was special. What she and her servant had was something more, more than anything Ikaria had ever had before. And Ikaria could never take a chance and ruin it, all over some sort of curious pleasure.

Besides, while inside Derek's mind, connected to his thoughts, feelings, emotions, and his sexual tension—combined with her heightened sense of the effects of the magic's intoxication—her life force *raged* with desire. Everything looked so good. Derek's lustful desires for the Queen made her want Emerald just as much as he did. Everything was available, so why wouldn't she take the opportunity? The beauty of the whole thing was that it wasn't her body doing all the work—it was Derek's. She was there for the ride, feeling the pleasures of his mind, present for every moment of the whole experience.

The fact was, if Derek had truly wanted to stop her from doing it, he could have. He had the power to do so. But he hadn't. She felt Derek's mind—the man had enjoyed it just as much as she did. Both of them drunk on the power from the Gift of the Black, and ultimately, they did what they did. And that was the end of it.

Did she feel guilty about it? No. She was no saint, and she had done far worse things in her life. Well… perhaps she felt *slightly* conflicted, considering she had felt a small connection with the Queen during her purification, before she was sent back to her time. But in a bizarre, twisted, sick fascination, and most curious way, she admired how Derek was so taken captive by one woman his whole life. Never had Ikaria seen that kind of dedication. In her opinion, the man deserved to be rewarded by bedding his fantasy.

Ikaria flipped her hair over her shoulders, not wanting to think about the matter anymore. She never liked it when she thought about men being so loyal to one woman. It made her relive her foolish memories of Cyrus. He was to be "the one" for her, the one to worship the ground she walked on. The one to make her feel like the empress she was meant to be. Damned, naive fool she was. Who was she to even think such an idea? He deserved not even one moment of thought from her.

A sudden metal sound came from the door.

A visitor. Her sister, no doubt. No one else had ever visited her. No one cared enough or even wanted to bother except the jailer to give Ikaria her daily meal.

Moments later, the soft sound of slippers shuffling on the hard stone floors.

"Well, well, well, if it isn't my pious *sister*," Ikaria called out. She didn't move, not even her eyes, to see her sister.

"You're on speaking terms with me now," Ayera said. It wasn't a question.

"I suppose I am. As you can see, there really isn't much to pass my time away, and I feel quite generous today," Ikaria said, rolling over on her stone bed, facing away from her sister. Her magical "prison," meaning her barrier, moved with her as she did, still encapsulating her fully. She really didn't want to talk to Ayera, simply out of spite. After all, she was the one who put her in this damned place. But talking to an actual person, and not herself for once, was quite refreshing.

"What brings you to my chambers? Looking for my advice as court enchantress? I told you not to come groveling at my feet," Ikaria continued bitterly. She managed to sweep her bangs out of her face, then rolled back, glancing at her sister.

Ayera stood just a few steps inside the cell, dressed up like one of her childhood dolls. Face painted perfectly, hair twisted and looped on the top of her head, while the bottom portion ran down the swell of her back like a river at midnight. Even the hair ornaments looked perfectly arranged.

"You acknowledge me as your sister?" Ayera said evenly. "According to your last outburst, you said you had no sister."

Ikaria ignored her. "Tell me. Is the 'world' celebrating your glorious win? Defeating your *dark* and *wicked* sister, the one who gained the Gift of the Black? The one who sought for a revival of the *evil* technology? Is there much drinking and dancing up in the courts? It's such a shame I am missing out in all the excitement, especially with those blond lords. The least you could have done was left me a playmate in here to pass the time."

"Sister, no one is celebrating."

"I don't believe you." Ikaria sat up instantly on her stone bed, glaring at

Ayera. "I'm sure Cyrus is drunk in his cups, his mouth devouring a bosom of a young serving girl."

"You are most incorrect, sister. We found Cyrus in your chambers. Naked, I should add, and I had him arrested and imprisoned."

Now that bit of information surprised her.

Ayera's words made Ikaria burst out laughing, wildly and uncontrollably.

Her sister? Imprisoning Cyrus? How Ikaria wished to see Cyrus's sneering face.

The more she thought about everyone surrounding the Emperor in his nakedness, all tied up, the more humorous it became. Her wild laughter bounced off the walls, her body rattling with amusement. Tears formed in the corner of her eyes, and she wiped them carefully.

"Oh, sister. I daresay you are almost as humorous as Suri," Ikaria managed to say in between her laughs. "What I would give to see that snake the way you found him."

"You will be happy to know he was most angry at you, cursing your name."

"Just cursing my name? Oh, I was expecting more drama from him," Ikaria said, now disappointed, leaning back against the wall once more.

"What ever did become of your servant Suri? We can't seem to locate her," Ayera said.

Ikaria gave herself a private smile. *Oh, my dear little Suri…*

"How should I know?" Ikaria shrugged. "I've been imprisoned this whole time. I may be powerful, sister, but not that powerful. You have plenty of gifted at your disposal. I'm sure a mere servant like Suri can be found."

Ayera sighed. "Forget I even asked about Suri. Sister, I came to ask you—"

"I told you, I'm not helping you!" Ikaria interrupted her. "Not now! Not ever!"

"But it is about the High Court!"

"The High Court! It's always about the damned High Court!" Ikaria shot up from her stone bed, stalking over to her sister, her violet eyes flaring. "How dare you! You think you can just prance on into my newly acquired chambers, wanting to make conversation with me, then proceed to ask me questions that will help *you*? Have you lost all your senses? I took you as naive, but never a damned fool!"

She stretched out her hand, her chains whipping wildly, shooting a burst of violet magic toward Ayera. But the energy hit her enchanted barrier, absorbing the blast.

"You see that, sister?" Ikaria continued. "That's what you have done to me! I was well on my way to defeating the High Court with that mindless green-gifted queen and a slew of cyborgs. But no. You just had to listen to that rotten priest and his raving mad ideas of the God of Light and the High Court, and stop me from entering that portal!"

Ikaria's heart hammered in her chest, pounding fiercely like in one of her throes of passion. But this was not that kind of passion; she was truly enraged.

Ayera paused, giving her a strange look.

"You… you were going to bring the green-gifted here? To our time?"

Ikaria neared her sister's face, yanking the chains with her. "That was the plan, until you kindly interrupted it," Ikaria spat. "I was about to wipe them off the face of this earth."

Why was her sister so naive? It infuriated Ikaria that Ayera was the empress of their sector—the one with no wit, no brains. It should have been *her.*

"That is why they didn't want to help me," Ayera said.

"What? What was that you said?"

Had she heard that correctly?

"The High Court didn't want to help me stop you," Ayera continued under her breath.

"Nonsense," Ikaria spat angrily, slapping the barrier as if it were a fly. She huffed away angrily, seating herself on the stone bed once again, holding her head up high as if the bed were a throne, and she were empress. At least she was empress of her own godforsaken prison cell.

There was an uncomfortable silence that clung in the air like a thick woolen blanket. Ikaria could tell her sister was formulating words but couldn't speak her mind freely. That is, to her, anyway.

Finally, after moments of stillness between them, her sister broke the silence. "Sister, there is someone on their way here to see you."

"Oh? Let me guess. Is it that bitch Belinda? Come to gloat over me? Take my blood?" Ikaria looked directly at Ayera. *Foolish girl.* "You know that is what they want, don't you? My blood. Violet blood."

"It is actually High Inquisitor Rubius. I assume he has come to restore order within this sector."

"Restore order," Ikaria mocked.

"Yes, sister." Ayera glanced at her. "You should know... this might be the last time you see me, depending on the outcome."

Ikaria paused at her words.

Outcome? Her sister actually doing something that would require her to stand up for something other than the High Court?

Oh, this was good.

Ikaria slowly glanced over her shoulder, meeting Ayera's eyes. "What is it you plan to do, sister?"

Ayera remained silent.

Ikaria could tell just by that action that Ayera was going to resist the High Inquisitor, one way or another.

Does she want to protect me? My blood?

Ikaria neared her sister, sweetening her voice. "Let me out of here, sister. You know very well that I can be a big help to you. I will personally take care of this High Inquisitor. You and I, we can clean up the High Court once and for all." Her persuasive words rang out like crystal, clear and true.

Indeed, if her sister was about to resist a powerful man of the High Court, who better to put him in her place than her?

Ayera wiped her eyes. "A persuasive argument, sister. You've always had a silver tongue." Ayera shook her head. "You must remain here to atone for your sins."

Surely, Ayera had lost her wits.

Ikaria scoffed. "My sins!"

"You nearly wiped out all of time with your actions!" Ayera said pointedly. "The very *least* I can do is keep you in here for the rest of your days! Regardless of whether we adhere to the High Court's laws and customs or not, I have already made my decision about you."

Ikaria snapped to full attention. Did she just say *whether* they adhere to the High Court's laws or not? Was Ayera planning on breaking away from the sectors?

Ikaria quickly neared her sister, coming face-to-face with her. "I am not accustomed to begging, sister, but for the love of the God of Light you hold so dearly to your heart, let me out of here!"

"No. And that is my final word." Ayera turned away, knocking at the door to be let out.

Frustrated, Ikaria slammed her hand against the personal magical barrier, and it vibrated with bright colors where her palm impacted the barrier.

The door opened, and Ayera quickly left through the second magical barrier, leaving her alone.

"Damn you!" Ikaria's words echoed as the door slammed shut.

She heard muffled words outside of her cell, and the padding of feet walking off.

Why? Her sister had finally gained an ounce of intelligence, and Ikaria was locked away, unable to aid her sister when she needed it most.

Damn her!

She needed to get out of this cell. Before her sister went and screwed everything up. Again.

***

Ayera saw Auron standing in the prison hallway, waiting next to her string of guards, when she exited her sister's cell.

"What is going on?" Auron asked, bowing as she neared him. "Our meeting was just adjourned, then I heard that you summoned everyone back."

"I am surprised to see you here, and not upstairs in the meeting chambers," Ayera answered.

"When I had heard that you went down into the prisons, I had to see if everything was all right. You had me worried. I know how Ikaria can get."

Ayera looked over at him, giving him a sympathetic look. "Thank you, Auron. I appreciate your concern."

"So why did you come down here?" Auron pressed. "Does it coincide with the newly summoned meeting?"

"High Inquisitor Rubius is on his way here to our sector," Ayera stated. "I just got word right after our meeting."

"Word? Was it an official message from the High Court?"

"It came to me in secret, and I had it burned immediately."

Auron's eyes met hers, holding his expression firm and strong. But to Ayera, she could see the worry dancing in his eyes.

"Please, Empress," he began, "don't tell me you are having second thoughts about your sister."

Ayera shook her head. "You do not have to worry about that, Auron." She paused, still distracted by her conversation with her sister. "Auron, this entire time, my mind could not stop thinking about why the High Court refused to aid us in stopping my sister. It's been festering inside me, and I've been wanting answers. All the times I have visited my sister, I was hoping to glean something from her."

Auron frowned. "It was a major disappointment to us all here in our sector, causing us to realize a great many things, Empress. Including myself. I am still coming to terms with it, even with our plans to break away from the High Court itself."

"Indeed. That is why I went to my sister. I'd hoped to get her to talk to me before the High Inquisitor came. My thoughts were, if I told her that the High Inquisitor was on his way here, it would maybe get her to open up to me, and I could possibly learn something that I missed in my prior assessments."

"I recall the last time she didn't speak to you at all. Did you get her to say more than two words this time?"

"I did," Ayera said, looking at him. Her head was spinning at what she had learned. Green magic. Violet magic. The two colors that the High Court didn't have, and Ikaria had been leading herself and the green-gifted queen straight into the time portal… on their way to the High Court, personally, to deliver their blood. They didn't even have to do any of the work. Ikaria had planned to do it all for them.

"It is very peculiar that the green throne now lies empty," Ayera managed to say, insinuating her thoughts.

Auron gave her a curious look.

"Please, keep distance while I walk with High Priest Auron," Ayera said to her guards. They bowed, then trailed back at a distance. When there was a good amount of space between her and the guards, Ayera turned to Auron, keeping her voice low. "I find it interesting that my sister had a green-gifted woman in captivity back in time. She told me just now that she was well on her way to bring this green-gifted with her through the time portal." Ayera stopped, looking up at Auron. "And now the green throne on the High Court sits empty…"

Auron's golden eyes went wide. "Green… the color that is void in this time."

"And you can count on the High Court not having any access to my sister's power either. That is, until *now*."

Auron paused, thinking. "Do you think that they had the means to stop Ikaria, even with her absorbing all colors of magic?"

Ayera looked at him. "I do. Why else would they not want to stop her?"

"And the green throne? Do you think the green-gifted woman of the past would actually aid them?"

Ayera paused. She knew nothing of that green-gifted woman. Would a seat on the High Court entice her? "I honestly don't know, Auron. You would know more than I would, being that you met the Queen personally."

He paused, contemplating. "I got the feeling that she wouldn't… though I couldn't say for certain," he finally said.

"It is a possibility that we have to keep in mind," Ayera said.

"What do you want to do about the High Inquisitor's visit?" Auron asked.

Ayera stopped, facing him. "Auron, I need your blessing, for what I am about to order the council to do has serious implications."

"Empress?" Auron asked, searching her expression.

She held her head proud and high, almost as if she were Ikaria herself. "The scales have been tipped out of balance for far too long, and it is high time we fixed that. All we've done the last two months is talk. Talked and talked and talked. No action."

Ayera was tired of it all. "I will order the court to prepare for the High Inquisitor's arrival. I want all our gifted summoned to our audience chamber, and every guard readied within this citadel. Every single one. We will give the High Inquisitor a welcome unlike any other he has ever had. I'm tired of lying down like a dead dog to everyone, whether it be the High Court, the Emperor, or my wayward sister. I am Empress, am I not? If the High Court is truly behind those losing their gift, I will protect our gifted at all costs, including my sister. The God of Light bestowed it to her for a reason, not to the High Court."

"I am glad that you still put your faith in the God of Light," Auron pointed out.

"Who else am I to put my faith in? Certainly not the High Court," Ayera said, nearing the council chamber. "We will inform everyone of the current situation."

Auron hinted a smile in approval. "Absolutely, Empress."

Ayera waved her hand at her guards, and they approached.

"Guards, gather any and all gifted, and ready the guard," she ordered. "The High Inquisitor will be here soon, and we must be ready to give him a proper greeting."

"Right away, Empress," both men said in unison, bowing.

They quickly turned away and went in separate directions. Courtesans approached her, and Ayera gestured for them to come closer.

"I want you all to assemble every lord and lady in the audience hall. I will be addressing everyone before we welcome High Inquisitor Rubius."

"Yes, Empress."

Ayera watched as everyone began to scatter through the citadel as she and Auron made their way toward the audience chamber.

She was done being a carpet for all to walk over her.

She was the Empress of World Sector Six.

And no one was going to take that away from her.

CHAPTER 15

Red

The airship was ready to depart as Rubius walked out onto the citadel's platform dock. Everyone was waiting for his arrival. The captain and his crew were standing by at the end of the makeshift bridge that led onto the ship, while the crew lined the sides of the deck.

Rubius passed by the captain and crew, and they saluted. As he crossed the bridge and walked onto the airship, the captain and crew trailed behind him, then scrambled to get situated for departure.

That irritating woman, Elyathi, was on the ship already, peering at the open sky at the far end of the airship's deck. She still appeared to have orange hair like she did in the High Court meeting instead of the blue as when he first had met her. From a distance, Rubius could see her sneaking a peek at him with disdain on her face.

Rubius couldn't help but think that he had seen Elyathi before. And if what the High Court said was true—that she had been working with them for years—she must have been in the court at one point, when he had entertained them with his harp. Still, something was bothering him about her, and he couldn't quite place exactly what. Besides, of course, her annoying personality.

I can't believe I have to work with her. What a joke.

Glancing at her for a few more seconds, Rubius then turned his attention back to the ship. It lacked a blue-gifted, and all that stood before him was non-gifted, except Elyathi at the other end.

"Where's the blue-gifted?" Rubius asked the captain as he walked on deck. Zaphod cawed in question as well.

"There were no blue-gifted to spare," the captain said.

"What do you mean, there are no blue-gifted to *spare*? Where are they?"

The captain shrugged. "Didn't ask."

Where was Dydrone when he needed him?

Rubius turned in the direction of Elyathi. "Hey, Lady, did you hear that? They don't have any blue-gifted," Rubius said, calling out to her across the ship.

"I won't respond to your lack of formality," she said loudly.

Rubius rolled his eyes. "Lady Elyathi," he said with more grace. "They don't appear to have any blue-gifted for our travels."

She came over. He nodded politely to her, inwardly gritting his teeth.

"So I heard." Her orange eyes glistened in the light.

"Perhaps, since they seem to be short-handed, maybe you can use your... blue magic?" Rubius asked. "That is, if you have it?"

He wondered how it was even possible for her to have blue magic, and then later, orange.

Maybe it has to do with the High Court collecting magics. They probably figured out a way to change between them.

"I apologize, High Inquisitor," Elyathi said, "but I am not skilled in transporting this ship throughout this dimension. We will have to travel the old-fashioned way."

"Wonderful," Rubius remarked. He hadn't slow-traveled by airship in months. "Why can't we just go? Me and you?"

"I do hope you realize that the world doesn't revolve around you," Elyathi stated, holding her head high. "As you can see, there is much more to take to World Sector Six than us. Like our *guards*, for example."

This woman made his skin crawl.

At least it will give me time to look over that tome...

"We will get you set up in the decks below," the captain said, interrupting. "The captain's quarters are at your disposal." He paused. "Unless you want to give them to the lady?"

Rubius looked to Elyathi, then swallowed his pride. "The lady should have them. I'm fine with lesser quarters."

Elyathi hinted at a cool, approving smile at him, then nodded. "Thank you, High Inquisitor."

Caught off guard by her smile, he said, "You're most welcome, my lady."

"Fine by me. I'll get you set up in the first mate's cabin." The captain waved for him to follow. As the captain led him down the ship's flight of stairs, Rubius squeezed by the tight-knit path, passing by first the captain's quarters, then coming to the first mate's cabin. They both entered, and Rubius took a look around. A nice, plush bed filled up half the chamber.

"I'll get your trunk stored in here. It will be about twelve hours before we arrive in World Sector Six. You need a meal, just go to the mess hall, and our cook will fix you something."

"Thanks," Rubius stated. "Also, have someone fetch me my harp. That is what I most care about."

"Sure thing, boss," the captain said, closing the door behind him.

Rubius took off his boots, then noticed a bottle of spiced liquor on the desk. He grabbed the bottle and popped open the flask, taking a drink. It was the best alcohol he'd had in a long time. Zaphod squawked as he took another drink, looking at the bottle.

"Yeah, yeah. I'm not going get inebriated, my friend. Just enough to put me to sleep. I hate traveling by ship. Sometimes I wish I was born violet, that way I could summon the adjacent power of the blue to travel on my own. I hate relying on others."

The parrot nudged him under his chin. Rubius responded to Zaphod's affection by petting the bird's head for a moment. After a few gentle pats, he then took Zaphod off his shoulder, placing him on his stand while he looked for a few crackers in the chest. Rubius found some, then fed a couple to Zaphod, who happily ate up the snack.

There was a knock on the door.

"High Inquisitor? I have your harp as you requested," said a gruff man's voice.

"Bring it here!" Rubius said.

The door opened, and one of the shipmates carefully placed the harp on his bed, then left, closing the door behind them.

Rubius ran his hands over the instrument, smiling. It was like being reunited with an old friend again.

He turned to his pack, then started rummaging through it, finding the tome that Lady Xui had given him. Making himself comfortable on the bed, Rubius started thumbing through the sections of the book, coming upon a page flagged by a soft, deep-green ribbon used as a bookmark.

At the end of the Millennium Era, before the great cataclysmic event, it had been written in several documents throughout the region that the reappearance of magic came into being. There also had been several "gifted" people recorded in the United Kingdoms archives as having magical abilities, but many of the records had been destroyed in the Apocalypse. Most documents were electronic, and have not been reactivated except in one instance.

However, there were a few handwritten accounts within that timeframe that have been discovered. It has been said that some in the Arcadian court before the Apocalypse had been gifted, and that a marriage union between a gifted king and gifted queen took place. The king was recorded as being gifted and was detailed as blue-gifted, and his wife the queen was described as green-gifted. Their names were lost in the records, and these were the only accounts found in those handwritten texts. These texts were found in proximity of the old Kingdom of Arcadia in several caves in the surrounding desert region, and are dated from 2380–2400 M.E., approximately.

Rubius read another couple sentences, but it mentioned nothing else about the queen.

Queen of Arcadia? he thought to himself. *It seems to fit…*

He thought back to years ago. There was a strange green-gifted man who appeared in his chambers, looking for a woman called Geeta.

That very name, Geeta. He had never forgotten it for some reason. Rubius seemed to forget everyone's names unless they were of some importance. But the name *Geeta*, that one stuck out to him the moment he had heard it uttered from that green-gifted traveler's lips.

That entire situation was all very bizarre, and at times, Rubius wondered if he had made the whole thing up, or if he was too drunk to remember. But he had not been drinking that day, or at least, not before that moment the man showed up. That man mentioned a queen with the white gift, and that she had a daughter. If that were the case, this Arcadian queen could fit what the green-gifted time traveler was saying years ago.

He felt certain this had to be the woman.

Rubius hadn't known why at the time, why he had let that green-gifted man go instead of reporting him. He would have been handsomely rewarded, perhaps even given a lifetime pension from the High Court, so he could live in comfort for the rest of his years.

He knew very well that the High Court sought out the colors of magic. He was no fool. But the fact was, he had no love for his superiors on the High Court, nor the thought of them having access to all the colors of magic. He wouldn't freely hand over information that gave them more power. That would be plain foolish of him.

The world was already dangerous enough as it was, with technology banned throughout the sectors, the earth being toxic, and the High Court being the ultimate say in many matters. But to give them more power? It would become much more dangerous than it already was. Besides… no one could find out about that green-gifted woman. No one. She was his deepest secret.

When he reflected upon the whole situation, Rubius cursed himself for even mentioning the green-gifted woman to the green-gifted time traveler. He had never told anyone about his dreams before, so why tell a random stranger? But just seeing the green magic from that time traveler made him desperate to understand his dreams. In a way, it was a good thing he mentioned it to the traveler, for if he hadn't, he would have never gotten a possible clue.

Why is there green magic within you? Does it have to do with the woman you seek? He recalled the green-gifted time traveler's last words. Those words had haunted him since, replaying in his mind every day. What did the man mean by those words? Rubius had wanted to ask so much more after the man spoke those words. But it had been too late. The time traveler had gone.

Over the years, Rubius had tried to understand what the man meant by his parting words. Why *was* there green magic within him? To hell if Rubius knew. He couldn't very well summon any green magic, nor could he feel any green magic dwelling inside of him. But Rubius felt for certain that whatever this "green magic" that was inside of him was, it had everything to do with his dreams pertaining to the green-gifted woman.

Rubius turned back to the book, rereading the marked section. *Are you truly the queen of Arcadia?* he asked in his mind, thinking of the green-gifted woman.

He set down the book next to him, picking up his harp, which lay gently in the folds of the pillows. Rubius ran his fingers over the instrument once again, then began to strum the strings softly within his jeweled fingertips.

Her song. The green-gifted woman's song. The one that made him think of her. Her melody had played over and over again in the back of his mind his whole life, invading his thoughts and dreams. Though it was completely mad of him to think that the tune was somehow connected to this green-gifted woman, he just knew deep down it was. There was magic behind each note of the song, like a spell that wove itself as he played, as if his heart were searching for her as he played.

This woman… he felt a desire for her, a burning passion that he couldn't quench. His soul ached for her.

But she wasn't real. She was just a dream.

The mere thought depressed him, but what else was he supposed to do? Even if and when he figured out who she was after all these years of searching for her, then what? It wasn't like he could ever be with her, whether she was a shade of his dreams or a woman living in the ancient past. But why did she continue to appear to him? Why him? Was she searching for him? Did she need help?

The time traveler's words echoed once again in his mind. *Why is there green magic within you? Does it have to do with the woman you seek?*

Rubius sang quietly as he played his harp softly, reflecting on the mysterious green-gifted woman. Her beauty. Her spirit… calling out for him.

His eyes began to get heavy and his body tired and weary. Adjusting himself on the bed, he placed the harp gently on the pillows next to him, along with newly acquired tome.

Before he knew it, the slight movements from the airship rocked him to sleep, the melody continuing to linger in his mind.

CHAPTER 16

VIOLET

Sunlight peered from behind the curtains as Geeta lazily opened her eyes, squinting. Her body ached from her work yesterday, and she just didn't want to move. Rolling over, she looked at the manuscript that lay on the floor, then groaned.

She had to finish it today.

Slowly sitting up from bed, Geeta wiped the sleep from her eyes, then pushed the top of her greasy hair out of her face. She idly walked to the kitchen and started boiling a kettle of water for tea, then started to walk over to her altar to say her quick morning prayers. As she did so, she absently kicked the fallen Yellow God statue, nearly tripping over it.

Pausing, she looked at it for a second, then bent over and picked it up. She walked over to the altar, laying it back in its middle spot between the Orange and Green God, face down.

She looked at the Yellow God laying in its spot a moment longer, then heard the kettle whistle. Breaking her gaze, she walked back to the kitchen and grabbed an empty mug. She set it down and rummaged in her cabinet for a tea bag. The box was empty; she was out.

Cursing herself for not having any, she turned off the kettle.

Was it so bad she was out of tea? She could eat at the diner. Maybe see Nym?

Geeta felt flustered at the mere thought.

Making a sudden decision, she quickly said her morning prayers, slipped on some clean clothes, and headed to the bathroom to finish getting ready.

She washed her face, then grabbed some hair glue, rubbing it into her hair with her head upside down, the blood rushing to her face. She felt around for her hair dryer, found it, turned it on, and began blowing her hair into the mohawk fashion. After that, she attached her jeweled bindi to her forehead. She looked at her new henna tattoo across her chest, smiling. The tank top she wore really helped show it off. Geeta added a few more necklaces and bracelets, then threw on her jean jacket, heading out the door.

When Geeta arrived at the diner, she immediately spotted Nym pouring a customer a cup of coffee, her brightly painted pink lips smiling playfully. Something about Nym was different. Her messy, bubble-gum-pink chin-cropped hair still framed her face, but her bangs were cut drastically short and styled neatly, framing her finely plucked dark eyebrows nicely. Nym's vibrant blue eyes stood out from under heavy black eye makeup as she looked Geeta's way.

Nym flashed her a smile from across the diner, and Geeta shuffled her boots awkwardly.

"Hey, Geeta," said Mike, one of the other waiters at the diner, coming into her view, blocking Nym.

"Hey, Mike," Geeta said.

He waved his hand, and she followed him to an empty booth.

"I need some tea," Geeta said as she seated herself.

"Sure thing."

Geeta frowned slightly at the knowledge that Nym wasn't going to be her waitress for today. *Can't expect her to always be my server.*

Mike came back, setting down a white coffee mug with tea in it. The diner's tea was basic, as most mid-level Arcadians didn't drink tea. Coffee was their thing. Over time, though, Geeta had gotten used to the taste of Arcadia's bland tea, and it did the trick with the caffeine.

"Sorry, I don't know what you normally order. Usually Nym has your table," Mike said. "What will it be for you this morning?"

"The number three special," Geeta said.

"You got it." He walked off again, leaving Geeta to sip her tea and watch all the customers. Behind her, there was a guy talking loudly, giving her a headache. She wasn't sure if it was the volume that drove her insane or just the annoying sound of his voice. Even his thoughts were blaring in her mind.

"...Sorry, man, that I couldn't call you back. The call dropped on my transmission device when I hit the wastelands. The signal kept blipping off and on like a damn light switch," said the loud man behind her.

"No worries, bro," said another man in his booth. "Must have been a sandstorm coming."

"Probably. I didn't remember seeing the weather forecasts about any sandstorms, but I wasn't paying much attention at the time. My girlfriend kept talking to me about some bitch at her work." The man sighed, slurping whatever drink he was having, also very loudly, and very annoying.

Geeta grimaced. People annoyed her; this man was no exception.

Mike came back with her breakfast. "There you are."

"Thanks, Mike," Geeta said. He left, and she slathered ketchup onto her cheese and mushroom omelet. She took a big bite, chewing slowly, her mouth delighted at the taste. Nothing was better than the diner's omelet.

Right as she shoved another big bite in her mouth, Nym walked by.

"Hey, Geeta," she said, smiling.

Geeta silently cursed the ketchup on the side of her mouth at that very moment. Quickly wiping her mouth free of food, Geeta swallowed hard.

"Hi, Nym," Geeta managed to say as she fidgeted with her necklace.

"Sorry that I wasn't your server. They put me in the other section for today," Nym said, still smiling.

"It's okay, Nym. Next time."

What a stupid thing to say.

"How's that translation work going?" Nym asked.

"Going well enough, I guess."

Stupid. Stupid. Stupid.

"That's good," Nym said, her bright-blue eyes twinkling. Nym's gaze lowered to Geeta's chest. "Nice tattoo work, by the way. Looks cute on you."

"Thanks." Geeta scratched the back of her shaved head nervously. "It's a henna tattoo."

"Henna? Sounds interesting. I should try it sometime."

"Yeah." Geeta's heart was pounding, and she felt like a complete wreck on the inside.

"I gotta run to table ten," Nym continued. "That particular customer gets grumpy if his coffee reaches the halfway mark."

"You better get to him, then," Geeta said. "You don't want to make him upset."

"I sure don't. Hopefully I'll see you sometime this week, yeah?"

"I'll be here."

Nym giggled while she flashed Geeta one last smile, then took off.

Geeta watched as Nym ran over to her customer's table, pouring the man coffee. She sighed. Why couldn't she make better conversation? She sounded like a flipping idiot. Why was liking someone so hard?

As Geeta continued to eat her breakfast, she caught a glimpse of Nym on the other side of the diner once again, taking a customer's order. What was Nym's type? Men? Women? Geeta could never could figure it out. Nym wasn't dating anyone and flirted with everyone.

I'm probably not her type anyway, she thought to herself. Though Geeta was still technically married to Vihaan, she'd considered herself free from him the moment she left her own time. Her marriage had been arranged at birth by her and Vihaan's parents, and it was not one she had ever wanted. Geeta wasn't even attracted to men, though once or twice, Geeta had seen a man that she had felt a slight attraction to. But most men were big, smelly, and too hairy. Women were much more easy on the eye… smooth, soft, and curvy. Nym was no exception. Where Geeta was flat as a board, long and thin, Nym was anything but. She was short, thick, and had extreme curves that filled out in the right places.

Back in time, Geeta had known for many years that Suresh was attracted to her; she felt it in her mind whenever they spoke at the temple, which had been often. In a way, Geeta probably would not have minded if she had been married to Suresh, if he had been arranged to be her husband instead. He was cute in his own sort of way. He was kind, and would make a decent husband. But things happened the way they happened. She was in Arcadia, and Suresh… Who knew where he was?

Maybe it was a fool's hope to think Nym would like her, but Geeta didn't want to just give up. At least, not just yet. Every time Geeta had seen Nym, it made her day. Just one of Nym's smiles, just one conversation between her and Nym… it fueled Geeta's insides. Yes, Nym was pretty cute, fun, and flirty. But it was much more than that. Nym seemed genuinely interested in getting to know Geeta every time she visited the diner, unlike anyone else in Arcadia. Not even her coworker Frank seemed as genuinely interested as Nym did.

And each time she and Nym had a conversation, there was a powerful spark between them. Perhaps Geeta was imagining it. If she truly wanted to end her misery in this whole dating game, she could very well just dive into Nym's mind and find out. But that was just *wrong*—Nym's thoughts were her own. Geeta could never and would never violate Nym's private thoughts. Ever.

Just as Geeta was paying the bill and about to leave, a male customer approached Nym, who was near the register, handing a ticket to the cashier.

"Hey, Nym. Looking cute today," the man said, getting close to her.

Nym clenched her teeth, not smiling. It was the first time Geeta had ever seen her not smile.

"After work, I'm going out for a drink," he continued, leaning close. Too close. "You should come with me. It'll be fun. What do you say?"

"I say that I'm busy," Nym said, not meeting his eyes, trying to brush him off.

What is it with men, anyway? Did the guy think that if he kept harassing her that she would finally succumb to his whims?

Geeta narrowed her eyes, waiting to see if the guy was going to leave or continue to harass Nym.

"I think your tough-girl act is pretty sexy," the man continued. His face was right next to hers, as if he were positioning himself to kiss her.

"It's not supposed to be," Nym said coolly. "Listen, Rex, I'm working. I'm busy, can't you see?" She pushed him away lightly.

Rex brushed his jacket off, looking nonchalant. "I hear ya, Nym. I'll swing by later."

Rex turned away, and Geeta relaxed a bit, seeing Nym doing the same. But in a quick movement, Rex turned back around and squeezed Nym's butt hard, then walked out quickly before Nym had a chance to say anything.

Nym looked mortified, her eyes wide with shock. Nearby customers had witnessed the moment too, making the situation even more embarrassing for Nym.

Geeta threw down a few bills to cover what she owed on her table, then sprinted past Nym and a few other shocked servers, pushing the door open wildly and exiting.

She spotted Rex immediately, walking down the main sidewalk strip of the mid-levels.

"Hey," Geeta called out.

Rex turned around. He shrugged, not recognizing her, and turned away, continuing to walk.

"Yeah, you," Geeta continued.

He turned back around, raising an eyebrow. "What do you want?"

"Leave her alone."

He snorted.

That snort infuriated Geeta. She clenched her teeth and marched right up to him, getting in his face.

"I said, leave her alone."

Rex laughed in an asshole fashion right in her face. "Oh yeah? Who are you? Her best friend?"

"Not at all."

In an instant, Geeta slapped him hard across the face, then clenched her hands into fists, her violet power flowing to them. She whorled her hands in a circular motion, and her magic exploded from them.

The violet force whooshed out so fast and so furiously that it knocked Rex's body back with such force that he slammed against the side of a food cart, making an audible smacking sound.

The cart spun wildly, hot dogs, buns, relish, ketchup, and mustard flying wildly all over the walkway and into the street as people dodged out of the way.

Ketchup was smeared all over Rex. He wiped it away angrily, still lying against the cart, his eyes wild with disbelief and anger as he tried to comprehend what had just happened.

"What in the *fuck*? What did you *do*?" Rex screamed as he tried to move from his spot, grimacing.

A crowd gathered, taking pictures, talking about the impossible things they'd just witnessed. Geeta turned around, seeing some of the diner workers within the crowd, pointing.

Geeta froze.

Nym was there, taking in the whole situation.

Suddenly scared of the possibly that Nym had witnessed her magic, Geeta took a step back. Sirens could be heard far off, getting louder. Within moments, the Arcadian authorities were in view, arriving on their aerial motorbikes.

"What happened here?" an officer asked, getting off his bike and approaching.

"She fucking hit me," Rex said, angrily pointing to Geeta, still trying to get up. A glob of ketchup ran down the side of his face from his hair. He grunted in pain, flopping back down on the ground. "After that, I don't know what the fuck she did. Some kind of…" He paused at the word *magic*, because he would sound crazy if he uttered it. "She pushed me into this cart!" he lied.

The police eyed him. "You are telling me that *this* woman pushed you that hard into the cart, sending it flying across the street?"

"Yes!"

He looked to Geeta. "You pushed him?"

Geeta looked at Nym in the crowd, then eyed the officer. "I suppose there is no denying it."

"You see? She said so herself!" Rex shouted, blood trickling down his split lip.

"He touched her ass," Mike called out to the authorities within the crowd, pointing to Nym. "He was harassing her while she was working."

Nym nodded.

The police looked back at Rex, then put away his device and turned to leave.

"Hey! Aren't you going to arrest her?" Rex yelled angrily.

"No. But I should arrest you. Next time, keep your hands to yourself. Looks like you got what you deserve."

The police jumped on his aerial motorbike and took off, and the crowd dispersed, leaving Geeta still standing in the middle of the sidewalk.

Geeta looked over her shoulder, seeing Nym's gaze on her.

The cart owner was yelling at her and Rex, but Geeta didn't hear any of it; her mind was on Nym. Had she witnessed everything?

She sure hoped not.

Geeta turned and walked away quickly before the situation got any worse.

All the way home, Geeta kept replaying the situation in her head. Had Nym seen her use magic? She groaned.

When Geeta returned to her apartment, she changed out of her clothes and into sweatpants, grabbed a drink of water, then situated herself in front of the old manuscript, sweating profusely.

How am I supposed to work when that just happened? she asked herself, sighing.

Geeta took a deep breath, then gave herself a good long stretch, arching her back, then snapped into a working position, hunched over the manuscript.

She sure hoped that she hadn't blown her chances with Nym.

Managing to clear her thoughts, Geeta picked up a pen, then started reading the next verse of the ancient poem in her own old language silently.

I see your soul across the sands of time,

Locked beneath the earth below,

Cycling through the lifestream flows,

Back to the desert you go…

Geeta started translating the words onto her translated paper, writing each word with care. She stopped at the word *desert.*

A strange feeling came over her.

Desert, the word read on the page.

Desert.

Something about those words…

Must have been the conversation I overheard at the diner. Something to do with the possible sandstorm?

Geeta contemplated a little longer, then continued to translate. As she continued her work, she felt an overwhelming sensation flooding her veins, and she became fixated on the word, unable to focus.

She looked back at the first verse, rereading it, ending at the word *desert.*

Desert…

In an instant, power jolted through her whole body, and she no longer could see the poem in front of her.

Violet flooded her vision, then it slowly melted into a pure golden color.

Is this retribution for my anger? she asked the Yellow God, her heart heavy with hurt and loss.

And it was as if the Yellow God heard. Her spirit felt lighter from the yellow light, making the heavy feeling disappear. A strong, powerful presence filled her heart in its place, and a healing wave rocked her soul.

Desert… the magic whispered.

Desert…

Back to the desert you go…

CHAPTER 17

ORANGE

The camp guards hurried all of the camp dwellers into whatever vehicle they had. There were an assortment of ground vehicles, some with trailer beds, others either motorcycles, dirt bikes, or four-wheelers. Those who were in the ground vehicles were all packed in like a can of sardines, squeezed in the beds of the vehicles.

Drew scoured the camp with his cybernetic eye, seeing if any of the dwellers showed up on his scans.

Just a few left.

"Is everyone just about ready to leave?" he heard Victor ask from behind him.

Drew nodded. "Eight humans and three cyborgs remaining."

Victor came up to him, looking around the camp. "And what about Telly? Have you seen her yet?"

"Negative. H-h-haven't seen her since. B-b-b-but my scans-s-s inform me she is in the lab trailer…"

"She needs to get moving," Victor stated. He turned, looking over the crowd of frantic people. "Reila!"

Reila jerked her head from behind the side of a military ground vehicle, looking at the two of them. Victor gestured to her, and she made her way through the camp, meeting up with them.

"Yeah?" she asked coolly.

"I need you to take one of the transports into Arcadia."

"That will be fun. We going to the palace again?"

"Yes," Victor said.

"Wonderful. This time, do I get to fight, or do I have to stay tucked in behind my seatbelt like a good little girl again?"

"Telly needs to deliver a message to the Queen."

Reila furrowed her brow, then snorted. "I could just go. No sense bringing baggage along."

Drew did not like her statement at all. In fact, it rubbed his circuits the wrong way, making him much more heated on the inside.

Drew stepped in front of Reila, flashing her a look.

Reila stared at him evenly. "No offense to your woman. Just saying that she would be of more help out here, is all, and I am much quicker working by myself." The woman was not afraid of him, unlike most other wasteland dwellers. He found that odd.

"As true as that might be, the Queen would heed her words over yours, with Telly being an Arcadian citizen," Victor pointed out to her.

"Fine." Reila shrugged. "I'll go find the scientist."

"My scan located h-h-h-her in our lab with Scion," Drew said.

Reila was about to walk away, but Drew suddenly felt a range of emotions flooding him all at once, causing him to grab Reila with his good hand.

Startled, Reila jerked her head in his direction as he yanked her close. His heart continued to flood with mixed emotions, strange feelings that felt foreign to him. The thought of losing *her*...

He jolted, then shook.

Reila eyed his hand. "Watch that hand, cyborg," she warned.

"Telly... D-d-d-do not let anything happen to Telly," Drew said, fighting back his shakes. He was... was he choking on his own words?

Malfunction.

He shuddered while Reila gave a crooked smile, shoving his hand away. "Don't worry, weirdo. I'll take good care of your wife."

"Not wife," Drew corrected her.

"All right," Reila said. "Woman."

He was about to correct her once again, but he didn't even know how he would identify his and Telly's coupling.

Drew watched Reila walk off, then she turned around midstep. "By the way, you really should fix that situation," she called out to him, then she turned and walked away.

Memories of them came to his mind. Broken, distorted memories. He had wanted to ask Telly…

Malfunction.

He wanted her to be his wife all those years ago…

Drew jolted.

"Get all of Garrett's weapons loaded from storage, and I'll meet you back here in ten minutes," Victor said, interrupting his thoughts.

"Five minutes," Drew corrected him. "I-I will be here in five minutes."

"That works too," Victor said.

Drew walked quickly through the camp. It was already abandoned; tents were packed away and the dwellings empty. Everyone was in their vehicles, waiting to depart as a group. Only a few stragglers ran to and fro, grabbing last-minute possessions.

What was he feeling? Loneliness?

Malfunction.

Anxiety?

Cannot process that request.

Telly was about to be separated from him, and all Drew could think about was that it made him feel *uneasy*. Telly had left him once before, back at the corporation, when she was transferred, but that situation was much different in structure. He couldn't compute this strange feeling of separation.

His circuits were a mess.

When Drew got to the dwelling where the camp housed all their weapons, Ryan, one of the camp's guards, was on standby, while two men were loading the trucks, going in and out of the building, emptying it.

"Garrett is already inside," Ryan told Drew. Everyone always told him where Garrett was. It was like that with Telly and Gwen too. It wasn't like he couldn't find them in a minute with his scanners if he wanted, but Drew was starting to realize that they told him out of friendliness.

As he entered the dwelling complex, Garrett placed three weapons in a man's arms. The man didn't flinch at the weight, even though Drew knew it was heavy.

"Don't drop any of these!" Garrett barked at the man. "The ones with an orange mark aren't stable yet. Only use the ones without the orange. Got it?"

"Dude, chill out," the man said.

As he left, Drew saw Garrett rub his hands over his hair in a nervous movement.

"I'm telling you, some cocky ass is going to accidentally use the orange-marked one and get themselves hurt. Then I will have to say I told them so," Garrett told him.

"They w-w-w-will all work. C-c-checked every one o-of them."

"But did you test it out personally? Like, press the button and see what happens?" Garrett pressed.

"No."

"Exactly!" Garrett said, waving his hands wildly, then turning back to the weapons. "It's going to happen, just you wait. Just because your processor told you it will work, doesn't mean it will. Human error, Drew. Human error."

Drew didn't reply to Garrett's unstable conversation; there was no point. The man was frantic, as humans would say.

Drew grabbed several of the weapons, loading more into his arms than the other guards. As he was about to exit the complex, Gwen appeared in the doorway, looking in at the both of them.

"Dad? Are we really in danger?" she asked, her blue eyes frightened.

"Y-yes. Did you see your m-m-m-mother?" Drew asked, pausing.

"Mom was still in the trailer gathering up the last pieces of important equipment. She should be out about now, and I saw Scion in one of the trucks."

"Good," Drew said, grabbing a few more weapons. "N-n-n-need to get o-on the truck."

"Me?" Gwen asked.

"Yes. Now."

"I'm… I'm just waiting for everyone to get on, then I will," she said, her eyes glancing in Garrett's direction. Garrett didn't notice her prolonged stare.

"D-d-d-don't wait. Y-y-you neee-need to get loaded onto it now," Drew urged her. "Almost-t-t… almost the entire camp is loaded."

"At least issue me my own weapon before I go," she stated.

Gwen… wanting her own weapon?

"No. Y-y-y-you have not been trained," Drew answered her.

"I've shot the camp's guns many times before!"

"Not in r-r-r-real situations. T-t-t-these are different. Not for you."

"I'm not a kid anymore, despite what you and Mom *think*," she argued, her voice having more of an edge than usual. Even Garrett stopped what he was doing, looking up at them.

What was he to do with her? Telly would just get upset and use a loud, stern voice and tell her no. But Drew… he didn't know how to respond. He never had to.

Making a decision, Drew walked over to her, then studied her with his cybernetic eye, scanning her face. What was she thinking? He calculated a solution. One she wouldn't like, he could already detect.

"I-I will let you shoot these w-weapons sometime, but now is n-n-n-not the t-t-time. Now get in the *truck*," he said in his most authoritative voice. This was the second time today he'd had to use an edge to his voice. He didn't like doing it; it was against his programming.

Gwen paused, her eyes wide open, giving him a strange look of disbelief. Finally, after eleven seconds, she said, "Fine." She glanced again at Garrett, giving him a lingering stare before taking off.

Drew looked over at Garrett to see his expression, but the man was already grabbing more of the specialized weapons. Weapons with his magic.

A few more men came in, collecting the remaining weapons, then he, Garrett, and the men walked out together to the vehicles.

Drew ran one last scan on the camp—all clear. Everyone was loaded on the trucks, Victor included. The only ones not loaded were Telly and Reila; they were standing off at a distance near one of the camp's air transports.

Telly caught his gaze from afar, then quickly ran over to him as Reila jumped into the air transport and started its engine.

"Drew!" Telly called out. She ran up to him, throwing her hands around his neck. Her body smashed into his as she hugged him tightly. He carefully wrapped his hands around her, ensuring he wouldn't scratch her with his mechanical hand. "Drew… Victor wanted me to go to the palace, so I'm going with Reila. But some of the equipment… the camp can't take it with them. There's no room."

"D-don't worry about-t-t… it," Drew reassured her. "Y-y-y-you must go and tell Q-Queen Emerald everything. The t-t-t-transmissions… Radio waves… being interfered with. Scion and… and the file. The dispatch unit. And the Olympian armies… They need to know everything."

"You really think the Olympian army stands a chance against the Arcadian armies? Arcadia has cyborgs too, you know."

"I cannot calculate that…" Drew paused, thinking about her statement. "I-I can only process that they are powerful… very powerful, Tell-me-lots."

"I know," she whispered. "I was just trying to be positive."

She leaned into him, and he felt the need to do the same. Drew trembled for a moment, and then the strange fear sensation returned to him. As he towered over her, he kissed her forehead and held her close, almost in a protective stance. A warm flood of emotions hit him; he didn't want to part from her.

"I-I love you," he uttered, the emotions coming straight from his heart.

There was a moment of silence.

"Drew…" Telly whispered. She moved her head, looking up at him. "That was the first time you've said that to me since your resurrection."

It was. There were memories of him saying it to her prior to his rebuilt body…

He shook, thinking of those memories.

In that moment, Telly went on her tiptoes, kissing his lips. The flesh of her warm lips stirred his insides, causing his circuits to spark a feeling… a feeling of desire… but yet… a feeling of…

Telly pulled away, then nudged him. Her eyes were an especially alarming pale orange, with the warm light of the setting sun capturing the orange depths. "You better take care of our daughter."

"S-s-s-she will be safe with the camp."

Telly paused. "Wait. What do you mean the camp?"

"I-I am not g-g-g-going with them."

"If you aren't going with them, then where *are* you going?"

"Staying."

"Staying where? Here?" she said incredulously. "You can't stay! You have to go with the camp. Stick to the plan!"

He couldn't. There was something stirring inside of him. He had his own idea on how to buy the camp, and Arcadia, more time.

"Come on, Telly!" Reila yelled across the campgrounds. "Everyone is leaving! We need to get out of here before we're spotted by that cyborg dispatch unit. I'm sure they have aerial transports!"

Telly looked to him one last time, hurriedly kissed him, then took a step back. Her light-orange eyes sparkled in the light. She was beautiful.

Malfunction.

"Whatever you are up to, you better make sure you stay in one piece. I trust you know what you are doing," she said. "It seemed to do us good last time you had some wild idea."

Drew smirked, nodding. "I… I… promise you it is the best chance to help… help the c-c-c-camp and Arcadia."

"I believe you, oddly enough," Telly said, returning his smile. She began to step away, the winds whipping through her short honeyed hair, hinted with pale-orange growth at the roots. "I'll meet up with you soon."

She blew him a kiss, then she turned away.

His heart sank inside his chest, and his nerves were once again running wildly through his circuits as he watched Telly hop into the air transport before it took off.

He stood there, watching her air transport disappear into the burning orange of the setting sun.

The more distance between him and Telly, the more his heart hurt, and his circuits ran frantically inside of him.

CHAPTER 18

BLUE

Derek arrived at the royal banquet hall with Silas trailing behind him. It was already packed with many birthday guests.

The hall itself was decorated exquisitely for the Queen's birthday. Instead of the silks and fabrics typically used for the late King Damaris, Derek had ensured that those fabrics were burned, as the old colors reminded him of how Derek ascended to Arcadia's throne in the first place. No, everything was decorated much how Emerald would love it. Soft lavenders, pale greens, and gentle pinks were woven throughout the hall. Elegant strings of lights wrapped around the pillars and hung from the ceilings, and flowers of all sorts were displayed, much like an indoor garden. Even the banquet hall's patio balcony had been heavily redone, with new plants and flowers, most of them blooming with all sorts of purples and pinks. All decorations that reflected the Queen's beauty, her elegance, and her soft spirit.

Though Derek had ensured that the celebration would be to the Queen's liking, he knew that all his effort wouldn't matter to her. But he still made the effort regardless. He wouldn't give up, no matter how much the brokenness that was between them was shattered beyond repair.

As Derek made his entrance, he spotted many notable guests within the crowd. He had invited many of the royals from the other kingdoms, hoping to smooth out any misunderstandings they had about Arcadia and the cyborgs. But he did not see any of them; only the lower lords from those kingdoms had shown up in their stead.

Out of them all, Derek had hoped that His Majesty the King of Illumina would attend, considering King Abdul made himself always neutral in any situation. But the fact of the matter was that as much as King Abdul Zahra loved a good party, most of the other kingdoms' parties were not close to his "taste" in activities, at least not in comparison to those that went on within his own kingdom. But Derek had still hoped to establish more of a permanent alliance between the two kingdoms, especially at a time like this.

Many of the guests who were dancing and drinking stopped their merrymaking and bowed before Derek as he passed by. Then came the whispers and faint gasps from the ones who hadn't seen him in many months.

Derek eyed them, while Silas's face didn't hint at any change. Derek still heard the whispers within Arcadia's court—whether it was from their lips or their minds. The guards, the servants, even the courtesans; they all were wondering the same thing—was he truly gifted? Was the Queen herself gifted as well? Was that why she had green hair? Did she dye it, or did she truly have green hair like the gifted in the folklore?

And now, his blue hair most likely confirmed all their suspicions.

There were a few lingering stares at his blue hair, but then finally, they turned away to enjoy the rest of the party, not wanting to stand out with their gawking stares.

Yes, everyone, see what I have become! A curse to society! I should just tell everyone what I am, then it would stop the frivolous rumors.

He seated himself next to the throne of honor, then immediately motioned for Silas to fill his glass, his servant obliging. Derek drank half the glass, then looked down at his jeweled fingers, staring at the glimmering effects. Emerald's seat was empty, of course; she wouldn't be seated until she had to for the dinner and the birthday toast. And when that was over with, she would immediately vacate it for the rest of the evening.

His stomach was in knots at the thought of seeing the Queen. Earlier in the day was a disaster. This evening, no doubt, would be similar.

"Well, that wasn't merely as painful as I expected," Derek muttered to Silas. Derek looked down at his drink, then his hands. They didn't have a single scratch on them from breaking the mirror. Another thing that was healed by his green-blue magic.

"It went well," Silas agreed, nodding.

He scanned the hall to see if his father and mother had arrived, but he didn't see them either.

They aren't coming, Derek decided. Another reason that confirmed Derek's suspicions about his parents—they were afraid of him. The only one who seemed to have stayed true was Silas. If it weren't for his servant acting the same around him, Derek would have lost his sanity and wouldn't have been able to keep it together to rule Arcadia.

At times, Derek thought about what Ikaria had told him about his father a couple months ago. When Derek tried to think back on the visits to Arcadia during his youth, he never recalled witnessing anything unusual between his father and Queen Elyathi. Perhaps that witch had lied to him. Derek wouldn't put it past him. But still…

He had wanted to confront his father about it, but what was the point? What good would it do if it were true? That his father had been having an affair? Then what? They were already having issues between the kingdoms.

Derek sighed.

Best that I not see them, he thought bitterly. He was already feeling more than deflated, and he wasn't sure how much more he could take from his parents. He couldn't face their gaze upon him, their realization of what their son had become. Not only that, they would ask a slew of questions about Emerald, especially his mother, and Derek was not prepared to answer any of them. How could he? She had been in seclusion most of the time.

Emerald's words still haunted him.

I don't know if I can ever forgive you…

He clenched his cup as his thoughts turned to Ikaria, darkening.

He would pay her back tenfold for what she did to him.

For what she *made* him do.

I am coming for you, witch! Derek thought. *You will be no more than a lost memory in time when I am done with you!*

There was a clearing of a throat, and Derek snapped out of his thoughts, glancing toward Silas.

"Yes?" Derek eyed him.

"I didn't hear you answer… I just wanted to know if you wanted to be served dinner now, or if we should wait for the Queen," Silas asked.

"I will wait for the Queen," Derek answered, and Silas bowed.

A man approached the platform just then, bowing before him. Derek motioned for the man to rise and speak. He was a well-dressed older man, with long gray hair and a neatly trimmed graying goatee. His ornate jerkin was decorated with several pins, one being the Olympia crest.

"Your Majesty," said the man started, "forgive me, but my name is Phillip de Stephano. I am Olympia's envoy, first in command."

Derek sighed inwardly, but outwardly he nodded to the man and gave him a faint smile. "Yes, of course. I was surprised that you wanted to come so soon for another round of talks between our two kingdoms."

The man laughed. "Who could miss the Queen of Arcadia's birthday celebration? I, for one, couldn't."

Of course you couldn't. You just wanted to ruin our celebration! Derek thought sarcastically. "Yes, it would have been quite unfortunate if you missed the Queen's celebration."

"And so here I am, ready to celebrate the Queen's twenty-fifth year."

"And so you are," Derek said smoothly, taking a drink, continuing. "Where is Ambassador Rickes?"

"He isn't feeling so well, so His Majesty King Renard sent me instead." Phillip flashed him a daring smile. That smile. It was *taunting* him.

"I see. He didn't get what Renard wanted, so he sent you instead?" Derek stated boldly.

Phillip gave him another smile, then motioned for Derek to join him. "Your Majesty, let us take a stroll around the hall. There is much for us to see, is there not?"

Derek gritted his teeth, then forced the biggest smile he could muster up. He already hated this guy. "If you insist," Derek said curtly. He grabbed his chalice, then got up from his seat and walked down the platform.

They made their way through the party, side by side. "So what is it? What will sedate your hot-headed king?" Derek asked, getting right to the point.

"Your Majesty, I think you already know the answer to that question." Philip smiled, talking a drink.

"We have already told Ambassador Rickes, and I will tell you the same thing—we will not be dismantling the cyborgs. Period. They are *people*, Ambassador. You can't just *dismantle* people. It seems to me, Ambassador, that King Renard has no regard for human life. And now he has gotten all the other kingdoms in an uproar over his ridiculous fears."

The ambassador eyes grew dark, but he still wore that infuriating fake smile. How Derek wanted to wipe that smug look off the man's face.

"You have to understand, Your Majesty, how any of us outside kingdoms feel about Arcadia having such a deadly weapon as the cyborgs. You are the only ones that have access to such power. And for you not to want to give it up? Well, we view your actions as a threat."

Derek swung around, getting in the ambassador's face. "Not wanting to give it up?" He leaned in further. "Not wanting to give it *up*?" he repeated again, this time more heatedly. He then dropped his voice into a sharp whisper. "You listen, and take note, Ambassador, the corporation is no longer producing cyborg units. All we have left is what remains. We stopped all production! Why? Because of you and your kingdom!" Derek's eyes flashed in anger. "And still, your kingdom prances around, stirring up the other kingdoms to rally to your demands. Well, I don't take kindly to that. We have kissed your king's ass long enough trying to make him happy, but he doesn't seem to care for our efforts. I will fight for my citizens, even if they are not your ordinary citizens. Now you go back home and tell that pompous prick *exactly* what I said!"

At that moment, Derek caught sight of Emerald from across the room, the people around her bowing.

He froze at the sight of her, the sight of his wife, looking so magnificent in her lavender gown and soft wavy green hair flowing like a river at her sides. Even the circlet that framed her head sparkled from afar, giving the Queen a shimmering aura. Just her presence calmed the anger that pumped through his heart.

Derek leaned away from the ambassador, straightening his posture.

Emerald caught his gaze from where she stood, as the people bowing allowed her to see him perfectly. She immediately turned away and moved toward her friend Haze, the palace photographer.

"Ah, there is the Queen herself," Phillip said, raising his eyebrow to Derek. "I must wish her a happy birthday after our little conversation."

"Yes, you should do that," Derek said, a bit more pleasantly than his tone a moment prior.

Philip didn't move, but he took another swift drink. "Before I go chat with the Queen, there is another matter that I have need to discuss with Your Majesty."

"Is that so?" He was over the ambassador and his false smiles.

"There have been the most unsettling rumors circulating within the Olympian court…" he said, his eyes turning to Derek's hair.

He wants to know about the magic.

Philips eyes lingered for a moment on Derek, then turned back to Emerald. "Rumors of people with special *abilities*."

"I think, Ambassador, that you have heard one too many bedtime stories. Especially in regard to *The Spectrum*," Derek said stiffly.

"I do not believe in bedtime stories, Your Majesty. However, my king does." The Ambassador turned his full attention to him. "There were videos circulating online before they were scrubbed. From the very heart of your city, showing incredible powers and unexplainable things. *Magic*, they say."

"Magic?" Derek snorted. "Come now, Ambassador, those so-called videos… all they showed were colored flashes in the sky. Nothing of importance."

"I would be inclined to agree with you, Your Majesty, but the power that radiated from those bursts of color…" Philip's eyes trailed right back to Derek's hair, as if he could see right through them. "Many in your kingdom boast of their king and queen being gifted."

"People can say what they want to say, but doesn't make it true," Derek shot back. "I do not see the point of this conversation."

"The point, Your Majesty, is that Olympia and its allies do not like being in the shadow of a kingdom with supreme power. After all, we are the United Kingdoms, are we not? And if one kingdom tips the balance, we must restore that balance, by whatever means necessary."

Philip shot him a daring smile, and Derek finally understood. Olympia truly wanted to see for itself if there was a gifted king and queen, if they had true power. They wanted to see what there were up against if they declared war.

"I am sorry that this visit was a waste of your time, Ambassador," Derek remarked, eyeing him evenly. "Tell your king to stop believing in fairy tales, and do tell him our terms regarding the cyborgs. It seems they become much more unfavorable every time we talk. Good evening." Derek turned away.

Philip bowed. "I had better leave His Majesty to enjoy the rest of the evening with his beautiful wife."

Wouldn't that be something? If that were only the case, he thought sourly.

Derek paced furiously through the crowd until it became an endless sea of people, dancing and drinking, all with cheer. All except him, and possibly the ambassador. The one thing Damaris was ever right about was keeping magic a secret from the other kingdoms. Tensions were already high with them knowing about the cyborgs, but magic… Derek could sense that war was about to be thrust upon them.

Derek approached the platform, where Emerald sat at the table, refusing a glass of wine. She caught his glance once again, pretending to make herself look busy.

Derek sighed to himself, then took a deep breath, approaching her. "My Queen," he said as he bowed low to her. She formally offered her hand, and he kissed it. She averted her eyes, and he let go quickly, taking his seat next to her.

Both sat there uncomfortably for several moments, until he broke the silence. "I hope you are having a good time."

She sucked in her breath, not saying anything.

Derek coughed awkwardly, then continued. "I am going away for a while."

The statement caught her attention. She glanced at him out of the corner of her eyes, not touching her dinner plate in front of her. "Where are you going?" she asked without emotion.

"Just away for some time. I will be appointing Councilor Emerys to take care of the kingdom's matters while I am away. You will be in good hands with him." *Much better than I could ever do, that is apparent.* He hated himself—and the sorceress—all over again for the situation that he was in with Emerald. She used to look at him with such adoration…

Derek swore he saw a look of hesitation on her face, but it was quickly erased, leaving the Queen to her blank stares once again. "He is a well-suited choice. I will rely on him for any matters," was all she said before getting up. Several birthday guests called for her to open her gifts, and she obliged, making her way to the present table.

Derek watched her as she moved. Again, she made that maternal hand gesture against her stomach.

Derek swallowed with heavy guilt. Further result of the terrible deed, and a sobering reminder once again that he was going to be a father. He looked down at his cup, and his stomach churned. As much as he wanted an heir, it wasn't supposed to happen this way. This bad dream never seemed to end, and Derek was sure that eventually he would be swallowed up entirely by this nightmare.

Emerald opened her gifts one by one as the crowd oohed and awwed over each one, clapping politely. Derek watched as she opened each gift. Emerald looked fuller, now that he was truly studying her for the first time in months. She did her best to look happy, but it was clear to Derek that her soul bled sadness, the one emotion that Derek was most familiar with due to his "gift." Derek knew she still longed for that dead man. He could feel it in her sadness, tucked away in her mind. He understood the severity of Emerald's situation—she was pregnant and had no one to turn to.

Emerald came upon Derek's gift to her, and she read out loud who the gift was from. She flushed, making eye contact with him, then looked away, unwrapping the gift. She pulled out a large gemstone necklace, glittering with one of the largest diamonds he could find. The crowd gasped at the size, the court women excited at such a marvelous piece of jewelry.

"Thank you, Your Majesty," Emerald called out rather stonily to him across the room. "I am honored." Her eyes sparkled with melancholy that only Derek could see.

Derek bowed his head to her in acknowledgment, then answered, "The honor is all mine, My Queen."

She casually handed the necklace to one of the servants to store it, then turned away quickly. She started talking to a businesswoman from the eastern sector as she unwrapped the next gift.

When all the gifts were done, Derek got up, excusing himself from the room. His head was swimming with thoughts of Emerald being pregnant, and he didn't want to think about it anymore. But as much as he didn't want to think of it, he wanted to know if others within the court knew. He *had* to know.

Emerys met him across the room, walking in unison with him.

"The party isn't over," Emerys stated.

"I'm done for the evening."

"I saw you and the ambassador were talking."

"The Queen…" Derek interrupted him. "She looks different, does she not?"

Emerys gave him a curious look as he followed him out of the hall, not understanding what Derek was getting at.

"The Queen always has a new wardrobe, Your Majesty. That's how women are," Emerys stated matter-of-factly.

"That's not what I mean," Derek said, continuing his pace. "The Queen isn't pregnant, by any chance, is she?" Derek did not look Emerys straight in the eye.

Emerys stopped midstep, stunned. "You think so, Your Majesty?"

"I am not by any means familiar with these kind of matters," Derek said. "But… have you heard anything?"

"Me?" Emerys laughed at the thought. "Not in the least. I leave that to the women of the court. I am the last to hear of things regarding those subjects." They started walking again, continuing down the hall. "Why don't you ask the Queen herself? That is… unless…"

"Never mind. Forget I even said anything," Derek said quickly. He didn't even know how *he* felt about the whole situation.

"And what of the ambassador? What did he say?" Emerys pressed.

"The same thing that Ambassador Rickes said last time, but with more words. And he insinuated that the Queen and I have magic."

Emerys was caught off guard, staring straight at him. It was something that was hardly ever talked about. And if it was, the conversation was over before it even began.

"What… what did you say?"

"I told him to stop believing in fairy tales."

Emerys sighed. "It was those videos, wasn't it? They got ahold of them."

"They did," Derek confirmed. "But there is nothing that we can do about it now."

Emerys's face turned serious, heavy in thought. "I do not like where all of this is going. It is as if they are seeking reasons to go to war with us, and getting the other kingdoms involved too."

Derek looked at him. "That is exactly where this is going. They sent him here to get an idea of what they are truly up against."

Derek set his hand on Emerys's shoulder, and the councilor frowned in confusion.

"Your Majesty? What is it?"

"I am leaving, and am placing you in charge while I am away. That is, you and the Queen."

Emerys looked shocked. "At a time like this? Your Majesty! Why? Our kingdom is in peril!"

"That is exactly why I am going." Derek paused, eyeing him. "I must change the future." Little did the councilor know that it was to get his wife back in good graces with him, but all would change, even his current situation… "Councilor, what I am going to do is help stop this war from coming to our doorstep." It was a half lie, but hopefully he bought it.

Emerys stood silent, then continued. "What do you suggest we do while you are away?"

"Make preparations for the Arcadian army to be dispatched at a moment's notice. I want us to be ready for Olympia." Derek gave Emerys a look. "And if it gets bad, then beseech the Queen to use her power. She will protect our kingdom. I will do what I can where I am going."

"She… she has that kind of power?" Emerys asked in a whisper.

"She can wipe out an army if needed," Derek said slowly.

And she would if the kingdom cried out to her.

Hopefully it wouldn't come to that.

Hopefully.

Derek gripped the councilor's shoulder in brotherly affection. "I will see you when I see you."

"Soon, I hope," Emerys said, bowing.

"Soon."

Derek turned away, then headed to the one place he could restart his destiny…

To the Queen's chambers.

CHAPTER 19

GREEN

From the corner of her eyes, Emerald saw Derek leave the party early. There still were many attendees in the hall, and her birthday party was not even close to being over.

Emerald breathed a sigh of relief.

"It looks like he's gone," Haze said from over her shoulder.

Emerald turned around to see her well-dressed friend in a puffed gold jacket with elaborate black designs. Haze wore heavy black eye makeup, gold painted lips, and his silver hair slicked back.

"Yes, thank goodness," Emerald said under her breath.

Knowing Haze, he had much more to say about Derek, but he bit his tongue, knowing that no good would come from him bad-mouthing the King.

Since that moment of their brief exchange within the halls, Emerald had grown fearful that Derek had suspicions about her secret. She kept running their exchange over and over in her mind, and each time, she became more convinced that somehow Derek knew, making her more anxious. Between her exhaustion from the pregnancy, keeping it a secret, and her anxiety about the situation between her and Derek, all Emerald wanted to do was hide and not face the world. Sleeping was best, because she could forget about everything.

"Can I get you a drink, My Queen?" Haze eyed her empty hands, interrupting her thoughts. "I haven't seen you indulge all night."

Emerald quickly shook her head. "No, that is not necessary, Haze. I'm about to retire."

"Well, before you leave, I have a little surprise for you. So make sure you don't flitter on by without saying goodnight." Haze gave her a small hug.

"Okay. I'll find you when I am going to leave," Emerald said.

"You had better." He wandered off, grabbing another drink for himself. He finished his wine immediately, then got to work taking more pictures of the socialites, ensuring no one was left out.

Glacia came up with a wineglass in her hand. "I got you a drink. I've noticed you haven't had a sip all night. You really need to… to take your mind off things." Glacia paused, offering her the glass. "You will find that it helps. A lot."

"I'm not in the mood." Emerald eyed her handmaiden, declining the glass.

What was with everyone offering her a drink tonight anyway?

"Are you sure?"

Emerald gave her a weak smile. "I am sure."

"We should have dressed you in a different gown," Glacia continued. "Your chest is spilling out way too much. Have your breasts gotten bigger?" She eyed Emerald's chest, then rolled her eyes in laughter.

Emerald swallowed, then pretended to playfully give her friend the stink eye.

"What? I'm just saying," Glacia said, laughing. "They do look a lot bigger for some reason."

Emerald had been worried about that. Her body was changing, and soon she would no longer be able to hide her secret. She was already paranoid that others had seen right through her.

But why couldn't she just tell people that she was pregnant? Why keep it a secret? Even her best friend, Glacia—Emerald hadn't told her. Why?

Emerald swallowed hard. A range of emotions flooded her, making her feel terribly sad.

She just *couldn't.*

She wasn't ready.

If Emerald uttered the words, it would make everything seem real. And right now, she just wasn't ready to deal with the reality of the situation. The pregnancy made her feel so isolated from everyone. Emerald was so lost, alone, and… *confused.* Pregnant, with twins. Her green gift of life told her so. She could feel them inside, their souls intermingling with hers. But the green gift had also told her something else, something even harder to process.

The life forces inside of her—they were from two different fathers. One from love, one from…

A sudden twist of pain and sadness hit her. Emerald felt a small tear form in the corner of her eye and quickly wiped it away with the tip of her finger, being careful not to smudge her eye makeup.

Glacia casually glanced over at her, then raised an eyebrow. "What is it?"

"What is what?" Emerald asked, trying to act normal, forcing a fake smile.

"You have a weird look on your face. Did I say something?"

Emerald quickly shook her head. "Not at all. In fact, I changed my mind. I'll take the wine after all," Emerald lied, holding out her hand.

Glacia smiled. "I thought so," she said, handing her the glass. "Do you want me to get any food for you? I need to go check on something for a moment. I'll be back and can swing by the snack table for you."

"No. I don't feel like eating anything," Emerald said.

"Okay, no food for you. I'll be back," Glacia said as she bowed, then wandered off.

As Glacia disappeared into the crowd, Emerald casually walked over to one of the nearby potted plants, then dumped her wine into the pot. As she emptied the glass, her eyes started to water. She felt empty like the wineglass; her soul was gone, and she felt like she was invisible. She was just an empty shell, walking alone in this world. Life felt meaningless and incomplete without Kyle. She wished that he was there, with her. He would have been her strength during her time of hardship. He would know what to say and be there for her.

But he was gone, and her secret was hers and hers alone to bear.

More tears formed, and she blinked them back quickly. A man cleared his throat behind her. Startled, she turned around. Standing before her was an older man with a graying goatee.

"Queen Emerald, what a delight to finally meet you," he said.

Emerald looked at him curiously, not recognizing him. "I'm sorry. You are…?"

"We have never met," the man said smoothly, and she breathed a sigh of relief. "I am Olympia's ambassador, Phillip de Stephano. Pleased to meet you," he said, bowing low to her, then kissing the top of her hand.

"Likewise," Emerald said.

"What a splendid birthday celebration. I am so glad that I had a chance to visit just in time." He eyed her and flashed her a warm smile. "And I daresay, you are more beautiful in person than any picture has claimed."

"You are much too kind," Emerald stated, nodding gracefully. All she wanted to do was get out of the celebration, and she wasn't in any mood to meet new people.

I must do my part as queen, she reminded herself.

"What brings you here, Ambassador?" she asked, trying to subtly find the nearest distraction.

Phillip gave a deep laugh. "Business with His Majesty, your husband."

Emerald mustered up a smile. "Well, I do hope your business and stay have been favorable."

The ambassador took a small drink, almost in a rehearsed fashion. "Our meeting has been quite… interesting to say the least." He took another sip, eyeing her hair, then turned his attention to her directly. "Have you ever read *The Spectrum*, Your Majesty?"

Emerald's heart suddenly beat fiercely, seemingly pounding through her chest. *Why is he asking me this question?* It was such a random question, one that no one ever asked. No one hardly believed in anything religious, including *The Spectrum.*

She gave him an inquisitive look. "What do you mean?" She was no longer looking for a distraction; she needed an escape. But there was no escaping the conversation at hand.

"His Majesty, the King of Olympia, he has a *fascination* with *The Spectrum.* And so I have been told that your father had the same passion for that holy book." He took another drink, then chuckled. "Me, I care not for such things. I find it rather dull reading material myself."

"It is rather dull," Emerald said, agreeing with the ambassador quickly. She did actually like reading it from time to time, but she would say anything at this point to get away from this man.

"So you have read it?"

Emerald felt flustered. "Indeed, I have. As you have said, my father had an interest in it. So did my mother when she was alive. You might even say she was quite devout in her faith."

What is he getting at?

"*The gifted.*" The Ambassador made a wild, sweeping gesture with his hand. "People with great power, bestowed with their power from the God of Light himself."

His eyes darted to hers, then he glared. His manner of expression made it seem as if he knew who she really was.

Emerald paused, unsure of what to say. All she knew was that she wanted to excuse herself. But before she could, he turned away.

"Myths," he said, continuing as he shrugged. "It is all myths. I don't know what has gotten into the King of Olympia, believing in such nonsense."

Emerald breathed, then took a step back. "I'm sorry you do not feel the same as your king. Though it does all sound very odd, there are poems and words of comfort in *The Spectrum*, pertaining to the God of Light. We all have difficult journeys in life, and sometimes one looks to a higher power for guidance."

"Interesting." The ambassador didn't sound interested at all in her words, but instead glanced once again at her hair, then darted to her eyes.

Why did she even go there?

Emerald nodded as she took another small step back, then quickly backpedaled. "That is, if you believe in God, or of any god, for that matter." She bit her lip. "I… I don't know really know what else to say."

"You need not say anything." He returned an odd smile, chuckling. "I wish you a very happy birthday, and many good fortunes to come to the Kingdom of Arcadia."

She held out her hand, and he kissed it in respect. "Thank you, Ambassador."

"Your Majesty." He bowed to her, then vacated his spot, walking into the crowd.

The whole conversation gave her a terrible feeling within her gut. Had she been more attuned to everything around her, and not solely focused on Kyle and the pregnancy, the conversation would have had her extremely worried and in a panic. But now, instead of making her worry, it made her more depressed, and was just another thing that kept her soul heavy.

She just wanted to hide from everyone and everything.

"We really should have dressed you in that silver gown," Glacia said as she came back up to her, bowing. She then adjusted the midsection of Emerald's dress slightly. "What was that all about?"

"I don't know."

"You have that weird expression on your face again."

"Do I?" Emerald eyed her friend.

"This is the second time now. Believe me, I know when something isn't right."

"It's like... he *knew* about me."

Glacia shrugged. "Well, everyone knows about you. It's hard not to know about the beautiful Queen Emerald."

She leaned into Glacia. "About *me*."

"Oh," Glacia said, turning serious. "What makes you say that?"

"He asked me if I believe in *The Spectrum*... and the way he was staring at me for a moment. I just... felt it."

Glacia remained silent for a moment, then spoke. "Even if he did, what would it matter? There are rumors in Arcadia that you and Derek are special."

Emerald shot her a look. "People are saying that?"

"Well, sure. *And* they seem to love the idea. So what if Olympia suspects it?" Glacia shrugged.

Thinking of her passing conversation with the ambassador just now, it made her suddenly think of her father's fears. All through her life, her father had constantly reminded her why they had to keep her gift a secret. Other kingdoms might try and kidnap her and access her power. And with her current conversation... it didn't sit right with her. At all.

Emerald turned to Glacia, sighing. "I don't want to think about it anymore. Let's go."

"We have to find Haze first," Glacia pointed out.

Emerald frowned in disbelief. "How do you know I have to go find him? He asked me when you weren't around."

Glacia laughed. "My Queen, since when is it possible to keep anything from me? I find out things too easily."

Emerald sniffed. "It's because you are nosy."

"I am not nosy!"

"I beg to differ," Emerald stated.

"Well, anyway, come on, let's go."

The two of them eventually found Haze and his partner, Troy, and the group of them wandered off to the grand hall's patio overlooking the very city.

Outside on the platform was a magnificent garden with new flowers in full bloom and a few tables and stone benches to overlook Arcadia's night lights. The air was fragrant, but the air had a slight chill to it.

"What's this all about?" Emerald asked, looking to Glacia, then to Haze.

"I wish I knew too," Troy said, shrugging. "It seems that these two are up to no good." He nudged her playfully.

Emerald gave him a small smile. "Since when are they ever up to any good?"

Troy laughed, then raised his glass, cheering her response.

"What time is it?" Glacia asked Haze.

"Almost time. You better hurry," Haze replied, taking a seat on one of the benches.

"Time for what?" Emerald asked, still confused.

"What is going on, you two? The suspense is killing me!" Troy blurted out. He'd definitely had one too many drinks.

At least someone is having a good time at my party, Emerald thought, smiling at Troy.

Glacia stood before her and handed her a small pink bag. Her eyes glistened with a sparkle of excitement. "I didn't have time to wrap it," she started, "but just look inside."

Curious, Emerald reached inside the bag, pulling out a cassette tape with the words SOME OLD SHIT written in permanent black marker.

"What is this?" Emerald glanced at it, then to Glacia.

Glacia smiled. "Remy gave it to me. The band found it in storage. They all thought you might like to have it."

Emerald gripped the cassette, her hands beginning to shake. She tried very hard to hold back her emotions.

In her hands, she held Kyle's voice. His *voice*.

Tears began welling up in her eyes, and her vision went blurry.

"You got ahold of Remy and the band?" Emerald said to Glacia. No longer could she hold back her tears; they came trickling down her cheeks.

Glacia smiled, looking proud of herself. "I had gotten his number awhile back, but that's another story. But yes, I ended up meeting him." Glacia smiled to herself, as if she were in a dream.

"Uh-oh, sounds like someone has the hots for this Remy character," Haze inserted, taking a drink.

"Most definitely. Just look at the way she melted at just the sound of his name," Troy pointed out. Haze and Troy nodded to each other, laughing, then clinked their wineglasses together.

After they took a drink, Haze looked down at his watch. "Almost time, by the way."

"Time for what?" Emerald glanced at Haze, then turned back to Glacia, lifting the cassette tape in front of her. "Glacia, this is old technology. I don't have anything to play it."

"Well, it's a good thing that I think ahead. I bought a tape player yesterday while I was out. It's already set up in your quarters. Cyndi got it all hooked up while you were here."

"It's about that time!" Haze interrupted, looking away from his watch. He grabbed Emerald's hand, then directed their interlocking hands toward the city before them. "There. Look over there."

Within seconds, hundreds of fireworks shot up in the air, painting the sky in red splendor. Some were grand fireworks, shaped as spheres, others shimmered downward like falling stars.

The bursts of red kept coming, like a beating of her heart that yearned for Kyle. Absentmindedly, Emerald clutched the cassette tape as if it were her own life in her hands, placing it against her heart while watching the vibrant bursts of red light across Arcadia.

The pain of losing him came back to Emerald all at once.

She began to weep as her friends sat there in silence.

Haze, not saying anything, put his arm around her, gently guiding her into him, holding her close, letting her cry into his puffed doublet. Glacia also put her hand on her shoulder, intermittently stroking her hair in comfort.

They sat in silence, watching the grand red display of fireworks until the very last one burned out, and the city's colors came back into Emerald's line of sight. The smoke from the fireworks hung over the city in a giant fog, the smoke soaking in the neon glow from the city below.

Emerald turned to her friends, her eyes still filled with tears. "Thank you," she whispered to them. "I needed that."

Haze and Troy smiled at her, then both got up from the bench and gave her a hug. "You're welcome. The fireworks was my idea, and the cassette tape was Glacia's. Happy birthday, My Queen," Haze said softly, gently wiping one of her streaming tears away from her cheeks. "I should think you would like the rest of the evening by yourself."

"Yes, I shall very much like to get to my quarters," Emerald said quietly, tightening her grip on the tape in her hand.

"Goodnight, sweet queen," Haze said, giving her a hug.

"Goodnight, my beautiful queen," Troy whispered, kissing her hand.

"Goodnight, you two."

They both bowed to her, then strolled back inside to the party.

"Do you need to say goodnight to your birthday guests?" Glacia asked as they both got up from the bench.

"No, I should think they are all having a good time without me," Emerald said, thinking of the tape that had Kyle's voice recorded on it. "I really want to hear this."

"Sure, let's go out the back way."

Glacia led her to a different door that was on the far end of the platform, leading them both back inside the palace. The hallway was much narrower here than the main hall, used by the servants to serve, so that they wouldn't be seen in the main hall at any palace function. This way was much longer, Emerald knew, but it cut the chances that Emerald would run into anyone and have to stop to chat.

They made their way through the servant halls, then came to a staircase that connected to the main hall. Luckily, there was no one there except guards, which relieved Emerald greatly.

Emerald and Glacia took her private elevator, then arrived at her quarters.

As Glacia opened the door, Emerald rushed across the sitting room and into her bedchambers, looking around for the cassette player. The other handmaidens ran after her, wondering what the commotion was about.

"Where is it?" Emerald called out, looking around.

"Right over here, My Queen," Cyndi said, pointing to her nightstand.

Emerald rushed over, inspecting the player. Cyndi came up to her, offering her empty hand, waiting for Emerald to place the cassette tape in her hand. Emerald hesitated, then finally handed to her.

Cyndi carefully put the cassette tape in the player to demonstrate to

Emerald how the contraption worked. After she inserted the tape, she pointed to the circular button on top of the player.

"Here. Just push this one when you are ready," she said, bowing. She and the other handmaidens quickly left the room, leaving Emerald to herself.

She hesitated, her finger hovering over the button.

A flood of emotions came over her again. She wasn't sure if she could mentally handle listening to it.

But she *had* to hear his voice. It had been months, and if she didn't hear his voice soon, she was afraid she would forget what he sounded like.

Kyle... I miss you...

Her fingers trembled for a moment, then she gathered her courage.

Emerald pushed the button.

There was a fuzzy, static sound, then suddenly erratic music burst into a melody. Emerald listened as her stomach knotted up, her face lingering by the speakers of the stereo player.

A minute of the band's music went by, and then...

It was Kyle's voice. His voice, which she hadn't heard for months.

His voice. She was listening to *his* voice.

As Emerald clung to every word, every pitch, she closed her eyes, imagining what Kyle's face would have looked like as he sang this song. Details of him were becoming fuzzy in her mind, like an almost-forgotten dream. He had been gone for a couple months now, and all she had were his pictures. But even so, the colors of the pigments were fading, and her memories were slowly dying in her sorrow.

Tears began to flow as Kyle's voice became more intense.

His soul lived on in the music. But he was gone. Gone forever in the lifestream.

Please, God... let me dream of him.

The tears kept coming.

And coming.

And coming.

They kept coming until Emerald cried so hard that everything in her body and soul ached of despair.

She was losing herself. Her soul was void without him.

His voice continued to sing...

CHAPTER 20

GREEN

Ghost Man… Could he be truly alive after all?

Extreme heat burned his body as he tried to regain his senses.

I must find that man Rubius…

Suresh faintly opened his eyes. A blaring red sun burned bright in the atmosphere, nearly blinding him. Hot winds scorched his dirty body as he lay on his stomach upon a rocky, dusty ground.

Did I choose the wrong portal again? No, I'm sure this was the one…

It had been like this for months now. Suresh couldn't seem to find the time portal that led to that red-gifted man Rubius he had met years ago. It was as if the portal was missing. At times, Suresh blamed his memory for serving him incorrectly. However, just recently, in his last travels in the time-space continuum, the time portal had made itself known again, and it was in the place that Suresh had remembered it to be. Had the gods tampered with the portals, only allowing Suresh passage to where they wanted him to go? That, indeed, was something he thought of constantly.

Suresh slowly lifted his head, which was scraped and bruised, and took a deep breath. Instantly, the air suffocated him; the spores in the air attacked his body and wreaked havoc on his lungs. The winds were like poisonous needles, shooting pain into his lungs.

Struggling with the inner attack within his body, Suresh held his breath, trying to focus on the life force that flowed within his soul. Within his mind's eye, he saw him tapping into the green stream of magic, which flowed like rushing waters.

The magic roared through his body, gathering in his lungs. As he took another breath, he felt the air attack him once more, and his flowing green magic countered its poison.

I must get out of here! he thought frantically.

His eyes scanned the land around him; it was nothing more than a barren desert laid to waste, littered with rocks and sand as far as the eye could see. The sun hung in the sky, burning bloodred within the thick, yellowish atmosphere. Through the poisonous clouds, Suresh saw many shadowy shapes skittering throughout. The shapes… they formed giant magnificent castles that floated in the sky, shrouded in the clouds.

I have to at least get to the skies above… he thought.

He closed his eyes, trying to concentrate on his analogous magic, the blue that sat next to his green gift. He let the blue take over his body, filling every ounce of his being as he breathed again.

The sharpness of the air attacked him again, filling his lungs, paralyzing his movements temporarily.

Quickly! he shouted at the blue magic.

An immediate sensation of the blue magic engulfed him as he choked on the air, his green magic temporarily suspending him as the blue magic took over. The blue magic vibrated through his body, and weakly, Suresh took another breath, unable to hold it for long.

Pain rocked his body as blue filled his vision. His body felt light as air, then he blacked out.

***

First, it was the tickling of the winds against his cheeks and the soft tossing of his hair. Then came gentle sounds with the breeze.

He could breathe. Cool, refreshing air filled his lungs. His green magic mixed with it, restoring and repairing the damaged flesh on his insides.

Slowly, Suresh sat up. There were no people around; he was alone. In fact, he didn't see much of anything except some old stone ruins and wisping clouds floating by, eye level to him.

He was on one of the floating islands he had seen from the ground below. How long ago had that been?

Gathering his strength, Suresh got to his feet and began walking toward the ruins. All were engraved with strange inscriptions. None of it looked familiar. They did seem rather ancient, similar to his homeland, but yet different, with peculiar symbols.

Must be an ancient tribe's written script from this part of the world, Suresh thought. He ran his hand over the writing, feeling the grains of the stone. Brushing his fingers away, he looked up in the distance at a large outline that blocked part of the sky. There loomed a large gleaming floating citadel, with an expansive bridge that linked the floating chunk of earth he sat upon to the magnificent structure.

Suresh felt the magics that were bound to the island he sat on, the underlying power that held its place within the sky.

This is the time where the man Rubius hailed from… it also had enchanted objects bound with different magics. It was a time without the strange technology, a time that was heavily laden with magic.

This has to be the correct portal. I am certain! he thought. *Perhaps the last time I happened to appear in one of those citadels instead of on the earth below.*

Suresh started heading across the expansive bridge toward the citadel. As he traveled, he saw several other bridges that led to the gargantuan structure, all connecting smaller islands to the main floating citadel. From what Suresh could tell, these islands didn't have impressive structures on the islands, but instead old ruins like the one he'd been on. Perhaps the people of the future had saved parts of the earth below, from their old civilizations… maybe even from the parts where he and Geeta were from.

Wouldn't that be interesting? he thought. *To see old temples from my homeland, thousands of years later?*

The walk across the bridge was long, but at least the cool winds were pleasant and the sun shone brightly, making the walk enjoyable.

As he neared the citadel, Suresh saw a grand entrance with guards posted, causing him to slow his walk to a complete halt. He absentmindedly reached for his hood, but he had forgotten that it was in tatters. He grabbed what remained of it and pulled it over his hair. It hardly covered it, as it had many holes, but it did hide the majority of his green hair. He made a mental note to himself that he needed a new cloak at some point.

Hopefully there aren't any blue-gifted here to discover me…

Though he had blue-gifted capabilities, any of them could overpower him. The blue gift was not his main color, unlike his green-born gift. And if he tapped into the blue gift, especially to halt time, some of them might not succumb to stopping with the flow of time.

Perhaps I'd best just dimensional jump, he thought.

Out of view from the guards, Suresh filled his life force with green-blue magic, flowing it within his soul. A vivid green-blue flash engulfed him, and then the dimensional time place appeared.

The world was frozen, but he had only stopped time within his current plane of existence to move around.

Suresh saw the world tinted in green-blue, so he moved quickly though the dimensional plane before he took too long, afraid that any blue-gifted might be nearby doing the same. He moved past the guards and into an oversized hall entrance, which split in different directions into smaller corridors.

Picking one, Suresh moved down the hall until he came upon many different doors lining the halls. Peeking into the first door, Suresh saw it was a bedroom with someone inside, stilled in time, reading a scroll. He moved to the next and the next, until he found one that was empty, and he slipped inside.

Relaxing for a moment, Suresh lifted the magic spell, and the world came back into full color. As he did so, a bright green-blue flash engulfed him. To him, it had taken several minutes in the dimensional world. To anyone else, it was just a split second in time, while he flashed from one place to the next.

Suresh glanced around at the room quietly and carefully, hoping to come across something that could replace his hood. He passed by an enchanted fire pit.

His heart soared at the sight of it, recalling a similar magical firepit in Rubius's study chambers.

Suresh walked past the firepit, heading into an adjoining bedroom. He listened for a moment, and after deeming it safe to enter, opened the door. Upon entering, Suresh smiled, seeing a dresser.

Running up to it, Suresh dug through the drawers, hoping to find another cloak or hood at least. To his disappointment, there was nothing but women's clothing, and he shifted the clothes back into place and shoved the drawers shut.

He looked around for a moment, noticing that the room he was in was in shades of golden yellows and some oranges. He slunk down to the floor.

He was tired. So very tired and weary. All he wanted to do was sleep.

But every time he thought of rest, he kept thinking about the green magic… of Queen Emerald's magic somehow tied to Rubius's soul. It was the same magic Suresh had felt in fleeting when the Ghost Man perished back in time.

Suresh had to find him.

I don't even know where to begin. The sky is vast, and there seems to be many of these islands.

Suresh studied the room again, this time paying attention to the color. He wondered what the colors of the hallways and rooms were, as he couldn't say, for he'd traveled when the world was tinted. He recalled Rubius's chambers… a parrot, a harp, fireplace… black, silver, and…

Red.

Just as he got up from his spot, he heard a noise. His heart thumped loudly, then his body froze.

It came again, but this time it was clear—it was a splash of water and a woman humming.

Oh, goddess of all that is good! he cursed to himself. Suresh definitely didn't want to be in the woman's room when she was done with her bath.

He frantically looked around, hoping to find an exit. There was no other door besides the one back to the main chambers and an adjoining patio.

Quickly, Suresh walked toward the main chambers, but he heard the main door open.

"Darling? Are you here?" a man called out from the main room.

"Yes, dear!" called the woman in the bath from Suresh's other side. "I'm in the bath!"

"Good! Shall I dirty you before you get clean?" he said suggestively, his voice moving toward the bedroom.

"Oh, you!" The woman giggled.

I have to get out of here!

In a panic, Suresh dove out of the room and onto the patio. He slid, then backed himself against the wall, making sure the man walking by wouldn't see him. A few of the woman's giggles came from inside, then louder splashes of water mixed in with several loud moans.

The suggestive sounds suddenly made him think of himself being wifeless. Everyone back in his time had said how much of a disgrace he was. He represented the God of the Green in his region's temple, and had been expected to marry and have offspring. *To flourish the land with magic,* said the high priest of the temple at the time, all before Vihaan became the high priest.

He always had loved and admired Geeta, and she knew his feelings for her. He would always feel that way about her. Back in time, she had often opened her mind to his so that they could talk privately through her violet mind magic, so he knew that Geeta had only felt comfortable around him, confiding in him a great many things. Suresh couldn't help it during those mental connections; he had allowed her to see how he felt, and surprisingly, it never scared Geeta away. If anything, it made them closer in their friendship.

But she was in an arranged marriage, and there was nothing he could do about it. Besides, Geeta always seemed… uninterested in him romantically, which made him wonder who Geeta truly felt for. That is, if she had ever felt anything for anyone. Vihaan had stolen the true joys of life from her. He was an evil man.

That all seemed like a lifetime ago.

Suresh heard a few more moans from the couple, which told him it was safe for him to move, as it seemed the couple were heavily distracted. Beyond the patio's railing, there was nothing but the endless sky with several floating islands. However, to his right, he saw an adjacent patio that led to another set of rooms. The patio itself was far from the one he was on, much too far apart to jump to.

Suresh held up his hands in front of him, then made them into fists. He felt the surge of the blue magic that mingled with his green flow through him, like a strong tidal wave. The power flowed through his body, bathing him in a greenish-blue power.

The world turned a greenish-blue, pausing. Time hadn't necessarily paused for the world, but it would allow him to move within the world and space, so he could reappear instantly to those on the outside.

Suresh began walking as if he were crossing a bridge between the two patios, but there being no bridge underneath him, he was moving through dimensional space with his weak adjacent blue magic, but it had been made much stronger with the consumption of Raghu's blue-gifted blood he drank years ago.

He reached the other side, standing on the other platform, then released the magic. The world appeared in color again, and movement continued around him. He looked inside the new set of chambers, which appeared empty.

Opening the door slowly, Suresh let himself inside. Another room, this one decorated in yellows with hints of oranges and golds as well.

Another yellow room…

He made his way through the chamber but paused as he came across an armoire. Opening the drawers, he pulled out several pieces of men's clothing, including a cloak. Quickly, Suresh changed into a new set of clothes, then threw the cloak over his shoulders and pulled the hood over his hair. It felt good being in clean clothes, especially ones so regal, though he definitely had to bathe at some point.

Suresh neared the exit and cracked the door open, peering through. There were no sounds, and the hallway seemed like it was empty. He slipped through the door, then walked down the hall, periodically peeking into the rooms, noting their colors. The hallways were designed in geometric pattens throughout, with orangish lamps, very ornate and beautifully decorated. Every so often, people would walk past him, eyeing him, but they made no other contact. He had been careful not to peek behind the doors when anyone was around, or if he heard sounds behind the doors.

After looking through many of the doors, he came upon corridors that were bathed in red colors.

Hopefully the High Inquisitor is housed in this structure.

A woman dressed as a royal servant walked past him rather quickly. At the same time, a man with ebony skin saw her and stopped her as Suresh casually strolled by.

"A summons came for Lady Vala," the man's voice stated with great concern.

"Summons, my lord? Who is it from?" said the female servant.

"World Sector Three. The *High* Court," the man said in a whisper.

Suresh turned slightly as he walked, looking back out of the corner of his eye. The woman exchanged a serious look with the man, then accepted a scroll, bowing. "I will take it to the lady right away."

"Thank you," the man said, then lowered his voice, barely enough for Suresh to hear. "And please, tell the lady to be careful. The blue-gifted that have been summoned…" His voice wavered.

"I know. Please, don't say any more," the woman said swiftly.

"Also, please inform the lady that High Inquisitor Rubius is now en route to World Sector Six." There was a pause, and the man's words struck Suresh.

Rubius! He was on his way to World Sector Six. Wherever that was...

Perhaps if he followed that woman, he could find out where to find this World Sector Six.

Suresh dared not turn back, so instead he turned down a side corridor, then peeked out to see the servant woman.

"My lady has been made aware of the High Inquisitor..."

They exchanged a few more words, then the servant nodded in understanding, making her way down the hall as the man went in the opposite direction. Suresh pretended to open one of the doors near him as the man walked by from the main corridor.

Be careful? The High Court? The servant had warned him to be careful and mentioned the High Court. It *had* to be Rubius's superiors that he had briefly mentioned to Suresh—superiors that he necessarily didn't agree with.

Worry washed over Suresh, and he felt like there was a great deal more going on then what he had heard. Blue-gifted... That man had wanted to say more, but the servant woman stopped him. And High Inquisitor Rubius... he had been sent to that World Sector? *For what?* Suresh wondered.

A hard, pulling sensation in his life force rumbled through him. It was like a warning and an urging at the same time, commanding him what he ought to do. It was like a tug at his heart, the same tug when he came across the white-gifted woman Elyathi many years ago.

Suresh walked back to the main corridor, watching the servant woman from a distance. Turning in her direction, he followed. He was much further back, to the point the woman did not detect his presence.

The woman took several turns through the corridors, then came to a large set of double doors. She walked inside the chambers and shut the door behind her.

Just moments later, Suresh approached the double doors, leaning in to see if he could hear anything. He did indeed hear voices inside.

For a moment, he thought to pause time for him to slip into the room without being detected, so he could find a hiding spot. But since he had heard that this so-called High Court was summoning all blue-gifted, he gathered this Lady Vala had to be a blue-gifted herself. And that in itself would cause her to be alarmed by his presence.

Instead of using magic, Suresh cupped his hands against the door, the sounds and vibrations allowing him to faintly hear the voices.

"I'm scared, Katrina!" said a female voice behind the door. Suresh could only gather it was the lady Vala that the servant mentioned.

"I know, my lady," said the servant girl. "But you have to!"

"Then you know if I go, you will never see me again. I mean, why does the High Court need so many blue-gifted in their service?"

"The summons doesn't say, mistress."

"It's a hypothetical question, Katrina. They don't!" the voice said loudly. "And my poor uncle! I'm so worried about him. I haven't heard from anyone from that sector ever since I sent them that message! With High Inquisitor Rubius on his way to World Sector Six, you know the High Court will now come down hard on all those who traveled back in time!"

These are the gifted who traveled back in time to help Geeta and the Ghost Man!

It all suddenly made sense. The High Court was coming down on those involved in the trip back in time. It seemed like they were to be reprimanded. Those who'd aided Geeta and the Ghost Man to stop the sorceress. They were in danger.

The more Suresh uncovered, the stranger things became. This man Rubius, who Suresh had seen years ago, was traveling to this World Sector Six. And this High Court, they were summoning blue-gifted, especially ones who had traveled back to help the Ghost Man.

Something was wrong. Very wrong.

There were footsteps behind the door, and Suresh immediately tucked himself behind the door. A second later, the door burst open, nearly slamming into Suresh. Footsteps echoed down the hall, and Suresh heard several more words exchanged between Lady Vala and her servant Katrina.

Now he felt at a standstill.

Should he go and find this World Sector Six and finally see if this man Rubius was indeed connected somehow to Ghost Man? What of these blue-gifted all being summoned… and possibly in trouble?

His heart sank, thinking of Lady Vala.

Suresh thought for several more moments, then came to a decision.

He could only hope he'd made the right one.

CHAPTER 21

GREEN

Darkness embraced her, the endless void of nothingness surrounding her presence.

Where was she?

Emerald stood within the void, unsure of her whereabouts. Fearfully, she held out her hand, trembling, blindly trying to feel around her. She had a strange sensation that she was high up in the sky, within the dark world, but there were no immediate clues to confirm that fact. She just *felt* it.

As her hands continued to reach out into the darkness, they brushed against cold metal. Tapping it with her hands, Emerald concluded that it was a metal railing, possibly to keep her from falling if she were truly in the sky. Her feet were cold and bare; beneath her feet was grated metal flooring, which was uncomfortable to stand on. Had she forgotten her shoes?

What is this place?

Clutching the railing, Emerald slowly took a step in front of her, then bumped into a person.

"Hey!" said a man in front of her. "Watch where you're going!"

"Sorry, sir," Emerald apologized politely. She couldn't get a look at him, as her surroundings were still in darkness.

Hanging on to the railing, she felt a sudden weightless sensation once again, then clutched the railing in fear. She peered into the darkness with confusion. Anxiety set in.

Taking a step back, she bumped into another person, this time with her head, and much harder than the first.

"Ouch! What do you think you are doing, lady?" exclaimed a man's voice from behind.

Her head throbbed from the bump. She rubbed it with one of her hands, the other still holding on to the railing.

"I don't know what I am doing," Emerald whispered in a soft cry.

What *was* she doing? Where was she, and how was she going to get out of there?

As the words left her lips, she saw a faint light from below. As the light became brighter, she peered through the darkness at thousands of black silhouettes eclipsing in the soft light. The silhouettes… they were people. Thousands of people in front of her. Thousands of people behind her.

Feeling suddenly overwhelmed and anxious being stuck in the sea of people, Emerald desperately looked for a way out. But there was none. Only the endless line of people, as far as her eyes could see.

And she was in the middle of the endless line.

Light gently touched her surroundings. Emerald started to make out shapes other than people. She was high in the rafters of some industrial building, and she was standing on a metal scaffold in the rafters. Heavy metal equipment hung from the ceiling, looking very much like stage lighting, their beams of light slowly intensifying on a platform below.

Clutching the railing, Emerald peered below, trying to see where the light was pointing to.

What is that line for?

The moment she asked herself the question, it was answered deep within herself.

It was the line to see Kyle.

Through the metal grating at her feet, Emerald could see that the platform was a stage, the lights brilliantly illuminating it. The stage was empty, but musical instruments were in place and microphones set up.

Kyle. He would be down there, playing at any moment. She felt it in her soul to be true. And if the line didn't move fast enough, she would miss his show.

Actually, the line wasn't moving at all, and Emerald felt trapped.

She just had to get to the end of the line.

"Excuse me," Emerald said politely to the man in front of her, tapping him on the shoulder.

"You again," he muttered.

"Yes," Emerald said. "When is the performance starting?"

He laughed. "Just about any minute now."

Her stomach sank, and her heart beat hard. "But I have to see him!"

He shrugged. "You and everyone else."

Emerald grasped his arm, shaking it. "But you don't understand. I have to see him!" Her voice trembled as tears formed. "I just have to!"

Her voice echoed, bouncing through the seemingly endless rafters. Then she heard music.

Frantically, Emerald darted to the railing, peering over it. Spotlights shone on the stage below, but she could only see outlines within the bright light.

She had to get out of the line!

Breaking her proper etiquette, Emerald started pushing her way through the people.

"Hey! Get back in your spot!" yelled a voice.

"What do you think you're doing?" called out another shadow.

Emerald struggled through the pushing shadows. "I need to get down there!"

"Then wait your turn!" yelled one shadow.

All the shadows started radiating a violet energy. Through their power, her body was being pushed back, back into place.

"I haven't seen him in months!" Emerald cried out.

The shadows kept pushing her back as she struggled against them. The overwhelming violet power was so intense that she stumbled to her knees, scraping her delicate flesh against the metal grating.

Then a voice, clear as crystal, smooth as glass, broke out in song. The melody, it was familiar. It was the same song that she heard before within her dreams.

The music… it transformed into a powerful feeling, and Emerald saw its violet brilliance pouring over her body, enrapturing her with its power. It was a spell, weaving her into a trance, wooing her and seeping into her soul, lulling her into a transfixed state.

No… I can't stay here, Emerald cried to herself. *I have to see him!*

Shaking her head hard to wake from the musical seduction, she sprung up from her bloodied, scraped knees, grasping the metal railing and peering over it once again.

Then Emerald saw him. Far below the stage, his voice continuing to sing as the instruments played their tune. He didn't look quite the same being dressed in royal fashions and his hair crimson from the gift, but it was *him.* His mere presence radiated from the stage, and she felt connected to his life force.

"Kyle!" Emerald screamed to the stage below. "Kyle!"

He didn't hear her, and continued to sing.

"Kyle! Come back to me!"

All Emerald heard was his music, and by the looks of it, he wasn't moving either. Could he hear her?

"Kyle!" Emerald yelled louder. "Kyle!"

At that moment, Kyle began burning with a bright violet magic, basking within its light.

With a sudden rush of violet energy, Emerald was locked in place. Tears of sadness, frustration, loneliness poured down her face.

"Kyle…" she cried softly.

Overwhelmed by his power, all she could do was weep while listening to him sing.

"Come back to me," she whispered, choking on her tears.

The violet power responded, holding her tight.

"Come back to me…"

CHAPTER 22

BLUE

It was deep in the night as Derek walked through the palace, bathed in blue from his time magic. Everywhere had a blue tint; even the air seemed to have a wash of blueness to it, all but him, of course, and anything he touched. The world had stopped with his magic, and time stood still.

In his hand he held a chalice, the wine inside swishing back and forth as Derek moved. He was slightly intoxicated, as he'd had one too many glasses of wine.

But too much wine was the only way he could pull himself through what he was about to do. For if Derek were sober, he would falter when seeing her face, and the whole plan regarding Ikaria would cease to exist. No, he *had* to do it.

Derek needed Emerald's blood.

Flashes of his past conversation with Ikaria came to his mind. How the blue-gifted couldn't survive time without consuming green-gifted blood. The blue gift was indeed flawed. Of course, he had consumed Emerald's blood months ago, for that was how he had received his blue magic. But that was when he first received his gift. Derek was certain that he only had his true blue magic inside of him, and that his adjacent green magic was nothing more than a spark. It was what Ikaria had referred to as "analogous," or just blue-green magic. Weak. To be sure, to have the full potential of the green gift and to withstand time, Derek knew he *had* to consume his wife's blood.

Just one more reason for Emerald to hate me if she ever finds out.

Derek came to Emerald's quarters, turning the knob. The door wasn't locked, so he let himself in. Did the servants always keep it unlocked, relying on the guards? He would have to make sure that was fixed when he returned.

As he entered the sitting room, Derek saw several of Emerald's handmaidens asleep on the sofas instead of in their own bedchambers, which were adjacent to the Queen's quarters. They must have had a good night at the party.

In the corner of his eye, he saw Glacia, Emerald's favorite servant girl. Just seeing the handmaiden's face caused a stir within him. Derek recalled how she'd eyed him during his wedding feast. He had wanted to get rid of her. He still did, for she cast disapproving stares at him whenever it was safe to do so. But he couldn't because she was Emerald's best friend. And as much as Derek felt terrible for even thinking those terrible thoughts, it was just another reason for him to go through with what he was about to do. Because if he did, the handmaiden wouldn't hate him anymore either, and he wouldn't have to worry about her at all.

Derek crossed the sitting room, then came to Emerald's bedchamber and opened the door.

Slowly, Derek slipped inside. He paused in the shadows.

There he saw Emerald in her bed, fast asleep.

Slowly, he approached. He hovered over her body quietly, studying her. Emerald's body lay still from his time magic, sleeping, frozen in her dreamlike state.

His heart began to beat in his chest, pounding hard. His nerves wracked him. His breath quickened.

Derek took one last long drink from his chalice, then placed it on one of Emerald's small end tables. The chalice turned blue as his fingers separated from the metal, matching the rest of the world's blue tint. He took a deep breath.

Emerald's face was so sad and heavy with sorrow. He could feel that sadness radiating from within her, eating away at her soul day by day.

Why did it have to come to this? Her mourning over some man she'd spent such a short time with? And Derek… caught up in some wicked witch's plan, now the center of the Queen's hate. All the secrets that lay between them, their souls shrouded in mystery, only drove the desires of his heart further. How he wanted to go back to how it used to be.

It all came down to this moment.

He was going to change his future. His and Emerald's future.

Derek stood over her, drinking her in with his eyes. He hardly ever got a chance to look at her, and now here she was, unable to pierce him with her scornful eyes.

His eyes lowered to her belly. To what lay within her womb.

Was it his?

"I'm so sorry..." he said in a whisper. Tears started to form as he gazed upon her body.

He touched her belly, and in that moment, a small feeling came over him—the feeling of *life*. It was that spark, that green magic that was faint within him.

In that moment, Derek was certain. The child was his.

Derek trembled, then his eyes trailing down to Emerald hands. They were clutching something.

Derek bent down toward her, inspecting it. There was a cassette tape, held tightly within her grasp. Even in her deep sleep, Emerald wasn't going to let go of that tape.

Seeing the tape inflamed him, and rage poured out into his being. For he knew instantly what was on that tape. It was that damn man's songs. It had to be.

Derek's eyes moved back toward Emerald's face as he leaned over her. "I didn't want to do this, but I have to in order to make things right," he confessed to her still body, his heart pumping wildly with jealousy at seeing the tape. "Right with you, right with the world. This man... he will live again, but you just won't know him."

That thought satisfied Derek immensely. Emerald would never know Kyle, because he was going to stop her from ever leaving the palace that night, and instead, he would whisk her away to York.

And this time, there would be no sorceress to interfere.

Derek unclasped his doublet, then reached inside into its secret pocket. An enchanted blade emerged, his hand shaking. Gently, Derek took Emerald's hand, raising it up. He turned her hand over, face up, and swiftly cut her skin.

He called forth the time magic from within his life force, flooding his veins with it, allowing the magic to pour out of him and into her blood. The magic worked through her body, allowing her blood to flow from her open veins. He watched the glowing liquid, then his lips met her open wound, kissing it gently.

His blood temperature rose at the touch of her upon his lips against her delicate skin. How he wished she would give herself to him, be his fully.

But it was never meant to be in this timeline.

This timeline. That was the key.

It would be completely different in the alternate… no, *new* timeline. Everything was going to change.

Derek felt Emerald's blood mix with his within his lifestream; new power of the green blood rushed through his body, overwhelming him until he collapsed on the bed beside her. A painful, almost erotic, sadistic sensation shot through his being, wracked his body to where his vision started to blur. Time was fading in and out, and the world was flipping back and forth between blue and full color.

His heart began beating faster and faster. Wildly, fiercely. All his senses started running wild within him. He felt the extremity of life, as if he had never truly lived life until now. The power from the green magic, it gave him vitality, pounding him through his being. He wanted to scream, run, jump to the highest mountain, fight the strongest man, punch a wall and have hard, wild sex all at the same time.

As he continued to tumble around on the bed, he rolled over, focusing on Emerald as she lay next to him. Her body slowly stirred, and the blood continued to flow.

Through his struggles, Derek shot out his hand, calling for the familiar analogous magic of the green that he had accidentally tapped into several times before. But this time, it was no accident. The magic made sense to him within his life force, and now he understood how to fully access it.

A bluish-green glowing wave flowed from his palm, and the power surrounded Emerald's cut hand. The magic worked quickly, repairing her flesh to its original state, until there was only a trace of dried blood near her wound, leaving no scar.

The beating of the magic continued to pound through his system, his senses in a heightened state. His body screamed for rough, wild sex, desiring the nature of its fleshy lust.

Derek closed his eyes again, trying to ignore his overwhelming desires and sensations, and focused on his breathing, picturing that place that gave him hope—the crystal throne room with Emerald smiling at him.

He opened his eyes, and indeed, the flow of time came to him through his magic, showing him exactly what he had been focusing on—that future throne room. The sun poured through the windows, and everywhere was polished marble and sparkling glass, with reflections of him and Emerald within that room. Sounds of praise and cheer came from that kingdom.

But there was one detail he hadn't seen before. A shadow standing within the room. A familiar shadow.

That shadow… She was beautiful and smiling at him, proud of his kingdom and of the peace.

It's impossible! Derek thought as he stared at the familiar face.

The face… it was suddenly surrounded by darkness. The darkness flowed to him, then *through* him, embracing him. The darkness was like Emerald's smooth, soft kiss. It enraptured him, just as Emerald had, as if she were in his arms, their love bound together.

The feeling swelled within his soul, and his magic mixed with its power.

The image still remained of the crystal throne room, but time was revealing much more. He was seated upon the throne, with Emerald next to him, smiling with her vivid green eyes. The vision of her leaned over to his image, gently stroked his face, caressing it with a tenderness that he had once seen in her. A few more moments went by, then she softly grasped his face, pulled her to him, and kissed him with tenderness. The flesh of her lips, the taste of her seductive kisses, like the finest wine that he could forever drink from…

She will be yours forever. Forever, and ever, and ever… the darkness whispered in his heart, as Derek felt her passionate kisses.

The guilt, the remorse, the sadness that Derek had felt these many months, it suddenly was lifted from his soul. He felt… renewed.

Renewed from the darkness.

I shall make you my champion… it whispered, the image and the feeling of Emerald softly fading away. His heart burned for her, renewed the fight to make her his own.

"Gladly," he answered. "If that is what it takes for me to win my bride back!"

There was a violent shock within his body. His heart pounded much harder than before. It kept pounding, hammering… until he could no longer take it.

To access my power, you must drink from hers, the darkness echoed.

With a sudden burst of force within his life force, the darkness evaporated, and Derek cried out.

The pounding of the magic was gone. Peace and tranquility poured over him.

As Derek caught his breath, he realized he was no longer viewing the flow of time. Instead, he was in the stilled world of Emerald's bedchambers.

He felt completely renewed. Body, soul, and spirit.

Derek rolled over, looking at Emerald as he caught his breath. He gently stroked one of her locks of hair, admiring her. How he longed for her, longed for her love and affection.

"I will see you in the past, My Queen," he whispered. "For we will have a happy future, and all shall be well."

He then dared himself, and kissed her lips. Her soft lips were ever so sweet on his, heightening his newfound senses.

To access my power, you must drink from hers… the voice echoed in his mind once again.

It wasn't Emerald the voice was referring to; he had just drank her blood. It was the face he had just seen in his vision, the proud woman who stood behind his future throne.

Closing his eyes, Derek lay his hands upon his chest, burning with the new powerful magic that flowed through his core. Bright-blue magic burned around him, enrapturing him within its power and light.

Then Derek felt a pull through the time dimension, the suction of the time force flinging him into the flow of time.

Lead me to the witch, he called out in his mind to his blue magic. There was a stirring within his life force as if in answer.

Then he was falling, endlessly, through all of time and space.

Falling to his destiny.

CHAPTER 23

Red

With sudden shock, Rubius jolted upright from his bed, gasping for air. He darted his eyes around wildly, scanning nothing but darkness, delirious and confused. He heard Zaphod fluttering around and cawing, probably startled from his sudden movement.

Rubius's heart pumped wildly in his chest, and he felt his blood flowing hard through him as he managed to catch his breath. Slowly, blues started filling into the room, then eventually grays. A flutter of red flew across his vision—probably Zaphod, still disturbed. After a few more seconds, the details of his cabin became clear.

Rubius haphazardly combed his fingers through his chin-length hair, then quickly tied it back out of his sweaty face. A few strands in front managed to fall slip out of the ponytail.

Come back to me… The words reverberated in his head, over and over again. *Come back to me…*

Rubius fumbled his hands across his nightstand, grasping for the liquor bottle he had been drinking earlier. He yanked it off the stand and popped the cork, downing half the bottle.

Come back to me…

The liquor burned down his throat and into his body. The harsh liquid mixed with the words like a slap, fully awakening him.

He heard her screams, calling out a strange name. It was as if she were in trouble or needed help. Rubius polished off the rest of the liquor as his parrot cooed in protest.

"I don't need another lecture right now," Rubius scolded Zaphod as the parrot perched on his shoulder. "If only you dreamt what I just did, you wouldn't complain."

Zaphod nudged him, with Rubius petting him in response to the parrot's apology. The bird cooed, then fluttered back to his spot in the cabin. At times, Rubius wondered if the parrot truly did understand his thoughts. Maybe it was because of his violet power mixed with his special attachment to the bird.

Why me? Why does she keep appearing to me? Rubius thought, wiping the sweat off his head. Throughout his entire life, ever since he could even remember his dreams, he would dream of *her*—this green-gifted woman. It had started when he was a boy, and they came every couple of years, but then it became more frequent as he became a man.

Perhaps he was causing the whole mess himself, dwelling on his strange dreams, thus causing himself to subconsciously re-dream of the green-gifted woman. But these dreams, they felt *different* from the others. It was one of the many reasons why he sought out answers, looking to see if this woman was real. And when the time traveler man appeared to him years ago, telling him of the white-gifted woman pregnant with a green-gifted girl… it solidified his suspicions that these were more than just dreams.

Shaking the empty bottle to ensure there was no more, Rubius chucked the bottle to the foot of the bed. He pressed his face near the airship's window, peering out into the night sky. The moon was full against the clouds. The ship had to be close to World Sector Six; it was nearly the middle of the night. Perhaps a few more hours and they would be at Six's royal citadel.

He needed some air.

Quickly throwing on his boots, Rubius grabbed Zaphod and perched him on his shoulder. The parrot protested for a moment with a caw, then made himself comfortable on his favorite spot on Rubius's shoulder.

"Let's go see how close we are," he said to his feathered friend. "I can't stand to be stuck in this cabin another minute."

As Rubius opened the compartment door and ascended to the deck, the winds picked up, rushing through his hair. The wind had an icy bite, chilling him to the bone. Not even his thick black jerkin could block out the cold. The wind. It gave him strength, vitality, and power. And that power made him feel so *alive*. It was as if the wind itself carried energy, refreshing his spirit.

It was eerily silent out on the airship deck; only the sounds of the high winds could be heard along with the creaking of the ship. The full moon cast its pale light upon the old wooden floorboards. Rubius could see a crew member up in the crow's nest high in the mast, looking out for any other airships flying close by, ready to warn the captain.

Rubius neared the ledge of the ship, staring off into the distance at the blackish-blue clouds highlighted by outlines of bright white from the moonlight. It spread out before him, as far and as vast as the eye could see. The full moon stood proudly above the clouds, majestically spreading its light before him.

"It's beautiful, isn't it?"

He whirled around quickly with Zaphod clutching his shoulder, both startled at the sudden voice. There was a soft movement in front of him, outlined in transparent orange. Slowly, an orange glow appeared within the outline, then a shimmering brilliance formed Lady Elyathi.

Great, he though inwardly.

"You here to criticize me?" Rubius said.

"I am never out to criticize anyone. You put that upon yourself with your poor decisions," she said, still shimmering with orange magic, becoming clearer until her full color returned to her.

Rubius snorted, then brushed off her statement. Perhaps it was her way to make amends, or to smooth out their rocky start.

Elyathi joined him next to the ledge, looking off into the clouds. Zaphod cocked his head curiously at her.

"Beautiful bird," she said with a soft smile on her face. "I meant to tell you earlier."

"Thanks. I'm rather attached to him. He goes where I go," Rubius said, then turned to face her. "Why couldn't I see you right away?"

"Because you are red-gifted."

"Well, that's apparent," Rubius said. "But I don't think I need to remind you that I do have powers of the orange and violet as well. I should still have been able to detect you." Elyathi knew that fact; she had even mentioned it previously.

"Is it true?" she asked. "That you are just as strong with the violet gift as you are with your given red gift?"

Rubius shrugged, thinking of the sorceress. "You will soon find out."

She gave him a glare, slighted by his statement. "You really are rude, aren't you?"

"I didn't intend for it to come off like that, Lady," Rubius said. "You see, I have never matched my violet magic against another. It will be a real test to see how I hold up."

Her dark glare melted from her face, then she nodded. "Forgive me, High Inquisitor. I thought you were mocking me."

Rubius shrugged. "It's fine. I get it a lot." He looked over at Elyathi, studying her. "You never answered my question, though. How come I couldn't see you with my orange gift abilities?"

"Because I am different." Elyathi didn't meet his eyes, just continued to look off into the distance.

"Different? You mean enhanced? Or is *blessed* the correct term? Blessed by the High Court?" Rubius was no fool when it came to the High Court and their "blessings."

Elyathi turned, giving him a serious look. "I am not blessed by the High Court, Inquisitor. I am set apart, above all others."

"Is that so?"

"It is."

"You mean how you were blue-gifted, then you now are suddenly orange-gifted?" Rubius eyed her. "What kind of magic is that, anyway?"

"A magic that was spoken in an ancient prophecy," Elyathi answered, sounding almost melancholy. Her long wavy hair suddenly caught itself in a gust of wind, sweeping itself in its stream, while her robes swept up around her. A glimmering flash caught his eye, then he noticed that the woman had several silver necklaces around her neck, each having a colored jewel attached at the end of it. But there were also two necklaces, both with empty vials attached at the end of the chain.

Acutely aware that he saw her necklaces, Elyathi grasped them and tucked them back into the folds of her robe as Rubius's eyes darted away.

The winds died down, and he felt her position herself toward him. Her orange eyes flickered in the dark as she looked at him.

"I do hope Belinda is right about you," she said. "To be honest, I voiced my opinion several times to the High Court in opposition of your advancement. Granted, you do have the power that suits our cause, but you do not have the heart."

"Don't have the heart?" Rubius said. "What's that supposed to mean? You think those other jokers have a heart? Because I can assure you that's not the case."

Unamused, Elyathi glared at him, her face still dead serious. "I have seen you, High Inquisitor. You are irrational, careless, and live for earthly pleasures." She neared him, her eyes burning with power. "To strive for complete holiness in this world is to keep the world at peace and harmony, to live side by side with the God of Light's laws, and to walk blameless. And to me, you don't seem to care much about anything, let alone any of the God of Light's laws, the established laws of the High Court, or even laws from the old citadel records. So listen up, and listen good. You had best shape up and devote yourself to the greater good." She neared him, lifting her chin high. "Otherwise I will take care of you *myself*."

"Do you mean 'strip away my power' like you mentioned in the High Court chamber earlier? Is that even a *power*? Just who in the hell do you think you are, anyway?" Rubius snorted. To think, him being lectured by some random gifted! He didn't care who she was or how powerful she was *supposed* to be. No one should talk to him like that. He was the High Inquisitor, for god's sake!

She narrowed her eyes. "I am the chosen one," she breathed, her voice almost musical. "You cannot go against me, High Inquisitor. You will lose sorely if you do."

The chosen one? What in the hell does she mean by that?

It took every ounce of energy for Rubius to harness his rage and not do anything irrational. His body shook, and every fiber of his being withheld his violet magic, which was ready to be expelled at a moment's notice.

Instead, Rubius clenched his teeth. "I have never been *lectured* by religious zealots throughout all my time on the High Court, and I will certainly not let it begin now," he stated sharply.

She narrowed her eyes, the orange in them burning. "Don't think you are all important just because you are High Inquisitor. It was no religious lecture. I seek a better world that will bring peace, and I need to ensure all those involved will do the same."

"You think I don't want peace?"

"I sure hope you do, High Inquisitor. For all our sakes." Her eyes softened, then she bowed. "I want what is best for everyone and our world." Before he got another word in, she said, "We will be arriving soon. I'll remain unseen while you talk to the Empress."

Elyathi began to glow in her orange magic, then faded away. He then heard four soft footsteps, then she was gone.

Rubius took a few deep breaths, trying to calm his anger. Elyathi pushed all of his buttons, whether it was intentional or not. The more they conversed, the more he did not like the woman. At all. But there was something that was bothering him. Why did she seem so familiar?

He turned his focus to Zaphod, then gently patted the bird as it nudged him. He took one last look at the night sky, then walked back to his quarters.

CHAPTER 24

ORANGE

Night had fallen on the wastelands, and all Telly could see was pure darkness out of the transport window, with the exception of the air transport's floodlights. She had forgotten how far out their wasteland camp really was from Arcadia. They had been flying for a good amount of time now.

The transport rattled, making Telly's stomach jump.

"How much longer until we reach Arcadia?" Telly asked through the transport headset, sick from the motion.

"Hard to say, considering most of our communication signals are jammed," Reila answered back. "By my poor estimation, we are still a long ways off. You might as well sit back and relax, city girl. Besides, we have to get clearance to enter Arcadia's airspace, and I can't talk to anyone until we are in range to pick up a signal."

"Did they give you permission last time you showed up unannounced?"

"Not at all. But at that time, the city was a shitshow with all the cyborgs and magic flying around like a damn circus, so we just flew through anyway. No one shot at us, so it worked out."

"Do you think Olympia is jamming Arcadia's communications as well?"

Reila shrugged. "I'm guessing most likely not. The only thing I know about radio shit is that jamming frequencies tends to be localized in one area. The jamming signal would only affect the area around wherever the jamming signal is coming from. With our camp so damn far from Arcadia, I doubt that they're being affected by it."

Telly shifted again in her seat and yanked off her headset, trying to find a new position that wouldn't bother her back. The cockpit was uncomfortable. The transport that Reila piloted was nothing like the transports in Arcadia, and it didn't help that the jerkiness of Reila's piloting skills made Telly queasy. That was saying something, considering she never got sick on flights. Telly wondered if Arcadia would even clear this contraption in their airspace, or whether they'd even be able to reach them to ask.

Telly glanced out the window once again, trying to take her mind off the motion of the flight. She wanted to ask Reila to pilot the air transport so that the ride was smoother, but Reila looked like the type who wouldn't want to hear that sort of feedback, so she held her tongue. Outside the window, floodlights of the transport highlighted the sand dunes as they flew over each one, making it seem never ending. Every so often, they would fly over a bonfire, which Telly knew had to be one of the many encampments within the wastelands. She and Drew had gone to several of those encampments before, looking for scrap parts to repair the cyborgs that had shown up at their own camp.

Reila yanked off her headset, then lit a cigarette, puffing it within her clenched jaw. A giant cloud of smoke filled the compartment, quickly making the atmosphere smoky. The cigarette smell was overwhelming, burning Telly's throat as she breathed and tickling her nose. She coughed hard, then sneezed.

Quickly scouring through the transport's compartment, Telly hoped to find a tissue or a piece of paper to at least wipe her nose, but there was nothing but soda cans and gum wrappers that littered the floor of the vessel.

"Do you mind?" Telly said as she wiped the edge of her nose with her sleeve, sneezing again. She fixed her glasses, out of place from the jerk of her sneeze.

Reila didn't look at her, but she took another deep inhale, then tossed the cigarette out the window and exhaled.

"Better?"

"I guess," Telly said, coughing hard once again. "Water?"

Reila yanked a canteen from the side of her thigh belt, shoving it toward Telly. "Here."

"Thanks." Telly took a drink. The warm water wasn't refreshing in the slightest, but it did help the itch in her throat.

"So what's the story with you?" Reila asked, her eyes fixated straight ahead, concentrating on piloting.

"What do you mean?"

"You know. About Drew and your daughter. How did that all work out? Was he a cyborg when you decided to get it on?"

Telly's jaw dropped, giving her an incredulous look. "Well, that is a personal question if I have ever heard one before," Telly remarked. "Do you go around asking people about their sex lives often?"

"Not at all. But with something like that, it's hard not to ask."

"The answer is no. He was a human before," Telly snapped. "You happy now?"

"I guess. So I take it he was a scientist before he was a cyborg? You guys worked together?"

Reila was not one to make small talk, especially with one like her. The woman liked to keep her conversations to herself for the most part.

Maybe she just wants to get to know me. Or maybe the whole camp wanted to know, and it's been talked about during drunken parties.

Slightly flustered, Telly continued. "I met Drew while working at one of Arcadia's labs, doing research. At the time, he was developing some new technology, and I knew that what he was working on was my kind of thing. Over time, as we got to know each other, we became involved. However, we dared not tell anyone at the corporation we were working for at the time, as we both could have gotten fired. So we kept our relationship a secret, and made it come off like we were partners in research.

"Soon after, I ended up getting pregnant. I had to tell the corporation because I had to take maternity leave, but I never told anyone who the father was. It was a secret between Drew and me. As far as anyone knew, including my coworkers, it was a one-night stand from someone I met at a bar. They believed me, and the lie quickly spread throughout the corporation, something which I wanted them to do to make our relationship safe.

"A few years after Gwen was born, Drew and I attended a work party that the corporation hosted. We took an air transport taxi home..."

Her voice trailed off, and Telly paused, remembering the incident. She recalled seeing the pilot's windshield plummeting downward, right toward a building. The heat of the flames erupting. Drew's body, mangled, pinned within the debris of the transport. The flames... they burned his body. She couldn't help him. She tried pulling him free, but the weight of the debris… Oh god, she couldn't save him!

Reila glanced over at her, remaining silent. Only the sounds of the transport could be heard humming through their aircraft.

Snapping out of her thoughts, Telly wiped a small tear from under her glasses, then adjusted them back into place. She cleared her throat, then met Reila's eyes. "After the air transport accident, I had Drew cryogenically frozen until the technology that we had developed was finalized." A tear ran down her face again as she laughed at the same time. "It's ironic, isn't it? The same technology Drew had been developing made him who he is now. And the worst part is, for all those years, I lied to my daughter, telling her that her father was dead. I never told her the *truth*. The only reason she found out about him was that he went to my apartment and found her. Can you imagine? Your own mother telling you that your father is dead, and come to find out, he's alive. I'm sure she will never forgive me for that."

Reila glanced over at her. "I would give you a hug, but I'm not the hugging type. Plus, if I did, you would have to relive another transport accident with my hands not being on the controls."

Telly wiped her tear, then laughed at Reila's statement. "Thanks."

"Don't worry about your daughter. Seems to me she's over it."

"That's what you think. But when no one else is around, she constantly argues with me about *everything*. It seems she argues with me more than not."

Reila half-smiled. "She's a teen. That's what they do."

"I never argued with my parents," Telly pointed out.

"And you're clearly not normal. You can't compare yourself to her."

"Excuse me?"

"She'll understand why you did what you did when she's grown up, and she'll thank you for it." Reila shrugged, putting her headset back on. "We should be there soon."

"Good. My back is killing me," Telly managed to say, straightening her position, kicking a few cans on the floor of the transport as she did so. "You know, it wouldn't hurt to clean this thing once in a while."

"Not my problem Garrett is a slob. You should know that by now. This transport is his, and I'm not his damn maid."

"You do have a point," Telly said, eyeing the trash. She shifted her legs, kicking the old cans again. A burst of rancid stench permeated the air around her, making her feel even sicker than Reila's piloting skills.

Telly turned her head to the side to avoid the smell, looking out her side window. There were red flashing lights forming a pattern; Telly could have sworn it was in a shape of a *V*.

She watched the strange pattern slowly increase in size, and the lights became larger and brighter.

"I wonder what that is?" Telly said, still gazing out the window.

"What is what?"

"That," Telly said, pointing to the red light pattern.

Reila looked over, then a look of shock hit her face. "Shit." Reila pressed a few buttons, then pulled a lever. The transport shook, then sped up.

"Reila? What is going on? What is that?"

"Trouble. That's what."

"What do you mean by trouble?" Telly began to shake.

"Olympia."

Panic washed over her, and Telly's heart rate increased. Dramatically. She looked out the window again. This time, the red lights were much larger. She turned back to Reila.

"Are you sure it's Olympia? How do you know?" Telly asked quickly.

"Olympia uses that particular flying formation with those colors. I guarantee that's the damn dispatch unit looking for that robot, Scion."

Just when Telly was about to look out the window again, there was a blast, then a loud burst coming from the back of the transport.

The transport jerked hard, and they began whirling in all directions. Telly's head slammed against the window, then the seatbelt locked her into place. Reila frantically pushed buttons and jerked the wheel in response.

Suddenly, Telly felt a drop in her belly as the transport lost gravity.

"Shit!" Reila screamed through the headset.

The transport continued to spiral out of control, the force of the motion so great that Telly's breath was sucked right out of her.

This can't be happening! This cannot be happening! Panic overwhelmed her, then out of sheer helplessness, she burst out crying.

"Please do something!" Telly begged Reila through her headset.

"I'm trying, but the damn thing isn't responding!"

With her face still smashed against the window, Telly saw a glimpse of the red lights from the Olympian transports as their rinky-dink transport tumbled hard. Over and over, the motion swirled, with Telly seeing the opposing transports in and out of sight.

There was another big blast, and the transport rocked violently. The engine blew loudly, roaring in her ears.

"Brace yourself!" Reila yelled.

The ground was coming up fast. Too fast.

They were going to crash.

And she was going to die. Telly closed her blurry, tear-stained eyes hard, accepting her fate.

If only she had power like Drew! If only she believed in magic in the first place, maybe she would have had the power to save them.

With another sharp jerk, their transport stopped tumbling, smoothly steadying itself in the air.

Confused, Telly opened her eyes and regained her senses, looking around. She turned sharply to Reila, and they exchanged looks, then Reila turned and looked out the front windshield.

"What in the hell…?" she managed, awestruck.

Outside of their windshield, there was a powerful purple blast of energy. Within the surging purple energy were the Olympian transports. The energy swirled around them, then with a shark jerk, the magic whipped violently in the air, causing all the Olympian transports to smash together. Telly flinched at the sudden devastation.

Upon impact, the ships burst into a giant explosion in the air. But this explosion was not normal fire… It was purplish-red, a massive fireball of an explosion, engulfing all the Olympian transports. Shards from the transports shot to the desert ground, all embraced with the purple magic. When each of the chunks of the machinery crashed, they exploded like bombs, debris ricocheting in every direction.

The violet fires roared, with machinery fragments littered all across the sands. Whoever had been piloting those Olympian transports, Telly was absolutely sure that none had survived.

Reila's transport began to shift softly, and they slowly landed on the ground. As their transport came to a halt, Telly saw an outline of a person standing against bright purple magic. The person's hands were outstretched, but they lowered them.

Suddenly, their transport landed, slamming into the desert sands. Telly shut her eyes quickly in response, still frightened by the whole experience.

A few moments when by, then Reila finally spoke. "Damn."

Telly opened her eyes. Directly outside the front windshield, some of the magical purple fires still burned, along with normal orangish-red fires rippling in the wasteland winds. There were no signs of Olympian survivors.

Reila tried to fire up the transport, but the engine wouldn't turn over. She shot Telly a look. "I don't like any of this. That magic weirdo scares me. And the fact that all of Olympia's transport scouts were just annihilated. Between this and Scion, we are going to be two very dead women." Reila fidgeted with her seatbelt, but it wouldn't release properly. "Really?" she snarled at the seatbelt.

Trying to unbuckle her own seatbelt, Telly realized hers was malfunctioning as well, keeping her locked in place.

"I can't get out!" Telly said.

"Just like I said. Very dead women."

The shadow came closer, still engulfed in a bright purple magic radiating. As the magic faded, a woman came into view. She had olive skin, a gaunt face, purple eyes and mohawk, and strange inked designs on her chest with a jewel in the middle of her forehead.

Recognition came to her immediately. Telly had seen this woman before; she had battled against the sorceress. Though Telly had never personally exchanged words with her, she knew that others had trusted her during that magical battle.

"I know her!" Telly said hopefully.

"Oh, good. Can you ask her not to kill us?"

"She's… one of us?" Telly said. It was an odd statement. *Us.*

"Can you get out?" the woman called out from outside the transport, her voice muffled.

Reila shook her head in response.

"We're stuck," Telly called out.

The woman raised her hand, and it glowed bright violet. With a sharp jerk of her wrist, the transport doors ripped open, and their seatbelts burned with magic, unbuckling themselves.

Sighing with relief, Telly plopped down from the transport, and Reila did the same on her side.

"I've seen you before, though I don't know your name," Telly said as she fixed her glasses.

"Geeta."

Telly looked around, seeing the massive damage surrounding her. The winds picked up, scattering the wasteland sands across the scene, flickering the fires and gliding the broken pieces of the transports across the ground.

Telly looked back at Geeta curiously. "How did you know we were in trouble?"

"I had a disturbing feeling from my prophetic magic. I decided to follow my instincts, and it led me here," Geeta said solemnly. "And it appears that my instincts were correct. Why were you being attacked?"

"I assume those transports thought we were carrying one of their missing cyborgs."

Geeta studied her. "Olympia has cyborgs?"

Telly nodded. "Yes. Armies of them. And they have magical abilities, just like Arcadia's."

"Magic? Are you sure?" Geeta asked.

"Yes, without a doubt," Telly reaffirmed. "Olympia is planning a massive invasion of Arcadia with their magic-infused cyborgs, and they intend to kidnap the King and Queen. Olympia wants their magic. The only reason we happened onto this was one of the Olympian cyborgs came to our camp. He is a free thinker, and has evidence that proves everything I just told you. He was being hunted by an Olympian dispatch unit."

"Ain't doing much hunting now," Reila said, eyeing the shrapnel.

"Where is this cyborg?" Geeta asked.

"Hidden away in one of the wasteland refuges. He should be safe… for the time being," Telly said. She then looked to Geeta. "We were on our way to see Queen Emerald. That is, until we were attacked."

Geeta met her gaze evenly. "Then we'd best be off to the palace. Now." Geeta motioned to both women. "Both of you, hold on to one of my hands," Geeta ordered as she held out her hands.

"A chance to hold a cute girl's hand? Sounds good to me," Reila said casually.

A smirk ran across Reila's face as Geeta quickly grabbed her hand. There was an odd pause for a moment, and Telly could have sworn she saw a little red in Geeta's cheeks, but as quick, it was gone, making her think she imagined it.

Telly hesitantly held out her hand, but then yanked it away. "Will it hurt? I've never experienced any other magic except orange…"

"You mustn't be afraid of the magic. Especially blue, for blue magic is the complement to your own color," Geeta said, her voice even and smooth as glass as she took her hand. Her eyes glowed a vibrant purple, eerily casting a violet light in the darkness.

Complement to orange? She wasn't even a true orange-gifted. She was… half.

Telly shifted. "But how are you able to summon blue magic? Yours is violet," she pointed out.

"That is true, but I will be summoning the power of blue, as it sits next to my own color in the Spectrum of Magic." She hinted at a smile. "And the fact that I've consumed the blood of the blue makes it easier for me to tap into."

As much as Telly was considered "gifted" herself, she was scared being around other gifted. They were so powerful, and she was *not*. What if she was washed away by their power? What if her body couldn't withstand that kind of energy?

"Your life force… it radiates fear," Geeta said, interrupting her thoughts. "Fear of its own power. If you would just let go of that fear, your magic might fully embrace your life force, and even unlock the full potential of your color."

Telly's eyes suddenly met Geeta's. "You think… I could get the full power of orange magic?"

Geeta shrugged. "I do not know for certain. I have seen many things in my lifetime, over the many centuries. And one thing I do know is this: If you fear the magic, you can never fully master it." She gave her a serious look, then nodded. "We need to go."

"This will be fun," Reila said in a smug tone.

Telly clutched Geeta's hand tightly, still feeling reluctant.

"And just to let you know, your body can withstand anyone's magic. That is a silly fear you need to let go."

Telly was stunned. "How… how did you know what I was thinking?"

"I heard your thoughts."

Before Telly could get another question in, violet-blue power flooded Telly's body, and the world burst into violet tones.

CHAPTER 25

YELLOW

Auron took one of the censers, lighting the incense inside. The smoke curled into the air, mixing with the cool morning breeze. He was alone, before any of the other holy brothers and sisters arrived at the temple. This was his time, as the light aligned itself in between the pillars for the break of day, reaching perfection.

Auron fell to his knees, then knelt in prayer, his words softly whispering from his lips like honey as he uttered the worries of his heart. He prayed for the Empress, for the people of World Sector Six, and what was to come of the visit of the High Inquisitor. He prayed in earnest, hoping that the High Court's anger had subsided, that they weren't truly upset at Ayera, that the High Inquisitor's visit was only to interrogate the Sorceress Ikaria. Nothing more.

As he prayed, Auron felt the burning light radiate from him, his gift flowing through his veins and into his heart, giving him some sense of peace. It was strange, ever since coming back from the past, when he had helped capture the sorceress, his life force felt different. But even though it was different, it was a *good* different. If Auron had to describe the feeling, he would say it was as if he was whole. It didn't make sense, but that was exactly how he felt.

Light footsteps sounded, and immediately, Auron released his magic, calling it back into the core of his being. As the magic faded, he opened his eyes to see the priests waiting to enter the temple for their prayers. It was safe to enter now. They came wisping by him, situating themselves in their normal spots, and began their daily prayers. After some time, their whispered prayers became louder as they uttered in their heavenly language, and soon the room was filled with prayers of all kinds.

During their prayers, there was a sudden loud pounding at the temple door, interrupting everyone. Their magic faded away, and the brilliant golden magic dissipated.

The High Inquisitor must have arrived, he thought. An unsettling feeling came over Auron.

Auron ran up to the door, removing the wooden barricade. As he opened the door, he found himself facing a set of guards in the hall.

"High Priest Auron," one said while they bowed. "The Empress has announced that the time has come."

Auron looked at them. "Tell the Empress we will be on our way immediately."

They bowed again and took off, while Auron turned back to look at the temple full of priests.

"It is time," Auron announced to them.

At once, they all rose to their feet, quickly vacating the temple in all different directions, knowing what they had to do and where to be. Then he was alone.

Auron took a last long look at the temple, his eyes resting on the Spectrum of Magic symbol.

God of Light, please protect us for what we are about to do, he prayed silently. He took a deep breath, purifying his soul with the fragrant incense and prayers that lingered in the air. Auron turned, heading to the temple door.

"High Priest!" a voice call out from across the room.

Auron turned around, seeing a young priest, around fifteen or sixteen years of age. It was the very same boy priest who had asked him the difficult question about the God of Light and sacrificing themselves before they had time traveled months ago.

How had Auron not seen the boy moments ago? He could have sworn he was alone…

The young priest ran up quickly to Auron. "High Priest," he repeated.

"What is it, young man?"

"Forgive me, High Priest, but there is something I must tell you," said the boy.

"Yes?"

"It's just… Well, I had a vision while I was praying," the boy said nervously.

"A prophecy?"

"I… I think so? I can't be sure since I've never had one before, but I believe so."

"Can this wait? The Empress has summoned everyone into position," Auron said. Now was really not the time to be talking about boyish visions.

The boy shook his head quickly. "No, I know in my spirit that… that I have to tell you this now!" His golden eyes met his. "I heard a word… a word that you need to know."

"A word?"

"Yes," the boy continued. "'Prophesy.' That is the word."

Auron raised his eyebrow. "Are you sure that this was a vision intended for me?" Auron asked, doubting the boy. After all, he was very young, almost too young to receive visions from the yellow magic. Most priests didn't receive visions until they were at least eighteen years old. This boy was at least two to three years away from that.

"I know that word was meant for you, High Priest," the boy said.

Auron paused, then moved closer. "Are you most sure?"

"Yes, High Priest. I know you are to 'prophesy.' That is all I know."

Prophesy. What was it supposed to mean? Maybe it wasn't a vision or prophecy, but what the boy thought in his head at the time of prayer.

"Thank you for telling me," Auron said, nodding at the boy. He patted him on the shoulder.

The boy beamed, then bowed. "Yes, High Priest. I hope it helps you!" The boy ran out of the temple.

Auron sighed.

Prophesy. It didn't make sense.

Auron took a deep, nervous breath, then hustled out the door.

***

The hall was silent but for a few low whispers between the lords and ladies of the court. The gifted, all that remained of World Sector Six, were hidden amongst the audience hall, scattered through the crowds of nobility where Ayera had planned on them being. No one hardly dared breathe louder than they had to. Someone could have dropped a pin onto the marbled floor, and it would have been heard throughout the audience hall.

Auron stood to the side of Ayera, still as anyone else within the hall, a firm expression on his face. He had to. It gave the other gifted a sense of strength, and the lords and ladies a sense of security for what they were about to do. But underneath his outward appearance, Auron's stomach was unsettled by his nerves. He never liked arguments, fights, and battles, and had always thought of himself as a peaceful man. Ironically, he found himself in those very situations a lot more lately.

Auron glanced over at the Empress. Ayera was seated on her throne, her face cold and without emotion. She looked the most ornate she had ever appeared in court. She wore a fiery red kimono beaded and embroidered in gold, with many sections of her hair looped and twisted at the top of her head, secured with jeweled ornaments. Even her face was heavily painted with bright makeup, like a warrior using battle paint to scare off the enemy in the ancient tales. Perhaps the Empress sought to prove to the High Inquisitor that she was determined to keep her throne and her sector. Even Auron thought Ayera looked intimidating.

Auron was impressed that Ayera showed no hint of fear, especially since she didn't even have a gift to fight against the High Inquisitor. Auron wasn't sure how powerful the High Inquisitor truly was, but for the High Court to send him alone, he must be extremely powerful. Auron himself was afraid of the magic they were about to face, and he couldn't help but marvel at her determination. Usually, Auron could detect some anxiety just from her slight movements or expressions. But now, the Empress showed absolutely none. She was willing to fight for what she believed was right.

While they waited for the High Inquisitor to appear, Auron prayed over and over again. As his words formed within his mind, he felt his golden-yellow magic flowing through him and subtly flowing over the Empress, cloaking her in its power. He had no idea why, but as he prayed, the barrier magic didn't appear how it normally did whenever he cast a protection spell. This time it couldn't be seen by the naked eye; he could hardly see the protection at all, only a glimmer every so often, reassuring him that it was there.

Suddenly, there was a creak in the doors. The sound thundered through the hall, and all heads turned.

The High Inquisitor had arrived.

Auron's heart began to hammer in his chest while he fought to remain still.

A few seconds passed, and then there was scuffling of boots against the marble floor, echoing loudly in the hushed hall. As the footsteps became louder, Auron could see the High Inquisitor down the aisle, approaching the Empress's throne.

The power, the presence that radiated from the High Inquisitor… it was as if it demanded one should look at him. As he neared, Auron could make out the man's features. He was handsome, with ruby-colored hair, crimson eyes, and pale skin, somewhere in his late twenties in age. His jerkin was made of the most expensive black fabrics and was left unbuttoned, revealing a violet silk shirt with many ruby jewels and amulets adorning his neck and bare chest. Even his fingers were adorned with red garnets and stones.

As the High Inquisitor came directly in front of the Empress, Auron froze.

Ghost Man?

Auron blinked in disbelief.

He continued to stare at the High Inquisitor, as if he had been struck across the face. The High Inquisitor turned to him, and their eyes met. Indifferent, the High Inquisitor's gaze then moved to Ayera. Behind the inquisitor, a slew of High Court guards came marching down the aisle, many of them gifted themselves. There were more than what Ayera and the Inner Council had thought and planned for. Not a good sign.

Ayera didn't rise from her throne, as was customary. Instead, she sat on her throne, giving the High Inquisitor a nod.

"High Inquisitor Rubius. We are honored by your presence," she stated, waving her golden scepter in the air, letting all those in the hall know that the court was now in session. More importantly, secretly letting everyone within her sector know to ready themselves.

The High Inquisitor snorted at her greeting, then flashed a smile, eyeing the court of nobles. "Empress Ayera, how nice of you to greet me with all of your court present. There really was no need for all of this." He waved his hand nonchalantly at the court. "I see that the Emperor is not present. I was expecting to be greeted by him personally."

"He is indisposed, High Inquisitor," Ayera answered.

"Is that what you call it?"

"That is precisely what I call it," Ayera stated firmly. "I found out he had been masking his gift. We only did what was necessary; there are strict laws in place for those who hide their gift. I believe that also includes any ruling figure. And since he hid his gift from this court, I did what any other ruler should do—imprisoned him and waited for judgment from the High Court itself."

"High Justice Belinda of the Red sent you orders to release him," Rubius stated.

Auron eyed the High Inquisitor steadily as he continued to take in his features. *It can't be him... can it?* he thought in disbelief.

Ayera held her head high and proud, continuing. "High Inquisitor, I am under the impression that it is law for the High Court to schedule a hearing for cases like these. I did not want to break any laws, regardless of an order from Belinda of the Red, unless a proper hearing was scheduled and a ruling determined by all of the members of the High Court. After all, those are the laws set in place in all the World Sectors, are they not?"

There were two heartbeats of silence, and the tension in the hall thickened immediately. Several of the High Court guards stood firm in their position.

Rubius sighed, then turned around absentmindedly, casually strutting around the hall. "Well, this is certainly something I did not expect. You have quite the spunk, Empress. I admire your zeal, but you know very well that any order that was directed by High Justice Belinda is an order from all the High Court. She speaks for us all, I'm afraid," Rubius's voice rose, ensuring that the entire court heard.

"Then why did all of the members of the High Court not sign the document? Especially when such orders break protocol?" Ayera rose from her throne firmly, her head held high, her gaze locked with Rubius's.

Auron turned to eye several of the gifted on both sides of the court aisle, then scanned to see where the High Court gifted were within their guard. A slight orange blurry movement caught his eye off to the side of the audience hall, then it was gone. Had he imagined it?

"Empress Ayera, unfortunately, you will not win this argument, and you should stop before you dig yourself deeper into a situation you can't arise from. You were *ordered* not to have your gifted travel back in time, but instead, you did so anyway, without heeding the counsel of the High Court. That, in itself, is a serious violation."

Auron swallowed his nerves as he narrowed his eyes, infuriated by the High Inquisitor's words. He stepped forward, positioning himself in front of the Empress. "High Inquisitor," Auron interrupted, "I had a vision of prophecy given to me from my yellow gift. You must understand, despite what Belinda has told you, or even High Justice Tyllos, all of time would have ceased to exist if we had not stopped the sorceress. If Ikaria had gone through the portal back into our time with her black gift, our world would have ceased to exist as we know it."

The High Inquisitor's eyes met his, and Auron felt the overwhelming power of his life force. *Does he not recognize me?* Auron wondered. *I can't believe that's not him…*

"As much as I respect your position as High Priest of World Sector Six, those were not the orders your sector was given. And unfortunately, it now has brought us all here together in this fine mess."

Rubius turned his attention to the Empress. "I understand you needed to do what you needed to do, and now I have to do what I have to do." Rubius moved toward Ayera, his body starting to burn with a glowing red power as he held out a scroll with a wax seal. "Empress Ayera, you are hereby under arrest by order of the High Court. You are stripped of your title, and I am to have my guards accompany you back to World Sector Three. You are to go before the High Court and stand trial for your blatant disregard for the laws of the sectors, and be at their mercy for judgment."

Ayera stood in her place, unmoving; she did not even blink. "I am sorry, High Inquisitor, but I will not be joining you, nor will I appear before the High Court," she shot back coolly. As soon as the statement left her mouth, there was an eruption of wild cheers and clapping from the lords and ladies, with a mixture of them hurling insults at the High Inquisitor and his guards.

The High Inquisitor moved around slightly, still burning with his power.

"You hear that, High Inquisitor? It is my people whom I speak for. We at

Sector Six feel that the High Court no longer has the right to make decisions for us," Ayera stated boldly, her words cutting through the cheering, pointing at him. "Which means your visit is *unwanted.* We will deal with the sorceress on our own terms, which means she will remain imprisoned until the lords of my court have decided what is to be done with her. After all, Belinda made it clear it was my responsibility, and I intend to follow those *brilliant* words of hers. Go back and tell Belinda that we at World Sector Six no longer adhere to their laws, nor are we a part of the World Sectors! This is *my* sector!"

More cheers erupted for the Empress, while jeers about the High Court echoed.

Rubius sighed, then narrowed his burning red eyes. "You really don't want me to use my powers. It is unpleasant, and you seem like a good girl, one whom I don't want to squabble with. Just come with me and avoid unnecessary bloodshed."

"I think you are mistaken, High Inquisitor. You don't want *us* to unleash our powers against you. Now get out, and we will spare your life. We've had enough of the High Court's ideas on how they think we should run this sector!"

"Don't say I didn't warn you," Rubius snarled.

Rubius shot out his hands, and a red-violet force of wind suddenly circled around the Empress, trying to lift her from her feet. Rubius's force vortex met with Auron's invisible shield, and the red-violet energy squeezed the magical barrier instead of the Empress herself. Many of the non-gifted lords and ladies ducked for cover, while the gifted of World Sector Six came forward, casting their spells, the entire court erupting into chaos.

Auron immediately funneled more power into Ayera's barrier of protection, the golden stream of light enhancing its durability, while Rubius angrily funneled more power into his vortex. All the while, Ayera stood her ground, her eyes flaring with injustice at the High Inquisitor. Both magics fought one another and became brighter, until they both exploded, shocking the ceilings, causing some of it to crumble.

Auron struck his hands together, quickly forming a new golden energy around Ayera while the World Sector Six gifted fought the High Court gifted. The two sets of guards clashed with one another, and soon the massive hall became a magical battlefield.

"Like I said, High Inquisitor, we will no longer be taking orders from you or the High Court!" Ayera yelled. "Get him!" She held her scepter out, pointing right at him.

Several of the World Sector Six gifted unleashed their magic. Flashes of lightning lit the room, while others hurled fireballs. Some attempted to freeze Rubius into position. Auron cast a stream of massive golden energy, along with the other allied yellow-gifted, creating circular bubble barriers around all the World Sector Six gifted. One larger barrier, basked in bright yellowish-gold, swirled around Ayera, stronger than the others. Auron continued to fuel her magical shield.

Rubius smirked, then closed his eyes. Red energy wildly swirled around him, and when he opened his hot eyes of fire, all the flames of the World Sector Six gifted were snuffed out—the ice was a mere puddle at his feet, and the lightning spells cracked back at them, hitting their protective barriers. With another sweeping movement, Rubius grabbed the air within his fingertips, forming a violet force within his grasp. Jerking his hands, the violet force shot through the protective barriers as the High Court yellow-gifted melted away the opposing protection, causing Rubius to gain hold of them. The violet magic surrounded the World Sector Six gifted, squeezing them while the magic lifted them off their feet.

Rubius turned to Ayera. "Give up. I really don't want to hurt them."

"Never!" Ayera yelled back.

Frowning, Rubius turned back to the enraptured gifted, crushing their bodies while they screamed.

Frantically, Auron said a quick prayer, then filled himself with holy light from the yellow gift. Pulling all the energy that burned through his heart and into his veins and mind, his entire body lit up as bright as the sun, radiating pure protective light.

Help my brothers and sisters! he cried out to the magic.

Releasing the swell of magical energy, it burst from his body, funneling to those who were entangled in the violet magic.

The violet magic melted off the trapped gifted like hot wax, freeing his fellow gifted.

The yellow magic… it countered the violet power!

The yellow-gifted of World Sector Six cast new barriers around their comrades, with the red-gifted joining in. Both magics worked together in harmony as the casters allowed their magics to coincide. The two magics became one, becoming an elemental barrier of magic.

"I've had enough of this!" Rubius called out.

The High Inquisitor channeled his magic, filled with hot red fire. High winds joined in with his magic, fueling the glowing red flames. Larger and larger, his flames funneled around him like a growing fiery tornado, crackling with a force so powerful that even Auron could feel its underlying violet energy.

The room became hotter, even within their barriers, and Auron looked over at the Empress. Her body began to sway and waver from the intense heat.

"Someone shoot some water or ice into the Empress's barrier!" Auron yelled out to a nearby red-gifted.

One of the red-gifted heard, and a blast of red water poured over Ayera, mixing in with her shield. It helped, but not by much.

Rubius continued to grow the fiery tornado. Many around the room became overwhelmed by the heat, even his own guards and gifted. But it seemed the High Inquisitor cared not. The flames continued to ravage the hall, growing in size and making the heat unbearable. The red-gifted cast their red watery and icy spells to counter the hellish heat and flames, but it was like throwing a glass of water into a giant burning fire—it was no use. Many of the red-gifted recast ice magic, funneling themselves into the yellow barriers to combine the people with cool protection against the hot flames, but it only helped momentarily. As the whirling fires grew larger, World Sector Six's yellow magical shields began to glow bright, trying to protect them from being burned or scorched by the intense heat while the red ice started to melt away into puddles of water.

The High Inquisitor surged more power into the fiery red magical tornado, and it grew throughout the entire room with a sudden, violet energy.

Shields started failing, and suddenly, they were burned up in the powerful flames.

The gifted screamed.

Weakened, Auron focused on Ayera. She was on the verge of collapsing from the heat. He quickly summoned more of his magic, pouring it over the Empress.

Through Auron's transparent shield, he could see the World Sector Six red-gifted had gathered together, summoning a massive red tidal wave of magical waters, hurling it against the High Inquisitor's flames.

The two elements met with a powerful crack, countering each other for a moment. Rubius swept up his hand, sending their massive tidal wave right back at the opposing red-gifted, drowning them in their own watery magic. Then, with another jerk of his hand, the red waters assimilated into one large body of water, collecting itself. His hand started glowing with violet magic, and at the same time, the World Sector Six red-gifted moved unwillingly into the water, pushed by a red-violet force. They became submerged in the deep pool of water held up by invisible walls, and they couldn't fight the High Inquisitor's force, no matter how hard they tried.

The High Inquisitor's crimson eyes flashed with his magic. Instantly, the flames expanded in the room, turning up the heat.

Auron was becoming weary from the heat, and his thoughts were jumbled. He knew that the others were being sapped of their energy and strength from the unbearable hotness of the room.

He's too powerful...

Trying to fight his weariness, Auron could barely keep his eyes open in the intense heat. It was smothering him, and air was nowhere to be found. Weakly, he funneled some of his protective magic into the water, where the gifted were being submerged, trying to give an air bubble barrier to his comrades to breathe in the water. The magic flowed slower than he would have liked, but it did weakly stream into the body of water.

Suddenly, the High Inquisitor's fires intensified, burning so bright red that they were almost white. Many of barriers broke and shattered, incinerating half the gifted within.

Auron looked to Ayera. Her barrier had burst, and she fell to the floor, weak from heat exhaustion.

"Do you surrender?" Rubius asked loudly.

There was no answer.

Shaking his head in disappointment, Rubius swooped with his hands. The Empress was then embodied within his pure violet magic, levitating in the air, her feet dangling like a rag doll. Fear mixed with anger flashed over her eyes, but she didn't say anything.

Rubius gave a look of disapproval. "I don't like it just as much as you do,

Empress, but no one can go against them. Not even someone like me," he said. "Call off this little charade. For the sake of your people."

Her face twisted with thought, and she frowned heavily.

"Don't give in to him," Auron called out to her.

Weakly, she rolled her head to the side, still feeble and fragile. "I am not giving up, High Inquisitor..." Her voice trailed hoarsely. "For the sake of my people, we will fight for what is right..."

"So be it." The High Inquisitor frowned. He clenched his palms, and the fires intensified. People screamed in pain from the sweltering heat. Others were yelling how they couldn't breathe. Auron couldn't either, nor any of the other gifted. It seemed the only one who could was the High Inquisitor himself, with exception of a few of the red-gifted.

Auron's heart began to darken as he took in what was happening before his eyes. How could the High Inquisitor do this to all these people? How could the High Court be so falsified hiding behind the God of Light? High Justice Tyllos and the other High Court justices cited many scriptures from *The Spectrum* to claim their authority, and everyone adhered to it. And for a while, all did seem well with them ruling over all the sectors, for it seemed everyone was at peace.

But it wasn't now. It was apparent to Auron that Ayera was right—they wanted the sorceress's magic. And that was exactly what he and the gifted from World Sector Six fought against, for no one should possess all the colors of magic. It was heresy! And they themselves were the ones seeking it. Their authority had been tainted.

Foreign, dark feelings flooded Auron's mind. They were... welcomed, filling his soul with the injustice, the despair, the wrath. Auron always tried to flee his dark thoughts when they appeared in his mind. But this time, he fed his dark thoughts, funneling the power that grew within his veins.

The dark side of the spectrum, the dark side of his yellow magic. Only once had he ever reached out for it.

And now again.

The dark-yellow magic burst through his body, his insides burning violently as he himself shook from the dark power. The darkness funneled out as he directed the dark magic with his hands.

Glaring at the High Inquisitor along with the High Court gifted and guards, Auron unleashed the dark magic with a giant rush of energy. The dark magic poured over the opposing men, crackling with flecks of gold, instantly encapsulating the High Inquisitor and his guards in dark-yellow translucent bubble barriers.

The High Court gifted screamed as the barrier began to rip their life force from their bodies, continuously crackling with the dark magic. The more they screamed, the more the magic vibrated in response, shaking the ground beneath their feet. The dark barriers… they were hurting them, not protecting them.

"Stop this madness, High Inquisitor," Auron called out hoarsely. The heat was getting to him, and soon he would be dead.

The High Inquisitor was about to cast a spell, but he was interrupted by a blue flash of light.

Auron blinked, then saw golden streams of bright-yellow magic counteract his dark barriers, freeing the High Court gifted from their pain.

Confused, Auron tried to see the source of the power, considering there had been no blue-gifted within their guard, nor were there any in World Sector Six.

Auron turned to the side and saw another bright flash; this time the flash was yellow.

A woman stood, encapsulated within yellow magic, her long wavy yellow hair flowing wildly as the fiery winds of Rubius's spell raged through the room.

The High Inquisitor looked back at her. "I thought you weren't going to get involved?" he yelled at her.

"You are taking far too long," she said, her voice almost sweet and musical.

The High Inquisitor snarled, then released his fiery tornado, letting the destruction take over the hall for all to be burned alive, including himself and the mysterious woman.

Auron instantly shielded himself from the flames, and his other comrades did what they could in time to protect themselves, whether it be with shields of ice or yellow barriers. The orange-gifted, God help them. Auron hoped that they were shielded by the others.

With a flick of the High Inquisitor's hand, the Empress was surrounded by red-violet magic, her body nearing him. Ayera fought and struggled, trying to escape the magic, her feet dangling and kicking aimlessly.

Several spells were shot at the High Inquisitor as he guided Ayera toward him. Red ice spikes, the earth moving and rumbling to impale him. With each attempt, it seemed that the High Inquisitor was able to counter them with his spells.

The Empress's body kept moving toward the High Inquisitor. Auron felt around the inside of his robes until he found it. His enchanted blade.

He started running toward Ayera. If he couldn't fight the High Inquisitor with his power, then he would do it the old-fashioned way, and perhaps the blade would cut through the violet magic.

The High Inquisitor, the strange yellow-gifted woman, and all the other gifted were focused on the Empress or each other.

Now was his chance.

He ran fast and hard… as fast as his hefty body could take him.

Suddenly, Auron felt a hand upon his, giving him a sharp yank. His body jerked hard, and he was whipped aside. He tripped and tumbled and slid to the side of the hall.

"You need to get out of here now!" a feminine voice whispered in his ear.

Auron looked around; he didn't see anyone.

Confused, he got to his feet. He was about to run again until he was pushed harder, this time toward the exit.

"That woman is dangerous, High Priest! If you value your gift from the God of Light, you must leave right now!"

"But the Empress…" Auron fought back.

The invisible hand grabbed him once again, jerked with a sudden movement.

"NOW!"

Auron started running blindly, letting the invisible grasp lead him out of the hall.

Then behind him, there was a bright white flash.

CHAPTER 26

Pure, bright white light. That was all Ayera could see.

Screams and cries of her people echoed through the hall. The High Inquisitor's magic was still wrapped around her body, squeezing her in its grasp. She was completely helpless. Why couldn't she have been born gifted like her sister?

Ayera felt the weight of her body shift within the forceful magic, then the white flash subsided.

As the magic faded, shapes and colors came into view. The High Inquisitor was directly in front of her, his eyes burning with a red glow as he narrowed his eyes at her.

Terror came over her. The look in his eyes, the fury that radiated from them… it alarmed her in every way, causing the hairs on the back of her neck to stand out. Ayera was powerless, and there was no escaping the High Inquisitor.

She gasped, then began to struggle once more.

From the corner of her eye, Ayera saw her sector's gifted writhing on the floor in pain, cradling their heads and rolling on the ground. Some screamed nonsense, others shouted out to the God of Light to make their pain cease. These gifted… they were her people, many were her dear and loyal subjects. Some had been in her service for many years, others had been around long enough that they'd served her father.

Ayera's eyes met Lord Jiao's across the room, his eyes empty of color.

Her heart burst with sadness; it was as if his soul was gone.

Standing over the screaming gifted strewn across the floor, the mysterious woman with long wavy hair stood silently, as if the screams didn't affect her. She no longer had her golden hair and eyes; they had changed to pure white.

A white-gifted woman? Ayera thought wildly. Her gaze fell on the screaming gifted, then it hit Ayera. These were the signs of the gifted losing their magic, the same symptoms as the plague.

This woman has to be behind the plague! she thought frantically.

Then an even more terrifying thought came over her. The woman had the power to take away her sister's violet magic...

More screams erupted from the World Sector Six's gifted. The sight of all her gifted drowning in their suffering; it was too much to bear. Ayera hadn't been frightened before the battle, but she was surely frightened now, especially with the white-gifted woman.

"What did you *do* to them?" Ayera called out to the woman, her eyes watering with tears.

The High Inquisitor looked just as stunned, as if it was quite possibly the first time he had ever seen the white-gifted's power. His face remained in awe, almost as if he'd been slapped. It looked like he wanted to say something, but whatever it was, he remained silent.

The white-gifted woman moved to stand behind the High Inquisitor, ignoring Ayera's question. She gave her a slight sympathetic look, then it morphed into a cold, calculating appearance. The High Inquisitor scanned all the screaming gifted, then turned back to face Ayera, giving her a hard stare.

"You were warned, Empress." He then turned to the mysterious woman. "I'll take her to the ship."

The woman nodded. "There are still several loose. I need to find them," she stated. "Also, I'll have you know that I have already released the Emperor. He should be presenting himself to you momentarily." She then tightened her grip around what looked like a necklace with a blue gemstone. Her body radiated blue magic suddenly, and within seconds, her hair and eyes were soaked in blue magic. Then, with a wave of her hand, there was a blue flash of magic.

The gifted woman was gone.

"Great," the High Inquisitor muttered to himself. He waved his hand. As he did so, Ayera felt her whole body move downward until her feet touched the ground. His power around her loosened, giving her some movement within the swirling, binding violet magic that streamed continuously around her body.

"Walk," he commanded.

"No," Ayera said defiantly. "I'm not moving."

Rubius sighed at her, shaking his head. "*Walk*."

"No. I *said*, I'm not moving!" Ayera shot back at him.

"He said walk, you little cunt!"

Out of the corner of the hall, there was movement from the shadows. A glimmer of pink and magenta stepped into the light.

Ayera bit her lip, then eyed the High Inquisitor, almost in a pleading sort of way.

"How the tables have turned," Emperor Cyrus spat, his eyes glowing a bright magenta. "My little cunt of a wife is still stubborn, even to the very end. It was the same with your cunt itself, you acting like it was the most precious thing in this sector." Cyrus walked over, nearing her. He reeked of stench from his confinement and was extremely dirty but for the simple clean robe he wore. He leaned in, his breath hot on her face. "Let me tell you something, *wife*. It wasn't even good. I had plenty better than you." A dark smirk appeared, and he laughed at his jab.

His words dug into her, stirring up hatred in her heart. Ayera couldn't stand him before. Now she hated him. How Ayera wanted to smack his face. But even if she were free, would she have?

His face still an inch from hers, Cyrus whispered, "I hope they decapitate your pretty little head. It would decorate the High Court's outside spikes nicely." He laughed again, then kicked her calves, causing Ayera to stumble to the floor. "Now walk, bitch!" He kicked her again. "Walk to your death!"

Rubius turned to him, throwing out his hands. A sharp red spike of ice whorled past Cyrus's face, the deadly spike nearly missing the Emperor's face by half an inch. Then a vibrant violet magic went hurling at the Emperor, knocking him back hard, his body hurling into a gifted that was already screaming.

"How dare you!" demanded Cyrus, getting to his feet, smoothing his clean robe as Ayera allowed herself a private smile.

"How dare *you* treat the prisoner in such a manner," Rubius said, his eyes glowing a hot red.

"You were just squeezing that bitch with your magic yourself," Cyrus argued.

"I had a purpose to that violence. You didn't," Rubius said curtly. "Now, do what you do best and warm that cold throne with your ass. I will deal with *my* prisoner how I see fit."

"And what of *my* gifted? I can't run a sector with them rolling around like that! What is wrong with them anyway?" Cyrus demanded.

"Looks like the plague hit them all at once." Rubius walked away, shrugging. "You better clean this place up. I am sure that the High Court will be wanting to visit soon after I am finished with this sector. Send word throughout the citadel that you are rightfully restored to the throne and the Empress is stripped of her title. And please"—he turned, glaring at Cyrus—"do make sure everyone knows who I am."

"I am *Emperor*, and *I* am in charge. I will be giving orders," Cyrus snapped.

"Is that what you tell yourself to sleep at night?" Rubius asked nonchalantly. "You are nothing more than a puppet for them, just the same as me. Don't you forget that, Emperor. Now, would you like to look at the High Court's decree? They made it very simple for even for one such as you to understand."

Cyrus's clenched his jaw, clearly insulted. Ayera smirked inwardly.

"Give it to me!" Cyrus demanded, extending his hand.

Rubius reached inside his pockets, then a scroll appeared in his hand. Cyrus snatched it, then hastily unrolled the document, reading it quickly. After a moment, he threw it back at the High Inquisitor.

"I am still reinstated as Emperor."

"And Belinda made me in charge of everyone, including you. Don't go screwing it up with your puffed-up pride." He turned to Ayera, the violet magic glowing brightly around her legs once again. "Come, Lady Galanos. Our ship awaits."

Her new title stung. She wasn't even worthy to be called by her first name. She was reduced to her surname. Her married surname.

"It's Lady *Suzuki*," Cyrus called out harshly. "She is not worthy to carry my last name. She can go back to her family where I found her. I am divorcing her as soon as the High Court approves it. That is, if she's still alive." His eyes darted to her, and he laughed.

His laugh was truly horrible, causing Ayera's heart to plummet to the pits of her stomach. Somehow, Ayera had a feeling that he was right. She would be dead soon.

"I'd rather die a thousand deaths than carry your name," Ayera yelled back.

"How poetic," Rubius commented from behind. "Let's go."

"I changed my mind, High Inquisitor," Ayera said to him. "There's no need to use your violet magic on me. I would be more than happy to leave this place."

"Fine by me."

His violet magic loosened, but only on her legs. Her body was still ribboned with bright violet magic, almost as if a magical rope were tied around her body, making her arms and hands immobile. She moved her legs as quickly as they would take her, following the High Inquisitor, walking past many of her gifted, who were still on the marbled floors screaming. Some were grunting in pain, while others shouted within their hallucinations. She continued to follow him until they were out of the hall and far away from her disgusting, lecherous husband.

Ayera's mind was racing. What had happened to her gifted? Did that white-gifted steal all the other gifteds' magic? Even the High Inquisitor had seemed surprised at her power.

"You are thinking of that woman, aren't you?" he asked in a surprisingly pleasant tone, a contrast to moments prior.

Ayera glanced at him as she walked. "That woman. She is the cause of the gifted losing their powers, isn't she?"

He didn't look at her, but Ayera could see it; he was definitely troubled by the white-gifted woman as well. He didn't answer her, and continued walking, saying nothing.

Of course he wouldn't answer. But his silence was telling.

Tears stung her eyes as Ayera was led through the citadel. Many of the citizens who had not been present in the hall, nor were aware of what had happened, paused at the sight of her being led out. More and more they gathered, whispering, pointing in shock. Soon, as she was being led down the main hall, it was packed as word traveled wildly.

She'd failed them. Everyone.

If only she'd listened to her sister.

Would Auron's prophecy have come true if she had believed Ikaria about the High Court and acted upon those beliefs? What if his prophecy was true, but it wasn't her sister that would have caused time ceasing to exist? What if it was the High Court's reaction to Ikaria's actions, one that had yet to take place, that caused the destruction of their world and their future?

That was a disturbing thought. And by the looks of it, the High Court was well on their way to getting her sister's magic. Unless, by some miracle, the God of Light intervened. But even now, no matter how she wished that to be, it seemed far too unrealistic.

From behind her, Ayera saw the many people of her sector following the High Inquisitor and the High Court guards as she was led onto one of the citadel airship platforms. At first, it was just a few lords and ladies. But as they marched out of the halls and onto the platform, Ayera could have sworn that it was all of the citadel's citizens. Some cried, others shouted.

"God of Light bless you!" some yelled.

"Release the Empress!" cried others.

"Down with the High Court! Damn them all to hell!"

The noise from the crowd became so great, even the High Inquisitor couldn't ignore it. He turned around to address them, and they all froze.

"People of World Sector Six! You all know who I am and who I represent. Or at least, you should know who I am. I am High Inquisitor Rubius of the Red, and I represent the High Court. This woman is no longer your empress, and she will be tried in the High Court for her actions. Your emperor, Cyrus, is restored to his rightful place. Good day!"

"We don't want that jackal running our sector!" a man in the crowd yelled in response. "Empress Ayera is our ruler!"

Rubius snorted at the man's remark. "That man has the right of it. Your husband is a jackal," he said to her under his breath. "Not like I have any say in the matter."

Ayera frowned. "That isn't even the half of it."

"I know."

Ayera exchanged a curious look with him as the crowd grew agitated and restless. Many chimed in about Cyrus, calling for Ayera as their leader, and started to hurl objects at the inquisitor. Rubius snarled after a tome slapped him on the face. He angrily flung the tome back at the crowd with his violet magic.

Ayera turned to the High Inquisitor as they walked past the crowd. "You won't be able to keep them under control, High Inquisitor. There's not much power you can exert over them," she told him. "They have will of iron, and will resist you and the High Court, even without me as their leader."

"Be that as it may, you'd best get on that ship now if you value your people's lives. I am not known for my patience, lady." He motioned toward the airship bridge, his ship docked at the end.

As Ayera looked at the ship, she was sobered by the thought of where she was going. Her stomach started doing flips, and she suddenly felt sick.

"What will happen to me, High Inquisitor?" Ayera asked, turning to face him. "Will they truly put me on trial?"

His crimson eyes glimmered a bright red in the sunlight, then a slight frown creased his face. "Unfortunately, your journey will soon end," he said with a little bit of heart underneath his icy tone.

Fear hammered her heart. She was going to be executed.

"I am sorry it has to be like this, my lady."

"I am sure you are," Ayera said, narrowing her eyes at him.

He gave her a serious look. "You might not think so, but I really am. I don't have the kind of power needed to fight them… especially *her*."

He meant it. What kind of man was this High Inquisitor anyway?

Without another thought, Rubius guided Ayera onto the planks, and they walked toward the airship. It couldn't be helped; Ayera shed a single tear. It streamed down her cheek as she walked.

She would be far from home, off in another sector, awaiting her death sentence. She was stripped of her title, reduced to nothing, and now her people were going to suffer. Some already had—their gift was *gone*. Soon the world would forget about her, and her people would be a mere memory, if that.

And her sister was going to be next.

CHAPTER 27

GREEN

Emerald woke to the sound of knocking.

Confused, she rubbed the sleep out of her eyes, then sat up in bed. Complete darkness surrounded her except for a hint of city light peeking through her patio door. It had to be in the middle of the night, but as far as what time it was, Emerald could not say.

Had she dreamt the sound?

She flopped back down in her bed, tired. Her soul felt heavy, ladened with sorrow from her dream.

Kyle. She had heard his voice…

The knocking came again, this time louder, with a voice accompanying it.

"Emerald, it is really important," Glacia said from behind the door. Glacia *never* addressed her informally unless she was serious. "Are you awake? There are important visitors that just have arrived at the palace."

Important visitors? In the middle of the night?

All Emerald wanted to do was lie back down in her bed and sleep. She really didn't feel like she wanted to deal with anything, let alone visitors; she had already put so much energy into seeing everyone at her birthday party.

Emerald sighed, then called out, "Come in."

The door opened, and Glacia went straight to her closet to fetch a change of clothes for her.

"Who are these visitors? Why can't Derek see them?" Emerald asked.

"I was informed that the King is gone on business."

"He has gone already?" Emerald asked curiously. Derek had only told her earlier that evening that he was going away on business. Emerald had expected him to go soon, but in the middle of the night? What kind of business would require him to leave so late like that?

"I don't know all the details, but yes, the King has left the palace. Anyway, Councilor Emerys is requesting that you come to the audience chamber immediately to see three women," Glacia called out from her closet, appearing with a simple gown. "Two of them are *gifted* women, I should add."

The word *gifted* slapped her awake. *Two gifted women? At the palace?*

"I must hurry," Emerald stated, getting out of bed and onto her feet.

"Let's get this on you." Glacia held out the dress, gesturing for Emerald to strip. Quickly, Emerald slipped out of her nightgown and into the dress. As Glacia zipped up the back, the stomach area was tight and uncomfortable, making it hard for her to breathe.

"We really need to get you some new dresses," Glacia said, fussing with the zipper. After a few more attempts, she got it zipped to the top.

It would have been the perfect time to tell Glacia. But she just couldn't find the words.

Emerald ran into the bathroom to brush her teeth, and Glacia quickly fixed her hair at the same time, then they left her chambers.

The walk to the audience hall seemed endless. Every footstep seemed like an eternity, while mixed emotions flooded Emerald's mind. The corridors were dark and still. *Who are these two gifted women? And why have they come to the palace? And who is the third woman?* Emerald thought as they walked together in silence. The halls were void of people and sounds except for the occasional guards passing by on patrol. Completely opposite of the dream she awoken from—the crowds of people, the eternal line to see him...

Her heart panged with a deep hurt. She tried to push the dream out of her mind as they continued through the palace corridors, finally reaching the audience chamber. Councilor Emerys was already inside waiting for her, standing to the side of her throne. Derek's throne was empty, of course, and Emerys was much too humble to take the King's spot, even though it was customary for someone in his position to do so.

"Your Majesty." He bowed, urging her to take her throne.

"What is going on? I was told there were three women who have arrived here at the palace, two of them being gifted," Emerald said, taking a seat, nodding to dismiss Glacia. The handmaiden bowed to them both and left the chamber. "Where are they?"

"Waiting in the presence chamber. They were adamant that they speak to you right away," Emerys added. "And honestly, I do not want to offend any gifted by telling them to wait until morning. I don't have the powers to counter them in case they get upset with me, unlike Your Majesty does."

Emerald looked at him, and they both exchanged a slight smile, the first smile she had exchanged with the councilor in quite some time.

Emerald nodded. "Let them in."

Emerys motioned to the guards, and the main doors opened.

Emerald recognized the two gifted immediately. The first who came in and bowed was Geeta; she recalled their brief exchange after Kyle's death. Geeta was dressed similarly to how Emerald had seen her months ago, plus a new tattoo design on her chest. The second woman, Emerald had seen leaving with Drew after the sorceress and the gifted returned to the future, but she couldn't recall her name. The third woman, Emerald wasn't sure if she had ever met her or not.

They all bowed, with the second and third woman doing so in a completely awkward manner. Then they all waited for Emerald to speak.

"Geeta," Emerald said in recognition, her eyes taking in the woman, "I have not seen you in several months. Your presence is always welcome here at the palace."

Geeta bowed, then darted her eyes to the empty throne. "Where is His Majesty?"

Emerys cleared his throat, while Emerald gave her a blank look. "His Majesty has left… on business," the councilor said. "I am here to help the Queen in matters of state."

"I see." Geeta raised an eyebrow, staring right into Emerald's eyes. Somehow, Emerald knew that the violet-gifted was not convinced, nor did she approve of Derek's missing presence.

Emerald's heart churned. She repositioned herself in her seat and continued, moving her glance to the other woman. "And… I have seen you before, but I have not been told your name."

"Telly Hearly, Your Majesty." Telly cleared her throat, bowing awkwardly again. She pointed to the third woman. "And this is Reila."

"You are most welcome here," Emerald said. "But it is strange for you make your appearance in the middle of the night. Please, what brings you here at this hour?"

Telly stepped forward, her eyes glowing a pale orange from behind her glasses. "Your Majesty, I don't even know where to start, so I suppose I should just get straight to the point: Arcadia is in serious trouble. We have reason to believe that Arcadia will be invaded."

Emerys shot Telly an alarming look. "Truly? Pray, tell us what makes you think this?" he asked.

"Since the freeing of the cyborgs from the corporation, I have been trying to incorporate the freed cyborgs back into a way of life. We frequently get cyborgs showing up to our camp for tune-ups, or just wanting to be with other cyborgs."

"You mean the wasteland camps?" Emerys asked.

"Precisely, er..." Telly's voice trailed off, not knowing Emerys's official name or title.

"Your Grace is fine," he finished her sentence.

"Okay, Your Grace," Telly said, then continued. "But just yesterday, a cyborg showed up at our camp." Telly's eyes radiated with her magic, and a serious look washed over her face. "This cyborg was not from Arcadia. He came from Olympia."

"Impossible," Emerys stated. "We are the only ones to have such technology. You must be mistaken. Perhaps Olympia stole several of the freed cyborgs and modified them."

"There is no mistake, Your Grace. Drew, the only true gifted cyborg, personally hacked into Scion's processor and talked with him about it."

"Drew?" Emerald blurted out.

Telly gave her a look, then nodded. "Yes, Your Majesty."

"Who is Scion?" Emerys asked.

"Oh, I forgot to mention that. Scion is the name of this Olympian cyborg." Telly bowed to Emerys, then continued. "Scion has proof of the development of the Olympian cyborgs within his database. He downloaded it illegally, might I add. The file was supposed to be encrypted, but he found a weakness in the file. Scion told Drew that there was a deal between our Arcadian corporation and theirs, a large sum of money transferred from an Olympian bank account to one in Arcadia. It is safe to say that the corporation here in Arcadia was compromised at one point, and managed to sell their secrets, and…"

Telly paused, then turned to Emerald, looking straight at her. "Your Majesty, I know you are familiar with Drew. And that means you know he is never wrong about anything. Well, anything that pertains to mathematics and scientific calculations." Telly paused. "I myself was in a transport en route to the palace to tell you, but it was shot down by an Olympian transport. If it weren't for Geeta here, I would be dead, along with my pilot."

Drew…

Emerald had developed such a fondness for him. He had been her protector when Kyle was away, and had tried to stop Derek…

Drew was one of the most reliable people that Emerald knew.

Emerald glanced at Telly, nodding. "I believe you, Miss Hearly, without a doubt. I've only known Drew briefly, but I'd trust him with my life."

Telly nodded, then flashed a small smile. Her face shifted. "There is another thing about the Olympian cyborgs, Your Majesty," Telly continued. "Since the Olympian corporation paid the Arcadian corporation for their technology…"

Reila, the third woman, sighed louder than she probably intended, crossing her arms out of boredom.

"I was getting there!" Telly snapped at her.

Geeta approached the thrones, walking between the two women as if to break up their spat. "The Olympian cyborgs are infused with magic!"

Emerald's heart dropped into the pit of her stomach. She felt sick. Very sick. Looking over to Emerys, she could see that the councilor's face had gone white.

"How?" Emerald blurted out. "How do they have magic?"

Telly eyed her evenly. "I believe during the transaction between the two corporations, that not only were our secrets sold but also… your blood."

She was reliving a past nightmare all over again. It was exactly like when she had first discovered her power being used for the Arcadian cyborgs and how they had been experimenting on the wasteland peoples. But this… this violation was on a much grander scale.

"And you think that Olympia was able to get magic from my blood?" Emerald asked. "Surely there can't be any other way for them to get magic… can there?"

"That is my personal theory. However, one thing Scion did mention was that there were unknown subjects believed to be sources of power. So who knows if they used your blood or these unnamed subjects. It could be either or. Regardless of the source of blood or power, the odds are stacked against them for the cyborgs to fully obtain magic. In the case of Lab 34 at the Arcadian corporation, Drew was one out of almost a *thousand* cyborgs that received your magic blood. So Olympia would have to have been extremely lucky, as they would have had only a couple of your blood samples at most to experiment with, knowing how accurate the Arcadian corporation was at logging blood samples. But with the technology of cloning, it's possible to copy the blood. It was something that the Arcadian corporation never tried. I don't think you can clone *magic*, but who knows?"

Emerald's heart sank further. Others now had magic, just like her.

"Did Scion say what kind of magic they have?" Emerald asked.

"Yellow magic, mostly. But there is supposedly a subject that has blue magic, though we personally didn't come across any, nor did Scion. It was only documented in one file that Scion read, but even that had been moved and deleted."

Emerys's expression grew dark, his face downcast. "Do all the Olympian cyborgs have this yellow magic?"

"I believe so, or at least, that is what Scion had said. They have been infused with this yellow magic much the same way that the Arcadian cyborgs have been infused with green regeneration magic. Though Scion made it clear that none of them are true spellcasters, they do have strong powers."

"How can we trust this data from Scion?" Emerys asked. "What if he was programmed to give us false information as a decoy?"

Emerald looked to him. "What do you mean, Councilor?"

"What if these cyborgs are from *another* kingdom, and they are encoded for us to think that they are from Olympia? What if the real threat is from another kingdom, and they want to see our two kingdoms squabble? Though, it does fit the picture of the Olympian envoys pressing our kingdoms for their terms." He began to pace. "But it doesn't make sense. Why would they ask us to dismantle our cyborgs under threat of peace, while they themselves are doing it? They would have the other kingdoms against them as well."

"I... I am getting a sense that this is just the surface of our problems." Geeta focused on Emerald. "Olympia is after *you*, Your Majesty."

"Me?"

"You and the King. Who else is rumored to have magic? Why else would they invade Arcadia? What I have learned over time is that if magic is involved in any sort of dispute, you better believe that the end goal is the acquisition of said magic."

"She is correct," Telly added. "Scion said that he and the other cyborgs were programed with orders—orders to capture you and the King."

Emerys shot Emerald a look, his eyes asking if she trusted Geeta's and Telly's word.

"You are wise not to fully trust us on a whim, Councilor, and to weigh each option," Geeta continued, as if she'd heard the councilor's thoughts. "You are wiser than most people I have come across in all my travels."

Emerys raised his eyebrow. "Was it your power that… that…"

"Yes." Geeta nodded. "I can hear thoughts from time to time, if they are loud enough."

Emerys cleared his throat, flustered. "I appreciate you coming to us, Miss Geeta, and your understanding why I must weigh each statement carefully. You must understand the position that I have been put in while the King is away. And for the Queen." He looked at Emerald. "Under her father's rule, I knew of our personal cyborg armies, but I never imagined this particular outcome, the possibility of cyborgs against cyborgs…" His eyes lowered. "I have many regrets in my life, one being that the Queen was never told of what her blood was being used for. It was forbidden to mention it during her father's reign."

Emerald looked to Emerys and offered him a sad smile. "It wasn't your fault, Councilor. We all know what kind of man my father was."

He bowed to her, remaining silent.

A monster was what he was. Her father had lied to her, kept her stowed away in the palace, and had been swayed by the sorceress as well. Or did he have a choice regarding the sorceress? Either way, he was most unkind.

Emerald looked to the three women before her, their faces all in varying forms of distress. The third woman, Reila, hid her expression well behind her tough attitude, but she couldn't fool Emerald.

Emerald's eyes then trailed to Emerys. "What is your counsel?" Emerald asked him.

The councilor remained silent. Emerald could tell he was pondering the whole situation, carefully assessing each detail. Finally, after several moments, he broke the silence. "If what these women say is true, then we must be ready. Before he left, His Majesty had ordered us to prepare the armies in case of a possible war between the kingdoms, to be ready at a moment's notice. I would request Her Majesty consider allowing our cyborgs to join the Arcadian armies once more." His dark eyes met hers. "I know they have been put through a great deal already, but we certainly cannot beat a whole cyborg army with human lives. We must have power behind our armies. That, I truly believe, is the key. We must have cyborgs fighting alongside our armies." He paused. "That is, only if Her Majesty wills it."

What did she will truly? Not to rule under these circumstances. Not to be Derek's wife. To have Kyle be with her night and day…

She refocused to the current situation. As a sheltered princess, and now a queen, Emerald had never been trained in these type of situations. What if she made the wrong decision? What if her decision cost many lives?

All she wanted to do was crawl back in her bed and forget that this was happening. She was no ruler. She could barely even manage herself! How was she supposed to manage a kingdom?

Geeta's violet eyes met hers, and she bowed lowly to her. "Your Majesty, forgive me for being forward, but Councilor Emerys is right. You must have power within your army. The Arcadian cyborgs would be a huge asset if Olympia did indeed march upon Arcadia."

"We must be proactive, My Queen," Emerys added. "Send out troops to the wastelands to show Olympia that we won't lie down for them. We need to be ready."

"Scion made it sound like it was urgent, and that they were coming soon," Telly added.

"We can gather the wastelanders, equip them with Arcadia's weaponry, and add them to our ranks. Those willing to fight, that is," Geeta stated. "I'd put my money on them being more than willing to help out, especially those who are in the path to Arcadia."

They both had presented decisions. Much better than she could ever make.

Just then, a thought came to her. Her eyes darted to Geeta. *She will be perfect.*

"Councilor Emerys," Emerald said, looking over to where he stood.

"Yes, Your Majesty?" he said, bowing.

"As of this moment, I am naming Geeta Protector of the Realm."

Geeta's head jerked up, her eyes darting to Emerald's as Emerys nodded with approval.

"I'm no protector, My Queen," Geeta argued. "I am ill-equipped to handle any matters of state!"

"But you are much more equipped than I, Geeta," Emerald said. "I know absolutely nothing of matters of state, and rely heavily on Councilor Emerys's advice, and that of the other advisors. What Arcadia needs is a gifted to help with this threat of war, especially if it is true what Miss Hearly says." Emerald paused, taking a deep but sad breath. "Geeta, I cannot… I do not have the energy…"

Everyone looked at her. All Emerald wanted to do was have a breakdown. She was tired, drained, and her soul was completely crushed. She just wanted to *disappear.*

More like not exist.

"I need you. Arcadia needs you," Emerald continued, her voice shaking. Tears started spilling down her cheeks. As much as she tried to hold them back to be strong, Emerald just wasn't strong. Not anymore.

She felt so inadequate.

Geeta stared at her for a moment, then sighed. "Very well. I will do my best to aid Arcadia in any way possible with the use of my gift," she said, giving Emerald a sad but reassuring smile.

Emerald wanted to return that smile when her own, but she couldn't muster up any bit of happiness. She had none left to give.

Emerald looked to two of her guards, then motioned for them. "Guards."

They bowed, approaching the throne.

"Please fetch me my staff," Emerald ordered. As much as Emerald didn't want to let it go because it was just one more thing that reminded her of Kyle, she knew it had to be put to good use where it was needed.

They both looked at her with eyes open wide. "Are you sure, Your Majesty?" one asked.

"Yes, you have permission to remove it from its place."

Geeta turned to her wildly. "Oh, no. I would advise against this decision! You might need it here, especially if Olympia is indeed after your magic. You need it to defend yourself."

"No. You need it as our protector. If the Olympian armies have magic, then you will need to amplify yours to help." Emerald paused, thinking of Kyle, of Kyle holding the staff. "The staff is not mine anyway. It is Kyle's, and since he's… he's gone, I feel it best that you should have it. You were the one who delivered it to him in the first place."

"I don't like any of this," Geeta muttered.

"I agree with the Queen," Emerys stated. "Anything that can stop the Olympian armies from reaching the city, we need to put to use. And if the Queen thinks the staff will help, you must take it."

"Geeta, do whatever you can to stop this whole thing peacefully if they show up at our borders," Emerald added.

"Peacefully," Geeta repeated, as if she knew it wasn't possible.

Somehow, Emerald knew it wouldn't result in peace either. "However, if Olympia wants no peace, then we must proceed," she continued.

Geeta wearily sighed, then bowed. "Yes, Your Majesty."

Emerald nodded. "We are indebted to you, truly."

Emerys turned to Telly. "Miss Hearly, if you can, please contact as many cyborgs in the wastelands as possible to join our ranks."

"That is, if they are willing," Emerald added weakly. "They have to be willing. We don't want to force them; they have already had enough force in their lifetime."

"There is one thing," Telly added. "The wasteland transmissions cannot reach the palace. As of right now, our camp has retreated to a safe location in refuge caves, but the camp's communications are cut off. I believe Olympia is blocking it somehow. That is the reason why we came here in person."

Emerys's face dropped. "I was not aware of this."

"I believe the reason why is that it is localized out in the wastelands, and not affecting Arcadia. It's only if one tries to contact the other that the problem arises."

"Can we somehow bypass it?"

Telly shifted. "I have been running through different scenarios in my head, and I think that we could devise something to send out a stronger signal than the one they seem to be blocking. But it's going to take time, and I need to get a team assembled. Quickly." She fixed her crooked glasses, then continued. "I am optimistic that once we are able to make contact with the other camps, I can gather many of the cyborgs to our cause. Who knows, perhaps I can scrounge up some additional wastelanders to the Arcadian ranks. But the thing is—they might want to fight Olympia in their own way."

"I don't care how they fight, we need all the help we can get," Geeta pointed out.

"You have whatever you need at your disposal, then," Emerys said. "Write up what you need and who you need with our advisor of technology. He will get you everything you require. We will give you lodgings here at the palace while you work on the device."

"Thank you, Councilor." Telly nodded. "But once the plan is in place and the device's development is underway, I must return to my camp. My daughter is out there, along with Drew."

Emerald looked to Telly at that moment with a sudden realization. Telly was much more than someone who simply knew Drew. She was Drew's significant other, and they had a daughter together.

Emerald blinked, then nodded in understanding to Telly. "I understand, Miss Hearly."

"Whatever you must do," Emerys said in agreement.

"Thank you."

"Then I will be off with Reila, then," Geeta said. "I will be awaiting the network's connection to the new satellite. Contact the camp when you are done. Please don't tarry. I'll do what I can out in the wastelands."

"I am quite efficient at managing my time. It'll be done quickly," Telly huffed with pride while Reila rolled her eyes.

Reila snorted. "I hope so."

The guards came in and bowed, holding the staff out to Geeta. Emerald watched as Geeta hesitated, then slowly took the staff from them. As soon as the staff touched her hands, it glowed a bright violet-white color, and swirling energy flowed around her.

Everyone in the room stood amazed and afraid at the same time; even the guards took a step back.

Emerald watched as Geeta took in the beauty of the staff. "It's like seeing an old friend again," Geeta said.

Emerald smiled sadly.

"I miss that old jerk," Geeta continued under her breath, then looked to Emerald. "I will do whatever I can to stop this, My Queen."

"I know you will," Emerald said. "Please take care. And give Drew my regards."

Geeta bowed one last time, then turned to Telly and Reila. "I need to know where the camp is."

"I'll draw a map," Telly said, then looked to Emerald and Emerys. "Don't be alarmed. I will need to use my magic for a second."

Emerald nodded, while Emerys looked at her curiously.

Telly closed her eyes, summoning her bright light-orange magic. Slowly, Telly moved her hands in front of her, almost like a child finger painting, but a bit more detailed. Transparent glowing orange imagery appeared in the air, floating right in front of Telly until it formed a large map about four feet long.

The illusion remained as Telly opened her eyes, Geeta and Reila coming up right beside her, inspecting the map.

"This map sucks," Reila said, studying the map. "I take it art was not your specialty."

"It was the best I could do," Telly huffed. "I doubt you could do any better."

"You really don't want me to answer that." Reila crossed her arms. "You're missing a major landmark here." Reila pointed to a part of the map. "And what about the this over here?"

Telly opened her mouth in protest, but Geeta cut everyone off. "The map's landmarks are sufficient. I'll figure it out." Geeta turned to Telly and Reila. "Just point to where the hideout is on here."

Telly ran her hands over the map, then zoomed in the image with the movement of her hand, the orange-magic illusion obeying her swipe. "Here. This is where the camp should be."

"Thanks," Geeta said. She nodded at Telly and held her out hand to Reila. "Let's go."

"Please," Telly called out. "Make sure he is okay."

"Don't worry. I know Drew will be fine. It's everyone else that I'm worry about," Geeta said. She gripped the staff, and it burned brightly with violet-blue magic. Her other hand held Reila.

In a flash, the women disappeared, and Telly wiped her hand across the orange illusion, as if she were swiping her hand across her tablet, clearing the air of her magic.

Emerald motioned to the guards. "Please show Miss Hearly to her new quarters. See that she has whatever she needs."

"Yes, My Queen."

"I will send word when we are reconnected to the wastelands," Telly said, bowing.

As Telly left with the guards, Emerald and Emerys stood alone in the chamber for a moment. Emerald felt deflated.

"Councilor, I cannot… I just cannot go on like this," Emerald said, feeling drained once again. A cramp lanced through her belly.

His gaze met hers. Did the councilor know about her? Could he see her dark secret through her eyes?

Worry spread like wildfire through her. All she wanted to do was not think about anything. That way she never had to worry. But the more she didn't want to think about everything, the more things kept piling on.

"My Queen, I understand that you…" He paused, then awkwardly cleared his throat. "…want to keep to yourself at this time. I see it in your eyes. I do not know what demons you face alone, but please know that I want the very best for you, and the best of… care." His gray eyes were sad, his face firm with worry. "I know that there is much going on in the kingdom right now, and I do not want to see you stressed. It is not healthy for you."

Sadness flooded her once again. Her heart ached.

"I will take on as much of this burden from you as possible," he continued. "Although I worry for this kingdom, I also worry about you. *You* are most important." He offered a sad smile, and Emerald's eyes went to the floor.

"Thank you, Councilor," Emerald said, softening her voice. "I trust in all of your decisions, and think it's best that I do not involve myself wherever possible. It is true what I told Geeta, that I feel that I cannot make any wise decisions right now. My head is full of confusion, my soul weary with sadness, and my body… Well, I am not well, truly."

"I understand," Emerys answered. "Please, get some rest, and I will keep you updated on all that is happening. You only need to say the word if you feel that I need to do anything different."

"Thank you," Emerald managed to say.

Emerys is such a good man, Emerald thought. *I wish there were more of them.*

Emerald rose from her seat, and Emerys bowed deeply to her. She nodded with approval, exiting.

Glacia was waiting for her outside the hall, rising to her feet from a nearby bench.

"You okay?" she asked as the two started walking.

"Yes, I just need to lie down."

Glacia remained silent. Her friend had already pointed out her sleeping habits many times, and Emerald was sure Glacia was tired of doing it.

Perhaps, it was Glacia's way of saying that she knew her secret. Perhaps not.

As the two of them headed back to her chambers, Emerald found herself short of breath, huffing. Glacia didn't say anything, but to Emerald, it was obvious that the walk had taken a toll on her.

I need to tell her... But when was it ever a good time?

The two of them neared her private lift, then Glacia stopped. "What in the *world*?" Glacia said.

Emerald turned, looking at where Glacia stared. There was a pile of clothes on the floor in the middle of hallway.

They both walked toward it curiously. Glacia gently kicked the pile, overturning lavish jewelry inlaid with large blue gems. The garb was extraordinary, all in teals, azures, and sapphire blues, ornately decorated with golden designs throughout.

"What courtesan would just leave their clothes in the middle of the hallway?" Glacia asked, bending over the pile, inspecting it. "What a careless slob."

It was rather odd. Especially since no courtesan was housed where they were at due to being close to her own personal quarters.

"When we get back, let someone know about this," Emerald said, her eyes flickering away. *Just one more thing to think about...* Her mind had had enough for one day.

"I will. So weird," Glacia said under her breath, eyeing it one last time before they got on the lift.

When the two of them got back in her chambers, Emerald went into her bedroom, lay down on her bed, and closed her eyes.

She was tired. So tired.

As she drifted off, she heard faint mumblings of Glacia on her communicator, talking about the strange set of clothes.

CHAPTER 28

YELLOW

The invisible gifted swiftly guided Auron through the many corridors of the citadel. He was also invisible, which made it difficult to see the steps he was taking. Auron didn't even notice when he had become unseen, but it was at some point while he was being hurriedly pushed out of the audience hall and led away from the High Inquisitor.

Auron remained silent as he and the mysterious gifted moved. Each time they came upon High Court guards, a small hand rested on his chest, silently telling him to stop and wait. Whenever the guards moved out of sight, the hand would move away from his chest and yank the sleeve of his robe, deeming it safe for them to move once again. He still had no clue who was at his side, only that it was a woman, since she had spoken to him back in the audience hall.

As they walked quickly through the citadel, Auron's thoughts were on the Empress. Ayera was going to the High Court to be tried for treason. Maybe even put to death.

His heart pounded at the thought. Auron had served her father, then her. What would he say to Emperor Ojin in the Realm of Light, where all the good souls lived eternally in peace? "I'm sorry I couldn't save your daughter" sounded pathetic. Somehow, just the thought made Auron feel worse.

How was it that everything Auron knew to be good was bad, and what was now bad was possibly good? The only constant that remained was that the God of Light himself was pure and holy. Steadfast and true. But his devout followers, they were the ones who seemed to have been corrupted.

Auron frowned. *If I live through this, I swear I will make it all as it should be!* He promised the God of Light in his mind.

When there was no one around and he deemed it safe enough, Auron whispered to the invisible gifted, "The Empress! We can't just let the High Inquisitor take her!"

"We will help her," the invisible woman's voice assured him.

"Where are you leading me?"

"Please be quiet. You will soon know."

They came to a spiral staircase that led downward, and Auron suddenly knew exactly where they were heading.

It was the way to the sorceress.

Auron was about to say something, but the invisible gifted rested her hand on his chest to give him a silent signal to follow her. With another tug on his sleeve, they descended quickly into the depths of the citadel.

At the bottom, there were more guards, plus a High Court commander.

The invisible gifted woman yanked him to the side, and they both stilled their movements.

"Emperor Cyrus spoke with his court," said one of the guards, "and he had any of those who spoke out against him or the High Court rounded up. They will be down here shortly."

"Good. Prepare spaces for the traitors," the commander said. "Where is the High Inquisitor?"

"I believe he is still in the upper ramparts of the citadel. I was told he was going to make his way down here soon."

"Thank you," the commander said, and the guards saluted him.

The guards dispersed, walking right past Auron and the mysterious gifted next to him. Auron held his breath, trying not to make any sort of movement.

It's a good thing we are invisible and they aren't orange-gifted, he thought to himself.

After another moment, the invisible gifted led Auron down a side hall of the prison. There were broken stones, shattered walls, broken-down doors, and cobwebs as thick as cloth. Everything was coated in gray from a thick layer of dust, making Auron's throat itchy and his eyes water. All he wanted to do was cough, but he held it in as much as he could, knowing that one sound from him could blow their cover.

This place looks like it hasn't been used in centuries, Auron thought. Oddly,

Auron hadn't ever been down this particular hall of the prison, nor had he ever noticed it before.

They came upon an empty cell that was unlocked. The invisible woman slid the door open very carefully, just enough for them to squeeze through. Auron was amazed—somehow the invisible gifted made no sound as she slid the iron doors open and shut. It seemed like an impossible feat.

Auron entered, and the door behind him shut.

At that moment, Auron saw a shimmer of orange from within the cell. Slowly, the invisible gifted woman took form from within the shimmer, and she materialized before him. Small, thin body. Black hair with a bit of orange hair at the roots, all done up in a bun with hair ornaments. Eyes that burned orange with bright magic.

Auron gasped in disbelief. "Suri?" he said, his mouth dropping in awe as he gazed upon the sorceress's servant.

"Greetings, High Priest. Though it is not a happy day," Suri said with a frown.

"I didn't know you had magic." Auron glanced at her, dumbfounded. "How? When?"

"I've had it now for several months, High Priest. I never intended to reveal it to anyone, but the situation has changed, and I am desperate."

"Is that why you pulled me out of the audience hall?"

"If I hadn't interceded, you would have lost your gift." Behind her masked face of calm was fear. She was just as frightened as he was, but she hid it well.

"Lost my gift?" Auron said, studying her as if he was seeing her for the very first time.

"Yes, High Priest. That woman was going to take your gift along with all the others there. I was in the hall, hoping to grab the Empress before the High Inquisitor got to her. But I was too late, and here we are."

Ikaria's servant… trying to rescue the Empress? Saved him from losing his gift? She must be desperate. Or maybe she was very different than her mistress…

Auron's eyes met hers, and he nodded in sincere gratitude. "Thank the God of Light for your help."

"Forgive me, High Priest, but the God of Light had nothing to do with me helping you," the servant pointed out. "I merely aided you because I need your help, especially since I couldn't get to the Empress in time. As much as the Enchantress doesn't like you, I cannot let the High Court representatives take any of our sector's magic away—for that is the ultimate wish of the Enchantress." She had a determined look on her face.

"Who *was* that woman?" Auron asked. "The woman with the long yellow hair?"

"I do not know who she is, High Priest, but I have been aware of her for some time. She works for the High Court, but beyond that, I don't have any other knowledge of her identity," Suri replied, her voice with grave concern. "But what I do know is that she has some kind of ability to absorb magics. Did you see the colored stones that she keeps around her neck?"

"No," Auron said. How could he? He barely had enough time to make it outside of the chamber.

"The woman has necklaces with transmuted gems, most likely from a gifted's blood, or quite possibly even from a gifted's life force. From what I was able to observe of the woman, she has different amulets, and she is able to swap between the different color magics using them." Suri's eyes glowed eerily. "She has red, orange, yellow, and blue-gifted blood. When in need of a different color of magic, all she has to do is lay her hands on the different gem, and she absorbs that magic. While everyone was back in time, I stayed here, and I became aware of her in the shadows of our court, lurking within our citadel. And after everyone had returned from back in time, I again caught a glimpse of her, on more than one occasion, always around the same time our gifted lost their magic. All my suspicions were confirmed when I witnessed her harvest our very own Lord Kako's magic."

It was the answer that he had been praying for all these years.

"Is she…" Auron began.

"The cause of the plague? Yes, High Priest. From what I have gathered, she has been in the shadows in our sector for years, slowing taking away the powers of our gifted." Suri's face darkened. "The Enchantress was right. She always *is* right. The High Court was behind the plague."

Auron swallowed hard. "I can't believe this," Auron said. "What kind of terrible magic is this?"

"White magic," Suri said evenly.

"White magic? But that magic does not exist in *The Spectrum*. The only true white magic is when one gifted is joined with their complement." Auron shook his head. "Are you sure she has white magic?"

"I saw it for myself. Before she took Lord Kako's power, she had white features—white hair and eyes. She used white magic to absorb Lord Kako's power, and when she did, her life force absorbed his magic, making her eyes and hair red. His red magic was transferred to her body, leaving him non-gifted and powerless."

Auron's eyes met Suri's. "How did you go unnoticed? When witnessing Lord Kako and this woman?"

Suri huffed. "I go unnoticed in the citadel most of the time, High Priest. Even before my magic, I moved in such a way that no one ever noticed me. I am unseen, and have always been that way. However, in the case of this woman, either I am stronger than her with orange magic, or she is less acquainted with the orange gift. I don't know how else to explain her not noticing me when I was in his chambers. Perhaps, it was my stealth. I do not know, but I am fortunate regardless."

All of this was becoming more and more terrifying. That woman, that evil woman, was the cause of the gifted losing their magic? And what of all the gifted that they left behind in the audience hall? Had they lost their magic while he and Suri were escaping?

Auron recalled a brilliant white flash. A shiver ran down his spine. "Suri, do you think this woman could have taken all of our gifted's power up there in the audience hall? I mean, it took years for the plague to attack our gifted, and that happened over time."

"From my assessment, I believe that her power grows the more she absorbs magic. The 'plague,' as it were, started off slow, but over time it became more rapid. And as of this moment, given that all of our gifted were in the same room as that woman, I would not doubt for one minute that we are now the only World Sector Six gifted remaining, besides the Enchantress."

Auron shuffled his feet nervously, kicking at some small pebbles. A gifted with the power to absorb magic, able to shift to different colors…

The Spectrum of Magic. Its fate now lay in peril. Magic was disappearing, all at the mercy of one woman.

Auron's mind raced, swimming with all the new information. Or more like drowning in it. Ikaria was in immediate danger, but so was Ayera. He began to sweat profusely, worried. As much as he needed to rescue Ayera, things would be much more severe if that powerful gifted woman got ahold of Ikaria's gift.

He now understood why Suri had brought him here. Auron didn't like it. Not one bit. But what choice did they have?

What am I thinking? Have I gone mad? Perhaps he had.

"Suri," Auron whispered.

"I know, High Priest. We will get the Empress, I swear it on my life," Suri said, her eyes suddenly glowing a bright orange in the dark of the cell. "But we must free the Enchantress first, at all costs," she said firmly. "Otherwise, the High Court will be much more powerful, with a new color added to their collection."

Auron cringed, but he nodded in agreement. "As much as I hate even think of freeing Ikaria…" His voice trailed off, and his gaze met Suri's. "I see no other option. I will help you free the sorceress."

Suri hinted at a cool smile on her usually expressionless face, then nodded. She turned to the door. "For now, we wait until the changing of the guards. Hopefully, it will be a red and yellow-gifted guard."

"And if not?"

Suri cocked her head, raising her eyebrow. "Then you'd best pray to the God of Light, because we don't have many options available to us."

Auron sighed.

The odds were definitely not in their favor. He'd best pray, for they needed a miracle for their plan to succeed.

CHAPTER 29

RED

High Inquisitor!" a voice called out from across the airship's bridge. Rubius took one last look around the deck of the airship, seeing that the guards were in position to hold the Empress who was being held inside. Satisfied, he made his way across the bridge, the wind ripping through his hair and tossing his cape.

"All the World Sector Six gifted are accounted for," one of the High Court guards said, bowing as Rubius stepped off the bridge. "That is, except for High Priest Auron. He still seems to be missing."

"Well, then what are you doing reporting to me?" Rubius grabbed the guard's collar, dragging him close. "Find him! This citadel is only so big. Perhaps you can ask the priests. They are known for telling the truth."

Rubius let go of the collar suddenly, causing the guard to stumble.

"Yes, right away, High Inquisitor! I'll have a unit question the priests." The guard saluted, along with several others, and they took off.

Just what I need, an earful from Belinda. I can hear her now, complaining about one silly gifted getting away, and she will continue to remind me even after the job is done. It was the last thing Rubius wanted, another lecture from the High Court picking apart his methods. Though he had no specific orders in regard to High Priest Auron, the man chose to fight the High Court, and had now marked himself a dead man. Rubius would have no choice but to jail the old man as well and drag him back to World Sector Three, along with the other rebels.

Wasn't Elyathi the one who was supposed to be finding the stragglers? Rubius thought, irritated. *This job is turning out to be more than I bargained for.*

Rubius eyed his guards behind him. "Did someone find out where the sorceress is being imprisoned while I was securing the Empress?"

"Yes, High Inquisitor. She is in the dungeons. They enchanted a special cell for her," one of his guards answered.

"Take me to her," he ordered.

The guard bowed and led Rubius off the receiving docks, and they entered the citadel's corridors once again, the other High Court guards trailing behind him. As they walked, Rubius's troubled thoughts returned to Lady Elyathi.

Lady Elyathi was *white-gifted.*

Rubius let it stir in his mind, tossing the idea over and over again in his head. It troubled him, for many reasons. It was odd that he had never heard of any white-gifted before, that was, until he had been visited by that strange green-gifted time traveler years ago. Rubius had asked the time traveler about his mysterious green-gifted woman, but the man didn't know who she was, only that a white-gifted woman back in time was once pregnant with a green-gifted child. A girl.

Could it be that Elyathi is somehow connected to the green-gifted woman I've been searching for? Could she be the green-gifted woman's mother? She is white-gifted, after all…

Rubius paused. How would that even be possible?

It doesn't make sense, he told himself. Elyathi was here, in this time. Here, with Rubius. If Rubius was correct on his theory that the green-gifted woman was indeed the old Queen of Arcadia going back thousands of years ago, then it wouldn't make sense that Elyathi could be her mother. Maybe the white gift appeared on rare occasions throughout time.

But what *if?* The question begged to be asked. If anything, maybe he could understand more of the white-gifted and get more solidified clues on the white-gifted mother. Maybe Elyathi had studied of the other white-gifted like her throughout time, and she had read of this woman who birthed the green-gifted child.

Rubius's head was spinning wildly. He'd never thought there would ever be a time that he had wanted to converse with Lady Elyathi. And yet now, more than ever, he had many questions for the religious nut.

What was also alarming was seeing Elyathi's power in action. In a second, she'd absorbed a whole audience hall of gifted's power. He shuddered. There was no way anyone could stand against *that* kind of power. And that thought sobered him.

He thought back to her words in the High Court chamber. *Strip away his power,* she had said. That is exactly what she'd done to everyone in that World Sector Six audience hall. Stripped away their power. Every single one of them. He swallowed hard. Rubius had already angered Elyathi in more than one way. What if she were to strip away *his* power right after she stole the sorceress's violet magic? What if that had been the High Court's plan all along? Or what if Elyathi acted on her own and decided to take away his power regardless of what the High Court wanted?

Rubius definitely had to be on his guard around that woman.

As the guard led Rubius through the citadel, many courtesans scattered across the halls like mice, quickly running to and from where they had to go. If they saw him, they bowed quickly, then scampered away. They were all scared, fearful at what was happening to their sector. He couldn't blame them, especially after that stunt that Elyathi pulled in the audience hall.

The guard led the entourage, descending to the bottom of the citadel where the prisons were housed. Stone bricks lined the corridors, along with heavy wooden doors with iron bars running across them. It was dank, with an old musty smell that made the air feel thick and heavy. The main corridor was a bit larger, and every fifteen to twenty feet, there was either a door to a cell or another corridor with more cells.

They walked until they came to the very end of the hall. Two World Sector Six guards stood in front of the door.

As Rubius approached, they bowed. "High Inquisitor."

"I have come to see the prisoner."

They bowed, then stepped aside, one grabbing a set of iron keys. As the guard shifted out of his position, Rubius saw violet magic radiating faintly from under the door, with hints of orange and yellow magic.

Violet magic?

Rubius looked at the guards. "Who enchanted this cell? And how is it enchanted with violet magic?"

"One of our very own orange-gifted enchanted this cell with the help of a violet-gifted," one of the guards replied.

Rubius's jaw dropped. "Violet-gifted? What violet-gifted? You mean to say there is *another* violet-gifted floating around this sector?" Rubius asked.

The guard shifted. "From what I was told, this violet-gifted came from another era. Appeared in our sector, then left again. I don't know much more than that."

Violet-gifted... from another time? This was getting more bizarre by the minute. Elyathi having the white gift, and now a violet-gifted from another time?

Rubius strongly suspected that both were somehow connected to that strange green-gifted time traveler.

Rubius neared the guard. "Do you know the name of this violet-gifted?"

"No, sir."

"Does *anyone* know who the violet-gifted is?" Rubius turned his head, asking the other guards.

"Quite possibly the Empress, perhaps maybe even the Emperor or his court," offered another guard.

Rubius huffed. Just talking to that jackass Emperor sounded like too much energy that he didn't want to expend. Rubius made a mental note to ask Ayera about it before the ship departed.

"This enchanted barrier... how exactly does it work so I know what I am getting myself into?" *More like if I need to use my magic against that woman.*

"It suppresses the magic inside the cell. This is the second level of protection," said the first guard.

"Second level of protection?"

"Yes. This is just in case the sorceress somehow breaks out of her first level of protection barrier. This barrier suppresses her magic to the confines of the cell, and her mind magic is suppressed to that area."

"Then what is the first level of protection?"

"It is essentially the same type of barrier, but with more color enchantments added to it. It surrounds the sorceress at all times; it's an enchanted transparent barrier that has most of the colors combined. It technically does the same thing as the outer layer barrier, but it keeps the sorceress's magic within that box."

"Most of the colors combined?"

"It was said that when our... when the World Sector Six gifted traveled back in time to stop the sorceress, every color of gifted was present. Some of them focused their magic to enchant the barrier. At times, the barrier appears to fade between orange, yellow, and violet. But other times, it looks prismatic. We assume that there are all colors present considering the prismatic effect, but theorize that some of the gifted funneled more power into the barrier compared to others. We cannot say for certain."

"And the barrier still surrounds the sorceress? When is it to fade?"

"No one knows, High Inquisitor. No one can say."

"So, could I use my magic on the sorceress? Or will the barrier block it?"

"From what I understand, you can use your magic on her by streaming your power into her barrier, but she cannot stream magic out of it—the barrier suppresses her magic. With the outer barrier in place, you will still be able to use your magic within the cell; your spells will be confined to the cell only."

"Excellent. Thank you."

"Most welcome, High Inquisitor." The guard bowed.

Rubius turned to the door. "Open it up."

The guard turned the iron key in the lock, and it made a loud clank. As the guard did so, Rubius hesitated. Behind that door was a woman who had been in the same time era with the green-gifted woman.

It was ironic that two people who could possibly have answers regarding his mystery woman were women who were in opposition to him. The Sorceress being opposed to the High Court and everything that had to do with it, and Lady Elyathi being opposed to his mere behavior. If anything, he could possibly get answers from the Sorceress...

The door to the cell opened, and Rubius slipped inside. As he passed through the outer barrier, the magic clung to him like a sticky gel. It hung on to him even as he moved. After a few more steps, the barrier gel released his body, snapping back into place. It left Rubius looking untouched, as if the gel had not just run over his body. The barrier radiated its magic brilliantly, running over the cell's walls and door.

As he fixed the collar of his jacket, Rubius saw the Sorceress Ikaria. She sat regally on the stone prison bed, as if it were her throne and the cell was her deserted court. Her back was against the wall, and her legs were elegantly crossed. She was a bit older than he expected—around late thirties or possibly early forties. She wore a revealing corset that exposed most of her well-endowed bust, with a long black shimmering skirt with slits up to her waist, hardly covering any of her legs or thighs. Manacles were clamped around her ankles and wrists. Chains were attached to her shackles with enough slack for her to move around in the cell.

A plain white robe was folded by her bed, untouched. Violet hair flowed down her back, puddling around her on the marbled bed, with some spilling to the floor. Surrounding her was the iridescent rainbow barrier, shimmering every so often. It subtly shifted in size in a very peculiar fashion. The sorceress's personal prison.

The sorceress's violet eyes immediately darted to his. An unusual expression appeared on her face for a brief moment, her glimmering eyes examining him, locked in a fixated gaze. Then, after several moments, her mouth twisted in a daring smile.

"So you are the High Inquisitor," she called out, sounding unimpressed. "For some reason, I had pictured you much differently. How disappointing for us both."

"Don't worry, you're not the first," Rubius said, shrugging. "I seem to disappoint everyone on the first meeting, especially when it comes to women."

Ikaria leaned back, then paused, her eyes lingering on him curiously. "You don't say? How unfortunate." Her face twisted into a frown, then she looked away from him, lazily observing her fingernails, the chains of her shackles jangling. "So I suppose you have come for my blood. Or perhaps to steal my magic by way of that phony plague orchestrated by your superiors."

"I personally haven't come for your blood, or to steal your magic."

"Oh?"

Rubius casually paced around the cell. "I've come here to have a little chat with you."

Ikaria snorted. "Well, you'd best go somewhere else for conversation, High Inquisitor, because I am not in a chatting sort of mood. Go talk to the Emperor instead. I am sure he can tell you all about me and this World Sector."

"The Emperor doesn't know what you know," Rubius said, nearing her. "Especially when it comes to the technology of the past. *Cyborg* technology."

Ikaria belted out a loud laugh, and it echoed through the cell. She threw her head back, then her whole body, howling with laughter, her hair tangling around her. She then rolled onto her stomach, peering up at him. "So Belinda wants to know about how to control the cyborgs that came through the portal, does she?"

"Indeed."

"And if I refuse? Are you going to 'get' inside my head?"

"That is the plan, yes," Rubius said.

With a swift flick of his hand, Rubius called forth the adjacent power of his orange magic, then poured it out onto a nearby empty food tray on the floor. Orange sparkles dusted the tray, settling onto it. Slowly, the tray morphed and jiggled as the orange magic glowed brighter, until the entirety of the object was wrapped in orange magic. The tray slowly formed into a paper scroll, inkwell, and a quill. With a flick of his wrist, Rubius commanded the magic to carry the newly formed objects toward Ikaria, then dropped them at her feet.

"I want you to record everything you know of the ancient technology," Rubius said, dusting his hands off as if his orange magic was dirtying his hands.

The sorceress idly grasped the scroll, then opened the inkwell, her magical barrier moving with her movements, allowing her to pick up the objects. She stared at him for a moment, then she raised the inkwell, purposely spilling it all over the scroll.

"Oops. My, my, how clumsy of me." Her eyes narrowed, then she chucked the empty inkwell against the prison wall, and the glass shattered upon contact.

Rubius swallowed his anger to remain calm. "I honestly don't feel like dealing with you, truth be told. So why don't you save all your *smooth* talk and just tell me what I want to know? Everything will go a lot easier. For you, and for your sister."

With the mention of her sister, Ikaria's eyes met his, but she remained in the same position, the translucent magical barrier slightly shifting forms.

"What about my sister?" She dramatically sniffed. "You going to get in her head too? See that she is a true loyalist to the High Court?"

"Get in her head? No. She is being sent to the High Court to stand trial."

For an instant, Rubius saw a hint of fear in her proud eyes. It was only a second, but it was all he needed to know.

"Stand trial? You mean to be executed?" she stated.

"Unfortunately, that tends to be the verdict of the high justices."

The sorceress sneered, but remained silent.

"Got nothing to say about your sister? No comment?"

Ikaria shrugged, then looked away. "What makes you think I care about her?"

"So you don't care that she will most likely be executed?"

"No, I don't," Ikaria said indifferently.

"I don't believe you," Rubius said, calling her bluff. "You know I have the power that could help spare her life. Give me what I want, and I will do what I can to see that she is spared."

Ikaria's head snapped up, and she angrily stalked over to him, the chains attached to her shackles snaking behind her, rubbing against the stone floor. Her eyes flared. "Do you see what she has done to me? Do you see this invisible prison that surrounds me?" She snorted, waving her hands around aimlessly at the cell, the chains swaying. "If what you say is true, then I say let her *learn* from her mistakes!"

Rubius inched near her barrier. "Don't you care what is happening? Your sister will be tried for treason. And you, your violet magic will be taken from you. Who knows, perhaps the High Court will have you executed too, like your sister."

"And there it is. Your lie exposed. You *have* come to take away my violet magic." Ikaria held her head high, narrowing her eyes. "Come and take it, High Inquisitor. Come see inside my mind. I'd like to see you try. You are just some no-name hack from the High Court. I hadn't even heard of you until my sister mentioned you, but everyone has heard of me."

Fury burned within his blood, and his life force started bubbling with rage.

"It won't be me, Sorceress, that you'll be crying to when they remove your magic," Rubius snarled. "I'm giving you a chance to redeem your sector! Just give them what they want, and you might just save your sister, perhaps even yourself."

Her eyes flared at him. "And what is the value of my life if I just give them what they want?" The sorceress stood, perfectly poised. "I am far more valuable than anything on this earth, High Inquisitor. Those fools don't deserve one drop of my body, my blood, or my knowledge. Go crawling back on your knees like the dog you are and continue to kiss Belinda's backside."

Her insult infuriated him, his heart racing while he shook with rage. With a loud snarl, Rubius marched right up to Ikaria's personal barrier. Channeling his rage, it spread throughout his body, transforming into magic as it flowed.

He grew the magic more and more until his hands glowed a hot red, burning with animosity.

With a sharp movement, he slapped his hands onto her barrier, then released his magic.

Red lightning filled the inside of the sorceress's magical barrier with glowing forked lightning, bouncing all over her barrier within.

Suddenly, the red lightning struck her, and Ikaria's eyes went wide with shock as she jolted, then slumped to the ground. A small tear of pain ran down her cheek as she clenched her teeth and closed her eyes. Even in her pain, she managed to hold on to her pride.

Not for long…

Satisfied, Rubius knelt down beside her barrier, trying to get a good look at her face. "You want to stop? Just tell me about the technology."

She managed to lift her head slightly, cracking open her eyes, her breathing irregular. "Oh, I could go all day."

"Suit yourself."

Again, Rubius pressed his fingertips against her barrier, the veins popping out of his hand from the tension of the magic flowing through them, waiting to be released with another onslaught of rage. Rubius released another wave of red magic; this time it flung out of his fingertips in the shape of ice spikes.

But what happened next surprised Rubius.

With a struggling gesture, the sorceress summoned her own blast of violet-red ice shards.

Her ice shards collided with his within her barrier, and both shattered to the floor.

Rubius shot her a look. "*How*?" he asked incredulously. "How do you have the red gift? No one told me you had that ability! Do you have the blue gift too?"

Ikaria glared at him weakly, then gave a cool smile. Turning her gaze away from him, she lowered her eyes to the shattered red-and-violet magical ice, heating her hands and placing them above it.

The ice melted into puddles of reddish-violet water within her box. Then the sorceress seductively bent down and licked the water off the floor, still weak with shock.

Rubius hovered over her, his gaze meeting hers behind her prismatic barrier.

"I asked you a question!"

"Oh? Didn't you know?" She slurped the water again, this time, her eyes intent on him.

He was the only one in the world who had magic outside his main magic. That is, that he knew of. And yet here she was, the same as him.

The sorceress took another lick of the water, then wiped her mouth with her hand. "Why don't you use your power and find out what other sort of tricks I have? Like I said, I could go all *day*. It's been awhile since someone has played with me."

Rubius sneered, then closed his eyes, letting the violet side of his life force flow through him. The jealousy, the underlying power that it held swept over him like a great overwhelming force, flooding his mind.

Clutching the sorceress's prison barrier without letting his fingers slip inside, he released the overwhelming forceful power of his mind, channeling it into hers.

With a sudden rush of violet power, Rubius's consciousness jumped into her mind. He found himself immersed within her twisted thoughts. Darkness was in every corner of her mind, highlighted with deep violets and neon purples. He couldn't make out the shapes of the insides, as it was too dark, and his consciousness felt… *sick* being inside of her.

Before Rubius could find a weakness within her mind, a roaring force attacked his consciousness, grasping at his.

Just as I thought… her mind whispered into his. *Well, this is going to be much more enjoyable than I originally anticipated.* Her mind echoed a deep laugh, and it reverberated through his consciousness. *We are going to have so much fun, you have no idea.*

Angrily, Rubius struggled within the confines of her darkened mind, trying to scan her thoughts for any means of escape. Shooting pains rocked his mind, scrambling his thoughts. A deep power squeezed his soul so tight it rendered him incapacitated. The darkness closed in on him, his consciousness paralyzed by her sheer power.

Just when he felt like the darkness was about to overtake him, Rubius was thrown out of the sorceress's mind, sending him back into his body.

Grimacing, Rubius stumbled, catching himself against one of the cell's walls. Blinking to gather his wits, Rubius still felt the wracking pains clenching his thoughts, but they were fading, as he was no longer linked to her.

"That was a neat little trick, High Inquisitor," the sorceress said, amused. Ikaria rolled over on the floor, lifting her head slightly. Her body was still incapacitated from the lightning, her movements jolting every few seconds, her chains making slinking sounds. But her mind was fully intact. "*I* am in control within this box. You will soon realize that you cannot go up against a violet-gifted, High Inquisitor."

Shaking with rage, he shot to her. No one got inside *his* mind. "You just marked yourself a dead woman!"

"Oh? Is that so?"

"You bet your ass!" Rubius snarled. "Don't count on me to lift a finger to help save your sister. And as far as *your* life goes, it's over. I should have your gift stripped right now. In fact, I think that's an excellent idea."

"I look forward to it."

Rubius clenched his fists tightly. He wanted to punch something. *Hard.*

Angrily, he turned away, knocking on the door. "Open up now!" he roared.

The door opened, and he turned to look at the sorceress one last time.

A smug look appeared on her face with a hint of insanity. "I do hope to see you again soon." She waved at him with a false smile.

Damn that bitch!

Rubius stormed out of the cell, and the door closed behind him. He grabbed the guard outside, the one who had explained the barrier to him, yanking him so hard that the guard tripped.

Rubius's nose smashed against the guard's nose, his eyes narrowing. "You told me her barrier suppresses her magic!" he yelled.

"It does! It really does!" the guard said in a panic, scared as he tried to pull away. "I swear it, High Inquisitor! I swear that's what they told me. Please! I'm just a mere non-gifted. I swear I don't know how it all works."

Angrily, Rubius flung the man away, sending him crashing against the stone wall with the help of his violet power.

He yelled in frustration, then hurled a ball of fire down the corridor. With another yell, he kicked another prison door, screaming. All the while, the guards remained silent, not making eye contact with him.

Then he stormed off before he let his emotions fully consume him.

CHAPTER 30

GREEN

World Sector Three. That was where the High Court was, according to the conversation that he had overheard. Suresh had no knowledge of where this World Sector Three was located within this time, but it seemed that Lady Vala did.

Since making the decision to follow Lady Vala, Suresh had been doing so across the chasm of the time dimension, keeping a safe and discreet distance from her. He didn't want to alarm her by any means, and he maintained his travel carefully so she wouldn't discover him.

Very faintly, Suresh could see Lady Vala's path glittering and gleaming with her magic, stretching far across the sky dimension. It was very similar to the space-time continuum's magical paths. Curiously, Suresh had only seen these magical paths emit from the blue-gifted within the worldly dimension a handful of times. It always showed up in the space-time continuum. But in the real world, frozen in time magic? Suresh could only recall seeing it two other times.

Lady Vala has to be special... Suresh thought. *Or perhaps very powerful.*

Suresh continued to travel across the cloudy sky, the world stilled in his green-blue time magic. He maintained his speed, stepping foot on the sparkly path of Vala's glittering blue magic as he moved across the light atmosphere. Far ahead in the distance rose large grand citadels. All of them gleaming with grandeur, carefully sculpted. Amongst the citadels was a prominent structure. It had to be the main citadel, possibly where the High Court was housed.

Suresh marveled at the beauty of the citadels, especially the preeminent one. He couldn't remember the last time he had seen architecture so beautiful. The temple from his home time was beautiful, but nothing compared to what lay before his eyes. As he traveled closer to the floating structure, Suresh saw more of its intricate details. The citadel was almost overwhelming in how large, radiant, and magnificent it was.

As he approached the citadel's airspace, Suresh saw a shadow coming toward him. He paused, watching the shadow approach him.

It was a man, traveling in the opposite direction as Suresh, away from the citadel. If they maintained their same travel speed, they would eventually cross paths. Suresh pulled up his newly acquired hood, covering his hair.

The man continued toward him, then suddenly stopped, looking at Suresh almost in alarm.

Suresh returned the look, each wondering if one was a threat to the other.

The man. He was blue-gifted.

Suresh knew what the man had to be thinking—that if he was animate in this time-frozen world, then he had to have blue magic too.

They continued to study each other, until the man broke the silence.

"Looks like you're on your way to the High Court," the man said with caution. "Did Belinda summon you?"

Suresh wondered what he should say. It was interesting that the man knew about the summoning of the blue-gifted.

He is traveling in the opposite direction of the High Court, Suresh noted. Was he evading the High Court?

"No, my friend, I am on an... errand," Suresh answered, choosing his words carefully. "Though I have heard that the High Court has summoned blue-gifted."

"That they have been," the man said.

"I think it's strange that many of the blue-gifted have been called to court," Suresh said. "In fact, I am on my way to visit an old blue-gifted friend of mine that I haven't seen in a while." He felt bad about fibbing, but he didn't want the man to think he was an enemy.

The man relaxed a little. "I would have been in the clear, but some High Court blue-gifted woman found out about me when she went to retrieve my friend back in World Sector Five. I just happened to be drinking with him when she found him. That's when she noticed me. She asked me if I had been summoned to the High Court. I didn't know what she was referring to at the time, and thought she was just being polite." He looked irritated. "I thought it rather odd that she couldn't travel with my friend's harp, her being blue-gifted. I thought she was just too prissy, so I offered to deliver it to my friend's living quarters at the High Court citadel. That's where I was just at—the High Court citadel."

The man sighed. "That was a big mistake. After I dropped off my friend's instrument, I went to visit some friends. They told me of the rumors of the blue-gifted being called to the High Court to serve. To serve what? I had no idea. I left the citadel before my official summons went out. But I know it is only a matter of time before they come after me, especially if they're reminded of me."

"That is unfortunate, my friend."

"The name is Dydrone."

"Dydrone," Suresh repeated, nodding at him.

"My friend with the harp—he had told me of the blue-gifted rumors before, but I never really paid attention to them. I was always focused on what was going on in my life. Never did care for rumors. That's all they were—rumors. Turns out that I should have been paying closer attention."

Suresh studied him. "Where are you off to, then?"

"I plan to lay low for a while," Dydrone stated.

Suresh gave him a half smile. "I understand your discretion."

As Dydrone was about to take off once again, he gave Suresh one last look. "Your eyes. They are green. But you have time magic."

Suresh jolted in alarm, taking a step back.

Dydrone eyed him. "I don't know who you are, but you'd best be careful, especially going into the lion's den." He paused. "And you need to cover your face much better. Make sure your eyes are well shaded by your hood." He looked over his shoulder again. "I need to get moving."

"Good luck, Dydrone."

"Thanks, friend."

"I'm Sur—"

"Don't tell me who you are," Dydrone interrupted. "I don't want to know. The more one knows of unique or powerful gifted, the more dangerous it is. For both of us." He glanced at Suresh. "And I can definitely tell you have something going on, something that is most dangerous to know about." He nodded. "Good day."

Suresh nodded back, and the man took off, burning in bright-blue magic, almost as fast as the speed of light. Dydrone's magic burned across the sky like a blue shooting star until it flashed away.

Looking back toward the citadel, Suresh realized something. Lady Vala's path. It was gone. It must have faded while he was talking with Dydrone. His stomach sank. How was he going to find her?

Determined, Suresh continued to move toward the citadel. A sick, dark wave of disgust came over him. Suresh trembled for a moment, then swallowed. There was something not right about the citadel. Was it about the blue-gifted being summoned? Lady Vala?

The hair on the back of his neck stood on end. Something definitely wasn't right. But *what*?

CHAPTER 31

BLUE

Vala stood outside on the welcoming platform of the High Court citadel, where the airships docked. She didn't usually fly on airships, being blue-gifted, but she didn't want to look out of place when first arriving to the High Court, so she made sure she appeared at the main docking platform. This was her first time at the High Court, and she wanted to carry herself like a true lady of the court, though she was anything but at times.

The buildings, the architecture... it was all that she expected and more. The grandioso of the High Court structure was one of the most remarkable towers she had ever seen. It stood higher than all the other surrounding structures that composed the citadel. Pure white-marble walls capped golden spires, with gold scroll designs inlaid throughout the citadel itself, and all along the citadel were marbled staircases leading up to the main entrance, with many people robed in different colors going every which way to their daily activities. In the middle of the outside courtyard was a sculpted statue holding the symbol of the spectrum, representing the God of Light's pure power in the form of an orb.

Vala breathed nervously, then pushed her anxiety aside. She arched her back and held her chin high. It always gave her strength when she acted like she was in charge and in power, for if she appeared like that to others, it gave her more courage to be bold, especially in trying times at court. This time would be no exception. She would need all the strength she could get.

In the back of her mind, Vala focused on what Katrina had overheard from the high lords at her court—no one had seen or heard from the blue-gifted who had been summoned to the High Court. No one knew what had become of them, nor could Vala make a viable guess as to what had happened to them, but Vala had a deep fear that it wasn't good. She knew her recent actions were going to face the consequences. After all, she and several other gifted had violated the decree of the High Court, and she'd aided her uncle anyway. Especially now knowing that the High Inquisitor was making his way to World Sector Six. Most of all, she worried for her uncle. He was the only family she had, and the thought of losing him was unbearable.

Hopefully Uncle is all right. Perhaps I can lay a convincing argument at the feet of the High Court about the whole ordeal, Vala thought. She always did in any other situation. She had a gift in the art of persuasion and could give a convincing argument to any of the other lords of the court. They usually always assented. Silver tongued, they called her.

Vala took one last look at her surroundings, then started up one of the main stairways that led to the citadel's entrance. It was a beautiful day. The sky was at peace with the gentle clouds. But Vala felt anything but pleasant. With each step, her nerves shook, but she kept reminding herself to not let her fear get the best of her.

It was more than obvious where the High Court was situated within the citadel. There was a path that was much more grand than all the others that branched out. Vala followed that path and reached the top of the stairs, then passed the main archway, walking down the main aisle that led into the citadel. There were a good amount of guards stationed sporadically, their eyes following her without the motion of their heads.

As she neared the entrance, she saw courtesans working and fluttering about, noticing her approach.

One of the High Court secretaries bowed. "Lady Vala, The High Court is expecting you. Please, have a seat while I inform them of your arrival." He gestured to an elaborate carved marbled bench just outside the entryway.

Vala nodded, then sat down, watching as the secretary disappeared behind the oversized double doors. They creaked loudly as he did. As she waited, Vala noticed the fine magical woven tapestries of all the different high justices. They all had a slight glow to them and were very vibrant in color. Her eyes scanned each of them. Belinda looked like a goddess, her slim, perfectly sculpted face surrounding eyes of glittering red gems. Long perfect cascading curls flowed down her sides. Tyllos, on the other hand, looked rather decrepit. Vala chuckled at the thought of Tyllos looking rather ill. She didn't think much of the yellow justice, as whenever he visited her sector, he seemed rather arrogant.

There was a vacant spot on the wall, a slight discoloration on the wall where a tapestry should be. One justice was missing from the wall—High Justice Oriel.

Vala frowned, thinking of the High Justice's recent death.

How quickly they removed his portrait, she thought. *Why wouldn't they keep it up? They kept other deceased people's portraits hanging in the halls.*

It was rather odd.

She continued to scan the paintings of the important figures until she spotted the portrait of an extremely striking man, one with the red gift. She'd always had a fancy for the red gift, and that included red-gifted men.

Vala eyed the description. *High Inquisitor Rubius.*

Her eyes darted to the picture once again. *So that's the High Inquisitor? Handsome man.*

She fidgeted with her gold-plated necklace, then fixed her circlet, making sure that the main jewel felt centered on her forehead.

Just then, the secretary came back to the receiving chamber, bowing. "The Justices are ready to receive you now, Lady Vala."

Vala bowed in return, then followed the secretary. As they stepped through the double doors, Vala felt an immense power and rush of energy flowing within the room. It rattled her life force violently, causing an overwhelming sensation through her core. Vala felt dizzy from the powerful energy, and suddenly her legs buckled, causing her to nearly fall to the floor. Luckily, she caught herself in time, then composed herself. Never in her life had she felt that kind of extreme power.

As she walked toward the center, Vala saw the justices, all but the deceased High Justice Oriel, seated on their thrones of power. Behind each throne was a large jewel encrusted in their high-backed throne, almost appearing to float above their heads.

Vala approached a golden circle that was engraved on the floor, assuming that is where she was supposed to position herself. As she stepped foot in the circle, she fell to her feet, bowing so low that her forehead touched the polished marbled floors.

"Lady Vala," called out High Justice Belinda. "You may rise."

Vala immediately got to her feet, then nodded her head in acknowledgment.

Belinda's eyes sparkled as her painted red lips parted into a smile. "How good it is to see you. How long has it been since we last spoke? I daresay it's been several years."

That overwhelming power hit Vala again, and her body sickened with the rush of it. She blinked for a moment to regain her senses, and the power fled, leaving her feeling as she should.

"Yes, I believe it has been several years, High Justice," Vala answered steadily, eyeing all the justices, lingering at Oriel's empty spot. "I was very sorry to hear about High Justice Oriel. May he rest in peace." Vala bowed in respect.

"Truly unfortunate," Belinda said. "We are missing one of the greatest blue-gifted to have ever lived."

"Why have you removed his portrait?"

The high justices shot her stares like poison darts. Vala remained poised, unmoved. She shouldn't have blurted out that last question, but it couldn't be helped.

Belinda let out an audible "hmph," and Tyllos frowned.

"This one has quite the mouth on her." Nyrden smirked, turning to Belinda. "Quite discourteous, don't you think, Belinda?"

"Most discourteous," Belinda answered, her eyes never leaving Vala.

That woman... Vala shivered as the justice stared at her but remained silent.

Belinda's eyes lingered on her, then she began to speak. "Do you know why we have called you here, Lady Vala?"

Vala shook her head. "I must admit, I do not, High Justice."

"Now, more than ever, we need of the someone to replace Oriel's vacant position. Someone with talent."

Vala's gaze met hers instantly. "You are not recommending I sit on that throne, are you?"

Nyrden laughed. "Dear heavens, no," he said. "A flittering, ill-mannered gossip like you? Never."

His words were like a punch in the gut, angering her. Vala gritted her teeth inwardly, but outwardly, she maintained her posture, not even flinching.

"You see, Lady Vala, we have a bit of a dilemma, one that deals with the past," Perserine said, entering the conversation. "It deals with the precise time when you visited the past."

"The time of the battle with the Sorceress Ikaria?" Vala asked.

"Precisely. There is a certain gifted who resides there. I am sure that you saw her at some point, or even interacted with her. The green-gifted named Emerald."

Vala's attention snapped to meet Perserine's gaze. She knew exactly who Emerald was—she was the gifted who cleansed her before they departed back to the future. Queen Emerald had immense power, almost as much as the sorceress.

"Queen Emerald was able to drain one's life force," Vala stated to the court. "She was indeed a very dangerous gifted when her mind was compromised by the sorceress."

"So you can understand how powerful her gift is, and how much we could benefit from her being here, in our present time," Perserine said in return.

Her words echoed in Vala's ears, and Vala finally understood what they were asking of her.

"I might have this wrong, High Justice, but are you asking me to travel back and acquire the gifted queen's blood?" Vala asked incredulously. "I mean, not to question you or anything, but I do believe that this goes against any teaching held in *The Spectrum*, does it not? Have you talked to my uncle about this? He is quite the expert when it comes to the laws of the holy book."

"We are not asking you to take her blood, Lady Vala," Belinda said smoothly. "We are asking for you to bring *her* here." She eyed the green throne. "That way, we can have a true green-gifted sitting on the green throne."

Vala couldn't believe what she was hearing. "But what if Emerald doesn't want to come here? What if she wants to stay in the past? What if she can't even survive in the future?"

Vala thought for a moment. The green-gifted queen could actually survive with the green blood, come to think of it. But this whole thing was absurd!

"I can assure you, she will want to," Belinda answered, turning her attention to Borgen.

Within a blue time flash, High Justice Borgen burned brightly for a moment, then the flash died down, and he held a sealed document in his hand. He motioned for Vala to come forward, and she did so, taking it.

"Give that to Queen Emerald," he said. "That should convince her."

Studying the sealed scroll for a moment, Vala glanced up at Belinda. "You know that one has very little time in the past before they deteriorate. What if I cannot find the Queen in time before I die? You are asking me to risk my life to try to convince this green-gifted to come to our time, and we are not even certain she will want to come."

"You have your orders," Belinda said with finality. The other justices stared at her evenly.

Everything about the situation was *wrong*. Had they lost their minds? Disrupting the very flow of time itself? It was complete madness! The High Court wanting a green justice… wanting to bring another gifted to this time. Strangely, back in time, the Sorceress Ikaria had wanted to bring the green-gifted queen through the time portal as well, but her attempt resulted in failure because of Vala and the other gifted.

Why would the High Court and the imprisoned sorceress have the same goal?

Vala held her head high, staring straight back at Belinda in defiance. "You must understand, High Justices of the Court, that I have always been willing to stand up and fight for a cause that I believe in. But this? Risking my life just to have a green justice on the throne? For what? Removing one gifted from one time to another? Surely even you know that it would alter the flow of time? It would disrupt what the God of Light intended for our very future," Vala said passionately, staring at them evenly. "I'm sorry, High Justices, but I cannot help you. This is complete and utter madness, and I will have no part in it."

Suddenly, a sharp wind hit struck her body, knocking Vala to her feet. She slid backward, hitting her head hard against the marble.

"You have no choice in the matter, Lady Vala." Belinda's tone was icy. "This is your punishment, *lady*. Or did you think you would get away with your insolent behavior? You *knew* of our court order not to help the other sectors. And yet you rallied gifted in the other sectors."

"But my uncle…"

"Your uncle has been labeled a traitor and deemed a heretic!" Belinda snapped. "And now you are going to pay the price for your foolishness!" Belinda snarled at her.

"What was I supposed to do? Let time cease to exist?" Vala countered hotly, rising to her feet. *Boy, no wonder people have been disenchanted with the court with this kind of attitude...*

"Silence!" Belinda roared. "You *will* help us."

Before Vala had any chance to react, Belinda snapped her fingers. That same overwhelming power hit her, but this time it was much stronger. Vala went to take another step back, but she was overwhelmed. Time rendered her still from the waist down. From behind the pillars that surrounded the room, orange-gifted guards who served the High Court came forth, closing in on her.

Vala's eyes went wide as she tried to counter the time magic frantically, but it was much stronger than hers.

"What is going on?" The four orange-gifted guards grabbed her, holding her in a death grip. "What are you doing?" Vala shouted, struggling. She couldn't feel her legs...

"You see the man on your left?" Nyrden called out.

Vala's eyes jerked to the side to a man with a large needle; it looked similar to what the strange orange-gifted lady in the past had.

"He is going to infuse you with a concoction. If you foolishly decide to hide in the space-time continuum, think again. Its poison will slowly seep through you, and you will eventually die."

"I'll just find Queen Emerald and have her heal me!" Vala shot back.

Nyrden barked out a loud laugh. "Are you so confident that she can heal poison? Especially *this* poison? I wouldn't be so sure if I were you." He laughed again, as if the whole situation was amusing.

"If you choose not do as we command, then you will die, along with everyone else in your sector," Belinda said coldly.

Vala froze in position, her face dropping. "What?"

"You were the reason everyone else defied our court order. You and your uncle. Now, because of your lack of steadfast faith in the court, you have led your whole sector down the path of unrighteousness. And for that, we must purge the sectors of sin." Belinda paused. "That is, unless you redeem yourself by setting it right."

Vala shook her head in disbelief, taking a step back. "You would kill a whole sector? All because of my actions?"

"We do not make idle threats," Belinda said. "Your sector *will* perish if you choose not to return with what we want. So you see, you either die in the past or die here. And your sector will go down with you. The choice is yours."

Vala's eyes shot all over the room, her heart pounding. "Punish me all you want, but leave the people of my sector out of this!" she screamed, struggling. "I take full responsibility! Leave them alone!"

High Justice Nyrden laughed. "It's a little too late for that."

High Justice Borgen interrupted. "You still have time to redeem yourself and your sector. That is, if you find the green-gifted queen and bring her back here, just before you die," he said in an eerily friendly tone. "Only then can we counter the poison with an antidote, and your sector will remain safe. Best hurry."

Without warning, Vala felt a sharp jab in her side, then pain shot through her. The guards let her go, and she doubled over onto the floor, rolling around clutching her body.

"Get up," Belinda said coldly. "The clock is ticking, and you have very little time. And just so you know, the more you tap into your power, the quicker the poison will work through your body. So you'd best only travel there and back. We will even be nice and summon you a portal."

Vala wept silently. Her people… her sector. The fate of their lives were all on her. Her body wracked with pain, she began to shake. Through her tears, she saw Borgen standing before her summoning a time portal. Its blue magic rippled with power.

"What are you waiting for? Get up and go!" Nyrden stood over her, then kicked her hard, sending her sliding several inches.

She didn't know what to do. She was still in shock over what was happening.

"Get up!" he yelled.

Vala started crawling toward the portal, the pain still gnawing at her side. Belinda, Tyllos, and Perserine looked on while Borgen moved out of the way.

Belinda gestured, and the four orange-gifted came forward. They pulled Vala to her feet, then threw her into the portal.

The world started melting before her eyes. The world around her fell apart as time began forming. Then time dropped, and she fell endlessly through time and space.

Pain filled her veins, and her tears wouldn't stop. She had never been one to cry, but the shock of all of this was all too much to bear.

Friction whipped Vala around, then her body tumbled on a hard surface, rolling until it came to a stop.

She took a deep breath, pain shooting into her lungs. Stars, galaxies, and blue portals filled the sky as skittered stars formed under her body into a path.

She was in the space-time continuum.

New tears were shed, some in anger, some in fear. Vala was unsure of what to do. She couldn't let her sector die because of her. But helping the High Court, especially now, at this point… she didn't want to help them.

Oh, Uncle, what would you do? she cried out in her thoughts.

Her uncle. Vala hoped and prayed with all her heart that he was okay. Did the High Court have him as well?

She grimaced, swallowing hard. Her life couldn't end like this. Vala was convinced that she was going to be a great woman of the court, and wise like her uncle one day. Plus, all those things she had said about the God of Light not making her a red-gifted. Would God punish her? It had only been a half joke, but still, she hadn't repented.

With one big movement, Vala vomited, spewing bile from her body. Her body kept trying to purge the poison within her bloodstream, but it just couldn't shake it.

Wiping the bile from her mouth with the hem of her garment, Vala weakly shifted away from the mess, not wanting to smell it for fear of heaving again.

What am I going to do?

She looked down at the parchment, at the seal on the paper. Would Queen Emerald truly want to read this message? The Queen seemed so kind, and High Justice Belinda was rotten to the core. Was Nyrden bluffing about Queen Emerald unable to heal the poison from her body? Or was it something more than poison?

Vala struggled, managing to get to her feet, limping quickly past a vast number of portals, feeling their time connection to her spirit.

Who did the High Court think they were? Gods? They were representatives of God Himself, but they certainly were not acting godly.

Vala winced but kept limping down the starry path until she felt the presence of where she had been before. She stopped in front of a rippling portal.

It had recently been activated; it glowed a brighter blue than normal. The portal to the Queen's time. Someone had been there before her.

Maybe I am not the first blue-gifted sent on this mission.

The other blue-gifted. Maybe they, too, had been injected. Vala could count on the High Court threatening their loved ones, just like they did with her.

Vala's eyes went wide with fear. The blue-gifted. They were all after the Queen.

Struggling, Vala weakly rose to her feet, then glanced at the portal with determination. She had to get to Queen Emerald. Either before the other blue-gifted did or before she died of the poison.

She had to save her sector.

CHAPTER 32

Red

The sounds of Rubius's boots echoed across the sterile, marbled floor as he marched into the dining hall. Only servants remained, waiting to serve him. Whether Emperor Cyrus had ordered the lords and ladies to remain in their quarters or they were frightened of what was happening, Rubius couldn't say. At least he didn't have to deal with the Emperor during his meal. He'd had enough of that man for one evening.

The servants immediately came up to him, bowing as he sat down hastily, kicking a chair out of the way to seat himself.

"Dinner! And someone get me my damned bird," Rubius ordered one of the servants. They all scattered, rushing to serve him.

He ran his fingers through his hair in frustration, feeling the sweat upon them. How had the sorceress gotten inside his head? Wasn't that the point of the magical barrier?

Out of the corner of his eye, Rubius saw one of the servants approaching with a chalice of wine. He immediately snatched it and took a long drink. The wine was terrible, but it did the trick to numb his anger. There was still lingering pain from the sorceress getting inside his head, like a shard that had been hurled at him within his thoughts. His head just didn't feel *right.*

He heard a familiar caw. Rubius glanced over his shoulder at a servant girl stood with Zaphod perched on her arm.

"Come here, you old coot," Rubius called out. He winced at his movement, his head still hurting.

Zaphod leapt off the girl's arm, flying across the room, then hovering next to Rubius as he made a spot on his shoulder for him. After a moment, the bird took hold of his jacket, then perched on his shoulder.

Rubius gave Zaphod a reassuring pat as dinner was placed before him and his chalice was refilled once again. He drank the wine given to him as Zaphod sat cooing and cawing every so often. How was he to do his job if the sorceress had access to his mind? Rubius sneered into his cup, taking another long drink, the pain still lingering in his head.

That barrier only seemed to contain her magic in the physical world, Rubius tried working out in his mind. *Perhaps she was able to use her magic when I entered her consciousness because it wasn't technically in the physical world...*

Rubius paused. That had to be how the sorceress did it. There could be no other way. Convinced that was the case, Rubius continued to mull over his situation.

Now how am I supposed to extract that information? It was going to be harder than he thought. And what was even more disappointing was that he didn't get a chance to ask the sorceress about the green-gifted woman. It was clear the sorceress wouldn't be telling him anything, and it would be just another thing to pry out of her if he truly wanted to know.

Pain shot through his head once again, and Rubius grimaced. His thoughts felt muddled and fuzzy. It was as if something in his mind had snapped, and his whole body was now *different.*

After taking another drink of wine, he started in on his dinner. Zaphod cawed.

"You hungry too?" Rubius asked the bird in a soothing tone, trying to take his mind off the pain. He reached into his pockets and grabbed a handful of seeds, then placed it on the table. The parrot hopped down, then began pecking at them.

Rubius felt a sudden shift in the room. There was a presence here, one that annoyed him greatly.

Great. Just what I need.

"Did you find that priest?" Rubius called out irritably.

"I searched everywhere for him," said Elyathi's voice as an orange glow appeared before his eyes.

"My guards couldn't find him either." Rubius sighed.

"He'd best not have vacated the citadel." Elyathi came into full view, bathed in orange magic, then it flashed away, revealing her true form—white-gifted.

She gave him a look, and suddenly it struck Rubius *why* she looked so familiar. He couldn't believe it. Elyathi looked very similar to the green-gifted woman in his dreams. Not only her face, but her eyes, save for the color.

Why hadn't he noticed it before?

What if? What if Elyathi was that white-gifted back in time who mothered the green-gifted woman? But how would Elyathi have gotten to this time? She does have access to the blue gift, but is it possible?

His eyes lingered for a moment, then he coughed. Pushing the thought aside, Rubius shrugged. "So what if one gifted gets away? That wasn't our job."

"Maybe it wasn't your role," Elyathi said, "but it was mine. We must find that priest."

"If you say so. I will have my guards do what they can," Rubius said. *As long as it keeps you off my back.*

She nodded with gratitude. "Thank you, High Inquisitor."

Rubius glanced at her, noting more similarities with Elyathi and the green-gifted woman.

Dare I ask her?

He decided he had nothing to lose. Gesturing toward an empty seat, Rubius asked, "Are you hungry?"

"I am," Elyathi said, nodding. Immediately, servants pulled out a chair for her, and she gently seated herself at the table.

"Get her some dinner," Rubius called out to the servants. They nodded, walking quickly out of the hall. He winced again from another shockwave of pain.

Elyathi raised her eyebrow. "Are you okay?"

Rubius rubbed his head. "Yeah, I'm fine." He took another swig of wine, trying to ignore the pain.

"You said that your bird goes wherever you go, High Inquisitor, and I see that it's true. Most of the times I see you, that bird is beside you," Elyathi stated as she eyed Zaphod. "You must have a love for animals."

"I guess," Rubius said, taking a bite of his food. "I never had an opinion of them either way, but as soon as I came across Zaphod, I formed an instant connection."

"Zaphod. It's an unusual name, no?" Elyathi asked. "How did you come up with that name?"

Zaphod. How *had* he come up with that name?

"I don't know. I guess it just came to me on a whim," Rubius answered.

"Just like most everything you do," Elyathi commented, taking a sip of her wine. "It is fascinating you take a loving interest in simplistic things such as your parrot companion, and yet I have heard whispers of your cruel behavior to those you interrogate."

Rubius put down his glass, snorting. "Listen, it's not my fault that those people put themselves in their position. Do you think I delight in what I do?"

"From observing you, I would say yes. I think you rather enjoy it," she said.

"Well, I don't revel in it at all."

Elyathi looked at him intently. "Then why do you do it, High Inquisitor?"

"Because I get paid. End of story." He leaned back in his chair, taking another drink.

"So you are a man with no beliefs, no ideals, no great causes."

Rubius leaned far over the table, meeting her steady gaze. "And what of you, Miss High and Mighty? Miss *Justified.* Do you delight in *stealing* a person's gift from them? Sucking away their soul from them? Tell me. You think what you do is more justified than what I do? Did you not hear their screams when they were losing their power? Or do you somehow manage to have selective hearing?"

She remained in her same position, narrowing her eyes at him. "What I do, High Inquisitor, is for a greater cause. And if it means I have to extract every single gifted's magic from them, I will do it."

"What greater cause?" he asked incredulously. "The High Court's cause?"

"I need not explain to you. I would be wasting my breath."

"Please. Enlighten me."

Elyathi's eyes continued to pierce him, then to his surprise, she answered. "To build a better world, starting with the promise of the prophecy," she answered.

"Prophecy? What prophecy? To build a better world? I hope it includes gambling and drinking," Rubius retorted under his breath.

Elyathi seemed to take offense as she leaned back in her chair, unamused.

"This is why I do not like you. We are very different. It's unfortunate we have to work together."

"You're telling me," Rubius said as she sighed. "I was only joking."

"Crude humor leads to a corrupt heart."

She is even more of a religious nut than the whole High Court combined.

Rubius took another drink as Elyathi started in on her food. A slight movement… it reminded him of *her*. Similar face shape, eyes, long wavy hair…

Elyathi was suddenly aware he was staring, then her eyes narrowed. "Do not get comfortable looking at me, High Inquisitor. I don't like it."

Rubius rolled his eyes, sloshing the wine around in his cup. "I wasn't looking at you in that manner."

"Then how were you looking at me?" The whites of her eyes glistened, as if daring him.

He had to ask. It was his one and only chance.

"Lady Elyathi, do you have a daughter?"

Elyathi shot him a death glare, putting down her fork. "How dare you! Your statement is offensive on multiple counts!"

That stunned him. "Offensive? How!"

"Let me make something very clear, High Inquisitor, I would never introduce my daughter to you, *ever*, knowing what kind of man you are!"

Rubius shot up from his seat, nearing her face. "You are really something, aren't you? I was not insinuating anything of the sort! All I asked was if you had a daughter, and it seems I was correct, because you do not deny it."

Pain shot through him again, causing Rubius to flinch. He took a deep breath, then sat back down. He rubbed his head, trying to dull the sharp pain.

Elyathi watched him, narrowing her eyes. "It is true, I do have a daughter," she said in a low soft voice. "What I would like to know is *how* you know. Did Belinda tell you? Or was it Tyllos?"

She has a daughter… and the High Court knows of her daughter? His heart raced at the revelation.

"Is she green-gifted?" Rubius asked boldly. His voice came off slightly desperate, but he tried to hide it as much as he could. He had to know.

"I will ask you again, High Inquisitor, *how* do you know of her?" Elyathi asked firmly again.

I know it sounds nuts, but I dream of a green-gifted woman and can't stop thinking of her, he wanted to say. Confessing his dreams to Elyathi, whom he really didn't like, seemed like a bad idea. But what else *was* there to say?

"You wouldn't believe me even if I told you," Rubius said.

"Try me."

Rubius studied the whites of her eyes. *It's like what the green-gifted time traveler said… a white-gifted.*

Elyathi made no movement, awaiting his answer. In her eyes, he could see her anticipation.

He took a deep breath. This was it. His only chance.

"For as long as I can remember, I've had strange dreams, ones that always show a green-gifted woman," he started. "Many years ago, a man appeared in my chambers. A green-gifted man. A time traveler from the beginning of time. He was searching for some 'Ghost Man.' I asked him if he had ever seen a green-gifted woman in his travels, and he told me about a white-gifted woman who was pregnant with a green-gifted child two thousand years ago." Rubius paused, looking at her in desperation. "I know this sounds crazy but… do you know this man? Are you that very same white-gifted woman he was referring to? Is your daughter truly green-gifted? Could she be the one that I have been dreaming of all these years?"

As each of his words unraveled his story, Rubius watched as her face displayed an array of emotions, twisting until it hardened. Then Elyathi's eyes met his, giving him her full attention.

"I will only tell you this *once*, High Inquisitor, and we will speak no more of this matter, as I do not like to relive my past," she began sharply. "I do indeed have a daughter who was born thousands of years ago. Am I from the past? No, this is my true time. I was stolen away as a young child by a group of rebels that dwell on Earth's surface, all because they were trying to 'protect' me. I was the 'chosen one' of the greatest prophecy of all time, the one who would reshape the planet to its destined glory, restore magic to the heavens. These rebels believed the High Court to be false and believed that I was to be the one to destroy the High Court, according to their *twisted* version of the prophecy. To 'protect' me in my youth, a blue-gifted rebel traveled here and took me to a foreign time, leaving me out in a desert wasteland. Before I traveled back in time, the rebels made a promise that they would come back for me when the time came. Time came and went. No one came.

"When I reached womanhood, I was married off to a king with a cruel heart, locked away and only let out when he needed to satisfy his deep sexual appetite, or when he wanted to release his anger. For many years, all I knew was that my worth was in my beauty. My husband liked to show me off like a prize for all of the world to see, otherwise keeping me locked away like a precious doll, a plaything for his manhood. I was never physically beaten, but I was beaten down by his actions and words—every moment was an eternal prison. Everything he gave me was to look beautiful for *him.* My body and beauty became my prison, and soon I became nothing.

"My husband made sure that I was his, and no one else's, and he was allowed to do whatever he liked with me. I cried day and night; tears became my comfort. I was rarely allowed to see my daughter. Can you imagine that, High Inquisitor? Not being allowed to see your own daughter? All I had to hold on to was the written promise within *The Spectrum*—the God of Light's sacred written words of comfort.

"Through my tears, I prayed. Prayed for help. Prayed for a new life. Prayed to be anywhere other than where I was. And finally, help came. Two blue-gifted sent by the High Court found me, and brought me back to my true time." Elyathi paused, then took a deep but heavy sad breath.

"My only regret was that my daughter was left behind, back in time. I had been locked away in my chambers, unable to get out for many days. When the blue-gifted appeared to rescue me, they were about to perish, and had nothing left to spare for me to get my daughter. They quickly killed one of my maids and transformed her to look like me, for they had orange magic deep within their life force. They staged my death—a suicide.

"When I met the High Court, I begged for them to return and fetch my daughter. They agreed, and they sent out more blue-gifted for her, but the portal was missing. It was like that for many years, but now the portal has been restored. She will be brought to me, and I will finally be reunited with her, and I will be able to fulfill the prophecy that was meant for me. I will have all the colors of magic represented as a testament to the God of Light—with the help of my daughter and the wicked sorceress's power. Earth will finally be made anew in the God of Light's glory."

Elyathi eyed him, then leaned in close. "And when that happens, I will ensure that you have *nothing* to do with my daughter, whether it be on this earth or the new. Dreams or not, I know how the world works, High

Inquisitor, and what men truly want with young women. She is a *pure* soul, unlike yours."

Rubius sprang to his feet, meeting her gaze. "I'm *sorry* about your terrible past, lady, but why do you project it onto me? I am not what you think I am."

"Do not lie to yourself, High Inquisitor. Actions speaks louder than words. I have seen only a glimpse of your behavior, and it was far more than I needed to see, lest I remind you."

Enraged, Rubius clenched his fists, shaking furiously. "Just who do you think you are? You know nothing about me!"

Elyathi stood. "I know enough about you to make a full assessment." She leaned in. "You might be able to charm the others on the High Court with your looks, or your honeyed words, or your sweet songs, or even your immense power, but your soul toes the line of darkness. You have a blatant disregard for the God of Light. All you care about is yourself." She raised her chin. "If I ever catch you near my daughter when she arrives, I will personally castrate you by taking away your power, and I will wear it upon my neck as my most precious jewel, to remind all those who try to defile my daughter, to show them what happens to those who try."

"Damn you!" Zaphod flew away as Rubius yelled. He shook with rage. If he ever wanted to punch someone, it was now. Elyathi *infuriated* him. Rubius didn't know her daughter, but he was angry. She was making decisions for her daughter without her say in the matter.

"You make decisions for your daughter? How do you even know what she wants?" Rubius challenged her. "Sounds hypocritical to me."

"I know what my daughter needs in life." Elyathi eyed him evenly. "Good night, High Inquisitor. Tomorrow, when I see you, I will pretend this conversation never happened, and you'd best act the same, because I will never speak of it again. Like I said before, I do not like reliving my past."

"How can I pretend this never happened when you've insulted me so?" Rubius snapped, ready to throw his chalice across the room.

"It's very easy. I did it for many years with my husband. You tell yourself that the conversation never happened, then you believe those words. And then they become a new reality," she said smoothly, then nodded to him. "See you in the morning. Perhaps I shall come with you when you see the sorceress again." She grabbed an orange gem around her neck, then sucked in its power, her hair and eyes turning orange. Then she started fading into the orange magic.

"I think not," Rubius called out.

"You want to change my opinion of you? Live according to *The Spectrum.* Perhaps then we can get along after all."

Living according to *The Spectrum*? That was the last thing he would do.

I don't care what she thinks of me, he thought angrily.

Rubius heard her footsteps trail away until they were no more, and her presence was gone from the room, leaving him alone once more.

Before, he'd thought Elyathi was crazy. But he hadn't realized the extent. Prophecy? A new earth? Representing all the colors of magic? The woman was a lunatic—more so than the High Court.

He shuddered at the thought of that woman having that much power. A fanatical religious zealot with absolutely no forgiving bone in her body?

What was even worse was that he was infatuated with that fanatical religious zealot's daughter.

CHAPTER 33

YELLOW

Cries came from the next room, and muffled voices tried their best to soothe her. Auron paced frantically around the room, feeling sick.

The door opened, and immediately, Auron turned to look. A priest appeared in the doorway, then bowed.

Auron ran up to meet him. "How is she?" Auron asked quickly.

"Not good," said the priest. "There have been complications..."

A scream from his sister came from behind the door, and Auron's and the priest's eyes met.

"What kind of complications?" Auron pressed, grabbing the priest. His stomach was doing flips. "My sister and her baby, you must make sure they will be okay..." His voice wavered.

"We are doing everything we can. Please continue to pray, High Priest. Fervently, might I add. Your sister needs all the prayers she can get at this time," he said sadly.

The priest bowed, then hurried back into the next room where his sister's screams continued, shutting the door behind him.

Auron blinked, holding back a few tears as his memories faded away, leaving him in the present silence of the empty cell.

Vala... She was the only family he had left, a gift left by his sister before she departed into the realm of light.

Worry came over him just thinking about his niece. If World Sector Six was turned upside down, what of her current sector? Was she in grave danger too? The mere thought unnerved him.

Brother… you can't tell anyone. You mustn't. No one must ever find out. Ever… His deceased sister's words reverberated loudly within his mind. It was as if they were freshly spoken.

No one must ever find out…

Auron never liked to hide the truth; it was deceitful to do so. But this truth could do so much harm to everyone. The only detail Vala had ever known about her birth was that she was the result of a one-night coupling, and that her mother didn't know who the man was. Auron always felt awful telling Vala that half truth, but what else could he say? To even whisper who her real father was—a high justice—would have been treasonous. If word got out, it would be the biggest scandal that ever occurred in all the World Sectors. People's faith would be shaken, and some might even turn from the God of Light. Even then, if people didn't believe the truth of the matter, his sister, Auron, the priests involved, they would be mocked and flogged, and quite possibly hanged for making such a wild accusation. Luckily, Vala never pressed him any further, though Auron could sense there were several times that she wanted to ask him more about it. But now, with the High Justice dead, it made him worry about Vala all the more.

The only regret he had was paying Lady Penelope to raise her instead of doing it himself. But he had already taken the priestly vow, which included him dedicating his life to solitude, to focusing on the God of Light.

Auron sighed sadly. At least he had been able to see Vala grow up, spend time with her when life allowed. Most importantly, at least she knew him to be her true family, and he got to be an uncle to her. That, he was most thankful for.

The door to the cell quietly opened, then slipped shut, interrupting his thoughts.

"It seems that the God of Light must have heard your prayers, High Priest," Suri's voice reported quietly to him. They posted a red and yellow-gifted guard."

Auron shoved his unnerved thoughts about Vala aside and focused on Suri's words. He couldn't see her, as she was still bathed in her invisible magic from scouting.

"They just got settled. We'd best hurry," she continued.

"What if the High Inquisitor comes?" Auron asked, getting to his feet.

"Then he comes, priest, and we are all in trouble," Suri's voice called out.

There was a pause, then Auron saw a glistening of orange magic in front of him, and Suri's image formed within the power. Then Auron saw her completely. Her eyes were closed, her hands palms up in the air lightly, orange magic pouring out of her hands. It flowed like a glowing orange river, swirling in the air.

The magic moved, then came at Auron, wrapping itself around him. Within the brilliance of power, Auron watched as it settled on his skin like sparkling dust. He then looked over at Suri. The orange magic had enveloped her as well, shimmering like stardust, and their bodies began to transform.

Auron watched as Suri took the form of a man. The power warbled her skin, changed the shape and colors of her traits, until she looked like the High Inquisitor himself.

Auron quickly looked down, but he saw nothing. He was invisible.

Suri eyed him through her new set of eyes, satisfied. Once again, she poured magic over her neck, and it settled in her throat.

"Don't talk," she said, her voice coming out like a man's voice. It was so close to the High Inquisitor's voice that even Auron believed it was his with just the two words she spoke.

"Just follow me and you won't be detected," she continued.

Auron waited while Suri cracked open the door.

"It's clear," she said.

Auron nodded, and they both slipped outside the door.

They entered the side corridor, then turned, going down the main prison corridor. The hall was empty except for the set of guards stationed outside Ikaria's cell. It was just as Suri said—a red and yellow-gifted guard.

The two guards immediately saw the High Inquisitor approaching, or rather, Suri approaching, and they bowed.

"High Inquisitor!" they both hailed, bowing again.

"I need to speak to the prisoner," Suri commanded with a voice of authority.

She's good, Auron admitted to himself. Better than almost any other orange-gifted in their sector that he had witnessed.

"Yes, High Inquisitor, right away!"

One of the guards fumbled with the keys, obviously nervous that the High Inquisitor was in front of them, opening the door quickly.

The guards bowed, then moved out of the way, letting Suri and Auron pass.

They stepped inside the cell, and the door quickly shut behind them, making a deep metal scraping sound. Translucent colors of magic clung to the both of them as they passed through the protective barrier—Geeta's barrier, which she enchanted months ago. Auron took a long look at the barrier, impressed by Geeta's magic on display.

As the sticky gelatinous magic barrier pulled away from him, Auron felt Suri's magic melt off of him. He looked down and saw his body; he was visible.

Auron felt a pair of eyes on him, and he looked up. There, across the cell, was Ikaria. Her wrists were locked in manacles, her body bruised and her hair ragged.

Their eyes met, and suddenly, a strange powerful feeling stirred within his life force. It was almost as if the sorceress had sent a powerful force blowing against his soul.

His body wobbled for a second, overwhelmed by the strange sensation, but then quickly composed himself.

"Well, well, well, look who we have here. If it isn't High Priest Auron himself. Did you come expecting a confession? Because rest assured, priest, I will do no such thing." Her gaze shifted to Suri, who was still disguised as the High Inquisitor. "And how are you, High Inquisitor? Didn't have enough of me today? Back for more? Believe me, I have plenty of games that we can play."

"Enchantress," Suri called out, her voice wavering from the High Inquisitor's voice to her own.

Ikaria's face froze. "Suri? Is that you?" Ikaria said, surprised, the rattling of her chains echoing.

"Yes, it's me, Enchantress," Suri breathed.

The image of the High Inquisitor morphed in front of them, giving them a shimmering glimpse of Suri's true self.

"Oh, my dear Suri," Ikaria said desperately. "I have missed you so much."

Suri blushed at her words, then bent down toward Ikaria, moving her hands around the magical barrier, studying it with her hands. After a moment, she shoved her hands through the barrier, touching Ikaria's shackles.

"Enchantress…?"

"Yes, they enchanted these chains." Ikaria narrowed her eyes. "Violet, blue, red, and orange magic." She shook the chains angrily.

"I am sorry," Suri said, lowering her head. "I am an utter failure to you, Enchantress. I did not know about the chains. If I had known, I would have been fully prepared."

"Oh, Suri, you could never disappoint me," Ikaria said.

"We must get you out of here before the High Inquisitor comes back," Auron said, kneeling down, inspecting the chains himself. Suri was right; Auron could feel the power radiating from them. What was he or Suri to do?

"Or worse, that woman," Suri said. "She is constantly walking the corridors."

"What woman?" Ikaria asked.

"Enchantress, I believe I have found the cause of the 'plague.' It is being orchestrated by a woman from the High Court. She has the power to take magic from a gifted's life force. Permanently. The Empress confronted the High Inquisitor with the gifted in our sector, but then that woman showed up. Now the Empress has been captured and taken away, and I am quite sure that the high priest and I are the only ones left in our sector that remain with the gift. That is, besides you, Enchantress."

Ikaria's face shifted through a range of emotions, and Auron could have sworn he saw her eyes water for a split second. Then she snarled, grabbing the collar of Suri's robe and pulling her face closer. "Suri, listen to me, and listen quickly. The High Inquisitor is indeed sending someone to collect my blood. And by the sound of it, sooner than I anticipated," she said, pausing. "We cannot let that bitch Belinda, nor anyone else from the High Court, have my blood or my gift."

"That is why we have to get you out of here," Suri pressed.

"With what power? I am stuck in here within these barriers and chains. Even if I were free, I would still have this godforsaken barrier around me at all times. How would I be able to help?"

"But we cannot leave you here."

"You, Suri," Ikaria continued, ignoring her. "You and that priest have the ability to move as you like. With you two, we still have a chance."

"A chance at what?" Auron interrupted.

Ikaria looked up at him, then bit her wrist quickly.

Mortified, Auron shook his head. "What are you doing?"

"Something that I should have done long ago," Ikaria said, turning to Suri. "Transmute a vial, now."

Without hesitation, Suri took out a small stick from her hair, then pressed her hands together, quickly summoning orange magic. The stick melted into a bright-orange blob, then shaped into a vial small enough to fit in her hand.

"No! Absolutely not!" Auron said sharply.

"I never asked for your opinion, *priest*," Ikaria shot back, then turned to Suri. "Quickly."

When the vial had finished forming and the magic had wafted away, Ikaria snatched the vial out of her hand, then let her blood flow into it, making sure it was full. She then shoved the vial back into Suri's hands.

Suddenly, his rescue plan with Suri had become a nightmare. The last thing they needed was Ikaria's blood running around.

"Sorceress, you are playing with fire," Auron said in disbelief. "I thought you much more clever than this!"

Ikaria flashed her violet eyes at him through her barrier. "It is my guarantee, priest."

"Guarantee for what, exactly?"

"Have you been not been paying attention? Let me recap for you in case it slipped from your mind. There is a woman out to take my magic from me."

"And you think Suri running around with a vial of your blood is a good idea? That woman and the High Inquisitor are in this very citadel! It is highly probable that Suri and I will pass them in the halls."

Ikaria shook her head. "You couldn't find a more secretive person than Suri. That is why she is perfect."

"Do not worry, High Priest. I never fail in my mistress's commands," Suri assured him.

Somehow, none of their assurances made him feel any better.

Ikaria turned to Suri. "Suri, would you be so kind as to get my sister out of her little predicament? I will not tolerate the High Court making a mockery out of her."

"I am yours to command, Enchantress," Suri said, bowing low. "I will not fail you."

"Good girl," Ikaria said smoothly. "I know I can always trust in you, my dear Suri." Ikaria gently nudged the back of Suri's neck, with both of their foreheads slightly touching each other, in some sort of strange embrace. Ikaria then pulled away. "After you save my sister, leave this sector. Get that vial of my blood as far away from this place as possible. Guard it as if it were me. Even if you have to go to the earth below and stow it away in the hideouts. Do you understand?"

Suri nodded, taking a necklace she had, then transmuting the chain until it made a loop so it could hold the vial. Suri secured the vial, then shoved it into the neck of her clothing.

Auron felt a pang of worry. If they left Ikaria in the cell, she would have her magic taken away from her by that woman and the High Inquisitor.

"What about the High Inquisitor?" Auron blurted out. "How are you planning to fend him off? What about that woman?"

"Don't worry about me, priest. I am always one step ahead."

"In here? One step ahead?" Auron asked incredulously. "I should stay here in hiding. To protect you."

Suri raised her eyebrow slightly. "No, High Priest. That would alert them right away. We need to get to the Empress."

"Suri is right, priest," Ikaria added. "As much as your words touch me, you must leave me here. Alone. I can take care of myself."

Suri turned to Auron, then gestured. "We must leave before it is too late and that woman finds us all."

"One last thing," Ikaria called out.

They both looked to her, pausing.

"Yes, Enchantress?" Suri asked.

"You haven't drank my blood."

Auron snapped at full attention, shooting her a look. "What did you say?" he asked.

"Come here, Suri."

Auron marched past Suri and right up to Ikaria, his eyes meeting hers behind her barrier. "After all the cleansing that Queen Emerald did for you? You would think that you would have learned your lesson!"

"How dare you lecture me, priest! You yourself go on and on about the God of Light and obeying the High Court. And here you are, trying to break me out like a lowlife convict."

"That is different!" Auron fought back.

"Oh? I like to think otherwise," Ikaria said.

"Blood consumption is wrong!"

"It is right when you have no other options, priest," Ikaria spat, then turned to Suri. "Now, Suri, drink quickly. I promised my blood to you, did I not?"

"You did, Enchantress."

"Come claim your reward. Besides, someone else should have the power of the violet besides that arrogant ass inquisitor."

"Suri, don't do this," Auron begged. He couldn't believe it. After all that he had been through, Ikaria was at it again. But this time she was dragging her servant into it.

"I'm sorry, High Priest, but the Enchantress is correct, as always." She turned away from him, then knelt before Ikaria. The sorceress offered her wrist, awaiting Suri.

Suri's lips met the sorceress's barrier, then her lips passed the barrier. Suri began to lick the blood off her wrist gently, as if Ikaria was a delicacy. More and more, Suri tasted Ikaria's blood, becoming more passionate and wild. Ikaria laughed, a perverse, wicked laugh, as if she delighted in it.

"I can't believe this," Auron said, circling around the room impatiently.

What should he do? Stop her? Fight them?

A small flicker of thought came to him. If that woman did indeed take away Ikaria's magic, there was still a chance to counter that woman's spells. The violet blood in that vial given to Suri, it was true what Ikaria had said—it was a guarantee. She would need it if her magic was taken from her. He could see the sorceress's plan now. With Suri having violet magic and safeguarding Ikaria's blood, it gave them a small chance to help set things right in their sector, including rescuing the Empress.

Suri suddenly thrashed to the floor, writhing in pain. She bit her lip, trying not to scream.

Ikaria watched as Suri tossed and turned on the floor, making no noise, then turned to Auron. "Always the good servant."

"I can't believe this…"

"If it vexes your soul so greatly, why aren't you stopping us, priest?" Ikaria asked.

"Good question."

Ikaria hinted at a cool smile, as if she knew his thoughts. "It's survival of the fittest, priest, and I always survive."

Auron looked to Suri, still writhing in pain.

"How long will she be like this?" Auron said anxiously.

"A few minutes. Perhaps more," Ikaria said. "Don't worry. You shall soon be on your way out of here, leaving me to my own devices once again."

Auron looked at her. "You really think you have a chance against the High Inquisitor?"

Ikaria laughed. "Oh, yes. He is the best chance I have."

What is that supposed to mean?

They both watched as Suri rolled and struggled on the ground, her whole body pulsating with orange magic, almost like a heartbeat. When Auron could no longer take it, he turned to Ikaria.

"Sorceress Ikaria… did you notice how much the High Inquisitor looks like the Ghost Man?"

Ikaria didn't move, remaining still, looking at Suri in pain. "Isn't that interesting? How one could look so similar to another person across the chasm of time?"

"Do you think…"

Suri stopped her movements, breathing heavily.

"You'd best be on your way," Ikaria interrupted him, pointing to Suri. She laid a hand on Suri, then stroked her hair. "It is time, my dear Suri. Go get my sister. Keep my blood safe."

Suri breathed hard, then nodded. "I shall succeed, Enchantress," she said breathlessly, almost in a sexual manner, causing Auron to look away uncomfortably.

Auron heard Suri getting to her feet, then looked over. Her legs were shaking as she closed her eyes, starting to summon her orange magic.

For a moment, Auron's eyes met Ikaria's, and once again he felt the strange stirring in his heart. It was as if his soul didn't want to leave her. Strangely, Ikaria's eyes seemed to tell him the same thing.

Orange magic settled on him and Suri, bathing them in its power. He disappeared into thin air, and Suri once again became the High Inquisitor.

As they slipped through the door, Auron turned back to see the sorceress one last time.

Her violet eyes were locked on him, as if she could see his life force within his invisibility. Within her brilliant violet eyes, he could feel the depths of her emotions.

Auron knew then.

She had felt that strange connection too.

CHAPTER 34

The ground transports came to a halt, and everyone started to filter out of the beds of the vehicles.

Victor waited until it came to his turn, hopping down from the back.

"Everyone get inside the caves quickly," he ordered them.

The people complied, grabbing their own bags and supplies, walking along the path leading into their evacuation caves.

I hope Telly and Reila are with the King and Queen by now, he thought. He was anxiously awaiting for what the palace had to say about the matter. Would they send an army out to protect their part of the wastelands? Would they strike first or wait until Olympia made a hostile move? Victor assumed that the King or the members of the council would do something. He knew that at least the Queen was on their side and would urge the King and his council to do something. It was already decided in Victor's mind: If the King and Queen sent an army out in the wastelands as backup, Victor and his camp would do whatever they could to help. And if they did join, he could rally the other camps to help. Whether the camps liked the "big city" or not, they relied on Arcadia being at peace, for as long as it was, their camps would be left alone, for the most part.

Victor saw Garrett and a few men unloading the specialized weapons and guns, with several of them passing them off to other wasteland wanderers to carry to the refuge.

"Easy, easy," Garrett said to one of the men, handing them a weapon. He turned, noticing Victor. "Have you seen Drew?" he called out to him from the bed of the vehicle.

"I thought he was with you," Victor answered.

"No, the last I saw him was in the complex. I assumed he hopped in another vehicle with Gwen."

Victor sighed, already forming a scenario in his head. Gwen had gone with others before him up the path.

Drew just had to get a fool of an idea! he cursed to himself, then turned to the remaining stragglers. "Has anyone seen Drew?"

"I saw him back at camp," a woman said. The rest of them shrugged before heading up the path.

Dammit.

"I can go find Gwen and ask," Garrett offered, grabbing one of the weapons.

"Don't worry about it. I'll ask. Just finish unloading quickly and head up," Victor answered him.

"Sure thing."

Victor headed up the path, hiking up the switchbacks of the dusty path. With each bend in the path, it became more difficult. His legs began to ache and burn. Man, he was getting old. His body wasn't what it once was. This path used to be no problem. Now it was strenuous for him, painful after just a little walk. He was only fifty-five, and this path was nothing like the other paths in the surrounding mountains. And he was in decent shape for his age. But a little part of him knew he was in denial—his body couldn't take the physical activity like it once had. He *was* older now.

As Victor continued, old memories bombarded him. He had been on this same path many times before, but mostly during his childhood and teenage years. He passed by a familiar boulder, one of the more unique ones along the trail, and Victor had always spotted it every time he walked the path. It made him think of *that* time…

It had been when he was evacuated with his camp in his early twenties. Elyathi had been with him as their camp made their way into the refuge for several weeks.

Victor's thoughts darkened. His father had been hiding Elyathi from Prince Damaris… no, the newly crowned King Damaris of Arcadia at that time. No one knew the true reason why the camp was being evacuated, only

Victor and his father, who was the camp's leader at the time. It was said that King Damaris went mad, killing his own father for the throne, and was searching for the "perfect" bride. The King had caught word of Elyathi's beauty and became manic over finding her. But more importantly, it was said that the King was becoming more obsessed with *The Spectrum* day by day, and it was widely whispered that he was in search of magic.

Those in Victor's old camp, Victor and the elders, knew who Elyathi truly was. Or *what* she was. And for that, they *had* to keep her safe from King Damaris.

Victor recalled Elyathi's white eyes sparkling in the sunlight that day, almost like a pearl. So prismatic, as if the full spectrum was in the very depths of her eyes, radiating from her soul.

Why are we retreating to the refuge? Is our camp in danger? Elyathi's words reverberated in his mind as Victor stared at the boulder. Those were her words, spoken at this same place, but during a very different time.

I don't know exactly what the situation is, but my father suspects so, Victor recalled fibbing to her. *He is taking extra precautions just in case.*

Elyathi hadn't known what was happening at that time, how King Damaris was in hot pursuit for her as his bride. Word had traveled to the other kingdoms about Elyathi's beauty, and many princes and rich lords went searching for her. But King Damaris was determined to find Elyathi first and have her as his own. He was doing everything in his power to have her. Victor's father made a promise to the blue-gifted man who had appeared with Elyathi. He promised that the camp would take care of her, protect her from any danger. And all these fanatical suitors… the camp was always trying to protect her from them too. And Elyathi? She never knew what was truly happening at the time. She was innocent as a dove, always dreaming of being swept away by true love. At that time, she never would have understood the true scope of the situation—how dangerous it was if one of those kings, princes, or lords found out who she really was. And especially the King of Arcadia…

Victor looked at the boulder once again, pausing.

Elyathi had been so close to him as they walked by that boulder, closer than ever before. She had always lingered around him during his teenage years; they had been close friends. But that time, by *that* boulder, she was much closer than before, and Victor had suspected at that moment she liked him. He had always liked her, that was certain. But did that make him as bad as the men pursuing her?

He never did sort it out. A damned fool, he was. For everything. *Would've. Could've. Should've.*

Victor frowned, trying to forget the endless list of regrets he had in his lifetime. There were too many.

He came to the entrance to the caves, dodging the rock outcroppings and squeezing his way through the narrow entrance. Inside, lights had already been placed throughout, with many of the wasteland wanderers setting up additional equipment. Men with guns were at the entrance, with the campers filing their way into the next cavern's corridors, which led to different rooms.

"Victor, there you are. I've been looking for you," Ryan said to him as Victor passed through the first chamber.

"What is it? One of the campers need more supplies?" Victor asked, inspecting the setup as he passed by.

"No, it's not that," Ryan began. "We aren't the only ones in the cave."

Victor looked directly at him. "What?"

"Yeah, one of the northern outposts was destroyed. Get this. That dispatch unit thought their cyborg was in that northern outpost. So the dispatch unit shows up, and the wastelanders told them that the cyborg trailed through their camp, nothing more. Well, the dispatch unit didn't like that, so they started tearing apart the camp. And when that wasn't good enough, they started killing the campers. Several of them escaped and hid, then made their way here."

Victor frowned. It was the first of more to come. Turning to Ryan, he said, "Get them something to eat and drink. Something hard."

"Aye-aye," Ryan said, walking off into the next chamber.

Victor sighed, closing his eyes for a moment. Perhaps if he opened them, all the world's problems would be fixed, and he could live out his days in peace like he had hoped.

Somehow, he didn't think it was going to be that easy.

CHAPTER 35

Orange

The camp was empty, almost as if life from within had exhaled its last breath.

Dead. All seemed dead.

Drew paused, examining his thoughts. How could an encampment be dead?

Malfunction.

Seeing the camp in its current form… it was… sad.

Malfunction.

He shook his head. This was his home now. He had to protect it, because that was where happiness was—being with Telly and Gwen, here, within the camp. And he was not going to let anyone destroy his home, nor the new happy memories that were attached to this place.

Wandering through the camp, he made it to his and Telly's makeshift lab, climbing the three metal stairs. Pushing open the door, Drew saw the contents inside strewn across the floor. Garrett did not possess the human ability of organization and order. Drew often wondered how a man like Garrett could break complex, elegant coding when it came to the mind of a computer, but outside, he was what Telly would call a "slob."

Drew shook his head again at this thought.

Shifting through the trailer, Drew gathered a few supplies that he deemed important and put them in a small knapsack. Water, rations, a few electronic gadgets, small tools, and one of the newest weapons he and Garrett had been working on—a modified handgun with magical capabilities at the frequency of 488.

Garrett must have forgotten about this, Drew thought.

Drew picked up the weapon, gripping it. The weapon was easy for him to shoot with his good left hand in case the circuitry shorted out in his body. If he somehow encountered the dispatch unit that had magical power, Drew figured that he would need a backup plan if his body was hindered.

After he was satisfied with his supplies, he exited the lab. Drew looked around at the camp one last time as he descended the trailer's metal stairs, calculating his next move. Eyeing the giant boulders around the camp, Drew then looked down to the rocky soil mixed with sand under his feet. His circuits vibrated with approval for what he was about to do.

Drew headed to the outskirts of the camp, putting a good amount of distance between him and the camp. He stopped, bent over to his knees, and laid the palm of his hand against the wasteland's terrain.

They were coming.

Olympia was coming.

He paused, thinking for a moment. Why did he care if Olympia was coming? Why did he feel solely responsible for protecting Scion and saving Arcadia?

His thoughts turned to Queen Emerald. Admiration stirred in his heart just thinking of the Queen. She had been so kind to him when he was with her in the palace. Since his resurrection, she was the only other person who had ever treated him like a human besides Telly and Gwen, making him feel like an elevated being. Even more than that, Emerald went out of her way to try to heal him and restore his voice. She didn't have to do that, especially after he had tracked her down, chasing her through the entire city of Arcadia. But she did so anyway because she was so…

Kind.

Malfunction.

Drew shook, his hand rattling in the sand.

It was his time to help her once again. Emerald would need him. Drew felt indebted to her, so he would help in any way he could.

Closing his eyes, Drew began to draw upon his power, which resided deep down, past his circuitry, in his soul. Instead of channeling the joy he felt for Telly and his daughter, Drew channeled a different feeling. Thoughts of being tied to the corporation, thoughts of being used by the violet witch who once held the gauntlet, thoughts of King Derek taking advantage of the Queen when she was compromised…

Drew made a guttural sound, roaring deep within his throat. Fury filled his veins like burning fire, then poured into his outstretched hand like furious lava that gave no leeway.

Opening his eyes, Drew saw orange-red magic glowing brighter and hotter, then it poured out from his hand, spreading onto the sands of the wastelands. He funneled more power, and it shifted across the desert until the entire campground glowed bright orange-red.

Grunting, Drew kept funneling the power. The energy drained him of his life force, but he couldn't stop. The power kept colliding between him and the ground, flowing back and forth, demanding to be released. He held on, sending mental orders through its energy.

Suddenly, it was as if there was a giant orange-red wind in the center of the camp, blowing at the ground wildly to the perimeter of the glowing campground. Sand, dirt, and rock wildly tore through the camp, forming at the outskirts. It gathered together in a massive formation covered in the magical dust, wind, and rock, growing in size until the entire camp was a full-sized desert mountain.

Satisfied, Drew shifted his feelings to his own true magic, and it filled him with a joy that he loved experiencing. He thought of home. With Telly. With Gwen.

With a sharp jerk of his hand, Drew clenched his palm shut.

Instantly, the mass was covered with bright-orange magic, flashing brightly, blinding him.

As the light faded, Drew gazed upon his new creation: a newly formed mountain transmuted with the help of his orange magic. It was hollow inside, as that was how he'd made it, keeping the camp's housing and equipment intact. It was thick enough that the Olympian cyborgs would have a hard time detecting it. If anything, they would be confused by the new rocky mass.

Drew smiled at his work, then wiped his brow with his good hand. He yanked the canteen from his hip and took a small sip, trying to conserve the water.

Good. It is good, he confirmed to himself.

There was fast movement in the distance that flashed within his cybernetic eye. Scanning his surroundings, Drew caught the direction of the movement. He focused in on it, then zoomed in.

His heart pounded as his circuits shook.

There were ground vehicles heading in the direction of where he was standing. Eight vehicles.

It had to be the team looking for Scion.

At least Scion is safe for now, he thought.

The mass of vehicles came closer as Drew shifted himself against one of the rock outcroppings of the new mountain. He had to warn the other camps in the path to Arcadia. Olympia was coming.

Drew summoned his magic, bathing himself in its power. The magic embraced him, making him disappear into the landscape of the rocks as he shifted back. Though his illusions would fool the humans, they wouldn't fool any cyborg, especially ones with heat detection.

Drew heard the transports roll to a stop, then the sound of men and metal footsteps. There were murmurs and shouts, then sounds of guns being drawn.

"What is going on?"

More footsteps. Drew remained frozen against the rock.

"Commander, there was a strange reading on my device. I could have sworn it detected one of our cyborg units, but it doesn't make any damn sense!" said a man's voice. "This mountain was not on any of our topographical maps. There was supposed to be an encampment right *here*," his voice said in disbelief.

"I want every one of you to lick this place clean and dry and find me something! Even if it's a piece of shit, I want to know about it!" ordered a strong, deep male voice.

"Yes, Commander," the men said.

The men started to spread out around the rocks.

Carefully keeping out of their line of sight in case of heat detection, Drew moved quickly and systematically around the giant rocky mass. Out of the corner of his eye, he saw some of the men scan the desert sands, finding trash and other small metal objects from the camp's outskirts. There were cyborg units with them. Olympian cyborgs.

They wouldn't be fooled long.

As Drew shifted around the next set of rock outcroppings, he heard a strange sound.

"Detection. Cyborg detection," shrieked one of the Olympian cyborgs in a mechanical voice. "To the east. Coordinates 24.36."

Drew's circuits stirred within him.

"Did you find our fucking robot?" the commander demanded.

"No. Arcadian make and model," chanted the cyborg.

Drew heard other sounds of cyborgs.

"Well, what are you all standing around staring at me for? Get me that cyborg!" the commander shouted. "It probably knows where that piece of shit Scion is hiding!"

Move! Drew told himself.

With a burst of energy, Drew ran from his hiding spot into the openness of the wasteland, creating an orange-red mass of energy under him. His illusion wore off as he became enveloped in his own magic.

"He has magic!" shouted a soldier.

"I *said*, GET ME THAT FUCKING CYBORG!" shouted the commander.

There was a mass sounds of confusion, weapons, yelling. Drew couldn't make out what else was said because he was already airborne, flying high in the atmosphere above the camp.

The sound of weapons firing rang out. Summoning his orange-yellow magic, a hardened shield poured quickly over his body, enveloping him in its power.

The bullets struck his weak shield, breaking the magic flow instantly. The broken orange-yellow shards littered the ground below but stopped the bullets, keeping him safe for the moment.

Pulling the orange magic within his life force, Drew went invisible and headed north, flying as fast as the winds could carry him. There were camps out in that direction that needed to be warned of the potential ground army marching upon Arcadia. That is, if they hadn't yet experienced this small reconnaissance group trying to recover Scion. Besides, he couldn't go directly to where his own camp was hiding out anyway, not with the Olympians aware of his presence. He would be putting their lives at risk.

Below, Drew saw the vehicles branch off in different directions—two moved east, two to the south, two to the west, and two north. Two of the vehicles that were traveling east were heading down the road leading to the caves his camp was at. The chance of the Olympian military dispatch unit finding their hideout was under 2% probability; that particular road split into many different directions, making it unlikely anyone would pick the same sequence of turns.

But something in his heart didn't feel right.

Drew continued to fly until the vehicles became small specks on the horizon; they had been fooled by his magic, and he was too far out of reach for the cyborgs' detection.

He was safe for now.

Landing on a nearby rock outcropping, Drew planted his feet, then grabbed his handheld satellite transmission device.

Turning it on, Drew dialed into the frequency that the camp would be on, hoping to get a signal.

Static.

Frustrated, he put the radio away in his knapsack and studied the vast open wastelands before him. He took a drink of water from his canteen, then scanned the wasteland in a 360-degree view, taking all details in with his cybernetic eye.

To the north, he saw it. And it was vast.

The Olympian army.

Drew shook. Thousands of ground vehicles created one large horde, moving in an almost inhuman fashion. There were men, machines, cyborgs… all traveling in the same direction.

Toward Arcadia.

Something caught Drew's attention immediately. In the midst of the horde was a contraption jutting out from a massive vehicle. Some kind of communications tower, but altered…

Was a human on top of the tower? Drew scanned the tower more thoroughly, zooming in as far as he could with his cybernetic eye.

No, not a human… a child. Boy. Eight years in age. What was a boy doing on top of a communications tower?

Malfunction.

Drew jolted.

He continued to study the boy on top of the tower. He could see goggles attached to the child's face—a VR headset of some kind, with wires and cables coming from the headset. The boy was still in his chair. Maybe he was asleep?

Drew shuddered, confused at the logic of it.

That tower has to be the cause of the disabled communications.

But why the boy?

Drew quickly summoned his magic once again, rendering him invisible. He took off, heading toward the same direction that the Olympian army was heading. He had to warn the camps that were directly in the army's way, then go protect the Queen.

They were coming.

Olympia was coming.

CHAPTER 36

YELLOW

Colors of the spectrum swept over the land. The ground shifted and quaked, then violently split apart, the other pieces of earth falling as the ground under him rose, causing Tyllos to tumble to his knees. He clutched the edge of his piece of earth, watching as the new world took form.

All the colors met one another in harmony. Forming, shifting, molding. Across the expansive chasm of dreams, time, and dimensions, they all came together as one.

New kingdoms formed, six in total, each one basking in a pure color.

Far in the distance, Tyllos saw a brilliant light. A pure, bright light. He could not pinpoint the source, but he felt each color of magic within the light. Together, they created white magic, and its power flooded the earth.

Within the white light, Tyllos saw the creator of the new world.

There were shadows behind this creator, and Tyllos couldn't see any details within the shadows. But these shadows burned with magic, each one a different color of the spectrum, their power flowing into the creator.

Tyllos smiled as the world took shape, watched as it turned into a new beautiful brilliance. Mountains rose up from the seas while new life and new technology teemed across the virgin lands. Kingdoms rose up into power, a multitude of people singing praises of their new life and new world. Tyllos saw no presence of magic; only the leaders of the new kingdoms held that power. And the praises. Oh, how the people glorified the new kingdoms!

As Tyllos gazed onward, the creator of the new world's light burnt out.

Lead me to you, a voice whispered in his mind.

Tyllos looked to the heavens still rumbling, the clouds forming new shapes at super-human speed. In the sky, he saw the remnants of the floating citadels, all of them melting away like candle wax, dripping onto the new earth below.

I am here, the voice called out.

A vision filled Tyllos's mind—a clear picture of World Sector Five. Tyllos had seen this place before. It was an outpost of the royal citadel, a prominent one that housed many of the gifted in that sector.

"We will come for you," Tyllos called out, smiling to himself.

His heart delighted at all that he saw, and he began to laugh and laugh and laugh. The echoes of his laughter ripped through the earth, echoing for all to hear.

"What is so amusing?"

The burning bright yellow from Tyllos's eyes faded, and he shook his head.

"Did you not hear me? I asked what is so amusing."

Tyllos suddenly became aware that he was in the midst of a vision. He blinked a few times and saw the details of his chambers around him—the plush velvety chairs, golden tables, gold and silver ornaments, walls of crystal, and countless golden bookshelves and glass cases housing extremely rare books, tomes, and scrolls.

"You are lucky that I saw your power radiating from under your door," Belinda's voice called out. "If you had blinded me, I would not have been happy." Belinda's footsteps scuffled across his quarters, and she seated herself across from him in one of his velvet chairs. Tyllos's manservant came in and filled two chalices for them to drink, then left.

Tyllos gazed at Belinda as she took a sip from her chalice. She grimaced. "I forgot that you prefer sweet wine."

He chuckled. "And you prefer the bitter ones."

They exchanged smiles as he took a drink.

"What did you see?" Belinda continued, sitting up perfectly straight in her chair. "It must have been quite something for you to laugh like that. I haven't heard you laugh like in many, many years, and we've known each other how long?"

"Too long to recall?"

She swirled the wine in her chalice. "I seem to have lost the concept of years as well. I blink, and each time I age, it seems I am a new person."

"Luckily, your body and beauty remains just as the day we first met."

"Perserine is a true blessing. None can match her skill when it comes to the art of body sculpting," Belinda agreed, taking a sip of her wine. "So, do tell of what you saw."

"You will be delighted to know that we will succeed with our plans," Tyllos said.

A smirk curled at the corner of her mouth. "Good. And what of our other plans? The yellow-gifted and blue-gifted? Did you send the prophetic dream as we discussed?"

"It was already sent into the stream of visions. I sense that it has been received."

"When you see Borgen, ask him to scry that time. I want to ensure that the men have already established themselves back in time."

"I will have him confirm," Tyllos said, eyeing her. "What of the cyborgs? Have Nyrden's disciples made any progress getting them revived?"

Belinda's face darkened. "Unfortunately, no. The High Inquisitor had best pull through. Otherwise, there will be serious repercussions."

"Absolutely," Tyllos agreed, taking another sip of his wine. The taste was refreshing; he couldn't understand how Belinda didn't agree. "This morning, Borgen informed me that Lady Elyathi has wiped World Sector Six's gifted clean." He paused. "That is, except for High Priest Auron. He seems to have gone missing."

"Auron has become quite the pain."

"Indeed, he has," Tyllos said. Auron always had to be so righteous and just, and Tyllos hated him for it. Everything had to be by the book. The man had no imagination.

"After Auron is found and Ikaria's power gone, Elyathi will go to the next sector."

"It's nice that she has finally learned how to use her abilities to their fullest extent."

"It is rather quite nice," Belinda said. "The more she uses her gift, the stronger she becomes. Perhaps when she reaches the next sector, it will take no time at all. That is what I am hoping for, anyway."

"I think we can plan for that," Tyllos said, taking a drink. "Also, about the current vision. There is someone we need to retrieve in World Sector Five."

"Someone?"

"They are the key; we will need this person to achieve our ultimate design."

"Who is it?"

"The vision didn't show me. I couldn't even say if they are a man or a woman." Tyllos took another drink, then turned to look out his tower window at the courtyard gardens below. "This person… they are somehow tied to Elyathi's power."

"Should we send Borgen to retrieve this person and bring them here?"

Tyllos paused, thinking about his vision. "I am not sure how this mysterious gifted person would take to Borgen. I suggest we send Elyathi."

Belinda scoffed. "I am sure she is squabbling with the High Inquisitor this very moment. It's disappointing, really. I didn't have high hopes for the High Inquisitor, but I did think he would have made at least some progress by now." Belinda paused, then her eyes lit up in thought. "Perhaps this mysterious person could be the one to overpower the sorceress instead of the High Inquisitor." Belinda's fiery eyes met his. "If your vision is indeed correct, and this person is the key to our plans, then Elyathi must meet them right away. The sooner the better, for us all."

Tyllos nodded. "I'll have Borgen send word to Elyathi immediately, and she can go meet this mysterious person."

"It is settled, then," Belinda said, nodding to him. She smiled, then took another drink of her wine, making a puckered again face. "Really, Tyllos, I don't know how you can stand to drink this." She stood up, then smoothed her long locks of crimson curls into place and walked away.

She paused for a moment, glancing over her shoulder. "Soon, my friend. It is almost within our grasp." Her face hinted at a smile.

"Indeed," Tyllos answered, smiling back. "It can't come soon enough."

Belinda departed his chambers, leaving Tyllos alone in his chair. He sat far back, nestling himself in the velvet, then glanced back out of his window, gazing across the courtyard and into the cloudscape.

Soon, all would be changed.

He would finally be the god of his own yellow world.

And that thought delighted him.

CHAPTER 37

RED

He was flying forward. So fast, faster than any magical wind that had ever carried him before.

Rubius glanced down. He sat on a small, stiff seat. His hands were spread apart, gripping metal bars attached to a machine. Two wheels, one in front and one behind, were attached to the machine. The wheels spun fast, and the machine's engine roared loudly.

What was happening?

The grounded machine drove wildly forward and wind ripped through his cape and hair. Rubius was on a crowded street in an ancient city. Massive buildings rose as high as the sky itself, glittering with vivid colors in the night. The tops of the structures disappeared into the darkness, hidden from the naked eye. The buildings weren't enchanted with magic—the lights came from an array of machines and technology, dotting the grand city. It was nothing like he had ever seen.

Exhilaration, excitement, and a hard thrill pumped through his veins, filling him with a kind of energy that he had never known.

Are these the machines of old?

The machine continued to plow forward, and Rubius neared a crowd of people on the side of the street. Instinct kicked in, as if he knew how the machine worked. He veered away from the crowd quickly, then rode into a lane marked on the street with glowing lights. Putrid smells of old food, urine, feces, and other foul stenches entered his nostrils, mixed in with the smells coming from small restaurant carts that lined the street and alleyways.

Suddenly, Rubius heard more sets of roaring mechanisms. Two other machine drivers closed in and pulled up on each side of him, and several behind him. Their machines looked much more powerful than his.

The gang of the riders came closer to him, giving him hardly any room to drive except forward. The closer they got, the more powerful the vibrations of their machines were.

"Look who it is!" yelled a man with facial tattoos off to his right. "It's that baby-back bitch!" He laughed loudly, closing in on Rubius.

The gang burst out in laughter with the man.

"How about a race, little bitch?" the man taunted him.

"I don't know how to work this!" Rubius yelled, feeling overwhelmed.

"Did you hear that? The vagina doesn't know how to work his bike!"

They all roared with laughter again, stirring up rage in Rubius's soul. He didn't even know these people, but they infuriated him.

"What is your problem?" Rubius yelled at them.

"Are you deaf, pretty boy? I said fucking race me with your shitty bike, you pansy-ass pussy!"

A knife glinted, then the man threw it at Rubius.

Rubius made a sudden movement on his bike, swaying his shoulder. The knife just missed him.

"I can't wait to give her a good hard fuck!" The man roared with laughter. "I bet she's wet right now, waiting for me!"

"Who?" Rubius yelled out in confusion.

The tattooed man ignored Rubius and neared him, the other man on the other side of him doing the same.

Suddenly, he kicked Rubius hard. Upon impact, the "bike" swerved to his left, almost plowing into the other rider. The rider on the left took out his own knife, then violently swung it at Rubius's chest.

Rubius punched him hard before the knife made contact, causing the man to lose control of his machine. The man veered off, and seconds later Rubius heard a crash.

"Ryker!" called out the tattooed man.

Another rider pulled up next to Rubius in the place of the absent one. The tattooed man was still on his right.

What am I going to do? Rubius thought wildly. *If I was not on this machine, I would beat that man to a bloody pulp!* But he was on the machine, and for some reason, he felt glued to it, and his magic felt absent somehow, far away from this ancient world.

All he could do was go forward. Nowhere else. How he wished that the road had shifted.

As soon as he had that thought, the world began to contort and morph right before his eyes. The roads began to form different paths while the old ones crumbled behind him, twisting and tangling with each other like a giant complex puzzle that could never be solved. But he drove on, his road remaining constant.

As the paths shifted, the main road split, and the tattooed man veered off to the one on the right. It led him upward, while the man Ryker took a completely different road to his left, twisting into a maze of buildings.

"I'm gonna fuck you up!" roared the tattooed man.

In the distance, between two towering buildings, a twinkling star fell from the sky. The star was most unusual; it was green in color, so vivid and so intense that it radiated life from its light.

Deep in his heart, Rubius felt a stirring within his life force. That green star… he knew in its green brilliance was the green-gifted woman he had been searching for.

And she needed help now. Otherwise, her fate would end terribly.

Hold on!

Rubius quickly twisted the right-hand grip, somehow knowing that doing so would make the contraption go faster.

The bike rumbled, and the road disintegrated into dust as his back wheel left it. The maze of buildings and roads shifted again, this time entwining with each other with complexity. It was like one big ball of roads and buildings, all in chaos, and he had no way of knowing how to get to the falling gifted woman.

"Help me!" her voice echoed across the sky.

"Dammit!" Rubius cried out. "I'm coming!"

Trusting his instincts, Rubius took the next road that led off to the left. It took him upward onto a ramp that twisted inside a hollow building and then out again. He was high above the ground, and the road kept sloping upward.

A giant machine-like vehicle blocked the road, much too large to pass. Frantically, Rubius spun off to the right, weaving through another hollow building and out again. As he continued, another machine fell from the sky, and this time it exploded in front of him.

Squeezing the bars' levers and pushing down with his toes, Rubius caused his machine to stop suddenly. He was about to backtrack before realizing that the road behind him was crumbing to dust.

What am I going to do? Rubius thought in a panic.

Looking up, he still saw the woman falling in the nighttime sky, enveloped in her green magical light, almost as if she were in slow motion. The world began to rip apart wildly and form a new maze.

Rubius's heart hammered in his chest. His body ached and was drenched in sweat. Nothing mattered except her. He had to save her.

Twisting the machine's handle at full force, Rubius began driving across the building's rooftop. There were no roads now to take. He was stuck on that rooftop.

There were buildings around him, and one in particular was closer than all the others. It was a stretch, but he could make it, or at least die trying.

Turning his bike, Rubius furiously rode toward the opposite building at full force. He braced himself just before driving off the edge. Then he was airborne with the machine, riding the winds wildly to the other edge of the building.

Midair, Rubius had to face a hard reality—he wasn't going to make it to the other side. He was going to come up short.

He yelled out in a frustrated snarl, then gritted his teeth and closed his eyes. Rubius waited for death to embrace him.

He waited.

And waited.

Death did not come. Instead, his whole body jerked on the machine.

Rubius suddenly opened his eyes and saw that his bike had landed on a long glassy bridge, with people walking inside. His bike was still moving, and he was in one piece.

Realizing he still had control, Rubius instantly took charge of the bike, riding off the glass bridge. He fell just a few feet and landed on another road, this one clear of obstacles.

Focused, Rubius maneuvered his machine through the endless maze, letting his heart guide him to the falling gifted woman. The roads became clear, and the path more apparent.

Rubius came upon a clearing. The falling green light was closer to him than before. He was finally getting close to the woman, but not as close as he wanted to.

"Hurry up, you damn thing!" Rubius cursed.

Making the bike go as fast as he could, Rubius rode furiously, weaving through the paths. Up ahead was an oversized cement wall, which ended the road. Rubius looked around, and there were no other roads around. It was just him and the twisted road he rode on, and the gifted-woman falling to her death. And he was going to slam into the wall if he didn't do something fast.

Was this it? Was this how everything was supposed to happen? There were no other roads, no exit, and it was like he was attached to this machine, and Rubius had no way off it.

As his bike moved furiously toward the wall, Rubius saw a burning violet flash to the side of him. A woman with a strange purple hairstyle with a staff in her hand appeared, flying at the same speed as him.

"Use your magic, you idiot!" she called out to him.

"Don't you think I would if I could?" Rubius yelled back at her. "I can't feel my magic!"

"You are in control of this dream!"

"It sure as hell doesn't seem like it!" he argued. "I'm stuck on this thing, and in about a minute I will be dead, and so will that woman!"

"Focus on your life force!" the purple-haired woman yelled back.

"Focus on my life force?"

"Don't make me repeat myself!"

His heart beat wildly, and his energy was spent. He wasn't even sure if he could muster up any magic at this point.

Focus on my life force...

The wall was coming closer to him by the second.

Rubius breathed. He still felt the green-gifted woman's life force near him, shining deep within his own soul. There was love and life within it, reaching to the depths of his being.

Help me... her soul called out to him.

Then his magic ripped through him like a flood.

Narrowing his eyes, Rubius focused all his magic and might, calling forth the power of his red winds and combining them with his violet force. With a hard jolt in his mind, Rubius released his power over his bike.

As fast as lightning, the machine jerked up high in the sky and over the wall. With another swift movement, it flew back down on the other side of the wall. As the tires of the machine touched the ground, it peeled away against the smooth road.

Rubius heard the woman's screams as she continued to fall aimlessly, and saw the shadows of her long wavy hair flying wildly around her. Suddenly she was falling faster than before.

"No!"

Leaping off the bike toward her, Rubius called forth his powerful elements, letting the thrashing winds funnel around him like a vortex. As his body soared toward her, he saw all her delicate features. Pale skin with piercing, glowing green eyes, wild with fear. Her emerald-green hair was entangled around her, while her simple lavender gown flapped wildly, her body mostly exposed from the fall.

His heart quickened at the sight of her. At that moment, it was as if time slowed or even stopped. She looked at him desperately, reaching out to him. He did the same, reaching out, wanting to save her from her impending doom.

As their hands were about to make contact, her soft pink heart-shaped lips whispered, "Come back to me, Kyle." Her eyes sparkled with tears. "Come back to me!"

Rubius desperately tried to grab her hand, but the more he reached for her, the farther apart they became.

"I'm trying!" Rubius called out to her. "Believe me, I am fucking trying!"

With that, his power died out, and his life force gave way. He was falling, endlessly falling.

As he plunged into the darkness, Rubius saw the beautiful woman burn with her green magic, then she flew away like a shooting star. Her burning green light flared into the nighttime sky, far, far away from him.

She was so far. Far, far away.

He couldn't save her. No one could.

Instead, he fell to his doom.

***

Rubius shot up from bed.

His heart hammered in his chest, the pounding sound filling his ears. His eyes stared at the wall of his temporary guest quarters, but he didn't see it. In fact, he didn't see anything around him. Instead, he saw his dream as he replayed the details in his mind.

The green-gifted woman… she was falling, calling out to him. But it wasn't his name. She called him by another name. Kyle.

What does it all mean? These dreams had to mean something significant, given the fact they kept coming to him.

Rubius made a sudden gesture, startling Zaphod. His bird cawed in response.

"Sorry about that," Rubius muttering to his parrot. He stumbled out of bed, still slightly disoriented from the dream, running his hands across the desk for his flask. After finding it, he took a long swig, then wiped his mouth hastily.

Who is this Kyle? Why did she call me by that name?

On the desk where the flask was, Rubius noticed the old book Lady Xui found for him, the one mentioning the green-gifted queen. Running his hands over the book, he opened it, flipping to the page where it mentioned the Queen of Arcadia, rereading the small passage about her.

Is it you who haunts me, Queen of Arcadia?

His hand lingered on the page, his eyes focusing on the word *queen.* Thinking of the woman… his heart ached with a deep longing for her, as if he was bound to her in some way, and she to him. But why? And how?

Why is there green magic within you? Does it have to do with the woman you seek? That was the very last thing that strange green-gifted time traveler had said to him before he disappeared. Even though those words were from years ago, they still haunted Rubius. Somehow, what the man asked him had convinced Rubius that his dreams of the green-gifted woman were tied to his destiny.

That is, if he truly believed in destiny.

Rubius looked down at the book again, rereading the passage about the Queen of Arcadia.

What are you trying to tell me?

Taking another drink, Rubius plopped down on the chair, then situated himself by the desk, which was already in disarray. He shifted through the messy stacks of papers, reaching for a quill and parchment, and began to write.

He felt confused, and… what else was it? Frustrated. Frustrated that he longed for some woman who was nothing more than a figment of his imagination. Or if she was real and somehow tied to his destiny, she did not even exist in his present time. How was he supposed to go about his life when this kept happening to him? How was he supposed to enjoy a woman fully when in the back of his mind, all he wanted was this fantasy woman?

And that sorceress. She had changed him somehow… opened a part of his mind when they had exchanged magical blows. Oh, he'd had dreams of this green-gifted woman countless times before visiting the sorceress. But this dream… it had been so *real* and so *vivid*. Never had his dreams been this clear. It was as if a fog had been lifted from his mind, and everything he had been dreaming about was undeniable. His desire for this green-gifted woman hit him harder than ever before, and the thought of her fully consumed him.

And there was absolutely nothing he could do about it. It was terribly frustrating.

Damn that sorceress!

Rubius finished up scribbling his note, signed it, then sealed it with his mark. He set down the note, then placed several other books on top of Lady Xui's book so the servants who walked through his temporary chambers wouldn't see it.

Rubius walked over to Zaphod, then fed him a few crackers, stroking the bird's feathers.

"You behave while I'm out," he told the bird.

Zaphod cawed in response, and Rubius laughed.

"Don't you give me any lip! That crazy zealot already gives me plenty."

Rubius quickly changed into a new set of clothes, stuffed the letter in his pocket, and took one last drink. He turned to the door and exited his chambers.

Outside, guards standing watch saluted him.

"High Inquisitor," they greeted him.

"Gentlemen," he replied. He headed down the hall, making his way through the citadel, back to the sorceress.

Suddenly, he felt a shift in the wind around him, and a presence approached.

"Have you been drinking wine?" asked a woman.

"If you must know, it's brandy," Rubius snapped, knowing who stood next to him.

"It is much too early for that."

"And it's much too early for me to hear any sort of judgment," Rubius huffed. "What do you want anyway?"

"I have been summoned to go away for a short time," said Elyathi. She was invisible, and it seemed that she wanted to keep it that way.

"Good. Perhaps I'll make some solid progress with you gone," Rubius said.

"I will be back, High Inquisitor. It is something that won't take up too much of my time."

I wish it would, he thought to himself. "When will I see you again?" Rubius asked, still pacing down the hall, his cape flowing behind him.

"Perhaps a few days? I cannot imagine any more than that."

"I guess I will see you when I see you."

"Yes, you will. Goodbye, High Inquisitor. May the God of Light favor you while I'm away," she said.

He would have responded to her statement, but what was the point? Elyathi would just make some ridiculous argument, and he didn't want to deal with it.

"Goodbye, Lady Elyathi," he said in a low voice.

Rubius continued to walk, until he felt Elyathi's presence no more. She was gone.

As Rubius continued to walk toward the dungeons, he passed by several courtesans and other staff in the halls. He recognized one of World Six's couriers. Feeling secure that Elyathi was truly gone, he stopped her.

"You there," Rubius called out to the courier.

"Yes, High Inquisitor?" The woman bowed in greeting, coming up to him.

"I need you to deliver a letter," he said, pulling out the sealed envelope. "To Lady Aurora in World Sector Three's court."

"Yes, High Inquisitor," the courier said, accepting the letter.

"For her eyes *only*," Rubius added firmly.

"Absolutely, High Inquisitor."

Rubius gave her several coins from his purse, and she bowed, hastily heading down the hallway in the opposite direction.

He continued through the citadel, his thoughts still on the green-gifted in his dreams. He needed *her*. His body. His mind. His life force. Everything within him craved her. And if he couldn't have her, he needed something to replace what he couldn't have. Something to pacify him. What else was he to do?

Rubius came to the spiraled staircase that led to the bowels of the lower citadel, where the sorceress was housed. He paid no mind to all that was around him, or those who wanted his attention. His thoughts were entangled from his disturbing dream.

Kyle. That name kept echoing in his mind, over and over again.

Rubius gritted his teeth. He wanted to hit something in anger, but he managed to keep his patience. He couldn't be looking like a fool when he was about to see the sorceress for the second time. He needed to focus.

Rubius reached the sorceress's cell and took a deep breath, trying to forget his thoughts. The guards unlocked the door, letting him inside.

As soon as he stepped inside, Rubius eyes met the sorceress's. She lay lazily on her bed, her legs straight up against the wall, her breasts nearly spilling out of her top. She was clearly unaffected by his presence. Or if she was, she was acting indifferently. Her wrists and ankles were still bound, hair slightly matted, and she looked a little more shabby from their recent spar.

"Hello again, High Inquisitor. I'm so glad you came. I was starting to get bored without any company." She gave him a half-crooked smile through her prismatic barrier. "Though, I must say, you don't look well at all. Those dark circles under your eyes don't suit you."

Rubius stormed right to her, standing outside her barrier, snarling, "What did you *do* to me?"

"Whatever do you mean?" she asked innocently, her hands pressing against her chest mockingly, the chains jingling.

"You know what you did!" he roared. Rubius suddenly took a step back, feeling dizzy.

"Oh my. You really aren't yourself today. Perhaps you should consider pushing back this scheduled visit until you are feeling up to it." The sorceress shrugged. "That is, if you ever feel like yourself again."

His eyes darted to hers, looking intently. "So you *did* do something to me." Rubius narrowed his eyes. "I ought to just forgo finding out the information and just do what I ultimately came here to do," he snarled.

"Well, I must say that I am in the mood for a little excitement, High Inquisitor. As you can see, I don't get much action these days, so I welcome it."

"Unfortunately for you, my help is not here, so taking your power is not an option. *Today*," he emphasized.

Kyle... Her voice rang in his head.

Rubius hovered right next to her barrier, weighing the option of using his magic or not, especially concerning the violet power. Normally, he would have cleared anyone's head by now, but this was completely different, especially knowing that the sorceress had a way to jump into his mind.

Kyle...

Rubius paused, looking straight into Ikaria's violet eyes.

"Is it true that you came in contact with a green-gifted woman?" he asked.

Curiously, the sorceress raised an eyebrow, almost in delight. Then she laughed, rolling over on the bed flat, her breasts still somehow managing to keep themselves inside her corset. "Did Belinda tell you to ask me nicely? Or did you have a sweet dream of a girl and are trying to chase some tail?"

God. Between this woman and the Lady Elyathi, he was seriously going to lose it.

"*I* want to know. Belinda doesn't even know I know about her," Rubius said.

The sorceress eyed him again, almost frozen, as if calculating her thoughts. "What have I to gain if I were to give you information? What is in it for me?"

"You are a prisoner."

"Oh, come now. That doesn't mean a thing. After all, you are the one practically begging me for information."

"Saving your sister doesn't appeal to you?" Rubius shot back.

"No. It doesn't. I say let that bitch rot in the pits of the High Court prisons."

"We can go all day at this, but honestly, I am an impatient man. And for you, sorceress, my patience is at an end," Rubius snarled. "If you don't want to tell me about the green-gifted woman, fine. But the cyborg technology? Now is the time to talk."

"Come get the information from me. I *dare* you."

Rubius's dream flashed in his mind again, and he winced. The sorceress… she'd done something to him again.

Kyle… come back to me.

Or was it the green-gifted woman? Had she changed him?

It made him angry. Really *angry*.

"What's the matter, High Inquisitor? Is something bothering you?" the sorceress mocked behind her magical barrier.

"Enough! Whatever you did, I will *wreck* you like you did to me!"

With that, Rubius summoned forth the power within his soul, the gift of the red, running rampantly through his spirit. With a great multitude of red magic mixed with his orange residing gift, he hurled it through her barrier.

The floor underneath the sorceress's stone bed transmuted itself to a batch of hot coals, all spread out within the entire area of her barrier and beyond.

The sorceress looked surprised for a split second, but she remained seated on her bed, raising her head high and proud. She gathered her hair, ensuring none would spill on the hot coals.

"What do you plan to do with me? Burn the information out of me?" she taunted him, eyeing the hot coals in the corner of her narrow slits as they turned a hot white. Sweat beaded on her brow.

Rubius flashed her a half smile. "That's exactly what I am going to do. I don't care about you, honestly, but now you just made it personal."

With another stroke of Rubius's hand, the fires under her bed turned up the heat, intensifying. The room became hotter, and through the heat wavering within her barrier, Ikaria's body began glistening with heavy sweat as the coals intensified. The white light of the coals brightened her face, and Rubius could almost see the fear behind her masked face.

One by one, the sorceress began stripping herself of her garments, drenched with sweat. With each one removed, she stared at him, her eyes unwavering, ready to prove that she could beat him at his own game.

Why isn't she using her adjacent red magic to cool my fire? She used ice magic earlier…

The sorceress leaned back after she was naked, the sweat gleaming down her curvy figure. She laughed.

"You find this funny?" Rubius asked.

"I find it truly amusing."

"What? You trying to withstand my fire? You trying to prove something to me?"

"That you don't *know*."

"*What* don't I know?" he yelled.

The sorceress flashed him a look of delight, then laughed in the fiery heat, the highlights of her face pouring with sweat. Rubius could tell her eyes were weakening, as her body made sluggish movements, no doubt overwhelmed from the intense heat. She then rolled her head deliriously against the wall behind her, laughing again.

"Tell me!" Rubius roared.

"That sweet, precious green-gifted..."

Rubius's head snapped to full attention as Ikaria's eyes slowly closed as if going to sleep.

Why is she choosing not to use her water or ice magic?

"Damn you! What about her?" he roared. He shot a blast of water to the sorceress's face, hoping to wake her from the heat, but the sorceress looked as if she had already passed out.

She wasn't moving.

He hesitated, wondering if what he was about to do next was the right option. Making a quick decision, Rubius made a sharp jerk of his hands. The hot coals were instantly snuffed out. He gathered all of his magic, the magic that ran next to his red gift. The violet magic filled his being, and he submersed his inner being within it.

Then he forced himself into her mind.

The moment Rubius felt his consciousness enter the sorceress's, pain exploded in his mind. A squeezing, suffocating sensation overwhelmed his spirit, strangling him, preventing him from doing anything. His vision went dark, and all he saw were swirling black stars.

Bravo, High Inquisitor... thinking that you could play me for a fool. Her voice laughed within his consciousness.

He had made a very wrong decision.

Cursing himself, Rubius fought back with all his power. He fought against the pain, but it rattled him, shaking his consciousness. He tried to push Ikaria's presence back in his mind, but his magic and his stream of consciousness were fuzzier, like everything was losing a sense of reality.

A startling force rocked his spirit hard.

He heard laughing echoing over and over again.

Rubius's mind's eye opened, seeing outlines in all shades of violets. The darkness consumed the violet outlines, but within moments, the outlines became clearer, and he realized what he was looking at.

Staircases. As far as the eye could see. They were headed in all sorts of directions. Some were going east, some west, some up, some down. There were even ones that went upside down and sideways. It was a giant labyrinth of stairs, all highlighted in violets. They all had a sense of familiarity to them.

Am I inside my own mind? Was that even possible? To see the inner workings of his consciousness? Wasn't it only reserved for seeing other's people's minds with the violet magic?

Rubius's eyes followed the many stairs. They all led to shut doors. He guessed that they were all locked.

A glimmer of green light caught his eye.

Looking up, far above, Rubius saw vivid green light coming from a cracked door. It was the only one that was slightly open in the whole labyrinth.

The door creaked slightly as it opened a sliver more. The sound of the creak echoed throughout the maze, and its green light shone on the nearby staircases within the expansive maze.

I know who you are searching for, the sorceress's voice could be heard echoing in the maze. *She's right inside…*

Just hearing the sorceress's mocking voice angered Rubius, flooding him with rage once again.

He hated playing games.

Rubius gritted his teeth, then filled his being with his violet magic. The maze began to shake from the force coming from him, rattling all the stairs and doors. The force built up, shaking violently, as if he were about to release an earthquake upon the maze to rip it apart.

Without warning, Rubius was knocked to his feet. His head slammed against one of the stairs. Hard.

What's the matter, High Inquisitor? Are you afraid to face her and discover what you have lost all these years?

"I'm not afraid of you, or anything!" Rubius roared.

Suddenly, Rubius felt a soft presence radiating from the opened door, brushing against his soul far across the chasm.

She was there, the green-gifted woman…

Rubius jumped to his feet and sprinted toward the light, determined to find her. Perhaps it was a trap set by the sorceresses herself. Regardless, Rubius had to know.

More and more, Rubius worked through the maze, his soul pounding. Every stair, every step that he became closer to the cracked door, made him feel more alive.

Rubius kept running, until finally, he found the staircase that led up to the slightly open door, its green light glowing from behind it. Cautiously, Rubius approached the door, waiting to see what would happen.

There was a low humming sound that came from behind the door. Rubius didn't hear the sorceress, nor did he feel her presence at that moment. But he felt the green-gifted woman's spirit, stronger than he had ever felt in his dreams prior.

She was inside, waiting.

When he deemed it safe, Rubius grasped the door handle, trembling with nerves. It felt solid, and the door had much weight to it. It was still cracked open, but not enough for him to slip inside.

With all his strength, he yanked on the handle. It didn't budge, so he yanked it again, this time with more force behind his pull. The door still did not move, so Rubius summoned up a blast of force, attacking the door, shattering all contents of it, leaving it wide open for him to enter.

A familiar wave of feelings flooded his consciousness, hitting him hard. Stumbling for a moment, he gathered his composure and walked through the opening.

Low humming became louder as he passed through the entrance, heading into a world that was submersed in blues mixed with violets. Strange tubes ran down the walls of the oversized room where he was. There were small tubes, large tubes, and...

Machines. The humming sounds were from *machines.*

Joining the humming sounds were other mysterious sounds of clicks. The machines blinked sporadically in all sorts of colors and patterns throughout, and bizarre pictures flashed across flat surfaces. It was as if the machines were communicating in their own language.

Fascinated, Rubius continued to walk, then stumbled for a moment, catching his balance.

His foot had caught on something on the ground. Rubius looked down and saw within the violet-blue hue that there were cords on the floor running in the same direction of the tubes. Looking up, he saw a faint green light behind a mass of tangled tubes, cords, and machines.

Following the direction of the cords, Rubius ran down the hall, ensuring he didn't trip on the cords. The humming becoming louder as the green light became brighter. The tubes and cords became more dense, thicker, and he tried to push them away.

It seemed the closer he got to the green light, the thicker the cords were. Rubius fought and fought, pushing and pulling.

Then he froze.

Within the tangled mass, her body was before him, radiating green light. The green-gifted woman was contained within a giant glass tube, trapped and encapsulated. She remained frozen, her hands gently crossed across her chest, in a deep sleep. Or more like a deep spell. The cords and tubes all led to her, running through to the glass capsule.

There was a shift within his mind, and Rubius felt the presence of the sorceress next to him.

"I don't understand," Rubius said quietly, pressing his face and hands against the glass.

You've been searching for her for many years, no? the sorceress's voice said within his mind.

Rubius touched the glass, staring. He soaked in every detail of the green-gifted woman. He'd found her, but they were once again kept apart. Just like every dream he had ever had of her.

I have a proposition for you, one that you will find to your liking, the sorceress said. *I will tell you everything you want to know in exchange for freeing me.*

"If you do know what I want to know, I could just continue to pry it out of you," Rubius countered.

And continue to make a fool out of yourself by failing? I think it a terrible idea, and a complete waste of time.

"How do I know you're not lying?" Rubius asked.

It's just a risk you have to take. Tell me, High Inquisitor, is she worth it? The woman who has been haunting your dreams all these years?

How did *she* know that the green-gifted woman had haunted him? The sorceress's words echoed in his head, enticing him. He could finally get the answers.

"Who is she?" Rubius asked, as his hands ran across the glass.

Wouldn't you like to know? the sorceress's voice murmured.

His eyes were fixated on the green-gifted woman, her magic stirring his soul. "How can I trust you? How do I know what you say is true?"

I will tell you one thing, and only one, so you'd best listen.

"You have my attention."

She is a remnant of World Sector One's past. The once great Kingdom of Arcadia. Queen of the ancient kingdoms. There may even be remnants of her empire still standing.

There it was. Her words confirmed what Rubius had suspected since reading Lady Xui's book. It lined up. Rubius studied the sleeping woman, leaning against the glass. *So close...* he thought.

"What is her name?" Rubius asked.

I have said enough. Like I said, if you want more, you need to free me, including my barrier.

Suddenly, the world around him melted rapidly, and Rubius felt a forceful jolt, his spirit shooting hard. Rubius blinked. He was back inside the sorceress's cell. He could feel the leftover heat from the smoldering coals and the scent of fire damage.

The sorceress remained naked, lying across the stone bed. Her face rolled over, and her eyes opened slowly.

"So what will it be, High Inquisitor?" she said softly, struggling with her words. She was completely exhausted from the heat.

What would he do? Just seeing the green-gifted woman within his mind, so close...

But Elyathi—she had warned him. If Lady Elyathi were to find out that he had aided the sorceress in any way, she would be his bitter enemy. Perhaps the High Court would order for his magic to be removed.

Rubius snapped out of his thoughts. "I have a job to do! I don't barter with prisoners."

"Suit yourself. Your loss," the sorceress said weakly.

She passed out.

Rubius paused, wondering if he should attempt to jump back into her mind. But the woman loved to play games, and he had already been fooled twice. How much of an imbecile did the sorceress think him to be? Shame on him if he fell for her trap again...

Rubius studied the sorceress for a moment, her barrier vibrating with prismatic, translucent colors. What was he going to do?

He did an about-face, then pounded on the door to the cell. "Let me out!"

The door clicked open, and he hastily walked out, his cape trailing behind him as they bowed.

He walked down the corridors, his mind even more muddled than before.

World Sector One…

Perhaps he would do exactly what the sorceress had suggested.

He would go see the remnants of the Queen of Arcadia's empire himself.

CHAPTER 38

YELLOW

Auron followed Suri close behind as they hurried through the citadel. They were both invisible from her magic; Auron couldn't see her or even himself. To reassure himself, he held on to the hem of Suri's robe as they moved, in case he lost her. Auron prayed every moment that they wouldn't run into any orange-gifted High Court guards, the High Inquisitor, or worse, the powerful gifted woman.

Perhaps now they had a chance to rescue the Empress with Suri having consumed violet magic. It was a fool's hope, but at least it was something.

It still made Auron uneasy. Suri consuming Ikaria's gift. But in a strange way, as Auron prayed in his mind while they were making their way through the citadel, a feeling of assurance came over him. It was a brush with the divine, making Auron feel that the God of Light had approved their decision. Perhaps not everything was black and white, spelled out precisely as it was in *The Spectrum.* Maybe God Himself allowed instances in times such as these. Even Empress Ayera had stated this belief to him—that sometimes things weren't black and white. It was ironic that her words now held true to the current situation to rescue her.

As they moved through the halls, he felt Suri's hand press against his body from time to time, signaling when they needed to stop. Every time they did, High Court guards passed by soon after. Auron had to admit that Suri was even more practiced at being unseen in the shadows than he had originally gathered. It was as if a sly but artfully graceful snake guided him throughout the citadel. Her skills in the art of evading and avoiding detection were incredible.

As they turned down one of the corridors that led them closer to the airship platform, Auron felt a sudden pulling sensation deep within his chest. It was as if his heart… no, his *soul*, was being slowly draining away from him. It was such a strange, overwhelming feeling, troubling his life force greatly. But what? It had started after he left the sorceress's cell.

The troubling thought came over him again. *Did we make the right decision to rescue the Empress?*

They finally exited the citadel and made their way to the outside airship platform. There, the High Court airship remained docked.

Thank the God of Light, he breathed with relief. *We still have a chance!*

"High Priest," Suri whispered. "There will be gifted guards. You will have to be ready to cast protection on me."

"I will have your back," Auron replied.

She gently tugged on his arm, giving him the silent signal to get moving. The two of them headed toward the bridge that adjoined the High Court airship, then started to cross.

Immediately, Auron saw several High Court gifted guards patrolling the ship from the deck above. There were orange-gifted amongst them.

"Two gifted heading this way!" one orange-gifted called out in alert.

"It's High Priest Auron! Seize him now!" yelled a second orange-gifted.

"Cast your shields now, High Priest!" Suri said.

Following Suri's commands promptly, Auron held his hand out, as if telling everyone to halt. Out of his outstretched hand came his protective magic, flowing rapidly around them with golden power, forming a translucent golden circular barrier. As he did, the shimmer of Suri's orange magic faded, leaving them exposed to the naked eye.

A red-gifted guard flew toward them in the air from above, while two yellow-gifted came running onto the bridge.

The red-gifted sent a blast of magical red ice toward Suri and Auron, pelting Auron's barrier. As soon as the red ice made contact, Auron's golden shield intensified.

Another burst of ice came, this time in the form of ice shards. But the ice shards sunk into Auron's shield, cracking it.

The red-gifted whooshed by in anger, then summoned another round of ice shards, hurling it into their barriers once again.

Auron's shields shattered like broken glass. Auron swallowed, seeing more guards heading toward them on the bridge. He and Suri were surrounded by at least ten guards. Another shot of magic came from the flying red-gifted; this time it was a huge gust of red winds raging with fury.

Suddenly, underneath Auron's feet, the bridge took a new form, twisting like putty. The bridge morphed smaller and smaller until it settled as a rope.

Auron was standing on a *rope* stretched from the platform to the airship.

All was sky under his feet. He *hated* heights.

"No… no, no, no!" Auron cried out in panic.

"Don't be fooled," Suri said. "It's an illusion. Hurry, cast another shield. The red gust is coming!"

All Auron could think about was dropping to his death. His horrifyingly big feet teetered on a tiny tight rope, nothing but pure clouded sky below.

Sweat, fear, and panic pumped hard through his body. He couldn't help it; all he saw was the tightrope, and he flailed his hands to keep balance. Even the rope swung wildly as he moved.

"Hurry, High Priest!"

"Get me off this thing!" Auron yelled frantically.

A red blast of wind hit them hard, causing the rope to swing hard and wild. Auron thrashed back and forth, his whole body swinging wildly with the movement of the rope as he frantically tried to maintain his balance.

He was going to fall.

With a loud burst, Auron cried out at the top of his lungs and clenched his eyes shut. He couldn't take it anymore.

"High Priest! Focus," Suri said firmly. "It is not real!"

Please, God of Light…

Auron opened his eyes and immediately saw a wall of ice heading toward them. But behind that wall of ice was something even worse—the airship was departing.

It was leaving. And the Empress was leaving with it.

There was a loud crack, and Auron turned back. Suri had blasted a wave of deeper orange force toward the red-gifted man, pummeling him through his own summoned red ice, then slamming him back against the ship. The wave of ice stopped, leaving Auron to balance on the thin tightrope once again.

Auron glanced over to Suri, bathed in her new deep-orange magic. In her hand she held an enchanted dagger, and she plunged it right into an orange-gifted's chest.

She had broken the illusion spell, and the bridge could be seen once again. Auron fell to the bridge with gratitude, almost wanting to kiss it.

"We have to move!" Suri said.

She turned away, heading further down the bridge. Auron moved with her, refreshing the shields on them. The bridge started to shake as the airship pulled away from the dock.

"My mistress will never forgive me if I don't get on that ship!" Suri yelled as she knifed another orange-gifted effortlessly.

That same strange sensation that came over Auron once again, causing a huge stir in his life force. It felt like… he *needed* to be with Ikaria. Auron paused.

Suri looked over her shoulder, meeting his gaze.

"I… I can't leave the sorceress," Auron called out.

"But the Enchantress said—" Suri said.

"It doesn't matter what that woman said. My life force is telling me otherwise," Auron argued. "I need to go back!" Auron's heart fluttered when the words left his lips.

Yes. He *had* to go back.

Suri eyed him for a moment, then nodded. "Do what you must. I will free the Empress."

Their gaze broke as the bridge rattled violently. The airship fully split from the dock, leaving a huge gap of airspace.

Suri cried out and bolted for the ship. Reacting quickly, he jolted out his hand, shooting one final magical blast to Suri, enveloping her with a refreshed barrier of protection as she continued to sprint.

Suri burned with a deep-orange brilliance. The magic swirled around her body from head to toe. Then Suri jumped with a powerful force, impossibly crossing the huge gap. Suri got closer to the airship, but her jump was a little short, and she missed the deck. She slammed against the side of the airship and quickly grabbed onto one of the window ledges.

Swiftly, as if it were nothing, she gracefully crawled across the side of the airship, using the window ledges, then made her way up the side ladder until she reached the deck.

Auron's jaw dropped. What Suri just had done was truly amazing.

Turning away, Auron sprinted across the airship bridge, then glanced back just in time to see a blast of orange magic coming from the airship. It seemed that Suri could indeed handle herself.

With a sharp gesture of his hands, Auron funneled another wave of golden magic, sending it surging directly at Suri's barrier. He poured more and more of his energy toward her, praying for her safety. Far off, Suri's barrier radiated brilliantly with power.

That should hold for several more moments, Auron thought. But what was Suri going to do? Kill everyone on the airship and turn it back around? Somehow, he had a feeling Suri might do exactly that. By the looks of it, she was certainly capable.

A blast of orange magic funneled around Auron, pouring over him brightly, then turned him invisible.

Suri. She was returning the favor.

Auron turned to look at her. Theirs eyes met across the distance. Both nodded in gratitude, then went back to facing their current situations. Auron finally reached the end of the airship bridge.

He had to get back to Ikaria. He had a sinking feeling that if he didn't, something far worse would happen to their sector than what was already happening.

***

Suri used her new force ability and flung her enchanted dagger straight into a yellow-gifted guard. On contact, the force flowing around the dagger made it twist and turn in the guard's chest, carving out his flesh.

He screamed, then flopped over, dead.

She turned around. There were two more guards coming toward her. Suri kept her face frozen and emotionless. The violet magic was pure ecstasy. Just like the Enchantress herself. So pleasing. She was doing this all to please the Enchantress.

With a graceful sweeping gesture, Suri raised her hand toward the guards, then narrowed her eyes.

The Enchantress. They will pay for what they did to her!

With a snap of her fingers, the guards' bodies were smashed together with her dark-orange magic. An audible crunch rent through the air as their bones snapped. The guards screamed.

Just as she was about to turn invisible, she heard a voice.

"Watch out, miss!" yelled a boy.

She quickly turned and saw an enchanted sword about to slice her, but it bounced off a new, golden barrier surrounding her.

The sword scratched the barrier, making an ear-splitting sound. With no time to waste, Suri lifted her hand, summoning her new violet ability mixed with her orange magic.

Deep-orange magic surrounded the guard, encasing him. Suri connected the magic with a deep feeling in her heart. She couldn't fail the Enchantress. It was not an option.

The magic crushed the man's body, and he slumped over, adding to the body count. Suri paused, evaluating the situation. It was silent on the deck. She had taken out all the guards in this section, and the others below hadn't heard the commotion. But they would be up on deck eventually.

She reached inside her robes, reassuring herself that her mistress's blood still was secure around her neck. Tucking the chain next to her heart once again, Suri took a small breath. She didn't have long.

Suri turned and saw a yellow-gifted young man with golden hair and shimmering yellow eyes, perhaps sixteen years of age. He was dressed in his daily priestly vestments, long and white and embroidered with gold, and the pendant of the spectrum hung on his neck.

"Where did you come from?" Suri asked, her face without expression.

"I had a vision that I needed to be here. So I came," he said. "Somehow, when I came to the docks, I felt a strange sensation, and then I turned invisible. I don't know how I did it, but it happened, and I hid here, waiting for a sign." The boy smiled, looking excited. "Must have been the God of Light intervening."

Suri eyed him. "You accessed your analogous magic."

"Analogous?"

She heard sounds coming from below.

"Do not worry about it now, young priest," Suri said.

As she was about to go invisible, there was a blast of violent red wind that hit her hard. Then there came a loud vibrating rumble within the airship. Lightning started shooting from the sky, and the ship jerked violently back and forth.

Suri gained her footing, but with the ship jerking like this, she wouldn't hold her stance for long.

The ship began rocking harder, slamming her and the yellow-gifted boy against the mast. Then, after a few more hard jerks, the airship swayed almost completely to one side, causing them to roll down the deck and hit the railing.

They knew we were here and waited for us, Suri thought.

Clutching the railing firmly, Suri swung one of her legs over it to secure steady support. The yellow-gifted boy clung to the railing tightly, fear radiating from his eyes.

"I don't know if I can hold on!" the boy exclaimed.

She couldn't fail the Enchantress, but Suri admitted to herself that she wasn't sure if she could hold on either.

***

Ayera slammed into the side of the airship's wall. Her hands were shackled, and her body was pulled as far as the locked chains would allow as the ship completely turned on its side. Objects within the compartment hit her in the face and body hard. Loud but muffled yelling came from outside the locked door. Was she being rescued?

What is happening?

"Help! I'm in here!" Ayera called out loudly.

She slammed her chained wrists against the wooden boards of the airship, making as much noise as she could.

"Someone help me!"

There was more commotion, and the ship tumbled further, causing her body to twist in the chains to her side.

Was her sister out there? Coming to rescue her? Only Ikaria had the kind of power to turn a whole airship… unless it was the winds of a red-gifted?

Maybe Ayera had been wrong about her sister…

She could only hope.

***

The airship kept rolling, and it seemed like it was not going to stop until it rid itself of Suri.

Suri and the yellow-gifted boy continued to cling to the railing for their dear lives, dangling like puppets.

Below them, there was nothing but sky, clouds, and an occasional small floating island. Suri called upon her new power, and it flowed over them, trying to keep them in place. But Suri's energy was spent; she had used much of it on the deck, and the violet power was still new to her. She felt the energy holding them, but then it weakly started to pull away.

The boy looked at Suri once again, this time his eyes watering with tears. "I think I am going to die," he said in a defeated tone.

Suri's arms burned. She couldn't hold on much longer.

"I cannot die, young priest. For if I do, I fail my enchantress," she said in a murmur. "If I will not die, neither will you."

The boy gave her half a smile, then doubled his effort with his grip.

The ship gave a sudden, sharp jerk. With the force of the violent movement, Suri and the boy were torn from the railing. The two of them were falling.

And falling.

And falling.

CHAPTER 39

VIOLET

"Over there," Reila said, pointing to a large rock formation within the violet while she was latched onto Geeta's hand.

About time, Geeta thought.

The rock formation was far off, but at least now Geeta knew where she was going and had an actual landmark to target. Telly's map was an utter disaster, and nothing was even close to being accurate. And since Reila hardly ever went into Arcadia, the woman was unfamiliar with where they were going until they hit the wasteland stretch.

"Are you sure?" Geeta asked. "It looks like every other rock formation we passed."

"I recognize the area. Especially that shape on the top of the rocks," Reila said, nodding.

Geeta grasped the staff tightly while Reila held her hand, flying gently with Geeta's movement. The woman pretended that she wasn't amused, but Geeta knew Reila was thrilled at the sight of her magic.

As they flew closer to the rock formation, Geeta saw something strange in the distance. It was hard to make out the exact details since everything was in violet-blue hues, but it was expansive, a dark formation across the desert plains.

Wonder what that is?

A strange, unsettling feeling came over her, and Geeta changed course.

"I'm not sure if you misheard me the first time, but the refuge is over there." Reila pointed back to the rock formation.

Geeta ignored her, continuing to pull them in the opposite direction.

"Seriously, what are you doing?"

As they moved closer and closer, the details became clearer and more precise. Geeta stopped cold when she realized what the dark formation was.

Reila's eyes went wide. "Holy shit!" Reila exclaimed. "That robot was telling the truth..."

There, at the base of one of the mountain passes, was a large army. No, large wouldn't even begin to describe it. There were legions of soldiers and cyborgs, with oversized ground vehicles and weapons. There were camps set up, the soldiers paused in time.

"Why the hell do they have a communications tow—" Reila said, then stopped herself, her eyes full of knowing. "The interference..."

Geeta's eyes looked to where Reila was referring to and saw the tower jutting out within the camp.

Strange that they have a chair on top of the tower, Geeta thought. It appeared empty. At least, for the time being. *What is the purpose of it? Who would actually be seated there?*

"I know you're having fun with our little detour of sightseeing, but if you don't mind, I'd like to get to the refuge now. Especially since there's *that* out there," Reila said, giving Geeta's hand a little yank. "Besides, all this purple is hurting my eyes."

"Yes, we're going now," Geeta said, turning away from the sight.

"Good."

Geeta infused her body with her analogous red-violet winds, while the staff in her hands turned almost a bright red. The winds began to rip through the women with power, causing them to take flight within the violet world, sending them back in the direction of the refuge. They reached the landmark Reila had identified as being the point of interest, then moved in closer.

"Land there," Reila called out, pointing to a small path. Geeta wouldn't even have spotted the path without Reila saying something. It was completely hidden, even from an aerial viewpoint.

They landed, and Geeta drew her magic back in, it dissipating around them. The world turned back into full color—the sun hot with orange and yellow hues and the rocks a golden reddish-brown color.

Geeta let go of Reila's hand as the woman took out a cigarette, then lit it. "Up this path," she said, walking off.

They both headed up silently, with Reila's puffs of smoke blowing into Geeta's face, causing Geeta to grit her teeth. Normally, she would have said something, but it didn't matter.

There was a series of clicks, and Geeta saw guns surrounding her and Reila.

"Don't move," said one of the men.

"Believe me, if I wanted to take you out, you would be dead by now," Geeta said.

"Ryan," Reila said coolly, "get that gun out of my face before I decorate your face with my fist. Stop dicking around."

"Didn't see you, Reila," said Ryan as they lowered their weapons.

"I don't know why Victor keeps putting you on guard duty," she continued. "You're terrible at recognizing our own camp members."

Ryan gave an embarrassed chuckle, scratching his head.

"We need to see Victor."

"Did you talk to the King? What did he say?" Ryan pressed.

"None of your business."

"Why are you such a bitch?"

"Why are you so annoying?"

Another guard smirked, and Ryan waved to them. "Fine. Have it your way. I'll take you to Victor."

"Don't think just because you're being nice to me means that I'll sleep with you tonight," Reila said.

Ryan's cheeks burned, and Geeta snorted.

"Who said anything about wanting to sleep with you?" he asked.

"We'll see when night comes," Reila remarked.

The other men laughed, then the group took off, walking into the entrance of the caverns. Reila walked next to Geeta, both of them squeezing their way through the cave's corridors and chambers.

"Ever since I got drunk and slept with him six months ago, he keeps hanging around me," Reila said casually, obviously referring to Ryan.

"I see," Geeta said. "Perhaps you should stop making suggestive statements. I'm sure he will stop at some point."

Reila looked at her teasingly. "Where's the fun in that?"

Geeta rolled her eyes and sighed.

The cavern narrowed, causing them to follow each other in a single-file line. As they moved further into the caves, they twisted around tight corners and squeezed through cramped areas. Geeta barely managed to get the staff through certain areas. At times, there were large rooms with equipment. Wastelanders were already setting up camp or working on devices. What fascinated Geeta was that there was a system of lights in place throughout the caves—they were using modern technology to light the chambers and paths. There had to be a generator somewhere, or some other source of power, to light up that many spaces, which impressed her.

The path opened up to a large underground chamber, big enough to be its own canyon. On the side of the grand cavern was an underground river, providing the refugees with fresh water. There were many people spread out by the waterway, already setting up their supplies. The area had been split up into different zones—the armory over to one side, supplies toward another, and other chambers with various purposes.

Their group kept walking toward the center of cavern until they reached a decent-sized tent, lit with an electric lantern inside.

"Victor," Ryan called out. "Reila's back from Arcadia."

A hand pulled back the opening of the tent flap, and then an older man stuck his head out, his eyes meeting hers. The man, who had to have been this so-called Victor, had deep ebony skin and long black dreadlocks peppered with some gray. He was dressed in a tunic with loose pants that were tight around the ankles, with worn boots weathered from use.

Victor's eyes met Geeta's, and he let out a small gasp. Then he gave her a knowing look and waved Geeta and Reila inside.

The two women moved through the flap and stood near a small square table surrounded with floor pillows.

"I am Victor. Leader of this camp," he said, nodding for them to take a seat.

"Geeta." She nodded back, flopping down on one of the pillows. She set the staff down on her lap.

"You're gifted," he stated, glancing at the staff, then moving his gaze back to her eyes.

"I am."

"She showed up when I was about to crash," Reila explained. "Olympia tried to shoot us down. If it weren't for her, that scientist and I would be dead."

"You have my gratitude." Victor nodded, and Geeta returned the gesture.

"I did what any human being would do," Geeta said. *That is, what most people should do.*

"What news of Arcadia? Do they know of our situation?" Victor asked them.

"They do. The Queen has ordered the Arcadian army to be dispatched into the wastelands. They will also secure the perimeter of the city with soldiers."

"What of the cyborgs?"

"The Queen has also ordered the reassembling of the Arcadian cyborg units. That is, if they want to help," Geeta said.

"You forgot to mention the part where you were named Protector of the Realm," Reila added smoothly.

Geeta shot her a look, and Reila shrugged.

"Protector of the Realm," Victor murmured, studying her.

Geeta suddenly felt uncomfortable. She was no protector. She couldn't even prevent Kyle's death. And what of Nym? Nym was inside Arcadia, and soon there was to be an army invading…

Geeta swallowed hard at the thought of Nym being in danger.

"I am sure with your gift, you will be a great asset to us out here. Perhaps we will be able to eliminate the threat before it arrives at Arcadia's doorstep."

"There's something else you won't like, Victor," Reila said. "On our way here, we spotted the Olympian army. They're not too far from where we are right now."

Geeta's thoughts immediately went back to the communications tower. Victor frowned and looked at her curiously.

"What is it?" he asked.

That empty chair… Geeta met his gaze. "There was a tower among the Olympian army."

"A tower?"

"It looked like some sort of communications tower," Reila said. "Probably why we were having interference issues. The Olympian army has been fucking with our signal. Don't know how they're doing it, but they are."

"But there is something more than that," Geeta interrupted. "At the top of the tower, there was a chair. It was empty at the time, but it was obviously made for someone to sit up there."

"Maybe it's made for His Royal Ass, the King of Olympia," Reila said sarcastically.

"No," Geeta said gravely. "I suspect whoever sits on top of that chair is *how* the tower actually interferes with communications."

"So you think, perhaps," Victor suggested slowly, "it is for a gifted?"

That was exactly what she was thinking. Turning to him, Geeta asked, "Did that cyborg of theirs ever say what magics the Olympians have access to?"

"Yellow, I think. But he also mentioned something about magic shifting through dimensions, though I do not what kind of magic that is."

"Blue magic."

"Blue magic?" he repeated.

Why would they have a yellow-gifted, or possibly a blue-gifted, sit at the top of that tower? That wouldn't cause any interference. That doesn't make any sense.

Everything about the situation troubled her greatly.

"Can I talk to the cyborg?" Geeta asked, breaking her thoughts. "Is he here?"

"You can. He's with a man named Garrett in another section of the refuge." Victor paused, sighing.

Geeta heard Victor's thoughts and the scope of the situation. Magic within another kingdom, the spreading of magic in the wrong hands. He was fearful but hiding it well.

"I know your thoughts, and indeed, this all troubling," Geeta said.

Victor looked to her, surprised. "You know my thoughts?"

"That is a part of my gift," she said. "I don't like this just as much as you do. Magic has torn many kingdoms apart throughout time. Even at the birth of civilization, there was always discord." Her eyes met his. "That is why the gods stripped humans of their gifts long ago and the world was void of magic for several millennia. Too much chaos."

"And yet it has surfaced once again."

"It always seems to find its way back into the hands of humans," Geeta said. "Perhaps the gods aren't done with us yet."

She got up from the pillow, with Victor doing the same. "Take me to this Olympian cyborg," she said.

He nodded, and they vacated the tent.

***

The cyborg was resting when Geeta arrived in the chamber that he was housed in. It was a chamber that had been designated for stockpiled weapons, equipment, and some survival supplies. Geeta even spotted a couple of devices that looked like EMPs. Much of it was still randomly spread out throughout the cavern.

They sure have a good stockpile, Geeta thought, eyeing all the weaponry.

The cyborg was on the floor of the cavern lying on a blanket, a machine next to it, with cables running back and forth. Sitting next to the cyborg was a man with dark skin and facial tattoos similar to a circuit board. That had to be Garrett, the one taking care of Scion. Standing over Garrett was a teen girl with blonde hair.

As Geeta and Victor approached, Garrett looked up at Geeta. The teen girl left the room without a word. The man gave Geeta a once-over, probably noticing her violet hair and eyes, then his eyes landed on the staff, which was slightly glowing.

"That staff," he said, rising to his feet. "That was my buddy Kyle's staff."

"It still is," Geeta said. It would never be her staff. It would always be his. Geeta met the man's eyes. "The Queen ordered me to take it, though I didn't want to."

"Gotcha." Garrett smiled sadly, then sat back down next to the cyborg, typing into a small handheld device for a second. "There, much better," he commented, satisfied.

"Garrett," Victor said. "This is Geeta, the new Protector of the Realm for Arcadia."

"Protector of the Realm?" Garrett whistled in surprise.

"She wants to talk to Scion. Can you wake him?" Victor continued.

"I can, but I'm still running some scans on him, so he might be kind of grumpy." Garrett adjusted the machine's knobs.

"Just wake him," Victor said pointedly.

Garrett shrugged, then patted the cyborg on the shoulder. "Hey, Scion, someone wants to talk to you." He gave him a hard shake.

The cyborg stirred, then gently opened his eyes, revealing a soft yellow glow. Magic radiated from them, and immediately Geeta felt a sense of love and devotion from them.

Protection magic...

Scion sat up, his eyes scanning Geeta, causing the hair on the back of her neck to rise. He then paused, waiting for her to speak in the uncomfortable silence. Apparently, the cyborg still had much to learn regarding proper etiquette.

"Scion, I'm Geeta," she said, breaking the silence. "I'm here to help stop the Olympian army from reaching Arcadia's border. I have to ask you a few questions so I know what I'm dealing with."

"Greetings, Geeta," Scion said mechanically. His eyes scanned her systematically, his head cocked to the side as he looked at her curiously. "I will do the best I can to help you, though please do not be alarmed by my movements. I think like a human inside, but I cannot help the mechanics of my actions."

"I understand," Geeta said, sitting down next to him.

Well, at least he knows he's odd...

Scion sat there, unusually still, causing a shiver to run down Geeta's spine once again.

"I am sorry, Miss Geeta. I don't mean to make you feel uncomfortable."

Geeta's mouth dropped, almost in amusement. He detected her awkwardness? Geeta then burst out in laughter.

Scion cocked his head. "What is so amusing? Did I miss a joke?"

Geeta shook her head while Garrett raised his eyebrow. "It is nothing, Scion. It's just... I have always been the one to 'read' people's thoughts, and you are the first to 'read' mine."

"That is amusing, Miss Geeta."

For a moment, Geeta thought that the cyborg would give her a smile, but it seemed his face wouldn't comply as much as he wanted it to. He did laugh awkwardly.

"It was your face that made me aware of your hesitation."

"I'll try to be more forgiving of your mechanics." Geeta nodded. Turning serious, Geeta leaned closer to him. "Scion, on the way to the camp, we discovered the Olympian army is already on the move. At the center of the army, there was a communications tower. Do you know anything about it? There was a chair at the top."

Scion processed her words for several moments. "Troubling. Very troubling."

"It is. What of the communications tower, though?"

"I do not know of any communications tower, nor am I aware of any design when I was hooked up to Olympia's network. I am sorry, Miss Geeta."

Geeta frowned. "Victor told me that most of the Olympian cyborgs are infused with yellow magic, and possibly blue magic? Is that true?"

"Yellow magic? Yes. Blue magic? I cannot confirm that."

"You mentioned shifting through dimensions, no?"

"That is correct. But I was only aware of the possibility of a human subject with that ability, not a cyborg unit."

Geeta looked to Victor and Garrett. "Blue magic. Could be very dangerous with the wrong person. We already have enough trouble with King Derek, which is a whole separate issue. But two, possibly?" She sighed, turning back to Scion.

It still didn't explain the communications tower. Blue or Yellow magic wouldn't be needed for it.

"Any other powers that you know of?" Geeta pressed the cyborg.

"None that I have been made aware of," Scion offered.

Perhaps I'm mistaken, she thought. *Maybe it is for a commander with a special device?* "Thank you, Scion," Geeta said as she got to her feet.

"I am sorry I could not assist you further, Miss Geeta."

"You've already helped Arcadia more than you know, and we appreciate it," Geeta said, bowing to him. "By the way, why do you call me Miss? Do you call everyone else by proper titles?"

"No, Miss Geeta, I do not. Only you."

"Why me?"

"Your mannerisms are refined for a human, and you carry yourself like someone with great importance."

Geeta raised an eyebrow.

Garrett chuckled. "I'm starting to like this guy."

Proper? Hardly, she thought. Though, she had been a high priest's wife at one time in her life. But she'd sworn that she had stripped herself of that life completely.

"Thank you, Scion," Geeta said again, nodding to him.

"You're welcome, Miss Geeta. I hope my information was useful to you."

Geeta eyed him one last time, then left the chamber, Victor next to her.

"What are your thoughts? What are we up against, truly?" Victor asked her.

"More than what we can handle," Geeta said bluntly.

"Even with your power? And what of the King and Queen, and even Drew and Telly? They have magic, lest you forget."

Geeta turned to him. "The King is gone, the Queen doesn't have the will to fight, and only the gods know where Drew is. Even with Telly as a 'tinted' gifted, she is at the palace, which does us no good here. Me against an army of magical cyborgs? That's not my idea of a fair fight."

As the words rang off her lips, she grew frightened, and realization set in. But she had to hide it, otherwise the others would see her fear, and what good would that do?

Victor raised an eyebrow. "What do you mean the King is gone? Where did he go?"

"No one knows, not even his own advisor. My guess is that he disappeared into the flow of time. To do what? Who knows." But then an idea formed as to why the King would disappear into time. And that train of thought was even worse. But she didn't want to think about it at the moment; there was already too much going on.

Victor remained silent, walking next to her.

Geeta turned to him. "I… I didn't mean to sound negative. It's just… concerning that all this is happening when Arcadia is at its weakest."

"No need to explain yourself. I understand," Victor said. "Just know that we wastelanders will do whatever we can to help. I have already talked to everyone within the refuge while we were waiting on word from the palace. They all are ready to fight. When it comes their homeland, they do not take kindly to anyone marching across *their* lands. We may not be gifted like you, but we are true desert warriors, and we don't fall down easily."

Geeta smirked at his statement. "Good. Because I'm going to need all the tough-as-nails people I can get." She paused, then looked to him. "I need to use the women's room and at least eat a ration of food before we plan out what is next."

"Bathrooms are over there, and the rations are over there," Victor pointed in two directions. "Tell Chris that I sent you for the rations."

"Be back shortly," Geeta said, turning away. She headed down the path toward the bathroom area, passing many wasteland people going to and from the underground river.

As she walked through the cavern, she noticed that the same teen blonde girl she had seen earlier with Garrett was peering at her curiously.

Geeta turned to call out to her, but the girl took off, so Geeta headed to the bathrooms.

CHAPTER 40

From across the cavern, Gwen saw several of the camp's highest-ranking men go into Victor's tent, along with other elders from other encampments. Moments later, the violet-gifted woman entered as well, and the glow from inside the tent illuminated a portion of the cavern.

The violet-gifted woman was pretty, Gwen decided, even with her boyish clothes. How she wished *she* had magic. Ever since she found out about her dad and her mom having magic, Gwen wanted to be just like them. Gwen had asked her mom several times to consider injecting her with her dad's blood to see what would happen. But as usual, her mom didn't want to hear about it.

Wish I could be someone important, Gwen thought. It seemed the harder she tried to help out with the camp, the more everyone pushed her away. Everything was "too dangerous" for her. She was "too young." On and on and on…

I am seventeen!

Gwen clenched her teeth. She knew how to shoot a gun, and she wasn't afraid of the Olympian army. It wasn't fair. The boys her age were helping out, and yet the camp treated her like an ignorant, weak city girl.

It made her mad.

And Garrett… He was nice to her, but even Gwen could see that he thought the same as others. Though Garrett had stuck up for her at times when no one else did. She liked Garrett more than just a friend, and it was hard to hide her feelings from him. Gwen was pretty sure Garrett had to know by now, but he never said anything, and she never brought it up. Maybe, just maybe, Garrett would like her if she tried hard enough.

Flickering came from within the tent while she waited in the shadows. Voices rose higher, some sounding rather heated. Finally, after some time, the group filed out of the tent. The violet-gifted woman looked over in her direction, and Gwen could have sworn that the woman saw her, even in her hiding spot.

The woman passed by, then Gwen heard men calling out within the cavern.

"Assembly in fifteen minutes in the main chamber!" their voices echoed throughout each of the chambers. As they continued to call people, everyone started to file into the main chamber, Gwen included.

The crowd gathered, everyone packing in tightly. Gwen looked around, hoping to spot Garrett. The whole camp was there, including other wastelanders from other camps that had recently shown up. They had all given the same news—Olympia had marched on their camp and destroyed it searching for their missing cyborg. It amazed Gwen how many people were already here. More than she had thought.

More people must have come during the night. There had to be nearly a thousand people within the chamber.

Victor walked through the crowd, and they parted for him. Gwen spotted Garrett behind him with the pretty violet-gifted. The crowd started to get rowdy, everyone talking, muttering, and yelling anxiously.

Victor made his way up front to a rocky platform. He stood above the crowd, and raised his hands, gesturing for silence.

"Quiet down, everyone!" he said.

Some people hushed, while others grew louder and more antsy. A bright blast of purple-red magic flashed above the crowd, shooting to the other side of the cavern and into the stone wall, crumbling it.

The crowd was silenced immediately, stunned by the sight of magic.

"He said, *quiet down*!" the violet-gifted woman said angrily. "We don't have time for chaos, so you'd best listen up if you want to save your lands!"

"Who is she?" asked one of the men from the crowd.

"Is that a true gifted? Does the Spectrum of Magic really exist?" called out another person from the crowd. Gwen noticed that person wasn't a wastelander from her group.

Victor raised his hands again in silence. "Listen, everyone. By now, you are all aware of what is happening in our homelands. Olympia is coming! They intend to conquer Arcadia and kidnap the King and Queen. They are also anxious to find their runaway cyborg, who is with us now."

"Who cares about Arcadia? They don't give a shit about us!" a woman called out from the crowd.

"In the many years past, I would have agreed with that statement," Victor answered the man in the crowd. "But Queen Emerald is very different from her father. She is the reason the cyborgs are free, and that the laws of the wastelands have been lifted, restoring our freedoms back to us! And for that, are we not obligated to help the very one who gave us back our freedom?"

He turned to scan the crowd. "Whatever your thoughts are about Arcadia, I cannot change them. But if Olympia succeeds in taking over Arcadia and capturing the Queen, then I can guarantee you things will get much worse for you. Look at what they've done already. Destroyed several of our encampments. Isn't that why many of you are here? Can you imagine if they got ahold of the Queen's magic? What do you suppose would happen?"

"So it's true!" one wastelander called out. "The Queen of Arcadia does have magic. Just like the cyborgs!"

Geeta nodded at the statement, and the crowded murmured with excitement and fascination. Victor raised his hands, trying to quiet everyone.

"What do you suggest we do, then?" called out another man. "How can we fight against their technology?"

Garrett approached Victor's side, facing the crowd. "Our camp has devised specialized weapons to combat magical capabilities. Many haven't been tested out, but I am confident that they will work and be useful for our fight against Olympia."

"What kind of weapons?" asked one of the other camp leaders.

"Magitech weapons, I like to call them," Garrett answered, standing proud.

The crowd gasped and whispered, looking to each other.

"Magitech?"

"Technological weapons infused with magic," Garrett said. "Much like the cyborgs that Arcadia and Olympia have, these weapons are infused with magic that I extracted from one of our very own gifted within our camp, though it is not at the same full power as the donor—these weapons have different capabilities. Some have fire magic; others have lightning or ice powers. There are a few with blasting shields of protection as well. Though we cannot guarantee this will stop the Olympian army, it will cause them to slow their roll to Arcadia's doorstep."

The crowd appeared energized now, cheering at Garrett's words.

Victor hushed everyone again. "I have a devised a plan with Arcadia's new Protector of the Realm," Victor said, pointing to Geeta. "We will lead our own army using these magitech weapons, and station ourselves sixty miles from Arcadia's border. By then, Arcadia should have reinforcements to meet us, and we can hold off the army, hopefully sending them back to where they came from. We ask that every able man and woman join us, and we'll assign certain people to stay behind to protect the refuge with our elderly, sick, and children."

Victor scanned the crowd. His gaze met hers, then continued to move over the crowd. "Everyone has one hour to eat and recharge, then you're to head to the armory to ready yourselves. Garrett will issue the magitech weapons that we have. We don't have enough magic-infused weapons for everyone, but we will make sure everyone is armed with something. For those of you getting the magitech weapons, Garrett will go over the functions with the user when issued the weapon. If you know how to shoot, you should be in good shape. You'll be divided up into groups so each one has at least one magical weapon per group. The rest of you will have to rely on the firepower you have brought with you, and stay with your assigned magitech weapon user. Now, go! Get ready! We'll meet up outside near the circular formation, and Arcadia's Protector of the Realm will port us. It takes a lot of power for her to do so, and the portal can only be open for so long before it closes, so you'd best be prompt."

The crowd cheered. Gwen felt the excitement too. Now was her chance to show people that she could be one of them, to prove that she could be as good of a fighter as her peers.

Gwen weaved her way through the caves to where she had her supplies, energized by the situation. Quickly changing into better clothes, she pulled her hair back into a ponytail, packed a side pouch with a few rations, and grabbed her canteen to fill.

After doing that and eating a last-minute strip of beef jerky, she walked to the armory. *I hope I'm one of the people they issue a magitech weapon to,* she thought excitedly. After all, she had worked on them with Garrett.

As she stood in the weapons-issue line, she spotted Garrett with several of the camp's men walking down the line and selecting men to arm them with the magitech weapons. Other men were assigned standard heavy artillery. Victor was with the violet-gifted woman, making last-minute orders and overseeing everyone getting ready.

When Gwen was near the front of the line, Victor walked by. When he noticed her, he stopped. "Gwen, your mother would have my hide if you were to come fight with us," he said.

Gwen felt her cheeks turn red. She eyed the people around her. "You said any able man and woman was to come, so here I am," Gwen said logically.

"I'm afraid that I can't let you come. We need people here to take care of the elderly and children," Victor stated.

She couldn't hide her disappointment. Again, they were treating her like a child.

"I don't *want* to stay behind with the others. I *want* to help out," Gwen spat angrily.

People in line started to stare at her as she looked around out of the corner of her watery eyes, embarrassed.

"I appreciate your willingness, but I just can't take you with us," Victor said in an even voice. "If something happened to you under my watch, your mother and father would never forgive me."

"Why are all the boys my age allowed to fight?" Gwen shot back. She angrily wiped her tears away, hoping no one saw. "I know how to use the weapons, better than most of the camp. I helped work on them with my parents and Garrett!"

"I don't doubt your skills," Victor said calmly. But his steady words only made her more angry. "Both your parents aren't here, and I can't allow you to come without them knowing about it."

Gwen jerked her head toward the violet woman, pleading silently for backup. The woman gave her a soft look of sympathy, then sighed.

"Please!" Gwen pleaded with her. "Don't you have anything to say about this?"

"Unfortunately, I'm going to stay out of this."

People in line started to whisper, making her feel even more small and deflated.

"I'm really sorry, Gwen. I hope you understand," Victor said with finality.

Garrett looked up from what he was doing in line, and their eyes connected.

He heard, she said to herself. Garrett had heard the commotion, which made her feel like even more of a child around him. *He probably thinks I'm stupid,* she thought angrily. Her throat tightened, and she couldn't stop the tears from flowing. *He'll never like me now. Why would he? Everyone acts as if I'm a useless girl.*

Turning away quickly, Gwen bolted from the line and ran. Where she was running to, she didn't know, and she didn't care. All she felt was the warmth of her tears stinging her eyes, blurring her vision.

"Gwen!" Victor's voice echoed behind her.

She ignored him, running as fast as she could.

"Gwen!"

It was too late. She kept running, pushing people out of the way, and didn't stop until she came upon a small empty chamber with no one around. She squeezed in, the space barely big enough for her.

I dare them to find me now!

Bitter tears continued to flow down her cheeks. Her soul felt sick. No one understood her. All they saw was a stupid teenage girl.

Just the thought of everyone talking about her back in line made her let out a loud cry. She fell to her knees, curling into a fetal position.

I hate them!

Yanking her hip pack off, she hurled it across the rocky chamber, still weeping. She wasn't going to help the elderly or the children. *They can help themselves,* she determined out of spite.

For a long while, she sat in the cave, crying softly until she no longer had tears. She looked up, taking in all the rock patterns on the ceiling of the cave. All the chaotic noises died into soft murmurs, and soon, silence settled in.

Gwen continued to lie there in silence, her thoughts running wild. She didn't need anyone to tell her what to do. She could handle herself just fine. She had so far!

Wiping away the remaining tears from her face, Gwen rolled over and crawled to the entrance of the tiny cavern. She peeked out, seeing a few children playing off on one side of the cave. On the other side, an older woman sat outside the armory area.

Good enough…

Looking back at her pack strewn across the cavern, Gwen snatched everything up, fastened it quickly around her, and slid into the shadows.

CHAPTER 41

Blue

In a flash of light, the time drop ended.

Derek's body crashed against a hard, rocky surface, then rolled several times until he came to a stop. Fortunately, his padded doublet and plush cape softened the blow somewhat, but his body still felt battered and bruised. At least he wasn't injured.

I have control over time magic, but it treats me like this? One would think that it could at least set me on my damn feet! he thought bitterly.

He groaned in pain. Taking a deep breath, Derek tried to clear his mind, then called the green magic, the magic that resided next to his blue magic. He wasn't sure if it would answer him; it always came to him when he injured himself, not when he actually thought he'd need it.

To Derek's relief, the magic answered him, sending a small healing wave throughout his body, enough to take away most of the pain. He got to his feet and brushed off the remnants of dirt and ran his fingers through his royal-blue curls, setting them back into place. As he was doing so, Derek saw several men and women approaching him with caution. They were all dressed in outlandish fashions. Derek thought them gaudy and quite ridiculous.

Straightening his posture, Derek's gaze locked onto the person closest to him, a man with orange hair and orange eyes.

They had magic, like him.

He paused for a moment, wondering if they were going to be hostile. Hopefully that wasn't the case.

"Who are you, friend?" the man with the orange hair asked.

At least he called me friend. That is a good start.

Derek answered him. "I came here in search of the Sorceress Ikaria."

The man narrowed his eyes, and the others positioned themselves around him. "What sector are you from?"

"I don't even know what that means," Derek answered.

They inched closer to him.

"I'm not from this time," he added quickly, "and I have no idea where I am right now."

"Not from this time?"

"Yes."

The orange-gifted man stared evenly at him.

"Can you not tell from the color of my hair and eyes that I have magic? A magic that has the power to travel through time? Why is that so far-fetched?" he asked them in annoyance. "I'm from the past. If I'm not mistaken, I believe several of you or your comrades traveled to my time to capture..." *The witch,* he wanted to say, but he held his tongue. "...the Sorceress Ikaria."

The magical guards closed in on him, almost in a semicircular formation.

"Indeed, several of our people did travel with Lady Vala back in time. But what, may I ask, is *your* business with the sorceress?" the orange-gifted man pressed.

Derek scoffed. "Business? What business *don't* I have with her?"

"You need to get permission from the High Court. No one sees her unless they are granted access. Especially now. Many of our people are under tight watch with the high justices, especially after the recent string of events."

"The High Court?" Derek spat. "I don't care about them. All I care about is getting to the sorceress!"

"You cannot," the man said, narrowing his eyes. "It would be a danger to everyone in our world, especially if she were to be released from her prison."

"You are mistaken. I don't want to release her. I want to get rid of her once and for all!"

"Be that as it may, we cannot let you pass. The sorceress, she is very powerful. Going up against her, you *will* fail. And if that happened, then it would unleash a whole other set of problems," the man said. "And we cannot let you jeopardize that for your vengeance."

"Then, unfortunately, you've just made an enemy," Derek snarled. "I will not stop until the sorceress is lying dead in her grave. That, I have sworn. And if you want to protect her in a prison still alive, then so be it!"

Derek shot out his hand. Blue magic streamed out of his palms wildly, wrapping itself around the orange-gifted man, pausing him in time. Derek turned to the others, directing his magic to flow to the next gifted.

The ground below him roared, then the earth shot up, encasing him in hardened rock, bathed in red magic. More flashes of different colors followed, and more encasing rock formed around him, capturing him in place. Derek's feet felt glued within the rock, and there was no flashing out of it with his blue magic.

He was stuck.

Angrily, Derek looked up. The world wavered and morphed into a frozen world, filled with nothing but ice and snow. Hard, icy winds mixed with snow pelted his face so fast and so hard that all he saw was white. Snow landed on his face. The hardened rock that held him felt like solid ice.

"What did you do?" he roared through the vast empty plains of white.

There was no answer, only more frosty winds, this time carrying ice.

This has to be a trick! There's no way they ported me!

The cold settled in his bones, and he felt as if he were succumbing to the elements.

This has to be illusion magic from that orange-gifted man. Just like that damn robot.

Derek snarled, then he closed his eyes. He filled his heart with dark rage, wrath pumping through his heart. He channeled his jealousy. It was the same feeling as when Emerald called out to the robot for help the time he had put the circlet on her head. How that had angered him.

The jealousy, the hatred... it flowed through him. The rage converted to sheer power, swirling violently through his entire being as his body was enveloped in blue-violet light. As the light grew more intense, a powerful force rattled the rock that entrapped him. More and more, the power fueled his magic, until the rock that held him prisoner shook violently.

The wind start drafting upward, carrying the icy snow away from him in chaotic motion. The white of the snow flickered in and out of existence as he continued to funnel his magic through his core.

With a ruptured force, the rock shattered, pieces scattering wildly as the icy world melted before his eyes.

Derek saw the gifted fly backward from the explosion. Some tried to dodge the debris while others attempted to cast their yellow-magic shields. But all Derek saw were yellow sparks from their hands before they crashed against a stone structure.

Before they got ahold of themselves, Derek lifted his hands, filling them with blue-violet power. As he did, the gifted levitated with his movements, until he smashed his hands together. Several of the gifted were grasped tightly within his blue-violet magic, then they came crashing together in sync with his hands.

"Tell me where the sorceress is!" Derek yelled at them.

"Do not do this!" said a yellow-gifted woman guard. "We're on the same side!"

From the corner of his eye, Derek saw several gifted that had evaded his magic casting spells. With another sharp swipe of his hand, he flung them onto their bellies, sending them sliding against the rocky gravel of the path. Derek made sure he pushed them far, far away.

The gifted guards struggled to get up. Those who'd slammed against each other started to freeze in time, with Derek allowing time magic to wash over them.

He had the perfect moment.

Slowly, he focused deep within himself, allowing it to pour out into the world. The skies, the ground, the people… all began to fade into blue tones. The actions of the guards became slower and slower.

"Derek?"

That voice. He stopped.

"Is that truly you?" the familiar voice continued.

Derek turned around, and a woman materialized before his eyes. He stood there, soaking in her image in disbelief. She had long blue hair and icy glimmering eyes, but her looks… they were the same.

Pure shock ran through his body. "Queen… Elyathi?" Derek hesitated.

The older yet timeless, beautiful queen stood before him, a burning blue aura surrounding her.

"What… how…?" Derek fumbled with his words, confused. The Queen had died years ago. But here she was, standing before him… with magic too.

Suddenly, the future vision came to his mind. He had seen *her*, there, in his future. At the time, he'd thought he was imagining it.

But this… There was no mistake. Time never made mistakes.

"Finish your time spell," she said softly.

Still in shock, Derek nodded. With the flow of time bubbling inside of him, he began to drain it from his heart, letting it seep into the world. Slowly, the world finished turning blue, until everything radiated a bright-blue light.

When the world was completely paused, Elyathi looked to him, then gave him a sweet smile. She closed her eyes. Slowly, the blue from her hair drained like water, revealing her true, pure white wavy locks of hair.

She opened her eyes. Her pupils were pure white with a hint of icy blue outlining them.

Her eyes… they are white. Derek recalled Elyathi's eyes were always a light blue. Had that been a trick?

Her startling eyes gave him an electrifying look, then she turned to the gifted frozen in time. She laid a hand on the nearest gifted, the orange-gifted man who Derek had spoken to first.

It appeared like nothing at first, but then Derek saw an orange light radiating from the orange-gifted's body. It burned brighter with each beat of Derek's heart, then it began funneling out of the man's body and into the palm of Elyathi's hand, until there was no more orange magic left in the man. All the orange features that the man had were gone—at least, that Derek could determine within the blue world.

The man had been completely drained of his magic. It was severed from his life force. During the magical transaction, Elyathi's hair had soaked in the orange magic. Derek reeled back. She now had the man's magic!

Queen Elyathi glanced at Derek, this time with burning orange eyes. Derek's heart began to beat wildly. Surely, this wasn't the Queen Elyathi he once knew… was it?

Derek watched as Elyathi yanked a chain from her neck, then drained her newly acquired orange magic into one of the many empty vials that hung from her neck. The orange color flowed out of her, returning her to her white form. She then walked over to two of the gifted, cutting their skin with a dirk from her dress pockets, then filled two vials with their blood. After filling them, she took their life force.

Derek stood in awe of her incredible power.

One by one, the former Arcadian Queen drained all the gifted of their magic and placed it into her empty vials. After she'd finished, she stuffed the vials back into the bustline of her dress. As she did so, Derek saw two larger vials that were empty. The gemstones around her neck shone in an assortment of colors.

"I'm finished, Derek, so you can release your magic anytime now," Elyathi said, walking over to him. She laid a hand on his shoulder, and Derek's heart beat fiercely with alarm as his gaze moved to her hand.

"I would never take your power, Derek," she assured him with a sad smile. "Only those who stand in our way."

Derek took a deep breath, still dumbfounded that Elyathi stood before him. Did she ever look like an older version of Emerald. It was uncanny, especially since he hadn't seen the Queen in years.

"I… I cannot believe you are alive," Derek managed to say.

"Yes, I have been alive all this time," Elyathi answered. She put her arm around him, then embraced him sweetly. He felt her hand over his hair, fixing his curls just like a mother would, admiring him with her stark white eyes. "When they told me I needed to retrieve someone here in this sector, I never expected that person to be you," she said breathlessly, giving him a warm, loving smile. "The God of Light is truly on our side." She hugged him gracefully once again.

Derek's cheeks burned slightly. "How did you get here? What happened back in Arcadia? I thought you were buried ten feet in the ground!"

Elyathi smiled softly. "Come. Let's leave this place, and we will talk."

Derek smiled back, then nodded.

"You can lift your time spell now," Elyathi reminded him. She grabbed a faintly glowing blue gemstone around her neck. The glowing power surrounded her, filling her with magic. Her eyes and hair turned blue.

As she did so, Derek released the tension within his life force, and the flow of time returned to the world, restoring everything back to full color and full motion.

The gifted, or those who *were* gifted, dropped like rocks, screaming in pain on the ground. They writhed in agony, yelling out nonsense and torturous cries. It was almost as if they were going mad from losing their gift.

Moving his gaze slowly to Elyathi, he met her eyes, and she gave him a private, subtle smile, then held out her hand, waiting for him to take it.

Derek accepted, taking her hand firmly. She clutched his hand tight in return. Her hands… they were so cold and so frail.

The screams and cries all around them continued, filling Derek's ears. Elyathi remained impassive, indifferent to their suffering.

Her hand squeezed his, and suddenly, brilliant blue magic surrounded them both, bathing them in its power.

Derek felt the sadness radiating within the magic—Elyathi's sadness. A sadness so sick and severe that Derek wanted to shed tears for her right there.

Then, in an instant, they were swept away in the blue dimensional magic, and the screams could no longer be heard.

***

The world around Derek materialized from the time-dimensional flash. Elaborate furnishings and sculpted marbled designs appeared around him; he was in someone's grand quarters.

Elyathi gently let go of his hand as the world around them stabilized. A servant was changing soft purple bedsheets, then jumped at the flash of magic.

"Lady Elyathi," the maidservant said, bowing quickly. "You frightened me. I was not expecting you."

"Yes, I had to come here urgently. Please send word to the clerk of the court to expect me."

"Right away." The maidservant bowed and immediately left the room.

Derek suddenly felt a wave of exhaustion, and his legs began to shake. He was exhausted, having only spent that amount of magic just a few times since receiving the magic. He needed more practice if he was to do that again. Or more power.

Elyathi gave him a knowing look, his face probably giving away his exhaustion. "Have a seat, Derek," she said, motioning to one of the sofas.

Derek did so willingly. Once seated, his eyes wandered around his surroundings, marveling at how lavish the old Queen of Arcadia's quarters were. Most of the chairs and sofas were silver, with cushions in a light lavender color. Translucent drapes hung from the ceiling, wisping in a light breeze from the open windows. The jewel-lined windows overlooked a marvelous courtyard with a fountain outside. The silver alone, along with the gemstones inlaid in many of the designs, was worth more money than he could even imagine, and far grander than any room in Arcadia.

"Queen Elyathi, have you been living here in this era? Are these your quarters?" Derek began, unsure of what to say. He was still in total disbelief that the Queen was, in fact, alive after all these years.

"Please, Derek, I do not want to be called Queen." Elyathi smiled softly. "It is a time that I wish to forget. People refer to me as Lady, but you may simply call me Elyathi. I need no title around you." There was a sadness behind her eyes; Derek felt it flowing from her life force. It was the same sick, deepening sadness he'd felt when they were immersed in her blue magic.

"Yes… Elyathi." Derek lowered his gaze, nodding.

She gave him a genuine smile and continued. "But to answer your question, yes, I have been here in this era since my disappearance."

All these years?

Derek turned to her. "We all thought you died. There was a funeral. All of Arcadia mourned you."

"It lightens my heart to know that I was missed. I do hope it was a heartwarming funeral."

"Unfortunately, my family was *barred* from the funeral." All because of Damaris. How he hated that man. The old king of Arcadia was just as bad and evil as Ikaria.

Bitterness came over Elyathi's face. "Of course. *He* was always irrational."

"Indeed he was. I had my own issues with Damaris," Derek added.

Elyathi began to tear up. "I hate that man. I *hate* him with every fiber of my being!" She started to pace around the room, probably to hide her tears from Derek. She poured herself a glass of water from a nearby pitcher. "I wasted years of my life with him. *Years.*"

Derek remained silent. What could he even begin to say to her to comfort her?

"I wish that he was *dead*," she continued, then turned to him with bloodshot eyes, taking a drink of her water.

Derek almost jumped back at the sight of her eyes, at the stark contrast of redness against her white pupils. "The worst of it is that my Emerald is back in time with him!"

Derek shifted in his seat, then cleared his throat. "Well, you will be happy to know that Damaris is dead. Ikaria killed him." *For my wedding present,* he wanted to add.

Elyathi's face lit up, and her tears stopped flowing. "Truly?"

"Yes. He's been dead for over two months now. That is, if you go by the time I just came from."

"How did he die? And Emerald? What of her?" Elyathi pressed. She took another drink of her water, then set it down, joining him on the sofa, sitting next to him. Her eyes were eager as she waited for him to speak. How would he even begin to tell her what had happened? It was all a mess.

"I don't even know where to begin…" Derek started.

"It doesn't matter where you start. I truly want to know everything."

Derek took a deep breath. What would Elyathi think about *everything* that had happened? Should he omit the worst of his own part in it?

No, he had to tell her. Everything.

Derek gazed at her tear-stained face, then he began.

"I am sure you were aware of York being barred from Arcadia years ago, ever since…" Derek paused, feeling awkward, considering Ikaria had told him that Elyathi had been having an affair with his father. "Since Damaris declared it for whatever reason," he said firmly.

Elyathi's eyes hardened. "The *supposed* affair," she said bitterly under her breath.

Supposed?

He paused, unsure if she planned to say anything of the matter, but she remained silent, waiting on him.

"Right." Derek cleared his throat. "Well, I'm sure you were well aware that I am in love with your daughter. I have been as long as I can remember, and always wanted to marry her. Even when we were excommunicated from the Arcadian court, I fought with my father vehemently to make my intentions known to Damaris and Emerald, but my father refused, and for many years he kept trying to persuade me to marry royals from other kingdoms. I flat-out refused each choice my father brought forth.

"After many years of being barred from Arcadia, Damaris finally gave York permission for a visit. My father gave me his blessing, so I visited the Arcadian court, making plans to propose to your daughter, hoping to marry the woman of my dreams, and also that our alliance could be restored to what it once was.

"Upon arriving at court, I found out almost immediately that Damaris had no intention of negotiating a marriage for Emerald. He'd deceived me. You see, he'd led me to believe otherwise. I proposed to Emerald in secret, and she agreed to marry me. We were in love, and I swore to her to do anything I could to make our marriage become a reality."

Elyathi's eyes softened, and a warm smile came upon her. "I always knew you loved my daughter," she said. "You were always so attentive to her. I saw it for many years as you two grew up."

Derek's cheeks flushed, burning with embarrassment. It was odd confessing his love to Emerald's mother. He lowered his eyes, still feeling the heat from his words. "Indeed, I had, and I could never hide my affections for your daughter." He coughed uncomfortably, then continued. "Unfortunately, Damaris found out about my secret proposal, and he forbade us from seeing each other. He put me under house arrest, and your daughter ran away into the heart of Arcadia. I found out later that had been Damaris's plan all along—to trap me in Arcadia to spite my father."

Elyathi eyes flashed with anger, but she said nothing in response.

"During that time, the Sorceress Ikaria started appearing in my thoughts and mind," Derek continued. "She… she also took hold of Damaris, possessing him. Through Damaris, she named me his heir, then killed him after my marriage to your daughter."

"You married Emerald, then?" Elyathi asked, struck by the news.

Derek paused, taking a deep breath. Sweat formed on his brow. How could he even begin to explain to her what had happened? Would Elyathi understand his perspective? Would she hate him just as much as Emerald hated him?

"Yes, but under horrible circumstances," he answered her.

Elyathi leaned in, confused. "I don't understand. Please, tell me what happened."

Derek began to sweat uncomfortably, and he shifted again in his seat. He ran his fingers through his curls, then wiped his brow.

It has come to this. He swallowed, then manned up.

"When Emerald ran away, she met a man in the lower levels of Arcadia. She was found and returned to the palace, but she declared she was in love with…" Derek clenched his teeth in anger, fighting his rage. "…with some *scumbag*!" he snapped. "A man who lurked in Arcadia's most dangerous clubs, with a history of drugs and public intoxication."

Elyathi looked mortified. "Emerald? After everything you did for her?"

Derek's anger rose in him, unsettling him just thinking about that man.

"Yes! She broke off our engagement and made it known that she would rather be with him than me. The whole time, the sorceress's magic…" He bitterly clenched his fists, shaking hard. The anger mixed with a deep sadness, causing his heart to sink, and he became sick all over again at the thought. How he hated what had happened. Tears welled in his eyes, and he shook with rage.

"What? What happened?"

Derek looked straight into Elyathi's white eyes. Her face. It looked so innocent, weighted down by the world. It looked the same as Emerald had looked ever since the incident.

Gathering courage, Derek continued, meeting her gaze. "That witch… she… she took control of my mind! She possessed me with her violet magic. I couldn't control my own body—only at certain times when she chose to give me control. But ultimately, she was the one with authority over me! Under her power, I married your daughter against her will."

Tears rolled down his face. Elyathi's eyes welled up with her own.

"The horrible thing is, I *wanted* to marry your daughter, and so I didn't really fight it. Not truly," he continued. "Whatever the witch held in front of me in my mind, it was like it was far better than reality, and I *wanted* it!" He struggled with his words as his throat tightened.

Then he began to sob uncontrollably. Derek didn't care at this point. What he said was true.

A blue-violet force came gushing out of Derek's soul in a wave that rocked the room. Chalices, pitches, tables, chairs rattled violently at the force.

"Derek?" Elyathi's soft voice said, trying to meet his eyes.

His stomach did jumps. He felt sick. Ashamed. How could he not be?

"I swear! It was not me!" Derek cried, clutching the arm of the sofa.

"Derek? What are you talking about?" Elyathi pressed. "The marriage?"

Derek shook his head, and new tears formed. "The witch…" he whispered. "The darkness that the witch instilled in me… the black magic mixed with her possession… I felt completely out of control when it came to *my* mind and *my* logic. In my mind, I was subjected to her twisted logic, her desires, her lusts… It was *my* body, but *her* mind!" he cried out. "She made me do it!"

Elyathi paused, then realization came over her face. Her lower lip quivered, and for a moment, Derek swore that she was going to jump up and suck away his power… or possibly his life. But what she did next, he did not expect.

"That evil, unholy, foul, despicable *hag*!" she said as if it were a curse. Her voice lowered to a dark whisper. "I knew the sorceress was a corrupt soul, what she was capable of, and the diabolic evil that flowed through her. I knew that she lived for her vile lusts and wicked pleasures. But this…" Elyathi clenched her jaw, her eyes flashing with wrath, sparkling with tears. "This… this is unforgivable. And for that, I will *destroy* her. I will take the sorceress's magic, then take her life! She will be crushed and reduced to nothing more than blood and bones for what she made you do to my daughter. That I swear!"

Derek found courage, looking up to meet her gaze, her cool look. In her eyes, he saw a burning love and admiration for him.

"I… I wasn't sure if you would believe me," Derek whispered, still shaking from his confession. "It was my body the witch used…"

"I believe you," Elyathi breathed. "I completely, wholeheartedly believe every single word you have confessed to me. I know you. I know who you are, and I know your heart."

At that moment, Derek felt her gentle hands on his cheeks, wiping away his tears. She hugged him, holding him in comfort. They wept softly in the silent room, their stifled tears the only sound, until he pulled away, looking at her.

"That is why you have come, isn't it?" Elyathi said in a steady, justified tone. "To change what happened."

Derek nodded, and his eyes narrowed at the mere thought of the sorceress. "I swear, I will make everything right. I already have a plan to make sure that your daughter will never suffer what she has suffered. If it weren't for that sorceress witch, none of it would have happened. I would never had been pushed, manipulated, and possessed. I did everything the witch forced me to do. And I have hated myself ever since."

A flood of emotions hit him all over again, and guilt filled every ounce of his body. It hurt what had happened. It hurt *bad*.

Their eyes met, as if they both understood one another.

"Elyathi, that is why I must rid time itself of Ikaria," Derek added. "She has damned everything, including me. I have seen different outcomes in the flow of time, at a point where I no longer wanted to live. But the flow of time also showed me something that renewed me. One possible outcome in another time and place, with Emerald and myself ruling happily, side by side, in a new kingdom. And Emerald… she loved me as she once did. We were together." He paused, thinking of Ikaria. "And I can tell you, that *witch* was not in that outcome."

Elyathi studied him for a long time. "I know exactly which outcome you speak of." She rose from her spot, then held out her hands to him. "You were meant to be with her. I have known it ever since you both were little. My daughter, infatuated with some drug-induced man… that is *not* her future! Those types of wretched, debauched men—they prey on vulnerable women! She is no more than a *toy* to those types." Her eyes met his evenly. "Together, we will change everything… it will be as if it never happened, that I promise."

He felt another pang of guilt. What she said, men preying on women, he had preyed on Emerald. But he was mind-controlled under the dark influence of Ikaria. She used his vessel for her own nefarious purposes…

Derek lowered his eyes. "Even after all that I have told you…" He trembled at his own words.

"Do not blame yourself," Elyathi said softly. "I do not. Darkness takes shape in many forms, and it has its way with us when we cannot fight it. It has been said in *The Spectrum*, and I know it to be true." She paused, gently touching his chin, lifting it. "The sorceress was the face of darkness—she welcomed sin, evil, and wickedness with an open heart. And she was the ultimate reason for what happened; you had nothing to do with it. What she did with you was *detestable*… using you as a mere joyride for her debauchery. And for that, she will pay!"

Derek paused, reflecting on her words. There was truth to those words. It *wasn't* his fault. All this time, he had been blaming himself and Ikaria. But why should he ever have blamed himself? It really was all the witch's fault. Her lusts, her evil desires, her dark mind possession. She'd pushed him! She *made* him. She *forced* him. If it weren't for her, none of it would have happened.

It was as if a burden lifted from his soul.

Derek took a breath, almost as if it were his first breath of life.

His brokenness… it was as if the pieces had come together in his soul, restored.

"There are people I would like you to meet," Elyathi said, interrupting his thoughts. "I think you will find them to your liking."

He knew exactly who she was referring to. "Is it the High Court?" Derek asked.

Elyathi looked surprised. “You know about them?”

“Ikaria told me all about them.”

“I’m sure it was all twisted, coming from her lips.”

“Everything that came out of her mouth was perverse,” Derek answered in agreement.

A thought came to him. Something Ikaria had told him. The High Court was after Emerald’s blood.

“Elyathi, there was something Ikaria told me. She said that the High Court was after Emerald’s blood.” He looked at her. “Tell me that isn’t true.”

Elyathi shook her head, then smiled. “The sorceress was indeed correct. They were after her.”

Derek’s face dropped. “But… why?”

Elyathi maintained eye contact with him for a moment, then moved to her window. “I have missed my daughter all these years, and it is long past time she was brought back to me. The High Court has been attempting to bring her back here. The time portal had been hidden to us… but now it is available, finally, after all these years.” Her voice softened. “With the help of Emerald’s blood, you and I, we can both achieve what we seek.”

Her words… everything about them surprised him.

“Truly?” Derek asked, curious.

“Absolutely. It has been prophesied in ancient manuscripts. One with the power of the white gift will restore magic to the heavens and create a new earth. One who erases our past transgressions, creating a place that can take away our sorrows and memories we no longer wish to remember. A place where time itself meets as one. One timeline.”

One timeline?

His thoughts shifted to one of his visions in the flow of time. The unfamiliar kingdom with Emerald at his side.

Was that the future Elyathi was referring to? He sure hoped so.

His train of thought shifted to Emerald. She had been left behind all this time. How could a time portal be hidden from the High Court? He didn’t understand it.

“Why couldn’t Emerald come with you when you left Arcadia?” he asked. “I don’t understand about the time portal being gone.”

Elyathi’s voice lowered. “When I was found in the palace by the High Court gifted, they had little time to spare, and they had to bring me back before they perished. As far as the time portal being hidden, there was a gifted who was concealing the portal's whereabouts. This blue-gifted, only he could make the portal that led to Emerald known to certain gifted who traveled within the space-time continuum." She sounded bitter.

"But this blue-gifted is gone now," she continued, "and we have found the portal. The High Court has been sending our blue-gifted back in time to retrieve my daughter." She paused, clearly aggravated. "But they haven't made it back. None have, as they have no idea how to find Emerald once they enter the portal. They end up perishing in that time."

She glanced at him, and her gaze melting into kind eyes. "But you, Derek, you don't understand how truly lucky it is that our paths have crossed. You are the link to Emerald; you have the power to bring her here. And it is apparent that you have already consumed her blood to stay alive in this time, yes?"

"Yes…" He was reluctant to admit it. "But I drank your daughter's blood without her knowing. With the mess that Ikaria has created back in our time, Emerald…" He choked on his words. "She wanted nothing to do with me."

She gave him a motherly hug, comforting him. Did it ever feel good to have someone understand what had really happened and not judge him by his dark deeds under the witch's influence.

"Elyathi…" Derek paused, looking to her. "How do you exist in this time if you don't have green blood? Or should I say, how did you survive back then?"

Elyathi smiled at the question, nodding. "Do not all colors of the light spectrum equal white? I have a little bit of each color in my life force. It is fully awakened each time I connect to a gifted's magic. But the magic remains dormant in my life force." She paused, eyeing him evenly. "That was how I remained fully intact back in Arcadia. The green magic of my life force sustained me. And those who brought me back in time must have known that as well, for they were well aware of certain prophecies regarding the white-gifted, the one to restore peace to the new world." She looked to him, taking a drink of water gracefully. "You must come with me and meet the High Court. I know for a fact that you could use their help, and they could use yours."

"If it means ridding the world of Ikaria and changing the past," Derek said, "I will gladly go to them."

"You will find them most agreeable."

Derek paused, thinking about what Ikaria had told him about the High Court and the disappearance of magic. The witch was right about that; Derek had witnessed Elyathi herself stealing those gifteds' magic away firsthand, and he knew she was aligned with the High Court.

"Why do you steal magic from others?"

"It pertains to the prophecy I mentioned earlier."

"But why?" he pressed.

"Because man is not meant to be trusted with great power. Many times in earth's history, the gifted sought to become greater, while the common man killed for power. There have been wars because of magic. Even the Lord of Darkness fought the God of Light to get more power, almost destroying heaven and earth. It causes nothing more than chaos with the colors distributed amongst humankind." Her eyes watered, then she went on. "Think of all that took place, even in your case. What would have happened if Emerald had not been born with the gift?"

Derek thought hard. *Everything would have been different.* "I guess the events in time would have been much different."

"Precisely." She leaned in. "Damaris wouldn't have kept our daughter locked up the way he kept me locked up, there would have been no experiments on her, and the sorceress would never have been after her. She probably would have been sent to York, and you would have had a grand wedding."

"What makes you think that Damaris wouldn't have kept Emerald locked away? He kept you confined to the palace. Was it because of your magic?"

"He never knew of my gift… His reasonings were very… different." Her face trembled, and her eyes began to water. "Regardless, the gift should be taken from this earth and entrusted to those who can re-form our world into something better without it."

"Who do you trust? This High Court?" Derek asked.

"I only trust myself," she said firmly. "However, I do think the High Court has the right idea of taking away the gift and only giving it to those willing to submit to their laws, those who are obedient. Only a handful of people to fully strive for the utopia we seek."

"Is that why you work with the High Court? Because of this utopia?"

"Yes… and no. I was stolen from this time, and I waited for almost my whole life to come back. You see, the tribe that brought me back in time left me, abandoned me out in the wastelands. They promised they would come back for me." Her words became bitter. "But no one came. I was left to be found and tormented by the King of Arcadia. I was warned by the earth-dwellers from this time. They told me of the High Court and how evil they were, that they were the ones I needed to hide from.

"But it turned out my saving grace was the High Court. They were not the evil ones; it was the earth-dwellers who stole me who ended up being the evil ones. And because the High Court rescued me back in time, I owe them my servitude." She kept her face even. "But even though I side with them, I am not blind to humankind, including the gifted. Anyone can become corrupt, and innocent hearts can turn dark. As I see it, most all gifted have no light left in their souls. And as a penance, I gladly take away their gift, working to fulfill the ultimate prophecy to mankind and the gifted."

Derek absently shifted back from her, and she caught sight of him. "Do not worry, Derek. I won't be taking your gift. Your heart... though it is burdened with heaviness, I do feel the purity that lies within your soul. We will change everything."

Derek nodded, feeling hopeful, and also relieved. Her face gave him the drive to set things in motion to make the new utopia a reality.

"When can I talk to this High Court?" Derek asked.

"I sent my servant ahead. We can go after I finish my tea."

He nodded.

"And Derek," Elyathi said.

"Yes?"

She leaned toward him. "Do not mention the new world as one timeline."

"Why? I thought you said that's a part of the High Court's goal?"

"The new world and fulfilling the prophecy, that is their goal," Elyathi said. "But one timeline... that is something entirely different."

Derek paused, then nodded. "I will not breathe a word of it. I promise you."

She smiled warmly at his response. "I know you won't. You have always been so devoted and loyal."

Derek flushed red, feeling the burn in his cheeks.

Elyathi noticed and sought to reassure him, holding out her hand. "You know what, I don't need my tea. Let's go meet the High Court, shall we?"

"I am ready."

He took her hand, and a vibrant blue magic enveloped his being. His soul was uplifted. Everything was falling into place for what he had foreseen.

CHAPTER 42

RED

Rubius had made up his mind during dinner. It was decided. In the morning, he would leave and go see for himself the remnants of World Sector One. Maybe, just maybe, the sorceress was telling the truth, and he would find some sort of clue to confirm his far-fetched dreams.

He felt spent. Tired, exhausted, and confused. After only two confrontations with the sorceress, he was getting nowhere with her. He was *supposed* to be getting inside the sorceress's mind, not the other way around. Belinda would call upon him soon, no doubt, if he wasn't making any progress. Rubius was willing to bet that the fanatical Lady Elyathi was reporting his every failure.

It's a good thing she's gone now, he thought. *Gives me a chance to go check it out.*

Rubius entered his quarters. Zaphod made a squawking noise, reminding him that he had been left alone all day. Rubius felt a pang of guilt; his companion was hungry and lonely.

He walked over to his parrot, stroking his crimson feathers, then pulled out a handful of seeds.

"Yeah, I know," Rubius said to the bird as he ate. "Sorry, my friend."

He heard Zaphod's appreciation through his thoughts, and the bird cooed in response from the affection, continuing to eat. Rubius couldn't hear and understand any other animal's thoughts; he didn't know if the violet gift allowed humans to hear animals' thoughts like it did for people. But somehow, with this bird specifically, he could understand Zaphod's thoughts.

They weren't in clear, precise sentences, nor did they have structure like human language. It was more like a feeling of words jumbled together. Rubius had heard Zaphod's thoughts the moment they met, and he knew then that he had to have Zaphod. Rubius knew, deep down in his life force, that Zaphod was his bird, through and through. Luckily, Zaphod's previous owner was hurting for coin, and Rubius hadn't gambled his away at that moment in time, so it was an easy transaction.

After Zaphod finished a handful of seeds, Rubius loosened his boot laces and shook them off. He threw his cape to floor, poured himself a large chalice of wine, and downed it. Looking at the bed, Rubius was reminded of how truly exhausted he was. He plopped onto the bed, then looked up at the ceiling while sinking into the soft blankets.

"I was wondering when you were going to come back to your quarters," said a female voice.

Startled, Rubius jolted up, his eyes carefully scanning the room.

Why didn't I didn't see her when I entered? He could only guess why. His mind had been so muddled from recent events.

"Lady Aurora. What are you doing here?" Rubius called out.

Before his eyes, the image of a young woman came into view, surrounded by a dazzling orange glow. After the power settled, she flipped her long orange hair back behind her shoulder, flashing him a sweet, seductive smile, her eyes sparkling.

"What do you mean, what am I doing here? You sent for me," her voice mocked softly, like crashing water in a raging ocean. "It's been awhile, hasn't it?"

"Yes, it has been awhile," he admitted. He had dropped off the message for her early in the day, and here Aurora was, by nightfall, standing before him. *That was quick. She must have some good connections with a blue-gifted.*

Aurora came stalking toward him in a very predatory sort of way. She stood before him, running a finger down his face lightly. Her finger reached the bottom of his chin, and she gently tapped his jaw, leading his line of sight upward.

Her well-endowed bosoms were right in Rubius's line of sight, the cut of her dress revealing a good portion of them.

It couldn't be helped. Rubius looked and was immediately aroused. An image of the green-gifted woman came to his mind. Rubius averted his eyes from Aurora.

"I missed you," she breathed as she ran her hands down the front of his shirt, burying it inside the neckline. Her fiery touch rubbed against his chest as she knelt in front of him to meet his gaze. Her hand never left the inside of his shirt, and she began caressing his chest playfully. He wanted her, but he was also extremely confused. Her hand grazed across his skin, stimulating him.

His dreams… the green-gifted woman. He couldn't get her out of his mind. Rubius had called Aurora because he wanted sex badly. But now, with her being here, and with his dreams suddenly feeling real…

Rubius glanced down at her hand on his chest hesitantly, then lightly pushed it away. "I… I made a mistake."

"I don't believe you. How many times have you said that to me, and yet you continue to sleep with me?" Aurora smiled, her orange eyes burning with desire.

"We haven't been together in a while, and I have wanted you," Rubius stated. "But in truth, I think this time, I can't go through with it. I think…" A thought of the green-gifted woman flashed in his mind. "…this time it's different."

"I've missed your body terribly," Aurora said, leaning in. Her cleavage was practically spilling out of her dress and into his face. The sight of her breasts, along with her provocative words, make his loins ache. It had been a long time…

Because of his dreams.

"Look," Rubius said, patting her away gently, "I said I made a mistake, and I am sorry that I have wasted your time. You know that our arrangements have always been about personal needs, nothing more. I just wanted you out of sheer convenience, and this time was no different. My heart's just not in it."

She leaned into him, but Rubius pushed her back softly. "I'm serious, Aurora. We can't keep meeting. I swear, I'm done."

Aurora eyed him with a captivating glance, then took a few step back. She started glowing with her orange magic, bathing herself within its power. The orange energy flowed over her body, running over every inch of her skin, her hair, her eyes… the slow transformation of Aurora melted away, forming a new woman.

It was *perfect.* It was the exact image of the green-gifted woman.

Rubius stopped all movement, staring.

"You want to be done when you can have this?" she whispered.

The image of the green-gifted woman was irresistible, tempting every sensation in his body. The long wavy, emerald-green hair flowed at her sides, her porcelain skin and bright-green eyes; it was the exact image he had seen in his dreams. And her lips, they were perfect. So, so kissable. Rubius could not see a hint or glimmer of Aurora's orange illusion magic. Aurora must have gotten a power boost from the High Court.

It was as if the green-gifted woman was standing there before him, in the flesh. Rubius's heart began to pump wildly.

Aurora knew exactly how to fashion herself to him, for he had once allowed her in his mind so that he could show her what the green-gifted mystery woman looked like. It was like this with all the other orange-gifted women he fooled around with. But Aurora, she never made a mistake. She was flawless… No, it was the green-gifted woman who was flawless.

It was as if Aurora was nowhere to be found, and the green-gifted woman was truly there…

Ever so slowly, the green-gifted woman reached for her bodice and began loosening it, then dropped it to the floor. Her perfect round breasts were exposed, and Rubius went hard. The sight of her pink nipples against the creamy-white color of her skin made his cock throb. Her nipples were the same color as her lips, soft and desirable. He fought the urge to bite his fist.

She continued to strip off her clothes, each piece dropping to the floor until she was fully nude and standing before him playfully. Rubius wanted to tell her to get out, but the words wouldn't form.

"You don't even have to touch me. That way you won't feel so bad," her soft, flirtatious voice said playfully, as she ran her hand down her neck. It traveled in a downward motion, brushing over a hardened nipple, then lower to where her womanhood was.

Her eyes… those captivating, entrancing eyes. Rubius's mind was one big cesspool of confusion, and he just wanted to sink deep into it.

The image of the green-gifted woman walked slowly to him. His heart continued pumping wildly in his chest, his brow beaded with sweat. He reached into his jacket for his flask and immediately downed what he had. Whenever he was in doubt, Rubius took the bottle, for it made him think more clearly.

The green-gifted woman stood in front of him, her thigh lightly brushing against his leg, making Rubius lose all sense of reality. She magnificently tossed her long tresses back, revealing every aspect of her flesh, tempting Rubius to indulge in his desires.

Rubius wanted to explode.

Her eyes locked on his, capturing his desire, his lust. She ran one of her hands upward to her breast and squeezed as the other hand toyed with her lowers.

He couldn't take it anymore. Obliging his lustful cravings, Rubius loosened the laces of his pants, slipped his hand inside, and gripped his hardness. The green-gifted woman smiled deviously at him, continuing to passionately play with herself as he stroked his member.

"I want you inside of me," she begged loudly.

Her voice. It wasn't her voice. It was Aurora's voice.

Rubius snapped out of his fantasy. He went limp, and quickly removed his hand from his pants. He became angry. Really angry. Angry at her. And angry at himself for letting himself be fooled.

"Get out," Rubius growled. He started lacing up his pants hastily.

The image of the green-gifted woman melted away, and Aurora stood before him, just as naked as her illusion. The sight of her only added fuel to the fire.

"I don't think you really mean that, do you?" Aurora shot back. "I know what you like, and it's not like we haven't done this before."

"I'm going to give you one more warning." Rubius narrowed his eyes, his body shaking with rage. "Get *out*."

Aurora grabbed her clothes off the floor. "What's with you? You could have *any* woman at court, and yet you indulge in strange fetishes over a fantasy woman who doesn't exist!"

Rubius grabbed his flask and threw it at Aurora, purposely missing her. "I said, get *out*!" he roared, getting to his feet. Rubius grabbed another chalice, pouring wine in it and slurping it. "If I wanted a whore, I could have hired one!" he said, pointing to her.

"You treat me like one, do you not?"

Rubius stormed around the room. "I never want to see you ever again!" he shouted, taking his chalice and throwing it to the other side of her, hitting the wall.

"You are a pompous prick, you know that?" Aurora yelled back as she hastily threw on her clothes.

"I always told you that I was," Rubius shot back. Whether she heard his response, he would never know, as the door soon slammed shut, leaving him in silence.

All he wanted to do was punch a wall. Burn something or decimate things with his magic. Aurora had always agreed to their sexual excursions *willingly.* She'd pushed him, begged him, and like a damn fool, Rubius gave in almost every time, because he had needs to fulfill. But this was the very reason why he *didn't* want to give in to her—she was a body, nothing more, and he knew he couldn't give her what she wanted from him. A commitment. And this time, it didn't feel right. He had made a mistake sending for her, and seeing her in person, he knew they were done. Permanently.

All he really wanted was whoever the hell the green-gifted woman was. The Queen of Arcadia, who no longer *existed.*

Why did he have to be in love with a dream?

Zaphod cawed in the corner, interrupting his thoughts. It was as if Zaphod knew what he was thinking. At times Zaphod seemed to understand him more than he did. The bird probably figured his master was becoming more unraveled by the hour. And his pet was right. Soon there would be nothing left of Rubius's mind, considering he was being consumed by his burning desire for a fantasy.

Rubius walked over to Zaphod, then set him on his shoulder, petting him. He grabbed his harp, seating himself in front of the fireplace, gazing into the sparkling orange flames as he situated himself to play the instrument.

Kyle... That's what she'd called him. *Who is this Kyle?*

He closed his eyes, playing the melody that he always played when thinking of her. The song flowed through him, and the words came out of his lips, like weaving a spell. She needed to hear his song, his desire for her.

In a sad way, Rubius knew it would be all in vain; she would never hear him. But that was what he desired in his heart, for the Queen of Arcadia to hear his words. Zaphod snuggled his feathered head against Rubius's cheek as he played and played, all while staring at the magical flames.

In the morning, he would go see for himself the remnants of World Sector One.

CHAPTER 43

VIOLET

Ikaria groaned in ecstasy as she climaxed. She breathed heavily, then shuddered, rolling her eyes back from the pleasure. Removing her sticky fingers from her lowers, she lay there, catching her breath.

Lying on her back on the stone bed, Ikaria focused her eyes, blinking a few times. They were still blurry from doing the nasty deed. How she hated pleasuring herself. It was far more enjoyable for a man to pleasure her than for her to do it herself. Most of the fun came from the man's pure enjoyment, his lust for her flesh, his hard desire. But what else was she to do? She was bored and hadn't been played with in months now. She would even go so far as to settle for one without blond hair—that was how desperate she was. If only she had orange magic, then she could at least conjure up an image of one while pleasuring herself.

Ikaria lazily held out her hand, touching her magical barrier, studying it as if it were the first time seeing it. She almost admired it.

Finally, she had found a weakness in the barrier. Her mind was the key. The magical barrier did indeed suppress her magic, and it had allowed the High Inquisitor's magic inside the barrier to harm her as he saw fit. But the magical barrier could not suppress her consciousness from jumping into his, because there was no *mental* barrier, only a physical barrier. One couldn't possibly enchant a mental barrier; it had to be enchanted into the human consciousness, which was impossible in itself.

She had finally found a flaw in her magical prison, and she'd used it to her advantage. The High Inquisitor had established a link between their minds, creating a clear path straight to his consciousness, bypassing that physical magical barrier. Though the High Inquisitor was gifted himself, and though it had always been hard for Ikaria to seep into a gifted's mind, she had done it. It seemed his mind was *damaged.*

Ikaria laughed to herself. It was all too much. The High Inquisitor held a secret. A secret he didn't even know he had. She had seen his identity—his *soul*—through his complex mind of labyrinths and mazes, all made up of lost memories. And those memories had woven the many stairs and locked doors that made up his consciousness. It was all one big giant puzzle woven intricately together. But within that labyrinth of his mind was a door, only one, that had been opened just a sliver. And in the moment Ikaria had been deep inside his complex mind, she had used her magic, yanking on that opened door with her violet force, trying to get inside. The door cracked open a hair more, just enough for Ikaria to see the shadow of a certain memory of his past life.

She fully intended to use that memory to break him. She was already well on her way to doing so. She had planted the seed, and she could tell from the last time she saw him that he was a mess.

Love is so disheartening at times, Ikaria thought indifferently. But she had to rely on that thought. The High Inquisitor would see that what she had told him was accurate, and slowly, he would consider the notion of breaking her out of her musty cell.

Ikaria's thoughts turned to her sister. Such a fool she was. Ikaria always knew she would have been the better ruler. It inflamed her that her dunce of a sibling made World Sector Six look so weak. Their father would have been rolling in his grave if he knew the recent chain of events. What a shame. But even with her hatred of her sister, Ikaria still had feelings for Ayera. After all, they were blood. What she had told Suri and Auron was true; she could not stand the High Court to make a mockery of her family, even if it was her sister, who she'd despised at many times in her life.

Ikaria had no choice but to act like she didn't care what happened to Ayera in front of the High Inquisitor. She did it so that they wouldn't make it harder on Ayera. If Ikaria had shown an ounce of care on her face, she knew very damn well they would harm her sister while they held her. Or, if they were to execute her, they would do so much sooner than intended if Ikaria showed any sort of affection. After everything was done and settled, then

Ikaria could lecture Ayera about how wrong she was, and how right *she* was. Then she would take her rightful place as empress and make her sister serve her.

But first she had to get out of her godforsaken box.

Suri had best have gotten to the airship by now, unless that bumbling priest somehow convinced her otherwise.

How she hated that priest. Auron was nothing but trouble.

Suddenly, there was a click, and the door opened for a brief moment, then shut again.

A man walked through barrier. It clung to him like gel as the door was shut behind him. Ikaria groaned. As the magical gel pulled away and sprung back into place, Ikaria looked upon the man she hated most.

"Isn't this a sight," Cyrus said, as if he had been the one who contained her himself. "The disgraced sorceress, suppressed. Her power contained in this little enchanted barrier." His magenta eyes glowed as he gave a haughty laugh.

"Well, if it isn't the pathetic Emperor himself," Ikaria said unenergized. "Tell me, was it cold in my room all those hours until they found you?"

A look of anger came over him as he stomped neared her barrier, towering over her. "You should talk." He raised his head highly. "It was a good thing we were never married, you and I. You are nothing more than a glorified *whore* that caused nothing but problems."

"A whore? Is that what you call it?" Ikaria snorted. "I personally like to call it a woman with options. Really, Cyrus, you were always so unoriginal." Ikaria looked directly at him. "You always had to compensate for your incredibly small manhood. I'm sure you left all your little sluts completely unsatisfied. At least I am well-endowed." She ran her hands across her large breasts, almost in a taunting fashion.

Cyrus gritted his teeth, his eyes flashing with hatred. "Do you know how much you humiliated me?"

Ikaria rolled her eyes. "Humiliated you? Why don't we revisit all the things you did to me, and then my sister. You will find an incredibly long list. It's quite extensive, really."

"Leaving you to marry your sister was *nothing* compared what you did to me."

"I have to disagree with you."

"I am your emperor! You will address me as so!"

"You are foolish to think I would ever address you as such. You are nothing more than a coward, hiding behind the High Court like a dog, sniffing for scraps," Ikaria spat sharply.

Cyrus neared her barrier, almost within reach.

Ikaria looked at him indifferently. "What are you going to do? Use your pathetic pink magic on me? Not even the High Inquisitor could get me. Did you see his face as he left? I found it quite amusing."

"I'm not going to use my magic on you. No. Instead, I am going to humiliate you. You always thought you were in charge. You will soon learn that I'm in charge, and always will be in charge, and there is *nothing* you can do about it."

Cyrus quickly unlaced his breeches, then pulled out his manhood, fully exposing himself.

Ikaria laughed. "What do you think you are doing? Put it away. I find yours most uninteresting." She waved nonchalantly.

He gave her a dark smile, then he was standing over her. He start urinating. His urine stream went through the magical barrier like nothing, splashing directly on her face.

For a moment, she was too shocked to do anything.

He was *urinating* on her. She blinked, then she came to her senses. He'd urinated on her. Wrath ripped through her life force. He'd urinated on her.

He was going to regret ever being born.

Ikaria unleashed her fury in the form of a burst of violent time magic, halting any motion within. Time had stopped within the barrier, including his urine stream, but she remained animated.

Surprised, Cyrus leaked the last of his golden stream, with the remainder of it stilling of motion when it entered her barrier time-capsule. Then, with another burst of magic, with her wrath underlying her power, she froze his time-halted urine stream, and it became one solid form of ice.

Cyrus hastily laced up his breeches. "You bitch!" he roared at her. "Since when do you have other magics? I thought you were stripped clean of all other powers?"

Indeed, she had been stripped of her powers at the cleansing of Queen Emerald. But what the arrogant ass didn't know was that when she was purified, her blood was renewed, and she was now how a gifted should be… with analogous powers.

"Answer me, you disgraceful cunt!"

"Why don't you come inside my little personal bubble and tell me how you really feel," Ikaria snapped. "I *dare* you."

"You won't have any magic left once the High Inquisitor and that white-gifted is done with you!" Cyrus threatened.

"Oh? I'm so frightened," Ikaria mocked sarcastically. "Do you see me trembling with fear?"

The mere thought of her last encounter with the High Inquisitor made her burst out in laughter, and it echoed through the cell. She even rolled over the frozen urine, but it mattered not.

"You laugh? You think this is a joke?"

"You know damn well I think you're a joke." Ikaria looked at him, then narrowed her eyes. "But mark my words, you will be sorry for what you just did to me."

"You will never get out of here." Cyrus laughed haughtily. "You don't even have a fool's hope. Just you wait for that white-gifted. You will be sorry you were ever born with magic, you little cunt!"

"Oh, I will get out of here, you can count on that. After I crush the High Court and all their little lemmings, I will come for you. I will hunt you down personally. No matter where you go, where you hide, I will find you. And you will regret you ever crossed paths with me." Ikaria breathed, sucking in the smell of urine. Even his urine stench was disgusting and vile. "I will make you relive your worst moments over and over again. I will be your ultimate nightmare, that you can be sure of."

Cyrus stared at her for a moment, and Ikaria caught a glimmer of seriousness on his face. Then he smiled. "That is, of course, *if* you still have your gift." He turned away, about to leave. "Who would be the pathetic one then?" He turned back to her. "I wonder, where is that servant of yours? Suri is her name? Oh, that's right. We just locked her up in these same dungeons. If you are lucky, maybe you will hear the bitch scream your name."

Ikaria forced herself to make no sudden gesture, but her stomach sank.

He has to be bluffing, she reassured herself.

Cyrus gave her a knowing look, then laughed, knocking on the door.

Before he exited, he turned back, saying, “I will make sure Suri is *well* taken care of.”

He raised his chin high as if he had won, and walked through the magical barrier. Ikaria heard the guards open the door. He laughed all the way down the corridor.

Suri… Had she indeed been captured? Ikaria's mood darkened.

No one would dare harm Suri.

Yes, Cyrus had urinated on her, and she would see him pay for that disgusting deed. But harming Suri? If the bastard harmed her servant in any way, Ikaria would be his personal *hell.* She would castrate that man. Take his manhood and *burn* it in front of him. Perhaps she would eat it, or better yet, make *him* eat it. Then she would kill him. A slow death, one she would enjoy moment by moment, with the help of her adjacent blue magic.

That she vowed with every ounce of her life force.

Cyrus would pay.

CHAPTER 44

GREEN

Let's get you changed." Glacia came marching into Emerald's quarters, all the other handmaidens trailing behind her.

"Why?" Emerald asked, removing her circlet from her head. Emerald had just finished her dinner with Emerys, and all the talk of what was happening had made her even more distressed than before.

"We are going out," Glacia announced.

Emerald gave Glacia a stunned look, almost scoffing. "I can't go out. There are so many things happening at court. Tensions with the other kingdoms are high, especially with Olympia. With the arguments about the cyborgs and an army that could be at our doorstep at any moment… you want me to just abandon the palace for evening to enjoy myself? I cannot do that, Glacia," Emerald said, her voice tense. And she wanted to add *because I am pregnant and don't have the energy*, but the words stayed in her head.

"That is exactly why you need to get out," Glacia said pointedly. "Everything that is happening is getting to you, and your judgment has become clouded. You are overthinking every single situation, and now you cannot think straight because you are so stressed out. You need to step away and clear your thoughts."

"Glacia, I appreciate your concern, but it would seem utterly reckless of me as a queen to go out and try to enjoy myself." She took a deep breath, then sighed, gazing into the hazel eyes of her servant. "I can't… I just can't."

Her eyes began to tear up, but Emerald sniffled them away quickly.

Inside her womb, she could have sworn there was movement. Perhaps it was a cramp…

"You need a break from *everything*, My Queen. Including a break from *life*," Glacia fought back. "I cannot watch you waste away into nothing day after day, seeing your heart and spirit broken. You are becoming an empty shell with no spirit left, and it breaks my heart seeing you with no joy, and no dreams! You won't even *be* a queen if you have no spirit left to fight!" She stepped forward, giving her a serious glance. "Your people need you. They need a leader! And here you are, locked away in your room, just like how your father locked you away… but this time it is by your choice."

Emerald's eyes darted at her.

Glacia paused, and her face softened. "You need to breathe, and you need to laugh. It's good for you. After you clear your head, then you can step up and *lead*."

Was Emerald truly becoming nothing? Just an empty vessel? The more she assessed Glacia's words, the more they resonated with her. She hadn't cared about anything since Kyle died, her soul fractured. Making it through every day was a chore, and her energy was slowly being drained from her.

Emerald's eyes met Glacia's, and her best friend laid a hand on her shoulder, smiling sadly at her. "I am worried about you…" Glacia's voice trailed off. "Please. It's only one evening. There is nothing better than music to cheer you up. And I'm not referring to his music," she added quickly. "You need to laugh and enjoy what life has left for you. Tomorrow, you can think about all these imposing issues with the kingdom. But it will be with a clear head."

Emerald looked to her other handmaidens, and they all gave her sad but hopeful smiles. Emerald could see the worry in all of them. Her eyes trailed back to Glacia, then she nodded.

"Okay, Glacia. I will do this," she said.

Glacia smiled brightly, excited. "You won't regret it, promise."

"But I will have to bring several guards with me just in case," Emerald said. "I can't just go out by myself, especially right now, while things are playing out."

"Of course. But they don't have to be wearing palace uniforms, do they? That will really cramp our style. And that'll just bring attention to us."

"I will ask them not to," Emerald said. *What is Emerys going to say about this? He's probably going to have a heart attack.*

Her handmaidens ran to their bedrooms excitedly, talking happily. Glacia smiled at Emerald, then motioned for her to turn around so she could help her get changed. Glacia unlaced her bodice, then she stepped out of it, heading over to her walk-in wardrobe.

Emerald lightly brushed her hand across the portion of her closet dedicated to unique fashions. It had been a while since Emerald stepped inside her own wardrobe. At one time, she'd proudly collected any outfits that were unusual and unique to her, even though she never wore any of it. That was, except for the time she left the palace and met Kyle. Now, her unique collection of garments just hung in her closet, collecting dust, forgotten.

Sifting through the clothes, Emerald pulled out a shiny purple corset with a matching miniskirt and a pair of high boots. The outfit reminded her of the lower levels when she was with Kyle. As much as she would love to wear it, it would be uncomfortable in her condition. She set them back in their place and picked up a tight but stretchy silver mini dress. One sleeve puffed out wildly; the other side left her bare. She looked at her shoes, thinking that all of them looked rather high for her tired feet, but she chose to brave a high pair of silver heels. After all, she was only a couple months pregnant. What was the worst that a pair of heels could do to her?

She slipped on her outfit, then went to her mirror, tossing her hair up in a high ponytail, securing it with a big matching bow. She decorated her bare arm with a silver armband, then chose large dangling earrings. Her eyelids she colored with several bright eye shadows. Magenta lipstick finished the look.

Emerald glanced at her reflection. All dressed up. Her eyes darted to her hair color. She could try and change it to disguise herself. She had done so in the past, just by sucking in her life force and focusing it deep within her core. But what of the new life forces inside of her? What if she sucked theirs away as well?

No, I dare not try, she told herself. *I am queen now. Why should I have to hide who I am?*

As she glanced at her reflection one last time, she saw her handmaidens behind her in the mirror. She turned around. They were all dressed up for the evening with similar attire.

"Glacia, please inform the councilor that we will be leaving with several guards for a few hours," Emerald ordered. "Tell him not to worry."

Glacia nodded, then quickly disappeared into the sitting room, probably dialing her device.

When Glacia finished the transmission, the group left her quarters, walking through the halls until they reached the royal receiving platform, which was only used for the king, his court, and special envoys and royalty from the other kingdoms.

As she entered the royal air transport, Emerys came running up to the vehicle with several guards.

"My Queen! What is going on? What are you doing?" Emerys asked, out of breath.

"I am going out for the night."

"At a time like this?" Emerys exclaimed incredulously.

"It is precisely why I am getting out," Emerald said.

"Pardon me for saying so, but are you out of your mind? First the King goes off to who knows where, and now you are going out with your ladies to go have fun? What is going on with this kingdom?"

What *was* going on with the kingdom? And did she have the heart and strength to make a difference?

Emerald sighed, her thoughts flickering between the loss of Kyle, the betrayal of a friend who crossed a line, and the imposing doom of the kingdom.

"Councilor, I cannot bear the... the sadness that lingers within these walls. I have to breathe."

He eyed her with his steel-gray eyes, and the two exchanged unspoken words. After a long pause, he sighed, then finally bowed. She held out her hand for him to kiss it in reverence. "Yes, My Queen. Just, please, be careful."

"I am taking several guards."

He shook his head. "The Inner Council will be up in arms when they hear of this."

"Tell them not to worry."

Emerys shot her a glance. "That won't go over well, Your Majesty." He sighed. "I... I am worried for you. You are the remainder of our kingdom, and I couldn't forgive myself if something happened to you."

Emerald smiled at him. "It seems everyone is worried about me."

"Yes, we all are, Your Majesty."

"Councilor, I will be fine. I highly doubt anyone could hurt me. I have magic, do I not?"

"That you do," he said doubtfully.

"Just a few hours. That is all," Emerald said. "I promise not to make you worry for too long."

He stared at her, then bowed lowly. "Yes, My Queen. Please send word when you return."

"I will," she promised.

He moved off to the side of the platform with his string of guards, watching as her air transport took off. She looked back at all her handmaidens, who were all giggling, excited for their nightly adventure. They had never experienced a night together outside the palace, and they were thrilled.

A cramp hit Emerald's stomach, but she did her best to ignore it. "Where exactly are we going?" she asked Glacia.

"Somewhere in the mid-levels. I have a surprise there waiting for you."

Emerald raised her eyebrow. "Surprise?"

Glacia smiled brightly. "Nuh-uh. I'm not saying anything. You'll just have to wait and see."

Emerald looked out the window, watching their transport being submersed in the city, flying across the sky. Neon lights filled her window, and other flashes of color streamed inside. Cyndi sat on the other side of the transport, tapping her window excitedly.

The transport wove through the city toward the southern sector. After about twenty-five minutes or so, the transport lowered itself in the tangled mass of skyways and buildings, landing on a platform in the mid-levels, just like Glacia said. When it came to a complete stop, the door flung open, letting out the guards first, then the women. Three men surrounded Emerald, and the other handmaidens had two guards with them.

Emerald followed Glacia, who led them down the main strip of the platform. They passed by shops, bars, nightclubs, and restaurants, all busting at the seams with business. Endless flashing advertisements glowed brightly throughout the platform. Crowds of people went to and from the mid-level shops. Several of them stopped and stared at her, and some whispers questioned if she was the true Queen of Arcadia who passed by them.

Glacia stopped in front of a nightclub, its bright sign shining in hot blues. Lines of people waited outside, and the city advertisements' lights shone on the group.

"I have everyone on the guest list," Glacia said proudly.

"Not like that would even matter. We have the Queen with us," Celeste whispered with a giggle to the other handmaidens.

"Come on," Glacia continued, waving to them excitedly.

They approached the front of the line, walking past everyone. Emerald's undercover guards approached the bouncer, exchanging some heavy words with the huge man. He nodded, gesturing for them to go inside.

They entered a dark room completely illuminated by pink neons. Across the room was a dance floor with platforms throughout the venue. Women hardly dressed in anything danced seductively on the platforms, and the floor was packed with people dancing and drinking, enjoying themselves.

Glacia led them to a bar lit up in neons, painting the whole atmosphere in blues and violets. As they approached, Emerald recognized several guys sitting there, and her eyes lit up.

Glacia ran over to the familiar faces, then kissed one of the guys. Emerald stood dumbfounded.

Glacia had kissed… Remy?

Emerald blinked to make sure she hadn't imagined it, but it was true. Glacia positioned herself right in Remy's arms.

"This is your surprise!" Glacia exclaimed, pointing to Kyle's former band members and friends. Diego, Remy, Kamren… they were all there.

"How…" Emerald approached them, looking between each of the band members and Glacia.

"Em! How the hell have you been?" Diego said, taking a drink from a paper bag while slapping her shoulder in a friendly gesture. He stopped. "Oh shit. I forgot you're royal and all that shit." He leaned in. "Do I have to say 'Your Highness?' Because I'm pretty fucking wasted right now, and I'm feeling pretty fucked." He laughed, taking another drink.

Emerald shook her head, smiling at him. "No, no, please don't. I don't want to be addressed like that. Not here."

Diego smiled. "Good. Cause I'll forget to say that shit anyway." He looked at her hair, eyeing her. "Green hair. Looks fucking dope. I still can't get over the fact that you're a royal and stayed at that shithead's place. Kyle was always one lucky son of a bitch."

Emerald looked down at the sound of his name, and Kamren punched Diego's arm.

"Why do you have to go and open your damn mouth?" Kamren said. "Can you fucking use your brain when it matters, shithead?"

Diego got in his face. "I miss that asshole just as much as everyone else! He was my best bud, or did you forget about that? Besides, I'm drinking this to remember him," he said sharply to his friend, raising his paper bag. He pulled out a bottle of whiskey, showing everyone the label. "*This* was my man's favorite poison. I'm drinking to him tonight."

Emerald bit her lip nervously, and her handmaidens all seemed shy around them, all except with Glacia, whose hands were all over Remy's body and her head on his chest.

"When did you two happen?" Emerald asked Glacia and Remy to defuse the situation.

"Long story short, I called the band when you were…" Glacia stumbled. "Er, well, I was looking for Kyle at the time. I happened to call the band and talked to Diego, then Remy." She looked up at Remy, and they both smiled. "After… the whole wedding…" She faltered again, clearly having a hard time with her choice of words. "After the whole situation, I called the band back to see if I could get ahold of Kyle's music. I met with Remy a few times, one of them to get the tape for your birthday." She smiled at Emerald, then at Remy. "Then the rest is history."

"And you are just telling me this now?" Emerald asked.

Glacia paused. "It's just…I didn't want to parade myself dating in front of you… But since it has been a couple months now, I didn't want to keep it from you any longer."

Glacia was right. Emerald would have been sad to be constantly reminded of Glacia's happiness, and it possibly would have made her even more depressed. Glacia was trying to be considerate of her feelings. Besides, she was hiding her pregnancy from her best friend. Was there any difference?

"I understand," Emerald said, giving them an approving smile.

At least someone found true happiness, she thought. Emerald couldn't think of anyone who deserved it more than her best friend.

"Well, I don't know about you all, but who wants to get smashed with me?" Diego butted in, looking at all the other handmaidens. They all giggled.

"I'll take that as a yes." He led them to the bar to order them all drinks.

Remy turned to Glacia. "I'll go get us some too."

"Sure," she said, playfully slapping his behind. He blushed, then turned away to join Diego and Kamren at the bar with the girls. She looked at Emerald. "I hope you aren't mad at me," she started.

Emerald looked straight at her. "I'm not, at all. What kind of person would I be if I was?"

"You mean it?"

"Of course, Glacia." Emerald smiled. "I am truly happy for you."

A twang of jealousy stung her, but Emerald quickly put it out of her mind. It was more from just seeing her handmaidens and the guys together.

It hurt.

Glacia smiled. "Good. I was a little nervous telling you. I thought by coming out here with us and seeing some familiar faces, you could enjoy yourself. Besides, the guys were constantly asking how you were doing. They missed you too, believe it or not."

"They did?" Emerald asked, surprised. She had missed them too, but she wasn't sure how much of an impression she made on them.

Emerald's feet hurt, and she started getting cramps in her stomach again, so she sat. She noticed Remy eyeing Glacia from the bar. "Go have fun with Remy." Emerald waved to her handmaiden. "He's waiting for you."

"Come over with me."

Emerald shook her head. "I need to sit for a second. I'll join you in a few minutes."

"I'll at least go get you a drink. What do you want?"

She thought of the growing lives inside of her and smiled slightly. "Just water for now, thank you."

Glacia smiled, then took off, joining the group across the room. They had already started drinking. The girls were flirting with both Diego and Kamren, but it looked like they were more taken with Kamren. Diego was trying his hardest, but his intoxication was clearly not helping things. Glacia returned for a moment with Emerald's water, urging her to dance with the group. Emerald politely declined, using the excuse that she just wanted to take her surroundings in first, but the reality was she had no energy. Pregnancy was far too exhausting.

Slinking into a nearby barstool at the counter, Emerald saw her guards position themselves close by. Emerald watched as Glacia returned to Remy.

They could hardly take their hands off each other. Emerald laughed inwardly. Remy hadn't seemed like the kind of guy to display affection in public; he had always been so rigid about the band. It was interesting seeing a different side of him when he was with Glacia.

Emerald turned her attention to the dance floor, her eyes trailing to the racy women dancing on the platforms. She was enamored by their dancing. However, their perfectly shaped bodies made her feel all the more unattractive. She had already gained weight from the pregnancy, and was started to feel insecure about her new body. Her stomach wasn't as flat as it was before, though her corsets still managed to hide her weight gain. But her breasts were larger, as Glacia had so kindly pointed out. Watching the women made Emerald feel inadequate as a female, and so alone. Men and several women ogled over the dancing women as they ran their hands over their bodies seductively, teasing the men. Had Kyle ever frequented clubs like this one? If he did, had he been enamored with these kind of women, just like how these men were?

Emerald knew that she could never compare to them; she had not even the first clue on how to dance seductively. She was graceful in many ways, but she simply didn't have the confidence. She wouldn't even have the nerve to stand up on the platforms, expressing her sexual side like that.

Her eyes scanned back to Glacia. Her handmaiden was in the throes of passion, making out with Remy back in the corner of the club. She saw Remy's hand slide up Glacia's thigh, then averted her eyes to Diego and Kamren, who were leaning in and talking to her other handmaidens. Kamren seemed especially taken with Cyndi, while Celeste and the other maidens laughed with Diego.

It was a mistake coming here, she told herself. The happiness, the upbeat music… it all made her feel worse. Seeing everyone either in the throes of passion or flirting made Emerald's heart burn for Kyle all the more. It hurt so much and so deep within her soul that she couldn't do anything about it.

Emerald missed Kyle terribly. She would never love again, nor would she ever feel the beating heart of a man next to hers, or even express herself physically with another man. Never would she flirt with another, never would she bestow a smile of affection, because no one could replace Kyle. He was gone, and all she had left of him was what was growing inside her womb.

Her heart sank with sadness. It ached in her bones, causing her to feel dizzy. Her head was spinning, and her tongue felt dry. She was dying of thirst. Then she realized that she had not drank any of her water, and the heat within the club was overwhelming her.

Emerald hurriedly grabbed her water, drinking the whole glass in one go. From just those movements, her head spun harder, and her vision began to blur. Her heart began to race as she looked in Glacia's direction.

Through her blurry vision, she watched Remy and Glacia exchange wild kisses. They were so sensual and intimate.

Kyle...

Emerald's body was shocked by a flash of heat. She tried to move her mouth to call out for help, but it refused to work. Her head was spinning so fast that all she saw was dimming blackness, deep and dark as the void of life itself.

She was no longer on the barstool. She was falling. Her back hit the floor hard, and she smacked her head.

The last thing she remembered was the music.

The beat of the music...

CHAPTER 45

Red

Bright neon-pink lights pierced the sapphire-blue atmosphere, while shocking, electrifying azure lights illuminated the floor. A heavy layer of smoke blanketed the air, soaking the haze with light. Every so often, flashes of light appeared, lighting up silhouettes of scantily clad women dancing. There was music with a steady, low beat. The melody sounded so strange, like nothing Rubius had ever heard before. It was as if the music was coming from machines.

Rubius looked around, confused. He had no idea where he was, or what kind of place he was in. Never in his life had he seen anything like it. Before him was a metal counter, and he was seated in front of it. The sheen of the metal reflected the blue lighting as a man handed glasses of drinks to customers, taking sheets of paper in exchange. Shadows of people stood around, some in bright colored fashions, others in a black leather with metal adornments on their clothes. Rubius looked down at his own clothing, noting he was still in the normal expensive garb he always wore at court, along with his large amulets studded with rubies. Would the people near him notice his fashions?

"Drink?" asked the man behind the counter.

"Huh?" Rubius looked at him, confused.

"You want a damn drink or what?"

"I… I don't know," Rubius replied.

"Listen, buddy, if you can't make up your mind, then make room for those who can," the man said curtly. The man then turned to another man next to Rubius, who was waving small pieces of paper.

"You look like you could use a drink," said a feminine voice on the other side of him.

Rubius turned. A woman with short cropped black hair stood there, her lips painted magenta, flashing him an alluring smile. She wore very little, and what little she did wear was very tight, and very revealing. The woman was attractive enough, he supposed, but she paled in comparison to the green-gifted woman in his dreams.

The green-gifted woman. Was she here?

"I'm looking for someone," Rubius answered the woman. "She might be here."

The woman gritted her teeth. "Of course you are," she said bitterly.

The man at the counter poured two drinks, both of them glowing a vibrant green. She slid one over to him, slammed her own glass of liquid, and smirked at Rubius, daring him to do the same.

Rubius looked at the pulsating green drink. It reminded him of the green-gifted woman. He had to find her.

Rubius pushed the glass away. "I can't. I told you, I have to find someone."

"It's *her*, isn't it? I just wasn't good enough for you, was I?"

"Excuse me?"

"You can't even remember her name," the woman commented. "You were always such an ass."

"I don't even know you, lady!" Rubius said heatedly. "If you know who I'm looking for, then by all means, tell me! What's her name?"

"You think *I* would tell you her name?" The woman sneered, pulling out a small box, revealing a thin rolled-up paper that was stuffed with something, then she lit it on fire. The woman inhaled the smoke from the tube, then exhaled it, the smoke gathering in the thick air.

"I would hope so," Rubius replied. "Look, I don't know what I have done to offend you. I have no idea where I am, and I don't know how I ended up here." He paused. "But… thanks for the drink." He got up.

The woman raised an eyebrow, then shrugged. "Many people come looking for someone in a place like this, but they never truly find them. Especially if they don't belong here."

Rubius narrowed his eyes curiously. "What do you mean I don't belong in a place like this? What is this place?"

"You aren't meant to be here."

"Well, no shit. I stick out like a sore thumb." He paused. *What kind of word is* shit *anyway?* he thought to himself. Did he make that word up? Where were his manners?

She took his full drink, then hurled the liquid at him, splashing it all over his face. "That's not what I am talking about, dickface. I'm talking about this *time*," she said as he wiped his face with his sleeve. "You have to stay in your own time. It's dangerous for you if you don't."

"What…?"

"Well, look at who it is! My man! How the hell have you been?" a voice interrupted.

Rubius turned around to find a strange man his age next to him. The man had dyed blue hair, similar strange fashions as the rest of the crowd—a black leather outfit studded with silver.

"Getting along with Sonja, I see," the man said, eyeballing him. "What the fuck are you wearing? You look like a fucking joke. I mean, since when did you get all fancy and shit?" The man took a drink from a flask.

Rubius looked at him strangely, then turned around to see if the man was talking to someone behind him. But there was no one there, only people dancing in the crowd.

"Are you talking to me?" Rubius asked, confused.

"Well, who the fuck did you think I was talking to? That jackass in the crowd? What the hell is wrong with you, anyway? Did you go do a line and get spun out?"

"You know me?"

The man laughed again, then lit a smoke stick, inhaling from it. "Of course I fucking know you. You're my best friend, asshole."

"Best friend?"

"Well, I ain't your fuck buddy, that's for sure."

Rubius stared at the man, trying to recall his face. "Just who exactly do you think I am?"

"Is this a trick question?"

"I'm serious. Who am I?"

"*Who am I* is not the question you should be asking me. The question is, do you know who *you* are?"

The man pointed to a giant mirror behind the counter, gesturing for Rubius to take a look. In its reflection, Rubius saw the crowds of people dancing in the colored smoke and the men giving drinks out to the crowded people at the counter. And he was in the center of it, with his so-called "best friend" behind him, taking a drink.

"Am I supposed to be seeing something?" he asked this friend of his. "What am I looking at?"

"Dude, just take a look, will ya?"

Rubius looked at the mirror once again, but this time, instead of seeing himself in his royal garb, it was gone, replaced with black leather like all the others. He wore silver metal jewelry, and what was more bizarre was that he had white hair. The only thing he recognized was his face and his red eyes. But deep down, he felt his soul stir. Seeing that image made him feel… *different.*

Looking away from the mirror, Rubius looked down at himself. Just like his reflection, he was wearing the black leather clothes and silver jewelry with many silver spikes attached. His heart lurched.

"That's fucking better," the best friend said.

Rubius turned fully to the man, almost in a panic. "What the fuck is going on? Do you know what is happening to me?"

"Like Sonja said, you're not supposed to be here," the man reiterated.

"Sonja?" Rubius looked over at the woman.

"Fucking dick," she said, and she threw another drink at him. Apparently Rubius was supposed to know this woman, and she didn't like the fact that Rubius kept questioning who she was.

He looked back at the man. "What the hell is that supposed to mean, that I'm not supposed to be here? I don't even know where *here* is! Why do you people keep telling me that? Why do you have to be all cryptic and shit?"

"God, and you are always calling me clueless. It means what I said. That you aren't supposed to be here." He paused. "But *she* called you here."

"*She*? You mean the green-gifted woman?"

"You are a hopeless fuck, you know that? *She*. You know *she* has a fucking name, or did you forget that too? Here, have a cigarette, maybe that will screw your head on straight."

The man shoved the "cigarette" in Rubius's mouth, then lit it with a flame.

Rubius's head spun with confusion, and his life force raged. Something was happening, like a friction of forces within. He felt completely lost.

He turned quickly to the man. "She called me here? Where the hell is *here*? Am I in a different time? Or is this a damn dream? God, tell me her name at least!" What was with his speech? It all seemed to come out naturally, much more than his courtly speech. It was that shift… a shift in his soul, connected to his life force. It happened right when he looked into the mirror. He felt like… like he wasn't Rubius, or he was living someone else's memories.

The man laughed, took a drink, and puffed his cigarette. "This is her world. These are the fragments of her mind… all of her thoughts, wishes, dreams, and memories. We are all taking part in her dreams on another plane of existence." He paused to take a drink before continuing. "But I think part of this is fragments of your mind too, giving this world more detail."

"So I'm in a dream world? My mind mixed with her mind?"

"Well, yeah. When you dream, your souls meet in a place where human bodies cannot go. Both your minds are there together. Your soul is here, on this plane of existence, while you sleep, so your body tells you it's a dream. But it's her magic bringing you here," the man said, taking a drink. "God, I sounded fucking smart there for a minute." The man smiled, looking proud of himself.

"And you, whoever the hell you are, wherever you are… you are here too, with me?"

"Diego, dipshit. I have a name."

"Okay, yeah, whatever, Diego. So your mind is here with me?"

"Naw, dude, I'm just a shadow, a memory from *your* mind. Only your two souls are here. I'm just playing the damn puppet like everyone else. You should feel fucking special."

Rubius's heartbeat quickened. He was really in a different time and place, and yet not a normal plane of existence.

Was it blue magic that had called him here? Did she have adjacent powers too? Or was it a combination of someone's lost memories trapped inside of him, unleashed when the sorceress got inside his head?

Rubius turned quickly to the man. "What year is it?"

"2384 M.E. Wait, I keep forgetting it just changed to a new year. 2385. Damn. Time flies."

2385 M.E. I'm in a different fucking time…

"Damn, you lucky bastard. Just in time too."

"Huh?" Rubius questioned, inhaling smoke from his cigarette. Rubius followed the man's gaze, trying to see what he was exactly looking at. He didn't see anything of interest, only people dancing in the haze on the floor, all lit up in the colors of the spectrum. On the far side, there was a different level of small platforms, with women dancing on each one, as if they had been put on a pedestal for any man's enjoyment, dancing provocatively.

"Dude, check it out," the man said, nudging him, pointing.

Rubius followed his finger to one of the silhouettes on a platform. He froze in place.

Basking in bright-green light, bathing in its beauty was the woman. The green-gifted woman. His heart raced at the sight of her, and he became paralyzed, frightened, and excited all at once.

She was on display for all the world to see, dancing as if she hadn't a care in the world, making him flustered at the sight. Her long green wavy hair flowed down her back against her thin frame as she moved, almost as in slow motion, allowing Rubius to feast his eyes on glistening full breasts barely contained in her corset. The luscious curve of her ass teased him from her skimpy bottoms. But even in her amply revealing clothes, she wore it with a strange sense of elegance, making all the other women look like complete trash.

If he could, Rubius would have had slapped himself to not be so obvious, but her movements had killed his ability to think clearly. It was like a spell had come over him, and there was no coming out of it.

Her intoxicating green eyes glanced directly at him, and his soul shook with shock. She danced for him and him only, and she desired no one but him.

His blood began to burn. Watching every movement of her body made him sweat with desire. Oh god, his body and his soul had craved hers for all these years… He just wanted to drink in her form and ravish her until he was bone dry.

He wanted her. He had always wanted her.

She smiled at him, almost as if she could read his thoughts. In their connection, he felt her longing for him too. And within that longing was a sense of sadness.

The bright-green light faded to a hot pink, then purple. She ran her hands across her body as she danced, lightly brushing her neck as she arched her back, accentuating the curves of her body. She threw back her head as she moved, exposing her neck, her wavy locks of hair kissing her skin as she ran her hands through her tresses. As she did, her well-endowed breasts perked upward, making them even more round and more tastefully inviting. Rubius could see her hardened nipples poking through her top…

God, if only he could stuff them in his mouth. His raging hard-on agreed.

She locked eyes with his and raised one of her eyebrows, almost in a dare, as she touched her nipples through her shirt, then slid her hand down her tummy, then lower. Rubius broke out in a hot sweat as he trailed his eyes to her where her hands were leading his gaze…

She stopped at the top of her tight little shorts, then she reached inside, grabbing the strap of her undergarment. She smiled at him and gave her strap a teasing yank.

Rubius's mouth dropped, his cigarette nearly falling out of his mouth, causing him to break his focus from her. He quickly grasped it with his fingers, then looked back at the platform.

She was gone.

He panicked. *Where did she go?* He had to get to her. Rubius plowed through the crowd, his mind and heart on one thing. He knew she had to be there, just on the other side of the dance floor. The only thing that kept them apart was a crowd of people.

I can get to her!

Rubius's heart raced as he fought his way through the crowd. It seemed when he made progress, more people crowded front of him.

"Dammit! Will you people move?" he snapped at the new people in front of him.

It was as if they never heard him. They continued to dance and drink. Light flashed, and for a split second, he spotted her in the crowd, further off across the room.

He pushed through the crowd desperately, knowing that he had very little time to get to her. She would be gone at any moment. Rubius pushed with more force. People flooded the floor, making it impossible to get to the green-gifted woman. He was in the midst of a sea of people, and they kept coming, pushing them further and further apart.

There was another flash of hot white light.

She was gone.

Rubius looked quickly around him, scanning the crowd, but there was no hint of her. He summoned his power, sending it ripping through his life force. He shook with rage. He'd been seconds away from being with her! It seemed his dreams were just one cruel trick after another.

He yelled in frustration, but it was no use. The crowd thickened, parting him from the green-gifted woman. There were too many people, and he was lost and alone.

Lost in a sea of people, rippling like the ocean.

Lost in a sea of time...

CHAPTER 46

GREEN

The sounds of light rain pattering on the palace turrets greeted Emerald as she groggily opened her eyes. She didn't want to move, nor did she think she could. She had absolutely no energy.

She managed to sit up, feeling something foreign attached to her arm. Emerald looked down and saw an IV, and a tube ran to a nearly empty bag of fluid hanging from a metal stand.

What happened to me? She looked at the IV, feeling confused. The last thing she remembered was being at the nightclub with her handmaidens, and then she'd blacked out. After that, she had no idea how she got back to the palace.

Her thoughts turned to Emerys, and she sighed. She had told Emerys that he had no reason to worry. The councilor was no doubt fretting this very moment.

As Emerald sorted her thoughts, realization hit her. A doctor had to have put the IV in her. Did they know about what grew inside her womb? Panicked, Emerald grasped the covers, pulling them to her chin, almost in hiding. Her head pounded while a wave of nausea hit her.

Kyle… Emerald had dreamed of him again. But this time, she had *felt* his life force, his presence near hers. In her strange dream, she had danced for him—boldly and erotically, she might add—just like those dancers at the club she had seen. And in her dream, she'd seen Kyle's desire, his longing and aching need for her. They had been so, so close. Just being in that proximity of him again caused her to be in complete ecstasy, even if it was only a beautifully sexual dream. It was so vivid, so bright, and this world she awoke to was anything but that. Now, being awake, reality showed its ugly face, and a deep hopelessness settled in her bones once more.

Kyle was gone forever. There was nothing Emerald could do to change it.

Nothing.

The thought made her soul ache. Tears streamed down her face as she began to weep. Kyle. He had joined the many souls of the lifestream, flowing their way to their final destination. They would be parted forever until she passed into the lifestream as well. Oh, she had tried to resurrect him with her life magic, but it only proved what a failure she was. And as wonderful as his presence in her dream was, it was just more of life being cruel to her. All her life, Emerald had dreamed of finding true love. And when she had found her complement… the soul that *completed* her, he had been taken away from her. How Emerald hated her life. Hated herself because she didn't have the power to stop herself from draining Kyle's life force.

It was all her fault. She didn't want to live in this world anymore.

More tears came, and her dark thoughts continued to linger in her mind. Slowly, Emerald got out of bed, pulled the IV tube out of her, and walked toward her patio window. She laid a hand on it, feeling the coolness of the glass while watching the rain spatter against the panel, feeling the small vibrations of the rain under her fingertips. How she wished it was Kyle's arm that she touched.

Kyle, why? Why couldn't I resurrect you? she asked herself bitterly. *Why didn't I have the strength to block the sorceress's control of me? How was it that I harmed you…?*

Emerald slammed her hand against the glass panel, rattling it. She hit it again in a crying fit of rage, so hard that all she saw was a blur of tears as she fell to the floor crying.

He was no more.

Emerald heard the click of her bedroom door. She turned around and saw Glacia with a doctor lingering in the doorway.

"You're awake," Glacia said, noticing her on the floor. "Oh my god, are you okay?" Glacia rushed over to her, putting a hand on her shoulder.

Emerald looked to the doctor in the doorway, then quickly wiped her eyes. "Yes, I'm fine," she lied. "I'm just still tired." Glacia helped her off the floor and onto her feet while Emerald gestured for the doctor to come in. "Why do I have an IV?" she asked the doctor as he approached.

"You were severely dehydrated and dangerously low on electrolytes. I actually came to check on you and to see if you needed a new bag of fluid. Also, we ran a few tests on your blood." The doctor looked at Glacia. "Perhaps I should talk to you privately?"

Pain ran through her. She knew exactly what the doctor was going to say. Emerald's eyes met Glacia's, and she saw the worry in her handmaiden's face.

She told me her secret, which was hard for her to do, Emerald thought. *I owe her the same.*

"She can stay, Doctor," Emerald said.

The moment had finally come. Everyone would know. After this, her dark secret would become reality to everyone. Including her.

"About the blood tests… we ran basic blood work, but one of the test results came back positive." The doctor hesitated, then continued. "You are pregnant, Your Majesty."

Glacia didn't flinch at the doctor's news, remaining impassive.

"Your Majesty, did you know?" the doctor continued.

"I did, Doctor," Emerald said, burning with shame. "With twins."

The doctor's mouth dropped, and this time, Glacia's eyes went wide.

"Your Majesty, how could you possibly know that?" the doctor asked incredulously. "We haven't even run an ultrasound."

Emerald frowned. "I have life magic, do I not, Doctor?"

The doctor's eyebrow lifted curiously, then he nodded. "I am not familiar with 'magic,' Your Majesty, but I suppose that is as valid a reason as any." The doctor gave her a reassuring smile with a tense face. "With twins, you run many more risks than a normal pregnancy. We must monitor the babies at least twice a week, if not more, considering what happened last night."

There was another knock, and Glacia opened the door. A nurse stood there with another IV bag in the doorway.

"I think Her Majesty will not be needing another bag of fluid at this time," the doctor said to the nurse.

"Yes, Doctor." The nurse bowed to Emerald, then left the room.

The doctor focused on Emerald. "Your Majesty, please, get some rest. And *eat.* You must eat. With your electrolytes low as they were, it is apparent you are not eating enough. I know that most food will make you feel nauseous, especially during the first several months, but you have two growing inside of you. I can prescribe you some anti-nausea medicine."

"That would be fine, Doctor," Emerald said softly. She was trying really hard not to weep.

"I'll leave you to rest," the doctor said uncomfortably. "And I'll have the nurse bring in the medication shortly."

"Thank you."

A few seconds later, Emerald heard the door shut, but she still sensed Glacia inside, lingering.

Emerald went back to the window, staring out at the rain. "Did you know?"

"I figured it out a while ago," Glacia said in a quiet voice.

Emerald slowly looked over her shoulder, giving her friend a sad look. "Why, then, did you offer me wine?"

"I… I was just trying to act normal. For your sake. I knew you wouldn't drink it anyway."

Bitter tears ran down her cheeks as Emerald turned back to the window, leaning her head on the rain-covered glass. Fog blossomed where her mouth cried out, and she slowly slid to the floor, her hand still dragging against the glass.

"My Queen…" Glacia started. "I… I'm sorry about hiding me and Remy."

"I'm not upset about that," Emerald said. "I must admit, I was slightly jealous, but only because I have lost my love."

"I feel like I made things worse for you. If I hadn't pushed you to go out…" Glacia's voice trailed off.

Emerald ran her hand against the drizzled glass, then fell back to the floor, crying. "I hate my life, Glacia. I *hate* it!" Emerald shouted. Her face streamed with hot, fresh tears.

Glacia remained silent while the pounding of the rain continued outside.

"Why is life so cruel, Glacia? *Why*? What have I done to deserve all that has happened to me?" Even though the question was posed to her best friend, she was really asking herself. "My whole life, my father kept me locked away. I barely saw my mother, barely knew her, and then she was taken from me to join the others in death.

"And Derek… the one person I trusted for so many years." More tears fell, then Emerald shot a glance at Glacia. "I trusted him, Glacia! *Trusted* him! Do you know how much that hurts?"

Glacia parted her lips for a split second, but Emerald continued before she got a word in.

"There is nothing left between me and Derek. Even with all that has happened between us, I could've possibly managed to move on. But my soul… my other half. He's gone forever. And I cannot move past that. I do not have the strength!"

Glacia remained silent, her own eyes welling up with tears.

"And what's even more cruel is that I see him in my dreams," Emerald continued. "Glacia, he is there! I feel his life force in my dreams. He is… so real. His soul is searching for me." Emerald shook with deep sadness. "Don't you see, Glacia? How can I possibly live my life? What do I have to look forward to? War with the kingdoms by day, royal parties at night? I care nothing for them. All that lies before me is pure desolation of my heart. It is shattered into a thousand pieces, and I cannot even manage to pick up one."

"But your people!"

"Sure, I love my people, and I do care for them. But that is not enough to live for."

"I care!" Glacia fought back. "I care for you. And your other handmaidens. We all care. And what about your babies? You are going to be a mother. You have plenty to live for."

Emerald scoffed through her tears. "My twins? One will grow up having a father, and one won't. And the man I desire will not ever see his child," Emerald said bitterly.

Glacia gasped. "How do you know that? Is it even possible to have twins with two fathers?"

"It is possible because it has happened to me. I feel both fathers' life forces within me, growing inside the twins' bodies." Emerald looked at her, her vision a blur. "I don't have any soul left within me to raise two children, especially knowing that one of their fathers is gone. And every day, I will have to lie to Derek's face about one child's true heritage. I don't like lying; it hurts my soul. To go through life with one big lie in my heart… I just can't do it."

"Why don't you tell him the truth?"

"And then what will happen to that child? Do you think Derek would allow that child to grow up in the palace? Or even in Arcadia?"

Glacia frowned, knowing she was right.

"I think not," Emerald whispered in a hush. "It would be best no one knew. Including the other handmaidens."

"I will not breathe a word of this," Glacia promised softly.

Emerald turned around, meeting Glacia's gaze, then started to sob all over again. "I'm sorry, Glacia," she said lowly. "I don't mean to burden you."

Glacia leaned over her, brushing her back gently, trying to calm her. "You don't ever have to be sorry." Glacia bent over her, lifting her chin. "I wish I could bring you comfort. But please, know that we all care about you. You may feel that no one cares for you, or that you have nothing to look forward to, but know that we are here for you, and will do anything and everything for you."

Emerald gave her a weak smile, then wiped the snot from her nose. Glacia ran and grabbed a few tissues, then set them in Emerald's lap.

"I'll let you rest for an hour, then I'll bring your lunch up," Glacia said.

Emerald nodded in a daze, blowing her nose and staring out the window as she heard Glacia leave the room.

Emerald continued to watch the raindrops trickle across her window. Rolling dark thunderclouds formed in the sky. White lightning flashed, the sound of rumbling thunder following soon after.

The rain. It was all that was left of Kyle in this world. Emerald saw him in the sun. She saw him in the snow. She saw him in the rain, the storms, and on and on and on. It was all that was left of his spirit besides the paintings that hung on her wall. And his ghost in her dreams.

He was so real there, especially in that last dream. He was *there*, with her. In her other dreams, she could hear his voice resonating in her soul. His song captured her mind like a spell, calling her from across the chasm of time and space. All she wanted was to be with him. In this world, Emerald had no way of seeing him. But in the dream world, he was there.

Was waiting for her.

Wiping away her tears, Emerald crawled across her bedroom floor, then made her way into her bed, sobbing into her pillows. She didn't want to live anymore in this world. She wanted to live in her dream world. For that was where Kyle was. The deep sadness in her spirit worked through every inch of her body, settling into her bones, seeping into the depths of her life force.

Forever. I want to live in the dream world. To see him forever…

Power softly came over her, lulling her into a tired state. Her mind became tranquil, and her tears subsided. Her spirit submitted to the power of hopelessness and anguish. The soft power pumped through her heart, flowed to her veins, then gently poured over her body, encompassing her with a soft green-blue glow.

She began drifting away in a dreamlike state. As her soul was gently swept into her sullen state, she heard Kyle's song. It played like a beautiful, powerful spell within her mind.

That melody. That sweet melody.

His voice.

It echoed across time and space, and Emerald closed her eyes and drifted off to sleep.

CHAPTER 47

It was near dinner, and Emerald had to eat. The doctor had told her so. Glacia was going to make Emerald eat, whether she was in the mood or not.

Earlier, Glacia had brought the Queen's lunch to her. She knocked, but there was no response, so she left the lunch outside Emerald's bedroom, not wanting to intrude. But now, she was worried.

Glacia, with a fresh dinner tray in one hand, then knocked on Emerald's bedroom door with the other.

"My Queen?" Glacia called out.

No answer. Just the sound of the rain pattering on the rooftop of the palace turret.

"Hello?"

She knocked again. Silence.

Boldly, Glacia entered the bedroom.

All was still. The room was dark, as there were no lights on. Rain pattered against the windows. A strange, eerie green-blue light was coming from the bed.

What is that light?

Cautiously, Glacia moved toward the bed until she realized where the light was coming from. She gasped.

Emerald. She was radiating with magic. But it wasn't her normal green magic that Glacia had seen a few times, nor was it that strange deep-green magic either. No, the Queen was basked in a brightly transparent blue-green magic.

Why is her body doing that?

Glacia's stomach turned a little, knowing that this was not normal for the Queen. She had never encountered anything like it in all her years of serving her.

"My Queen?" Glacia said quietly.

She had hoped her voice would wake Emerald, but the Queen did not stir. Emerald lay still on her back, her hair draped to her sides, her eyes closed. The only movement was the gentle rising and falling of her chest as she took slow, deep breaths.

Glacia bravely laid a hand on Emerald's skin to see if the magic did anything to her. Nothing happened.

"My Queen," Glacia said again, shaking Emerald this time.

Emerald didn't move.

"*Emerald*," Glacia said, shaking the Queen hard. "Emerald!"

The Queen didn't wake. Instead, the magic glowed brighter in response, until it burned Glacia's eyes. Glacia jumped back, startled at the sudden brightness. She shielded her eyes as her body trembled with fear.

Slowly, the magic faded back into a soft, faint glow, leaving Glacia in the darkness once more. Scared, Glacia shook, but then she took a deep breath, bravely moving toward Emerald once again.

"Emerald! Please! Wake up!" Glacia cried as she gave the Queen a violent shake.

Emerald breathed faintly in response, but the rest of her body remained lifeless, like a corpse.

"Oh my god!" Glacia screamed, trembling in place. "Oh my *god*!"

Suddenly, the door burst open, and several other handmaidens came running in.

"What is it?" Celeste asked.

"The Queen…" Glacia cried out, pointing. "I think… she's in a coma!"

Celeste ran up to Emerald, then trembled at the sight of the blue-green glow. She shook her head in shock, then starting bawling. The other handmaidens shook with fear along with her, then they all cried along with her.

"What… what are we going to do?" Celeste cried.

"Send a transmission to Councilor Emerys now," Glacia ordered. "Cyndi, run and fetch the councilor in case he doesn't pick up. Someone send a transmission for Councilor Lysander. Another call for the doctor. I will stay with her in case anything happens."

"Right away," Celeste said through her tears as she and the other handmaidens quickly ran out of the room.

Glacia looked at Emerald, and guilt overwhelmed her. She shouldn't have taken the Queen to see Kyle's friends. This was all her doing.

"My god, Emerald. This can't be happening. Please, wake up," Glacia pleaded. She sat down next to Emerald, feeling her head. It was quite cool, though her body seemed colder than usual. She threw the blanket on Emerald, then went into the closet to get another.

There was a click at the door just as Glacia grabbed the spare blanket in the closet.

"What did Emerys say, Celeste?" Glacia said as she walked out of the closet. "Did the others get ahold of the doctor—"

A strange man with blue hair stood four feet from her. Glacia's eyes went wide, then she screamed. In a panic, Glacia threw the blanket at the man. The blanket hit the man lightly, and to her surprise, he slumped to the floor, coughing blood. A flash of blue magic came from his body, flickering like candlelight.

Without a second thought, Glacia screamed, grabbed the nearby glass pitcher of water and hurled it at the man as he vomited profusely. The glass pitcher missed the man's head and hit him on the leg, shattering and tipping him off balance. He cried out as his hands hit the floor, crunching the shards.

With her heart hammering in her chest, Glacia ran to grab a water glass, ready to throw it. Celeste came bursting through the door. She saw the man and began screaming.

"Get out of here!" screamed Celeste to the man.

The man weakly looked at her, then spewed more blood and bile. "I'm already dead… it's too late. I'm too late…"

Glacia froze in place. "Late for what?"

Then he went still, and no answer came. He was dead.

Both the girls looked at each other, then grabbed onto one another, still frightened. With her heart pumping wildly, Glacia let go of Celeste, then tiptoed to the man. Glacia felt Celeste latch onto her arm again, shaking with fear.

Before their eyes, the man's body began to give off blue smoke then it began to dissolve. The fragments of his body wisped in the air like a puff of dust blown in the air.

Taken aback, Glacia gasped, staring at where the remains of the man should have been. His body was completely gone. The only evidence he had ever been there was his foul-smelling vomit, blood, and a pile of rich azure garments and sapphire jewels that had adorned him moments ago.

Both girls looked at each other, wondering if they'd seen the same thing.

"Oh my god," Glacia whispered. "Did you just see what I saw?"

"What… what just happened?" Celeste asked. "Do you think this has anything to do with what's going on with the Queen?"

"I… I don't know," she answered.

Glacia nudged the pile with her toe, and a few rings fell from the pile, causing her to jump back. The pile… it was just like the pile she had discovered in the palace hallway with Emerald.

Just then, Councilor Emerys and Lysander came in with a string of guards. As they entered the room, they all stopped dead in their tracks.

"What is going on here?" Lysander asked with a grimace, noticing the vomit and the pile of clothes.

"A man…" Celeste started in a panic. "H-he… was here, then he just… *disappeared*."

Emerys's eyes went wide with alarm, and he ran to Emerald. He placed a hand on her forehead.

"She's cold. Much too cold," he said, worried. He shook her, but the Queen was nothing more than a limp doll.

"I went to fetch another blanket, Councilor, while Celeste was calling for you. That was when this man showed up," Glacia said. "He had magic."

Emerys's dark eyes met hers. "Then what happened?" he pressed.

"He just started spewing blood and vomit. He tried to use his magic, but he died before he got a chance."

"What color was it?" Lysander asked quickly, his face wrinkled with dread.

"Blue, Councilor. The magic only flashed for a second before he fell to the floor. He said he was too late."

"Too late?" Emerys repeated.

"Yes. Those were his exact words. Nothing more," Glacia said, biting her fingernails.

Emerys looked at Lysander. "See what's keeping the doctor," he ordered.

"Right away." Lysander pulled out his communication device.

Glacia cleared her throat.

"What is it?" Emrys asked.

"W-well…" Glacia stammered. "I'm not supposed to say anything, but I think the Queen would forgive me in this case."

Emerys raised an eyebrow. "What?"

"The Queen… she is…"

"Pregnant."

Glacia looked at him anxiously. "You… you know?"

"The King suspected," Emerys said, turning to Lysander. "Did you speak to the doctor?"

"He's on his way," Lysander confirmed. "I told him to hurry."

"Good," Emerys said, then eyed the vomit. "I'll get people to come clean the Queen's quarters."

He walked over to the pile of clothes, picking up a sapphire amulet. The councilor was clearly disturbed. His face was tinged with distress, but the man hid it well.

"Councilor Lysander, we are in much more danger than we thought," he managed to say, clasping onto the amulet tightly.

"Agreed," Lysander answered, his voice booming. "Somehow, Olympia has already infiltrated the palace."

Glacia gasped.

"We must call a meeting. Now," Emerys said. "Convene the councilors, and call more guards to this room!"

"Yes, Councilor," Lysander said.

The two men waited until the additional guards were stationed in the room with Emerald. The palace cleaning crew came in, disinfecting everything that the vomit touched.

What would happen to Emerald? Would the doctors be able to wake her?

Glacia's stomach sank. Somehow, she knew it had to be a spell.

But who would be able to break it?

CHAPTER 48

YELLOW

Under the cloak of Suri's magic, Auron moved swiftly through the citadel. There was a loud commotion down the hall, and Auron moved quickly behind a large statue. He really needed to avoid any orange-gifted from the High Court.

"My lady," Auron heard a man say, "are you okay?"

"I'm *fine*," said an angry feminine voice. "Please summon me an airship immediately. I want to get as far away from here as possible."

"Right away, my lady."

"Please, let me lead the way," said another man's voice.

"I can fetch you a fine glass of wine," offered a third man.

Suddenly, the people speaking were in Auron's line of sight, and his heart pounded. The young woman was orange-gifted. A swarm of men doted over her. Luckily, the woman was so distraught that she wasn't paying much attention to anything around her, including Auron.

Auron quickly moved around the statue and out of the woman's sight as she stormed off with the string of lords behind her.

Auron breathed, loosening the tension in his neck. What should he do? How would he get to Ikaria? He had no real plan, no idea, no solution. Even if he did, how would he break her out of her cell? And what about her magical chains? And her magic barrier? Before, he'd had Suri. It seemed she was one step ahead of everyone, methodically thinking up a plan, carefully weighing the options. Now, it was just him. What could he possibly do to fool the guards to get into Ikaria's cell?

I can't do what Suri did, he thought.

What could *he* do? Nothing. Not with his magic he couldn't. If he couldn't, who could help him get into the sorceress's chambers? An idea flashed in his mind, and Auron quickly headed to the upper ramparts of the citadel.

After climbing the stairs, he moved into a small elaborate hall, quickly crossing the corridor where a good portion of the high lords resided. Turning this way and that, Auron found the chamber door he was looking for. He listened for a moment, then deemed it safe to enter.

He entered and closed the door behind him, standing in Lord Nyko's empty chambers. He'd hoped to find the lord. But Lord Nyko was gone. The lord's chambers were void of his presence.

Should he wait for the lord to return?

He stood in silence, taking in all the surroundings. There were shelves upon shelves of books and tomes. Some of the books' material looked questionable. He recalled that the lord had stood up for the sector to return to the days of technology of the ancients.

Lord Nyko must be still dealing with what's going on in the halls below.

Far worse, perhaps the High Court had found out Lord Nyko's stance on technology. Auron shivered, thinking about the fate of his sector and the current state it was now in.

There was a click at the door. Perhaps Lord Nyko was retiring for the day. Auron turned to the door, then took a step back, still invisible, awaiting for the lord to enter.

The door was flung open, and a swarm of guards entered—non-gifted High Court guards. The guards immediately started to ransack the chambers.

"I want any and all evidence brought to me!" commanded a voice.

Auron knew that voice. It was the Emperor. Sure enough, Cyrus entered observing the guards tearing through the chambers.

Evidence of what? But deep down, Auron knew the answer. Fear pounded through his veins. How was he going to get out of there, especially with all the guards? Looking around the chambers, Auron knew he had nowhere to go. He certainly couldn't fit under Lord Nyko's bed. Even if he could, the guards would probably go under the bed too, searching for any "evidence."

Auron did the only thing he could do. He flattened himself against the wall as quietly as possible. Luckily, the guards were making so much noise that the occasional sound from his movements was masked.

As the guards continued to dig through the chambers, Auron worked his way toward the doorway, hugging the wall. He prayed in his head the entire time that Suri's spell wouldn't run out…

Cyrus stood close to the doorway, and Auron paused.

"Your Majesty! I found a trove of artifacts hidden in the next room!" called out a guard.

"I knew it!" Cyrus boomed. "Arrest this lord, and any other disobedient citizen found with any sort of ancient evil! Whether it be machines, technology, books that contain that sort… it was all supposed to be sent to the High Court! It has no place in my sector!"

"Yes, Your Majesty!"

Cyrus stormed into the other room, where the discoveries were being made. The doorway was clear. This was the time. Now or never.

Hurrying, Auron dodged through the opened doorway and out of the chambers.

As he exited, Auron tried not to make noise. The further away he got, the faster his pace became. More High Court guards marched down the corridors, and Auron's heart pounded at the sight. More chamber doors of important lords were flung open, some were loudly arrested for "treason" and "disorderly conduct," while others complied completely. Soon, all of the living quarters of the lords were emptied, with the hallways flooded with objects, from books to scrolls, notes, and documents to technological artifacts…

Thoughts of what Geeta had said about ancient technology flooded his mind. *I do see them for what they are—tools. It's what the person does with those tools that makes it bad or good,* she had said.

She was right. Had the God of Light ever stated in *The Spectrum* how technology was evil? Not one statement pertaining to that matter was ever mentioned in the holy book. It was, in fact, the High Court that had deemed it evil, and over the many centuries, they made many laws in regarding it, all while writing lengthy articles on the evils of technology.

Over the course of the last two months, it had become more apparent that the High Court was twisted. Their hearts were hardened, especially against one so devout as the Empress Ayera. They made her out to be the evil one. Including Auron himself. According to them, his faith was out of line.

Seeing the flood of objects, books… these people, these friends of his… they were good people, despite their flaws. They might not be the most devout, or the most faithful, but they tried their hardest to stay in line with the God of Light while embracing the idea of ancient technology. Auron knew their hearts. They weren't wicked people. It was one more reason to get the sorceress out of her cell. World Sector Six needed Ikaria.

Auron hurried down another hall, wondering if Emperor Cyrus had ransacked Lord Jiao's quarters yet. He had to find out. Jiao could be one of the last ones who could help him.

As he made his way through the citadel, Auron saw that the halls became emptier the farther he traveled to his destination. He came to the hallway leading to Lord Jiao's chambers, and it was completely vacant.

Breathing a sigh of relief, Auron headed down the hall, stopping at the lord's doorway. Behind him, Auron heard noises. Looking over his shoulder, Auron spotted High Court guards starting their purge down the corridor.

Turning quickly, Auron opened the door to Jiao's quarters and entered. Inside, Jiao jumped from a seat in his study, startled at the sight of his door opening by itself.

"Who's there?" he called out, throwing down a quill.

"It's me, High Priest Auron," Auron said.

"Auron? Truly?" Jiao said. "Is it true? That you got away before that woman took our gifts?"

"I did," Auron said quickly. "You don't have much time. The High Court guards are coming this way to arrest you."

The lord's face turned dark and serious. "I'm not afraid of them. I stand for the Empress. Let them arrest and make a martyr out of me. I would be honored. For what they did to me, stripping me of my beloved orange gift, I will die standing against them and everything they stand for!"

The words were encouraging, renewing Auron's drive. "Then we have the same mindset," Auron said. "I am in dire need of your help."

Jiao nodded. "Anything, High Priest. But first, I need to know that it is actually you. I have lost my gift of seeing the unknown, so I do not trust my naked eyes."

Auron grabbed his amulet of the God of Light, then grabbed the lord's hand, pressing it into his palm.

"Can you feel that? My amulet."

The lord smiled. "How is it that you are invisible?"

"Suri."

"I knew it. Clever one, hiding her gift. Always liked her. I would have taken her for a wife if she hadn't been so infatuated with the sorceress." He pondered for a moment. "How long will her spell hold on you?"

That was a good question.

"I truly don't know how much time I have," Auron answered him. "It could fade at any moment."

"Then I must hurry, for your sake. How can I help you, High Priest? What do you need of me?"

"I need to free Ikaria."

Lord Jiao smiled brightly, then laughed. "About time someone came to their senses. The sorceress is like a sleeping dragon in the tales of old. If you awaken her, she will tear you apart."

"That's why we need to release her." Auron swallowed hard. He never thought he would be doing this, but here he was. "I need to get inside her cell and unlock her chains, but I do not know how to unlock them since they are enchanted."

"They are unlockable. However, I am not sure about her magical barrier. That will be your greatest difficulty." Jiao went over to his desk, rummaging through his papers until he pulled out a box.

Loud sounds came from behind the closed door, and both men startled. The door remained still. Jiao returned his focus to the box, opening it and producing a set of keys.

"Prison keys," he said, holding them out for Auron. "I don't know which one is hers, but it's on that ring. All of the keys are there."

Auron took them quickly, placing it in his robe pockets. As soon as he did, the keys became invisible.

More noise on the other side.

"You must get out now while you can," Jiao said. "I will stall them."

"Thank you, Lord Jiao."

"May the God of Light be with you."

With that, Jiao threw the door open and rushed into the hallway. Auron sprinted in the other direction, shouts rising behind him.

He couldn't look back. It would tear him apart inside. He happened to look down. The orange magic around him was starting to fade.

No! he told the magic. *I need you!*

The magic hummed through his body, and Auron felt it renewed. He frowned in confusion. Had he made that happen?

With no time to wonder further, Auron turned down the next corridor.

CHAPTER 49

RED

Rubius rummaged through his wardrobe, throwing on his favorite jerkin haphazardly as Zaphod flew around his chambers wildly, startled by all of the commotion.

That dream. She was *there*, with him. His heart thrashed in his chest.

And seeing that image of himself in the mirror… His head hurt, and his heart was a mess. What was happening to him? He was *losing* himself… Losing himself to a dream girl.

Rubius threw open his door, about to leave, but he stopped when he saw his guards. "Take care of my parrot. I expect him to be in perfect health when I return," Rubius said sharply.

"Yes, sir," they said in unison.

Rubius quickly marched down the hall, many of the World Sector Six courtesans actively avoiding him. Some looked away, others did an about-face and went off in a different direction before he neared them.

Outside, in the citadel gardens, the air was crisp and cool. There were no guards, no people in the section of the gardens he was in. Just the whisper of the wind, the clouds wisping by in the blueness of the sky.

Closing his eyes, Rubius took a deep breath, focusing on his life force, which burned with anguish inside. He was losing himself and the chance to find this woman. It was now an obsession. He had to find her. He was convinced that she needed him, and he needed her. It was crazy. Everything was spiraling out of control, and everything that he knew to be true had been turned upside down.

All he cared about was finding this woman.

Rubius channeled his frustration, and the anger that resonated deep inside swelled. His burning desire, his pent-up energy, coursed through his veins, flooding him with wanting.

He closed his eyes, calling forth red wind. It answered his desire and flowed around him, whipping in a continuous direction. He was airborne.

Opening his eyes, Rubius felt the vibrant red magic wind, waiting to be commanded.

It's been a long time, my friend, he told the wind. He couldn't recall the last time he'd summoned it to fly. It had been a long time. Why hadn't he done this sooner?

Rubius's body levitated up into the sky as he called upon the orange magic within his life force, making himself invisible. He wouldn't fool any orange-gifted if they saw him, but it should do for any others.

Looking through the clouds below, he saw the vastness of the earth. His heart stirred again.

Take me away from here! he commanded the wind.

The wind obeyed, and he flew furiously across the endless plane of clouds, in the direction of World Sector One. The wind ripped through his hair, its icy, piercing touch shocking. But he cared not; he had to keep moving.

What would he find in World Sector One? Something to confirm what the sorceress said was true? Then what? What would he do with that information?

Rubius continued to fly across the sky, passing many different floating citadels and fortresses. Some islands had gardens and statues, others had just a single tower as private housing used by the middle and lower classes of the sectors, who didn't reside in the main citadels. Some were abandoned, and their structures crumbled and eroded over the centuries, long forgotten.

After hours of flying, Rubius was getting tired, and his energy was spent. He stopped at one of the abandoned islands, resting for a brief period before resuming his flight.

He flew and flew for hours, taking breaks when he could. Day became night, and night became day, until finally a patch of earth below teased him from a small opening in the thick clouds, a barren, sandy mass of land.

World Sector One.

Diving under the cold fluffy atmosphere, Rubius headed to the surface.

As Rubius descended through the clouds, he felt a violent energy ripple through his body. It was as if the earth was telling him it was sick.

A strong, powerful gust of wind from a violent sandstorm ripped through the air, pelting his face, forcing him to close his eyes. It was powerful, ripping through his body and soul. Another shock of the earth's tainted energy hit him, and suddenly Rubius lost all concentration.

His red wind gave way, and his magic dissipated. The lack of magic caused him to plummet. Rubius yelled in fury, calling upon his red magic once again. It funneled over his body, but his wind was not as powerful as the sick, violent one tearing through the earth's atmosphere, causing him to fly aimlessly. Rubius continued to fight against the strong current, battling the power of the earth's winds. He funneled every ounce of energy into not falling; he had to try to remain steady so he could at least get to the ground safely.

Another thrash of wind hit him hard, causing him to lose his concentration once again. This time, however, Rubius could not stop himself from falling. Endlessly falling, while sands in the air pelted his face relentlessly.

Winds to my side! he called out in his mind.

Rubius mustered his strength, summoning his violet magic along with his red, creating a cyclone around him. The violet magic forced his body downward at a safer rate. The cyclone winds created a wind barrier, and the sand now had a hard time coming through. The magic continued to take him downward, closer and closer to the earth's surface.

As Rubius neared the ground, another wave of nausea hit his soul. But as soon as it hit, it stopped, leaving him able to take in more of the world.

Glancing at his surroundings, Rubius understood why everything was so harsh. He didn't see any grass, trees, lakes, rivers, like how he had seen paintings in the many citadels throughout the World Sectors. Instead, the surface was red rocky dirt, just a pure…

Wasteland. It was an endless wasteland. The surface consisted of reddish-orange sand glistening in the hot sun. Harsh winds blew furiously throughout.

But there was something else. Far off, there were decayed structures. Remnants of a fantastic city, its tallest buildings rising high up to the sky. Rubius's heart pumped wildly at the sight.

There was hardly anything left of the structures, only what seemed like steel frames of its remains. They were all either twisted, toppled over, or snapped, with sharp steel spikes pointed at the sky.

Harsh winds continued to rip along the earth's surface, and the sun was hotter than Rubius had ever felt before. In all fairness, Rubius hadn't had to endure much heat while up in the sky.

Finally, he landed on his feet. The earth groaned in pain beneath him. There was a dark energy in the soil, humming with wrath. The earth was angry.

It wanted *revenge.*

Just then, there was a loud rumble, and the earth shook violently. The surface glowed a deep, dark-red energy, and a violent red gust hit him. Rubius called forth his own red wind to counter, but this was much more powerful.

As his wind made contact with the violent dark-red gust, he was jarred where he stood. The ground shook with fury once again. Like a fierce punch to the face, the wind hit hard, and Rubius could no longer keep a foothold on the ground. It was just too powerful.

The violent red wind swept over his body with such power that even Rubius felt small against the elements. He was supposed to be the master over them. Instead, the wind had mastered him. Its power could not be contained.

What am I going to do? he thought as he fought the opposing force. He took a breath, and like a flood of poison, it streamed into his lungs. Rubius coughed, then took another breath. He was choking on the air.

Looking in the direction of one of the steel structures, Rubius started to crawl toward them, but the violent force of nature made it difficult. It sapped him of every ounce of his energy, and his muscles were already tired. With the force raging against him, Rubius was sure he'd be swept away in the storm.

"You can't be out here in this!" yelled a strange muffled, mechanical voice within the sandy winds. "The sandstorm is coming!"

Is that a machine?

"What?" Rubius yelled, squinting as he gasped for breath.

Several hands grabbed him, and suddenly Rubius was being dragged against the rocky ground.

"Don't open your eyes," the mechanical voice said, fighting the sound of the roaring winds. "And whatever you do, don't breathe."

Sounded like a good idea to him. At this point, Rubius didn't even want to try; the wind felt like a thousand knives. Then a mask was slapped onto his mouth, covering his nostrils as well. Air flowed within the mask. Clean air.

Rubius took a breath, keeping his eyes shut. He was still being dragged, but then he was lifted up and loaded onto something. He didn't know what, and frankly, he didn't care. He just wanted out of the sandstorm.

Whatever he was loaded on started up with a loud roar, and vibrations rumbled under him. And then they were off.

CHAPTER 50

ORANGE

Telly grabbed another tool, handing it to the technicians wiring the new transmitter device. It was cold on the rooftops of Arcadia, especially this time of year. Arcadia just had broken a record for snowfall two months ago, and the chill hadn't let up. Her breath frosted the air, and she huffed her warm breath into her cold hands, then rubbed them together.

What I would give for a pair of gloves right now.

Satellites were not her area of expertise by a long shot, but she was doing whatever she could to assist the team in creating the amplifier for the new satellite tower they were installing on the Multicorp building. Hopefully they would soon be able to send a strong signal out to the wastelands that wouldn't be blocked by the Olympians.

"Hand me that cable over there, will ya, Telly?" called out one of the technicians, pointing to the wires and cables strewn all over the place. It looked as if a transport exploded, junk littering the rooftop. It was hard to find anything in the mess. It was almost as bad as Garrett's trailer. Almost.

Telly tiptoed through the piles of wires, finding the cable that was needed, then walked back to the technician and handed it to him.

"Thanks," he said, inserting the cable into the box.

Jonathan, her old boss, walked up, handing her a cup of coffee. "Thought you could use this," he said, his breath frosting the air.

Telly smiled, taking the cup. "Much appreciated." The warmth felt great on her icy hands.

"How much longer until this contraption is up and running?" he asked, taking in the device from where he stood.

"Shouldn't be much longer," Telly said, taking a sip of her coffee. "They said two days at most, but it looks like they'll be done in the morning."

"Are you staying after this is all over? You know we all miss you at the corporation. Could still use a brilliant mind like yours. Even Drew."

Telly shook her head. "I have to get back," she said firmly, turning to him. "My daughter is out there. So is Drew. And besides, I'm rather useful out there. I've become attached to the camp."

"Really?" Jonathan looked surprised.

"Yes, really. I know I'm not a big outdoorsy kind of person, but it's home to me now," Telly said. "I consider the camp my family."

"Well, if you change your mind, you know where to find me," Jonathan said wistfully.

"I will keep that in mind." Telly paused, taking another sip of her coffee. "You know… you were right."

"Right about what?"

"About *The Spectrum*. It was true, even though I didn't want to believe it at the time. I still don't… but in a way, I can't not believe…"

"You don't have to say anything," he offered, smiling. "Just enjoy your coffee."

She smiled back knowingly, and they turned to the technicians, walking over to join them. As they helped assemble a few more parts, a transport flew over, then landed on the rooftop. A palace guard hopped out and ran up to her.

"Telly Hearly," the guard said, yelling over the sounds of the transport. "You need to come to the palace. Now."

Telly and Jonathan exchanged looks. Her hair whipped in her face, and she turned back to the guard. "What is it?"

"Councilor Emerys needs you."

"I just spoke to him this morning," Telly said.

"He has asked for you. Now!" The guard started pushing her away from the tech site.

"Hey! What's the big idea?" she barked at him, shoving away from him.

"I don't mean to be rude, miss, but the Queen is in trouble," he said quickly. "We have to get back to the palace quickly."

Telly's heart raced. Had Olympia already made it to the palace? "Is she okay? Has she been kidnapped? Please, tell me what has happened," Telly yelled over the sounds of the transport's engine, following him onto the vehicle.

"No kidnapping, ma'am. I'll let the councilor fill you in," the guard said as they seated themselves.

The ride back to the palace was short, but it felt like an eternity to Telly. She sat nervously, chewing on her nails while her stomach did flips. Drinking that coffee earlier didn't help at all, the caffeine mixing with her nerves.

The transport landed at the palace's royal receiving platform, and Telly followed the guard quickly into the palace. Emerys met them at the door.

"Telly, please, come quickly to the Queen's chambers," he urged, gesturing quickly.

"Councilor, what has happened?" Telly asked, half running to keep up with his pace.

"The Queen… she won't wake up."

Telly's heart jumped at the statement. "Won't wake up? Is she dead?" Telly blurted out. "Oh god, please don't say that, Councilor!"

"She's not dead, but it's as if she's… under a spell," Emerys said, his dark eyes darting to hers.

Spell?

Telly's mind reeled. What could she do about it? This was not her area of expertise. She didn't have anywhere near the power the other gifted had. What could she do with her piddly magic? It hardly allowed her to do anything.

"There is something else as well…"

Telly looked at him, sucking in her breath. "What is it, Councilor?"

"There was a person with magic who appeared in the Queen's chambers."

Telly paused, and her mouth dropped open. "A person with magic?" she repeated.

"He appeared in her chambers, then moments later, disintegrated right in front of the Queen's first handmaiden," Emerys continued. "I'm afraid that Olympia has found a weakness within Arcadia." He looked right at her. "We need someone to wake the Queen. She has the power to deal with these infiltrators. Or if she does not wake… perhaps you can at least protect her."

"Councilor, I'm not sure I am the one you should ask for assist—"

"You have magic," he interrupted. "Maybe there is a chance you can wake her. There were doctors who looked at her earlier, but this is beyond… anything normal."

"I don't think you understand. My power has limits. I am not strong like the others," Telly stated.

Emerys stopped. "We have no other options besides Geeta, and she is in the wastelands assembling our army. All I'm asking is that you see what you can do, or give us ideas on what to do. Please."

Telly swallowed. It felt like a dry lump of bread would not go down her throat. Finally, Telly nodded, then straightened her glasses. "I will see what I can do."

He nodded with gratitude, then gestured. "Please, let's hurry."

They made their way up the Queen's lifts, then into her chambers. Her quarters were some of the most luxurious rooms Telly had ever seen. If it hadn't been such an inopportune time, Telly would have sat and stared at all the wonderful carvings, paintings, and decorations that made the Queen's chambers feel so inviting. But now was not the time.

One of the Queen's servants bowed to her. "Telly, I presume?"

"Yes," Telly answered, nodding to the girl.

"I am Glacia, the Queen's first handmaiden. This way, please." There were other handmaidens in the sitting room, all of them anxiously waiting or pacing, some were crying.

Glacia led Telly to the Queen's bedchamber, leaving Emerys behind with the other handmaidens. Upon entering, Telly stilled, and a shiver ran down her spine.

A brilliant glow radiated around the Queen, softly pulsating between greenish-blue and greenish-yellow. She lay still on her bed, as if sleeping peacefully.

At first, Telly thought her eyes were playing tricks on her, but the colors continued pulsating around Emerald's body. Strangely, the setting was serene, almost like Telly was witnessing a scene in a childhood storybook.

"When did this happen?" Telly asked, cautiously approaching Queen Emerald.

"Sometime in the night," Glacia answered.

Telly hesitantly reached out to touch the Queen, waiting to see if the magical barrier affected her. It didn't, and Telly was able to reach a hand through the transparent barrier and touch the Queen's hand.

Emerald's pulse was there, her heart still beating. So slowly, though. Near the Queen, there was an IV machine, though the Queen was not hooked up to it.

"Why is there an IV?" Telly asked.

"Early yesterday evening, us handmaidens and the Queen all went out to a nightclub," Glacia said.

Telly jerked her gaze to the handmaiden, but the girl wouldn't meet her eyes.

"She… the Queen fainted at the nightclub, so the guards brought her back here, and the palace doctors put in the IV…" The handmaiden paused. "You have to understand, I've known the Queen all my serving life, and I have never known her to faint. She doesn't even get sick. Not that I can remember, anyway."

Telly looked to her, surprised. "Never?"

"No, Miss Hearly. Anyway, the Queen woke up sometime in the middle of the night. She was awake, coherent, and depressed. Said she didn't want to live anymore. Cried a lot. I didn't mean to make her cry…" Glacia's voice shook, then tears welled in her eyes.

"Make her cry?"

"It's all my *fault*." The handmaiden started sobbing.

"Why would the Queen's depression be your fault?"

The handmaiden's hazel eyes peered into hers. "You see all these paintings around here, Miss Hearly?"

Telly looked around. They were all of a certain man, every single one.

"The Queen misses the man in those paintings. But the problem is that he's dead, and that is all the Queen thinks about, night and day."

Looking at the paintings in more detail, Telly realized she recognized the man—he had electrocuted Drew during the battle with King Derek's advisor when Drew went haywire on her. In a way, that man had saved her from Drew being under control of the gauntlet, and he'd also saved Drew from himself.

Telly shuddered at the thought.

"Anyway, at the club, I was with my boyfriend… and happy. And the Queen… well, she was lonely." The handmaiden broke into new sobs, resting her head on the Queen's stomach. "It's my fault she's like this!"

Telly ran a hand over the Queen's one more time while listening to the ongoing sobs of the handmaiden. She felt bad for the poor girl. But what was she to do for the Queen? It was exactly as she'd told Emerys—she didn't have the kind of power Emerald needed. The only real assessment she could give was that the Queen appeared to be in a comatose state, but nothing in Telly's power, nor apparently the power of technology or modern medicine, could help awaken the Queen.

"Can... can you do something? With your magic?" Glacia asked, sniffling hopefully.

Telly shook her head. "I'm sorry. I can't."

Geeta needs to be here, not me, Telly thought. Geeta was worlds more powerful than her. At least Geeta would have an *idea* of what to do. Telly was worthless. Completely worthless.

"And what of the babies? What will happen to them in her state?" Glacia continued, tears flowing down her cheeks.

Telly's eyes darted to the handmaiden. "Babies?" Her gaze flicked to the Queen's stomach, somehow expecting to see a baby bump. It still looked flat to her.

The Queen is expecting twins?

The handmaiden nodded. "I figured that the councilor would have said something."

"He didn't," Telly said flatly. "How long has she been pregnant?"

"I don't know. The Queen only told me tonight, but she gave no details. But given her symptoms, I would assume two months..." The handmaiden trailed off, then cleared her throat before continuing. "The doctors discovered the pregnancy when they ran blood tests after last night's incident."

Telly glanced over at the Queen once again, realizing the severity of the situation. Emerald's face was in a dreamlike state, a permanent sadness on her face. It was as if the Queen didn't want to wake from or face the reality of her life. Who could blame her? She had lost the person she cared about most.

And now the Queen was pregnant. Not only with one baby... but twins.

Poor thing. That's a lot to take in for someone so young. The Queen probably knew and didn't want to tell anyone. It was a very real possibility, especially since her first handmaiden didn't know everything. The whole situation was overwhelming, and Telly wasn't even the person it was happening to.

"Go tell the councilor that he needs to have Geeta return to the palace immediately. Whenever the new transmitter device is fully operational, send word to her ASAP. Unfortunately, there is nothing I can do."

"Yes, Miss Hearly," Glacia said, wiping away her tears before going into the sitting room.

In the silence of the room, an eerie feeling ran through Telly. She looked around for a moment. Everything was unusually still. Like colored water running out of a faucet, the world became colored in blue tones.

What the…?

A bright flash of blue light shot toward Telly. Acting upon instinct, Telly dodged out of the way, then tapped into her own magic, sending it flooding into her veins. Her body was covered in her pale-orange power, and she went invisible immediately.

Telly ran to the side of the room, trying to get a sense of what was going on. Her breath caught. A man in rich blue robes was running toward the Queen.

Oh no, you don't!

Telly ran toward the man, grasping his cloak and yanking it hard. The hard jerk caused him to trip, and he landed flat on his back, yelping out loud.

"Where are you, orange-gifted?" he screamed as he rolled over onto his stomach. He yanked an enchanted dagger from his belt and got to his feet, turning around wildly every which way, the dagger pointed outward, as if to threaten Telly. It was clear he couldn't see Telly. He made a full circle, then gave up and ran toward the Queen.

Telly hurled herself at the man again, and this time they both tumbled to the ground. She wrestled with him, both of them rolling, tossing, and turning. Somehow, they managed to roll into the sitting room, knocking over end tables and lamps.

The two of them continued to tumble until they both smacked against a solid wooden coffee table. There was a loud crack as the man hit the back of his head against it. His head rolled in confusion, and the world began flickering between blues and full color.

He couldn't maintain his time spell.

Out of the corner of her eye, Telly saw the handmaidens' bodies flickering, pausing, and moving as if in one of Drew's video games going berserk. But this was no video game. It was time stuttering, holding them in place in spurts.

The blue-gifted man felt around aimlessly, trying to grab Telly, but she still remained unseen with her magic. They tossed around a few more times, then by chance the man found her neck and latched onto it with all his might. He began to choke her.

Her body began to shimmer orange, and she was visible again. Frustrated and overwhelmed, Telly reached out a hand weakly. Orange power roared out of her palm and out of the room as she struggled.

Hide her! she ordered her magic.

Then Telly could hear all of the handmaidens screaming; they had become unfrozen as the man's time magic faded, and the world was once again in full color.

The man, noticing that his spell had dissipated, narrowed his eyes at Telly and smacked her hard in the face. He jumped off her, making for the bedchamber. Telly rolled away, wheezing and trying to catch her breath. Her neck felt mangled.

Get up! she told herself.

Struggling, Telly managed to get to her feet, then ran after him into the Queen's bedchamber. Inside, Glacia was next to the empty bed, frantically looking for the Queen.

"Where is she? Where is the Queen?" the man yelled at Glacia.

"I don't know," Glacia cried, confused.

"Bitch! I need her now!" he screamed, flashing his dagger.

Telly looked around and saw one of Queen's hair sticks on the vanity. She grabbed it.

"Last chance!" he roared. "Tell me where she is!"

"Please don't hurt me," Glacia cried out. "I don't know!"

"Then you will die!" The man swung his enchanted dagger toward her, guided by his blue dimensional magic. Just as the dagger was about to hit Glacia, Telly lunged at the man, plunging the sharp hair stick deep into his side.

The man screamed, and the enchanted dagger dropped to the ground, its spell broken from the man's sudden severance of his spell.

Telly jumped onto him again, her weight knocking both of them to the ground. Knowing that this man could freeze her in a moment, she knew a second was all she had.

With a hard jerk of her leg, Telly kneed the man in the balls as hard as she could. He cried out in pain, doubling over. With a flick of his hand, he summoned his blue magic, pouring it over to his dagger. It levitated in the air, turning. Then it flung itself toward Telly.

Telly moved. It missed her chest, but it lodged itself in her shoulder. She cried out, and her mind went blank. All she could think about was the pain in her shoulder. She lost focus of everything around her, including her spell around the Queen.

Emerald lay visible on the bed once more.

The man's eyes met Telly's. He looked at Emerald, then back at Telly. He burst with vibrant blue energy, and it swirled around him. Then that energy came toward her.

Telly was going to be his next victim. Pushing through the pain of her wounded shoulder, Telly pulled the dagger out of her flesh. Grimacing, she leapt toward him and jammed the dagger hard into his chest.

"You bitch!" he screamed.

Looking straight into the man's crystal-blue eyes, Telly's heart beat wildly as she pushed the dagger further in. "Who are you?" Telly asked, shaken. "Did you do this to the Queen? Is this why she is like this?"

"You think I would tell you?" He spit on her glasses. Blood gurgled out of his mouth, then his eyes began to fade.

Telly grabbed him, shaking him by his clothes. "Answer me! Are you from Olympia? Who sent you?"

The man smiled smugly, then narrowed his eyes. Slowly, his eyes flickered closed, more blood shot out of his mouth, and his body went limp. He was dead.

Glacia let out a scream.

Telly let go of his collar, and he plopped unceremoniously to the side of the bed, then bounced off, falling to the floor like a heavy knapsack.

Suddenly, her injured shoulder exploded with pain, as if her body had just remembered that she was still hurt. Her arm went limp. She took a few deep breaths, but with each one, her shoulder burned like it was on fire. Trying to push through the pain, she inched her way to the corpse to inspect it.

"I need a vial, jar, anything…" she called out to the handmaiden, her eyes still locked on the dead man.

The handmaiden's footsteps faded out of the room.

I wonder if he is from Olympia? Telly thought as she waited. *Has to be. Scion said they had the power to move through dimensions!*

They needed Geeta back here at the palace. Heck, *she* needed Geeta.

The man's body began to bubble, and Telly jumped back at the sight, startled. The corpse was disintegrating before her eyes, rapidly decaying. The body dwindled down to bones, then crumbled into dust. Finally, the dust puffed up into the air. All that remained were his clothes and jewelry, piled on top of each other in a lump. Her mouth dropped open in horror.

Glacia returned with a vial, but it was too late. "What…? Where is he?"

"Gone…" Telly said, stunned. She turned to the handmaiden. "Where is the councilor? We need Geeta to protect the Queen. I'm talking right this very moment."

"Right away," Glacia said as she scrambled out of the Queen's bedchamber.

Another wave of pain shot through her shoulder. Telly grimaced. Geeta would actually be able to protect her. Telly's power was pathetic. She had gotten lucky stabbing the man, but even then she'd missed his magic entirely.

There was really only one explanation. Olympia had found a way inside the palace. Until Geeta got here, they were the only ones who could protect the Queen.

And she had no confidence they'd be able to do that.

CHAPTER 51

ORANGE

Twenty point two miles off in the horizon, there was a flash in the wavelength of 400 nanometers. Violet in color. Drew considered the coordinates of the flash, then summoned his orangish-red wind, heading off in that direction.

As he flew closer to where the burst of light had been, Drew saw many wastelanders gathered in the area of the initial flash. Several miles to the south of the group, the Arcadian army approached. By the looks of it, the Arcadian army was on their way to aid the wastelanders.

Drew's cybernetic eye scanned the perimeter. Several outposts were being set up across the area. Groups of militia were being formed and stationed all around the perimeter of Arcadia, to protect the kingdom from all fronts. Even on the major roadway that led from Olympia to Arcadia, there was a slew of people gathered, ready to protect Arcadia's borders.

Something caught his attention.

Right behind the wastelanders' camp was a swirling violet light. A portal of violet magic wavered with energy as men walked out of a portal, joining the crowd. He recognized a few of the men—they were from his camp.

Terminating his scans, Drew filled his circuitry and veins with orange power, and it vibrated within him. Reaching further within, he called upon the power that lay next to his original—red. The orangish-red wind took ahold of him, and he was airborne.

Drew flew to the newly installed encampment, then hovered over it. Men were yelling at him. He couldn't understand what they were saying since they were all yelling at the same time.

He was about to drop into the crowd when the sound of gunfire erupted. Quickly, Drew formed an orangish-yellow shield, sending the bullets ricocheting just in time.

Then, more bullets.

"Stop!" a man's voice pierced the commotion.

Victor's voice.

"Stop shooting! He is one of us!"

The gunfire stopped, and Drew landed on his feet, crouching over from the impact. His shield still fully surrounded his body, the color vibrantly illuminating the crowd. His legs felt weak, as if his circuits needed adjusting. He was overdue for a tune-up. At some point, he would have to get Telly or Garrett to change out some parts.

Grimacing from the pain in his legs, Drew made it into a full standing position, staring as Victor pushed his way through the crowd, along with a woman with a staff in her hand.

"Drew! Where were you?" Victor said. "Why didn't you come with us?"

It was human nature that people needed to know everyone's comings and goings, and Drew had mostly learned to ignore it. But this was Victor, and by the expression in his face, Drew could tell that the man was genuinely worried.

Drew cocked his head. "Needed to protect the remnants of our camp."

"But why?"

Because… it was home… Cannot let my home be destroyed.

Drew shook. Victor wouldn't understand his logic. Even Drew didn't understand it. "Also… w-w-w-wanted t-t-t-tooooo… to give you more time to reach the refuge," Drew said. "Important-t-t-t… important information left behind. Couldn't carry everything with us. N-n-n-needed to keep-p-p-p… keep it safe. Hid it with my magic," Drew said.

It was true, but really, he'd wanted to keep his home safe and intact.

The woman with the violet eyes stared at him. His circuits tingled.

Victor noticed. "Drew, this is Geeta. Queen Emerald sent her here to help stop the Olympian armies."

Drew scanned her. The only data that registered in his databanks was that he had seen her a few months ago for a few brief moments during the struggle against the future sorceress.

"So this is the cyborg with magic?" Geeta asked breathlessly. She walked around him curiously, making his circuits stand on end. She noticed this and paused. "Sorry. I didn't mean to make you feel uncomfortable. I still can't get used to technology mixed with magic. It's unusual, yet curious."

Malfunction.

He shook. "It… it is acceptable for you t-to stare," Drew acknowledged.

She glanced at him, and Drew could have sworn he saw a smile on her face, but when he scanned her expressions, nothing came up.

"A cyborg with attitude," she said, raising one eyebrow. "I think we will get along."

The woman was strange. Hard to read.

Malfunction.

"N-n-n-neeed-d-d… need to warn camps. Olympian a-r-r… armies are coming! Spotted them out in-n-n-n… in wastelands," Drew continued.

"We know," Victor said. "Follow us."

Geeta walked in front of the group as Victor walked beside him. From the crowds, Drew heard excited, invigorated talking, some showing each other their new weapons. It was the magitech weapons he had developed with Garrett. The camp had dispersed them.

Geeta led them to an open tent that held a few Arcadian military men, along with a few wastelanders.

"Who is this?" one of the prominent men asked from within the tent.

"This is one of ours. One with magic," Victor said pointedly.

The man looked at Drew. "A machine? Is this the…"

"Yes, it's the one Victor told you about," Geeta said, turning to Drew. "Drew, this is Duke Uthgard. He is Arcadia's military advisor on the Inner Council."

Drew nodded, and the man smiled.

"I can see why the Queen wanted to save you cyborgs," said Uthgard. "Such fascinating minds." He turned to everyone, addressing them. "We need to start evacuating the southern camps." He turned on a device, and a map appeared. He pointed to a specific area. "It won't be long until the Olympian army will be here, and you don't want to be caught in the crossfire. The city border guard has already been instructed to let in the wasteland folk, but only for a certain amount of time. They have to get moving quickly."

"I'll have one of my men spread the word in their camp," Victor offered.

"Good," the Duke said. "And as far as communications are concerned, I received word from one of the landed transports that the new device back in Arcadia will be up anytime now. So hopefully our personal devices will be able to make transmissions soon. Estimated in two hours' time. Let's hope it works. With us spread out all over the damn place, we'll need it." He took a breath, then glanced around at the group. "Once connected, I have men assigned to communicate to the outer camps about evacuating. They aren't in the line of fire, but it's best to be safe."

"Hopefully they won't run into any trouble," Geeta said doubtfully.

Drew's circuits gave him a strange feeling. He shook.

The violet woman looked over, then approached him. "You all right there?" she asked, raising her eyebrow.

"I… I will help evacuate the camps."

"We could really use your help on the front," she said pointedly.

"Neg-g-g… negative. Must help those without proper defense," Drew argued. Those people didn't have magitech weapons. They would need his help most.

The group looked at him for several beats, then Victor shrugged. "No use telling Drew what he can and can't do. He's going to do it anyway."

The Duke snorted with laughter, slapping Victor on the back in agreement, while Geeta flared her nose in protest, her silver nose ring looking predominate.

"Fine. Let the cyborg help out, since he is so determined," she said, crossing her arms. "But once you are done, we will need your help at the front. I have no idea what we are up against, but I have a horrible feeling. Especially with that strange tower."

Drew cocked his head at the statement. He knew exactly what Geeta was talking about. He had seen that very same tower—and who sat in its seat.

"The Olympian army is carrying around a portable tower," Geeta explained to him, not realizing what he knew. "My guess it has to do with your communications being down out here. There is a chair at the top of the tower. I'd venture to say it's for a gifted."

"You ar-r-r-re correct. For human ch-h-h… child," Drew answered.

Geeta's mouth dropped. "Are you sure? A *child*?"

"Affirmative. S-s-s-saw the child with my scans. A boy."

Geeta huffed, shaking her head. "If this boy is gifted, then we are in for a world of hurt."

"Why do you say that?" Victor asked.

"Gifted children do not understand their gift fully. They can unleash their full powers unintentionally, and are unable to control their magic once they do so." Her eyes darted around the group. "We will be playing a dangerous game with fire."

"Well, let's hope this boy child isn't some magical being," Duke Uthgard said.

"We can't count on that," Geeta said, sighing.

Drew calculated her words. A gifted child. Fully unleash their powers. Those people in the surrounding camps… they needed to get to safety.

"I… I will help the camps get to safety, then m-m-m-meet up with you, Miss Geeta," Drew stated.

Her face shot up. "Why did you call me Miss Geeta?"

Why had he called her Miss? He had never called anyone else Miss before. Had he?

"You… you seem… p-p-p-polite?" Drew said, coming up with the first statement that came to mind.

Geeta growled, stomping off.

"W-w-what? D-d-d-did I say something wrong?" Drew asked, looking around, confused.

The men just laughed.

CHAPTER 52

YELLOW

Please, don't take him!" she cried out. "Please, please, just leave him be!"

"Shut up, bitch!" an officer yelled back.

"You can't take him!" she cried out.

Children's cries could be heard with her screams. His children. The woman ran up to the officer, pointing her gun.

"Don't do it, Darcy," he told her. "Keep the kids safe."

"You can't leave," she cried. "You won't be yourself anymore!"

"Put the gun down, bitch!" the officer yelled at Darcy.

More soldiers surrounded them. Behind the group, he could see men and women of his camp being shot, the ones who resisted. Other men were being led in shackles, loaded like transport cargo onto a military vehicle.

"Darcy, just listen to the man. Just put the gun down," he called out to her.

"No! These assholes can't take you!" Darcy screamed.

Just as Darcy was about to pull the trigger, shots were fired.

It was too late. She was terminated. Darcy was terminated. She slumped to the ground as his kids screamed.

Darcy. She was gone.

He turned to the commander, and rage filled him. He shook. They killed his wife. They *killed* her. But what happened next, he couldn't process.

The commander pulled a gun out and executed his children like sheep ready for slaughter. They slumped over their mother, dead like their mother.

They killed his children.

They killed his *children.*

He screamed. Screamed with all that was left inside him. His rage transformed into pure wrath. He was going to kill them. Terminate and abort their lives for what they'd done to his family.

Endorphins kicked in, and he broke free from the metal bindings and grabbed a large rock from the ground, his breath heavy with intense grief. With a swift, violent movement, he leapt at the commander and slammed the rock against his head. Brains and blood went splattering while a loud crunch echoed in the camp.

They'd killed everyone he loved. They were gone.

Over and over, he slammed the rock against the commander's head while men yelled at him to stop.

They killed his Darcy. They killed his children. His *children.*

There was a burst of fire, and his body felt like a thousand bees had stung him at once.

They killed his children. His *children…*

Blood.

Noise.

Blood.

White noise.

Yellow.

He coughed.

Scion opened his eyes. His ears picked up a trickle of water from the cave's stalactites mixed in with the low mumblings of people.

He looked up at the cave's ceiling at the delicate stalactites. There was much beauty to be found everywhere, but he had been robbed of beauty a long time ago. The only beauty he saw was in the numbers that he calculated in his mind. But even the numbers did not bring him joy like how his family did.

He did not like sleeping. Every time he did, he saw his wife's and children's faces, causing his heart to hurt. And with every dream, more and more of his memories returned to him.

They had killed everything that he loved. They were gone. All gone. His wife. His children.

Scion struggled to sit up. It was difficult, but he finally managed to prop himself up. The machine that was connected to him beeped. It told him that it didn't like him moving.

Olympia. They needed to be stopped. Miss Geeta, she would need help. Miss Geeta… she was similar to Darcy. Tough. Strong. Fearless.

He paused, listening to the soft mumblings within the cave. Another drip from the cave's ceiling. He would help Miss Geeta. He would stop Olympia. He had made it this far, warning the others. But it wasn't enough. He needed to help the others.

Olympia needed to be stopped.

They killed his children…

***

Drew approached the southern camp from overhead, radiating with his orange-red wind and orange-yellow barrier magic. Below, the wastelanders of the camp gathered together, in awe at the sight of him.

He landed firmly on the ground, his magic continuing to flow around him. Immediately, the campers drew their guns, aiming at him. They didn't shoot, but Drew could read from their expressions that they felt threatened. They watched him cautiously as he remained unmoving in his spot.

"I… I am h-h-h-here to help you. Must evacuate. Olympian army on t-t-t-their way. North, twenty miles," he warned.

They remained unchanged.

"Who the hell are you to tell us to leave our homeland?" a wasteland dweller called out, reaffirming the position of his gun.

"Y-y-y-you must leave now. Your life will be forfeit if you-u-u… you stay," Drew urged.

"Why?" called out another voice. "Why is Olympia suddenly looking for trouble with Arcadia?"

How was he going to convince a resistant crowd?

"B-b-b-because…" he started.

"Because they want Arcadia and the Queen for themselves," called out a voice, finishing his sentence.

Drew turned around, seeing the gifted woman in the frequency of 400 nanometers.

Miss Geeta. Gratefulness came over him. At least Miss Geeta had the correct words in her to persuade them.

"Thought you could use some help," Geeta said, a cool smile gracing her lips.

"B-b-b-but… but you are to be with the others," Drew countered.

"It's only for a moment, and I'll be on my way back in an instant. Besides, most people will heed the words of a human rather than a machine. No offense."

Drew nodded, then attempted to return the gratitude with a smile, but it came out wrong. She raised her eyebrow.

This woman is hard to understand, he thought. For Drew, most people were hard to understand in general, but he couldn't understand a half of percent of Miss Geeta's personality.

Many of the members of the camp whispered wildly with fear. An old woman appeared from the crowd. She looked worn down but sturdy at the same time.

"It is true, then, the rumors," the old woman said. "The Olympian army is coming this way. A transport came through here a day ago. Said they saw a bunch of foreign transports, but didn't say much else." The old woman walked up to Geeta, her gaze running the entire length of her body. "The gifted are real, it seems."

"We are no children's story, that I can guarantee," Geeta said to the woman. "You need to move everyone out of here. They are on their way to Arcadia, and they are not being friendly in the process. They desperately seek a cyborg of theirs and are searching all the camps as they make their way across the wastelands to Arcadia."

"We have no cyborgs," the old woman said.

"Tell that to them. They won't believe you," Geeta said. "Get as many guns on your people as you can. Drew, the cyborg you see here, will take the elderly and children to safety."

The old woman whipped around to look at everyone while they stared at her blankly. "You heard her!" she barked. "Arm yourselves. Those who can't fight, gather up and make your way to the refuge!"

"Arcadia is closer," Geeta argued. "Why not go there?"

"My people ain't going to no stinkin' city," the woman spat. "We've always gone to the refuge in times of trouble. Always." She grabbed a weapon from one of her guards.

"What are you doing?" Geeta asked.

"Fighting. What are you doing?"

"Fighting."

"Good. Then we're on the same page." The old woman loaded her magazine. "Don't be fooled by my age, girl."

Geeta shrugged. "Whatever you say. I'm not going to stop you."

"Tim! Get your ass over here!" yelled the woman.

A man jogged over. "What is it?"

"Gather the old folks and children. That cyborg fellow is going to help them get to the refuge. Stick with him and help."

Tim looked at Drew, eyeing him. "That thing is going to help us? Doubt it."

The woman slugged him across the face. "That wasn't a request."

"Yes, ma'am," he said, suddenly changing his tone of voice. He rubbed his head as the old woman trudged off.

From Drew's assessment, the woman packed a solid punch.

"I'll round up the people," the man said, turning to Drew. "Not sure what you can do."

"Protect," Drew said.

"I sure hope you can *protect*," the man scoffed. He jogged off, yelling throughout the camp for the elderly and children.

As Drew waited, Geeta came up to him. "Hurry to the caves and meet back me with the others as fast as you can. If I happen to clash with that army, I'm going to need some assistance."

"I will," Drew said. "It-it's that… I want to protect people. As m-m-m-many as I can."

"I know," she whispered.

Tim came back with a group of elderly and children. Thirty-one people to be exact. They all stood in front of him, waiting for him to say something.

Except words weren't coming to him.

Malfunction.

"Hey. Cyborg. They're ready," Tim said, slapping him on the back.

Geeta turned to him. "I'll summon a portal," she offered.

Drew nodded. "Thank you, Miss Geeta."

Geeta closed her eyes and stretched out her hand, and it glowed with purple energy. She moved her hand in a circular motion in the air. As she did, her magic trailed behind it, creating a swirling magical vortex.

She opened her eyes, satisfied. "There you go. Should be the location of the caves," she said.

The crowd of elderly and children gasped in amazement, their eyes wide with wonder.

"Everyone into the portal," Geeta said.

"Will it hurt?" asked one of the children.

Geeta crouched down next to the little girl, placing a hand on her shoulder. "Don't be afraid, sweetheart. It's like riding a transport."

The little girl smiled, and one by one, the group started entering the portal.

When half the group had entered, Geeta turned to Drew. "I'm going. See you soon, I hope."

Drew nodded, then he caught a cool but subtle smile on Geeta's face as she turned, then flashed away in her violet-blue magic.

CHAPTER 53

WHITE

I will mark my chosen with a sign for all to see. Pure white light, the combined powers of my perfect holiness. Behold, my children, for the hour is coming when I will make the chosen one known. They will gather each color of my perfection, and the heavens will rejoice! When you see my chosen, be ready, for the earth and the heavens will gleam like the first ray of light that came into being.

—The lost writings of *The Gift of the White*
Author unknown, 2765 B.E.

Derek walked beside Elyathi as she led him through the High Court halls. The clutter of her necklaces of transmuted blood gems and empty vials jingled as she moved, and every so often, she held the gems in the palm of her hand to reassure herself that they were still with her. She could still feel the pulse of the life force radiating from her transmuted gems; they had life within their veins.

Derek remained silent as they walked. Elyathi glanced over at him. He was amazed at the citadel and his new surroundings. She remembered the first time she had seen the High Court citadel. Everything was so beautiful, from the enchanted objects to the ornateness of the structure. Derek's eyes occasionally wandered to hers, and she flashed him a reassuring smile, which he quickly returned. But behind those eyes, she could see the sadness that burdened his soul.

Her mood darkened. Why was darkness so vile that it corrupted the innocent? Her daughter, put through an unspeakable evil, one so heinous that it made her sick to think about. And that very same evil, used a vessel—Derek's body—to commit a horrendous sin. And in that sin, she was sure that her daughter's soul lay in fragments, hurt beyond all repair, and Derek now was the face of her daughter's tormentor.

That sorceress would burn in hell for all eternity for what she did to her daughter, and how she used her son-in-law's vessel for her means of revolting pleasure.

Derek had always been so virtuous and devoted to her daughter for as long as she knew him. And the sorceress ruined him, just like how she ruined and *defiled* her daughter. Derek did all that he could to rescue her daughter from Damaris. In fact, she recalled all the times she'd seen Derek and Emerald together when they were in their teens and early twenties. She had witnessed firsthand how much he cherished her daughter—she was his world. And now, seeing Derek after all these years, it was apparent that those qualities had never been lost. But what was lost was his spirit; the sorceress had broken it with her wicked deed.

What she had said to Derek was true—she believed every word Derek said. If Derek had been lying about what happened to her daughter, then why would he do everything in his power to change the course of time and rid the world of the sorceress once and for all? No, he was innocent, just like her daughter. Both were innocent.

Elyathi clenched her jaw, and a small tear formed in the corner of her eye. The sorceress was pure evil. And she would eradicate that evil.

She wiped the corner of her eye gently, and Derek took notice.

"My lady, are you all right?" Derek asked quietly.

Elyathi quickly removed her hand from her eye, then felt a bit flushed. "I'm quite all right." She turned fully to look at him, then gave him a reassuring smile. "Do not worry about me, Derek."

"But I do worry," he said slowly.

She knew what he was thinking. He was worried about whether she blamed him for what had happened to her daughter.

His eyes shifted down to the floor. "If it is about what I told you earlier—"

"Derek," she said, interrupting him.

He glanced at her, shame was in those eyes of his.

"I spoke the truth back in my chambers. You were used. The sorceress used you to defile my daughter. She will pay for her sins, and the new time will restore what once was."

"I wish for that more than anything," he said.

"It will be so, because I know so. For I am the chosen, am I not?"

His eyes lit up slightly, then he gave her a soft smile. "You are, my lady."

He looks exactly like Samir, Elyathi thought. They looked almost identical, father and son, except the color of Derek's eyes and hair, which were blue of course. The last time she had seen Derek, he was just a young man of twenty-one. Now, years later, he had filled out into a much more mature, grown man, and he very much looked like the King of York.

Thoughts of Samir flooded her mind. That *day*, the one when Damaris came storming into her chambers. He'd discovered their secret, but it wasn't the secret that Damaris thought it was. For much of her life, Elyathi wished it had been true, her and Samir. But it wasn't right. She was married, and so was he. It was forbidden. It was against the will of the God of Light, and in accordance with *The Spectrum*, one must keep their body pure, only devoted to their spouses.

But inside, she couldn't help but have secret feelings for him. Whenever Samir came to visit Arcadia, Elyathi hung onto his every move—for he was like wood to her fire. Every glance, every word was like adding a log to her eternal flame, lighting her darkened world. She wrestled with her desire for him and spent many countless nights awake with tears. How unfair her life was, never to be loved, cursed to spend it around the man she so desperately desired, all while married to a man who imprisoned her body, soul, and spirit.

Whenever Samir visited Arcadia, he never looked at her more than he had to, and he never gave her more praise than anyone else at court. In fact, it was much less than anyone else at the Arcadian court parties and events. But thinking back, Elyathi concluded that perhaps Samir *had* secretly desired her in return. There had been hints, but nothing ever was ever said. If it had been said, it would have been a sin in the God of Light's eyes. No, Samir was only there to rescue her that day. They had a plan...

It was such a tragedy that it was never carried out, escaping to York with her daughter. But it all worked out in the end—she was rescued by the High Court's gifted, and now Derek had appeared to her. Everything was finally going in her favor, and the God of Light was shining his rays of power upon her. Derek had the means to bring Emerald to her. And with her daughter by her side, they would acquire Ikaria's blood. Then, they could finally form the new earth and restore magic to the heavens where it belonged.

The justices would never truly understand the God of Light's ultimate purpose or his ultimate design, for only Elyathi, the chosen one, could fully understand the prophecy. Elyathi kept many things to herself, for it was between her and God, and not for the High Court to fully understand the commands given directly to her. They were serving their purpose to the God of Light by aiding the cleansing of the earth. They were given their positions on earth by God Himself, and Elyathi could see the blessings God was bestowing onto them just by their success.

The new earth. *One* timeline. It would bring her much joy, for she would have no memory of the hell that Damaris put her through. It was stated in the Chosen One prophecy, and even hinted at in *The Spectrum*, that all tears would be wiped away. Maybe, in the new earth, her spirit would allow her to freely love once again.

Elyathi smiled to herself, and Derek glanced over at her. It was apparent he was nervous. Poor soul. More the reason why he was so good. He cared.

She gave him another reassuring smile, and Derek loosened the tension in his face. His eyes, they were so bright. But she could also see the pain in them. It very much reminded her of her pain that she had suffered for many, many years…

They came upon the court clerk's desk. He immediately rose, bowing to her. "Lady Elyathi. How the light shines in your presence as always!" he complimented. "Your servant came and told us that you would be paying the court a visit."

"Yes," Elyathi said. "I hope that the court has cleared their schedule. I have returned from my given task."

"Of course, my lady. The High Court will always make time for you. They are already waiting for you," the clerk stated, bowing.

"Perfect," Elyathi said, then she turned to Derek. "Let's go."

Elyathi could see his nerves were back in full force as he bowed to her. The doors opened, and Elyathi walked into the High Court audience hall with Derek trailing slightly behind her. All the high justices were seated on their thrones. Except the green throne, which remained empty because of Oriel's death.

Oriel deserved to die, Elyathi thought bitterly. *Keeping my Emerald from me!* The justice was probably burning in hell for his actions, for going against the will of the High Court, and ultimately *her*. She was the one destined to restore the world to its glory. He had gotten his just punishment. For no one stood against the God of Light and his chosen one.

One thing that was most curious to Elyathi, however, was that the green-gifted time traveler had been shielded from the flow of time. Borgen had never come across him. And as for Tyllos, he had no visions of that man either. Elyathi knew he existed, for he had been the one to heal her during the last days of her pregnancy with Emerald. She had told the High Court about the man, for he had the green gift too, and he seemed like he would be a good fit on their court and to fulfill the prophecy. And ever since she told them about the time traveler, the High Court had been actively searching for him through their scrying. For if the man was still traveling, he should have been accessible in the flow of time. But it seemed that Oriel had been hiding this man from them in the space-time continuum. For many years.

Now the green-gifted time traveler could and *would* be found. He would aid them freely, Elyathi was sure of it. He had a good heart, just like her; she could sense it. He seemed like the kind of man who would have the deep conviction and spirit to fulfill the prophecy, just like her. In a sense, Elyathi felt that he was a kindred spirit… very much like her childhood friend Victor. So sweet, so kind.

Elyathi stood before the justices, with Derek behind and off to the side. The High Court made a gesture, and the two of them bowed deeply. Elyathi looked back at him for a moment, smiled at him, and turned back to meet the justices' gaze.

"Lady Elyathi," Belinda greeted her, nodding her head in respect. "How good it is to see you back so soon." Her eyes trailed to Derek, and she smiled delightfully. "Is this the one?"

"Indeed," Elyathi said.

She looked to Derek, making a slight movement to him, signaling for him to step forward. Derek did so, standing before them. He looked so regal, even more so than the justices themselves.

"What is your name?" Borgen asked. "I am aware of all blue-gifted, but I have not met you, sir."

Elyathi smiled. "You haven't met him because he is not from here."

The justices exchanged glances, then looked at Derek curiously.

"Where are you from, blue-gifted?" Tyllos asked.

Derek ran his fingers through his deep-blue curls, then took a deep breath. "My name is Derek," he said. "I am King of Arcadia from the past, 2385 M.E." He kept his gaze steady on them.

They all leaned in at full attention. "So you are from the time that the Sorceress Ikaria interrupted, are you?" Tyllos asked. "If you are still standing here, that means you have consumed the blood of the green, have you not?"

Derek paused, then lowered his eyes. "Indeed, I have. I was not exactly happy about it, but if it meant killing the sorceress, I had to. I did it happily."

Elyathi could see the marvel in their eyes as the High Court eyed him for a long moment. "He is my son-in-law," Elyathi said, breaking the silence. "Married to my daughter. Which means that now is the time to get my daughter. He has the means to retrieve her."

Belinda and the other members of the High Court smiled. "This is beyond good news. Now we can halt the plans involving our blue-gifted," Borgen said with mild enthusiasm. The old man hardly ever got excited over anything. Unless, of course, it had to do with their ultimate plans.

"Yes, I quite agree. Now is as good time as any to get her, especially with our blue-gifted dropping like flies trying to do it themselves." Belinda eyed him, then continued. "What I would really like to know is: Do you have your analogous or adjacent magics, Derek?"

"I have some abilities of the violet and green," Derek answered her. "They grow stronger each day. Especially the violet."

"So you can get inside one's mind, then?"

"I'm... I'm not sure. I haven't tried, in all fairness. I have summoned the violet force several times, but I have never tried using the ability in the mental realm." He paused. "However, there have been times when I think I have accessed it. On accident."

Belinda gave a cool smile. "That seems promising. With some study and practice, I feel confident that you can grow in that magic." Belinda's face turned serious. "Why have you come to kill the sorceress, Derek?"

Derek's cheeks reddened, and his expression grew dark. "Because she interfered and altered the course of my life and the lives of others who reside in Arcadia, causing irreparable damage," he stated angrily, his eyes shifting. "I will do anything necessary to fix it—to change time, as you will. To do that, I must get rid her *permanently*." He stepped a foot forward. "I have been told by the witch herself that she did not like you, and wanted to see your downfall."

"Those were her words?" Belinda asked, almost in jest.

"Something to that effect," Derek said. "I swore to myself that I would cast her from existence once and for all. Tell me, is it true? Do you wish to be rid of her?"

"She has been a thorn in our side from day one. First her father, then her. And now, it seems her sister has picked up on her insolent behavior," Belinda said. "We need her blood for our purpose. After that, once her power is removed, we could care less what becomes of her. Personally, I think it would be fitting to execute her along with her sister. We could finally be rid of that whole family."

"Then I devote myself to your cause," Derek announced. "I will help you. Whatever you need, I am yours. But it comes with a price. You must let *me* kill her!"

He sounds just as passionate as Samir was in his early years, Elyathi thought. She smiled at the justices, exchanging a pleasing glance with Tyllos.

"I like your son-in-law," Nyrden said, chuckling out loud. "Much more than that ass Rubius."

Elyathi twisted her smile into a frown at the name. He made a mockery of the High Court and all they stood for.

"You will find him much more suitable to our cause than the High Inquisitor," Elyathi offered. "Perhaps, High Justices, you might reconsider the offer given to the High Inquisitor. Derek here has much potential, and is much more aligned with our goals than that of Rubius, who cares nothing for the court. That man only lives for his selfish ambitions."

The justices looked to each other, then nodded in agreement. "Speaking of the High Inquisitor," Tyllos stated, then turned to Derek, "there is a matter that perhaps you can help us out with, and in turn, it would lead to the sorceress's head on a spike."

"Anything," Derek said ambitiously.

"You see, we sent another gifted, this High Inquisitor Rubius, to extract some information from the sorceress. Like Lady Elyathi stated, he is not aligned with our future vision of this High Court."

"You want me to get the information from her mind?"

"Yes," Tyllos said. "Finish the High Inquisitor's job. Once we have the information, Elyathi will take care of Ikaria's gift."

"Then, after we collect Ikaria's blood and life force," Belinda said, "we want you to travel back and bring your wife to this court. We will seat your wife on the green throne. In return, you will get your own dimensional kingdom when the earth is reborn."

"Dimensional kingdom?"

"Yes. But we will talk more about that later," Belinda said.

Elyathi saw Derek shift uncomfortably. "I can try to get you that information. But I must remind you, I am nowhere near as powerful with my violet magic. Like I said, I've only accessed it a few times. And the sorceress, she has a way of twisting your mind to her will. Also, about the Queen Emerald. I don't know if my wife would come here willingly."

"You hear that, Borgen?" Nyrden blurted out. "That's why I have not married. Too many problems."

Borgen rolled his eyes and sighed, as if they had discussed it recently.

"Do not worry about getting Emerald here," Elyathi interjected. "We will discuss that when the time comes." Her eyes met his icy-blue ones, so crystal clear. Full of sadness and sorrow, hurting her soul. She felt so terrible for him.

He maintained their eye contact, then he turned to Belinda. "What information do you need?"

"We seek information regarding technology and the cyborgs," Belinda said. "The Sorceress Ikaria was given the information when she unlocked the black gift."

"You don't need the sorceress, High Justices," Derek offered. "There are many people from my time that can give you what you need. They are knowledgeable in the sciences and technology. Just take the power away from the sorceress and be done with her! I can bring you people who can help you. Perhaps I can do this when I go back and get Emerald."

"Considering that you have the means to bring them here, that is a good suggestion. However, they won't be able to survive unless they themselves are gifted, and they must have drank green-gifted blood. I doubt that there are ones who understand the sciences who are gifted, no?"

"There are, in fact. Two of them. One is a full orange-gifted, the other is light orange," Derek stated.

"Only the full orange-gifted would be able to consume the green blood and have it work," Borgen answered. "Tinted gifted are blessed with only a hint of power, and cannot take on other powers."

"Then I will get him for you. You will be delighted to know he is a cyborg himself."

Belinda and the others smiled, then nodded to Elyathi. "Excellent. Bring him here, along with your green-gifted wife. But first, you must help Elyathi get the sorceress's life force. You will have to paralyze her mind and her body to hold her still while Elyathi drains her power."

"I will do everything in my power to do so," Derek stated boldly.

Elyathi glanced over at Derek. Yes, he would need more power. She smiled to herself. Elyathi turned to the court. "Let me give him some of my power," she offered. "I have seen the sorceress in secret, and what she can do. Derek will need it."

"Granted," Belinda said. "Now go back to World Sector Six. Tell the High Inquisitor that he has some help. If he complains, send him back here. I would like to talk to him anyway."

"I will." Elyathi smiled haughtily just thinking of the High Inquisitor's face once she told him.

The High Court got to their feet. Elyathi bowed, with Derek following suit.

"I hope to hear of your success very soon," Belinda said.

"It *will* be done, for it is the God of Light's will," Elyathi answered.

"Godspeed to you and your son-in-law. You are dismissed."

They bowed to the High Court once again, then exited the chamber. The clerk looked up as they walked by, then went back in his documents.

"What did you think?" Elyathi asked, looking to Derek.

"It is only a first impression, but they didn't strike me being one way or another," Derek said, eyeing her. "But if you fully trust them, then I am willing to work with them. Especially if it means that I get to take care of Ikaria." He smiled darkly. "I can't wait to see the look on her face when she loses her magic. It would be… poetic justice. She bestowed power to me, and I will aid in taking hers."

"Yes, I agree." Elyathi smiled. How she'd missed Derek, missed seeing him grow into a man. A man with great power.

"When are we going to see the sorceress?" Derek asked eagerly.

"Very soon. But first, we must go back to my chambers."

***

As they returned to Elyathi's chambers, Derek felt his spirit strengthened. It was as if everything that he had envisioned in the flow of time was actually becoming a reality. Ikaria would be reduced a mere memory. And Emerald...

Thoughts of Emerald filled Derek's mind with delight. Her glances at him, filled with desire. She would truly be his this time.

Conflicted thoughts echoed in his mind, until it became apparent what he truly had to do. Initially, Derek intended to kill the sorceress and return to the time when Emerald had loved him. But with his vision of the future, with Elyathi sitting behind his throne and Emerald in loving adoration of him, it was clear that it was his destiny to work with the High Court in order to achieve his heart's desire. Of course, he cared not for the High Court; they were but a means to an end. But Elyathi trusted them, and they had the same mindset—to rid the world of that witch. And if that was what they wanted, Derek would gladly take part and help them, for Elyathi believed in him.

Emerald... He was to bring her to this future after he was done with Ikaria. How would she fall in love with him, like how he had seen in the flow of time? Derek still couldn't figure that part out. But he believed that this was what he was supposed to be doing—helping Elyathi and the High Court. Perhaps Emerald would forgive him and consider him a friend and a lover if he reunited her with her mother. Whatever the variable was, Derek knew that her love would be restored to him. Time itself had told him so. They would be together, and she would have his children.

He gave himself a private smile, delighted at the future prospects. His thoughts turned to what kind of "power" Elyathi was to give him. He would soon find out, he supposed.

Elyathi's servant greeted them, and they stepped inside.

"Please, leave us alone," Elyathi ordered her servant.

Her servant complied, leaving the receiving chamber as Derek seated himself at a table near one of the windows overlooking the gardens. Sunlight burned brightly across the citadel, and the breeze was brisk, but not too chilly that it made Derek cold.

"Is this about giving me that power you asked the High Court permission for?" Derek asked.

Elyathi scanned her chambers, then opened a small compartment, grabbing something. "Yes, it is," Elyathi answered. She had a small enchanted dirk in her hand.

Derek eyed the dagger but did not flinch. Elyathi noticed his gaze fixated on the dagger, then smiled.

"Do not worry, Derek. This will hurt me far more than it will hurt you," she said softly, coming to the table and seating herself across from him.

She rolled up the left sleeve of her dress, baring her forearm. Derek saw several scars on her arms, then shot her a look, realizing what was going to happen.

Before words left his lips, Elyathi sliced her arm quickly, flinching in the process. Blood immediately began to flow, glowing as it bled from her limb. The blood pulsated light in sync with her heartbeat, or so Derek assumed. Elyathi stretched out her arm, inviting him to receive her gift. Her power was there, all within the contents of her blood.

Derek watched, almost in curious fascination, as it trickled down her arm and splattered on the table. "The first time I drank gifted blood was pure torment," he said hesitantly. "It..." His voice trailed off as he lost himself in his thoughts, recalling the last time he drank Emerald's blood. His time visions and his senses were heightened, almost erotic. "Let's just say it made me more aware of my body," Derek confessed to her.

"Those who drank of my blood looked more than satisfied," Elyathi reassured him. "You should know that I do not often freely give my blood. Only those worthy of the cause are granted access. Not even the High Inquisitor, the one whose job you will finish, has been this fortunate."

She gestured once again, glancing at her bleeding arm. Then her empty white eyes met his, sparkling like prisms.

"Now please, take my blood."

Derek felt awkward as he took Elyathi's arm and lifted it to his lips.

She noticed his hesitation and smiled. "I understand how reserved you are. You can just dip your finger in my blood and have a taste, like all the others, but you won't get as much power as you would drinking directly from my beating life force," Elyathi stated. Just then, a dark smile washed over her. "However, I truly wish for you to drink directly from me; that is my heart's true desire. The High Court does not know what I just told you, nor have they drank directly from my life force.

"But you, Derek, I feel your soul. It is as if I have found a part of myself in you, a part that was broken, lost, and damaged many years ago. But now, with you here by my side, it's as if my soul has been healed." She paused, giving him a bright smile, her eyes lighting up like the heavens. "*You* are most worthy. So please, I urge you to drink as I have offered. You will need as much power as you can to master the violet magic. It will help us force that sorceress into submission, and ultimately, it will contribute to reshaping the face of the earth."

Her words rang in his ears. Never had anyone praised him as much as she just had. Yes, he had been praised for his hard work in court when he was the Prince of York for all his youth. But this, it was beyond anything anyone had ever told him.

Elyathi… She made him feel important, special, and… *powerful.* Derek raised her arm up to his lips, then pushed them against her arm, the coppery taste flooding his mouth.

At first, Derek's instincts told him to pull away. After all, his mouth was on the arm of his *mother-in-law*, a woman he had known since he was a child. It made it all so terribly awkward. But as the blood mixed with his saliva, it suddenly slipped his mind why he hesitated in the first place, and with each swallow came *power.*

The coppery taste changed moment by moment to sweet honey.

And he wanted more.

Derek began to drink viciously, and he could feel the blood mixing with his life force. His heart pounded in his chest and hammered in his ears, but he cared not. It was a fierceness of his own, awakening his spirit. Through his mind, he saw his life force, blue in color, becoming more intense in hue. But also, deep within his innermost being, he saw the darkness surrounding the blue. They flowed side by side as if paired yet inseparable.

The power pounded through him, and he wanted more and more. It was like he had an appetite that could not be filled. The more he tasted the blood, the more power flowed through him, making him feel almost as if he had the power of God Himself.

No one could stand against him. *No one.*

"Derek?" Elyathi's voice asked within the darkness. "Is your life force becoming stronger?"

He didn't want to pull away from the power. It was addicting. He couldn't get enough. He had to pull away to answer the queen. But the power…

He kept drinking like a leech that could not stop. Derek wanted *more.*

Elyathi's words echoed in the darkness in his mind. "Yes. Fill yourself with my power. I want to *crush* that woman."

Drink… commanded the darkness. *Drink…*

CHAPTER 54

GREEN

Suresh waited behind an oversized white-marble pillar, watching the many people wearing colored robes go by. There were some dressed in plain garb, but from what Suresh had gathered, those were people who were just visiting the High Court, and not a part of the citadel itself.

I need to get out of these clothes, he thought. *It would be best if I didn't stick out like a visitor.* He secured his hood, ensuring that none of his forest-green hair was showing.

Suresh waited until the courtyard seemed mostly empty, then casually walked away from the pillar, acting as if he had somewhere to go.

Where was he going to find Lady Vala in this citadel? The place was monstrous. So many buildings that made up the citadel. Wings, chambers, courtyards, halls… it was *huge*. Since Suresh arrived at the citadel, he had been trying to keep his ears open to hear of any whispers regarding Lady Vala, or even anything to do with the blue-gifted being summoned. But somehow, since Suresh didn't know anyone personally, the task was proving to be difficult.

But he had to. Something was not right—he could feel it deep within. It was the same feeling when he had been traveling toward the citadel earlier; there was a darkness present within the citadel. And the more he moved around and within the fortress, the more disturbed his own life force became, and the more convinced he was that Lady Vala and the other blue-gifted were in trouble.

Suresh crossed the courtyard, taking in the blooms of the gardens and the sculptures handsomely placed throughout. The gardens were sorted by the color of their blooms, creating a full spectrum of color. Spherical symbols had been carved on the pillars, and the sculptures of men and women held those symbols in their hand.

Must be their religious symbol, Suresh told himself, studying it as he casually walked by.

Sitting in the gardens was a red-gifted woman clothed in red, reading a tome by a fountain. As he passed her, he heard footsteps behind him.

"Lady Tyranna," said a man's voice.

"Can't you see I'm reading?" the woman answered.

There was a pause. "Sorry, my lady," apologized the man. "But my master sent me."

"Did he now? Well, it had best be good, considering I'm at an excellent part of the story."

"I apologize, my lady. Lord Goya needs to speak to the High Inquisitor. He said you might know his whereabouts."

The High Inquisitor?

Suresh's heart pounded. The High Inquisitor. The one he had been searching for along with Lady Vala. Suresh kept walking casually, but at a much slower pace, heading toward another pillar in range of them.

The lady snorted. "I haven't been keeping track. Did you try his quarters?"

There was a pause, and from where Suresh was positioned, he could see the man shuffling his feet. "I have never been to this citadel before, so my lord told me to seek you out."

"I see," she said, then eyed him with irritation. He was blocking her sunlight, casting a shadow on her book. He noticed, then moved off to the side.

"See that corridor over there?" she said, pointing lazily. "He is housed in that section. I doubt he is there, though. I heard he returned from World Sector Five, only to be sent out again by the High Court to another sector. But with the High Inquisitor, everything is by chance. You may have luck."

"Thank you, Lady Tyranna," the man said, taking off.

Could it be that Suresh would face the High Inquisitor once again? What would Suresh say to him after all these years? *He warned me that his superiors were searching for green magic…*

Again, Suresh hesitated, and that strange, dark feeling twisted within him. He had come to the High Court citadel because of Lady Vala, and all the strange rumors regarding the blue-gifted. He knew there was something wrong. And yet, the High Inquisitor could possibly be within the citadel, and even involved in some way. Maybe, just maybe, the High Inquisitor would know what was going on; the man had confided in Suresh many years ago. If Suresh found him now, maybe the man would confide in him once again—especially if he was who Suresh suspected him to be.

That feeling returned to him again.

I'm already here, and if it's a possibility that he is as well, I need to at least try and seek him out, Suresh thought. It was his main objective, after all. But the woman had said that he might be already gone …

Either way, Suresh had to know for certain. He waited a few moments, then moved quickly in the direction that the woman had pointed to. He crossed the remainder of the gardens, seeing the manservant far ahead of him. With Suresh following far behind, he came to another grand door. Suresh entered, then looked to his left, then to his right.

The manservant was gone. Suresh stood for a moment, unsure of where to go. This part of the citadel was laid out in a circular fashion, curving to frame the gardens. Suresh saw a few people approach down the halls, all of them wearing red.

Good. I must be in the right place. He walked toward them casually and passed by them, trying to study each doorway. Most doors were uniform, with larger doors spread out intermittently between the smaller ones, leaving Suresh to believe that the bigger doors were for people with more importance.

He came to a set of stairs, which seemed infinite, spiraling up till the tops of the structure were so far off that it was blurry.

I am never going to find his chambers, he thought, overwhelmed at how many floors there were. Suresh climbed many more sets of stairs, and soon, he became tired. Somewhere around the thirteenth or fourteenth level, he saw a bench and plopped down on it, resting for a moment.

While he was catching his breath, two women walked up the stairs. Each step they took, Suresh heard the echo within the towering stairwell.

"I have heard he is out right now," said one woman as they passed Suresh, not giving him a second thought.

"He had better not be. He owes me money," said the other.

"Doesn't he owe everyone money?" said the first woman.

Suresh could no longer see them, but their voices bounced through the stairwell.

"Yes, but he always pays me."

"What makes you so special?"

"Because I get the High Inquisitor the information he needs in a timely manner," the woman said matter-of-factly.

At the mention of the High Inquisitor, Suresh bounced up from his seat, then started up the stairs after the women, following them from a distance.

"What kind of information? For one of his interrogations?" the first woman asked.

"Best not to ask me anything more."

"You were the one who brought it up."

"Yes. And this is where I end the conversation." The woman laughed. "You know how he is. I don't want to get on his bad side. He's such a hothead at times."

"And a drunkard."

"And don't forget easy on the eyes."

"That too."

The women laughed and continued to chat while Suresh listened. The women changed topics to other things happening within the citadel, nothing that struck him as important. Suresh continued to follow them, trying to be light on his feet so the women didn't realize they were being followed.

When their footsteps stopped, Suresh studied each landing, gazing down the halls to see if he could see them. After a few more flights of stairs, he spotted them disappearing down the main hall of that particular level. Suresh waited at the landing a few moments, then walked down the hall after the women.

The women stood before a doorway, and one of them knocked. Suresh hid himself down the hall in a doorway entrance, hoping that whoever's chambers those were didn't come bursting out and knock him over.

Finally, a door opened, and Suresh heard the women's voices.

"I am here to see the High Inquisitor," said one of the two women.

"He is out on business," said a voice, which Suresh assumed belonged to a servant.

"I have what he requested."

"Yes, my lady. He informed me by courier that I should expect you. One moment, please."

There was a pause as the door shut. Suresh heard the door open again a minute later.

"This is for you," the servant's voice said.

There was another pause, then the woman said, "Thank you. Tell the High Inquisitor I look forward to being called upon for future work."

"I will relay the message, my lady."

The door shut once again, and Suresh heard the women's footsteps approaching. His heart pounded. He couldn't be discovered here. Quickly, Suresh funneled the green-blue magic within him, and the world stilled. He walked down the hall until he was behind the women and tucked himself away in another doorway, then released his magic.

The world moved again, and he watched the women walk down the hall toward the stairwell until he could no longer see them.

Suresh sighed, plopping down on a nearby bench. He was there, just outside the High Inquisitor's quarters. But there was no High Inquisitor. Suresh turned his thoughts to the blue-gifted woman. Lady Vala. A stirring in his heart tingled deep within. If anything, Suresh could at least try to find her.

Suresh stood, then walked back down the hall, descended the stairwell, and crossed the gardens once more. He came upon another adjoining building, and this one was much grander in stature, with many robed people and guards. He adjusted his hood once again, ensuring that his hair was covered completely and his eyes shaded.

Suresh was about to turn away, but one of the guards caught him. "You there," the guard called out.

Slowly, Suresh turned around. "Yes?"

"Aren't you the new guy they sent for?"

Suresh couldn't think of an answer quick enough to respond.

"Yeah, they told us that you were the nervous type. Get over here, and Henry will show you to your new chambers."

A servant came forth from behind the guard, then nodded to Suresh, gesturing for him to follow.

"I…"

"I understand how your nerves can be," the servant said. "To serve the

High Justice herself, in any capacity, is quite unnerving. But you will get used to it." He gently pushed Suresh forward. "But don't ever provoke the justice. Her wrath is something that everyone should be scared of. Even the other justices are afraid of her," he whispered.

Suresh didn't say anything, avoiding eye contact. He nodded, his heart pounding. The servant Henry led him to a small set of servant quarters, then entered a simple bedroom with a red robe laid out.

"Get changed, and then I will go over everything with you."

Henry left, shutting the door behind him.

What am I going to do? Suresh thought quickly. *I've got to get out of here!*

Suresh changed into the robes, ensuring that the new red hood covered his hair while he tried to devise a plan. There was a knock at the door, and Suresh quickly thought of what he needed to do.

Calling forth his green-blue gift, he flashed from his place to outside the chambers, stopping time as he did so. The world was held still in his blue-green power, but he knew it wouldn't be long before it became undone. He was no master of time and space, and using his analogous blue gift was tiresome.

Running down the hall, Suresh saw everyone locked in time. He came to a subsection of the citadel. Knowing that there were probably blue-gifted within the citadel, he didn't have much time left within the blue world. If he kept it frozen too long, it would cause alarm among the other blue-gifted, and he had already paused time for far too long.

Suresh came to a set of stairs heavily guarded by non-gifted. He passed them by, staring at them curiously, wondering why there were so many guards. He took the stairs, descending into the bowels of the citadel.

A set of guards stood in front of a small door. These were gifted, but luckily, none had the blue gift, so they remained frozen in time like the others.

I hope no one notices, he thought desperately. Through the greenish-blue tinted world, Suresh spotted a door that wavered with several enchanted magics. Reaching out a hand, he felt a magnetic pull from the magic that guarded the door. He pushed on it, but it remained firmly locked. His eyes fell to a heavy iron padlock.

It must be enchanted so no blue-gifted can appear inside...

Looking at the stilled guards, Suresh searched them until he found a set of keys. He unlocked the door, returned the keys to the guard, then went inside.

Why didn't they post any blue-gifted guards? Maybe it had something to do with the blue-gifted being summoned to the citadel. Suresh closed the door behind him and turned around, releasing his time spell, returning the world to motion and full color. He breathed a sigh of relief, then looked at his whereabouts.

He froze, staring at the sight before him. Shelves as high as the ceilings appeared in a circular design, just like the citadel layout. In the center of the room shone a pale beam of light straight down, softly highlighting the many shelves.

But it was what was within the shelves that made Suresh stare in disbelief. Countless glowing vials adorned the shelves. Vials with *gifted* blood. But there was also something far more disturbing on the shelves, making Suresh's life force tug with an overwhelming force.

Many of the vials contained pure, bright light—pulsating *life.* Suresh took a step back, shaking his head, feeling suddenly sick and horrified, realizing what it was.

Those vials…

They held the gifteds' *life force…*

CHAPTER 55

GREEN

The sounds of night awoke Emerald. But these noises weren't the familiar sounds of Arcadia that she always heard from her patio window. It was a strange, musical sound traveling on a breeze. It streamed softly through her window, rocking the curtains gently.

The gentle breeze tickled her face, toying with her senses.

Emerald sat up, pushing back her covers. Her room was unusually dark. Normally there would be all sorts of colors of the spectrum dancing around her room, coming from the city outside. But now, only a green light from the illuminating palace panels shone through her patio window. The green highlighted the objects in Emerald's room with an eerie green glow, giving a strange, almost ominous feeling.

Emerald looked down, noticing that she was in an evening gown. Had she fallen asleep in it? She couldn't recall. How long had she been sleeping? It felt like an eternity, though she knew that to be impossible. Emerald tried to recall the recent string of events, but her mind drew a blank.

I must have been sleeping a lot longer than I thought...

Emerald sat, taking in the green light coming from outside. Her soul felt crushed, and her spirit gone. All that mattered was Kyle, and he was no more. The thought of her never being able to touch him again sank her spirit far beyond the depths of despair. But in a dark, twisted way, Emerald welcomed the anguish. It was the only thing that brought her comfort.

Outside her patio window, Emerald caught a twinkling in the sky. Still sitting up in bed, she watched the twinkling and its white brilliance for quite some time. Was it a star? Emerald hardly saw stars above the city sky. Every night, the city was cloaked in a thick haze, and the bright lights dominated the night sky, leaving the stars hardly seen by the Arcadian citizens. But for some reason, on this night, the city was much darker than usual, making the stars shine ever so brightly. Especially this star…

Rising from her bed, Emerald walked across her bedroom to her patio. It was far too quiet, even for the middle of the night. She heard no handmaidens stirring in the next room, not even Glacia's snoring.

What is going on?

Transfixed by the twinkling star, she went to pull the handle of her patio screen door, but immediately stopped. There, at the edge of her patio, was an iridescent staircase, glowing with all colors of the spectrum. It was pure magic, glistening and glowing with pure radiance.

It was beautiful.

Emerald's eyes trailed up the stairs, which led far up into the heavens above. There was no end to the staircase; it just disappeared into the sky. In the distance, strange castles floated in the sky.

Floating castles in the sky?

Frightened but curious, Emerald opened the patio door, stepping barefoot out onto the cool patio. As soon as she did, a little squeak came from her patio floor. She looked down and saw Rosie's rat, Zaphod, scampering near her bare toes, squeaking.

"Zaphod?" Emerald said, looking at the rat curiously. "How did you get here?"

The rat squeaked at her in response, then stood on his hind legs, squeaking again.

"I'm sorry, I don't have any food," Emerald said, bending down to meet him. She nudged the rat, rubbing its little head gently.

The rat squeaked again, then scampered to the magical staircase, then looked at her. Did Zaphod want her to follow him? Emerald rose, inching near the magical staircase. She felt a compelling urge to touch it.

Hesitantly, Emerald laid her hand upon the first stair; it was as smooth as glass but as strong as steel. A powerful yet peaceful wave of energy radiated from the stairs, overwhelming her. Its power seeped into Emerald's hands, then transferred into her body, deep into her soul, stirring her life force.

Her core began beating fiercely, flooding her with immense power. Faster and faster the power flowed through her, and Emerald began to tremble, shaking with fear and intense anxiety. Her heart beat wildly in her ears, as wild and free as the first day she knew she was in love with Kyle.

Kyle. His life force… He was at the end of the staircase!

Kyle! I'm coming! her soul cried out.

Quickly, Emerald pushed a chair over to the edge of the patio, then stepped on it, bringing herself level with the staircase. She caught a glimpse of the city below, but it was nowhere near as overwhelming as it had been the time she had escaped from the palace. This time, everything seemed so serene.

She placed her bare foot on the first magical stair, then took a full step off the patio chair. As soon as her foot landed on the first step, the rainbow colors swirled vibrantly in the translucent staircase, humming with its spectrum magic. Zaphod was ahead a few steps, making a little squeak. He climbed a few more stairs, then waited for her, squeaking once again.

It seems he wants me to follow him.

Emerald ascended to the next step, and again, with Zaphod running just a bit in front of her. The magic radiated wherever she placed her foot, the stairs glowing with brilliance. She looked up again. The magical stairs disappeared into the clouds.

Is this real? Maybe this is just another dream? she asked herself.

Did it matter whether it was real? Kyle was at the end of the stairs. She *knew* it. And these stairs would lead her to him. He was up there, waiting for her. She was sure of it.

Emerald's heart hammered with excitement as she continued up the stairs, knowing that she was on her way to see Kyle. With each step, the staircase glowed brighter, while Arcadia shrank below her. Soon she was so high that Arcadia was nothing more than a patch of glittering lights within a dark, vast world.

But above her, the floating castles in the sky became brighter and more in focus. In fact, Emerald hadn't even realized there were so many of them. The castles bobbed up and down slightly, as if lazily wading in water. Under her feet, the staircase began to hum more loudly, and it was a melody that she had heard in her dreams.

The melody. She knew it.

It was Kyle's song.

Emerald starting climbing the stairs at a much quicker pace as the melody became stronger. A voice began singing with the melody, echoing through the skies. It was *his* voice. He was singing to her.

"Kyle!" Emerald cried out to the skies. "I'm here! I'm coming! Please wait for me!"

Immediately, Emerald picked up the hems of her long, trailing dress, then went into a full sprint up the stairs. She ran and ran, up the endless staircase, and it felt as if time itself was making a mockery of her, keeping her apart from her love, the complement to her soul.

The melody became stronger, clearer, its tune resonating deep within her life force as his voice, clear as crystal, seeped into her mind.

"Kyle! I'm here! Please, don't go anywhere!" Emerald yelled out.

Emerald suddenly noticed as she ran up the stairs that the floating castles were more detailed, and much larger. But what made her heart leap was that she saw an end to the staircase. There was an end…

Emerald ran as fast as her tired body would allow her, with Zaphod running just as fast, always just slightly ahead of her. Her legs felt like heavy stones, and her limbs ached, burning like fire. But she didn't care; her heart knew that Kyle was waiting for her.

The voice continued to sing as she was finishing her ascent. The end was visible. Breathlessly, Emerald continued.

At the top of the stairs was a large door. It opened, and behind the door was imagery wavering with magic. It was as if what lay beyond the door were a portal to another world.

Just then, a familiar silhouette stood before the door, leaning against the frame, singing. Zaphod scurried up the stairs, then sat at the feet of the silhouette, squeaking. Tears of joy welled in Emerald's eyes at the sight. "Kyle!" she screamed.

The shadow of Kyle did not move but continued to sing. In his hand was a harp, and he was playing it.

"It's me!" Emerald yelled at him. "It's me, Em!"

Kyle stopped singing abruptly, and he lowered his harp. The shadowy figure of Kyle paused for a moment.

"Kyle!"

He turned away, entered the portal, and left Emerald and Zaphod outside, alone.

"No, Kyle! Please, don't go!" Emerald cried out.

He was gone. He'd left her. She screamed and burst into tears. He'd left her. Did he not recognize her? Her eyes went straight to the wavering portal—the door to the other world remained open.

"Kyle!" she screamed.

Zaphod squeaked with alarm, then ran inside the portal. Running as fast as she could, Emerald stopped at the door, standing in front of it. With barely a thought, Emerald followed Zaphod, dashing into the portal.

CHAPTER 56

ORANGE

Geeta's calculations on where to end the portal were inaccurate. The group of them had been dropped off in the middle of the wastelands, and they had still many miles ahead of them to the refuge.

"Some magic portal," Tim said to Drew, grumbling.

Drew's circuits told him to remain silent. No use in making matters worse by agreeing or disagreeing with the statement.

The group moved much slower than Drew would've liked. So far, it had been approximately sixty-eight minutes of the group traveling, and according to his calculations, they had about another hundred and thirty-three minutes to the refuge.

After sixty-six minutes of traveling, they all came upon a rocky ravine. Drew could hear several children asking how much longer it was going to be, with the older humans reassuring them they would be there soon.

Turning to Tim, Drew said, "We m-m-m-must move quicker."

"Try telling that to the old people," Tim replied. "These old folks gotta sit for a moment."

Drew saw several of the older children trying to help a man well beyond his age. The man looked exhausted. Several members of the group passed around water canteens while others begged to take a break. Weariness was on every one of their faces, and their eyes were weak and sleepy.

As much as Drew wanted to keep going, he relented. "Fi-i-ive… five minute break," Drew announced. They all made audible sighs of relief, immediately plopped down on the scattered boulders, and drank and ate from their rations. Watching all the humans drink and eat, Drew decided he was thirsty too. He took a small sip from his canteen, delighted at the refreshing feeling.

Refreshing. Feeling. Joy hummed through his circuitry. It was pleasant.

As they rested, he heard rushing sounds in the sky overhead. The sounds were getting louder and louder. Drew looked up, scanning the sky, trying to target where the sound was coming from.

Warning, his processor alerted him. *Aerial transport close in proximity.*

Suddenly, a military air transport came into view, bearing the markings of the Olympian army.

"Shit," Tim said under his breath.

The group screamed, every person fleeting in multiple directions.

"S-s-s-stay… stay within m-m-m-my barrier!" Drew called out.

Quickly, Drew called upon the power of his nearby orange magic, and yellow encased the group within his protective barrier. Those who ran off came back, gathering inside the translucent orangish-yellow barrier. Funneling two of his powers combined, orange and yellow, the group began to shimmer, then slowly disappeared within his protective shell.

Cyborgs began dropping out of the transport, falling to the desert ground. They aimed their arms at the group while casting yellow magic, sending it shooting out like a sharp laser beam. It sliced through Drew's barrier, and the group came back into view.

The wasteland children screamed in terror while the old people used their guns. Sadly, their aim was far off.

"Surrender, and you won't be harmed," called out an amplified robotic voice.

"Never, you assholes!" Tim yelled before Drew got a chance to respond.

Gunshots erupted. Tim fired at the foreign cyborgs, along with the old-timers. Their shots missed entirely, but one of Tim's bullets landed right in the heart of one of the cyborgs' chest. It hardly affected the cyborg at all; his chest was entirely metal.

Drew's circuits twisted inside. The group couldn't fight these cyborgs. There was a .05% success rate, and that was with Drew rounding up his calculations. The Olympian cyborg drew a grafted gun from his mechanic arm and fired at Tim. The bullets shimmered with an intense yellow power, then went straight through Drew's barrier like butter, landing right in Tim's chest.

Tim screamed in a curse, dropping to the ground. Several of the elderly ran over to him, and the cyborgs closed in. Calculating quickly, Drew recast a protective shell around the group. This time, each person had their own individual shell mixed with an invisible power.

"R-r-r-run!" Drew yelled to the group.

Through his detection ability, he saw orange outlines of people escaping wildly in the direction of the hills. Though the cyborgs could detect the humans by heat, if they were far enough away, perhaps they would be able to stay safe for some time.

He turned back to Tim, trying to prop him up.

"Don't bother," Tim said, panting for breath as he pushed him away. "Just help the others and blast the shit out of those assholes!"

More gunshots. Bullets crashed against Drew's protective shell, which slowed down the bullets. Several hit him in the back, while most sunk into Tim's body. Tim made a guttural groan, then went still.

He'd stopped breathing. Tim. Dead. He was dead. Life no more.

Malfunction.

He had no life. Drew shook. Angry. He was angry. In a furious rage, Drew whipped around to face the Olympian cyborgs. Fire gathered in his hand, burning and growing until it was the size of a small human. With sudden sweeping jerk, Drew released the orange-red fireball from his hands.

The fire blast engulfed the group of cyborgs, searing their bodies within a large hellfire. With another swing of his hands, Drew fed the hungry fires, growing them in size until all of them were inflamed, along with the Olympian transport.

Within the fire, Drew saw a bright-yellow light encasing them, protecting them from the growing flames. They had been damaged from his initial blast of fire, but they had quickly cast shields of protection around themselves.

They were coming toward him.

As they moved, the cyborgs held out their hands in unison, summoning a large barrier around them all. The magical barrier engulfed the flames as it made contact, snuffing them out with their new yellow magical barrier as it grew in size.

Frustrated, Drew charged toward the cyborgs, summoning the power of the winds under him. Flying up to meet them, Drew extended his mechanical hand, swiping at the magical barrier, funneling his magic into his hands. The circuits of his mechanical hand vibrated, glowing with vibrant orange-yellow magic. When he met the oversized barrier, he swiped at it with his power. It was as hard as metal. He gave another hard swipe with his metal hand, then his human side came into play, and he began punching the barrier with his other hand.

The barrier made a loud crack, then shattered, the golden magic dissipating into the air. Taking advantage of the situation, Drew quickly filled his veins with more orange-red magic, this time as lightning. He funneled more magic into the lightning, forming a giant blast of chain lightning. He sent it cracking to each of the cyborgs.

In the distance, another aerial transport landed, and armed Olympian military men joined the fight. He hoped that the elderly and the children were far away by now, because now it was him against twenty-two bodies. Not good odds.

He had to do something, otherwise he would be terminated just like Tim back there.

Think Drew, think!

His circuits hummed.

Placing his two human fingers on his head as if in concentration, he closed his eyes. Within his mind, he pictured a violent earthquake of great magnitude, shaking the ground under their feet.

As he concentrated, the ground began to rock and groan. Harder and harder the earth shook, and then he felt the vibrations under his feet. The earth wanted to erupt with anger—it told him so.

Throwing out his hands, Drew clenched his fists, and they burned a bright orange-red. Then he released the furious energy.

With a loud quake, the earth split apart where the Olympian men and cyborgs were. Everywhere around them crumbled. The Olympian men ran in confusion as the earth trembled, while others fell into the crack's depths. Their transport fell sideways through the splitting earth.

The ground continued to quake violently as Drew took off, heading in the direction of the refuge, still invisible. With his magic, he saw several of the elderly and children in the distance. Turning away from the scene, Drew flew toward the hills where the wastelanders had gone. After spotting them in a shimmer of light, Drew landed near them, still keeping them invisible.

"What happened to the cyborgs?" asked one of the teens, seeing his magical shimmer.

"O-o-o-on-nly have s-s-s-short amount of time," Drew said to the group. "Continue east." He pointed to the ridge of the mountain crest. "There... m-m-m-make your w-a-a-ay there."

The group nodded, then ran off, still bathed in his protection. Drew turned back to stall the Olympian military men and cyborgs. But just then, his radio came to life.

"Drew! Can you hear me? Drew!"

His heart soared at the sound of her voice. He grabbed his radio, clicking the button. "T-t-t-tell-me-lots," he said.

"Oh, Drew," her voice said, flustered. "No time to chit-chat, but I have the communications back up. Is Geeta with you?"

"N-n-n-negative."

She groaned. "Drew, I will try to reach out to the others in the camps, but if you see Geeta, tell her she must come to the palace now. The Queen is in danger! She is in some kind of magical coma. Not only that, but now there are blue-gifted trying to kidnap her... or harm her, I don't know I think Olympia found a way inside the palace. Please, you have to find Geeta. I barely managed to fend off the last attack. I got lucky. But my luck is wearing thin, and I'm not sure what will happen the next time."

Drew clutched the radio, shaking with emotion. The Queen was in danger. Telly had to fend off an attack. If anything happened to Telly...

"Drew! Did you hear what I said?"

Drew put the device to his lips. "Y-yes. Will find Geeta. Now."

"I will be on standby waiting for her. Meanwhile, I will be next to the Queen. Please... take care."

"Yo-o-o-ou... you too, Tell-me-lots."

Turning toward the direction where he last knew Geeta had headed, he took off.

***

"Communications are back up," Geeta heard one of the camp men say.

"About time," Duke Uthgard grunted. "Get your team on the devices and send out transmissions to evacuate the outskirt camps. Tell them Arcadia is open to them, but not for long. They are more than welcome to join us out here if they so desire."

"Yes, sir," the man said, turning away and to give orders.

Geeta grabbed one of the radios, then turned to Uthgard. "I will keep watch at a distance. I'll let you know if I see anything. Hopefully I'll be able to slow them down."

"Good. Our teams are prepared, and the rest of the Arcadian army will be here soon."

"They'd best be, because I have a feeling we haven't much time," Geeta stated, walking off with radio in hand.

What was taking the Arcadian army so long to arrive? She stalked off, passing many of the gathered wastelanders as she walked to the outskirts of the camp.

As Geeta reached the open desert, she stopped. The hairs on the back of her neck stood on end, and goose bumps pricked her skin. Dark energy flowed through the atmosphere, while the ground coursed with evil below her feet.

In a split second, the camp's tents collapsed. Guns were crushed in men's arms. The communications device in her hand shook violently. She looked down at the metal as the device morphed and twisted, busting the device entirely.

What in the world…

Cries of agony rose up from cyborgs within the camp. Looking around desperately, trying to figure out what was happening, Geeta saw the camp men running back and forth in a panic, trying to understand what happened to their weapons. Then she looked over her shoulder.

The color of the sun shifted, turning a deep crimson color, almost the color of burning blood. Geeta gasped, taking a step back. Voices around her cried out in confusion. More metal within the camp twisted and writhed as if they were living snakes, destroying much of the camp. This time, however, Geeta saw the dark power embracing the metal.

Dark-red magic! Turning, Geeta ran through the camp, seeing many of the metal parts around her contorted in different positions and items scattered throughout. The tent poles were bent, some of the camp's guns were warped, and metal devices lay strewn around everywhere, wrecked. Geeta could even feel her metal earrings wriggling and writhing, as if worms were trying to escape her earlobes. Cyborgs stared blankly at the sky, their metal parts contorting, many of the parts jutting out of their bodies. Their skin started regenerating from their infused magical blood, but Geeta knew that their circuits had to be a mess inside.

Garrett came running up to her. "What the hell just happened?"

"Dark magic."

"Dark magic?" Garrett repeated.

Geeta looked at the sun. It was still a dark, deep crimson. "Magic from the dark side of the spectrum. Dark-red magic." Her eyes met his. "Can't you feel the negative energy flowing around us?"

"I don't know anything about that, Miss Geeta," Garrett said. "All I do know is it gives me the fucking creeps."

Geeta whirled around at the mention of *Miss*. "You too?"

Garrett just shrugged sheepishly. Geeta would have chastised him, but there was no time for that.

Duke Uthgard ran up with some of the Arcadian men. "Miss Geeta, there is a report that the Olympian army is close."

"I know," she snarled. She didn't need a report to tell her that. All anyone had to do was look at the sun to figure out that everything was coming to a head.

"Gather everyone now," Duke Uthgard said to one of the officers. "Hopefully there are some weapons that are still useful."

Garrett turned to them. "I'll run through the camp and make sure everyone has a working weapon. I'll grab a few men who are handy and fix what we can quickly. Hopefully our magitech weapons are still working."

They better be, Geeta thought. "If Drew happens to show up, have him transmute the weapons that don't work. That will save you time."

"Got it," Garrett said.

He was about to take off, but another wave of violent energy hit the camp. Geeta's body swung limply, then she fell to her knees, grimacing. She looked up after a moment. Everyone was staring down at her. Apparently only she had felt that power.

Garrett looked at her, about to help, but Geeta waved him away. "Go," she said.

"You sure?"

"Yes, just hurry!" Geeta snapped.

At that, Garrett ran off, looking back at her for a moment before disappearing.

The world went dark. There was a beat of silence. Eerie silence. Then bursts of screams, cries, and yells filled the air, echoing across the sky. Geeta looked around wildly for the sun, but it was as if all the light had been snuffed out.

Cries came from men and machines, filling her ears, while the *rat-tat-tat* of gunfire erupted. Summoning her violet magic, the light from her energy lit up the darkness like the brightest star in the sky. In that moment, she saw it—a giant sandstorm embraced by dark-red magic.

It was heading their way.

"Everyone get ready!" Geeta screamed. Grasping her staff, she reached down to the depths of her life force, pulling everything she had within her. Power ripped through her body like a violent storm, her insides vibrating with energy. It hummed and tore through her organs as if peeling away the insides of her body.

Not yet! she told the magic. She funneled more power throughout her being, then pushed everything she had into her core. A loud scream tore out of her as she released her magic. Magic streamed from the staff as well.

The violet force ripped through the camp, tearing toward the dark-red energy. It gathered into a purple sandstorm, and a violet barrier covered the entire camp. Geeta kept screaming, filling her soul with the increasing power from the staff. Her violet magical force swelled to meet the incoming dark-red sandstorm.

The two storms collided, shaking the ground. The earth split open.

"Fire!" yelled one of the camp officers.

Around her, magitech weapons opened fire at shadows within the storm. They approached with incredible speed, becoming clearer as they neared—the Olympian cyborgs coming at them in full force.

Several of the magitech weapons blasted the cyborgs, unleashing orange-red electrical storms upon them. Geeta barely had time to marvel at the fact that they worked.

Geeta plunged the staff down into the ground, pouring violet-red magic into the earth, stabilizing it under her men's feet. An orange shimmer began glowing next to Geeta, and she drew back, but then Drew materialized next to her.

"Finally! What took you so long?" she snarled at him.

"Queen… S-s-s-she is in trouble," Drew said, almost unusually calm.

Geeta looked at him in alarm. Before she could say anything, a bullet pierced her upper arm. She cried out, then grunted. More bullets tore past. Through the storm, Geeta saw an influx of Olympian cyborgs and men storming through the camp.

She wasn't going to let them get the best of her. Groaning, Geeta funneled some of her life force into the wound, finding the bullet lodged in her flesh.

"OUT!" she ordered the bullet. Her violet magic forced the bullet out of her arm, flinging it back toward the Olympian army, lodging it into one of their men.

Geeta quickly sent a small healing wave over her wound to dull the pain and stop the bleeding. Shifting her power, she then funneled violet magic into the staff. It shot back out, amplifying her magic tenfold. All at once, she felt control over hundreds of human minds. They were all awaiting her orders.

Throw down your weapons! she commanded.

Far off, she heard the opposing army yell out orders, and in the midst of the chaos, men threw down their weapons. A few cyborgs did the same. She breathed, relieved that she had control. The staff sparked in response. She had used much of its power.

Without warning, Geeta was yanked by her chain necklace as if she were a dog in a collar. The wave of dark energy hit her again as her body was dragged across the sand. Choking, Geeta reached for her necklace, trying to rip it free. But the energy was locked around it tightly and wouldn't release itself from around her neck.

Gasping for breath, she formed a spell in her mind, hoping to counter the dark magic. Just as she was about to cast the spell, her necklace was yanked again, and her body was thrown across the rocky ground. Tumbling, she rolled over, smacking her head hard against a rock.

Her vision blurred, but she was still able to make out shapes amongst the speckled white stars in her line of sight. The communications tower with the chair was in view, but this time, that chair had a body in it.

Geeta squinted hard. There was a little boy in the chair, no more than eight years old, if Geeta had to guess. Attached to his head were massive electronic goggles, with a plethora of wires attached to them. Under the lens of the goggles, dark-red energy radiated. That had to be his magic. Wires from the goggles jutted out and wrapped around his chair, leading down and around the communications tower. Underneath the boy's goggle strap, Geeta saw black hair sticking out.

The boy screamed and cried nonsense. When the boy screamed again, another dark wave of red magic, wove through the encampment, twisting and contorting not only metal, but rocks, sand… everything that was of the elements shifted wildly.

Geeta watched as Drew materialized in front of the boy, then smacked him on the face, giving the boy a bloody nose. The boy stopped crying, and suddenly, the sun shifted back to its normal state.

Geeta wasted no time. She grasped the staff in her hand, then stumbled to her feet, still off balance from the fall. The staff flickered slightly, its power not fully charged. Trying to quickly gather her thoughts, Geeta was about to cast a barrier over the camp, but someone beat her to it. She squinted at a brilliant flash, and then the largest, most vibrant barrier she had ever seen swelled up and surrounded the camp. Scanning the area, she saw Scion far off to the side. He looked to be in poor condition, still not fully healed, but his determination radiated from him as if he had never been injured. Pouring out from his hands was the magic built into his cybernetics—yellow barrier magic.

"Assist me, Miss Geeta," he called out. His voice had strength and resolve behind its edge.

Without hesitation, Geeta funneled her protection magic, combining her powerful energy with Scion's. Drew noticed and assisted them both, funneling his own protective adjacent magic into the golden barrier, reinforcing it.

Geeta quirked a smile toward Scion, and he gave her a nod. But their little moment of triumph was short-lived.

A man had just finished climbing up the communications tower to the boy. He did something to the wires, but Geeta couldn't say what. The boy started crying and screaming, fully consumed within his dark-red magic. Then he burst into crimson flames at the top of the chair, still screaming, and the shadowy man jumped back down the ladder.

Geeta heard the earth groan. She funneled more magic into the staff, then poured it into the barrier. It was just in time, as another dark-red sandstorm crashed against the barrier, and the opposing cyborgs and men hit the barrier like flies, dropping hard.

"H-h-h-have to get to the Queen!" Drew called out. "She is… she is…" he stuttered. "Under a spell! P-p-p-palace needs you!"

Geeta shot him a look. "Needs me? Under a spell? What do you mean?"

"W-will not wake up!" He flashed her a look with his cybernetic eye. "Also blue-gifted!"

Geeta frowned, still casting her magic against the army. "Blue-gifted? A blue-gifted is after the Queen?"

Drew nodded.

Geeta snarled in frustration. It had to be the blue-gifted that Scion had talked about. Olympia had gotten to the Queen, or they were about to. The palace needed her, and for good reason—she was the only one who could combat a blue-gifted. Telly couldn't fend off a blue-gifted, not with her tinted magic. But Geeta was Protector of the Realm. She had to be *here*, helping to stop the Olympian army. How was she supposed to be in two places at once? And what about this spell that the Queen was under? Had Olympia cast a spell on her?

Geeta clenched her jaw. Arcadia needed more gifted. "Where are my gods?" Geeta screamed in frustration. She wasn't talking to anyone, more to the wind, hoping that a higher power would answer her. "How am I supposed to single-handedly stop everything?" she roared.

Drew looked to her as if wondering if he was supposed to answer her, but she raised her staff.

"It was rhetorical!" she snapped.

Outside the barrier, the magic-infused cyborgs glowed with yellow power, using their grafted guns to laser the protective barrier. They were on the move again, leaving a line that concentrated on melting the camp's barrier.

Scion blasted at them with his gun, then cast another barrier around the group. This time, it was much weaker. The cyborg had given it his all the first time, and now he looked just as weak as he did in bed back at the refuge.

Geeta's barrier melted before her eyes. More men joined, waiting for the barrier to fully disarm. Drew sent a shockwave of lightning through the barrier, electrocuting the men outside. They shrieked in pain.

She had to do something. Geeta's eyes shifted to the boy. That kid was somehow Olympia's golden ticket.

She waved the staff, shifting from protection magic to forceful magic. She searched deep within her emotions, seeking out bitterness, thinking about Vihaan, her evil husband who she'd left back in time. All those times he'd ridiculed her. Beat her. Made her feel like *nothing*.

The magic around her turned from violet to dark violet. Its powers rocked her insides, making her feel wrong. But she let her hatred consume her anyway. She had to do it.

Releasing the dark magic, Geeta shot her consciousness into the boy's. Just as she landed in the boy's mind, her consciousness was met with pain, hurt, sadness, and anger, all at once. There were so many images, dreams, nonsensical thoughts… all overwhelming her spirit. None of them made any sense. It was so overwhelming that her mind started to scramble. She was losing herself.

Geeta flung her consciousness back to her body, then she tumbled hard in the dirt. She looked at the boy. Even with the thick goggles glued to his face, she could see tears streaming down his face as he continued to cry and scream.

Red-violet magic surrounded her as her body lifted up off the ground. Grimacing, Geeta gripped the staff, whipping her magic together with all her might, then she released the violet force, and it collided against the boy's. Hers was more powerful, and the boy was knocked off his seat on the tower, the goggles peeling off his face. She fell back to the ground, landing solidly on her feet.

Geeta looked up just as the boy fell to a small platform on the tower, lower than his seat. His face was fully exposed for Geeta to see. He had smooth, elongated narrow eyes like simmering embers of an evil fire.

He gave her an odd look, as if stunned or confused. She shuddered, then turned away, knowing that the boy was only stunned momentarily. The Olympian armies continued to plow through the wastelanders, who blasted their magitech weapons in return, but with the magical barriers of the Olympian cyborgs, it hardly affected them. Many of the camp's weapons were damaged because of the metal-bending spell from the boy, and it was only a matter of time before he recovered enough to cast more dark magic.

A man was about to get shot by one of the cyborgs, but Geeta quickly deflected the blow, funneling the magic through the staff.

The staff!

The magical charge was gone. Geeta could sense its power was drained. It was of no use. Yelling in frustration, Geeta chucked the staff to the ground, running her hands over the sides of her head. Several of the nearby wastelanders saw her but continued to fight. One had his chest sliced open from a cyborg blade.

"I don't know how much more we can hold on," said one of the wasteland men.

That made Geeta angrier.

"Where is the rest of the Arcadian army? Aren't they supposed to be here?" yelled another man.

"Most of our weapons are ruined!" said another man.

Before she could answer, the metal around them began to glow a deep red, and it all started creeping toward the wastelander men, sliding over their bodies.

Geeta turned. Multiple copies of Drew charged toward the communications tower. The metal embraced the men, then started warping around them, gripping their bodies.

No!

Geeta flashed her hand, channeling her force magic, trying to counter the squeezing of the metal. Harder and harder, she flowed her powers. The hatred in the dark magic… it was so strong. What was she to do? She tried getting into the boy's mind again, but it was so scrambled that she couldn't gain a footing inside. What she needed was more power. More reinforcements.

Then the idea came to her. She didn't like it at all. In fact, it was a terrible, reckless idea, but she was running out of options.

"Drew!" she screamed, getting to her feet and running through the fighting.

She passed men in the camp entangled within their melted guns. Others had working weapons, but they were sent crashing into the cyborg barriers. Bodies were everywhere, while blasts of power flashed across the armies.

Geeta summoned her violet-red wind, taking flight and hovering over the crowd. "Drew!" she called out.

One of the thousands of copies of him looked over at her and came close.

"I need you to distract the boy!" she called out. "As long as possible. And I need you to cast a barrier over our men. A shell. I need enough time to run through the camp!"

Drew's cybernetic eye flashed, and he nodded. "Affirmative," he said mechanically.

"I will assist with the barrier," Scion said as he trudged up to them. The cyborg looked beat to all hell—he had not been in any shape to begin with, and the fighting had only deteriorated his health further. "Let me worry about the barrier. Drew can focus on the distraction."

Geeta eyed him. "You sure you have enough power?"

"Yes, Miss Geeta. I am at thirty-two percent capacity."

Whatever I can get, I suppose. She nodded to him. "Do what you can."

Scion held out his hands, funneling a beam of yellow light, pouring it over the wastelanders. The golden barrier formed a half dome, encircling the people.

Geeta released her magic, falling into the barrier while Drew took off in the direction of the tower. She landed, spotting Victor, then ran over to him.

"We need more gifted," Geeta said to him urgently.

"That would be helpful," he said, pulling the metal off him while reloading his weapon.

"Gather the men. Now."

It was as if Victor had been slapped, because his eyes went wide, and he snapped to full attention. "Don't do this Geeta!"

"I have to, Victor!"

"We can't keep multiplying gifted among us! What will our world be like if we keep doing it?"

"I agree. But the world has changed," Geeta said. "The gift chooses the *right* people…"

"But they could turn out *wrong*," Victor countered.

"That might be true, but that is a chance we have to be willing to take."

Geeta didn't move her eyes from his stare. She could hear his thoughts wrestling back and forth within his mind. Finally, Victor opened his mouth, about to protest, but Geeta was quicker. She flung out her hand, summoning a dagger from one of the men's belts. The dagger glowed with violet power, then flew to her hand, and she clenched it tight.

"Geeta! Please, don't," he argued.

Ignoring his pleas, Geeta made a swift swiping motion, and the dagger cut the palm of her hand. Her glowing blood poured out of it.

Garrett ran up to them. "I don't know how much longer we can hold out. About half of our weapons are damaged. The normal weapons, that is."

"I am recruiting more gifted," Geeta answered him.

"No!" Victor pushed her arm down. "Don't do this!"

"Garrett, gather everyone under this barrier! Drew is buying us time," Geeta said, ignoring Victor as she looked at the barrier being melted by the opposing force. On the other side, Drew's copies were holding them off.

Garrett's mouth dropped at the sight, but he then took off.

With a flick of her wrist, Geeta sent a wave of protection, reinforcing the barrier over them. She turned to see men running to her, Garrett following them.

"One at a time. Now," Geeta ordered.

Victor stood in a protective stance between her and the camp members. "You cannot do this! You saw what happened last time at Arcadia's palace. It is dangerous for so many people to receive the gift. Wars throughout history have been fought over magic—you said so yourself! Now you want to repeat history all over again? You think now is dangerous, what will happen ten, fifteen, twenty years from now?"

"Arcadia needs help! They are powerless. You saw that boy. Someone has to combat the darkness. They have a red-gifted, a yellow-gifted, and quite possibly a blue-gifted, giving all these cyborgs power." She thought of her husband. "The King is gone, and the Queen needs me. That leaves Drew."

"And Telly!"

"A tinted gifted, Victor," Geeta corrected him. "Do you see what's happening? I cannot help Arcadia by myself. Neither can Drew."

From above, the opposing cyborgs started coming through Scion's disintegrating barrier. Geeta flashed Victor one last look, yanking her arm in front of him.

"What will it be? You are a leader, are you not? Will you let your men die because of your obstinance?"

The camp went silent, everyone staring at them.

Anger flashed across Victor's face. He took a deep breath. "Fine." He stepped aside, then turned to the camp members. "Form a line, quickly! One by one, everyone will taste the protector's blood."

The gathered wastelanders nervously looked at each other.

"You heard Victor. Hurry!" Geeta shouted, holding up her bloody arm.

Garrett moved toward her, his eyes lowered. "What if none of us get the gift?"

Geeta shrugged. "Then we are screwed."

The wastelanders still remained still, looking at each other.

"What are you waiting for? Come on!" Geeta screamed. "We don't have much time!"

Finally, one man walked up. He glanced at her, and with a nod from Geeta, took a taste of her blood. The group watched the man. Nothing happened. Right after, a woman stepped up, doing the same. Nothing happened to her either. Quickly, one by one, each of the armed campers tasted Geeta's blood—all with no results.

As the line dwindled, Geeta saw a crack in the barrier. Turning to the remaining people, she yelled, "Hurry!"

The last of the campers tasted her blood just as the barrier made an audible loud crack, ringing in their ears.

"Looks like no one was favored," Victor said to her.

"We're not done yet," Geeta snapped.

"I don't want it, Geeta. There is too much that comes with it!" he countered.

There were screams behind them as a wastelander was blasted.

Geeta turned to Victor. "I don't want to force you, Victor. Please, don't *make* me," Geeta said through her clenched teeth. "Just think of all those out there who need help. Think of the Queen! You might not even get the gift anyway."

Another audible crack came from the barrier. Geeta understood Victor's hesitation, almost too well. The man was very wise. Much good could come from magic, but just as much evil could come from it. He had seen firsthand—the sorceress, the cyborgs…

Geeta laid on hand on Victor's shoulder, then whispered, "I understand, Victor. I know you what you face deep within."

Victor paused, remaining silent within the chaos. There was almost no time left. Another scream, and a cyborg appeared through the cracked barrier. At the sound, Victor grasped her arm, then quickly tasted her blood.

Satisfied, Geeta turned to the cyborg, hurling a giant ball of fire at it.

More cyborgs came flooding through, and the wastelanders began blasting the Olympian army. Overhead, Drew was changing and shifting their surroundings to at least fool the humans, casting lightning across the cyborgs. Scion was shooting small protective barriers around those who needed it, but they were only as strong the cyborg's condition.

"N-need to get to the Queen!" Drew yelled to her.

"I can't leave them here like this!" Geeta yelled back to him.

He flashed her a look of irritation, then took off.

Suddenly, a man's yell echoed through the camp. Dark clouds formed around them, and then a violent earthquake split the earth beneath them.

There was a sudden shift in Geeta's life force, and it was as if her power was... *gone.*

Victor screamed. Cyborg shields instantly went down, and their magics ceased. Drew, who happened to be mid-flight, dropped like a swatted fly, crashing to the ground.

Then a giant magical explosion ripped through the land. Victor continued to scream and writhe on the ground. Geeta froze in awe and shock.

She had never seen *that* color of magic before.

CHAPTER 57

Gray

"Soul of my soul, why do you embrace darkness while you seek the light? What harmony can there be between the pure of heart and the corrupt of spirit? Why do you teeter between life and death? For the mixture between the two becomes the imbalance of the heart, and the two will be at constant war, hoping to dominate the other until one is no more."

—excerpt from the poetic verses "The Light"
Phoenicis Opila, 1432 M.E.

Night embraced him like a sweet lover, just how he had envisioned Elyathi embracing him in his dreams. Shadows of his sadness, pain, hurt, dark thoughts, and emotions swirled around him, haunting his heart like they had all these years of loneliness.

The image of her formed inside his mind; she was like an angel in the darkness. Her pale skin, her long snow-colored hair, and her bright white eyes. How he had loved Elyathi. He loved her in his youth, and he loved her to her grave.

She stood silently, her long wavy hair rippling in the darkness. Shadows of wickedness wove in and out of her locks of hair, then wrapped themselves around her body, then her neck. Victor closed his eyes, not wanting to face the darkness that those shadows contained. It was the darkness that lived inside his heart.

"Just let me be," he whispered to the memories.

His skin prickled as he felt a cold touch run across his arm, then down to

his chest. The coldness was icy, so much that it burned. The sensation clutched his heart, squeezing tightly. All the horrible memories that he desperately wanted to forget came flooding back like roaring waves in the ocean.

He didn't want to feel them. Not any of them. Victor's heart stirred as the darkness tried to consume him. He opened his eyes to the image of Elyathi opening her arms as if to embrace his darkness. At her welcoming, the darkness wrapped entirely around her, and she was no more.

"Why?" he cried out to the nothingness.

Only you can handle this magic, said a powerful voice within the darkness.

"I don't understand," Victor said hoarsely.

I deemed this magic forbidden, but I am granting it to you, said the roaring voice, rippling like thunder. *No one else can wield its power, not even if they consume your blood. To use it comes with a price. I created a perfect magic to restore unity to this world, one to embody all light, to embody the pure of heart, but it went astray, and it is now lost forever, as you have just witnessed. The prophecy will no longer result in truth of her, but instead, only lies. You will combat this deception.*

Victor's heart ached with a wave of hurt and immense sadness that settled in his bones.

Elyathi…

Elyathi had told him many years ago that there was a prophecy written of her, and that she would restore balance and unity to the world.

But it doesn't make sense. Elyathi died years ago!

The voice heard his mind, because it answered. *It is not as you think.*

"I don't understand," Victor called out. "Elyathi is dead!"

The goodness in her spirit is dead, changed and morphed into a twisted soul. But her body, and what is left of her soul, is very much alive. I have waited far too long to restore the earth to its former glory, but I can wait no longer. The Lord of Darkness's evil prowls like a lion upon the earth. Evil is readying itself, so we, too, must be ready to fend off the wickedness.

The dark shadows floated toward Victor, then hovered over him, like wisps of black ink slowly dancing in water. Rolling black storm clouds filled the skies and surrounded him, crackling with power and force.

"Who are you?" Victor asked, taking in the awesome but frightening sight. He expected to see something, but there was nothing but the dark, rolling clouds in the sky and the whirling shadows.

"I AM WHO I AM," boomed the voice. It was like pure music. This time it spoke with clarity, and not in Victor's mind. Thunder roared and lightning cracked in the sky, while a dark wind blew against his face, swirling all around Victor, inviting him to a dark dance that he did not want to indulge in. It blew hard and furiously. His skin didn't protect against the wind, and it blew straight into him like a surge of electricity.

The dark clouds, the shadows of his memories, the lightning… all of it formed a colorless beam of light. Their combined power struck him like a boulder against his body, knocking the breath out of him, piercing though his heart.

Victor fell limply to the ground, or what he thought to be ground, because all he saw was blackness from the power, twinkling with gray sparks. He lay there, gasping for breath.

Finally, air was restored to his lungs, and his vision slowly returned. A powerful jolt of energy, like a light switch that had been flipped on, brought sudden awareness to his life force. There was *magic* beneath it. Had it been there all this time?

The light faded, then turned into a gray hue. A bright, glowing gray. It was impossible. The light was colorless, and yet it was there… The colorless light ebbed away at Victor's life force, sucking away all the magic that surrounded him. Ravenous. *Hungry.* Victor somehow knew it wanted more magic. It wanted all the magic that thrived in the world—it had been waiting an eternity to snuff out everyone's power. All except its own.

Victor screamed once again in his darkened world. The power grasped his life force, tugging at it. "Am I the bringer of death?" Victor called out. "Is that what I will be?"

No… That is the dark side of the green. You are… special. Never have I allowed anyone like you to exist. You are to snuff out the magic of those who choose to use their magic for evil. To counter their spells, to wipe them away.

Thunder rumbled in the air, and the dark clouds sped up, forming hastily in the sky.

"I never wanted this!" Victor cried out.

"That is why I give it to you," the musical voice said as the heavens shook above him. The voice was so beautiful, like the sound of rushing water. Victor could listen to that voice forever if he dared.

A loud rumble underneath him completely shook his life force. Then,

Victor's sight adjusted to the darkness. Through the clouds, Victor saw a barren land that resembled the wastelands. Endless dunes, void of color. Everything was monotone, all in shades of gray. More details became apparent, and he could see the shadows in great detail. No, it was as if he could see clearly for the first time in his life. But it was more than that—it was as if he could see the darkness within his own *soul.*

Would he see the darkness in others? The shadows, the clouds, the gray sands… There was an underlying darkness that had to be eradicated.

Overwhelmed by the magic, Victor felt another deep tug within his core. The power consumed his entire being, eating away at his soul, until he felt his life force inching away into the lifestream…

Elyathi. You are alive… His heart twisted. *Why did you turn from the light? Why did you turn…*

Darkness surrounded him once more, and he began to weep.

Why…

The gray consumed him as tears fell from his cheeks.

CHAPTER 58

VIOLET

Victor remained lifeless, dead to the world. His magic seeped out of him like a raging river, pouring out over the land as the wastelanders continued to fight. At the same time, Geeta felt her magic squelched from her life force.

His power, his gray magic… It was as if his magic had disabled all other gifted from casting spells, or even tapping into their life force. Cutting them off from their magic.

Hopefully temporarily, Geeta thought.

At least now it was more of a fair fight without magic. As both armies fought with a sense of confusion, the wastelanders picked up the old guns of the fallen Olympian army. Even the magitech weapons appeared to be useless around Victor's magic.

Geeta looked to the far back of the Olympian army. They were able to summon their shields.

So… Victor has to be in the same vicinity as the gifted to disarm them. Geeta saw the Olympian communications tower moving toward the back of the army. *They are trying to move away from Victor so the boy can use his magic!*

Turning quickly, she spotted Garrett nearby. "Get a ground vehicle, now!" she yelled at him.

"For what?"

"Just do it!" she snapped.

Garrett ran off, and Duke Uthgard appeared next to her.

"So much for the Arcadian army," Geeta chided him.

"They were supposed to be here!" he fought back. "I was expecting them any minute now. We need more weapons. All of our equipment looks like damn metal putty!"

"If they happen to show up, have them follow Victor's vehicle," Geeta said. "He is leading a charge."

The duke snorted. "How? He's passed out cold, and that damn power of his is out of control."

"Precisely."

"So how is he exactly going to lead a charge?" Duke Uthgard pressed.

"You see that?" Geeta pointed at Victor. Gray magic continued to flood the area, with Victor burning bright gray at the center of it. "*That* is going to stop their spells."

The duke's face turned serious, hesitating. Geeta could sense he wanted to argue, his thoughts flickering on the absurdity of her idea.

She leaned into the duke's face. "Just have them follow his lead."

Duke Uthgard eyed her, then shook his head in disbelief. "You'd best be right about this, Miss Geeta."

He stomped off just as Garrett drove up in a vehicle. Ryan was with him too. The vehicle only had room for two.

They are going to need fire power...

"Tie Victor to the front," Geeta ordered.

"Are you shitting me?" Garrett remarked, looking at her as if she was crazy.

"Do it!"

Garrett looked dumbfounded, but Ryan ran and grabbed cords. When he returned, the men tied Victor's lifeless body to the hood of the vehicle, securing him. Drew came limping up, many of his mechanical parts sticking out.

"You must have been a cat in your past life," Geeta said to him, eyeing his damage. "I swear you have nine lives."

Drew attempted a poor smile, then grunted. "N-n-n-not my t-t-t-time to die."

"I'll say," Geeta said, leaning in. "Drew, I need to you to go with Victor. Drive this army back to Olympia if you have to, with our army behind us. His power... it stops everyone's magic."

"I-I-I can sense the void," he stuttered.

Geeta nodded. Her magic was still gone as well. It was painful not being able to sense her life force.

"It is only temporary, I think. I hope. We have to hurry before Victor's magic stops. We gotta move now," Geeta said. "Make sure the camp is safe. I'm going to the Queen."

Drew nodded, then turned to the vehicle where Victor was tied, his gray magic enveloping him entirely, continuing to radiate from his body. Garrett jumped in the vehicle next to Drew, while Ryan hopped into another ground vehicle next to the group.

Just then, Duke Uthgard returned. "It appears your words were like a lucky charm. The rest of Arcadia's army arrived," he said.

"Good. Have them follow that truck and stay close behind. They need to clean up the backside of the Olympian army," Geeta said, then looked to the duke. "I have to return to the palace. The Queen needs help."

The duke snapped his gaze at her. "What happened?"

"She is under a spell," Geeta said evenly.

"A spell? What kind of spell?"

"That's what I'm going to go find out." Inwardly, her stomach churned. "Please take over the assault. Just do what I said, and I think we will come out on top."

"Will do, Miss Geeta." He gave her with a serious look. "Please keep the Queen safe."

"I'll do whatever I can."

The truck started, and the wastelanders got into their vehicles, with the duke following suit. Geeta watched as the entourage took off. The Arcadian vehicles and the men inside of them started to gun down the Olympian army from behind. From the looks of it, it was just as Geeta had thought—it was going to be a rout.

As the entourage of vehicles moved north, she deemed it safe enough to cast her dimensional magic. She embraced her violet-blue magic, allowing it to pour over her body. The wastelands faded into violet-blue before her eyes.

CHAPTER 59

Gwen remained toward the back of the crowd, her face hidden by her helmet. The group around her took off on their vehicles, so she did the same, starting her dirt bike. Everyone had been instructed to follow the vehicle that had Victor tied to it. They said that they were going to lead a charge against Olympia.

It was pretty messed up having Victor strung up on the front vehicle, dangling like a dummy. A thousand things could happen to him. But Gwen could understand why they were doing it.

Luckily, so far, no one she knew had seen her fighting with the other wastelanders. If her dad saw her, or if her mom found out once it was all over, Gwen knew she would never hear the end of it. She tried to stay far back in the fight so no one would spot her, and kept her helmet on just in case. Even when Garrett was gathering the camp for a brief moment during the fight, and Scion cast a barrier over everyone, she remained hidden behind one of the vehicles, waiting to see what was going on. She didn't know why Garrett was gathering everyone at the camp at the time, but then she saw with her own eyes that everyone was ordered to take a taste of that violet woman's blood in the hopes someone would get magic. But no one did except Victor.

I wonder if I would have? Gwen thought. Her dad had magic, and even her mom had some to an extent. She had always assumed that she would get magic, probably orange like her parents. And now she'd missed out on the opportunity to find out, and all because she wasn't supposed to be there in the first place.

Revving the dirt bike one last time, Gwen put the visor down on her helmet, then made sure that the magitech weapon was securely strapped to her back—she had managed to snag it off a dead wastelander. She then tapped the side of her holster, feeling the weight of the handgun.

Check. All good.

A wave of her nerves came over her, but she pushed them aside. *Real fighters aren't scared,* she assured herself. Somehow, her words did not assure her at all.

Clouds of dust plumed around her as the vehicles took off, leaving her behind. Gwen took off, following the group. She was decent at riding her dirt bike. She'd picked up the hobby pretty quick over the last couple of months, being out in the wastelands. *I'm better than some of the other boys,* she thought bitterly, still angry about being ordered to stay behind.

She kept her eyes focused on the sprawling group in front of her. Arcadian military vehicles thrummed behind and above her, chasing the army. Up ahead, the circular gray light of Victor's vehicle shone brightly. Many of the wastelanders were gunning down the Olympian soldiers that stood before them, catching them from behind.

Every now and then, Gwen saw some of the Olympian cyborgs clashing with the wastelanders and a few Arcadian cyborgs. The cyborgs used their sheer strength and normal grafted weapons—that was all they could use due to being disarmed by Victor. All around Gwen, battle cries rose from the wastelanders, renewing their strength and fury for the fight. The wastelanders who weren't driving vehicles were piled up in the backs of open vehicles, shooting and screaming. Others rode their dirt bikes and all-terrain vehicles, chasing down the Olympian army.

In the distance, Gwen saw the strange communication tower, swaying back and forth as it moved. She'd seen what the boy did to the camp, especially her father. He was a mess, but he'd still managed to fight, even while half dismantled. That made Gwen angry.

No one messes with Dad!

The boy would pay. Olympia would pay. She may have been young, but she would show them. The wastelands were her home now, and she would fight just as hard as everyone else. She would prove she could do it.

Her nerves jumbled her stomach again. Would her magitech weapon be an equal match to the power of the boy?

I guess I'll find out when I get there, she told herself.

Taking a deep breath to release her nerves, Gwen narrowed her eyes, setting her focus on the tower ahead of her. She twisted the handle, kicking the dirt bike into high gear, making it go faster. Speeding through the group of ground vehicles, Gwen remained focused, determined to make it to the front. But there was too much dust being kicked around, making it hard for her to see, causing her to slow down. She did manage to make it slightly ahead of some of the vehicles.

The wastelanders kept up the chase, with the force of the Arcadian army behind them. They crossed the western wastelands, with many of the fighters firing back and forth. Bodies littered the trail while cyborg parts spread across the sands.

Suddenly, a string of vehicles slammed on their brakes, spinning out wildly. Gwen veered off to the side of the stopped vehicles, then continued to drive past them.

Dad is up there… I have to see what is happening.

She wove in and around the vehicles, leaving them in the dust. Some of the vehicles were still moving, but many had come to a stop with their drivers asking what was going on.

Why did they stop?

As soon as Gwen had passed a good majority of them, she saw why. The vehicle that Victor was strung to had stalled, and her dad was untying Victor. Another vehicle pulled up next to them. If Gwen had to guess, they were going to tie Victor to the new one.

As Gwen neared, she hesitated. She could stop and help them. If she did, everyone would know that she hadn't stayed behind in the refuge like she was supposed to. But if she kept going, no one would know, and she could get that boy. He was so close…

She made up her mind. Gwen approached her dad, Victor, and Garrett. It was as if her dad knew, because he looked directly at her, cocking his head. His cybernetic eye flashed as she sped past.

There's no fooling Dad, she thought. *Even with my helmet on.* She turned her focus to the retreating tower in the distance. *He has to be stopped.*

Gwen twisted the handle into high gear, gaining speed. With several minutes of hard and fast riding, Gwen managed to catch up with the tail end of the Olympian army. She smiled to herself inwardly, applauding her riding skills. Olympian men in the open ground vehicles saw her, then pulled out their guns, aiming at her.

Reaching for her holster, she yanked out her gun, doing the same. As she made the movement, her dirt bike swung wildly, so she gripped both handlebars again, her handgun smashed in between her clutched hand and the handgrip of the bike.

How can I shoot while driving?

The Olympian men fired their weapons, and suddenly, Gwen was scared. She braced herself, hoping that they somehow would miss. The moment came and went, and she was not shot. Instead, Gwen saw a bright orange-yellow shield encasing her.

"Dad!"

Blinking wildly, Gwen looked to each side. On her left, her father was driving a camp dirt bike like a pro. It was almost laughable. She had never *once* seen her father drive anything in the entire time she'd known him, but here he was, driving like a champ. Apparently his circuits knew what to do.

From where she was, even Gwen could see that her dad was in poor shape. Many of his parts were jutting out of his body while his mechanical arm had almost no flesh attached.

Gwen realized that her dad had used magic. *We must be far enough away from Victor.*

"G-G-G-Gwen!" he yelled.

More gunfire, but the bullets bounced off their shields. A few of the Olympian cyborgs started blasting their yellow powers against the shield, trying to melt it away.

Gwen lifted the visor of the helmet. "Dad! We gotta get that kid! We *have* to!"

His cybernetic eye flashed in understanding.

Giving him a satisfied smile in return, Gwen snapped her visor back down, then sped up, both their barriers lightly renewed by her father's magic. They drove through more Olympian vehicles, gaining on the communication tower. Olympian cyborgs shot at them from the vehicles while their drivers tried to box them in. But each time they got near, her father blasted them with magical fireballs or waves of lightning or made the earth give out under them, sending them off course or smashing into each other.

Her dad was pretty cool. Much cooler than her mom, that was for sure.

After another round of her dad's crazy-big fireballs blew up some Olympian vehicles, a clear path opened up—directly to the communications tower.

Gwen looked over at her dad, but he jumped off the bike.

"Dad!"

Suddenly, her father was airborne, basked in orange-red magic. Magical winds rushing under him, giving him flight. He flew near her. Gwen breathed a sigh of relief, then turned her attention back to the tower.

But then her father started to glow an intense orange-red, almost pure red. Instantly, his flying speed increased.

Gosh, he flies fast! she thought, amazed.

He flew ahead of her, then threw out his hand. A fireball grew rapidly in his palm, building to the size of a vehicle. He swung his hand downward, releasing the magic. The giant fireball came crashing down on the army that surrounded the communications tower, engulfing everyone in flames.

Screams and shouts erupted, all coming from within the hellfire. Gwen pulled over just before the ring of fire, then hopped off her bike. She yanked her magitech weapon off her back, cocked the weapon, and approached the flames.

Her nerves were kicking into high gear. She swallowed hard, gripping her weapon tightly. As the flames died down, Gwen saw charred bodies. There was no sign of her father, but she knew that he liked to hide with his magic.

Through the smoke, a dark, glowing red moved closer from within, and a shape formed.

It was the boy.

Her body shook, with her mouth dropping.

No way! Gwen thought wildly. She'd known it was a boy, but he was so young! Maybe eight years old? Could she really shoot an eight-year-old kid?

The boy was wearing some kind of electronic goggles attached to a headpiece—like a headset gamers used for online games. He yanked it off and looked in her direction. Their eyes instantly connected. His eerie dark-red eyes gave her the creeps.

Oh my God! I can't kill a little kid, she thought frantically, overwhelmed with panic.

She shook even harder, fear running through her body. Gathering her courage, Gwen aimed the gun, seeing the boy in the line of the crosshairs of the scope.

She fired.

A roaring blast of red streaming flames shot out toward him, completely engulfing the boy within a ten-foot firestorm. A terrible wave of remorse hit her, but Gwen continued, holding down the trigger. She was still shaking, but she tried to remain calm. After all, that boy had screwed with her father. He'd tried to kill all of them.

After holding down the trigger for several minutes, Gwen deemed it safe to release it. The flames were hot, so she moved backward to escape the heat. It was so intense that her face felt like it would melt if she stayed that close any longer.

To her horror, the flames that engulfed the boy grew larger and taller, then shifted into a deep, dark red. They flickered unnaturally. Gwen felt her body being yanked away in flight. It was her invisible father; she could feel his flesh and machinery around her as they flew to the side.

The dark fire shot out at them in retaliation, and her dad cast a last-minute shield.

"What…?" Gwen said, shocked. "What *is* he?"

"Unnatural…" her father said as they dodged the flames.

Her heart pumped hard in her chest, and suddenly she realized just how stupid she was to have chased after the boy. And now she and her dad were going to pay for her recklessness.

A new power suddenly enveloped them, and her father's orange-red wind shifted to dark red, flowing all around them, sending them to flying back toward the ring of fire where the boy stood.

The intense heat burned her skin. Her skin wasn't really on fire, but the heat sure made it feel like it. It was hot. Too hot.

"Dad! The heat is too much for me!" she cried out.

"I kn-n-n-now," he said.

He dropped her, causing Gwen to fall nearly fifteen feet to the ground. She landed hard, so hard her body made an unnatural crunching sound. Turning over to the side weakly, she groaned. Her body was shot with pain. She caught a glimpse of her dad being drawn toward the fire against his will. Gwen skimmed her gaze to each side of the fire; the Olympian army was close.

Move! she told herself.

Weakly, Gwen managed to crawl through the ash and dead bodies, searching for anything that could be of use. There was nothing, but then she looked down at her handgun, still in her holster. Not knowing what else to do, she pulled out the handgun and aimed.

If this doesn't work, I'm dead. Through the dark-red flames, she saw her dad swing wildly at the boy. The boy's narrow eyes glowed a scary red as his short black hair stood on end. He screamed at the top of his lungs as tears trickled down his cheeks.

"I don't want to be here! I wanna go home!" he screamed.

What?

"I don't want to be here," he repeated, continuing to cry. His power intensified around him, the dark-red energy humming and circling him.

As he screamed, the metal in her father's body bent and snapped, and her father grunted in pain. His body was twisting unnaturally before her eyes as he continued to try to get close to the boy.

Dad...

Her dad kept fighting as the metal in his body burned deep red, twisting. She gritted her teeth, then cried, seeing the damage done to her dad.

The boy screamed and cried out again. "I don't want to be here anymore!" He gripped his face, flailing and crying.

Gwen could see the pain on the boy's face. *Does he know what he's even doing?*

It made everything worse, and she felt horrible. It was as if he was trapped in some kind of nightmare. Tears rolled down her cheeks, then she aimed her gun steadily. When she had him centered, she closed her eyes and pulled the trigger. The crack of the shot rocked her ears, and she opened her eyes.

The bullet hit the kid right in the chest. It completely missed his heart, but it knocked him to the ground.

Off to the side, her dad slumped over too, free of the boy's magic. Her father looked to her, then tried to give her a reassuring smile. "I'm-m-m-m o-o-o-okay."

Then he passed out.

"Dad!"

Gwen threw up, sick with nerves and over what she had just done. Just as she was about to get to her feet, she bent back down, vomiting two more times.

She'd just shot an eight-year old. Her body felt sick and weak.

There was another scream from the boy. Suddenly, metal wrapped around her, yanking her toward the communications tower. Another cry from the boy, and more metal wrapped around her, this time locking her to the tower itself, securing her in place.

Gwen struggled, but it was no use—the metal secured her fully, and she couldn't budge. The Olympian army surrounding them, some gathering around her father.

"Get this cyborg onto one of our vehicles, and get it back to Olympia immediately. Make sure he stays alive!" commanded one of the Olympian men.

"You stay away from him!" Gwen yelled at them, struggling against the tower.

They all laughed at her as four men grabbed her father, lifted him up, and started heading for a vehicle.

Something caught her eye. A bright gray light was approaching. Apparently, the men saw it too.

"It's them! Move the boy before they get close!" yelled one of the Olympian men.

"Hurry your ass up and secure that cyborg! We can't lose him!" yelled another.

They hurried her father onto a vehicle while they readied the communications tower to depart. A bright gray flash of light, followed by a dark-red blast of color, forced Gwen to close her eyes, and the sound of a blast filled Gwen's ears.

As the flash subsided, Gwen saw Garrett on the back of an open ground vehicle, holding a launcher. Victor was still tied up to their vehicle, his body pulsating with his gray magic. Was it fading away? Gwen couldn't tell. Cyborgs were strewn all around, not moving, their human sides yelling in confusion. The Olympian soldiers tried to attack, but none of their equipment was working, and their vehicles were stalled.

Garrett flashed her a smile, then quickly got out of the vehicle with some other men. Far behind, the Arcadian army approached.

It's the EMP launcher! Gwen thought wildly. Garrett had been working on a new version with a few guys in his spare time. He'd been proud of his latest one, saying it had come in handy when he used it in Arcadia. He also had said something about how old the wasteland vehicles were, and how they wouldn't be affected since they were made with old technology, compared to the new vehicles used by modern armies.

There was mass confusion. The commanders, soldiers, everyone was completely distracted by Garrett's EMP.

"They have my dad!" Gwen yelled to Garrett. "In the big vehicle over there with the insignia!"

"Got it," Garrett yelled back. The wastelanders surrounded the area, the Arcadian army closer.

"Sir, the communications vehicle is still up and running!" yelled an Olympian soldier.

"Looks like the boy saved our ass. Get him out of here," an Olympian commander yelled to the scurrying soldiers.

Gwen saw Garrett pull her dad out from the vehicle. Everyone was still distracted. Then Gwen felt a vibration, and the tower started to move. Soldiers were hopping onto the communications tower vehicle. She was being driven away. Garrett locked eyes with her; they were thinking the same thing. The tower and the vehicle it was attached to was somehow unaffected by the EMP. Was it because the vehicle that it was attached to was of old technology? Was it shielded by the boy? She did see a burst of deep red before the blast…

Gwen screamed, but it was too late. Her screams were drowned out by the roaring hum of the vehicle as it took off at a rapid pace. There was already a good amount of distance between her and the Arcadian army. Gwen could still see Victor burning in his gray light. Wastelanders fought Olympian army stragglers left behind to fend for themselves.

More and more distance was put between them, and Gwen continued to scream. No one would hear her, but she screamed in frustration anyway. She tried with all her might to move again, but the metal had pinned her tight. The wind ripping through her ponytail, and the aches and pains of her body began to throb as her adrenaline subsided.

The tower vehicle kept driving and driving, until the gray light was no more, and all Gwen could see was open desert. Above, through the metal bars, Gwen saw the boy, his strange gaming-goggle headset strapped onto his head once again. He was still crying. They were softer cries, so it seemed that the boy was calming down. Where she had shot the boy in the chest, it looked like he had already been temporarily bandaged.

Gwen's heart dropped.

"Don't worry. Your dad will come for you," an Olympian man joked from the vehicle below.

Everything seemed to speed up in fast motion as a swirling blue light encompassed them. The speed of the vehicle, traveling through the wastelands, even the men were in fast-forward mode. It all made her dizzy.

Gwen closed her eyes, sick from the motion. She thought of her mom.

Mom is going to be so pissed… I'll never hear the end of it.

That was, if she ever saw her mom again.

CHAPTER 60

GREEN

Suresh stood amongst the glowing vials, stunned at the overwhelming amount of gifted blood and the sheer number of how many gifteds' life forces were contained. They burned wildly with power. There was no doubt they didn't want to be contained.

How is this possible? To contain one's gift, one's raw life force... It was impossible! But here he was, standing among a vast number of life forces contained in bottles, swirling with the energy of their color.

As Suresh walked by the vials, he noticed a small collection of gems on the shelves—a handful of reds, oranges, yellows, and a couple blues. The gems slowly pulsated their respective colors, like the beating of a heart.

These are the only gifted colors in this time era.

Turning, Suresh saw that the vials were labeled and cataloged. The ones with liquid blood pulsated like the gemstones, radiating with a warm glow. Others looked like as if the life force within the blood had disappeared due to being dried out from age. He couldn't believe what he was seeing. Life forces. Gifteds' blood. It was sickening.

This is unnatural! These people are vile. How could they do such a thing? Suresh thought in disgust.

He paused for a moment, swallowing hard. It was such a hypocritical thing for him to think about these people being vile, considering he had consumed his fellow comrade Raghu's blood years ago. But this... this was far worse than him consuming the blood of a gifted. Wasn't it?

A wave of nausea hit him, and he began to sweat profusely. Being in a place like this disturbed his soul, sickening his innermost being. Suresh looked up at the vials once again. There was a pattern to how everything was cataloged; they were in color order of the spectrum, and each of the vials had names. There were also empty spots on the shelves, with names engraved on a plaque where the vials would sit. Hundreds of vials were housed in the red, orange, and yellow sections of the shelves. It was the same with the gemstones. When Suresh's gaze came to the green section, it was completely empty.

Suresh stopped, his heart pounding. The foremost inscription in the green section read: *Queen Emerald of the Millennium Era. Born 2360 M.E.*

The High Court knew of Queen Emerald. They wanted her blood and her power! Or worse… her life force.

He had to get out of here.

No wonder the High Inquisitor warned me many years ago of his superiors. I might have been rendered powerless if they had found me.

As Suresh was about to use his time magic, he heard heavy breathing, as if someone was struggling for air. Suresh paused in the middle of his spell, then dropped his hands as a man slowly stumbled out of the shadows and into the light. The man gazed at him, then flopped to the floor. Suresh could tell the man's face was supposed to be ebony, but it was tinged blue from lack of oxygen. Dark-blue veins popped out along his face and neck. The man had piercing blue eyes and hair that matched. He was gifted.

The man looked at Suresh, and their eyes met. He could feel the man's weakened life force.

"I have been watching you, Suresh," the man struggled to say, gasping. "Watching you for a very *long* time. I have been waiting for this moment to meet you…"

The man sucked in his breath, then his eyes rolled back, his mouth foaming.

He was dying.

Suresh rushed over to the man, laying a hand on him. Suresh filled his spirit with his power, the healing magic of his life force. After surging healing magic throughout his body and gathering it in his hand, Suresh unleashed his power.

Like a strong wind, the magic worked quickly. The man continued to struggle to breathe. With each breath, the man became more stable by the second, and his face changed from a sickening blue back to his original skin tone, a deep ebony.

Life was restored to the man's eyes. He stared at Suresh and held up his hand calmly. Suresh moved back slightly, not sure of the man's intentions. He was still shaking from the amount of energy spent on healing the man, and his face was pouring sweat. His clothes were soaked.

"I am not going to harm you, Suresh, though many in this citadel would," the man said mildly. "Thank you for giving me a second chance." He slowly sat up, facing him.

"How do you know me?" Suresh asked, seeing the man in more detail. He was older, well dressed—wearing some of the finest robes Suresh had ever seen—with a long silk azure cape embroidered with gold banding. Various blue jewels adorned him. Whoever the man was, he was no doubt of significant importance.

"I have been scrying you in the flow of time for years now. A green-gifted time traveler," he said, studying Suresh's face. "I have never seen one like you before, one who shouldn't be traveling… one who has consumed magics."

"I did it because—"

"I know why you did it."

"You do?" Suresh neared him. "Who *are* you?"

"My name is Oriel. I am one of the six high justices on the High Court."

"High justice?"

Oriel nodded. "I have been in my position a long, long time, regrettably. This is truly a dangerous time for you to be in. As you have probably noticed from this room. For many years, I have been shielding you from my counterparts, the other members of the High Court. But one of them spotted you recently, and now your life, or shall I say, your *gift*, is in danger."

His words reinforced Suresh's anxiety. People were actively searching for him. Maybe they even had a spot especially for his gift.

"There is something I must do in this time before I leave," Suresh told him. "I must find the High Inquisitor, Rubius. It is imperative that I find him."

"Ah, the High Inquisitor. Or should I say, *Kyle Trancer*?"

Suresh froze, stunned at the man's words. "You *know* about his past life?"

Oriel nodded, then slowly leaned against the wall to support his weakened frame. "Yes. One of the many times when I was scrying time to search for the green-gifted Emerald, I came across him. When I saw him in the flow of time, I couldn't believe it—the man Kyle in the past had the same *soul* as Rubius in this present time. I watched him carefully, studying him nearly as much as I studied the green-gifted queen. And that was how I found you.

"At first, I thought of telling the others about my discovery of you, for we were all searching for the Gift of the Green." He paused, then frowned deeply. "When I first saw you in the flow of time, I was very… different. I didn't tell the others about you because I wanted your blood all to myself, to succeed the others."

"Then you are my enemy," Suresh declared.

"At one time, yes, I would have been. But as I near death's door, my soul groans restlessly. I have not walked the path of righteousness to enter paradise, and to be quite honest, burning in the fires of hell for all eternity doesn't sound quite appealing to me. I had hoped to escape death with the blood of the green, to find a way to live endlessly on this earth, but I have reassessed everything." His eyes watered with tears. "That way leads to endless darkness."

Suresh took in his words, his thoughts swimming. His eyes then trailed to the countless vials and glowing gemstones, and the life forces within them.

"What happened to all these gifted?" Suresh asked, pointing to the vials. "Did you kill them all?"

The man shook his head. "Not at all. They are all very much alive, unless they died of old age or natural causes."

"And the stones? Are those… transmuted?"

"Yes, from the life forces themselves," Oriel said. "At first, we wanted blood, to consume and distribute powers to others. But as you can see, blood dries up over time, so we came up with a more elaborate idea. We made sure that we got the blood, then we started transmuting it so we had enough. If it's about to dry up, we just transmute more, so that we can still bestow powers to other loyal gifted. Some we had converted to gemstones, though it is extremely difficult to do. There is only one who has the ability to do so, and she is an equal to the High Court."

Suresh couldn't believe what he was hearing. The future… the world… it could be destroyed because of what they were doing. "And the powers within the vials? I don't understand."

"There is a gifted who can absorb one's gift," Oriel said slowly. "But she can also completely take it away. These life forces are all her doing."

Suresh held his breath and went cold. There was only one person he could think of who could do all of this, but she was back in time. *It can't be her. She seemed so kind. Was she made to do these terrible things against her will?*

"Please, tell me, is this person Elyathi?" Suresh blurted out, recalling his brief meeting with her years ago.

"Indeed, it is." Oriel's eyes met his. There were no lies behind them.

"Is she harmed in any way?"

"Harmed?" Oriel half-smirked, shaking his head. "Not in the least." His eyes turned dark. "In fact, she is the reason for this madness. At first, we on the High Court set out to find each color of the gift, wherever and whenever in time that was. We had planned to consume each color, so that no one had the power to overthrow us once we unlocked the Spectrum of Magic. We were already the ultimate authority on earth, but what if the gifted people rebelled? To ensure our survival, we continued to outlaw technology, just like our predecessors, keeping it within our grasp and out of the hands of the people. All the while, we were on a quest to find each color of the spectrum, and aligning with many of the other gifted who were extreme supporters of our court. They thought they were doing God's work. In many ways, so did we.

"Then *she* came. We had finally found Elyathi after many, many years. We all knew about the white-gifted child. We had been searching for her for years. You see, Elyathi was from this time originally, taken away as a child by a small opposing group on earth's surface. This rebel group convinced a blue-gifted to take her back to another time so she could be as far away from us as possible. But we found her. Or I should say, *I* found her.

"After Elyathi was retrieved and brought back here, she vowed to help us in any way she could. In fact, she was so dedicated to our goals that she was the very one to come up with the idea to take away the gifteds' magic. She has such strong faith in the God of Light, much more than even the priests, I daresay. However, her faith is so fervent that she has become an obsessive zealot for the God of Light. She and the other members of the High Court—including me at one time—we all wanted to purify the world of magic, believing in the one true prophecy, which stated that magic should be returned to the heavens and foretold a new earth.

"We also believed that only one gifted person should remain on earth to represent each color of the spectrum. Over the years of having Elyathi with us, our plan has changed into something greater—when we called upon the new earth, we would reshape the face of it to our liking. We would transform it into kingdoms of color, with each high justice ruling over their own respective kingdom of color."

"But why?" Suresh said in disbelief.

"The ancient prophecy speaks of the God of Light's chosen one, one who will reshape the earth and restore it to holiness and balance. It is written that this chosen one has the Gift of the White, and only one throughout time will have this gift. By aligning ourselves with Elyathi, we were sure that we were aligning ourselves with ultimate power, and that God Himself was going to bless us with invincibility by fulfilling his ancient words."

"Elyathi…" Suresh whispered. "I just can't believe this."

Oriel nodded. "She is very aware of this prophecy, and takes her role very seriously. We recovered several ancient texts that have a spell written only for her. Only she can read and understand it."

"What is the spell for?"

"To shape the new world," Oriel said softly.

Suresh's eyes went wide.

"The only thing Elyathi has said is that during the casting of the actual spell, all colors of magic must be represented. The magic will be cast, focused to her, and she will do the rest."

"If this is a prophecy," said Suresh, "then wouldn't this be a good thing? To better our world?" And yet, somehow he didn't think so.

"Search your heart, time traveler. What does it say to you?"

Just thinking about everything Oriel said felt sick and wrong, that he knew. "I don't like this prophecy, especially given the current circumstances. I am not familiar with the God of Light. I only know of my gods, and yet I doubt that this"—he gestured around them—"is what the 'God of Light' intends."

Oriel nodded in agreement.

"If this happens, no one would be able to overcome the High Court's authority," Suresh said, his eyes narrowing. "And you wanted to be a part of this?"

Oriel's eyes fell to the floor. "As I have said before, I am ashamed of my past, time traveler. That is why I am here now. To warn you." He stood up with much effort, locking eyes with Suresh. "I am doing what I can to stop this, but I need more help. You must send Rubius back to Queen Emerald. With him lingering in this time, he is another means to retrieve violet magic."

"But he is red-gifted," Suresh pointed out.

"That may be true, but he possesses the full potential of the violet gift."

Suresh felt lost. "But I still don't understand. His blood would still have the red gift," he said, still trying to follow what Oriel was getting at.

"Extraction."

"Extraction?"

"If the High Court cannot successfully get the Sorceress Ikaria's blood, they are going to experiment with Rubius to try and remove his red magic, making him a pure violet-gifted."

"They… they can do that?"

"They don't know it yet, but I have seen in the flow of time that they will be able to, with the help of Elyathi."

Suresh thought about all that Oriel had said, trying to come to terms with everything. He sighed. It was all overwhelming.

"You mentioned Ikaria and the violet magic… why don't you have violet magic now?" Suresh continued. "Didn't the people back in time help send her back here to this time?"

Oriel smiled slightly. "Indeed, but she still proves to be difficult. We have been trying to get her blood for many years."

"Why hasn't Elyathi retrieved the blood? It seems like she has the means to do so."

"Elyathi can draw out one's life force and absorb it, but if she isn't linked to a color, then she is powerless." Oriel eyed Suresh. "We suspected that Ikaria knew how to use her gift for many years but had been lying about it. Elyathi wasn't as strong then as she is now. Before, she was very weak with her gift, and years ago, Ikaria would have destroyed Elyathi had she known about her. But with each life-force extraction, she grew stronger in her gift. And now she knows it too well. Especially now that she has access to the other colors we collected."

"I don't believe it. Elyathi doing all of this," Suresh said sadly.

"I am sorry to even speak these words, especially knowing that a lot of it is my fault."

Suresh shook his head. "It's just… I always wondered if she was going to be okay, being that the one and only time I met her, she was so kind of heart… but sad. It doesn't seem like her to do these awful things."

"But in Elyathi's eyes, she is justified," Oriel said. "She whole-heartedly believes she is doing God's work."

"Even if the High Court makes Rubius into a pure violet-gifted, who's to say that he would partake in this madness? And what of the green magic?" Suresh asked. "I surely won't partake in this ritual, and I would think Queen Emerald wouldn't either."

"I agree," Oriel said. "However, I have foreseen several outcomes, none of them good."

Suresh paused, disheartened. The more Oriel spoke, the more dire the situation seemed. "Please, tell me. I must know!" Suresh uttered, his heart heavy with worry.

Oriel continued. "One possibility is that Elyathi will try to convince her daughter to help her."

"Emerald wouldn't do such a thing," Suresh said quickly.

"Well, this is her mother we're talking about. She might. And if someone had the power to control her will… it is always possible. As for the other outcomes, one calls for you being used the same way, controlled. And another, by extraction from another blue-gifted."

Suresh was stunned. "Using me? Another blue-gifted? Are they from your time? Is it Lady Vala?"

The man's eyes went wide, then his face went serious. "How do you know of her?"

"I happened to come across her. I overhead that she had been summoned here, to this High Court, because of her being blue-gifted. I was actually worried for her, and came looking for her here, even though I have been searching for the High Inquisitor. Something was not right…"

The man's face went pale, and he suddenly looked sick.

"Is it Lady Vala? Is she in danger?" Suresh pressed.

"If it is as you say, she is already doomed. I must go." Oriel bowed to Suresh, then began casting a spell. "I am sorry to cut it short, but please, you *must* get Rubius out of this time and protect Queen Emerald at all costs."

"Where can I find Rubius? I heard that he was possibly in World Sector Six, but I don't know."

"It is as you say—he is in World Sector Six. In the royal citadel." Blue magic started enveloping the man. "Keep your violet-gifted friend Geeta, and yourself, far, far away from the High Court."

"But who is the blue-gifted?" Suresh asked. "You never said!"

"King Derek of Arcadia. He must *not* travel to this place."

Suresh paused, his heart sinking. He'd briefly come across the King in despair, as the king was trying to kill himself. Suresh had stopped him. "I know of him."

"He is dangerous, almost as dangerous as Elyathi herself. Those two must not come across each other!"

"I promise I will do whatever in my power to stop this!" Suresh called out. "Where are you going?"

"To try and find my daughter," he answered.

Oriel's blue magic washed over him, and he flashed away in the blink of an eye, leaving Suresh alone.

He is Lady Vala's father? Suresh wondered before turning his thoughts back to the current situation. *Perhaps now she will have the help she needs.*

Suresh straightened, determined. He had to get to Rubius. After he found him, he would take him to Queen Emerald. She had to be protected.

I must get to World Sector Six.

Suresh started summoning the dimensional magic, taking one last look at the room, his heart full of sadness. The thought of Elyathi behind the madness of this room made his heart break.

Just as Suresh was about to release the blue-green magic, there was an orange flash in the room. Suresh whipped his head around but saw nothing, and released his spell. The world turned a strange color. It was not frozen in green-blue for him to move around like how it should have.

"Oriel? Is that you?" Suresh called out.

"The *traitor* is gone. It's a shame that I missed him. It's just me and you, *green-gifted*," said a feminine voice, chuckling joyfully.

Everything in the world began to melt like hot wax, all in shades of orange. Images and objects flowed down until there was nothing but a puddle on the floor, pooling, leaving him in an endless empty white space.

Suresh readied himself. "Who's there?" he called out.

Nobody answered.

Looking around frantically, Suresh knew it was the workings of an orange-gifted, and whatever he was seeing was an illusion. He closed his eyes, trying to think of the time magic. Maybe he could escape this time altogether. Filling his veins with power, he began to fill his life force, but as soon as he released it, the spell was countered.

Then his body was whipped around. A metal object scathed him, clipping the edge of his clothes. His thoughts went wild. He was being attacked! Quickly filling his body with his dark-green ability, Suresh searched his surroundings, trying to sense the other life force presence, but it was impossible with all the other life forces contained in vials. But one was much stronger. It had to be the gifted in the room.

Focusing on that source, Suresh did what he should not ever do. But he was desperate. He funneled his dark-green magic out in the direction of the source, and it streamed out of him. Sweat beaded on his body from the sheer power.

He felt his magic as it started to drain the source, giving him more life from the mysterious caster's power. The world of illusion slowly melted away, restoring Suresh to his real surroundings. A woman with short orange hair lay writhing on the floor, his green magic sucking away her life force.

She looked at him with burning orange eyes and screamed. A bright-orange flash of lightning startled Suresh. His magic went cold as she charged toward him. The woman whipped out her hands, revealing knives hidden in the sleeves of her robes. With a burning orange glow, the knives morphed into long swords. She jumped in the air, swinging her swords manically at his body.

Suresh shot up a hand, releasing a weak protective barrier. Her swords crashed into the barrier, shattering it, then she swung again. This time, Suresh quickly summoned his dark-green magic. It shot to her, distracting her long enough for him to roll out of the way.

The woman summoned a huge barrier that flashed with orange brilliance. It soaked in most of Suresh's magic, with very little getting through. The little that did weakened her, but not by much.

I have to get out of here!

The world started shifting in hues of orange before his eyes. Suresh said a silent prayer to the God of the Blue, then tried to summon his time magic. The world flickered between green-blue, blue, then dark orange, the colors fighting each other.

Then the world went a solid blue. It had to be Oriel helping.

The world was paused, but it wouldn't be for long. Suresh filled his body and spirit with his dimensional magic. The world shifted again, this time into color before his spell washed over him. As it did, he heard the orange-gifted woman's bitter words, "I'm coming for you, green-gifted!"

CHAPTER 61

VIOLET

The violet-hued world faded to full color as Geeta pulled away her time magic, landing right outside Arcadia's audience chamber. The guards stationed became animated as color seeped into them. The guards made an audible noise in shock as Geeta flashed before them.

"Where is the Queen? I need to see her now," Geeta said impatiently.

"Thank God you are here."

Geeta looked over her shoulder as Emerys came running up to her.

"The Queen…" he said, urging her to follow.

"Let's hurry."

They both exchanged nods and quickly started walking. The councilor led Geeta through the palace to the Queen's chambers, and he took her straight into the bedroom. There, a handmaiden stood above the Queen with a stressed look upon her face. She looked like she had been crying, her face puffy and her eyes slightly red. Next to the servant was Telly, walking in circles. Her hair was frazzled, glasses crooked, and she had bloodstains all over her clothes, especially near her shoulder, which was injured.

"How long has she been like this?" Geeta asked.

"About twenty-three hours," said the handmaiden.

"And the attacks?" Geeta eyed both of them.

"One in the night, then one today," said Telly.

"And they were blue-gifted?"

"Yes, though their bodies dissolved. Only their clothes remain," Telly said. "The first one appeared to the handmaiden, though he died before he was able to do anything. The second time, I was here, and he attacked me while trying to get to the Queen. But I was in the middle of fighting him when he melted right in front of me." She pointed at a pile of clothing, then grimaced from the movement, clutching her shoulder. "That is all that is left of him."

Geeta walked up to Telly and laid a hand on her shoulder. Telly looked at her for a moment, confused, then stilled. Geeta sent a wave of healing magic into Telly's shoulder, the power that came from Suresh's blood, which she had consumed years ago. She wasn't the best at healing, but she did what she could to mend the scientist's shoulder. Telly breathed a sigh of relief as Geeta's violet magic began to settle in her shoulder, then fade away.

"Good as new," Telly said, nodding. She moved her shoulder around as if she were straightening a kink. "Thank you for that."

"You're welcome."

Geeta went to the pile of clothes, kicking through a blue robe with her combat boots. An amulet with several large sapphires flopped out.

"This clothing, I've seen its like before. Can't remember where," Geeta said, studying them for a moment. She moved to the Queen's side. Just as she was about to lay her hand on Emerald, Geeta looked over her shoulder at the councilor.

"May I?" Geeta asked him.

He nodded.

"What are you going to do?" asked the maid. Telly put a hand on her shoulder for reassurance.

"I won't hurt her. Promise," Geeta said to the handmaiden.

She sat down next to Emerald on the bed, then gently rested both her hands on the Queen's forehead. Closing her eyes, Geeta called upon the power within her life force. It came at her beckoning, ripping through her violently, shaking her from within. Geeta grimaced as the magic poured through her body. *I need more of you!* she commanded the magic. *I must get inside her mind!*

The magic listened, releasing its energy, flooding her bloodstream, then funneling straight into her hands. With a sharp force of the energy jutting from her mind, Geeta unleashed her spirit into it, allowing her life force to jump into the Queen's mind.

She was in.

As Geeta was gaining her footing, she sat in silence, trying to grasp the situation. All was dark. All was silent.

"Queen Emerald?" Geeta called out.

Nothing but darkness, not even an echo of her voice crying out.

How can there be nothing inside her mind?

Just then, Geeta felt Emerald's magic hum inside the darkened world.

"My Queen!" Geeta called out. "It is Geeta! Your newly named protector!" Slowly, Geeta's surroundings began to form, taking the shape of the Queen's bedroom. Confused, Geeta sat there in the Queen's chambers. Had her magic worked? She didn't see any other people in the room with her. There was no chamber maid, no obnoxious Telly rattling off something or another. All was silent as Geeta took in the strangeness of Emerald's bedroom.

It was nighttime.

I jumped into her mind during the day.

Looking outside onto the patio, Geeta saw strange glowing lights. Curious, she walked over to the door, then gasped. A magical, glowing staircase radiating all colors of the spectrum led from Emerald's patio to the sky. She slid the patio door open, then walked outside cautiously, her eyes glued to the magical staircase. Her eyes followed the trail until she could see no more of it. It was as if the staircase went on forever into the endless starry sky, past the full moon, until disappearing into the heavens itself.

What in the world? Geeta thought. Usually, people's minds were nothing but doors, tunnels, and chambers, leading to different memories. But here, in the Queen's mind, it was a darkened shade that mirrored the real world. It was unlike anything Geeta had ever encountered.

An overwhelming energy radiated from the staircase—a powerful blue magic, like none she had ever felt before. The magic coming from it called out to her, weeping. Studying the staircase, Geeta paced on the patio, wondering if she dared take the stairs.

I could be trapped if I ascend, she thought. But then her thoughts turned to the Queen. Perhaps this was the only way to wake the Queen in real life. Making a decision, Geeta took a deep breath, then stepped onto the staircase, beginning her ascent. Step by step, Geeta made her way up little by little, each movement bringing her a little bit closer to the heavens. After some time, Geeta looked ahead; there was still no end in sight.

The stairs were endless.

A sudden wave of magic struck Geeta, draining her life force, causing her to falter. Her life force was leaving her and being filtering into the strange plane of existence.

Is this truly Emerald's mind? Or am I in some kind of dimensional spell?

Steeling her resolve, Geeta continued her climb until the city below was no more, and the only sight was wisps of clouds highlighted by the moon.

Shapes in the distance started forming, and Geeta recognized them. They were floating citadels, very much like the citadels Auron had resided in from the future.

The future.

It all fell into place. Geeta was heading toward the future on a different plane of existence. With each step, Geeta was traveling through another time and into a new dimension. But what she couldn't figure out was how Emerald's mind was tied to all of it.

Picking up the pace, Geeta sprinted up the stairs toward the sky. There, in the distance, Geeta saw a doorway, sealed shut. Finally, Geeta stood before it. Looking down for a moment, Geeta saw the earth far below the glowing stairs. *I better not do anything foolish,* she thought. *I could die in my mind… or in Emerald's mind, whatever this place is!*

A voice came from behind the door. It was Emerald's voice, crying out.

"Queen Emerald?" Geeta called out to her.

Emerald's voice didn't answer her, but Geeta heard more muffled yells from behind the door, very faintly.

"My Queen!" Geeta yelled, slamming the door hard.

"Kyle?" Emerald screamed from the other side.

Geeta jerked back at the mention of Kyle's name.

"Kyle, please, answer me!" Emerald continued, the Queen's voice reverberating inside Geeta's head.

Emerald was calling out to Kyle. Was Emerald locked in a dream? Or could she somehow see Kyle's spirit within the lifestream here, on this strange plane of existence? Geeta sensed a painful sadness surrounding her. It sapped her strength, her spirit, her life. Then Geeta realized Emerald's sad world would consume her and break her spirit if she stayed.

I can't be here! The Queen can't be here! Geeta thought wildly. Panic for herself and panic for the Queen rocked Geeta's core. She had to get out. This sadness had to be broken. Feeling violet energy burning through her body, Geeta called upon the force that fed her spirit with all her might.

With a loud roar, Geeta grasped all her violet magic within the palm of her hand, then hurled it at the door. The door rattled, but other than that, it didn't budge from its locked position.

"Emerald! You can't be here!" Geeta called out. "Your spirit will diminish from your sadness."

Nothing but the high-altitude winds answered her back. Pouring her burning energy through her life force once more, Geeta funneled it all through her conscious being. Violet light emitted from her spirit, and in a split second, Geeta was burning with a magical violet fire.

Geeta screamed loud and hard, then ran toward the door, unleashing the violet force from her spirit as her entire upper body made contact with the door. Instead of breaking through, Geeta smashed into it, then tumbled off the stairs.

She was falling. Falling in the utter sadness and despair that fed Emerald's mind.

***

Staircases. Endless staircases. Some went up, others went down. Some went sideways, and some went completely upside down. It was a maze, a giant puzzle that she had to solve. And Emerald was standing at the start.

The maze… It looked familiar. So familiar, in fact, that Emerald was sure she had seen it before. The labyrinth appeared to have been constructed during the ancient times. It consisted of stone steps, with twisted spires and columns lining the sides of the staircases. Some of the stairs had an end to them, leading to doors that were locked. In between the countless sets of the stairs and platforms were sharp dark spikes coming from out of the void, going every which way, as if to confuse any person who dared attempt the maze. Below the stairs, Emerald couldn't see any sort of ground below; it was a pure black endless chasm.

As she took in the details of the maze, it struck her why it looked so familiar. It resembled Kyle's tattoo. The "maze" of his life… Feelings of longing washed over her.

"Kyle?" Emerald called out.

No answer.

"Please, Kyle… Come back to me." Her eyes began to well with tears, and her sadness drained any life from her insides.

No! I cannot sit here in despair!

Pushing back her tears, Emerald turned around on the stone platform she stood on. As she turned, she saw the portal door that she had entered from Arcadia's skies, with the rainbow staircase. It remained open, wavering with magic, revealing the other dimension of Arcadia.

I can't go back to Arcadia. I saw Kyle go through the portal to this place. Emerald glanced back at the maze, studying it. *He has to be here.*

She suddenly remembered that she had been following Zaphod up the magical flight of stairs. Glancing around at the intricate maze, she saw no sign of the friendly rat.

What happened to him? she wondered. Emerald took a few steps, looking around once again. "Kyle?"

There was no reply except her own words echoing across the expansive maze.

"Kyle, please, answer me!"

More echoes of her own voice.

Emerald stood for a moment, waiting with the hope of seeing or hearing Kyle. But the emptiness of the labyrinth gave her no sign of him.

Glancing to the side, Emerald saw a locked door glowing with violet magic from behind. Magic peeked through the cracks, radiating and pulsating a brilliant violet, highlighting the nearby stairs. Muffled noises came from behind the door.

Why didn't I see this door before?

Then she realized why. It was the same door that led to the portal of Arcadia. While sealed shut, it looked as if it were a completely different door altogether.

Emerald grabbed on the handle, attempting to open it, but the door wouldn't budge, not even an inch. The muffled noises that she heard were gone. Perhaps she had imagined them. Emerald released the handle, understanding that it wouldn't help her open the door.

I'm not going back until I find Kyle, she told herself.

Emerald walked a few steps back toward the first set of stairs. As she did, she felt magic flowing under her feet. It was violet magic mixed with blue, working together in harmony, flowing through the entire labyrinth.

This place must be the crossroads of time, she thought. But even to Emerald, that statement felt wrong. It was almost as if she were in someone else's mind, and that many memories lay behind those doors.

Was she inside Kyle's mind? Was it her blue magic mixed with his violet, creating this place?

I must be inside, she decided. Emerald looked across the chasm of endless staircases. A feeling of angst came over her. How would she ever find Kyle in this place? The twisted staircases made her stomach feel all in knots, overwhelmed, with no end in sight.

Taking a deep breath, Emerald started through the maze, taking the first set of stairs. Every few steps, Emerald looked over the edge to see if she could catch a glimpse of Kyle, or anyone else. But to her disappointment, there was nothing but the maze gazing back at her each time.

She came to another platform, this time with three sets of stairs and two doors. Emerald yanked on both of the doors, but they didn't move. Violet magic flowed over them, keeping them locked tightly. Selecting the middle set of stairs, she ascended to another platform with more locked doors and two sets of stairs. This time, though, the staircases veered sideways.

This is impossible! I won't be able to hold on as I move across them. I'm going to fall off, Emerald thought in a panic. Her eyes followed the sideways stairs, leading to more stairs that were upside down.

Emerald studied the stairs, then her heart stirred. An overwhelming feeling came over her. It was either continue through the maze or be lost forever in the maze, never finding Kyle. But it defied all logic—there was no way she could stand sideways…

Kyle… I will find you.

Taking a leap of faith, Emerald climbed onto the sideway staircase, she latched tightly onto the column and secured her foothold. The maze groaned like an earthquake in pain, and the world turned over on its side, the maze shifting and moving into a new puzzle. But more importantly, Emerald was standing upright.

It worked! she thought excitedly.

There was a fluttering sound, and Emerald quickly looked in its direction.

"Kyle?" she called out. "Are you there?"

The cawing of a bird answered her, echoing eerily across the chasm. Emerald looked up to catch a glimpse of the bird, but there was nothing but a red feather falling lightly before her, lazily making its way downward. She turned back, deciding to continue climbing the stairs.

As Emerald moved to the next set of stairs, she noticed all the stairs were completely upside down. But she did not hesitate, and chose one of them to ascend. Again, she grabbed ahold of the column that linked the upside-down staircase and the platform she stood on. The maze world shifted for her, this time groaning louder. The staircases twisted; some split apart and made new sets of stairs, rocks and gravel falling from the split. She could hear the pebbles bouncing off the stairs and spikes, then falling into the chasm below.

How am I supposed to solve this maze if it keeps moving? Emerald thought, her hopes dwindling and her heart dropping into her stomach. She wanted to cry, but she forced herself not to. Kyle was somewhere in the maze, and she had to find him.

Out of the corner of her eye, Emerald saw a bright-red fluttering moving in sharp contrast with the darkened maze. She spun around, catching sight of an exotic bird.

A parrot? It flew toward her, cawing. *This has to be the bird that the feather came from.*

The wings of the parrot created a soft red magical glow.

Red magic?

Something in her spirit moved, that familiar sense within the magic. *That bird has Kyle's magic!* she thought wildly.

Curiously, Emerald stretched her hands toward the parrot. The parrot flew to her, hovering several inches from her grasp. A wave of the bird's magic fluttered from under its wings, then surrounded Emerald, enrapturing her with its red intensity. An overwhelming sense flooded her veins and her spirit, and she felt Kyle's embrace from the magic. It felt right, and her spirit felt whole.

"Tell me, where is your master?" Emerald asked the parrot gently. "Where is he?"

The parrot cawed in response.

"Zaphod?" a voice called out from within the maze.

It was Kyle's voice.

"Kyle?" Emerald screamed. "I've been looking for you!"

Startled, the parrot flew off, its magic leaving Emerald.

"Kyle?"

No answer.

"Don't go!" she screamed again. "Don't leave me here alone!"

Her voice echoed back to her, leaving her to listen to her own cries of desperation. Tears stung her eyes and blurred her vision. Her heart sank.

"Kyle!"

No response. Emerald fell to her knees, crying. "Kyle!"

The maze began to crumble and shift, twisting itself all around Emerald. The world was closing in around her, crushing her hopes into nothingness.

***

She screamed.

Shooting open her eyes, Geeta saw the scientist right up in her face, the handmaiden shaking behind a curtain, and the councilor standing several feet back in the shadows of the room.

Geeta looked around, noticing that she was on the floor next to the Queen's bed.

"Did you see anything?" Telly asked. "Do you know the cause of her coma?"

Geeta blinked, gathering her senses. "Sadness."

The group of them sucked in their breath, their faces filled with fear.

"Can you wake her?" Councilor Emerys asked worriedly.

"Can't be done." Geeta looked at everyone. "I can't break into her mind. It's as if her mind is in another dimension."

She remembered hearing Emerald yelling for Kyle behind those doors. "Kyle," Geeta whispered.

The handmaiden came out from hiding behind the curtains. "Did you say Kyle?" she asked.

Geeta nodded. "He is the only one who can wake her." *And he's dead,* she thought glumly.

"If this Kyle is the only one who can wake her, then it is likely that the Queen will sleep until her death," Telly said, frowning deeply.

"I know," Geeta stared at them.

"And you are sure there is nothing you can do to wake her?" the scientist pressed. "Maybe try to convince her mind he's alive?"

Geeta shot up angrily. "There is *nothing* I can do!"

The handmaiden inched forward. "What about the babies?"

Geeta's mouth dropped open. "The Queen is pregnant?" she asked, dumbfounded. She shot a look to the councilor, and his eyes confirmed it was true.

Her hand immediately darted to Emerald's belly. Indeed, she felt life radiating from it. Two lives, in fact. How had she missed it before?

Removing her hand, Geeta shook her head and sighed. "This is much worse," Geeta said, looking to Emerys. "Those babies could be in danger. I was almost inside the Queen's mind; she no longer has the will to live. And that sadness could not only kill her, but these two life forces inside of her." Geeta plopped down on a nearby sofa, trying to think. With every thought, Geeta felt hope fleeing. "If her sadness doesn't kill her, it's quite possible these blue-gifted who are appearing just might… Unless they are trying to kidnap her."

"I know," Emerys said. "We don't know what else to do. It is ill timed that the King decided to leave."

Where was the King anyway? Why on earth had he not returned from his 'business' yet?

"Did the King ever say where he was going, Councilor?" Geeta asked.

Emerys frowned. "Only that he was going away to help stop this war from coming to our doorstep."

"Well, then I'd best pray to the gods he is doing something useful in all of this," Geeta said sourly. "From the looks of it, he is doing a terrible job."

Geeta looked to Emerys, his face downtrodden. She tried very hard to remain calm and focused. If she didn't, she would go haywire.

"I will remain here, guarding the Queen," Geeta announced.

"Good, then I'm going back out to the wastelands. My daughter is out there, and I am worried," Telly stated.

"I will call for a transport," Emerys stated. "Though most of the ones that handle the wasteland terrains have already been deployed. It will be several hours before one shows up."

"I understand. I will stay by the Queen's side until it arrives. And thank you, Councilor."

The councilor nodded.

Geeta looked to all in the room. "Everyone needs to get some rest. All I see is exhaustion. You are no help in any capacity if you don't rest."

Emerys hesitated, then finally submitted, bowing to her. "Yes, Miss Geeta. I will have my communicator on me, awaiting any further developments."

Miss Geeta.

"I'll rest over here while I wait," Telly said, plopping down on a nearby chair in the room.

With that, the councilor left, and the handmaiden too.

Telly crossed her legs, then closed her eyes. As she did, Geeta sat near the Queen. When all was still and silent in the bedroom, Geeta peered over at Emerald.

Emerald, you must wake up, she pleaded in her heart. *You must fight your sadness.*

Somehow, Geeta was sure Emerald had already succumbed to the despair. It was as if the Queen never wanted to return to the real world.

And that thought frightened Geeta.

CHAPTER 62

RED

Kyle!

Her screams echoed in his head.

Kyle!

His body vibrated as the heat radiated from hot metal he lay upon. He must have passed out on the strange ground contraption. It seemed he was still on it. How long had he been out? Rubius lay there, thinking of her voice. It was stronger than ever, and he had felt her presence. It was as if every dream, she came closer to him…

There was a sudden jerk, and his body bounced for a moment, then landed back on the hot metal. It had done that every so often before he passed out. Whatever contraption he was on viciously hit bumps on the surface as it drove, causing his body to jump. Rubius continued to keep his eyes shut during the ride, as sandy winds blew furiously against his clothes and bare skin, pelting him hard, even through his clothes. He was sure that his ears were full of sand, as his hearing seemed muffled. He continued to breathe through his mask.

What *was* he on, anyway?

He opened his eyes a crack, then realized what he was doing.

"It's not that time yet. Just a little while more, then you can open them," said the same man's voice that spoke to him earlier. It sounded like he wore a helmet, that or his voice sounded almost like a… *machine*. "We are almost there."

Rubius nodded as a gloved hand shielded his eyes, and he shut them once again. After what seemed like another twenty minutes, Rubius felt the driving sand stop, and the brightness from inside his shut eyelids went dark. The rumbling from the contraption echoed. It sounded like they had entered some sort of room.

The contraption came to a complete stop, and the rumbling ceased. Footsteps echoed loudly. Suddenly, his mask was removed, and sand went flying.

"Don't breathe through your mouth yet," said the voice.

Rubius took a deep breath through his nostrils. Bits of sand went up his nose as he did. Rubius sneezed, then coughed.

"We are going to get you into the showers. You were exposed to the elements and toxins, and you still have much sand on you," the man said, this time sounding completely human. "Don't bother opening your mouth or eyes until you are fully washed."

Rubius felt several pairs of hands on him, leading him not too far from where they were, or so he thought, then he heard rushing sound of water. Hands moved up and down his body, yanking his sand-crusted clothes off. They stripped him naked, then shoved him forward, his feet touching cool tile. Hot water suddenly sprayed all over him, soothing his sore body from the harsh sands. To some people, the water would have been considered scalding hot, but for Rubius, the heat was welcome, restoring his body and soul. After all, he loved fire and heat. The hot water peeled the sand away from every fold of his skin, including the sand sticking to his balls. He didn't even know how the hell sand got in his pants in the first place.

As the water washed the sand away, Rubius felt a familiar power seeping into his spirit. It made him feel… whole. When he deemed it safe, Rubius opened his eyes, then stood in disbelief. The water glistened a glowing green, sparkling vibrantly.

Green magic? That's impossible!

His heart quickened. Was the green-gifted woman here?

The magical waters continued to pour over him, all the while, his skin radiated with the green energy, as if the liquid itself was pure renewal. Another thought came to him. Perhaps instead of the green-gifted woman, it was that green-gifted man who appeared in his chambers years ago.

I wonder what became of that man? Rubius thought. *Did he ever find the Ghost Man he was searching for?*

Finally, the water stopped, and Rubius took a look at his surroundings, noticing a towel and a set of clothes for him on a steel bench on the other side of the shower area. Rubius grabbed it and dried off. As he did, he summoned his red wind, along with the fire that burned in his heart. Hot wind funneled around him until he was warm and completely dry. Afterward, he threw on the strange clothes, which consisted of light-gray loose linen pants and a matching tunic, and knee-high black leather boots. He then exited the shower.

Outside, in a small hall, Rubius saw long dark tunnels with dim lights going in both directions, with small side tunnels branching off intermittently.

"Better?" asked a man dressed in white linens. It was the same man who Rubius first heard talking; he recognized his voice. The man had deep-bronze skin with black painted eye makeup and several white markings on his face. Rubius knew why the man used the black eye makeup; it kept the sun out of the eyes as much as possible.

"I appreciate your help," Rubius said. "What kind of storm was *that*?"

"Sandstorm."

"I gathered that, but that one was different from any storm I have ever seen. There was *magic* in it." Rubius paused.

"I take it that you are from the skies." The man inspected him, eyeing Rubius's red hair. "All gifted born on the surface are required live up in the skies." The man gave him a serious look. "Here on the surface, sky dweller, we are faced with those magical storms on a constant basis. Why were you out there anyway? Sky people just don't come visiting us below. Especially the gifted sky people."

Rubius contemplated what he should tell the man. If he told the man about his strange dreams of the green-gifted woman, he would probably think he was delusional. But then again, maybe the man knew of the woman, considering the magical green water in the shower.

Rubius hesitated. "If I told you why, I'm not sure if you would believe me. I don't even know if I understand it myself," he said.

The man's dark eyes studied him, then he laughed. "I have heard many things over the years, and I find it hard *not* to believe what I hear." The man looked at him. "What do the sky people call you?"

Rubius wondered what name he should give, or even his title. *Do these people even know about the High Court?* he wondered. Even if they did, he doubted Belinda and the High Court had spies down here. But then again, maybe she did.

"Rubius," he finally said.

"It is a pleasure to finally meet someone from the skies, Rubius. I'm Thaddeus," the man said, then nodded. "Come."

"To where?"

"Are you hungry?"

Rubius's stomach growled at the thought. He hadn't eaten anything in the many hours he traveled. "Yes, food would be nice."

Thaddeus smiled, then led him down a long corridor that slowly descended into the earth. *He's never met anyone from the skies,* Rubius thought. *Who are these people?*

They came upon a large metal staircase spiraling downward, going deep into the earth. He followed Thaddeus, and many people joined them on different levels, everyone making their way downward. Every so often, people greeted Thaddeus, and all the people gasped when they saw Rubius's hair color, amazed that he was gifted.

The people had similar fashions to Thaddeus, dressed in white, tan, and gray linens. Most had tanned, deep-bronze, or ebony skin with painted lines on their faces. There were some who did have pale skin the color of ivory or pale gold, with blue veins running up and down their body. Did these people never see the light of day?

Thaddeus and Rubius came to the bottom of the stairs, and it led to a large room with many long metal tables. But it wasn't the room that impressed Rubius—it was the *machines*. These people had technology, pieces of equipment built within their structure, while others had weapons with them. Some glowed with green power, others with orange, and even yellow. He had heard of the ancients' technology—machines and weaponry, and had even seen fragments of it being brought up to the sky citadels from the miners and scavengers. But to see it displayed like this… Rubius was in pure awe.

They look like the machines in my dreams, he thought, reflecting on one particular dream when he saw the green-gifted woman in a glass capsule.

Thaddeus led him to one of the tables, sitting down. Rubius joined him.

"I should find the leaders so they can talk with you," Thaddeus said. "We get visitors every so often from the other fortresses to trade, which is nothing.

But a gifted?" He eyed Rubius. "They would be most interested in speaking with you. I know I am eager to hear where you came from."

"I have many questions for your elders as well," Rubius said. Suddenly, he got a good whiff of seasoned food. His stomach groaned loudly all over again.

Thaddeus heard, then laughed. "I'll get some food sent over to you before I fetch the elders."

Rubius nodded gratefully, watching Thaddeus leave. About a minute later, a man came up to him with a plate of food. Spiced meat with mushrooms, warm bread, and sweet beets. Rubius wolfed down his food, not having realized just how long he'd gone without eating. It tasted terrible, especially the beets, but it didn't really matter. It was food, and Rubius was starving.

After eating everything on his plate, Rubius licked his plate clean, still hungry. He looked around at the others taking their sweet time eating. Most were chatting, taking a bite of their food intermittently. He could tell they were trying hard not to look at him.

Dinner must be a more social event than getting the job done, he thought.

Rubius saw Thaddeus approaching with two men and a woman, all well advanced in their years. The elders looked extremely sturdy for their age. They had probably been physically active for most of their lives.

"Done already?" Thaddeus glanced at Rubius's empty plate, raising his eyebrows.

"I couldn't help myself."

Thaddeus laughed deeply. "We can get you more." He turned to the elders, gesturing to them. "Rubius, this is Elder Nile, Elder Moon, and Elder Stone."

The elders nodded at him, and Rubius nodded back. The elders took a seat across from him at his table, while Thaddeus sat next to him.

"A gifted here within our fortress," Elder Nile said curiously as more food was placed before Rubius. "We have never had the pleasure of such a visit. Pray, tell us, why are you here?" His voice shifted slightly, lowering. "Do you work for the High Court?"

"You know of the High Court down here?"

"Sky, land… it doesn't matter where one resides. They rule over everyone, do they not?" Elder Nile stated.

Rubius heard Elder Nile's thoughts talking loudly within his own mind.

An underlying hatred for the High Court. Oppression, fear, worry, and anger. These people didn't like the High Court one bit.

"Unfortunately, they do have their hand in every matter of the sectors. As for me, I could care less about them," Rubius answered them.

The elders exchanged glances, then Elder Stone smiled. "That is good to hear. Your circumstances would have dramatically changed if you'd said differently."

"I can understand. The High Court is very… challenging at times, to say the least."

"It has been almost a lifetime since I have seen a gifted," Elder Moon said, almost in a whisper. "And to see one again…" Her eyes teared up.

Rubius felt like he should apologize to the woman, but for what? For showing up in their fortress? "I didn't mean to bother you," Rubius started. "I came here hoping to find…" He paused, scratching the back of his neck nervously. "…a green-gifted woman."

Their eyes went wide, and Elder Moon made an audible gasp. His heart beat quickly at the looks on their faces.

"Do you know of her? Does she live here?" Rubius pressed, almost in a desperate tone. "I can sense her in this place. When I was in the shower, her magic was in the water. She *has* to be here… or at least somehow tied to this place."

Elder Moon glanced at the other two, then turned back to him. "She did live here. Two millennia ago."

Her words drained the hope from his body, but at the same time, it didn't surprise him. What had he expected? That the green-gifted woman was alive, here, in this time? He already knew from reading the tome from Lady Xui that the green-gifted queen lived in another time. But he'd still harbored some sort of false hope that *maybe* she would be here waiting for him.

It seems the sorceress didn't lie to me. What she said was accurate.

The elders remained silent until Elder Nile spoke. "How did you learn of Queen Emerald?"

"Queen Emerald?" Rubius repeated, looking at the elder. That name struck him, rattling his insides. His head felt muddled just from the sound of her name coming off his lips. It was sweet as honey and familiar as his own soul, as if he should have known it all this time. Her eyes and hair… the color of an emerald jewel. It matched her beauty, the mesmerizing depths of that gem. Why hadn't he uttered the words before?

Emerald...

His life force stirred within him... roaring with rage. As if the name had come to life now. Before, it was just a faceless name. Now...

Elder Nile nodded. "Yes, that is the name of the woman you seek. How do you know of her?"

Rubius pushed back the unsettling feeling, but his life force continued to stir inside his heart, answering him. "For many years, I have dreamed of this woman. She is always there, calling out for me. But recently..." He paused, thinking about the sorceress. How to word it? "I came across a violet-gifted, and she used her magic to get inside my mind. It was as if she unlocked a part of my mind, and somehow it tied in with this green-gifted woman. Queen Emerald..."

That name. It felt so right saying it. "And ever since that violet-gifted messed with my mind, I've been feeling a bit unhinged. She told me that the Queen of Arcadia was somehow tied to this place. I came searching for her... or anything that had to do with her. Queen Emerald's magic, I felt it in my dreams. And her magic is the *same* magic in your water. How is that possible? I must know!"

The elders hesitated and exchanged glances. After a silent exchange between them, the elders nodded to each other.

"We don't share any information concerning our technology with outsiders, but since you mentioned the Queen of Arcadia and the green magic, we will answer," Elder Stone said. "For many years—years before I was even born—this fort had been extracting relics from the earth in this area. Magical relics."

"Her magic is in the relics?"

Elder Stone nodded. "This place was first discovered by our ancestors while exploring. Centuries ago, the old High Courts of the time ordered the technology extractions in this World Sector. It proved to be quite difficult. They made a small fort here, but with the powerful sandstorms that blew through, the dark magic quaking the earth, and the extreme temperatures, many died. In fact, too many had died, and the old High Courts gave up."

"Then how are you here?"

Elder Moon smiled, inserting herself into the conversation. "Centuries after the old High Courts gave up, our people in World Sector Two's fortress came here with their technology. They developed the windstorm masks and outfits you saw, which make it easy for us to breathe when the toxic winds blow in. They can withstand some of the heat and sand, allowing us to scavenge."

"So you are saying that the High Court doesn't even know you are here?"

Elder Moon smiled with a hint of triumph. "Exactly. World Sector Two's fortress has given us reports that the records from the sky people over the centuries show that our ancestors were written off as dead out in the wilderness. When in reality, they made it here and built the fortress underground. So from the sky, no one would know we are here."

Rubius's thoughts returned to Queen Emerald. "But what about Queen Emerald's magic?" Rubius pressed. "How did you get the magic through the ancient relics?"

"We don't necessarily have her magic in the way you think," Elder Stone answered. "Queen Emerald's magic had been infused in ancient weaponry and technology. Over the many centuries, our people found these relics and developed technology that allowed us to extract that power and infuse it into new technology and weapons. We mainly found magical artifacts that were tied to green magic based on our location, but over the centuries, we have found a few relics containing orange, yellow, and red magic, along with many tomes and devices that have history encoded in them, explaining the history of World Sector One."

"And that is how you knew her name?"

Elder Stone nodded. "Yes. The ground that we are under is the old Kingdom of Arcadia. Some of these tunnels were developed as a sewer system for that kingdom, as we have come to find out from the devices discovered." His tone shifted. "Tell us, Rubius, what do the sky people truly think of the High Court?"

Rubius shrugged. "Hard to say. The High Court has everyone doing their bidding, whether they like it or not. Many like them, others do not."

Elder Nile interrupted. "Yes, but what do *you* think?"

"What do I think?" Rubius laughed it off. "Like I said, I don't like them personally. But what chance do I have against them? There is one of me, and there are six of them. They are extremely powerful, more than anyone else on this earth, they have an unimaginable amount of followers at their disposal, and they have an overpowered gifted. You can't even fathom her ability. She has white magic." He shuddered at the thought of Elyathi having the ability to drain his magic.

"White magic, you say?" Elder Moon said, frowning.

"Yes. If you upset her, she has the power to suck away any gifted's magic. *Permanently.* And I don't know about you, but I want to stay far away from her. And I have yet to meet someone who loves the High Court more than her. She is a complete fanatic."

More like a complete lunatic.

"I had thought it to be a rumor. The white-gifted," Elder Moon said softly, then glanced at the others. "The others must have failed."

Rubius eyed them curiously. "Failed? Who failed?"

She glanced at him, then gave him a sad smile. "You must be tired. We will let you finish your meal and get some rest. You are welcome to stay here for as long as you like. We would be honored to have a gifted in our presence."

"Thank you, elders, but I do have to get back to the skies. I only came here to see what I could discover about the Queen. It seems I have found clues, but nothing more than that." He sighed. "I plan on leaving after the storm blows over."

"We are sorry you didn't find the Queen Emerald you perhaps expected," Elder Moon said, her dark eyes gazing at him gently.

"I was chasing a whim, Elder Moon," Rubius said with a hint of disappointment.

She nodded. "Thaddeus will show you to a room, and you can stay for the night, waiting for the storm to pass. Should be clear by morning. But don't linger too long outside. The toxic winds will soon blow in once again."

"Don't worry about me."

"Good luck, Rubius."

"Thanks for everything, elders."

They left, and Thaddeus motioned for him to follow. Thaddeus led them back up the spiral staircase, then into one of the halls. He opened a metal door, showing Rubius a small metal room with a single bed, a toilet, and a large vent above, probably for air circulation.

"I'll be back in the morning with some rations, and then I'll take you outside the fortress," Thaddeus said.

"I appreciate it." Rubius nodded.

The door shut behind Thaddeus, leaving Rubius alone in the dim room. He plopped down on the bed, its hard surface uncomfortable. There was a constant hum from the technology that ran through his walls, probably the energy flowing to and from each room in the entire fortress.

But more than the hum, Rubius felt *her* magic. Emerald's magic. She was here. In the technology, flowing through the whole fortress. It was as if she were there with him.

As Rubius lay there staring into the darkness, he heard a knock. Curious, he walked over and opened it.

Elder Moon stood in front of him, bowing. "May I?" she asked.

Rubius shrugged, waving her inside. "What is it? You have more questions for me?"

Elder Moon slowly reached inside the pockets of her robes, then gently pulled out a necklace.

"What are you—"

The necklace Elder Moon held out had a large cut emerald gemstone. It glowed faintly as she held it out.

"I knew it," Elder Moon whispered. "As soon as I saw my amulet glow within the pockets of my robe earlier, I knew this was meant for *you*." She held out the necklace, gesturing for him to take it.

Accepting it, Rubius clutched the necklace in his hand. Instantly, the gemstone shone brilliantly, lighting up the room with green power. They gasped, staring at each other in shock.

Rubius could feel her within the gemstone. Much more than in the room.

Queen Emerald… is your soul within this stone? Have you left a piece of yourself behind, just for me?

Rubius took a deep breath, inspecting the beauty of the stone, then glanced at Elder Moon. "I don't know what to say."

"Don't say anything." She got up and walked to the door. She glanced over her shoulder, pausing. "Good night, Rubius. I do hope you find her."

Then Elder Moon left, shutting the door behind her.

Rubbing his thumb over the gemstone one more time, Rubius slipped the necklace over his neck. As the emerald landed directly over his heart, he felt life flow over his body…

I will find you, he told the gemstone silently, as if talking to the Queen directly.

He *would* find her.

To his death, he would find her.

CHAPTER 63

VIOLET

Geeta clutched the staff in her lap as she prayed to the gods. Some power had been restored to the staff, but it wasn't enough to be able to tap into it if needed. For the most part, the Queen's chambers remained silent except the whispers of Geeta's prayers and the footsteps of the handmaiden Glacia as she checked in on the Queen.

Her prayers didn't calm her; in fact, they did quite the opposite, making her more anxious, and more furious. Arcadia would be overrun with Olympian troops soon, especially if Emerald didn't wake up.

The Queen. She was locked away in her mind, away in some strange dimensional plane. All in search of Kyle. But he was dead. Emerald was in denial. And what was worse was that it seemed that she wouldn't wake unless Kyle was with her.

Geeta's heart fluttered. What was she to do? She couldn't keep this up forever, nor could the councilor. Geeta glanced down at the orb of the staff, thinking of Kyle. All the times they'd practiced together. All the times they'd argued. All the times he'd been an ass to her.

There was a twang in her gut. She lightly embraced the orb on the staff, sensing the energy slowly being restored. She recalled how the Queen had unlocked the true Spectrum of Magic, using pure white holy light, with the help of the Ghost Man. Kyle.

She missed him. Geeta closed her eyes again, trying to focus on the current situation, preparing her heart for her next round of prayers.

Someone screamed. Jolting, Geeta swung wildly in alarm, seeing a blue flash. Geeta's violet barrier over the Queen flashed brightly, and then Geeta saw a blue-gifted man before the Queen.

Another attack!

In an instant, Geeta cast a violet ball of lightning, hurling it at the gifted man. The man whipped out his hand, and immediately a blue-magical barrier encompassed him. Geeta's lightning cracked the barrier. It shattered, but the man remained intact.

The handmaiden ran over to the Queen, placing herself in front of the protective barrier. "You can't have her!" she yelled in defiance, holding out her hands.

"Don't throw away your life so easily, girl," the man said. He whipped his hands around, summoned a spell, and released it.

Powerful blue winds hit Glacia so hard that it knocked her off her feet, and she yelped as she was thrown like a doll.

He's using other magic, Geeta thought wildly. How was that possible?

As Glacia was about to crash against the bedroom wall, she used the staff to funnel a protective violet sphere around the handmaiden. Her barrier, with the handmaiden inside, hit the wall hard, then slumped over onto the floor. The world lost its color and was cast in shades of azure blue. Time had stopped, and everything went still, except the gifted man and Geeta.

"You should have been stilled!" he said, shocked when he saw that Geeta wasn't frozen.

Because of the staff, she wanted to say. He was right. She probably would have been frozen with the amount of power radiating from his life force.

"Are you from Olympia?" Geeta asked angrily. She quickly cast a dimensional spell, flashing before the Queen.

The gifted man ignored her. He waved his hand and released a blue blast of fire toward her, careful not to hit the Queen. Geeta countered it with violet water, dousing half of the flames and making colored puddles on the floor. Quickly turning around, she blasted water at the patio curtains, which had caught fire.

That man has much more power than any other blue-gifted, she thought. It was as if the man's power had doubled, or even tripled. It was *amplified.*

The man snarled, then summoned another time spell, this one flowing from his hand like a translucent blue ribbon. It looked like an arrow with a streaming ribbon, the magic targeting Geeta. She knew if it got to her, this time she would be stilled in time, and the staff might not be enough, given how quickly it was losing its charged power. Rolling out of the way, Geeta shot another barrier spell over Emerald. The old barrier had been fading.

"Emerald! You must wake up!" Geeta yelled.

Emerald remained silent in her sleep.

Another blue flash burst before Geeta's eyes, and a sharp pain shot through her side. Thick cold metal burned her while excruciating pain flooded her life force. She looked down. It was an enchanted blade, lodged deeply in her side.

Geeta crumpled to the ground, then rolled over, barely dodging a blue magic spell that blasted past her. She yanked out the enchanted blade with an angry cry. Geeta looked up, and to her surprise, there was not one blue-gifted, but two, both casting spells.

The second blue-gifted started funneling magic over Geeta's protective barrier, and it began eating away at the barrier, leaving the Queen unprotected.

These men do have multiple colors of magic!

Geeta shot her hand out weakly, funneling her own protective magic back into Emerald's barrier. As she did, the first gifted hurled a shock of electricity. It hit Geeta sharply, and she let out an audible yelp.

Geeta fell back to the floor, twitching uncontrollably. Her heart tripled in beats, and her mind felt disoriented. Their magic… they were just as powerful as Ikaria with her black magic.

"You must wake up, My Queen!" Geeta screamed, trying to get to her feet. "If not for your kingdom, do it for your children!"

A glowing blue ice shard flew across the room. Geeta weakly put up her hand, casting a violet barrier in front of her. Just in time, the ice shard lodged itself in her barrier, then disintegrated. From the corner of her eyes, she could see the other blue-gifted melting away Emerald's barrier, until very little was left.

Geeta screamed in frustration. "Emerald! Wake up!"

***

The maze stopped shifting, snapping into its new position.

Emerald wiped away her tears as she looked around at the new sets of stairs, getting to her feet. Slowly, she inched near the edge of her current platform, holding on to one of the columns while leaning her head over the edge, gazing across the endless chasm.

There was a flash of red in the distance.

It's that parrot I saw earlier! Emerald's eyes darted to follow the bird's course, then her heart skipped a beat.

Kyle!

He was there once again, standing by himself on a far-off platform.

"Kyle!" Emerald screamed, running toward the edge of her platform. "I'm here!"

To her amazement, he looked in her direction. Red, violet, and orange magic swirled around him, glowing brightly as the parrot landed on his shoulder.

"It's you!" he said, his eyes lighting up. He looked around, then started moving quickly up a set of stairs in her direction. "I keep seeing you in my dreams."

"Yes, it's me!" Emerald's heart soared, running toward him.

"But why do you keep calling me Kyle?" he asked, his voice echoing across the chasm. "Are you Queen Emerald?"

Her heart beat hard at his words. *How does he not know who I am? He doesn't even know his name?*

"That's who you are," she answered. "You are Kyle!"

"I am?" he asked, confused at her words. He looked to her, their eyes meeting across the maze.

"Yes! That's your name! Don't you remember?" Emerald cried out. "Don't you remember me?"

"I have seen you for many years in my dreams, but… are they memories or just dreams?" he called out to her. His voice wavered as he continued. "My mind… it's as if someone smashed it into a thousand pieces, leaving me with nothing but fragments of my mind. It's like my dreams with you are real and my current reality is… *wrong*." He walked down a few steps of the staircase. "Why do you keep appearing in my dreams?"

"Because I love you," Emerald called out, tears streaming down her face. "Have you forgotten about us?" Emerald burst into a run, ascending her current staircase to another platform. She made a hard left, taking a new set of stairs in Kyle's direction.

"I… I can't remember," he confessed, his voice echoing throughout the labyrinth. "But I feel it deep down that you are a piece of me, one that makes me complete somehow. I need you… I've always needed you." He started running faster through the labyrinth, heading down a set of stairs.

"I need you more than anything!" Emerald cried out.

A loud rumbling roared across the chasm. The maze began to warp and shift, twisting and turning the stairs in all different directions. Emerald slid, losing her foothold, then grabbed onto a column just in time. The labyrinth had twisted in such a way that there was nothing underneath her, just a void of pure nothingness with spikes reaching to impale her body.

Emerald looked toward Kyle, clutching onto the column for dear life. "Kyle! You have to remember us! I cannot go on in life without you. My soul will remain here with you if that's what it takes. I must be with you…" Emerald trembled as tears streamed down her face. Her muscles began to burn from holding on to the column, and each moment, she grew weaker. She attempted to swing a foot to the nearest set of stairs, but she missed, swinging like a pendulum, her body left dangling over the deep pit. "Please… I have to be with you…"

As soon as the words left her mouth, the maze roared violently, changing once again. Emerald embraced the column tightly until the new maze was revealed. As the stairs and spikes settled into position, Emerald remained dangling, clutching her column. She was getting so tired.

Looking down, she saw a new set of stairs, far below her feet. From the corner of her vision, she saw Kyle frantically running through the new maze, searching for a path to her. Then she noticed a spot in the maze that would intersect his path. Taking a deep breath, Emerald closed her eyes, then let go of the column.

I believe…

"Wait!" she heard Kyle yell.

Emerald fell. It was as if time was eternal, and her fall endless. As she plummeted, the spikes caught hold of her dress, ripping and shredding it, scratching her bare skin. But somehow, the spikes twisted out of the way to allow her to fall without being impaled. Further and further, Emerald fell down the chasm, and time was meaningless.

Emerald hit a new set of stairs with a loud thunk. Black stars filled her vision as she groaned. Her arms burned from holding on to the column, the scrapes on her skin stung, and several of her bones felt broken. Whether they were or not, she couldn't tell at that moment. Her dress was in tatters from her fall, and she felt the flowing fabrics on her armbands had been ripped from her sleeve. Everything that happened to her body mirrored how her soul felt—worn down, ripped, and useless.

As Emerald lay there, her vision slowly returned to her. The dark maze formed in front her of eyes—she was still in its depths. Grimacing, Emerald turned her head to one side, then the other. There was no sign of Kyle; her aim to fall directly in his path had been off.

Emerald looked up. Nothing but thousands upon thousands sets of tangled stairs filled her view. If Kyle was up there, she would never know with the countless steps blocking her view. Slowly, Emerald got to her feet. No broken bones, but everything in her body hurt. But she didn't care. She had to find Kyle.

"I promised you that I'm not leaving. I will find you!" she cried out.

Then Emerald got up and climbed the new set of stairs.

***

Geeta sent a healing wave of violet magic flowing over her wound, relieving her pain enough to allow her to be mobile once again. She got to her feet and whipped her staff in the direction of the Queen, casting a fresh wave of barrier magic over her. The staff flickered; its charged power was nearly depleted once more.

I don't have much left!

Out of the corner of her eye, a bright-blue ribbon of time magic flew at her, about to ensnare her within its trap. She dodged it quickly, rolling over on her side, getting completely out of the way. Then she funneled her own time magic within her staff and released it with a blast. The two time magics countered each other with a loud crackling sound, then a shockwave followed, shaking the entire room.

"She has High Priest Auron's staff!" one of the gifted men yelled to the other. "We can't conserve our magic any longer!"

"Our life forces will be shortened to seconds!" yelled the other. "Where are the others?"

"We can't wait for them. We have to finish this! We don't have much time!"

There was a blinding blue flash, so bright that Geeta had to close her eyes. As she opened them, she saw two more men with the Queen in their arms. Emerald remained lifeless, like a rag doll, her arms dangling limply as they carried her.

What was worse was that there was already a portal, swirling with bright-blue light, open for traveling.

"No!" Geeta screamed.

Swirling the staff in the portal's direction, Geeta shot out her time magic. The staff's magic mixed with the portal's magic, creating a giant blast centered directly into the portal. The portal wavered, then faded away.

"You shouldn't have done that!" yelled the man.

As he yelled, three of the gifted men funneled their overcharged magic together, then released it. A loud blast erupted.

Then silence.

All was still. Unusually still.

Geeta realized what had happened. Her face remained in the same position, and she couldn't move. She had been frozen in time.

Geeta wanted to scream in frustration. But no scream came. Nothing in her body responded. It was locked in time. Only the beating of her heart and her consciousness were aware. What was she to do?

One of the gifted men summoned another portal, while the three waited. The Queen remained in their grasp. Glacia was still lodged in the wall within Geeta's protective bubble.

Geeta's mind was still intact, as it was the only part that she had been able to shield before the blast went off. It allowed her to retain control over the major functions of her body. If she could figure out a way…

She felt the staff in her hands. There was only a small chance it would work, but she had to try.

I did it before…

Darkness infused her violet life force, laughing within her mind. It built upon itself, power gathering fast. Geeta's heart beat fiercely at the thought of tapping into the dark side of the spectrum.

The dark power grew so strong deep within her core, so violent and so powerful, that she could no longer contain its power.

Geeta screamed within her mind, unleashing the dark magic. Violet-black magic shot out from her body as she continued to scream within her mind. She heard her voice screaming as well, her body entirely bathed in the dark power. The man casting the portal rolled his eyes back into his head, and blood streamed down from his eye sockets like red tears. He went limp, plopping to the floor.

The gifted man holding Emerald screamed along with Geeta, until his head exploded from the force of her dark magic. Blood and guts shot all over the room, splattering everyone and everything. The Queen fell to the floor, remaining lifeless, her eerie green glow still embracing her.

The world shifted back into full color.

There was a loud whack. Red wine sprayed everywhere, and one of the remaining blue-gifted cried out in pain and slumped to the floor, unconscious. The handmaiden had regained consciousness and grabbed a wine bottle, cracking it over the gifted man's head. Glacia's triumph was short-lived, however, as the remaining gifted man pushed Glacia hard, causing her to lose her balance and trip. She landed on the floor next to Emerald with a loud yelp.

Geeta swung her staff in the man's direction, then realized there was no magical charge left in the staff. She had used it all. The gifted man crackled with bright-blue magic, and objects in the room began to rattle. Geeta ran toward the gifted man, summoning whatever magic she could deep within her core. She roared, releasing a terrible force upon him.

The man remained as he was, and a blue shield absorbed her magic. Her violet force did nothing to the man.

"I never wanted to do this, but I don't want to die either," he confessed.

"I don't understand!" Geeta yelled.

The man released his blue magic across the room, engulfing her within its power. What happened next was a blur. She remained immobile and confused. Blue flashes came into Geeta's vision, until slowly, she closed her eyes.

Then, just when she thought she was going to pass out, her body was free from its prison, and she slumped to the floor. She lazily opened her eyes for a brief moment.

A blue-gifted woman stood before her, fighting the blue-gifted man. The woman looked familiar, but Geeta's mind was all muddled. The woman glowed with intense blue magic, countering the gifted man's attempts to recast his time spells.

The two fought with their time spells until finally, the man fell to the floor screaming, then crumbled to dust. The woman looked over at Geeta, falling to the floor, gasping and crying. "I'm going to die," she sobbed. "I can't die yet… I have to fight them!"

"You're not going to die," Geeta heard Telly say. "Not today, anyway."

In a wave of dizziness, Geeta blacked out.

***

The maze just had finished morphing again, halting in a new position. Emerald heart raced, taking in the sight. Somehow, there weren't as many stairs and spikes this time. In fact, the spikes seemed to have disappeared during the last shift. It was as if the maze was opening up a more direct path to her.

Emerald turned her gaze to the staircase before her. No longer were there multiple platforms or splits of new stairs with confusing, twisted paths. There was only one set of stairs, spiraling up toward…

Kyle.

Emerald's heart burst with joy. She leapt up the stairs, sprinting as fast as she could. Kyle did the same, both of them running toward each other. With each step, they got closer. Her heart felt like it was going to burst with anticipation.

Running and running, Emerald finally neared the top, then paused. Before her stood Kyle, standing a mere ten steps away. Her emotions overwhelmed her. Passion, love, wanting, desire, need. Trembling, Emerald stood there for a moment, gazing at him. Kyle was everything she remembered. And yet, there was more to him, much more in his soul. There was more life within it; he had lived many more years. Her soul told her this, for he was her complement.

Kyle gave her a searching look as he moved toward her. The details in his face were as clear as crystal; his eyes were like sparkling rubies, dancing with fire in the light. Emerald's eyes began to well up with tears as she slowly climbed to meet him.

"Kyle," Emerald whispered. "I… I can't believe it's you." Tears ran down her cheeks as she held out her hands.

His fingers sparkled in the light, showcasing the many rubies and garnets that decorated his fingers. As their hands touched, their life forces collided, sending a deep awakening within her soul. She was meant to be with him. He was her other half, and she was whole again.

His touch... she needed it. She needed him completely. Kyle gently caressed the tops of her hands with his thumbs, their fingers intertwined. Her heart fluttered, and longing burned within her.

A look of recognition came over Kyle's face as if he had been struck. Perhaps it was her life force that had awakened his spirit...

"Em?" he said, his eyes searching hers.

Bursting into tearful laughter, Emerald fell into his arms, clutching him tight. "Yes! I'm your Em," she cried.

"I remember... I remember everything..."

He wrapped his arms around her waist, holding her so tight that she felt smothered. But she didn't care; she needed his touch. His body, his soul, it felt so warm, so real... and so *alive*. She wanted to be nowhere else but here, forever in his arms.

"I've been searching you my whole damn life..." He clutched her tighter, his hands trembling. "I had no idea who the hell I was until now."

Emerald grasped him tighter, then raised her chin, her eyes meeting his fiery gaze. His hand brushed the side of her head, then came to her chin, lifting it as he leaned in to kiss her.

"Em..."

The warm, inviting, soft flesh of his lips met hers, and she kissed him deeply in return. She ran her hands up his neck frantically, combing her fingers through his hair. He kissed her back feverishly, his lips dancing across hers.

As their lips parted, Emerald gazed upon him dreamily, running her hands down his chest. She kissed it lightly where his skin was exposed.

She wanted him. Every part of him. Nothing felt more right than being with him.

"Come back to me, Kyle..." she told him. "Come back."

CHAPTER 64

RED

"MOTHERFUCKING PIECE OF GODDAMN MOTHERFUCKING SHIT!"

Kyle jumped out of bed. His bed. His motherfucking bed. It wasn't his bed from Arcadia; it was some strange fucking bed he had slept in last night. He looked around the room. Where the hell was he?

Memories came flooding back, and Kyle remembered that he was in World Sector One. Where the wastelands used to be… thousands of fucking years ago.

"FUCK!"

Kyle flung out his hands as if punching something in the room, his hands glowing red-violet. Suddenly, the table across the room was surrounded by his magic, and it hurled itself against the wall, smashing into pieces.

I was never supposed to have left Em!

With another jolt of his hands, Kyle angrily flung a chair sideways with his magic, sending it smashing into the wall.

"FUCK ME!"

Kyle's eyes darted to the mirror, then he marched over to it, inspecting his face. He had the same facial features that he had in his old life, thank fucking god for that. But it was as if his reflection mocked him. That face represented his new life. The life of "Rubius."

Fuck the name Rubius! The hell kind of name is that anyway?

Kyle eyed the jeweled pendants that hung heavily on him, and he spotted the emerald necklace. It glowed brightly on his chest. He closed his eyes as he clutched the pendant, feeling Em's life force radiating from the stone. God, she was so close to him, but only because of a fucking stone. Kyle shook with fury at the thought. *I was never supposed to leave you, Em! I'm sorry I was such a goddamn loser! I promise I'll find my way back to you. I fucking promise.*

Kyle opened his eyes, seeing his image once again in the mirror. His hair was well-kept, pulled back in a ponytail.

"GODDAMMIT!"

He yanked out his ponytail holder and flung it to the floor. He grabbed his hair with one hand angrily, then funneled his fury in his other hand, sending magical hellfire through it. With one fast swipe, he singed his hair, and the cut hair fell to the floor. He brushed the loose hairs off, then looked back in the mirror. His hair looked spiky, very similar to his hair in Arcadia, though the ends were fried, and there was still a bit of length in the back.

He looked at himself again, his eyes glowing with red fury.

"FUCKING BULLSHIT!"

Kyle punched the mirror, shattering his image. Then he punched it again. Then again. He punched the damn thing until blood spilled from his knuckles, until there was no more glass. Then, when the glass was all over the vanity and floor, Kyle ripped it out and threw it to the floor. He tore off his shirt and hurled it against the wall.

Then, he heard a rap at the door.

"What!" he roared.

The door opened, and Thaddeus appeared in the doorway. His eyes immediately went to the mess. "What is going on, Rubius? Are you okay?"

"I'm not *okay*! I'm so goddamned fucked!" Kyle hurled a glowing red ice shard against the wall, enraged.

Startled, Thaddeus, dodged slightly to one side of the doorway.

Kyle gritted his teeth. "What year is it?"

Thaddeus gave him a confused look.

"For fuck's sake, what year is it?"

"4403 P.A. *Why*? Tell me what is going *on*!"

Kyle stared at him. "And this place… Where am I again?"

"Maybe I should call for the elders."

"Fuck the elders, just answer me! *Where* the hell am I?"

"World Sector One, Rubius! Have you lost your mind?" Thaddeus asked incredulously.

"FUCK!" Kyle hurled another summoned ice shard, sending it crashing against the wall. "Don't call me Rubius! I don't ever want to hear that fucking name again!"

"You lied to us? You aren't Rubius?"

"Hell no! I just… I just lost my goddamned mind!" Kyle ran up to him, clutching his shirt. "I have to get back to my time."

"Your time?"

"Yes! *My* damned time. The time when Emerald lived."

More dwellers gathered in the hallway, whispering and trying to take a peek inside his chambers.

"Move aside!" called a voice.

Kyle looked over as the elders walked into the room.

"Everyone, back to work." Elder Nile waved them away. Thaddeus was about to leave, but Elder Nile stopped him. "Not you, Thaddeus. You stay to escort him out of here after we find out what is going on."

"What has happened, Rubius?" breathed Elder Moon, her eyes assessing the damage that Kyle made. Her gaze moved to the emerald amulet, and she gasped. It was glowing even brighter than when she'd given it to him.

Elder Stone didn't look as forgiving. "We made you a guest in this place! How dare you, Rubius."

"He says his name isn't Rubius." Thaddeus shrugged.

"Yes, I'm not Rubius. I'm Kyle! My name is Kyle Trancer."

"Kyle?" repeated Elder Moon.

"Yes, Kyle! I'm not from this time. I have to get back to my time!"

"Your time?"

"Yes!" He flung his arms about. "Why does everyone repeat everything I say? Fuck!"

"What do you mean, your *time*?" Elder Nile asked.

"Listen, I know it sounds crazy, but I am from another time, and I was reborn into this time."

"Reborn in this time?" Elder Nile asked. "How?"

"This sounds a bit unhinged, if you ask me," Elder Stone commented. "People die, then they are received into the God of Light's realm or descend into darkness."

Kyle's face was hot from no one listening to him. How could he make them understand? "The hell if I know how I was reborn, but I *was*. I mean,

I'm having a hard fucking time believing it myself, as you can see by the mess I just made," Kyle said sarcastically.

"But why now? Why did you remember right now?" Elder Nile asked.

He thought about Emerald. His heart hurt and was spinning just thinking about her, back in time, far away from him. He felt sick knowing that Derek, that asshole, was back there with her, and who knew what the fuck was going on in Arcadia. He had to get back. In response to his thoughts, his amulet burned an even brighter green, and the elders noticed.

"Perhaps it is Queen Emerald's magic, which still resides within that stone, awakening his mind," Elder Moon suggested, pointing to the magical amulet.

Kyle looked at her. "I've got to get back to her, Elder Moon. The reason why I kept dreaming of Emerald is because I love her more than my own goddamn life. We were together back in time; she was everything to me. I was *supposed* to protect her. Instead, I was reborn in this godforsaken place, living as a new damn person, but I was Kyle all along, the whole time. My mind was confused as fuck, and I just couldn't remember anything until I came here. I am sure she used her magic somehow to reach for me in my dreams just now, and this amulet helped her spell. I just *know* it!"

"You mean a spell she cast thousands of years ago?" Elder Stone asked.

Kyle narrowed his eyes. "No. She just cast it. I know it. She still lives back in time, dammit. And I'm going to find her."

He shook with rage. How the hell was he going to get back to Emerald? He would have to time travel, but what blue-gifted would help him? They were all in cahoots with the High Court. And the High Court… that was a whole other issue. God, what a mess.

The elders remained quiet, while a few of the dwellers exchanged looks with Thaddeus.

"I believe you," Elder Moon breathed. "Every word you said, I believe you."

The other two elders shot her a look. "You can't be serious," Elder Nile said.

She nodded. "We have not seen a gifted in almost our whole lifetime, and along comes this one, inquiring about the ancient Queen Emerald." She looked at Kyle. "He had knowledge of the Queen that no one else did. How can you not believe him?" She smiled, then eyed her comrades. "The amulet speaks for itself."

The amulet continued to burn brightly, casting a green glow over the entire room.

Elder Stone relented. "He still messed up one of our rooms."

"I didn't intend to turn your room into a shithole," Kyle said, then looked down at his bloody knuckles. Damn, he'd hit them hard. "I… I just went ballistic. I would help clean up the mess, but I can't because I don't have time."

Elder Moon held up her hand. "It's fine… Kyle. You need to get back to your time. The sandstorm has subsided, but it will only be a clear for a few hours. You'd best be on your way to finding a blue-gifted to help you get back to your time."

Not a chance in hell any of them will help me, he thought. But then, a thought came to him. There *was* one person who could send him back in time. He would piss everyone off, including the High Court, but it was his only fighting chance…

Kyle looked at the elders. "I gotta go."

"Indeed," Elder Moon nodded. "Thaddeus, clean up his wounds, then take him out to the entrance."

"Yes, Elder Moon." Thaddeus nodded at Kyle.

Kyle snagged the ponytail holder off the floor, hastily tying back the hair that remained long from his hack job. He grabbed his inquisitor jacket and was throwing it on when he saw normal court clothes, already washed and dried, next to his bed. Not caring what the elders or Thaddeus saw, he stripped to get dressed, and they averted their eyes.

As he was about to leave, he turned to the elders. "The High Court… you should know that they want to fulfill some kind of crazy prophecy. Actually, it's more like the white-gifted's plan, the one I told you about earlier with the crazy-ass power. Something about reshaping the earth."

The elders went pale, and their faces dropped. He saw the fear in their eyes. He felt as bad as they looked.

"Truly?" Elder Nile said.

"How do you know this?" Elder Stone asked.

"The white-gifted loon told me herself. The High Court intends to collect all the colors of magic for their plan. And they only need two more—violet and green."

All of them exchanged looks.

"They must be stopped," Elder Nile said.

Elder Moon shook her head. "We'll have to activate our plan a lot sooner than we thought."

If I have any damn say, I will fucking put a damper in their plans.

"I will make sure those assholes don't get the violet magic," Kyle cut in. He narrowed his eyes, thinking about Emerald alone back in time. "And you bet your asses that no one will touch Emerald. Not if I have any say on it."

"They must not find out about this place," Elder Stone warned. "If they were to discover all the magical relics that we possess and figure out how to extract the green magic from them, it will make them one step closer to their plan."

"Don't you worry, elders. They won't get a damned word out of me," Kyle promised. "I'm going to fuck up their plans so hard that they won't even know what fucking hit them." Just thinking about Elyathi pissed him off. He was going to have to do something about that crazy-ass bitch. Unfortunately, she *was* Em's mother. *God, what a fucking nightmare. Can't get any more fucked up than that.*

"Godspeed, Kyle Trancer," Elder Moon said. "May the God of Light bless your path."

"God of Light, huh?" Kyle clenched his jaw. "All he's done so far is fuck me over by sending me here."

"Perhaps there was a reason… Maybe to save us."

"Yeah, whatever. I don't have to like it." Kyle turned away, following Thaddeus through the underground halls to a small room where they dressed his wounds. Then he followed him to a loading area where the vehicles were parked.

Thaddeus punched in a code, and a hatch to the side opened up. They walked outside, and Kyle looked up. They were on the side of a desert hill covered by metal ruins, which hid the entrance. Hot winds blew in the area.

Thaddeus nodded to him. "Goodbye, Rubius."

Kyle shot him a look.

"I mean, Kyle." He chuckled. "You really are something else. Go and do some damage for us to the High Court."

"Don't worry. They will be pissed as hell with what I'm about to do." Kyle tapped him on the shoulder in a friendly goodbye gesture. "Thanks for saving my life out there earlier, man."

"I would do it again."

Kyle turned away, walking around the metal debris and into the open desert. The mechanical door shut behind him, and he was left alone in the open wastelands. His old homeland. It was thousands of years in the future, but it was still his homeland.

God, it felt good.

Now I just have to get my ass back to Em…

CHAPTER 65

VIOLET

She sat in her favorite booth in the restaurant, drinking her tea. Conversations from the customers blended together with noises from the kitchen.

"There you are," Nym said, smiling with her bright pink lips as she placed Geeta's food in front of her. She was so cute the way she tilted her head slightly.

Geeta looked down at her food, nervous. "Thank you, Nym."

"No problem, doll. I'll be back in a jiff to see if you need anything else," Nym said, giving Geeta a private wink, then walking off to one of her other tables. She sat there, not eating.

"You keep staring at that greasy-ass food, you'll go blind," said a voice.

Startled, Geeta looked up to find Kyle standing in front of her. She sucked in a breath, her eyes open wide with disbelief.

There he was, looking the way he always did, with his lip curled into a snarl, his arms folded as he leaned back against the diner wall. His hair was a bit different, longer in the back, and his hair and eyes were his gifted color, burning red, just like his hot-headed personality.

"Kyle?"

"The fucking one and only." He shrugged, feeling his jacket pockets. He rummaged around, finding a pack of cigarettes.

"Yo-you're alive…" Geeta stammered.

"Well, of course I am. What the hell kind of magician do you think I am if I just go and die without putting an end to all this shit," Kyle said, lighting a cigarette and taking a drag. The smoke went all over the restaurant, and Geeta's eyes darted around.

"You can't smoke in here," Geeta said, still in disbelief.

"The hell I can't. Why you always got to dampen my day, huh? I know you have a thing against smoking, but god, Geeta, can you just leave me be for once?" Kyle found a stool and casually sat down next to her while Nym came back. She looked at Kyle, then turned to Geeta, smiling again.

"You need anything else? More tea?" Nym said with a flirtatious tone.

Geeta quickly looked back down at her food, feeling a bit flustered. Nym had that effect on her. She swallowed the big lump in her throat. "I am good for right now. Thanks, Nym," Geeta managed to say.

"Sure thing," Nym said with another private wink, then walked off once again.

Kyle eyed her, then turned to Geeta. "I don't know why you don't just come out and say it."

Geeta's heart stopped at his words. "What are you talking about?"

"Okay, so we're going to play this game?"

"What game?"

"Shit, Geeta, really? I figured it out a long time ago. Probably the first night we met. I dunno why you continue to act like you aren't interested." Kyle snorted as he laughed, the smoke coming out of his mouth.

"For your information, I don't want *any* kind of relationship," Geeta said curtly.

"Your loss." Kyle shrugged, putting out the butt of the cigarette on the side of the wall.

Geeta raised her eyebrows. "Don't do that!" Geeta snapped, storming over to him.

"Do what?"

"Why do you always have to make a mess of everything?"

"Well, fuck you too," Kyle shot back, getting up.

"Jerk," Geeta mumbled.

"Geeta?" said a voice.

"You heard what I said!" Geeta called out.

"Geeta, what are you talking about?" said a voice.

This time her body rocked back and forth, and everything went dark.

"Kyle… he's such a jerk," Geeta mumbled, her body heavy.

"Kyle?" said the voice.

She could hardly move.

"Geeta, are you awake?" asked the voice.

What was happening?

Kyle. He was there talking to her. But that was just a dream…

Suddenly, Geeta remembered. The Queen was being attacked! Geeta shot open her eyes, then quickly darted to her feet, startling everyone around her. She saw the Queen, still locked in her coma, the handmaiden, Telly, and…

Their eyes met.

A blue-gifted woman.

Geeta whipped out her hands to cast a spell, but Telly rushed in front of the woman, jutting her hands out to protect her. "Geeta, this is Lady Vala. She is from the future," Telly said. "She *helped* us."

Geeta stopped, eyeing the blue-gifted woman, then breathed a sigh of relief, lowering her hands.

"Nice to meet you finally," Vala said, bowing low. "I saw you once before, but we were in the midst of battle several months ago."

Geeta nodded, then felt dizzy. She nearly flopped to the floor, but Telly caught her, dragging her to a sofa while Glacia brought her a cup of coffee. Geeta took a sip, trying to regain her senses. Why did she feel so out of it after that fight?

It had to be the energy I spent within the Queen's mind…

"I take it Telly injected you with the Queen's blood," Geeta said to Vala. "Otherwise you would have disintegrated by now."

"I did," Telly said, nodding. "She saved all of us. It was the least I could do." Telly walked over to the Queen, checking on her. "Besides, she was dying. What kind of human being would I be if I just let the person who saved us die?"

Geeta gave Telly a small smile, then nodded in approval. "I would have done the same." Her gaze shifted back to Vala. "Why did you come to this time?"

Vala's hand trembled as she held her coffee cup, her face angry and sad at the same time. "The High Court sent me. Or shall I say *forced* me? They demanded that I retrieve Queen Emerald, bring her back with me to my time. I told them no, so they threatened to kill off the people in my sector if I didn't comply, and they injected me with poison. I was thrown into the space-time continuum and told that unless I returned with the Queen, I would never get the antidote and would die alone, along with my people." Vala gritted her teeth angrily. "They made it sound like their poison was more than something that could be healed by the green gift."

"In all fairness, you looked pretty bad toward the end there," Telly pointed out. "I gave you two doses of the Queen's blood."

Geeta focused on Vala. "Are you saying that these blue-gifted, the ones who were after the Queen, they are from your time?" she asked.

Vala studied her. "I do not know of all the blue-gifted you have encountered. But there were many that disappeared in my time, on the account of the High Court's orders." Vala paused. "It is safe to assume that the blue-gifted you have seen are from my time."

So Olympia isn't behind the attacks, Geeta thought. She sighed, leaning back into the sofa. "The Queen will never be safe."

Vala nodded. "Never. The High Court is bent on her returning to my time. They said that they wanted her to reside with them—they even have an empty throne waiting for her. A *green* throne."

Geeta raised an eyebrow. "Emerald? On their High Court? They weren't trying to attack her or take her blood?"

"That's correct," Vala confirmed. She reached into her dress pocket, pulling out a letter with a seal. "They told me to give this to the Queen. They said that it would convince her to travel with me."

Geeta snatched the letter from Vala's hand, breaking the seal.

My dearest daughter,

You will be most happy to hear that I have been alive and well these many years. I know you probably thought me dead, for when I escaped your time era, it was staged to look as if I had passed onto the heavenly realm. But alas, I have been in the future, and have thought and prayed about you in every spare moment. I know this is much to take in, but I ask desperately for you to return with the blue-gifted, to the future where I am. I have a place for you, waiting for your arrival. When you return to me, we will finally be reunited, and we can live in peace. How much I miss you, my sweet love. Please return to me! I will be waiting.

Your forever loving mother,
Elyathi, former Queen of Arcadia

A terrible feeling came over Geeta.

"What does that letter say?" Telly asked behind her.

"I am also curious," Vala added.

Geeta crushed the letter.

"Hey," Vala said, frowning.

Nothing made sense. Emerald's mother… lived in the future? And this High Court, using idle threats against this woman Vala. Hadn't they given Auron's empress problems as well? She only vaguely recalled. But she didn't like any of this one bit. Something wasn't right. Was it truly Emerald's mother who wrote the letter? Or was it a ploy to acquire Emerald's magic? Maybe all they cared about was green magic.

Suresh had better watch himself, wherever he is, Geeta thought.

"So? Are you going to tell us or not?" Telly demanded.

Geeta looked at Telly, then Vala. "This letter, it's from Emerald's mother. *Supposedly.*"

Telly neared her. "The old Queen of Arcadia? She died many years ago!"

"The letter says otherwise," Geeta mumbled.

"Emerald's mother?" Vala asked, dumbfounded. "But I got that from the High Court…" She paused. "Do you think her mother is on the High Court?"

"I don't know what to think," Geeta said, looking at the crushed letter once again.

"Well, as far as I'm concerned, the whole situation isn't right," Vala stated firmly. "That is why I opposed the High Court. I may not love my blue gift, but I am talented with it, and I know that one must not interfere with the flow of time. If I did what the High Court asked of me, I would be a heretic of the institution the High Court has maintained for thousands of years. That can lead to the very destruction of earth and time itself. No thank you. And

Queen Emerald's mother? I do not know of such person. I will not help those who align themselves with the High Court. I am *done* with them."

"I think that very wise," Geeta agreed. Geeta thought about her own situation. She had chosen to live in another time. Had she altered the fate of the earth just by doing so? She shuddered.

The handmaiden fetched a plate of cookies and biscuits for them, then served Vala coffee.

"Thank you. That's very thoughtful," Vala said to the handmaiden. She snatched up a biscuit and scarfed it down. "It all doesn't make any sense. Emerald is here, in this time, but her mother is from my time? If one were to live in another time, I suppose it's possible for that person to be accepted in their new era," she said while chewing her biscuit. "However, with how the events unfolded with the High Court… I just know they are up to no good. They said they were seeking the green gift. They already have so much power! I can't even imagine what would happen if the Queen Emerald joined them at court."

It would be an utter disaster, Geeta thought. Bringing Emerald to the future…

Geeta froze. Wasn't that what the sorceress wanted to do? To take Emerald to the future with her? And from what the priest Auron had told her, the High Court had not wanted to help him and his gifted stop the sorceress. Geeta broke out into a sweat just thinking about the mess she was in. No, that *all of time* was in.

Vala lingered near Emerald, casting a sad glance at the Queen. "I wish I could speak to the Queen. Do you know why Queen Emerald is in this state?" she asked.

Geeta shook her head. "I do not know, but when I went inside her mind, I saw Kyle. She is in deep mourning for him. I believe her sadness is what is causing this."

Vala frowned, then her eyes scanned the room curiously, getting up. "This Kyle you speak of, is he the one in the paintings on these walls?" She strolled over to the paintings, looking at them.

"He is. They were lovers."

Vala paused, staring at the pictures, then she stopped at one in particular, completely taking it in. "It's curious that this man Kyle looks just like the High Inquisitor Rubius in my time. I mean, I've only seen a painting of him too, but I can say the resemblance is uncanny."

Geeta's heart nearly jumped out of her chest at her words, then her dream came to her mind. Kyle's words echoed in her mind. *Well, of course I am. What the hell kind of magician do you think I am if I just go and die without putting an end to all this shit...* He had been there with her, with red hair and flaming eyes...

"Lady Vala, do you know much about the High Inquisitor?" Geeta asked quickly.

"Only a little. Rumors."

Geeta got to her feet, walking over to Vala in front of the painting. Kyle looked regal in that one, almost royal.

Vala took another sip of her coffee, then studied the picture. "I heard he loves to drink, indulge in wild parties, bit of gambling every so often. It's rumored he is one of the most powerful gifted," Vala said. "I don't know if that's true or not, but it's what I heard."

Kyle. He was alive. He was truly alive. Of course he was. Geeta burst out laughing, crying and slumping to the floor. Everyone in the room stared at her in alarm.

"Are you okay?" Telly asked, hustling over.

Geeta laughed again. He was alive. That jerk was *alive.*

"I'm good, thank you," Geeta said to Telly. "I... I just... this is great news." Geeta wiped her eyes, then got to her feet, walking over to the Queen, staring at her.

Hang on, Queen Emerald. I'll find him for you, Geeta told Emerald silently.

"What is it?" Vala asked.

"You say that the man in these pictures looks like the High Inquisitor, correct?" Geeta said.

"Near complete likeness."

"The High Inquisitor *is* Kyle," Geeta said.

Vala raised an eyebrow. "Excuse me?"

"Yes. It all fits together."

Geeta recalled Emerald casting her green magic on Kyle—they'd all thought it didn't work. Boy, were they all wrong. If Kyle was alive, and they successfully brought him to this time, the Queen would be awakened and saved. Olympia could be put back in its place, and Arcadia would no longer be in peril, and the Queen... she would have protection for herself and her kingdom. Strong and *powerful* protection with her complement by her side. And they would have the power to stop these High Court gifted from taking the Queen to the future…

"We need to bring this High Inquisitor here. Now," Geeta said urgently.

Vala laughed anxiously. "I don't think that is a wise idea. You see, the High Inquisitor works for the High Court. And given what just happened… they don't like me right now."

"Be that as it may, I believe it's the only way to awaken the Queen," Geeta said. "I would go and get that dolt myself, but the Queen is being bombarded with these attacks." Geeta paused. "Attempted kidnappings, I should say."

"Let's not forget what's happening out in the wastelands," Telly said.

Geeta shot her a look. "I have not forgotten." She turned back to Vala. "Please, you must go to the High Inquisitor and convince him to travel with you back to this time."

Vala paused, biting her lip.

"It is imperative! I am sure that the Queen will soon die if he is *not* brought back here," Geeta continued.

Vala hesitated. "I'm just not sure it can be done. The High Inquisitor won't just come with me on a whim."

Geeta laughed. "I am more than sure he will go on a whim." Geeta neared her, grabbing her hands. "Please. I would go in a heartbeat, but as you said, the High Court will keep trying to kidnap the Queen. I *won't* let them take her."

Vala stood in silence for a while, then sighed deeply. "My life would have been a lot easier if I was born with the red gift," she said, exasperated. Geeta smiled, and Vala hugged her. "I'll do what I can. Can you at least let me finish my coffee and biscuits?"

CHAPTER 66

RED

Day was becoming night as Kyle flew furiously through the sky. There were still several more hours of travel ahead of him before he reached World Sector Six's royal citadel. No matter how much he wanted to get his ass back to the sorceress, his energy was spent, and he was tired as hell.

I'll be a useless piece of shit if I don't get some rest, he thought. Especially dealing with Em's crazy-ass lunatic mother. Shit was going to hit the fan if he ran into Elyathi.

There was a piece of land floating nearby, and he decided to take a break. Kyle slowly let go of his red wind, and it obeyed, bringing him down gently to his feet. As he did, the long grasses on the island rippled under his feet and the flowers waved back and forth.

Kyle looked off into the distance. Not too far away was an old stone spire, probably once a lookout point when the island sat in the earth below. At least it was some sort of shelter. He headed toward the spire along a pebbled path, picking a few flowers along the way. He never was a flower-picking type of guy, but the beauty of them reminded him of Emerald.

As he neared the building, Kyle saw that the door on the spire was greatly deteriorated, so much that it was useless. He pushed the door aside, then entered.

Inside the bottom of the structure was a rotting wooden table, a couple of shitty chairs, and a fireplace that looked like it had been burned down by squatters. That is, if squatters even existed in this time. Over to the side of the room, a stone staircase spiraled up to the next level of the tower.

Anything is better than this shitty room, he thought.

He climbed the stairs, going up the lonely tower until he reached the top of the stairs, which ended at another door. This door was in much better condition. He pushed it open with a creak to find a small bedroom.

The bed was old and decayed. It had looked like someone brought their own blankets and used it many years ago before abandoning it. There was another fireplace, but this one actually looked usable. It even looked like it had been used recently, as it was charred and held leftover coals.

"Apparently there *are* squatters in this time too," he said under his breath. He inspected the bed and decided to skip it, and plopped down on the floor. He pulled the flowers he had picked from his pockets, then chose the one that most reminded him of Emerald, putting it back into his jacket gently. The other flowers he placed in his hand, then poured his orange magic over them. Slowly, the flowers transformed, reshaping themselves, their properties becoming different. As the flowers took another form, Kyle poured more of his magic into it, thinking about how damn hungry he was.

After the orange magic subsided, a small burrito sat in his hand. It looked like shit, but he hadn't had a damn burrito in… his whole damn new *life*, come to think of it. He had missed burritos. Kyle took a whiff, breathing in the spicy scents of beans and meat, then took a ravaging bite. As soon as his tongue tasted his concoction, he spit it out, coughing.

Fuck, guess I'm not cut out to cook with my orange magic, he thought sourly. He looked at the burrito again, thinking about just how fucking hungry he was, then decided he had to restore his energy. He snatched the burrito back off the floor, plugged his nose, and started wolfing it down. After three more bites, he threw the rest of it on the floor, coughing again. The aftertaste was even worse.

What I would give for a good smoke right now.

He hadn't smoked in his whole life here. There was nothing *to* smoke. But the memory of enjoying the smoke came flooding back to him, and the pleasure he got from it.

Emerald. God, she was what gave him the most pleasure. All he had to do was think of her warm smile, and it made him the happiest man alive.

Em… I'm coming for you. I'm coming back to you.

Tired, Kyle took his rolled-up shirt, then used it as a pillow, lying down on the stone floor.

I'm coming back, Em…

His eyes felt heavy, and his body lethargic. He didn't want to nap, but it was as if his body ordered him to rest, and he couldn't do anything about it. Before he knew it, he was out.

***

A door opened from far across the chasm. Its glistening neon lights lit up the darkness, embracing her skin in cool tones. Emerald wiped her tears away, then stood up.

All around her, the darkness formed a rocky path, leading straight toward the doorway. He was there. All she had to do was enter the door…

***

Colors danced off Kyle's arm as he began to notice his whereabouts. Hot pinks, electric purples, and neon green pierced the darkness and highlighted his surroundings. He sat in a small room, and the neon colors were coming from outside the window.

He was in Arcadia! Or was it another dream?

On the other side of the paneled glass was the city-kingdom in its nightly glory, the mega buildings lit up in a range of colors—from bright reds and deep purples to cool greens and blues. A cigarette was stuffed between his lips. He had really wanted a cigarette after that shitty burrito, and now he finally had it.

Damn, he thought. *I should try that trick more often.*

Kyle took a long, deep inhale, letting the flavor soak into the pits of his lungs, giving him instant gratification. God, it tasted so fucking good.

He sat in the room in silence as he enjoyed his cigarette, watching Arcadia as if it was the first time he had ever seen it. In a way, it almost was like the first time, since he'd finally had his memories restored to him. The city burned brightly with a multitude of colored lights, some twinkling, some pulsating, some steady with glowing signs. Brightly lit tunnels connected the mega buildings, with silhouettes of people going to and from the buildings, moving through a maze…

Maze! he remembered wildly, recalling his dream with Zaphod in the maze. *Fuck! My damn bird!* He hoped that Zaphod was still safe with the servant.

"I have been waiting for you..." said a soft familiar voice.

His heart stopped, and he froze in place.

"...waiting for you to come back to me."

Kyle's heart hammered in his chest, and his muscles involuntarily twitched with nervousness. He rose from his seat, turning around to face her. As he did, he saw her silhouette through the thick, smoky air, framed against an open door, violet light shining behind her.

"Em..." he whispered.

"Kyle," Emerald answered softly. As she moved toward him through the smoky haze, her features became clear. The cool light kissed her smooth, delicate face, while her vivid green eyes sparkled with life. Her long hair was done up in a ponytail, with long locks framing her face and rolling down the swell of her back. With every step she took toward him, his body trembled, and his heart beat fiercely.

After what seemed like an eternity, she finally stood before him, gazing dreamily up at him, their eyes meeting. Slowly, she ran her fingertips over his chest, then up to touch his cheek. Her touch felt so real.

Her eyes went to his cigarette, then she smiled, moving her gaze back to his. Without breaking eye contact, she gently grabbed the cigarette out of his mouth and pushed him playfully back into the chair. As she hovered over him, she bent down, exposing the tops of her breasts as she inhaled a drag. Her eyes danced with a secret look meant for only him. There was a hunger in her eyes, causing his senses to go wild.

With a graceful movement, Emerald lowered herself onto him, straddling his lap. She placed the cigarette to his lips seductively, waiting for him to take a drag, indulging in visual pleasure. Obliging, he took a drag from the cigarette while she held it for him, pushing her pelvis against his. He went hard instantly, his cock throbbing for her.

"I see you still smoke cigarettes even in your dreams," Emerald said as she ran her hands through his hair.

Kyle took the cigarette from his lips, smashed the butt of it against the side of the chair, and chucked it. "Em, am I really seeing you? Or is this just another dream? Because if it is, I don't want to wake up."

"I have always thought when we dream of people and places, it is meant for only the dreamer, and that it is private. But this place…" She looked around him, then locked onto his eyes, smiling. "This place proved that I was right! It is where our souls can meet as we dream. You and I, we are truly seeing each other's souls in another world, I am sure of it."

"So, because I am sleeping in reality, my soul was sent here to be with you?" Kyle asked. Her words seemed right.

"I think so," she said, her lips nearing his. "All I know is that this place is where I get to be with you. If I cannot be with you in reality, I know that I want to be with you here."

"It feels so real."

"It's because our souls *are* together, at this moment," she said as she patted him gently against the side of his cheek, then nibbled at his ear, kissing it softly.

"Is that what was happening the whole time? Were we in another plane of existence?"

"Yes, I've been searching for you between the dimensions of time and your mind… weaving in and out. I was lost, but now I've finally found you." She lowered her eyes. "Kyle, I don't want to go back. I just want to be here with you forever."

Her words made his heart yearn for her, made it burn with an emptiness that only she could fill. Kyle brushed his hand against her cheek, caressing her soft skin. His hands traveled down her to her neck, then slid down her back as her lips brushed against his ear, kissing it tenderly. He pulled her body close, feeling her every curve pressed up against him, sending a fury of desire through his body, pulsating with temptation. He couldn't even fucking think straight. Em was here, and he didn't want to be anywhere else.

"Oh God, Em," he said. "I missed you."

"I missed you so much it hurt," Emerald murmured softly.

Fierce desire was heavy upon her breath as she moved her gentle kisses from his ear to his neck, then paused. "I want you, Kyle," she said, leaning back to face him. She studied him for a moment, then glided her hands down his doublet, unlatching the clasps until his neck and upper chest was exposed.

She giggled softly. "You look so different with this outfit. This is not you at all."

"You think it's funny?" he asked quizzically.

Emerald nodded, leaning in to kiss his lower neck. "Yes, I do," she answered, kissing him again.

"It's not like they have a wide selection of clothes to choose from in the future. It was this or robes," he joked.

She laughed under her breath as she continued to kiss him, lowering herself until she was in between his knees. Her lips went lower and lower with every kiss, tugging more of his doublet until it was completely open and his chest exposed for her pure enjoyment. She kissed his belly button, then her face hovered over his lap.

Oh my fucking god…

She looked up from between his legs and smiled at him, gently brushing against his erect member with her hands.

Her touch… it was real. It felt like no dream. He felt the heat of her body, the hotness of her steamy kisses. He was horny as fuck, and seeing her all horny… he was going to fucking explode in his pants.

He bent forward and ran his hand down her backside, slipping his fingers inside her tight little shorts, squeezing her tight, firm ass. He pulled her up toward him and grinned. Em always had a nice ass.

She approved of his forwardness, moving back up to his lips, kissing him passionately. Her lips were addicting, and he couldn't stop kissing her if he tried. Oh god, he didn't want to stop. She rocked her pelvis against his, stroking his bulge against her sweet spot. Then she began grinding against him. He couldn't help but moan with ecstasy, rolling his eyes to the back of his head. It all felt so damn good.

Emerald stopped gently, then rose, standing above him as she tugged a corner of his open jerkin.

"Em," Kyle said, rubbing his hands along her wet thigh.

She smiled at him, that smile that made him crazy wild for her, then unlaced the front of her corset, exposing her perky breasts, giving him a preview, then slid down her sexy little shorts. For a minute, she let him give a good look at her, then she yanked off her loosened corset, standing fully nude for him to soak in.

"Oh my fucking god, Em…" he whispered, involuntarily giving his member a hard yank at the sight of her.

She unlaced the front of his pants, exposing his manhood, then climbed onto his lap again.

"I need you," she whispered in his ear, desire heavy on her breath. Her full lips kissed his, and he was ready to succumb to every urge in his being.

"I need you too..."

He let her have her way with him.

CHAPTER 67

ORANGE

Telly stepped off the transport, seeing the path to the refuge.

Thank God I'm back here, she thought. Every moment she was away from Drew and her daughter, she was on pins and needles. Between the attempts made on the Queen, and from what she had heard from Councilor Emerys of the conflict out in the wastelands, Telly was a ball of stress, and she didn't know how much longer she could take it. Right before she left the palace, Emerys had mentioned that Olympia had retreated from the Arcadian troops, but that didn't make her feel any more at ease. What if it was a ploy, and something bigger Olympia had planned was on the horizon?

I sure hope Vala finds that man Kyle in the future, Telly thought. It seemed that he was the key to awakening the Queen. And now, with everything going on, the Queen's magic was the ultimate weapon to stave off any attacks from Olympia.

Telly paused, then swallowed hard. *What if Olympia learns of the Queen's current condition? What if they decide to attack the palace directly while the Queen is under her spell…*

She shook her head. They had Geeta. She was strong with magic, enough to help protect the Queen and help Arcadia's armies if needed. Geeta was tough as nails, and Telly was willing to bet she could kick anyone's butt, including the toughest of men. But Telly couldn't help thinking about Geeta battling the blue-gifted—she was tough, but she wasn't invincible. No one was. Arcadia needed their queen. She had the power to put an end to this madness. Heck, Telly had witnessed Emerald draining life forces firsthand months ago. Her magic was something to fear.

She shuddered at the thought of the life-draining magic. She didn't want to be on the receiving end of it, that was for sure. Telly started heading up the path, her mind still lost in thought about everything.

As she made a switchback on the path, she heard engine sounds far off. Turning to see where the noise was coming from, Telly saw a group of vehicles driving toward the refuge. Even at a distance, Telly could see the make of the vehicles—all were from the wasteland camps.

Are they returning from the confrontation with Olympia?

Telly waited for them as they drove up. The ground vehicles rolled to a stop, then men started filing out the of vehicle quickly. They were from her own encampment.

"Where were you guys?" Telly asked them. "What happened out there? I heard there was conflict between our army and Olympia."

It was as if the men didn't hear her, or just flat-out ignored her, because they remained focused on unloading. The men yanked on something, and Telly saw it fall into their arms like deadweight.

It was Victor.

Her heart dropped. Instantly, Telly ran up to Victor, trying to inspect his body. Victor was breathing, but he was leaned over like a toddler who fell asleep after a long ride in a transport.

"What happened to him?" she demanded. "Why is he like this?"

Garrett appeared, and their eyes met. He lowered his eyes uncomfortably.

"Garrett! What is in the hell is going on? What happened to Victor?" Telly fumed, marching over to him.

"Telly..." he managed to say, then he turned around, pulling another man out of the transport.

"Drew! Oh my God! Drew!" she screamed, running over and pushing Garrett away.

Drew's body was all mangled, the metal in his body extremely contorted, making him look unnatural, posed like a broken doll. His eye flickered for a moment, his real, orange eye with magic. He blinked, then tried to speak, but it came out as a gurgle. Blood spurted out from his attempt.

A choked sob escaped from Telly's throat, then she turned around sharply to the men. "Get him to the machines. Get him hooked up!"

The men nodded, carrying him quickly up the path. Telly ran to follow, but a hand gripped her shoulder, holding her back. She turned to see Garrett. He trembled for a moment, hesitating.

"I don't have time for this! Neither do you. Drew is in critical condition."

"Telly… Gwen…" he said slowly.

Her heart stopped. She felt sick. First Drew. Now her daughter?

"No… No, no, no…" Telly said, as new tears formed in her eyes. Her body started to shake.

Garrett's eyes watered, and he rubbed the tears from them, confirming what she felt deep within.

"What happened to my *daughter*?" Telly screamed.

Garrett was about to answer, but another man answered first. "She drove off in front of the wasteland army to fight one of their gifted. Drew went after her to protect and save her, but their gifted… he made Drew how he is, and they captured Gwen. We couldn't catch up."

Shock, pain, anger, fury… all of these feelings came to her at once. Her daughter. Fighting. Against the Olympian army?

Her eyes went to Garrett. "Is this true?" she asked furiously, tears streaming down her face.

Garrett looked at her, ashamed, lowering his head.

She slapped Garrett across the face hard, then spun around to everyone, kicking up sand. "How could you let my daughter fight? She's just a teenager!" she screamed. She looked to Garrett again. "And you!" She jabbed his chest hard with her pointer finger. "*You* should have known better!"

Telly let out a loud, wailing scream again, falling to her knees in the dust. "Oh God! How are we supposed to get her back? How will we even know where they took her?"

She cried and cried. Garrett slumped to his knees in silence next to her. She threw up on a pile of rocks, sick with loss.

Garrett remained near her, still silent. Angrily, Telly grabbed a handful of sand, suddenly aware of his presence. "What are you doing?" she screamed to Garrett, flinging the sand at him. "At least go and help Drew!"

He didn't move.

She screamed loud and hard, a hundred nightmare scenarios running through her mind at once. She fell to the ground, rolling in the dirt. She didn't care. Nothing mattered anymore. Everything she cared about was damaged or gone.

How could she live with herself? Her daughter was kidnapped, taken by an army. And Drew, he had a long road to recovery. It was up to her.

Her daughter. Gwen. She was *gone*.

"Telly… I… I feel like the lowest piece of shit right now about Gwen. We told her to stay in the refuge. I swear to *God*, I knew nothing of her fighting until we saw her in the last few moments before she was captured…" Garrett's voice shook, and there was a long, awkward pause. "I need your help with Drew. I can't fix him alone."

More silence between them. Telly blinked away her tears, thinking of Drew. Yes, he needed her now. Telly stopped crying, taking a deep breath. Garrett was right. He couldn't do it alone. Drew needed them both.

"I'll go now and get him hooked up," Garrett said quietly. "After we get Drew stabilized, I promise I'll do whatever I have to do to help find Gwen."

Telly heard his footsteps in the gravel, running up the path until there was nothing but the sound of the wasteland winds blowing across the sands. Angrily, she grabbed another handful of sand, then flung it while she screamed through fresh tears.

She was going to unleash hell itself upon Olympia for what they did to Drew and her daughter. She would hunt down every single soldier that was responsible and slaughter them. Then she would find their gifted and kill them too.

"I'm coming for you!" Telly screamed into the wind, thinking of Olympia. "I'm going to hunt every single one of you bastards! You won't have any life left when I'm through with you!"

The winds rustled in reply.

***

White noise.

Static.

Malfunction.

Gwen… They took her! Must get back online!

Bright light was all around him. He couldn't see anything; it was too bright for his eyes to handle. Even his cybernetic eye's data couldn't process it.

"Only fifteen percent up and running," said a familiar voice.

Drew tried to process what had happened. All he remembered was Gwen. His body hurt all over, severe inscrutable pain that ran through his whole body. He was indescribably aware of his circuits in his body, the unnaturalness of his machinery.

"H-h-h-hurts," he said through his teeth.

"I know," said the voice. "Garrett is running more pain medicine through your tubes while we fix you up."

His eyes couldn't focus on anything. Everything was a blur and not registering in his data banks.

Malfunction.

He shook.

"Gwen."

Even with his circuits a mess, he felt completely lost. His daughter was gone.

"G-g-g-g…" He struggled with the words. Through the blur, there was a large, light shape above him. His body, his heart, it felt like a void. He didn't like this void. It overrode every emotion in his core. He knew he had organs and cybernetic parts within him. Why did he feel so empty?

The void feeling ran through him. He blinked with his good eye, and he felt a wet tear. Was he crying?

Gwen was gone.

He could hear a faint breath being sucked in, and the shape above him stopped moving. "Once you are whole, we will get her back. You and me," the voice said, determined.

It was Telly's voice.

"I-I want her back, Tell-me-lots," Drew said.

He shook, that pain of loss running through his body. It felt like his body was in a meltdown. But there was no meltdown, for he was here. Suddenly, a loud crash rocked the room. By Drew's calculations, the probability of a metal object having been thrown against the wall was 2:1. It startled him, causing him to jolt.

Loud, wailing sobs came from Telly. Over and over again, she cried out. Her cries echoed in his mind. And they didn't stop.

CHAPTER 68

WHITE

Derek's blue dimensional magic flashed away, revealing World Sector Six's citadel halls. Elyathi's hands were still intertwined with his, which allowed them to port together.

Elyathi looked at Derek, his eyes meeting hers in return. She then gently released his hand. "This way," she said, nodding her head in the direction of the prisons.

Derek bowed in return. There was a hint of nervousness she detected, but otherwise, he held his composure, just like a true king would. The power that radiated from his life force was vigorous, energizing, and robust. It made Elyathi feel like she had woken up from a dream, that she had been asleep for many years, and now suddenly, that power gave her *life*. But something else had happened when Derek drank her blood. Elyathi could *feel* her life force inside his body, and it was calling her close. The strange sensation felt like nothing she had ever felt before. She wasn't even sure what to make of it. But what she did know was that her spirit felt complete when she lingered near him.

As they passed through the citadel, the High Court and World Sector Six guards on duty saluted, greeting her and gazing curiously at Derek. They made no inquiries. Elyathi spotted a World Sector Six councilmen she recognized coming down the hall. She stopped, waved to him. "Please inform the Emperor that I have returned," she ordered.

"Yes, my lady." He bowed.

"Where is the High Inquisitor?" Elyathi continued.

"He is on leave, my lady," he answered, his gaze lowering to the floor.

"On leave? On whose authority?" Why was she even surprised? She already knew that the High Inquisitor was useless.

"I do not know, nor did I ask," he stated.

Elyathi's face darkened. "Thank you, Councilman." She waved him away, and he bowed in return. Turning to Derek, she said, "It's a very good thing you are here, Derek. You see what I have been dealing with? The High Inquisitor has been a thorn in my side from day one."

"It seems so," Derek said, following her down the hall. "But you need not worry anymore, My Queen. I will take care of the sorceress myself."

Elyathi met his glance, then breathed a sigh of relief. "I cannot tell you how happy I am that you are here, Derek."

"Likewise, My Queen. I feel like I finally have hope. Something I haven't felt for many years."

"Remember, Derek, I am no longer queen," Elyathi reminded him.

Derek flushed for a moment, then ran his fingers through his curls nervously. "I… I am sorry, Elyathi. It's just out of habit."

"It is understandable," Elyathi said.

"It's just…"

"Yes?" Elyathi eyed him curiously.

"I will always envision you as queen, even though you say otherwise," Derek stated hesitantly.

"Because you have known me as queen your whole life," Elyathi said.

"Well, that may be true, but there is more to it," Derek said. "The way you compose yourself, the way you move with dignity and grace. Your beauty. You walk into a room, and immediately, your presence demands attention. That is why I think this way. You, in essence, are the very vision of what a queen should be."

Elyathi's eyes darted to him, seeing nothing but pure radiance from the depths of his icy-blue eyes. He was being sincere. There was admiration coming from him. Had he always admired her this way?

There was a strange feeling once again, then Elyathi made a small laugh. "Derek, I appreciate your kind words, but really, I truly never want to be queen ever again," Elyathi said with finality.

"I understand." His ears turned bright red while his cheeks flushed. "I… I am sorry if I spoke too bluntly."

"No, no, no." Elyathi quickly shook her head, meeting his gaze. "You should always speak your mind, just like how you did back in my chambers. After all, you are my son-in-law, are you not?"

He smiled, then nodded. "Absolutely."

She returned his smile. "You cannot understand how much I am looking forward to seeing the new world, with you and my daughter in it."

"I eagerly await it as well."

They both made their way down to the dungeons, until they were outside the sorceress's cell. Standing there were two gifted guards with the High Court emblem on their armor.

"Lady Elyathi," the guards said, bowing.

"I need to see the prisoner," she said.

"Right away," one guard said. He immediately opened the door, and the two of them slipped inside.

As they entered and passed through the outside magical barrier, Elyathi's eyes met the sorceress's.

The sorceress's expression changed sharply to a look of awareness, then her gaze moved to Derek. "Well, look who we have here. You came all this way to see me? I am flattered," Ikaria said in a smooth tone.

A snake, that's what she is! Elyathi eyed her evenly.

"It's been a while, hasn't it, my dear Derek?" the sorceress continued. "Sorry that I haven't made myself more presentable. As you can see, I do not have the means to do so."

"Do not speak, *witch*," Derek snapped. "I don't want to hear you talk. Not another word. I have been waiting for this moment, and I will not have you ruin it."

"Can't say that I feel the same," Ikaria said indifferently. "How is the fair and beautiful Emerald these days?" The Sorceress Ikaria's eyes then darted back to Elyathi, peering right through her. "And if it isn't Queen Elyathi herself."

Elyathi paused. *How does she know me?*

The sorceress eyed her up and down, then hmphed. "How disappointing. You looked far more beautiful in Damaris's thoughts and memories. Now…" She paused, raising an eyebrow. "It seems age has kissed your face."

"How dare you!" Derek spat.

Involuntarily, Elyathi lightly brushed her cheek, thinking of the slight wrinkle near her mouth. Someone had actually said something negative about her appearance?

"Elyathi looks just as young as you, witch!" Derek snarled.

"I digress." Ikaria shrugged, leaning back against the wall. "I was only trying to lighten the mood. It seems everyone has lost their sense of humor nowadays."

"It is a pity that you will lose your humor too once you no longer have your magic," Elyathi stated coldly.

"I find it interesting, Queen Elyathi, that you work for the very people who wanted to experiment on your daughter and raise Damaris up to be a powerful, mighty king. One to rule all kingdoms." She tsked. "I daresay that you have your priorities upside down if you're essentially helping those who harmed you."

It was as if she had been struck deep down, and she felt rendered without emotion. Was it true? That Belinda and the others were behind Damaris's rise to power? Did they prop him up to be a powerful king? Had they seen her back in time all those years in submission to Damaris, before they rescued her? Were they the ones to push the initial experiments on her daughter?

Elyathi dropped her voice into a dark whisper, moving closer. "You're lying."

The sorceress laughed. "Oh, so you didn't know? Well, perhaps you should do more research before you align yourself to certain people."

Elyathi ignored her as she neared the sorceress's barrier. It wavered, becoming more erratic as she inched closer.

Just one touch, she told herself. That was all she had to do.

"Derek," Elyathi called out, narrowing her eyes.

"I am more than ready, my lady," Derek said smugly as he flashed a look at Ikaria. He began to burn with blue magic.

"Perhaps you are taking it out on the wrong person. It isn't my fault how he treated you," Ikaria shrugged, inadvertently scooting away from them. As she did, her barrier followed, still encompassing her.

Elyathi took another step closer. "No. You were not at fault about him," she said, lowering her voice. "But as for my daughter… you will regret ever being *born*."

"Your daughter? I don't recall anything I did to her," Ikaria said.

"You *used* me!" Derek screamed. In his hand, blue-violet magic burned, swirling faster and faster. "Isn't that right? You *used* me! I want you to hear it from your own mouth. Right here, right in front of Elyathi. Now!"

"Oh, that? Come now, Derek. Really. Are you still going on about that?"

The room began shaking as Derek's body radiated more vibrancy; the blue started shifting to violet.

Elyathi smiled smugly as she watched the sorceress squirm back in the corner. The sorceress was trying to look proud and resistant, but there was no fooling her. Elyathi saw fear in her eyes.

That's right, you little unbelieving little unfaithful roach!

"Why don't you calm down a little bit, and we can all chat about it? No need to get all heated about everything," Ikaria said smoothly.

"Stop talking!"

"You and I, we had fun together, did we not? Ridding Arcadia of Damaris once and for all? Ruling Arcadia? And your beautiful queen… I daresay it was the most fun that I ever had, especially the time spent inside of you. It was quite the experience," Ikaria said in a convincing tone.

"Did you hear that, My Queen? The wicked witch admits it!" Derek cried.

"Such an utterly disgraceful creature," Elyathi said, her voice darkening. "I had no doubt in my mind that the sorceress was the cause of your downfall. She is a wicked thing, and must be punished for her sins."

Ikaria scoffed. "Oh? You think you are innocent?" She laughed. "Lest you forget, *Derek*, you enjoyed it just as much as I did."

"LIAR!" Derek shouted. He stormed right up to her barrier, leaning over her. "You know what you did. You pushed me and *pushed* me. Forced me to do what *you* wanted me to do for you!"

"This is why I don't get involved with other people. So complicated," Ikaria uttered.

"I will *destroy* you and your disgusting *lies*!"

Elyathi's eyes narrowed. "Even now, she is trying to worm her way out of it, weaving one lie after another."

Derek had had enough. He slammed Ikaria's barrier with his magic, and it shot right through, holding Ikaria in place, freezing her in time with a powerful force. Derek kept pouring the blue-violet magic over the barrier, funneling it straight into the sorceress's heart. Derek's energy bathed the room in blue, with powerful, bright azure flashes highlighting their faces.

The sorceress could still move slightly, since she had some time magic within her, but it wasn't enough.

"Now, while I have her!" Derek said loudly.

Elyathi quickly jabbed her hand through the barrier. It wavered wildly, as she clutched the sorceress's forehead. She thought about how Belinda wanted the cyborg information. Then she thought of what Ikaria had just said. She didn't want to believe Ikaria, but everything began piecing itself together.

Forget about the cyborgs, Elyathi thought to herself. *I will have her power once and for all. Then I will talk to Belinda.*

Elyathi shot her life force straight into the sorceress's body; she could feel it within her heartbeat, flowing through her blood. Closing her eyes, Elyathi pictured the sorceress's life force beating brightly within her. With her own magic, she grasped the violet life force, pulling it through the sorceress's veins.

In the background, she heard Derek shout, but it mattered not—she had the violet power within her grasp. With a violent yank, Elyathi pulled it out of Ikaria, and the sorceress fell limply to the floor. The enchanted barriers shook violently, then shattered to the floor in thousands of magical fragments.

The violet life force floated like a glowing ball of energy in the palm of her hand. Grabbing one of her empty vials from around her neck, she placed the life force energy within it and corked it shut.

The sorceress writhed in agony on the ground. Magic particles from her barrier, and the room's barrier, stuck to the sorceress's skin as she rolled around.

Derek flashed a dagger, then looked to her. "Let's end this once and for all," he said. "I will not rest until she is dead!"

Elyathi held up her hand, touching the dagger softly, then lowered it. "No. We must take her to face the High Court. We must follow the commandments of *The Spectrum*."

"I don't like it," Derek said sourly. "I want to end it here and now."

"Do not worry, Derek. You will have justice. Believe me, she will be put to death. As it is written: Only the wicked shall perish…"

He studied her, then breathed heavily. "I do not agree with that one bit, but I will do as you say."

Elyathi nodded in approval, then called out, "Guards!"

They appeared in the doorway, gawking at the magical fragments.

"The prisoner is no longer gifted, therefore this prison is no longer required. Please accompany her upstairs to World Sector Six's airship docks," Elyathi ordered them. "She will be loaded onto the High Court's ship. I will be there shortly."

"Yes, Lady Elyathi," they said, bowing.

"Don't bother, I will summon a portal for you," Derek said.

Derek snapped his hand in front of him, and a portal appeared before them. The guards carried the sorceress's limp body through the portal, and it faded away. Elyathi grasped her newly acquired prize—the violet vial. The glass was cold in her hand.

She called upon her life force, asking for permission to embrace the new violet magic. It obeyed and flowed directly to the vial. Elyathi soaked in the power, then looked to Derek with her powerful new violet eyes.

At once, she was awakened by her new power. There was a familiar mind within the citadel. A man who needed to be set straight.

"We must take care of an unwanted guest before we depart," Elyathi said.

"I will do anything to aid you, Lady," Derek said, giving her a dark glance.

For a moment, she brushed against Derek's mind. It was by accident, for she didn't understand this new violet magic. But somehow, it let her do it. There was a stirring in her heart.

Derek gave her a curious look, as if wondering what she was thinking. Elyathi quickly dropped the thought from her mind, then held out her hand, waiting for him to take it.

The two of them connected hands. Her life force felt *strong*. And his life force… it was equally matched.

CHAPTER 69

YELLOW

A loud shattering sound came from Ikaria's cell. Auron's heart dropped. He had been waiting for the changing of the guard, hoping to use Lord Jiao's keys to rescue the sorceress. He had missed his chance last time, and remained hidden in the shadows. The changing of the guard was to be very soon, but then the white-gifted woman arrived.

He was such a fool. He should have stopped the white-gifted woman from even entering Ikaria's cell. But what would he have done if he'd tried? The woman would have had his magic by now, and then there would be no hope at all to rescue the sorceress. He had to get to Ikaria now. *Now* was the time. But he had the sinking feeling that he might have already missed his chance.

Please, do not let me be too late! he pleaded to the God of Light silently.

But deep in his soul, Auron felt that the white-gifted woman had used her power against the sorceress, and that he *was* too late. He had no idea how he knew, but he sensed it, like a part of his soul was missing. He didn't know exactly what was missing, but his life force felt split. And it hurt.

Auron ran toward Ikaria's cell. Up ahead, the guards disappeared into her cell. The doorway appeared to have been broken. Running inside, Auron stopped. Magical fragments of the prison's barrier lay scattered about. The sorceress was gone, and so were the guards.

She was gone. Ikaria was gone. His life force *hurt.*

Panicked thoughts flooded his mind. Why had he hesitated so much?

Why was he so weak? Why wasn't he as powerful against the others? What was he to do now? He felt angry. Priests weren't supposed to get angry, but he couldn't suppress the feeling. It was a justified anger. He couldn't let that white-gifted take away all of World Sector Six's magic.

Prophesy, answered a voice.

Prophesy? Auron thought.

Wasn't that the same word the boy had told him in the temple? He blinked.

Prophesy, it whispered again.

Prophesy? Prophesy against what? Auron asked the whisper in his head.

A loud rumbling noise startled him, and vibrations shook the citadel. Stones shifted in and out of place as grains of sand waterfalled onto the ground. The rumbling was coming from above.

Is Ikaria up there? Something in his life force told him yes. Auron ran.

And ran.

Toward the life force calling him.

CHAPTER 70

THE SPECTRUM

Kyle landed on the outside patio of his temporary quarters of the World Sector Six citadel, releasing the red winds from around him. He wondered if Elyathi was back yet. He hoped to God she wasn't.

First things first. Kyle quickly entered his room. Zaphod cawed, cocking his head curiously at him.

"Hey, Zaphod." Kyle walked over to the bird, picking him up. His heart twanged with a sudden, deep hurt. He loved this damn bird. They had been through many things together.

"I hope that asshole room servant fed you, at least," Kyle said as he stroked the bird's feathers, giving him a loving pat. He soaked in Zaphod's beauty as he ran a finger down Zaphod's body, as if seeing the bird for the first time. Only, it would be the last. His stomach knotted up at the thought.

"Listen, a lot of fucked-up shit happened. I don't have time to tell you everything, but I… I wanted to say goodbye."

Zaphod cocked his head again.

"I'm letting you go," Kyle continued. "You can go wherever you want now. Turns out I'm not who you thought I was all these years. Hell, I didn't even know until now. That's why I gotta go. Em's waiting for me back in time."

It was as if the parrot understood him, because Zaphod whistled in a grievous tone. Just hearing Zaphod's sadness broke Kyle's heart. "I know, it's really shitty of me. But if you come with me, you might get hurt, and I don't want that to happen to you."

He set Zaphod down as he reached for a half-empty bottle of alcohol, then took a long drink. Zaphod whistled madly, then cawed. God, he felt like shit abandoning his buddy. But what the hell was he supposed to do? The assholes in the citadel, either from the High Court or World Sector Six, might harm his feathery friend when he was gone, knowing that the bird was his.

I'm doing him a favor, Kyle reassured himself.

Kyle looked at Zaphod, and the bird cocked his head, cawing again loudly. Zaphod's eye stared at him, its depths looking glassy. Was Zaphod *crying*? God, he felt even more like a fucking asshole.

"Dammit! This is just as hard for me as it is for you!" Kyle shouted as his eyes started to water too. Did grown men cry over pets? Because he sure as hell felt like he was going to.

Kyle took another swig of alcohol, then put down the bottle, trying not to look at Zaphod. If he saw the parrot, he might change his mind.

It's the best thing for him. Besides, can an animal withstand time travel? Probably not.

Closing his eyes, not wanting to see Zaphod's cocked head, Kyle sent a surge of magic to the door, blasting it with ice shards mixed with violet force, shredding the wood. Zaphod cawed in alarm.

"Sorry, old friend. It's for the best. You can't be with a fuck-up like me. You'll get hurt." His heart twisted once again. A tear squeezed through his shut eyelids, and he wiped it away quickly. "Be good to your next master!" Kyle called out.

There was a sad whistle in response. Another tear rolled down his cheek.

Dammit all to hell!

On the other side of the doorway stood the High Court guards, stunned at the condition of the door.

"High Inquisitor Rubius, are you okay?" one asked.

"Does it *look* like I'm okay?" Kyle snapped as he quickly wiped the tear off his cheek.

"No. High Inquisitor?" he asked, confused.

"High Inquisitor," Kyle muttered under his breath as he ran off.

God, it hurt leaving Zaphod. He felt like shit. Kyle tried to distract himself from Zaphod, hurrying his ass down the main halls that connected to the staircase to the prisons. He just had to get to the sorceress. *Hopefully Elyathi isn't here, or didn't already fuck with the sorceress's power. Ikaria is my one-way ticket out of this hellhole.*

Kyle ran down the stairs that connected to the prisons, then down the small prison hall to the sorceress's cell. As he approached her cell, he came to a halt.

The door was shattered.

"Oh God, no, please, fucking no!" Kyle yelled, running past the shattered door and into the cell.

The stream of magic was gone from the cell, and there was no sound but the echo of his boots scuffing the stone floors. On the floor were thousands of shattered magical barrier pieces.

The Sorceress Ikaria was gone.

"Oh my fucking God, no! This can't be happening!" Kyle screamed. The sorceress was gone! How the hell was he going to get back to Emerald? Certainly not with Elyathi or the High Court, that was for damn sure.

"Fuck me!" he screamed, then kicked the magical shards, sending them flying all over the place. He kicked the broken door hard, then hurled a blast of fire against the wall. Anger huffed through his lungs as he tried to catch his breath. *Think, you asshole, think!* he told himself. Exactly how long ago did the sorceress leave the cell?

Kyle blinked. *Maybe she's still in the citadel.* He ran as fast as he could back through the prison and up the stairs, his legs burning. A thought occurred to him: If he found the sorceress, would she even send him back now that she was free? That had been his bargaining chip.

I'll deal with that once I get to that point, he thought.

As soon as Kyle entered the main hall, there was a bright flash, blinding the shit out of him. He squinted, then blinked hard several times, trying to get rid of the white light burning his retinas. As he focused at last, he blinked again in disbelief.

Just when he thought matters couldn't get any worse, they got worse. It was that motherfucking asshole. The one he wanted to beat the shit out of.

"The fuck?" Kyle roared, his voice echoing.

"You! What are you doing here?" Derek yelled in disbelief, his voice booming across the main hall.

"I should ask the same thing as you, you fucking piece of shit!" Kyle called out.

Next to Derek was Elyathi. With purple hair. With *purple* fucking hair. She either had the sorceress's blood or her life force. His life was becoming one big clusterfuck by the second.

"I thought you were *dead*!" Derek yelled, narrowing his eyes in anger.

"Sorry to disappoint you."

Elyathi looked to Derek, her violet eyes wide. "You *know* him?" she asked.

"*He's* the one I told you about," Derek said. "The one with your daughter."

Her eyes hardened, and she turned her attention back to Kyle. "You… I *knew* there was more to you than you let on!"

"Whatever. I'll tell Emerald you said hi," Kyle said sarcastically.

"If you think you are going to travel back to Emerald, you are *sorely* mistaken," Derek added. "Lest you forget, *I* control time. I will not allow the blue magic to carry you back."

"And I will not allow my daughter to be anywhere near your vile stench!"

"Vile stench?" Kyle scoffed, laughing as if it were a joke. "You of all people are going to lecture me? You should ask that asshole next to you what he did to Emerald!"

"What I did?" Derek's eyes darkened. "How about if you had done your *job* and interrogated that purple bitch properly? She *told* me all about you."

"What?" Kyle said.

"You heard me!"

"We all know who was truly behind Derek's misfortunes, *Rubius*," Elyathi said scornfully. "I'm sorry, High Inquisitor, but you are no longer needed to fulfill the High Court's orders." Her eyes twinkled as they narrowed, her dark-red lips curling into a deep frown. "An indulgent, lecherous creature such as yourself has no place here…"

She began to burn with violet magic. Kyle hoped to God she hadn't figured out how to use it, otherwise he was in serious shit. Now was the time to prove that all his training with Geeta in his past life, and all the years in his new life, using violet magic, had paid off.

"All right, asshole bitches, that's it. I've had enough of this bullshit!"

Jolting out his hand, Kyle filled his veins with the furious, violent jealous rage that burned within him. Every word those assholes said made him even more angry. A powerful blast of violet burst from his body, consuming him from the inside out, encasing him. He had to disarm Elyathi.

Get that fucking bitch! he said to the magic. Kyle swung his hand, releasing the pure, raw violet force around him, blasting it straight at Elyathi.

With a flick of his wrist, Elyathi's necklaces with the vials and gems snapped off her neck. Before she knew it, the vials crashed to the floor, shattering across the marble floor, the gems sliding every which way.

"NO!" screamed Elyathi.

The violet life force that had clung around her neck had been destroyed, and it was flowing rapidly out of the broken vial and dissipating into the air. Elyathi looked around frantically, shaking her head in disbelief. Elyathi's violet hair and eyes were drained of color, replaced with her white features. Finally, the violet life force streamed to the side for a few seconds, then wafted away in the blink of an eye.

The violet life force was gone.

Elyathi whipped her head in Kyle's direction, her white eyes glowing brightly with fury.

"YOU!" she screamed. "You've ruined *everything*!" she screamed.

"Like hell I did!" Kyle shot back.

"My Queen!" Derek warned.

Kyle saw a blue-violet flash, and one of her gemstone necklaces floated before Elyathi, basking in Derek's magic. Elyathi yanked the gemstone into her hand, her features turning red.

Quickly, Kyle shifted his energy to his main power, the power of the elements. Channeling the fires deep within his heart, he let out a loud yell, then roared at the two of them, shooting out strong, fierce flames like a giant blowtorch in their direction.

Derek slid out of the way with his blue magic while Elyathi viciously cast a red ice block where Kyle was targeting. The fires hit the wall of ice, melting it away, and water puddled around her.

Kyle pushed more fire, more rage, more fury into his magic. The hell if the fucking assholes were going to stop him!

The flames melted the ice faster as Elyathi added more ice to the wall, her mouth curving into a snarl behind the foggy ice, the stream of melted ice flowing through the hall.

"Do you know that Emerald is pregnant?" Derek sneered behind the ice.

In that moment of distraction, Derek swirled his hands sharply, and Kyle's fire turned blue, reversing itself onto Kyle.

Kyle summoned a spray of red water, fizzling out the reversed flames, getting himself wet in the process. "Are you sure the baby is yours?" Kyle taunted.

Derek's eyes narrowed. The haughty smile dropped from his face, replaced by a dark, angry snarl. He growled, then flashed in his blue magic. He was gone.

"Behind you!" called out a voice.

Responding, Kyle instantly moved to the side just as a flash of blue magic slashed past him. Then Derek appeared in front of Kyle, lunging at him, swinging wildly. Derek was fast, much faster than Kyle remembered. The punch landed hard on the side of his face. Either that or Derek sped up time for that punch.

Elyathi clenched her teeth, her fists shaking. "You… How dare you insinuate anything of the sort! You insult her innocent character by your corrupt words!"

Kyle's fury pumped hard through his body. He couldn't recall ever hating anyone more than he hated Elyathi now. "Maybe instead of slandering me, you should ask your daughter what she thinks about all this bullshit!" Kyle yelled. "Ask her what she wants!"

"I know what my daughter wants, and what is good for her. And it is definitely not *you*!" Elyathi snarled. "She has loved Derek ever since she first understood what love was."

"Things change," Kyle countered.

A blue blur streaked in front of him. Kyle quickly tapped into his violet magic, ready to fight back with a powerful punch. But then the blue magic… slowed down. Way down. Kyle could see Derek in slow motion.

What the hell?

Taking advantage of the situation, Kyle punched Derek hard on the face, using some of his violet magic to pack the punch. He punched him again in the side of the gut. It felt good punching the fuck out of that asshole.

Then the world flickered back to normal speed, and Elyathi was yelling at Derek about something. The world started to turn blue, its color running like flowing water over the world. Derek stood burning with his magic, screaming with rage.

The world went still again.

Fuck me! Kyle cursed.

He couldn't move. Time was stilling, coming to a halt. In the corner of his eye, he saw Zaphod fly in midair.

Oh God, no, my friend!

***

Derek continued to channel his magic, filling the void of his soul, sweeping it across the world like a furious flood. He was going to crush those who opposed him. The power that Elyathi gave him, the power that came from her blood, it was so potent, supercharging every spell. His soul felt on top of the world, and no one could stop him.

The world froze at his command as the magic poured out across the citadel, but he allowed Elyathi to move within the stilled world. Derek put his hands down, finishing the spell. Elyathi gave him an approving look. She scampered across the hall, leaning down. The vials had been shattered, but the gems were intact. Derek watched her retrieve her necklaces and clasp them around her neck.

She smiled, clutching them as if they were her lifeline. Then she turned and walked over to that *bastard*. Derek smirked, celebrating inside, knowing that Elyathi would take away Kyle's power once and for all. And then what? That bastard nobody would never be a problem again.

Another thought came to Derek—he could just kill Kyle after Elyathi removed his power, ensuring he would never have to see that has-been ever again. Derek laughed at the thought.

Just as Elyathi got close enough to touch Kyle, a brilliant flash struck her, smacking her hard across the face. She yelped as blue magic encased her, stopping her right in her tracks. Elyathi was frozen in time.

Derek whirled around quickly, eyeing his surroundings, trying to find the source of the opposing magic. It had to be another blue-gifted.

"Where are you?" Derek roared.

Another azure flash, and this time Derek saw streaming blue ribbon of magic heading straight at him. With a swipe of his hand, his body effortlessly slid ten feet over, moving within the current dimensional space.

The frozen world was letting up, and color started returning.

"Oh no, you don't!" Derek yelled defiantly. "Time will remain still!"

Channeling all of his energy, Derek fought with the opposing gifted, their two magics rubbing together, fighting like oil and water. But he was stronger with the power from Elyathi's blood. He blasted more power, mixed with the analogous violet magic, pushing the opposing time magic with more force. How he loved Elyathi's magic; it was like pure ecstasy. So mighty, so robust, heightening every sense in his body.

With another powerful blast of time magic, Derek's power won over the opposing magic. And suddenly he knew where the mysterious blue-gifted was. Targeting his hand in their direction, Derek streamed his blue-violet magic, snatching up the mystery gifted. A woman screamed as he flung the body toward him, sliding her hard against the marble floor.

He caught a glimpse of her face and snarled. He recognized the woman—smooth, dark skin, big gold jewelry, bright-blue eyes. He had fought her months ago back in Arcadia.

"I won't let you hurt the High Inquisitor!" she said fiercely, flashing out of sight.

"You shouldn't get involved with matters that don't pertain to you!" Derek shouted at her.

Derek felt her mind once again as she had flashed back into the room. Quickly funneling the jealousy within, Derek unleashed a forceful blow toward the woman. She slid sideways, then hurried to counter his spell, trying to stop it mid-blow. But being his magic was more powerful, it ripped through hers, then changed direction, slamming her against the wall. Her head hit the marble wall hard, and she slumped over, moaning.

In the corner of Derek's eye, that red-gifted bastard remained still within his magic. Derek held out his hand in Elyathi's direction, his magic streaming over her, releasing her from her frozen time state.

"What is going on?" Elyathi demanded. As she recovered fully, color returned to her, and her red features became predominant. She turned and saw the blue-gifted woman, narrowing her eyes. Another bright-blue flash rippled across the room and out the doors.

An old blue-gifted man stood before them, his robes fluttering hard in a magical wind that encircled him. He hurled a large ball of blue fire toward Derek.

"You hurt my daughter, now I will hurt you!" he roared.

Elyathi waved her hands up in a powerful motion, and red ice spikes shot up from underneath the man as an ice block encapsulated Derek. Her spell saved Derek in the nick of time, because when the fire made contact with the ice, both elements dissipated.

The man was levitating above the ice spikes; he had saved himself just in time as well.

"Oriel," Elyathi sneered. "I thought you were on your way to the pits of hell."

"I won't let you succeed, Elyathi," Oriel said.

"I am the chosen one by the God of Light. Nothing can stop me. You cannot change a prophecy," Elyathi said with finality in her voice.

"We'll see about that," he called out.

Oriel put his hands together, then he burst into blue flames that consumed him entirely. He yelled from within the fire as his body struggled. The old man tried to pull his hands apart, but it was as if they were locked together by the magic.

Suddenly, the world around Derek shifted.

What is he doing? Derek thought wildly.

Oriel managed to pull his hands apart ever so slightly. The dimension that they were in was being split, like a beam of light shining through a prism, separating into their own bars of color. Derek watched in awe as six dimensions fractured before him, the red one starting to dominate the others.

Derek couldn't believe the display of power he was witnessing. The world was still locked in time, as was apparent with the red-gifted man still frozen, but the dimensions, they were splitting…

This has to be within my power as well. He is exerting his power over the dimensions of time and magic itself! Derek thoughts hammered through his mind. *Do all blue-gifted have this ability? Or is he that skilled and powerful?*

The red dimension ripped through the world, encasing everyone within it. It was almost a void, with the exception of red stars and space. Derek could feel its emptiness waiting to be commanded and shifted into its own new world.

Is this how the new world will be formed? Derek wondered.

"Derek, stop him now!" Elyathi screamed, interrupting his thoughts. "We are not ready for this!" She ran toward him, her hair still red from the gemstone around her neck. All around her, the earth rumbled violently as she waved her hand at Oriel.

Derek summoned the blue magic, but it refused. To his shock, it fizzled and disappeared within his hand. Oriel's magic rippled and funneled around him fiercely, burning from a bright-blue to red, red from within the dimension. His robes fluttered as he stretched out his hands, the dimension spinning around them wildly. The stars shifted, streaming together and funneling into his hand.

Elyathi shot a fireball toward Oriel, but as it neared the former high justice, it fizzled out. Derek tried desperately to tap into his magic, but it was as if blue magic simply no longer worked.

"Derek!" Elyathi screamed.

With a burst of pure magic, Oriel shot a giant bolt of starlight directly at Elyathi. She used red wind to take flight, but it was too late. Oriel's starlight bolt hit her straight on. She cried out in shock before falling like a dead bird to the ground.

"Elyathi!" Derek screamed, running toward her. He grasped her doll-like body, shaking her. Seeing Elyathi struck, hurt… Derek cried out, tears of anger falling.

"You bastard!" Derek yelled in outrage.

Oriel began casting another spell, encasing his body in his powerful magic once again. Derek had to do something, and *fast.*

This is a red dimension, Derek thought quickly. *It seems this dimension is only affected by red magic.* But what of violet? It sat next to red in the spectrum. Derek had no power over red, but he certainly did over violet.

Derek flicked his hand, filling himself with all of his violet magic, letting it work through him. Elyathi's power bubbled inside of him, its powerful surge of energy encasing his life force, embracing his magic. The violet magic flowed through him rapidly, laughing, gathering, begging Derek to unleash its jealous fury. Flashing his eyes open, Derek saw his blue-violet magic streaming around him, but it wasn't blue-violet. It was pure violet.

With a sudden snap of his hands, Derek released the magic burst at Oriel. It wrapped around Oriel's body in an instant, ensnaring the old man and stopping his spell, binding him in place. Then it squeezed hard. Oriel gasped, struggling for breath. He shook his head in anguish.

"You will pay for what you did to Elyathi!" Derek yelled, narrowed his eyes. Then he squeezed his hand as hard as he could. The magic complied, mimicking Derek by squeezing Oriel's body. Derek thought about the flow of time and Emerald smiling at him. Their new kingdom... their world. Now, Derek was sure Emerald would desire him once again. Because he had Elyathi.

Derek crushed his hand harder, and the magic crushed Oriel harder.

Oriel cried out, rasping for breath. "Don't align yourself with her, Derek of Arcadia."

"You don't know what I've seen in the flow of time," Derek said. "Elyathi is a good woman!" Derek looked over at the still body of Elyathi, her breathing weak from Oriel's blow, her eyes staring at nothing as if she were blind. He had to save her.

Derek sent a dark wave of magic, filling his lifestream, casting it into the violet binding magic, squeezing Oriel so hard that even Derek's body shook from the power exerted from his magic.

Oriel cried out, this time calling out to the woman. "Vala..."

Derek squeezed more, the power raging through him like a violent storm. Blood streamed out of Oriel's nose, and his pores wept blood. The red dimension shifted and wavered the more Derek squeezed. It was slowly fading away, aligning back into place with the other color dimensions.

Derek roared again, sending another surge of violet magic to Oriel. The old man cried out once again. Bones snapped the harder Derek crushed him. He was like a god with Elyathi's blood. Nothing could stop him.

Derek gave Oriel one last good squeeze, and the world restored itself to its normal dimension. Holding out his other hand, Derek streamed blue-green magic out of his life force and straight into Elyathi, desperate to save her. The radiating blue-green magic flowed over her, and Derek immediately felt life being restored to her. Elyathi's eyes became clearer by the second, and her body mended perfectly.

Elyathi blinked, then took a deep breath, giving Derek a look of gratitude. She rose to her feet, then moved toward him, laying a hand on his shoulder as Derek froze the world in blue once again.

"Thank you, Derek. You are a true warrior," Elyathi said, her voice as soft as honey, her clear eyes searching his. "You know what I must do."

"Indeed," Derek said darkly. A warm feeling went down his spine from her words, mixed with a strange confusion.

Elyathi's face went stern, then she turned her focus to Oriel and walked toward him. A small grunt came from the blue-gifted woman. She attempted to get to her feet, but Derek snapped another violet stream around her, pushing her next to Oriel.

"Vala..." said Oriel with much effort. He struggled within Derek's violet magic as blood poured down his body, making it slick with blood. "Don't let the white-gifted touch you."

Vala started to cry as Derek tightened his grip around them.

Elyathi hovered over the old man. "You first, Oriel," she said stiffly.

"I'm sorry, Vala," Oriel whispered to her.

"Why?" she cried.

"Because... because I was never a father to you."

Vala's eyes went wide as Oriel shamefully met her glance. Then she let out a loud, hard sob.

"And you never will be. Your sins will not be forgiven," Elyathi said.

With that, Elyathi put her hand on Oriel, and her body burned bright white, blinding everyone, including Derek. Within the world of white, Derek heard Vala cry out, and a stream of blue magic wavered within the white world.

A red parrot came into view, diving toward Elyathi.

Then there were screams.

***

Zaphod bit the bitch, and bit her hard. Time was restored to him, and he could finally move his ass. But it was too fucking late. The old man was fucked. Elyathi had touched him with her magic. But Elyathi screamed and recoiled from Zaphod's bite, trying to slap the parrot as he fluttered by.

"Oh, no you fucking don't!" Kyle yelled. "You don't fuck with my bird!"

Kyle cast a huge-ass red bolt of electricity toward Elyathi. It struck her, and she jolted, stumbling into a nearby pillar.

"Elyathi!" Derek yelled.

Oriel screamed when Derek released the violet magic around the old man. He muttered asinine things while clenching his head and tearing at his hair. His body burned brightly with his magic, but it was fading by the second.

He was losing his gift.

"Give it back, you fucking bitch!" Kyle yelled at Elyathi.

Elyathi recovered and took a deep breath. She gave Kyle a cold stare, her eyes like poison darts. "Never," she whispered sharply.

Kyle clenched his jaw, trying to think fast. He had to save that blue-gifted woman Vala. She was still violet-bound with Derek's magic.

Let's see what this asshole thinks about this.

Searching deep in his life force, Kyle funneled his magic, searing his soul as his jealousy emerged. He hated the fact that Derek thought that *he* had impregnated Emerald. It infuriated the fuck out of him.

The magic grew more as Kyle fed his jealous rage, burning with power. With a sweeping motion, Kyle released the jealous magic.

The violet magic rocked everyone with a giant shockwave of force, whipping everyone off their feet. It pummeled through the building, shaking the citadel.

Vala rolled on the ground, free from the violet magic. But it wasn't Kyle's magic that freed Vala; it was Derek losing his concentration. She rolled over to the old man, who was still saying delirious things. She hesitated for a moment, then her eyes met Kyle's. "You must come with me. I have to take you to Queen Emerald," she called out.

Kyle's heart stopped at the mention of Emerald's name. He jerked his head, giving Vala his full attention. "You know of Emerald? Please, I need to get to her!"

"That is why I am here, to take you back," she answered.

Kyle felt suddenly invigorated. He had a way back to Emerald. He was going to go back to her!

"You aren't taking anyone anywhere, especially not to my *wife*!" Derek snarled loudly, then he shot up to his feet. "I won't let you touch her!" he yelled to Kyle.

"Still trying to control Emerald, huh?" Kyle shot back. "Well, we'll see about that, asshole!"

White magic funneled into Derek while he burned with his own blue magic. Elyathi was behind Derek, giving him a boost of power from her own, and it was as if her magic magnified his. He already seemed too powerful, but this…

Fuck! If that asshole froze time again, he would be double fucked!

Kyle ran, filling his hand with a surge of magic. A giant blue blast enveloped the world, and all went blue. But he still had movement.

I'm still moving? Kyle wondered in disbelief as he continued to run. With no time to waste, Kyle roared as he gathered all of his magic, then blasted a stream of fireballs, shooting them like mad at Derek.

In shock that Kyle could still move, Derek simply gawked at the fireballs that were about to make contact, but then a yellow shield went up around him, absorbing most of the magic. Some of the flames made it through, singing Derek's clothes and making him sweaty. He threw off his doublet.

Elyathi's hair and eyes were yellow with magic, then turned white again, streaming into Derek.

"Freeze him once and for all! I will take his power, and then we will be done with him *forever*. This is the last we will see of the High Inquisitor!"

Derek yelled in a furious rage, his hand outstretched as he gathered all the world's blue into it. Vala burst weakly with her own magic, struggling hard to counter Derek, barely holding him back, but he was too powerful.

The hell do I do? Kyle thought quickly. He could jump into Derek's mind, but that was too risky—if he was too busy dealing with Derek's mind, Elyathi would get to his body and take his magic.

As Derek and Vala continued to struggle against each other with their own time magics, Kyle's movements flickered like a crappy broken monitor. He was so frustrated that he couldn't counter Derek. Not only that, with each flicker, Elyathi was getting closer to him, no matter how hard Vala tried. Derek was too damn powerful with Elyathi's boost.

This shit had to stop! Maybe instead of jumping into Derek's mind… he could jump into Elyathi's. She was gifted, and it would be difficult. But he had to try.

Just when he had movement, Kyle tapped into his violet magic, readying his spirit to jump. But just then, Derek's magic won over Vala's.

"Motherfu—" Kyle screamed, but his sentence was cut off.

He was frozen once again.

***

An overwhelming feeling surged through Ikaria as she breathed. Her magic, her life force, had returned to her.

She laughed wildly. The guard that was carrying her stopped suddenly.

"Why is she laughing?" asked the other guard, stopping too.

Ikaria slid out of his grip, slumping to the ground, laughing. Oh, how she felt *alive*. She laughed and laughed, rolling on the ground. She wanted to make violent love to the ground she lay upon, because she had her violet power back.

"What's so funny?" one of the guards asked.

"Isn't it splendid?"

"What's splendid?"

In answer, Ikaria sent a violent surge of violet magic. It ripped through her body and went straight into the guards, gathering in their minds. With an upward flick of her fingers, the guards' heads exploded. Blood, guts, and brains, splattered all over and around her, covering her in blood and flesh.

"That is what is splendid. Such a shame you didn't get to see my violet power in its full glory," she said as she brushed some brains off her shoulder.

Ikaria felt a calling from within the citadel. A strange, forceful nagging at her soul. She needed to be joined with whatever was calling her. She paused for a moment. The airship her sister had been on seemed to have already departed. She could just leave the citadel and go after her. But Suri and Auron were already helping Ayera.

The power surged into her life force once again; it was the same feeling as when her eyes had locked with Auron's back in her cell. Somehow, Ikaria knew that Auron was back in the citadel. And he needed her help.

Helping that damn priest... I would never. But her soul told her otherwise. He was supposed to be helping her sister. Ikaria gritted her teeth, then quickly headed toward the entrance of the citadel. As she made her way through the halls, loud rumblings shook the citadel. Much magic was being unleashed in the heart of the citadel. Time was flashing in and out, but Ikaria remained free. Her adjacent blue gift must love her, because she had full movement, even without the consumption of blue blood. Just another reason that someone in the heavens, or below the earth, favored her.

As Ikaria neared the top of the stairs, a sharp grab on her arm put her on the defensive. She was about to cast a spell when a voice interrupted her.

"Thank the God of Light you are safe!" Auron said, appearing to her. Time seemed to be flowing again. "You have your magic back."

Ikaria stepped back, startled. Then she narrowed her eyes. "Auron! What are you doing here? You should be with my sister!" she snapped.

"I couldn't leave you," he admitted.

"Leave me?" Ikaria scoffed. "I am truly touched."

He yanked her close. "Can't you feel it?"

"I don't feel, priest."

It was a lie. She knew exactly what he was talking about.

"It's just like you, isn't it? Even now," he scolded her, then turned his attention. "We must stop Elyathi before it is too late."

Ikaria's eyes darkened. Yes, she hated Elyathi. More than the bitch Belinda herself. Elyathi had dared to steal her very soul. Her magic!

"You don't have to convince me, priest. Just keep your barriers on me, and I'll do the rest," Ikaria ordered him.

Just then, time flickered again, and Auron stilled. Filling her veins with her adjacent magic, Ikaria latched on to Auron's forehead, sending a wave of time into him. Color flooded his body, and he moved once again.

Auron looked to her, then breathed deeply. "Thank you, sorceress," he said.

"Enchantress to you," Ikaria snapped. "I don't know how long my time magic will hold up on you, so we'd best hurry."

They made their way up the stairs, then came upon the main hall. Derek was there, and behind him was Elyathi, funneling magic into him.

Ikaria smiled to herself, almost with a secret pleasure. *Well, this ought to be fun.*

High Justice Oriel was also there, screaming out of his mind while another blue-gifted woman tried to counter Derek's magic. And then there was the High Inquisitor… or should she say Queen Emerald's lover? He was struggling against the crippling effects of time. Elyathi was getting close to him, ready to take his power.

Ikaria paused. Perhaps, she should let Elyathi just take this Kyle Trancer's power. But between him and Elyathi, Ikaria hated Elyathi more, and she didn't want to give that bitch one ounce of satisfaction.

The things I do for others… I'm sure I will regret this at some point. Ikaria clenched her jaw.

Auron gasped. "Vala," Auron said anxiously. "We have to help her!"

"Such unfortunate timing," Ikaria commented.

Auron got in Ikaria's face. "What do you mean *unfortunate*? Help Vala!"

"I meant, priest, unfortunate timing… for *them*." Ikaria flashed her violet eyes at him, giving him a smug smile.

Auron's eyes met hers, and for the first time, he acknowledged her fully, nodding in approval. "Let's go," he said.

Auron ran toward Vala with Ikaria behind him. He reached out his hand to shield her, but Ikaria's violet magic shot past him, swooshing to Elyathi, knocking her to her feet hard. She slid far away from the frozen Kyle Trancer. Elyathi groaned, taking faint breaths.

"Lady Elyathi!" Derek cried out as he continued to fight against Vala's spells.

A sudden blowback of blue-violet magic knocked the wind out of Auron.

"Uncle!" Vala screamed as Auron tumbled across the floor, still maintaining the fight against Derek's magic.

Auron burned with his own shield, trying to take his breath as his body rolled to a stop. Ikaria felt their life forces intertwining together. As much as Ikaria hated the idea, she had to come to terms with it—for the magic chooses.

Auron. His life force had been constructed for hers. They were *complements*.

"Sorceress… do you—" Auron started.

"I need you to funnel your magic into me, priest. Now!" she cried. Ikaria did not want him to utter what she knew. No sense in giving him any ideas. Ikaria snapped her head back, gathering all of her magic from her core being. It flooded her veins with furious power.

A new surge of magic rose in her, embracing her spirit fully and completely. Auron's magic flowed over and around her, renewing her life force. His magic, it felt so… *right*. Her senses were heightened, so much that Ikaria was in pure ecstasy, like an orgasm that kept going on and on. Ikaria laughed at the heightened awareness of power, and she flashed her eyes open. She swiped her hand toward Derek, releasing her violet power.

Only it wasn't violet.

It was white.

The Spectrum of Magic.

Pure white magic rippled through the citadel violently, shaking it, as

Ikaria jumped into Derek's mind. It was easy; she had been comfortable within his mind months prior, and it felt like a reliable pair of shoes. And now, with the power of the Spectrum of Magic, the pure white light, it was like drinking a fine wine. So very sweet.

As Ikaria entered, she immediately noticed that Derek's mind had become much darker than before. If she could have, she would have swum with delight through his dark thoughts, relishing in them. But there wasn't any time for that. For now.

Ikaria took hold of his thoughts, then his mind. From a far corner of his mind, Derek screamed from beyond. Commanding Derek's body, she stopped his spells. Through Derek's eyes, Ikaria saw Vala fall free from the magic. She scrambled toward Oriel, and both of them flashed away.

"Derek?" Elyathi called out from afar, knowing something had happened.

Ikaria saw her own body through Derek's eyes. She shot a wave of magic to her own body, commanding it to cast a spell. Ikaria's violet force picked up Elyathi, clutching her, dragging her toward Derek's possessed body. Ikaria saw Derek's thoughts attached to Elyathi as she gazed into the white bitch's eyes. Derek had been having confusing thoughts about her, trying to tuck them away within his mind. But Ikaria yanked it out, gazing at Derek's conflicted thoughts in her shining vision.

I will have to file that away for a later use... Ikaria thought wickedly, amused.

Auron ran up behind her real body across the room, along with brilliant red magic. The red-gifted man, Kyle Trancer, who was finally free from Derek's spell, was about to hurl a spell at him. Ikaria jumped out of Derek's dark mind, opening the eyes of her own body as Kyle blasted electricity at Derek. She had made it back in her body just in time, as Derek jolted hard, screaming. Elyathi was still clutched in the throes of Ikaria's violet magic.

Ikaria narrowed her eyes. "Hello once again, Derek." Ikaria waved with mock friendliness. "It seems our paths keep crossing."

"Bitch!" Derek screamed back, spittle flying from his mouth. He then dropped to the floor, pained from the shock of the electricity.

"Now, now. Is that any way to treat an old friend?" Ikaria called out.

Kyle neared her, his eyes wild with fury. "Where did the blue-gifted woman go? Vala?"

Ikaria looked at him, then shrugged. "How would I know?"

"Dammit! I have to go back!" he said, grasping her shoulders.

Ikaria look at his hands, then shouldered away from him, raising her chin. "I'm not helping you. You missed your opportunity when I was locked up."

"I will remove *both* of you from time itself!" Derek screamed as he rose to his feet.

Derek started to cast a spell, and blue radiated around him.

Ikaria rolled her eyes. "Why are all men so dramatic?"

Kyle yanked her close, staring right into her eyes. "Honestly, I should kick your ass for all the shit you put Emerald through back in Arcadia. If it weren't for you, I wouldn't even fucking be here! But I'm willing to put that shit aside for one moment. Help me find Vala."

Ikaria stared right back. "No."

He snarled in her face and was about to say something, but was interrupted.

"Witch! It's time for you to face me! I will have justice," Derek yelled through his blue magic.

Ikaria scoffed. "Still going on about that?"

"Rapist! You wielded me like a weapon, and she's never forgiven me."

Ikaria shrugged. "She'll get over it. Eventually."

Kyle froze, gaping at Ikaria in shock.

"Go to hell!" Derek screamed.

"You will pay for what you did to Derek and my daughter!" yelled Elyathi. "Finish her, Derek! I will make sure the High Court understands."

Suddenly, objects within the citadel began to shake, like an earthquake gathering momentum. Things started to float, and everything that was supposed to have weight no longer did. Dark-red magic flooded Ikaria's vision. Metal bent, rocks shattered, everything was starting to go against its very nature.

"You fucking did *what*?" Kyle screamed, bathed in dark-red magic. "*You* were behind that?"

And then Ikaria was in the clutches of his red magic.

Well, that certainly wasn't the right thing to say…

***

Kyle was seeing red. Pure fucking red.

He couldn't fucking believe what he'd heard. He couldn't fucking *believe* it.

The fucking bitch!

The more he thought of the sorceress's words, the more it fucking made him rage. He choked back tears. She was the one…

Wrath poured into his soul. Not only had the bitch controlled Em all that time, allowing Em to marry against her will, to have Em drain all his life force away until he died… but *this*? She fucking did that to Em?

Kyle thought he might explode just thinking about it. He was going to *murder* that evil bitch!

Dark-red magic funneled around him, whirling wildly like a storm at sea on a colossal scale that no one had ever seen. The dark side of the spectrum pumped furiously in his veins—the wrath of the elements, beyond earth and from the stars and space itself. Foreign magic from other worlds came at his beckoning, straight from whatever the fuck dimension they originated in. The more they gathered to him, the more the citadel shook. The floors split and the walls shattered, everything crumbling as dust permeated the air.

The pure dark elements were within his grasp.

He was going to fuck that bitch up. Her and that blue asshole. Dark magic moved unnaturally through the floor of the hall, forming and shifting around the sorceress, locking her body in stone.

With a hard punch in the air, Kyle released another dark wave of magic. A red wind funnel surrounded the sorceress, then Kyle shot another blast of small crimson ice shards into the winds. He was going to encase the bitch in stone and let the icy wind slice her body, and into her innards until she was unrecognizable. She would die a slow death. She deserved it for all the pain she'd caused. Especially Emerald's pain and suffering.

"Stop this! I need her life force," Elyathi screamed.

"Fuck you and your fucking life force!" Kyle roared over the crashing debris.

"Ghost man! Stop what you are doing! You are going to hurt the citizens in the citadel!" another voice yelled. Kyle vaguely registered the distant sound of screams from other parts of the citadel.

He didn't give a damn. All he could see in his mind was Em hurt. What those asshole fucks put her through… His mind conjured up a hundred nightmarish scenarios, and his pain and anguish swelled as he remembered Em's face, the pain, her tears, her shame.

Kyle unleashed another furious wave of dark-red magic, sending it running throughout the citadel. The fortress shook violently once again. Kyle's magic ravaged the marble floor as it traveled to Derek and Elyathi. Walls, floors, and columns nearby rumbled, then split apart.

"STOP, GHOST MAN!"

Kyle looked out of the corner of his eye to where the voice had come from. Standing there was a *green-gifted* man. The one who had appeared to him many years ago.

His jaw dropped. Kyle couldn't believe it. Out of all the times and places, *this* dude shows up now, right as he was about to end the bitch once and for all. Kyle burned with renewed rage, the fires within him roaring as his angry soul cried out in anguish.

"Think, Ghost Man! Think of the people within this citadel," the man said firmly. "I'll take you back to her, but please, stop this madness!"

Take me back to her?

The citadel continued to shake, rumbling under everyone's feet. Kyle panted with heavy, angry breaths while the man's words echoed in his mind. He whipped around to face the green-gifted man. He stood miraculously unharmed in a room that was nearly unrecognizable.

"You will take me back to Emerald?" Kyle asked.

"He's not going back!" yelled Derek, whose leg was pinned under a fallen column.

"Shut the hell up!" Kyle roared before turning his attention back to the green-gifted man. "It's you… from years ago."

"Yes. I finally found you," the man said with a small smile. "Let's go." The man with deep-green eyes motioned with his hand, creating a time portal. "Please, let go of your magic."

He was finally going to see Emerald. His heart beat nervously and his hands shook. Emerald was waiting.

"Let's get you back to your love," the man continued, motioning toward the portal.

Kyle was so nervous. But why? He would finally meet the woman of his dreams… the love of his past life.

Emerald.

Kyle released his dark-red magic, and the world slowly calmed itself with each of his breaths as he flew over the debris and landed in front of the portal.

"No!" Derek screamed, still not managing to pull his leg out from under the column.

"Get in, quick," ordered the green-gifted man. "I'll jump in after you."

Kyle eyed the man, then nodded, flinging himself into the portal. Just as he did, Zaphod darted toward Kyle, cawing, entering the portal with him. The world began to spin green-blue around him and Zaphod, and Kyle saw a white flash from behind as he began his journey back.

***

Rocks, chunks of the citadel, split columns, everything was collapsing around Suresh. Even with the Ghost Man calming down before he jumped into the portal, the aftershocks of his magic remained, leaving the citadel in shambles.

The entire structure was about to give out from underneath them. A blue-gifted woman appeared, enveloped in her magic, trying to slow the destruction of the citadel while citizens ran wildly. Even the encased sorceress's stonework cracked and crumbled, releasing her from her temporary stone prison.

Suresh quickly lunged toward the portal, but a burst of white light enveloped him. There was no portal around him. There was *nothing* around him.

Nothing at all.

Nothing but white light.

***

There was a white flash, then it subsided. Somehow, Derek managed to free himself, and he and Elyathi were gone, leaving the citadel to split itself apart on all those left within.

People, *his* people, in World Sector Six were all going to perish. Vala was trying as hard as she could to slow the destruction, but she was exhausted and her energy spent.

Prophesy! yelled the voice in his head.

"Priest, can you cast an enchantment with your analogous magic?" Ikaria called out. She was covered with dust, remnants of the stone spell.

"Enchantment? Are you in your right mind, sorceress?" Auron shot back.

"Yes, I am, priest! You are complete in your life force, otherwise we wouldn't have been able to summon the Spectrum of Magic, you imbecile!"

Prophesy!

Prophesy? he asked the voice inside his mind.

Are you not a priest, blessed with the power of prophecy? Use your voice and speak words to prophesy! For that is what true prophetic magic is, is it not?

He stopped. Priests for many centuries thought of prophecies as visions. But in the tomes of old, writings not found in *The Spectrum*, the priests used to prophesy simply by speaking to their people.

Yes, it is, Auron answered the voice.

Then prophesy, my child. Quickly. Prophesy!

A flood of words came to him. "Sorceress, I know what to do!" he called back to her. "Funnel your magic into me. All of your colors. Quickly."

"It better work," Ikaria snapped.

"For those who are faithful, relying on the God of Light always works to their advantage."

"Wonderful. Is that your big plan?" Ikaria yelled. "Waiting for the God of Light? Because I can tell you, priest, that people have been waiting for him for thousands of years!"

"I am going to prophesy," Auron stated.

"You can't be serious," Ikaria scoffed. "You are just going to *talk* to the citadel?"

"Precisely," Auron said with finality. "Now be quiet and send me your magic. Now!" he boomed.

Ikaria shot him a look, then rolled her eyes. "Whatever you say, priest." She began to channel her magic.

Auron felt it. Her soul. Her life force. He felt it all deep down within himself, mixing within his life force. Her life force was so full of darkness. He closed his eyes, channeled his own power. His soul was the complete opposite—pure and holy against her darkness. More and more, Auron pictured his two adjacent colors, envisioning light in perfection.

Orange… Green… Yellow…

"Uncle, please hurry!" Auron heard Vala cry out. "The citadel is about to collapse, and I can't slow time any longer. My energy is spent."

Screams from the citizens filled his ears, and Auron heard running footsteps and the cries of panic. Still, waves of Ikaria's soul flooded in.

Blue... Red... Violet...

With a surge of heavenly power, Auron's soul became weightless. In his mind's eye, he saw himself bathed in pure holy light, and the heavens opened up before him. A beam of light shot down into Auron's soul, and pure *power* surged into him.

Prophesy!

Auron shot open his eyes, then his voice boomed, "I command you, stones of the citadel, to be *calm*!"

The citadel shook violently in response, roaring. Then a groan came from within the elements of the structure, as if they did not want to obey but had no choice. Ikaria laughed in disbelief. The stones calmed themselves, halting in place. With a surge of holy magic, Auron released it from his life force, and it went flowing to his mouth.

"Citadel of World Sector Six, you will no longer destroy yourself! I *command* you to keep those within safe from harm."

The light in his mouth burst forth, the holy white magic pouring out onto the citadel, mending the bricks and walls, pushing everything back together like a giant puzzle. Another surge of energy blasted out of Auron as he breathed, and the energy coated the citadel, painting it in white light, settling within the stones.

The citadel transformed itself into the most beautiful architecture he had ever seen. Gold, crystal, pearl, and white marble embellished every aspect of the citadel, gleaming with holy radiance. Auron breathed in the beauty of the new creation in awe and wonder. He fell to the floor in pure amazement.

Ikaria's mouth dropped open at the sight, amazed and astonished. Auron heard the citizens gathering around them, and the crowd began to cheer and cry out in praise. Then he felt the other half of himself near him, his complement.

"You were right, priest. The God of Light helped us, just this once," Ikaria acknowledged.

Auron turned, and their eyes met. He looked into her violet depths, searching her thoughts.

Then he passed out, spent of energy.

CHAPTER 71

RED

Green-blue magic streamed around Kyle's body as he fell endlessly. His spirit was faint, his mind weak, and his soul was fleeting. At any given moment, Kyle wasn't sure whether he was going to black out or die. To make shit worse, the green-gifted man wasn't anywhere that Kyle could see. The man had not come in after him as he'd said.

Kyle looked down at his hands, which were flickering on and off in a pale-green light.

What is happening?

Above him, there was a squawking sound. Kyle looked up as he continued to fall, his clothes beating at him in the wind, his necklaces hitting him in the face.

Zaphod made another sound, calling out to him.

"I told you not to follow me!" Kyle called out to him as they both dropped in the endless green-blue time tunnel. "I didn't want anything to happen to you."

Bright-blue magic encased them both, swirling around their bodies. As they continued to plummet in the endless stream blue magic and stars, Kyle's vision narrowed. The stars whirled around faster and faster, until his head was spinning.

I'm losing my damn mind! he thought as his thoughts became jumbled. He looked down and could barely see his body.

Storm clouds rippled far below in the endless sky. Then suddenly, the clouds swelled in size, rippling like a violent sea in a storm, turning a bright white as Kyle plummeted through them.

Zaphod cawed in alarm. With a hard, forceful jerk, Kyle's body was whipped in a completely different direction, shooting sideways. Zaphod fell through the blue magic time chute of space.

"YOU ARE NOT SUPPOSED TO BE HERE," boomed a commanding voice.

"The hell I ain't! I have to get back to Em!" Kyle yelled back.

Thunder rumbled in response. Just then, his body stopped. Instead of dropping down, his body shot up as fast as the speed of light. His body met a new set of clouds—pure white clouds, soaring through its soft mist. The mist sprayed him with restoring powers, refreshing his mind and spirit.

Then, with another hard yank, Kyle crashed against warm, hard ground. His body rolled every which way until he stopped.

"Fu…" he began to say, grimacing.

Then suddenly his mind was muddled. When he tried to say the word, the F word… there was a void in his mind. He couldn't even *think* of the word.

Groaning, Kyle opened his eyes to nothing but a white blur. It was so da… It was so bright that he had to squint.

Guess I have to have a clean mind as well as a clean mouth, wherever I am.

"Don't try and open your eyes fully yet," said a musical male voice. "Let me adjust them first."

A magical peace fell upon him, streaming over his body and running through his soul. Kyle's eyes tingled with a weird sense of delight.

"Now you can open them," said the soft voice.

As he did, Kyle saw a beauty that he had never known before, other than Emerald, of course. He gasped in wonder and pure awe. The land, the skies, the rolling hills, as far as the eye could see, there was color that he couldn't even describe, had ever seen before on Earth. A gleaming crystal city flourished with millions of palaces in the distance. Rolling hills of vividly colorful flowers swayed in the gentle breeze, while intense green forests ran off to one side. A peaceful river ran by him, coming from the direction of the city. The path below him was made of the purest gold, refined so bright Kyle began to tear up from the radiance. A feeling of peace flowed through his heart, and music could be heard softly throughout, as if all the plants, hills, city, and its souls sang with their life force.

Above him was a spirit. But this spirit was solid in form. The spirit had male features and was clothed in green garments, with glowing pale skin and vivid green hair and eyes. Six wings spread out behind his back, all in forest-green colors.

Kyle looked down at his body. It wasn't faded anymore, but restored and solid.

"Where am I?" Kyle asked.

"We are at the gates of paradise," the green spirit answered in his musical voice.

"Paradise? You mean I'm in heaven?" Kyle asked in disbelief.

"Yes."

Kyle jumped to his feet, looking all around in alarm.

"Did I die?"

"No. You have not died. Yet."

His time travel hadn't worked. Why hadn't it worked?

Kyle neared the spirit, trembling. "Then why am I here? Why did I not travel back in time?"

"That is a matter for the God of Light to answer, not for a mere servant like me," said the spirit. "Come, I will take you to him."

The God of Light? Kyle shuddered, thinking about how dirty he had been throughout his life. Throughout both lives, actually. What would the God of Light say? Condemn him? Tell him he was nothing more than a piece of sh… He couldn't even think of cursing in this dimension. He knew the God of Light could hear his every thought.

I wonder what dimension this place exists in? Kyle thought back about several conversations he'd heard the yellow priests discuss in the World Sectors during his life as Rubius. Some argued there were seven dimensions, others said ten; both numbers were considered perfect. What Kyle never had understood as Rubius was that if the numbers seven and ten were considered perfect holy numbers, why were there only six colors?

Kyle continued to dwell on these thoughts as the green spirit led him down the golden path. He couldn't help but take in the awesome beauty of the place. He could see why people wanted to come here. His heart felt restored, and his spirit renewed, and all the pain and suffering was nullified in a place like this.

It was absolutely awesome.

They neared the city gates and stood outside. The green spirit turned to him, then spoke. "You are the first human in several thousand years to enter these gates."

Kyle wanted to say something funny or sarcastic, but nothing would come out of his mouth. His heart wouldn't allow it in this place. Instead, he remained silent, following the green spirit.

They passed through many gates, each one being made from a different gemstone, as if each gate had been carved from the biggest gemstone that ever existed, whittled into the shape of a gate that surrounded the city. Twelve gates in total they passed through. He also noticed that the river at the entrance to paradise flowed through the city, leading into the very heart of it. The end of the river led to a center tower bathed in pure white light.

They walked through the city toward the tower, passing by a multitude of spirits in different colors. Some were in reds, some in violets, others in blues, and so on. He even saw spirits in other colors that did not exist on Earth.

"What colors are those?" Kyle asked the green spirit, pointing to the unknown colors.

"Those are colors that the God of Light made specifically for the heavens, and not for the human eye. I have given you a special vision of power while you are here so that you may view all that is before you. That way your mind doesn't get confused or drive you to the brink of insanity. If I hadn't, you would have lost your mind by now."

"I suppose that wouldn't be a good thing," Kyle commented nervously.

"There are colors that the God of Light has determined will make their way into the Spectrum of Magic at some point in time, but as of right now, He determined six colors to equal complete holiness, though it said it might be changed to seven at a predetermined time in the future of Earth."

"When will that be?" Kyle asked, thinking back to the numbers seven or ten.

"Only the God of Light knows that."

A new color of magic on Earth? That would be something...

"You know, the priests on Earth think seven or ten are holy numbers."

"In a way, they are correct, considering seven colors are in the works to complete the spectrum. But in their own thinking, they perceive white as a seventh color, so I can see why they would think that."

"What about ten?"

The spirit smiled at him. "That is not my place to discuss that any further."

Kyle wanted to press the spirit more, but he decided against it, knowing that the spirit wouldn't change his stance on sharing information.

The two of them neared the white tower. The light shining off it burned Kyle's eyes; it was so intense that he had to shut them. He felt a gentle flow of power over him, settling once again on his eyes.

"Please, you are okay to open them once again."

Prismatic colors filled his eyes as they entered the white castle, which gleamed with pure white light. Truth filled his heart, and Kyle was overwhelmed by the power the light radiated. They entered the throne room, and the green spirit fell to his knees. Kyle looked up at what the green spirit looked at, and saw Him.

The God of Light.

The God of Light's face radiated with pure white light. His eyes were fire, and his hair and beard were snowy white, both long and flowing. His feet were bronzed from the fires, and below him was a sea of glass. Surrounding him was a halo of rainbow power, its brilliance burning Kyle's eyes. He was seated on a throne of gold encrusted with gems of every color on Earth.

It was as if the secrets of Kyle's heart were laid bare and exposed in the room, and suddenly, Kyle felt insignificant. He fell to his knees, overwhelmed by the greatness before him.

"Rubius," the God of Light said.

"I know you are God and all, but could you call me Kyle?" Kyle said, his voice shaking. "After all, that was who I was originally. Or still am."

"If that is what you would like," the thunderous voice echoed.

Kyle felt the roaring power from the voice and felt the need to confess everything. It was as if the voice demanded truth from his heart.

"I… I haven't always been the best of person," Kyle started. "In fact, I really enjoyed the things that the earth had to offer. Lots of drinking, drugs at one point, women… that is, until Em, of course, getting into fights… I liked it all…"

"I know," the God of Light said, His voice the sound of a trumpet. "No need to confess. You are not here to be judged. Not yet."

"Then why am I here? Why couldn't I go back in time to Emerald? If you knew how much I love her, you would understand why I need to be with her."

Kyle stopped. He'd said *love*. Kyle had never said love on Earth. He came close to confessing his love for Emerald to Geeta once, but he'd never actually said the word. But here, it couldn't be helped. He couldn't hide the truth, not from God.

"You are not allowed to go back to your old life," the God of Light rumbled.

"What do you mean not allowed?" Kyle rose, anger surging in him.

"My will is done. I answered Emerald's prayer to keep you alive, and granted your rebirth with her magic. I have done more than enough for you, giving you a chance at a new life to right your wrongs."

Kyle couldn't believe it. He couldn't go back? That was unacceptable.

"Excuse me, God, but living a life without Em is not worth living!" Kyle said sharply. "Don't you understand? I have been searching for her my whole life as Rubius, and yet you say I can never go back to her? What kind of god are you? Is this some kind of cruel joke?"

Kyle realized he was being rude, but it was the truth, and he was *angry*.

"Kyle, you don't see the overall picture, whereas I see everything that is and is to come. It is not for you, a human soul, to understand my decisions."

"Well, I don't like it at all," Kyle said, flustered. "I mean, how can I go back and live my life as Rubius, knowing that Emerald is waiting for me?"

"Kyle," the God of Light said. Rumblings sounded from under the glass, sending Kyle stumbling to the floor. The spirits all looked at him curiously. "I *cannot* allow you to go back. If I grant your request, a great number of people will perish." His eyes burned intensely, piercing right through Kyle's soul. "Can you handle the weight of many people of Earth dying for your foolish desire?"

"I can!"

"Spoken like a true human," He said, His voice echoing in the throne room.

Kyle fell to his knees. "Please, send me back! You want me to stop drinking? Cursing? I will! Just send me back!" he begged.

"You will go back to being Rubius. There is much danger in that time, and you can do much good there. Elyathi must be stopped. As of right now, her dark heart remains unchecked. If you were sent back as Kyle Trancer, you would not do the world any good."

"But I would! I would protect Emerald with everything I have. Doesn't that count for something?"

God remained silent, piercing Kyle's heart with His fiery eyes.

"Please…" Kyle whispered. His heart hurt, and his head was spinning. "Please, God… I know I am not the best example, but please…"

"I have spoken. Green Spirit, please show him beyond the gates so he can return to Earth."

Green Spirit bowed, while Kyle stared at every spirit, including the God of Light, incredulously. The God of Light remained silent, nodding to Kyle. Kyle bowed, fury filling his heart.

As they were about to exit the room, the God of Light called out. "You have the power to do great good. Don't waste what I have given you and pursue your frivolous pleasures instead."

He meant Emerald. Emerald was not a frivolous pleasure. She was everything to him!

"Don't worry, I don't plan on it," Kyle muttered to himself as he was led by the green spirit out of the temple.

They walked through the bright prismatic city, his heart heavy with hurt. Music that softened his spirit played melodiously, but he didn't feel like giving in to its joy. What God would do this? Allow him to have his old memories, dreams of Emerald, have her within reach, but not be able to actually see her ever again? His heart was broken. And he couldn't do a thing about it.

"I don't believe this…" Kyle muttered. He didn't mean to say it out loud, but it came out anyway.

"None of us understand the God of Light's will, but in the end, you will see that His plan is perfect by design, and He saves you from hurt and pain," Green Spirit said.

"Well, I don't like it one bit."

"I don't think any human does, but ultimately, they come to an understanding."

Kyle couldn't imagine living his life without Emerald and being free of pain. It already felt like someone had stabbed him in the heart and twisted it until his soul was unrecognizable. His stomach felt weak, and all he wanted in his heart was Emerald. Just to hold her, touch her, like they had in his dream, in that strange dimensional plane of existence.

They came upon the edge of the paradise world, at an abrupt cliff that ended at red-brown clouds below the edge of the world. In front of him was a golden gate with a glowing blue portal, swirling with energy and magic.

"What's below the clouds? Earth?" Kyle asked, eyeing the dark clouds.

"It is the where the weeping spirits lie, where darkness reigns in the depths of the earth."

Kyle looked down at the edge, his stomach lurching at the height from where he stood. He glanced at the portal.

"Good wishes to you, Kyle. Or should I say Rubius? May the God of Light bless the rest of your days."

"Thanks, but I don't feel like well wishes," Kyle said truthfully.

"Do not be down of heart. If it is love you seek, there are many spirits waiting for affection in your current time."

I don't want anyone else, he thought bitterly.

The green spirit backed away, then stood waiting for him to step through the portal.

I can't accept my fate. What kind of soul mate am I if I just go back to being Rubius? He felt the anger run through him again. *I can't let Em live a life without me, and me without her. We are made for each other.*

His heart burned, knowing the truth of it. She was his complement, and they were meant for each other. And it was as true now as it was back in his past life. His spirit yearned for her. If God Himself wouldn't grant his request…

An idea struck him. Yes. It was the only way.

Looking back at the green spirit one last time, he called out, "Tell God that I am sorry."

The spirit gasped as Kyle ran. He ran hard and furious. At the edge, he jumped off the cliff.

Paradise quickly evaporated from around him, morphing into smoky red clouds as he fell endlessly. He fell and fell, plummeting to the depths. Smoke filled his lungs, and Kyle choked, gasping for breath. He continued to fight for air, but the atmosphere was nothing but smoke and sulfur, thickening moment by moment.

Red turned to brown, then all turned to black. The smoke thickened, and the air became icy.

Pure darkness was all around him.

And he kept falling.

Eternally falling.

CHAPTER 72

GREEN

Emerald sat in the darkness of the labyrinth, embracing its loneliness. The maze had returned again, all the stairs and spikes. They had disappeared when she saw Kyle, when she had touched his lips, tasted his life…

She had kissed him, felt his touch, his embrace.

Then, in the depths of this world, Emerald had found him within his memories of Arcadia. She had made love to him, and they were finally reunited. Tears streamed down her face as Emerald embraced the stone platform in the labyrinth, as if it were Kyle himself.

Where did he go?

They made love countless times within that plane of existence—in his mind within Arcadia. And after all of their lovemaking, Emerald had fallen asleep in his arms, not wanting to leave. Kyle was alive in her dreams; he said that he had been searching for her his whole life. And if this was where Emerald found his soul, within this strange plane of existence, this was where she belonged.

But when her spirit awoke from that special place, the place where they had entwined their hearts and souls, Kyle was no longer there, and she was in the maze once again.

She lost him. Kyle was gone.

She had lost him.

More tears kept coming, pooling around her on the cold stone platform. She had been crying for hours. Or had it been days? Or had it been years? In this maze, time was endless. How could one put a measurement on eternity, or within one's mind?

Kyle... where did you go?

Emerald's eyes welled with tears again. Her heart ached with pain. His soul had been on this very plane of existence, somewhere in this maze. But now it seemed detached, void...

Gone. Kyle's soul was gone. Emerald could no longer detect his presence. That thought terrified Emerald.

More time passed as she cried, memories with Kyle replaying in her head. She thought of her dreams with him, and her waking fantasies, ones that never came to pass. They would never come to pass.

Emerald screamed. The walls of the maze echoed her screams and cries. The stairs shook, the spikes crumbled.

The maze was falling apart. All was crumbling before her eyes. And it was going to collapse.

She didn't care...

Kyle was gone. His soul was gone.

CHAPTER 73

RED

Darkness. Pure fucking black. No, blacker than black. No shadows, no light.

The foulest smells of shit, decay, and death lingered in Kyle's nose as he lay upon icy, damp dirt. His fingers were caked with soil, and it was stuck underneath his fingernails. Goosebumps prickled his skin as he shivered violently from the hellish cold.

Kyle peered into the deep darkness, his whole body tense from the immense pain wracking his body from the fall. He closed his eyes, and there was no damn difference because of how damned dark it was. It was almost darker with his eyes open than shut. In the darkness he could *feel* torment and anguish. It was as if a million souls cried out from their lost hopes, dreams, and sorrow. Their silent cries deafened him, and as their sadness seeped into his soul, his spirit hurt deeply.

I'm in a nightmare, he thought. *A literal, fucking nightmare.*

When he decided to jump into the pits of hell, Kyle hadn't really thought about what hell was really like. He just expected he'd be able to march his ass up to the Lord of Darkness and make a deal with him. But this? He couldn't even see in this shit.

Kyle shivered hard, tucking his hands under his armpits.

I gotta fucking find that Lord of Darkness or whatever the hell his name is before I freeze my balls off.

The most rancid smell wafted into his nose. It was a combination of someone having the worst diarrhea after a spicy meal, vomit from three bottles of whiskey, and a dead guy who had been rotting in a back alley of Arcadia. Kyle jerked his head to the side, then vomited in the darkness, retching up everything he had. He was pretty sure he lost a lung in there. His body felt achy, like he had the flu, making his bones feel weak.

Groaning from the pain from the fall, the weakness from vomiting, and the shitty smells, Kyle struggled to sit up, but his limbs were immobile. It was as if he had no control or function over them. Within the darkness, he saw shadows, or outlines of shadows… if that even made sense. They were outlines, almost like invisible beings or spirits lurking in his presence.

Kyle tried to sit up once again, but a dark spirit hovered close above. Somehow, that was the motherfucker keeping him bound up and immobile.

"Listen, I need to talk to the big guy down here," Kyle said, not sure if the spirit would understand.

Suddenly, his body was wracked with pain, and he clenched his teeth.

"Did you hear what I said? I *have* to talk to the Lord of Darkness!"

The spirit floated weightlessly above him, sending him hard, vibrating waves of pain throughout his body and soul.

"Come the fuck on!" Kyle shouted as he writhed in pain. Clenching his jaw and closing his eyes, he tried to think.

Em… I have to see Em again!

He saw her eyes in his mind, as clear as the light itself. He had to get to her. Kyle searched deep within his life force, the color adjacent to his own. The violet flooded his veins, burning with rage and hatred for the spirit holding him hostage. The power swelled so much that he thought he was going to explode.

Opening his eyes, he burst with violet magic, and the dark spirit flew back into the darkness. His chest and his arms felt lighter, and he could move again. Kyle waited for a moment to see if the spirit would return, or worse, bring friends to torment him. As he waited, a faint glow began radiating from the green gemstone that hung heavy around his neck. The light was faint, but it was enough to see faintly in front of him. He hadn't noticed the glow when he landed in this hellhole. Was it when he thought of Emerald that the gem lit up?

It has to be, he thought. *It lit up when I talked to the elders about Em too.*

Determining that the spirit wouldn't return, Kyle managed to crawl up onto his arms and knees. Wet dirt squished through his fingers, but it no longer felt like wet dirt; it was thick and coagulated. He rubbed his fingers together, trying to figure out what it was, using the soft green light. It felt disgusting as fuck, like congealed fat from a greasy breakfast.

Then he realized what it was. Blood. Dirt mixed with blood.

What in the everlasting fuck? He quickly wiped his hands on the back of his jacket. *I gotta get my ass out of here.*

Kyle started to move, realizing that he was in some kind of dirt hallway. As he traveled down the corridor, he felt the cold radiating through his boots from the stones and frozen earth underneath him. He came to the end of the corridor, or so he thought, then squinted in the green light to study his whereabouts. Reaching out in front of him, his hand met a cinder block wall with dirt caked in between the cracks, like a basement cellar back in the wastelands.

Trying to get a better look at the wall, he summoned a small bright-red flame. Instantly, red outlines formed imagery around him. He was definitely in an underground room with a long brick wall running in front and behind him. Under his feet, streaming liquid flowed over the stones, and he jerked in alarm at the sight. It was the blood he had felt earlier.

Looking around him, he noticed the corridor split. Choosing a direction, he made his way down the next tunnel, his right hand resting on the wall, his red magical flame still burning in his left. As he moved forward, the air changed, making it heavier in his lungs and harder to breathe. He pushed himself farther and farther, not caring about the lack of air because dammit, he had to find a way out.

All of a sudden, there was no more tunnel. It was a dead end.

"What the hell?" he cursed loudly, pounding his hand angrily against the wall. It was a stupid-ass thing to do, because now his hand hurt like a bitch.

Turning back around, Kyle went back the way he came, but this time he went down the other direction of the corridor he hadn't traveled. He hit another dead end. Panic set in as Kyle waved his flame around furiously, desperate to find an exit.

There was none. This was fucking it. Only three corridors. He was buried alive in an underground room. Kyle yelled in frustration, long and hard, filling his hand with more fire, then hurling the flame at the dead end.

The fire glimmered on the wall for a moment, then died out, leaving him in darkness. *This can't be happening. It's not supposed to be like this.*

He bashed the wall violently. "Em, I'm sorry I'm such a fucking idiot!" he yelled.

God, his heart hurt hard. He knew who he truly was now. He remembered everything. And here he was, finally on the way back to see the love of his life and dreams, and then God Himself denied him. It was one big fucking cruel joke. And now, here he was, buried in hell somewhere.

His last hope of returning to Em was dead. Because if God said no, there was no one else with the power to help him besides Death himself.

"Em…" he whispered in the darkness, "I promise I will find a way."

The green jewel lit up again, this time brighter.

There was a sudden peace in his heart filling his void, renewing his spirit.

It was Emerald's life force.

"I'm coming back," Kyle whispered, clutching the amulet. "I will do whatever the fuck it takes, but I'm coming."

Kyle's heart hammered at the thought of not seeing Emerald again. He wasn't going to let that fucking happen. He was *going* to go back to her. Seeing the dirt and cinder block walls before him renewed his anger all over again. Furious, Kyle started ripping his fingers through the cracks of the wall, digging out the dirt, then trying to budge the cinder blocks. He managed to yank a brick out and hurled it to the floor. Sweat beaded on his brow, and his jacket became soaked. Yanking the clasps free, the jacket hung open to cool his chest while he worked to yank the wall apart, brick by brick. He was short of breath, as there was little oxygen in the room, and he was light-headed.

I better get the fuck out of here, and fast.

As he pulled several more bricks free, blood began oozing from the dirt. Startled by the seeping blood, Kyle jumped back, then watched with disgust as the blood continued to bleed from the wall. He resumed his digging, faster and faster, alarmed that he was going to be trapped in the room filled with blood. He was losing more oxygen, his head felt fuzzy, and now there were stars in his vision.

Pushing aside his light-headedness, Kyle kept digging and digging, but the earth kept flowing with blood, and he was getting nowhere.

"No!" he screamed.

His magic burned inside of him with pure frustration, running like stone through his veins. Kyle hit the wall hard once again in frustration, but this time, he released the red magic that burned in his inner being.

The walls shook and the earth rumbled underneath him as he unleashed a powerful red earthquake. More blood came, this time at a much more rapid pace.

"Fucking *no*!"

His voice echoed the word *no* off the stones, but his ears caught a strange pitch from one of the stones behind him. Turning around to inspect the stones, he carefully ran his hand across solid dirt. He kept feeling until he found the source of the strange echoing pitch.

Toward the back of the room, a set of stone steps led into a tunnel. It was a way out of the damned cellar.

Why the hell didn't I see this earlier?

With no time to wonder about the answer, Kyle squeezed inside the tunnel. Blood flowed down the steps as he made his way up, reaching the top of the stairs. The tunnel opened up, and air flowed around him, making it easier to breathe.

Kyle stumbled against a large object in the tunnel, catching himself mid-fall. Finding his balance, he summoned red fire into his hand once again, trying to take in his surroundings.

The red light shone upon thousands of dead bodies scattered all across the tunnel. The scene was straight out of a horror broadcast.

"Oh fuck!" he exclaimed, jumping back. He nearly ate it on a dead man's shoulder right next to his foot, the man's lifeless eyes staring right though Kyle and into his soul. Blood poured out of the dead man's mouth like a river. In fact, all of the bodies had blood flowing from their mouths, like an eternal clusterfuck of vomit and blood. Their bodies were badly bruised, cut, maimed, and decayed. But somehow, the blood was fresh.

This is beyond fucked up.

Then their eyes shot to him, as if they'd heard his thoughts. Terror seized him. He took a step back. More blood poured out of them, covering the dirt where Kyle stood. Within the boundary of his burning red light, Kyle saw the outlines of millions of dark spirits surrounding him from above.

Those were their bodies that lay dead on the ground. And they were *pissed.*

The dark spirits began to hover around him, sending him bad vibes.

"Look, I'm just passing through," Kyle managed to say. He grimaced as his heart thundered in his ears, overwhelmed from the evil that radiated from the multitude of spirits. "Believe me, I don't want to be here as much as you don't want me to."

Light... they whispered in his mind.

"How about this: You stay up there, I stay down here. We both can be happy that way," Kyle said, taking another step back.

Light... They hovered closer, moving in on him.

"Look, guys, I prefer if you would stay away from me. Far away. As much as possible."

His red flame started to dim. Kyle looked to his hand; his magical flame was being sucked away by the spirits. A steady stream of red magic left his hand and wafted to their dark souls. They began whispering things he couldn't understand. The feeling of their voices radiated agony, pain, sorrow, and eternal damnation. Whatever they said in their language, it made his heart hurt and his life force weak.

And they kept coming.

More strange mutterings. Words of sorrow. They sent a wave of anguish straight through Kyle's soul. Suddenly, Kyle knew what they were saying in their fucked-up language. Their words were overwhelming, but their thoughts and words were true. Kyle could no longer take it, shedding a single tear.

You are damned, they uttered.

"The hell I am!"

Love has no place here.

"Fuck you all to hell, motherfuckers!" Kyle cried, cursing them. "Just because you are fucked, sure as hell doesn't mean I am!"

Infuriated by their words, Kyle summoned as much anger as he could, fueling the flame in his hand. Reaching his fiery hand upward, he released the flames, the hellish red fires pouring out across them with his fury. The spirits shrieked in pain as he funneled more flames, this time on the bodies that were scattered around him.

Those bodies caught fire while the spirits that floated above burned brightly. It now looked like what everyone envisioned Hell to be—bodies burning up with massive fires engulfing everything.

With not a moment to lose, Kyle hurried through the tunnel, coming across another set of stone steps, running up them. At the top was a strange, eerie red glow. Reaching the end of the staircase, Kyle emerged into another part of Hell, or so he assumed. Before him was an expansive cavern of cool gray stone. Giant stalactites covered the tops of the cave, with large boulders scattered throughout on the ground. Between the boulders was a rocky path that led down into an eerie crimson glow far off in the cavern's horizon.

Screams erupted from the cave, echoing around him and directly into his heart. The spirits were angry that he still had a body, and they longed for theirs. Kyle grimaced at the pain in the screams, but as quick as they came, the screams were gone, replaced by a strange noise that resembled a crackling bonfire. A wave of heat came rushing in, removing the bone chill that had settled within his body, replacing it with an intense, scorching heat. His skin blistered just from the air. Normally, heat never bothered him, but this heat was otherworldly and unnatural.

The far-off reddish glow lit a path under his feet, paving a way for him. With no better option in mind, Kyle quickly followed the cavern's path, and it swirled down into the depths of the earth. The farther down he went, the brighter the reds became, mixed with glowing hot oranges and yellows and some violets. But the colors… they seemed all *wrong*, as if they had been severely tampered with.

Then he stopped.

Lakes of hellfire came into view, engulfing chained souls and decayed bodies that endured their eternal torture. Boiling pools of blood mixed with fire were spread throughout the giant cavern, with souls burning and screaming. Dark souls similar to what Kyle saw earlier were in charge of the torture, like overseers. They, too, were chained to the chasm, still able to carry out their vileness upon the other souls sent to Hell.

Kyle felt terribly sick with fear, vomiting into one of the pools of fire.

"This isn't the ring of Hell for that kind of thing," hissed a dark spirit.

"Ring of hell?" Kyle shook, trying to get a look at the thing that spoke. He couldn't define its shape, nor did it register to his eyes; he felt terrible just being close to him.

"There is a ring of Hell filled with all of the vomit of sins, but it is not here."

"Sorry… whatever you are. I couldn't help it," Kyle managed as the spirit neared him. "I need to find the Lord of Darkness. Then, just between you and me, I need to get the hell out of here."

The spirit laughed, amused at his statement. "We will see what the Dark

Lord has to say about that. Follow the path all the way to the end. You will find him there."

"Thanks, man... I think," Kyle said, unsure, turning away from the spirit. The longer he stood in the presence of the spirit, the sicker he felt, wanting to vomit all over again. He had to keep moving.

Turning away from the spirit, Kyle hurried down the path, descending further into the bowels of Hell. Hotter and hotter the heat and the flames became on each side of the path, but he did what he could to ignore it. He had to find the Lord of Darkness. It had to the be only way to get back to Emerald.

As Kyle ran, he noticed his surroundings changing slightly, and he knew that he was in a different "ring of Hell," with different sets of torture for the souls. The screams and sounds were just... *different.* He couldn't fucking look, because if he did, he knew what *his* eternal punishments would be from his past transgressions, and whether he'd be sent to Hell in the afterlife, he just didn't want to know at this point. All he saw in his mind was holding on to Emerald once again in his arms and kissing her divine lips.

Just when he felt like his body was going to collapse from all the pain he'd witnessed and the agony that seeped into his soul, Kyle caught a horrifying glimpse of a figure in the distance.

The Lord of Darkness.

Kyle gasped, nearing fainting at the sight.

There, on a great throne constructed of decayed human flesh, skin, and bone all sewn together, sat a large spirit. The Dark Lord had the body of a strong, powerful man. He was six times the size of any human, with grayish skin and an undertone of red-violet. Long black horns of that like an ox crowned his head.

Kyle wanted to puke all over again at the sight. Pulling himself together, Kyle took a deep breath, then managed to continue down the path. As he neared the throne, he saw the Lord of Darkness in much greater detail. The Dark Lord's eyes burned of the eternal damned fires, and he had fangs among his teeth, all rotting and yellow. Long black nails curled over the Dark Lord's elongated fingertips, and his feet resembled hooves of a wild animal, his ears like an ox. The smell of the Dark Lord clung to him like an overwhelming perfume—the smell of pure death and decay. The Dark Lord's entire body except his face was wrapped in chains, while his joints were shackled, his neck and arms all locked to his decaying throne.

The overwhelming darkness that radiated from the Dark Lord's soul almost caused Kyle to pass out, but instead, Kyle slumped down to his knees. He bit his lip, trying to hold down his puke.

"I would appreciate if you do not vomit in front of me."

Kyle choked back his bile, slowly rising back to his feet. "Believe me, I'm really trying not to," he said, clearing his throat.

The Dark Lord laughed, holding out his hand. A dark spirit came out of nowhere, handing him a goblet of red liquid.

"Drink, human?"

"No thanks, I don't think I'm feeling up to it at the moment," Kyle said. He had a feeling that it was blood from the tortured souls' bodies from one of the rings of Hell, and not Hell's finest wine. Again, another wave of nausea hit him, and he tried not to puke at the thought.

"So, you've managed to crawl your way through my domain, in the hopes of satisfying your desires for one woman," the Lord of Darkness said. It wasn't a question.

"Sounds about right." Kyle would have argued that he did a hell of a lot more than crawling, but this wasn't the time for details.

"Queen Emerald. Such a *pure* soul, uncorrupted by darkness." The Dark Lord took a drink, his black fingernails curling around the goblet's stem. "Men like you are not meant for pure souls like her."

"Not true!" Kyle shot back.

"What does your dark, troubled heart have in harmony with purity? Darkness and light are not made to be together. Even the God of Light made sure to split them, never to embrace one another."

"Well, I beg to differ, Lord of… whatever you call yourself. Our life forces, they were made for each other. If what you said were true, then we wouldn't be complements. And if that were so, then Em wouldn't have been able to summon the full power of the Spectrum of Magic—pure white magic—when kicking that sorceress's ass while I was in spirit form… before I entered the damn lifestream and ended up as a fucking new person!"

A dark wave of energy blew through Kyle, and he immediately understood that the Dark Lord didn't like the mention of the white magic.

"You have to understand," Kyle backpedaled a tad, "that I would do anything to see her again. To hold her against me…" He met the Dark Lord's hellish eyes. Man, they freaked him the fuck out. "I would do *anything*."

"And so you have. Dared to meet me face-to-face in the hope that I will grant your request."

"Damn straight! The God of Light said that allowing me to be reborn in the future was sufficient enough. But I just can't accept that answer."

The Lord of Darkness took another drink from his chalice. "And you won't have to. I will send you back to her."

Kyle paused at his words. "Really?"

"Indeed. You have my word, Kyle Trancer."

"Just like that? No selling my soul to you? I mean, wouldn't that be something you would want?"

The Dark Lord laughed, the sound bellowing through the chasms. It rumbled so loud, shaking the earth, that all of Hell stopped for a second, startled, before they continued on with their cries and torture.

"Your soul is very tempting. But no, I have a different proposition for you."

Kyle sighed in relief. "Good. I was honestly a bit worried about that, giving my soul to you and all. But I would have done it, if I had to."

"I know. And that is why I will grant your request."

"Thank you."

"On one condition."

Kyle looked up at him slowly. "What do you want of *me*? I don't have much else to give, considering you don't want my soul."

"Do you see these chains? I have endured them since my fall from the heavens above. I cannot say how long I have been chained here, Kyle Trancer, for days and nights are eternal here. But I can say for certain that it has been since the beginning of time, just after my fall."

"That's a long-ass time. No offense."

"None taken." The Dark Lord smirked, eyeing him. "I was once a beautiful being in the heavens, more beautiful than your mind can comprehend. I had seen all the colors of light, all of them radiating around me with such immense power, such *beauty*, that I have not seen anything like that since."

Kyle eyed the Dark Lord as he said that, seriously doubting this dude could ever have been anything close to good-looking. He looked like a literal rotting heap of flesh.

"And since my descent from grace, I have not seen the true colors of magic with my turned spirit. Just as your human loins ache to be inside a woman, my soul aches to see the true beauty of color. I have seen muted colors in my presence here in these pits of darkness, but it is not the same as pure color. I want to see color. Pure color from your life force. That, Kyle Trancer, is what I request in trade for your return to see your love."

"Really? That's it? All I have to do is cast some magic for me to bust out of here?"

"Yes, that is what I desire," the Lord of Darkness took another bloody drink from his chalice. "My minions feel the same as I do. In fact, all of us spirits down here long for the power of color. We hunger for it." The Lord of Darkness paused, his fiery eyes casting a look upon Kyle, making him shudder. "Use your magic to battle your way out of here against my minions to the edge of this plane of existence, and I will grant you your request, allow you to leave this place to return to your lover back in time."

Kyle narrowed his eyes, giving him a half smile. "Battle my way through the rings of Hell? You bet your ass I will. Deal!"

"Then it is done!" The Dark Lord smiled, baring all of his rotten teeth. He clapped his hands for attention, bellowing with laughter as all of Hell rumbled.

Kyle trembled under the force of the Dark Lord's laugh. Hell rumbled once again, causing the earth to shift under his feet. The pools of hellfire bubbled and roared, flaming wildly. In the corner of Kyle's eye, he saw a legion of dark spirits heading toward him. There was a clanking of chains; each spirit was holding one.

And they were all fucking coming for him.

Kyle looked back at the Lord of Darkness sharply.

"You said I had to battle my way out of here!" Kyle yelled. "Now you wanna chain me to your ass?"

"I am the Lord of lies, nightmares, and sadness. Why do you think the heavens cast me to these pits? Besides, this will make it more enjoyable for me to spectate, *human*," the Lord of Darkness stated, laughing. "You see, I crave your soul just as much as color. I would be delighted to have you next to me, bound for all of eternity. The things I can do with the power of your life force."

Kyle looked over his shoulder again, seeing more chains swinging. Where the hell did all those chains even come from?

"You'd best hurry, Kyle Trancer, for if those chains are fully bound and locked to your body, your soul is *mine*."

Kyle whipped around, understanding the critical danger that was heading toward him. He was seriously fucked. Tapping into the magic that flowed adjacent in his life force, Kyle summoned the power of his orange magic, and he glowed mostly orange with a hint of red.

With raging power, copies of his body appeared, scattering all around in the crowd of spirits. In each of the false illusions, he sent part of his life force, distributing a piece of himself to them. Then he went invisible.

Hell rumbled again while the Lord of Darkness bellowed behind him, delighted by the burst of color coming from him. For a moment, the souls were confused where Kyle's real soul was, as was the point of planting a piece of his life force within the illusions. He summoned his red winds, still invisible from his adjacent magic. His body was enraptured by his red magic, levitating in the air, then started flying away from the Dark Lord's throne and his inner ring of Hell.

Suddenly, the dark spirits saw through his illusions and turned in his direction, swarming toward him, chains in hands. They had felt his red magic under the illusions.

Dammit!

Kyle narrowed his eyes, keeping his eyes focused on the way out of Hell while shedding his invisibility. Spirits came straight at him from the front, while others came from the sides, and others were right behind him, practically kissing his ass.

Chains swung wildly in his direction. Kyle dodged them as he flew by, narrowly missing them. The spirits hissed loudly, while others uttered curses in their dark language. There was a yank on his leg, then Kyle found himself swinging off course, flung into the cavern wall, smacking into it.

The noise of hordes of spirits swelled around him. Spirits as far as the eye could see came at him from every direction. Jumping to his feet, he clenched his jaw, then gathered his red winds. With a burst of red light, the bright crimson winds whirled around him. He funneled some into his hand, forming a swirling orb that expanded until it covered him entirely, like a protective elemental shell.

The spirits uttered sounds at the bright-red light, crying out in their dark language.

"Come at me, bitches!" Kyle taunted them.

The spirits hovered at the edge of his wind shell, and Kyle smirked. He channeled more of his life force in it, adding some of his violet magic to it. The power around him grew until he couldn't contain it any longer. With a giant burst of reddish-violet light, the power exploded, and the red winds ripped through the crowd of spirits, knocking them far back.

He had a clear path once again.

Filling his hands with more red wind, he churned it around his feet, then he made a mad dash to the path. Kyle ran furiously up the path, past several rings of Hell that he had passed by earlier. Screams erupted, with spirits joining the chase. With each circle of Hell he passed, more spirits followed, realizing what was happening.

As Kyle neared where he first landed, spirits appeared before him, blocking his path. Kyle threw out a hand, shaking and shifting the earth under him. A chunk of earth jutted out in front of him, creating a temporary barrier.

With a whack, he felt the sting of icy cold metal around his leg. A spirit had shackled his leg. With a dark vibration, power radiated from the chain, and his spirit was weakened. Another chain ensnared him around his wrist before he knew it.

His power was draining from him, and his vision was fading. All he saw were dark spirits swirling around him, a multitude of chains coming for him.

"FUCK!" he yelled in frustration.

It was as if the spirits only were temporarily stunned by his magic. He had nowhere near the power he needed to escape every spirit coming at him.

Then it hit him.

He couldn't fucking leave Hell. The Lord of Darkness said he would *allow* Kyle to leave Hell if he made it to the edge. But the Dark Lord hadn't said he would personally *send* him out of Hell. He had to figure that out himself.

But how? The Lord of Darkness admitted to seeing some color in Hell, but what made him fall from the heavens?

White light.

Kyle's heart sank, knowing he'd doomed himself. He couldn't summon white light without Em. But the thought of Emerald made the jewel glow around his neck. The chains weakened him further.

"EM!" he screamed.

The spirits swarmed him. He kept blasting them, but they kept coming. And coming. And coming…

***

As the labyrinth continued to collapse all around her, Emerald suddenly heard Kyle's yells echoing loudly, rocking the maze as his cries reverberated straight into her soul.

Kyle!

He was in danger. He needed her, and needed her *now*. Her spirit felt it deep within. She had to get to him.

"Kyle! I'm coming!" Emerald screamed, getting to her feet. She darted up the nearest stairs, and it crumbled under her feet as she ran. Everything was about to collapse.

After running up a few more sets of stairs, Kyle's voice roared again, this time with such force that many of the labyrinth's stairs and spikes plummeted to the dark pits below. As the maze continued to crumble, Emerald looked around desperately, trying to see exactly where his voice was coming from.

Another shout.

It was coming from below.

Emerald shifted her eyes hastily, peering into the darkness below the stairs as rocky debris fell into the depths. Deep within that darkness, Emerald saw an eerie glow from within the void, almost like black pool of ice, and yet it was not frozen. Instead, it burned with energy, sparkling with magical flecks of black and azure. Through the streaming, flowing liquid magic, Emerald saw an expansive world filled with chaos.

This world was layered, with each dimensional layer going far into the earth. It was as if she could see one plane of existence, but also many dimensions all at once, as if light itself was split through a crystal, forming brackets of color. A wave of pain hit her, and she felt all the sadness and angst and hurt and sorrow radiating from that other dimension. Souls in torment were suffering different punishments—burning, beating, raping, vomiting, mutilation…

And she felt a part of her spirit down below with them.

Closing her eyes to try to drown out the sounds of the maze collapsing,

Emerald focused on that feeling—a fragment of her life force that called out to her. Her fragment. She could feel it in the clutches of…

Kyle!

Her eyes shot open, and Emerald saw that glimpse of green light coming from below. Once she saw that, Kyle appeared behind the dimension, bathed in red magic. A mass of dark spirits surrounded him, burning with fury, loathing, and hatred, closing in on him, soul chains in their hands.

Her heart hammered in her chest. He would be bound in Hell for all eternity… She was not going to let the Lord of Darkness take him.

The thought of Emerald using her blue dimensional magic made her anxious. She'd only used it a handful of times, and she still wasn't that practiced at it. And porting to Hell itself? Would she be able to do it?

She had to try. The dream was only possible through her blue dimensional magic. She could do this. Filling her soul with as much of it as her spirit could hold, Emerald let it flow through her body, filling it every inch of her being.

Please, take me to him! she cried out to the magic. *I can't lose him again!*

Her spirit body began to glow brightly with greenish-blue magic. It swirled around her. Closing her eyes, Emerald leapt off the platform, releasing her magic.

Winds ripped through her hair, and her dress flew wildly around her, whipping her face and body. Power burst through her spirit, causing her to cry out in pain. But it didn't matter. She had to get to Kyle before it was too late.

She opened her eyes as she fell, pushing the hair out of her face. Greenish-blue magic burned all around her with such intensity that it became a hot white in her eyes, blinding her.

As Emerald's feet made contact with the barrier to the other dimension, her greenish-blue magic shifted to pure blue for a moment, blasting a hole through the barrier and allowing her spirit to drop into the pits of Hell.

Her body burned bright green, the most vibrant green Emerald had ever seen in all her life. With a loud roar, the world shook violently.

***

A big blast of blue light tore through Hell, and a solid bright-green light followed, causing all the spirits to freeze.

Emerald! Her spirit had heard him! Emerald's spirit was in that light, glowing and radiating a hot white-green. Kyle's heart soared at the sight.

"*What is this?*" roared the Lord of Darkness with such hatred and wrath that all the spirits cowered as one. "How dare you enter *my* domain!"

The Dark Lord was pissed. *Good. That motherfucker is about to get his ass served.*

"Kyle!" Emerald called out from within the radiant green light.

"Em! You're here!" Kyle called back to her.

"I heard you call my name!"

The blasting beam of light faded, revealing Emerald's spirit alone, glistening with green magic.

"Don't let him leave here alive! His life force is *mine*!" roared the Dark Lord, his voice echoing throughout Hell.

"I won't let you have him!" Emerald cried, her voice as smooth as glass, clear as crystal, but strong as iron. Emerald's voice was angelic and pure. *God, she is so beautiful.*

"We will see about that, Queen Emerald of Arcadia!" roared the Dark Lord in reply. "You two will be my most favorite possessions when I am done with you. Kyle Trancer will be chained at my side for all eternity, with his lover right next to him!"

Hell shook again, and a horde of spirits flung their chains around him, ensnaring Kyle completely. He was so weak from fighting, but he wasn't ready to give up. The chain attached to him tugged hard, causing him to nearly stumble. The spirits wrapped more chains around him.

Kyle struggled, trying to freeze the chains with his red magic, but the dark metal absorbed his life force.

"You cannot—and will not—have him! I won't allow it!" Emerald firmly stated.

More chains wrapped around him, then he heard a clanking sound.

Fuck! They were going to connect him to the Dark Lord.

More hordes of spirits surrounded him, and soon all he could see was dark spirits and chains.

"Em!" Kyle screamed. A chain clunked hard against his head, and his vision blurred. "We have to…"

The words wouldn't come to him. He felt drained.

"Kyle!"

A rush of peace came over him, and his vision became clear once again. Green light embraced him, soaking into his body, healing his innermost being. Another wave of magic came over him like a gentle breeze, this time encasing his skin with protection with greenish-yellow power.

Kyle jumped up, whipping around to see Emerald. The chains already wrapped around him clanged.

The chains. Kyle sensed they weren't bound to the Dark Lord yet.

"Em!" Kyle yelled, "we have to complete the Spectrum of Magic. It's the only way out of this hellhole."

The Dark Lord roared from far below in the caverns, shaking all of Hell. "Soon those chains will be bound to me, and darkness shall prevail!"

"Light always defeats the darkness," Emerald called out in defiance. Her face was determined, and her spirit burned a glowing vibrant green. "Kyle, we can and will do this together. I believe in us."

"Hell yeah! Let's do this, Em!" Kyle yelled.

Another rush of green magic flowed over him, renewing his body and mind, restoring his power deep within his core. This was it. It was now or never.

Filling his body with violet magic, Kyle unleashed it against all the chains wrapped around his body. With a loud snap, he broke free, flinging them wildly to the ground. With another swoop of his hands, Kyle cast fire all over the spirits, while Emerald poured her life magic into them. It was as if Emerald had read his mind, because that was exactly what he needed.

"Suck my magic, assholes!" Kyle cursed at them.

Over and over again, Kyle unleashed the special soulfire that he and Emerald created, melting the spirits. They shrieked in their foul language.

"That's right, motherfuckers!" Kyle yelled at them, then shifted his focus to Emerald. "Em, now! Summon all your magic!"

A wash of healing came over him once again, mixed with protection and a shift in time. Closing his eyes, he pulled together every ounce of his life force.

Red. Violet. Orange. He summoned them all, and it burned his blood, radiating through his skin. A gentle, cool touch grazed his neck, sending a warm feeling cascading through him.

There, next to him, was Emerald's spirit, radiating with her power. She ran her glowing green spirit hand over his, their souls connecting. They were bathed in pure white light. She looked at him, and her lips parted into a longing, loving smile. Her eyes radiated with pure life, filling the void he had been missing his whole life.

God, he loved her so much.

"I love you, Kyle," her voice said within the light. "Come back to me."

"Em, I will never leave you ever again," he whispered.

They held their hands up, then silently, they released their white light. It shot out from them with a loud boom, disintegrating all the dark spirits around them. Then the white light shot up, creating a white portal.

From far behind them, Kyle could hear the Dark Lord roaring with fury, his chains rattling, making a horrendous screeching sound that made Kyle wince.

"You are doomed, Kyle Trancer! I will make sure of that!" the Lord of Darkness screamed. "For I am everywhere, in all things. You may leave this place, but you cannot escape the hold I have on the earthly world."

"We will see about that, fuck face!" Kyle looked to Emerald. "Let's get the hell out of here."

"Hold on to me," Emerald said. Her spirit form clasped onto his body, and he to her. Surprisingly, her spirit body had some weight, allowing him to hold her in his arms.

He was complete with her.

The white light wavered around them, and he felt his body being whisked away as fast as the speed of light, escaping the pits of Hell with the complement to his soul.

CHAPTER 74

Red

Peaceful sounds. A gentle breeze gliding over his body. Familiar sounds of vehicles. Transports… so many transports.

Kyle tried to move his body, but he was spent. A moment later, he felt little clawed feet hopping onto his back, tickling him. A squawk rang in his ear.

Zaphod…

A delicate, soft hand embraced his. A delightful, intimate smell of lavender lightly toyed with his senses.

Emerald. He was next to her.

Kyle's eyes shot open, rolling his head over to the side as Zaphod fluttered wildly in the corner of his vision. And there she was. Emerald, next to him, her hand in his.

He sucked in a breath, staring. She was more beautiful than he remembered, even in his dreams. Long green tresses framed her pale face. A soft pale-green nightgown clung to her figure, accentuating her womanly form as she lay in her sleep.

His heart soared at the sight of her. She was really there next to him. Kyle had never been one to believe in miracles, but this was a true fucking miracle. Of course, he did have to fight Heaven and Hell to get to her, so they'd earned this miracle.

As he continued to gaze in awe at her, Emerald's eyes slowly opened, as if waking from a peaceful sleep, revealing their green brilliance, causing his heart to flutter with adoration. Her eyes met his, and her soft pink lips parted in shock, trembling, with tears of joy welling in her eyes.

"Kyle?" she whispered. "Am I dreaming?"

He was overwhelmed with so many emotions that he didn't know what to say. He tried to form words, but nothing felt right.

Finally, the words came to him. "Em… I came back," he answered in a whisper. "I couldn't live my other life without you."

Emerald smiled brightly, then flung her arms around him in pure joy, gripping him tightly in a big hug, then she covered him in kisses.

"I've missed you so much," she said through kisses mixed with tears.

Kyle cradled the back of her head, running his fingers through her long locks of hair. Her tantalizing scent made his senses to go wild, and she kissed his firm lips once again, this time long and hard, stirring his insides with longing.

She let go slightly, her eyes looking away. "I'm sorry, Kyle," she whispered, trembling.

"For what?"

Emerald hesitated. "You died because of me," she said, her voice shaking. "I wasn't strong enough to fight the sorceress. I didn't have the power to stop myself."

Fresh tears formed in the corners of her eyes, and Kyle brushed the back of his hand across her cheek.

"Hey," Kyle said softly. "Hey."

Emerald looked up at him, guilt clouding her face.

He moved into her. "None of it was your fault. You hear me? None of it!"

"But I—"

"But nothing," Kyle said, kissing her forehead. "We all know the sorceress was behind it. Not you." *She was behind a lot fucking more than that,* Kyle thought darkly.

"I've just been feeling guilty about it this whole time."

"But there is no need to. Besides, I'm here now, right?" He smiled at her, and she did the same.

Suddenly, her face shifted down in an embarrassed and guilty manner. He heard her thoughts loud and clear with his violet magic. She was scared to tell him.

"I already know," he said softly.

"Kyle… the other one…"

Derek's child. Kyle's heart darkened at the thought. Especially after what the sorceress said.

That fucking witch.

Kyle pulled Emerald fully into his arms, resting her head on his chest while he kissed the top of her head and stroked her hair. "I know. And it doesn't change a thing. I will be there for you, and for them. Both of them, no matter what." He pulled her back slightly to look at her. "I love you Em, with every fiber of my being. I love you. And I always will. I will do everything I can to make you happy. I promise."

He had actually said it. The L word. Never in his life, *both* lives, had he verbalized it, but it was true. Emerald made him a different man. A *better* man.

"I love you, Kyle. I don't want to live another day without you."

"And you won't have to," he whispered, holding her close.

He brushed his lips against hers, the soft flesh he had dreamed of kissing for as long as he could remember. She answered his desire and kissed him back, the two of them entwined together. His heart quickened. He was finally back with her, and she was in his arms, where she belonged.

After their long embrace, they pulled apart, and a serious look came over Emerald. "Kyle, what are we going to do? I am a queen, in charge of a kingdom… still married to Derek."

"We'll figure something out," he said. He grabbed her again, holding her close. "Don't worry about it right now."

I am going to fucking pound the shit out of Derek. And if he ever came across that bitch-ass sorceress again, she wouldn't live to tell the tale.

"But what of my kingdom? There are things happening right now…"

"I will do whatever I have to do to keep you safe. Always. I promise." He touched her hair to soothe her. "This time it will be different. Together, we have the power to take on everyone and everything."

"I believe you," she whispered.

"Damn straight." He hugged her tightly. "Let's not think about anything right now. I just want to enjoy you." He smiled, and Emerald giggled.

He suddenly remembered something he had stuck in his jacket. Kyle sat up, rummaging around in his pocket while Emerald looked at him curiously. He pulled his hand out of his pocket and revealed the small flower that he picked—the flower that made him think of Emerald. It hung limply, nearly dried out as he presented it to her.

"I got this for you," Kyle said, then flushed with embarrassment. "Although, it's… not in the best condition. I promise it was in much better shape when I picked it."

Emerald giggled again, accepting it. She grasped it gently in her hands, then smiled. "I love it. I'll always keep it."

"You will?"

"Of course I will," Emerald said. "Because it's from you."

"They make terrible burritos, by the way."

She laughed, then held it gently to her heart before placing it delicately on her nightstand. "You'll have to tell me the story behind that comment."

At that moment, Elyathi popped into his mind. God. Should he even tell her? And then there was the High Court, working alongside her crazy-ass lunatic mother…

Later. Can't ruin the moment.

A squawk came from the corner of the room, and Kyle turned his head. "Come here, you stubborn feathery bastard!"

Zaphod flapped over to them, then landed next to him on the bed.

Emerald looked at the parrot curiously, then smiled. "I saw him in my dreams," she said. "Is this your pet?"

Kyle returned her smile. "Yeah, he was with me through thick and thin when I lived in the future."

"What's his name?"

He laughed. "Zaphod. I guess that name stuck with me in my new life too."

Emerald laughed too, and the bird whistled happily.

God, he loved this woman. Then Kyle froze, staring at his bird. "Wait… can Zaphod live in this time?"

Emerald eyed him, then Zaphod. Without a word, Emerald removed one of her earrings, then jabbed the tip of her finger with the post. "Come here, sweet bird," she called out.

Zaphod fluttered to her. Almost as if the parrot knew what to do, he pecked the small drop of blood, then fluttered away into the corner of the room.

Emerald smiled. “I think he will be okay now.”

“Thank you, Em. Thank you,” he whispered.

Kyle leaned over Emerald, staring into her vivid eyes, which radiated life. He gently brushed a few locks of hair away from her face, revealing her soft, smooth cheeks. He ran his fingers over her face and her lips, caressing them.

He kissed her deeply, pulling her body against his, then they fell down on the bed. He pressed himself into her warm body, and Zaphod squawked in the corner.

Suddenly, the door opened, and a woman’s high-pitched scream sliced through the air, startling them both. Kyle jerked his body upward, hovering protectively over Emerald as his eyes found a servant girl standing in the doorway.

“Oh my God,” the servant said, nearly dropping the pitcher of water from her hands. The servant girl turned to Emerald, then a look sheer joy came over her, and she ran to the bed.

“My Queen! You are awake!” she exclaimed, putting down the water pitcher. Her eyes darted to Kyle, and his cheeks burned with embarrassment. She inspected him for a moment, her lips pursing slightly, then her eyes went wide. “You… How…?”

“It’s a long story, Glacia,” Emerald said, then waved her hand. “Please, if you don’t mind, I would like to be alone for a while.”

“Oh, yes, of course, My Queen,” Glacia said, bowing quickly and flashing them a knowing smile. She darted out of the bedroom.

“Well, I guess one person knows,” Kyle joked, holding Emerald’s hand.

“Make that two,” said a familiar voice.

Kyle whipped his head in the direction of the voice. Geeta stood in shadows in the corner of the room, a slight smile on her face.

“Geeta?” Kyle said, stunned. He hadn’t seen her in… how long? “How the fuck have you been?” Kyle paused. “Wait, how long have you been standing there?”

“Enough to make me sick from all your sweet talk,” she said, stepping out of the shadows. “Revealing myself in the middle of all that would have been quite awkward.”

"Well, fuck." Kyle looked to her, and they both smiled. In her hand was the staff.

"Now that you are back, you have work to do. There is much to fill you in on," Geeta started.

Kyle sighed, exasperated. "God, Geeta, you are such a mood killer, you know that? My ass just woke up, and you're already rattling off about something or other. I mean, I just went through Hell, literally. I can't even come back to life without you busting my balls."

Geeta stared at him, then the corner of her mouth curled up. She turned to Emerald. "There is much to discuss with you, My Queen. Dire matters require your attention. I'll be waiting for you two for whenever you are finished getting *reacquainted*."

Kyle snorted. "Thanks."

"Okay," Emerald said. "We will be out shortly."

"And don't wait right outside the door," Kyle said.

"Sure thing, idiot," Geeta huffed. She paused, then gave him a true, happy smile. It was almost weird seeing Geeta like that. "It is nice to see you again."

"What's this?" Kyle jested. "Geeta has a heart?" But he'd missed her too. She was a cool chick.

Emerald nudged him to scold him, and Geeta rolled her eyes. Then she flashed away, leaving them alone.

Emerald's eyes glimmered with laughter, then she nudged him again playfully, pulling him into her arms. "Soon, everyone will know."

Kyle smiled, kissing her once again. He got up from the bed and pulled her up, gesturing for her to follow.

"Where are we going?" Emerald asked.

"I haven't seen Arcadia with my own eyes in years. I want to see if it still looks as shitty as I remember it," he said.

He led her out to her patio. He leaned over the balustrade, peering out at the city that was once his home. And was now his home once again. The flashing of the transports in the sunny sky, the gleaming buildings, and the gentle wisps of clouds brought a smile to his face. This was his time, his place. He was made to be here, with Emerald.

This was what heaven was. No singing flowers or weird-ass colors vibrating with strange power. It was with his woman, both of them made for each other. That was his heaven.

Emerald leaned into him, running her hands across his chest as he put an arm around her. They silently took the sight of the city in as they both held each other close, their life forces radiating in harmony.

He was back.

Above all, he was with Em.

CHAPTER 75

YELLOW

"Wake up, you fool!" The words echoed in Auron's head over and over. "Wake up!"

He groaned in response. He felt tired, and his body could barely move.

Then someone slapped him on the face, instantly revitalizing him. Auron shot up, opening his eyes. Before him stood the Sorceress Ikaria.

"How dare you slap me!" Auron said.

"How dare you use that tone with me, *priest*! Besides, we have more important things to do than bicker with each other."

"I'll take whatever tone I want with you, *sorceress*."

"Oh, is that so?"

"Yes, now please get out of my face," Auron said, groaning and rubbing his cheek.

"Fine by me."

Their eyes met, and there was a strange exchange between them. Ikaria almost looked relieved. Auron groaned once again, then looked around. He was in the citadel… the citadel newly formed by the power of his words.

He got to his feet, then glanced around, amazed. The gleaming gold, the shiny marble, pearls encrusted within the structure. It was heavenly.

The sorceress stepped into his view, breaking off his moment of awe. "We have things to do. You know, like go retrieve my sister? Which is what you were supposed to be doing instead of rescuing me."

Words from the heated battle came back to him. About her taking possession over the blue-gifted man.

Auron had to ask. Ikaria was, after all, his complement. He had to know.

Ikaria eyed him, then narrowing her eyes. "I know you want to ask me, so *ask*."

Could she hear his thoughts?

"I hear them, yes," she said as Auron shot her a startled look. "I only have so much patience, so you'd best ask now before the opportunity wanes."

Auron took a breath, then looked at her. "Was it true what he said? You made that man do things he didn't want to do?" Auron asked.

"You want a confession out of me?" Ikaria asked nonchalantly.

"I just want to know exactly what I am getting into, since our souls are bound together," Auron countered.

"I'm sure you would. Would you also like to hear about all the times I killed High Court spies? Or the many times I lied to everyone in court about my gift. Or how about all the times that I tied up poor, helpless men to do my bidding? I'm sure they liked it, but one can never know for certain."

Auron stood up, his eyes meeting hers evenly. "I do want to know about the green-gifted queen. If you expect me be your other half, then I *must* know."

Ikaria sighed loudly, then placed her hands on her hips, eyeing a blond man who walked by in the citadel's newly golden hallway. "What Derek said was true. I used his body for my pleasure, and yes, it was my idea. However, he wanted it just as much as I did, and he didn't stop me. He could have if he truly wanted to. We were both intoxicated with the dark magic, and everything seemed so… *right*." She shrugged casually. "There is nothing more to say. Black magic makes everything look so delicious, and in the end, it got what it wanted."

"And what was that?" Auron asked.

Her eyes twinkled bright violet. "Dissension." She paused, taking a breath, then placed her hands on her hips.

Auron was about lecture her, but he stopped.

"Well?"

"Well, what?" he retorted.

"I'm waiting for the 'holier than thou art' lecture."

"What you did was despicable," Auron said quietly. "Pushing that man…"

"Yes, yes," Ikaria said, trying to look indifferent. "If you keep bringing it up, I will sear your lips shut. I don't feel like chatting about it anymore. The subject is exhausting, and frankly quite boring. We all know I am no saint."

Despite her cavalier tone, Auron could see a hint of guilt in her eyes. In her soul, Auron could feel her shame in the deed, but she was too proud to admit such guilt.

Auron sighed, then eyed her. "I wasn't done yet, Sorceress."

"Oh?"

"I… I wanted to say that the God of Light… he allows everyone to be forgiven from their transgressions. All you have to do is ask."

Ikaria voice became serious. "Leave those sweet words for your young aspiring priests. Those words are not for *me*," Ikaria said firmly. She turned away. "Now, if you will excuse me, I must get ready. The High Court calls, and I mustn't be late. My sister is expecting me."

"But what do you plan to do?"

"I plan, priest, to walk right into their citadel and get my sister." She paused. "Oh, and destroy every single one of them while I'm at it. I have my greatest weapon now."

"And what's that?"

Ikaria glanced at him with her narrow eyes, then flashed a half smile at him. "You. Now that I have my true complement to complete the Spectrum of Magic, the High Court will not be able to stop me."

"You mean stop us."

Ikaria laughed. "That's correct. Us. As much as I despise you, priest, I will gladly accept your companionship for this particular mission. But don't think this union includes extra favors. You aren't my type."

Auron looked at her with disgust. "Absolutely not, sorceress!"

"I know. I can hear your thoughts, remember? Now, please excuse me, I must get ready to travel."

"I'm coming with you," Vala said, running up to them.

Ikaria glanced at her warily, but Auron nodded in agreement.

"They…" Her voice shook as her eyes teared up. "They threatened my people… and what's worse, they took my father's power." Her eyes flashed a bright-blue seething anger. "I must avenge him."

"How poetic," Ikaria said, sounding bored, then turned away. "Get your things packed and ready yourselves. We leave after I've had a hot bath and a nice long romp with a blond lord. It's been far too long since I've had either.

Perhaps I can combine the two and be ready quicker. Suri is already well on her way, and I assume she'll require some assistance."

Auron's mouth dropped open, but he held his tongue. *Perhaps one day she will change her ways.* Though he highly doubted it.

Ikaria stalked away, leaving Auron alone with Vala.

Where had Oriel gone? Auron had seen him in the heat of battle, but then the High Justice was gone.

"Vala, what happened to High Justice Oriel? Where is he?" Auron asked.

"I moved him somewhere safe when I had the opportunity," Vala said sadly. "I just checked on him a moment ago, then came back here. He is... sleeping now."

"What of his—"

"His magic is gone."

Auron's heart dropped.

Vala turned to him, serious. "Did you know, Uncle? About... High Justice Oriel?" Her eyes darted to his, welling up with tears. "My *father*?"

His shoulders slumped. "I did."

"Why didn't you tell me?" Her voice began to shake. "Why did he wait to tell me now?"

Auron laid a hand on her, then gave her a long hug. In his arms, Vala sobbed so hard she shook.

"I honestly didn't know that *he* knew," Auron said, whispering her in ear.

Vala broke from their hug, looking up at him with her piercing blue eyes. "Tell me."

Auron took a deep breath, then motioned for Vala to sit with him on a nearby bench. He began to recount everything. Vala listened quietly, taking it all in. The one-night union. The hidden pregnancy, sequestered in secret. Their lives in danger over the true identity of her father.

After he told her everything, Vala gave him a soft hug. For a long time. Then she started crying softly.

"The High Court will pay for this, Uncle. They will."

In the back of his mind, Auron thought of the Empress, sickened. Hopefully they weren't too late to save Ayera from the High Court.

I hope Suri got to her first...

CHAPTER 76

YELLOW

Yellow-green magic brushed over the orange-gifted's body, wrapping around her entirely.

"Please, lady, please wake up!" Jude said, frightened.

The woman remained silent.

God of Light, please hear my prayer!

He sent another wave of his yellow-green magic, which glowed softly as it soaked into her. The woman involuntarily took a deep breath, and life brushed her face.

Jude gasped, amazed. *I think the magic is going to work this time.*

"Praise the God of Light," he said thankfully.

It was hard using yellow-green magic. He didn't even know he had that kind of power; he'd just happened upon it by accident a month ago, sometime after the battle with the evil sorceress. After he discovered it, he began practicing every day.

Jude sat next to the strange orange-gifted woman, laying a hand on her heart. It beat normally. The woman was going to be okay. Sighing with relief, Jude lay down in the long grass, looking up at the sky, taking a rest. Above him were several floating islands, abandoned and vacant. After trying to rescue the Empress, he and the orange-gifted woman had fallen from the airship.

Luckily, he had cast his protection magic on them both while they fell from the ship. It was a good thing too, otherwise they would have been squished like a flattened piece of clay. They had fallen on one of the many scattered islands, which relieved Jude. He had heard that the earth's surface was dangerous, and he wasn't sure what he would have done if they had fallen all the way down there.

The orange-gifted woman let out a breath, almost as silent as the wind. But there was no fooling him—he heard her and knew she was awake. Jude looked over at her, smiling.

"Hi, lady! Are you awake?" Jude asked.

The woman sat up silently, her eyes keenly aware and sharp as ever. It was as if she had never fallen or been injured in the first place.

"The Empress," she stated.

Jude had always liked Empress Ayera. He didn't understand what the High Court's problem was with her. Yes, Jude had decided that he simply didn't like those people from the High Court. Their hearts… Jude could tell they were not good people.

"I'm going to help you, Miss," Jude said.

The orange-gifted woman looked at him, expressionless. "Is that so?"

"Of course, Miss. The Empress needs our help! We can't let them take her! She did nothing wrong, the way I see it. I can be a great help to you, with my magic and all. I've helped you so far, haven't I?"

"I suppose you have…?" She looked at him questioningly, her orange eyes glowing.

Why had she stopped talking? Then he realized why. She wanted his name. "My given priest name is Jude," he offered.

"Jude. Interesting."

"I don't like it, but I didn't have much say in it." Jude shrugged. "My old name is better, but I am not supposed to dwell on my old life. I'm not even allowed to mention it."

"I see." She got up swiftly to her feet, almost as graceful as a cat. "I'm Suri."

"Hello, Lady Suri," he said.

"I am no lady," Suri said. "I'm just a servant."

"Just like me. I am a servant of the God of Light. We are the same, you and I."

The woman looked at him, still without expression. Jude smiled at her, then got up, looking at the blue sky and soft breezy clouds. The sunlight was shining. It was the God of Light's day, no doubt.

"We just need to figure out how to get off this island," he said, staring up into the clouds.

Suri stood silently next to him, then grasped a vial attached to a necklace around her neck. "I assure you, young priest Jude, we will get off this island," she murmured. "I must not fail the Enchantress."

CHAPTER 77

Clean silks gently caressed her dirt-crusted cheeks, and the cushion of soft pillows hugged her face. Remembering that she was tied to the communications tower, Gwen opened her eyes, scanning her surroundings.

But there was no tower. Instead, she lay in an oversized feather bed with red comforters sewn with gold, and giant posts reaching to the ceiling. The room was furnished with elaborate sofas, delicately carved tables, and rich brass lamps that gave off warm light within the cold room. There was a window to the side, with hard snow falling on the other side of the glass.

Gwen looked down at herself. She was still wearing her dirty clothes from the fight out in the wastelands. How was it that she didn't remember anything from being out in the wastelands until now?

Jumping out of bed, Gwen headed straight for a door off to the side. She opened it, revealing a bathroom. Over her right shoulder, she saw another door, so she ran to it. It was locked.

Frightened, Gwen ran to the window, seeing if it could open. There was no lever, and it was completely sealed shut. Leaning her forehead against the glass, Gwen saw the city before her. The visibility was low with the heavy snowfall, but she could tell immediately that she was not in Arcadia. The building architecture was different.

Olympia. Running back to the door, Gwen yanked at the handle, shaking it violently.

"Let me out of here!" she yelled, pounding on the door. "Hey! Did you hear me? Let me out now!"

There was a click in the door, and Gwen stepped back. Several maidservants trailed in, followed by a well-dressed man in royal attire.

"I see you are finally up," he said in a chipper tone. His deep-green eyes matched his velvety jacket, with his dark hair flowed down his back. In his hair were several small braids woven with golden strings and decorated with jewelry. He was probably Garrett's age if Gwen had to guess. Maybe twenty-eight or twenty-nine.

She ran up to him, getting to her knees. "Take me home! Please. My parents are probably worried sick about me," she begged, starting to tear up.

The man gave her a slight sympathetic frown, then shook his head. "I am sorry, but you are our guest now."

"You mean prisoner."

The man laughed. "If you want to view it like that. You see, the King is *very* interested in your father. If your father complies with our demands, you will be on your way home before you know it. But until then, you will stay here with us."

"I don't want to be here!" Gwen said with a shaky voice, getting to her feet, meeting his gaze. "I want to see my mom and dad!"

"As I said, that depends entirely on your father," the man said. He turned to the maidservants, nodding to them. The maids approached her with fresh clothes and towels, bowing to her. "These women are here to provide you with anything you need. Clothes, toiletries, meals. And if you are on your best behavior, you might be able to dine with His Majesty and his adopted son."

Gwen made a sour face, trying not to cry again in front of the man.

"I'll leave you to freshen up, and I'll have a meal sent up to you. By the way, you may address me as Councilor Jason," he said. Then with a bow, he left her with the maids.

There was an awkward silence, and Gwen sobbed again, slumping to the ground. Moments went by, and her sobs subsided, tears still streaming down her face. Behind her, there were soft steps and the rustling of skirts.

"What is your name?" asked one of the maidservants softly, bending over to face her.

"Gwen," she answered.

"Here, Gwen, I have several fine outfits for you to choose from. I will take your measurements for new clothes, but you can wear these for the time being. The other maids are getting your bath ready. You will feel much better after you get cleaned up and eat something." The maidservant gave her a motherly smile, sending a twang of sadness through Gwen all over again. All she wanted to do was yell at the maid, but none of this was the woman's fault.

There was a soft knock at the door, and the maidservant raised an eyebrow. She went over and answered the door, and bowed as soon as the door opened.

In the doorway was a boy. The gifted boy.

He came in playfully, with a bright smile on his face. He had changed his outfit and was well-groomed, in similar royal attire as that man Jason. He appeared to be in perfect health, as if he had never been shot at all.

"Hi!" the boy said, running excitedly over to her.

"What do you want?" Gwen snarled at him, narrowing her eyes. The boy had caused so much destruction out in the wastelands, and here he was, smiling and saying hi to her.

"I'm so happy that there's another kid in the palace with me!" he said. His mannerisms were completely uncharacteristic from what she witnessed prior. "Will you play with me? I just got a new video game. I just showed Vihaan, but he didn't wanna play." The boy's bright-red eyes widened and sparkled, pleading with her.

Gwen glowered at him. "You just annihilated half the wastelands out there with your magic, captured me, and now you want to *play*? What's wrong with you?"

The boy looked sheepishly down to the floor. "Sorry. I don't know how to control my magic. Bryce gives me medicine to control it, but I can't help it anyway," he said, then his eyes looked back at her. "So do you wanna play my new game? It'll be fun!"

Oh, great, Gwen thought. *I've been kidnapped, and now I am a babysitter for a crazy kid.*

Gwen eyed his chest where she had shot it. She couldn't tell since there were clothes covering it, but it really did look like he didn't even have bandages.

"Are you okay?" she asked. "You were shot in the chest earlier..." Gwen didn't want to point out *she* shot him in the chest, since he seemed to be screaming and out of it at the time.

"I'm feeling good now! Raghu is really good at making everyone feel better," he said, smiling.

"Jihyun," said a voice with a heavy accent from the doorway. "You weren't supposed to run off without me."

"Sorry, Vihaan," the boy Jihyun said. "I just wanted her to play my new game with me since you didn't wanna."

Gwen looked over at the doorway, where a man stood, probably her mom's age, tall with olive skin. But what shocked her was that he had golden eyes and long *yellow* hair.

A gifted!

"Come, Jihyun, before your father finds out," the man said, standing in the doorway. "I am sure you will have plenty of time to play your new game with the girl. Let her get dressed and eat first."

"Okay!" Jihyun jumped up with excitement, turning to Gwen. "How long will you be?"

"I… I don't know?" Gwen said. "I'll tell the maid when I'm ready."

"Yeah!" The boy twirled with joy, then sprinted out of the room.

Gwen's eyes went to the strange golden man as he left the room right behind Jihyun. A shiver ran down her spine, and a weird feeling came over her. Gwen decided she didn't like the man. But the boy… She wasn't sure about him. *Yet.*

Turning to the new set of clothes on the bed, Gwen picked them up, holding the dress out in front of her. The dress was pretty. She hardly ever wore dresses except at special occasions her mom dragged her to. Thoughts of her mom and dad flooded her again. Gwen suddenly regretted all the nasty things she'd said to her mom.

"I'm sorry, Mom," she said quietly, her hands trembling. She dropped the outfit and fell face down in the pillows, crying again.

How she wished she could take all those words back.

"I'm so sorry, Mom…"

EPILOGUE

Suresh couldn't move. He hadn't moved for ages, it seemed. He was paused in a world that was void of everything. Pure white surrounded him.

Suresh had thought about it over and over again while he sat in the endless void. What had happened to him? He had been about to jump into the portal right after the Ghost Man. But he didn't make it somehow, and found himself being hurled to the earth with the debris of the citadel, and the next thing he knew, he was in this eternal white void. And his life force… it was as if Suresh had lost a part of it in the white void.

Slowly, the world began to take shape, forming around him. Years might have passed, but he couldn't be sure. Suresh couldn't understand the concept of time in this place.

A beautiful, magnificent room fit for a king or queen rose out of the white light until it was clear as day. Sunlight streamed into the room, highlighting the pearls and golds while fresh air streamed through a nearby window. Expensive furniture accented the room, decorated with soft lavender fabrics.

A beautiful woman sat in an elaborate chair, her eyes completely focused on him. She was just as beautiful as she was when Suresh saw her in her youth many years ago. At the time, she was in her twenties, about to give birth. But here, she appeared to be in her fifties.

"Suresh," she said gently. She rose from her seat and made her way over to him with such elegance, such grace.

Sudden realization hit him. His magic, his *blood*, was before him. His soul was a magnet to his own power, because his eyes knew exactly where to find it.

A vial containing his blood hung around her neck. *His* power.

"I have been thinking of you all these years," Elyathi said in a gentle whisper. She delicately grasped the vial around her neck.

Suresh frowned in confusion as he stared at her. Behind her, a man lingered. The King of Arcadia. The one who Suresh knew would alter the very fate of their existence, and time itself. Darkness permeated from him, only it was much darker than before, devastating Suresh's insides. The King of Arcadia was powerful. So powerful, in fact, that he radiated more power and strength than Elyathi herself.

"Queen Elyathi," Suresh said, shaking, "please don't take away my power!"

She laid a hand on him, and he flinched.

"Don't take my power! I don't want to lose it!" he repeated.

"Suresh," she said reassuringly, running the back of her hand down his cheek. "I am not here to take your power." She showed him the vial around her neck, bringing it closer to him. "I only took a small amount of your blood, that is all."

"Then why am I here?"

"You have been told many lies, and I am here to dispel those. You need to hear the truth…" Her words echoed in his ears. "But for now, please rest. I wish for your well-being."

His eyes felt suddenly heavy, as if her words put a spell on him, and that was the last thing he remembered.

THE SPECTRUM OF MAGIC

MAGIC GUIDE

MAIN MAGIC

Red = Elemental magic: earth, wind, fire, water/ice. *Emotion: anger*

Orange = Illusion and transmutation magic. *Emotion: joy*

Yellow = Prophecy and protection. *Emotion: love and devotion*

Green = Healing, restoration, life, renewal and revival magic. *Emotion: fear*

Blue = Time and dimensional space magic. *Emotion: sadness*

Violet = Force and control over mind and objects magic. *Emotion: jealousy*

TINT MAGIC

Light Red (Pink) = One magic only *(earth, wind, fire, or water/ice)*

Light Orange = One magic only *(illusion or transmutation)*

Light Yellow = One magic only *(prophecy or protection)*

Light Green = One magic only *(healing, revive, or rebirth)*

Light Blue = One magic only *(time or dimensions)*

Light Violet = One magic only *(control of the mind or force over objects)*

DARK SIDE OF THE SPECTRUM

Dark Red = Meteor, sun/moon/star magic, gas, metal, foreign elements. *Emotion: wrath*

Dark Orange = Permanent illusions and unnatural body transmutations. *Emotion: ungratefulness*

Dark Yellow = False prophecies and disarming protection. *Emotion: loathing*

Dark Green = Life-drain and death magic. *Emotion: terror*

Dark Blue = Summon magic from other dimensions, compress all time eras into one time. *Emotion: despair/anguish*

Dark Violet = Full possession over mind and body. *Emotion: hatred*

Please note: Magic is like an art. Some gifted are talented at casting magic naturally, others take years of practice to hone their skills.

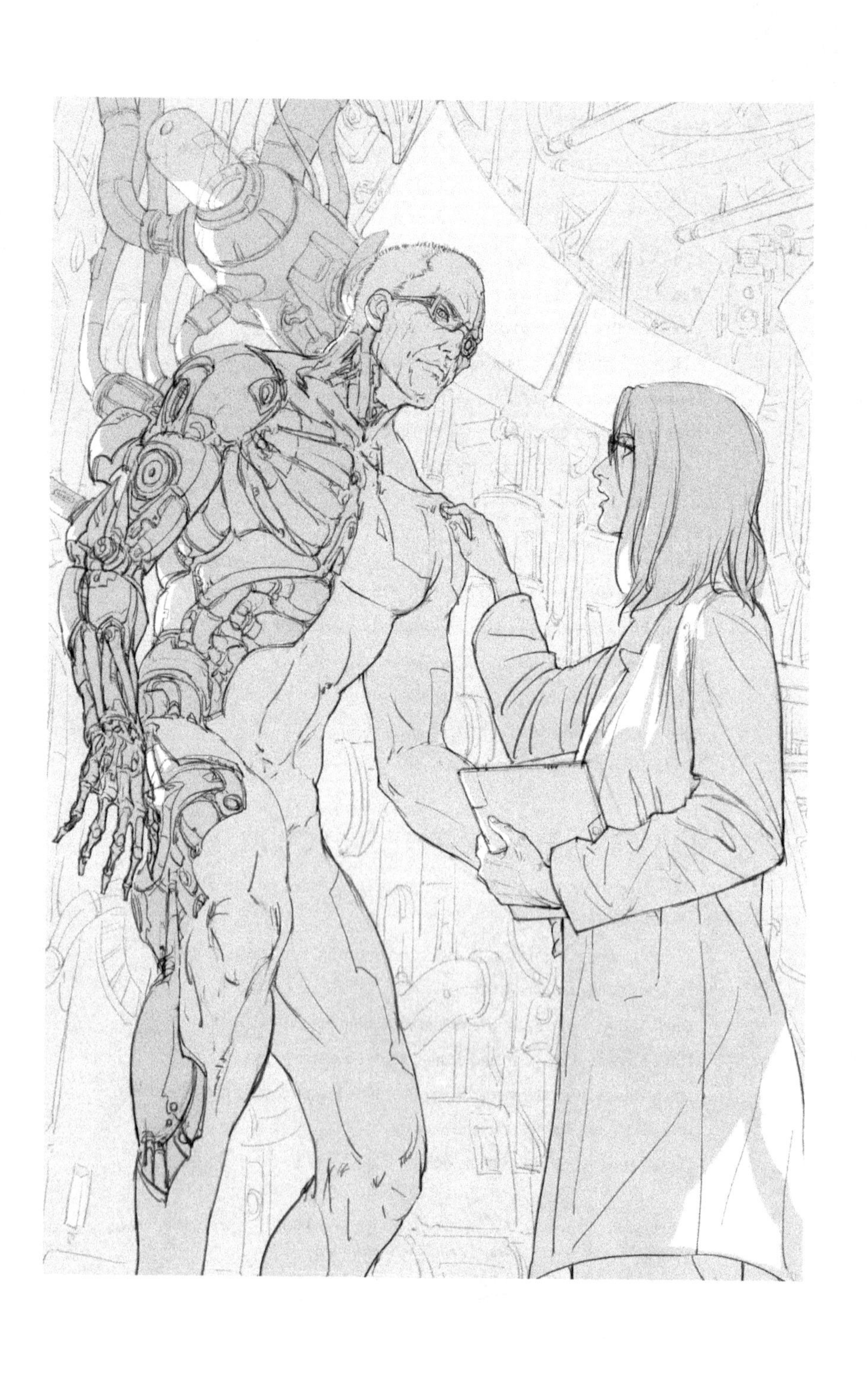

Color Complements

Color complements are opposite magics of the color wheel. When combined together, they can unlock the Spectrum of Magic. At the time of unlocking the Spectrum of Magic, both casters must summon their adjacent colors with their main color. This white magic that comes from completing the Spectrum of Magic is different from holy white magic.

Red + Green = The Spectrum of Magic (white light)
Orange + Blue = The Spectrum of Magic (white light)
Yellow + Violet = The Spectrum of Magic (white light)

No gifted can pair up with their opposite color. Only one person is made for the other. It could be a romantic love pairing, a friendship pairing, or a polar-opposite soul pairing.

Analogous/Adjacent Magics

Each gifted magic caster can tap into the two colors next to their main color to some degree. For instance, if the gifted has green magic, they have full capabilities of all green magic powers. They also have the potential to use small amounts of yellow (casting magic shields) and blue magic (dimensional magic.) Some gifted can practice and train to use the full potential of their adjacent magics.

Also, if the gifted uses an analogous magic, it manifests and a combination of the two colors. For example, Emerald's magic is green. If she uses yellow protection magic, her magic power looks greenish-yellow. If she uses blue magic, her magic power looks greenish-blue.

Black Magic/Blood Magic

If a gifted consumes the blood of another color, they absorb that magic, and their magic becomes a shade darker. If the gifted consumes two colors, their magic becomes an even darker shade of their color. If the gifted consumes all six colors of the spectrum, they unlock black magic, and their magic becomes pure black. See note about the power of black magic.

Holy/Unholy Magic

White = Ability to absorb a gifted's magic temporarily and drain a gifted's magic and lifeforce permanently.

Gray = ????

Black = Power of the gifted's heart's desire, magic of their choosing when black magic is unlocked, gifted's original magic power is increased 100 times their original power.

ACKNOWLEDGMENTS

Thank you to every single reader who has journeyed with me through The Spectrum of Magic. This particular book, Fragments of the Mind, involved a very different journey than the last book, Fragments of Light. This story was much more abstract, with explorations of the idea of dreams, dimensions, time, and the afterlife. It wasn't easy trying to solidify a story that mostly took place within the characters' minds and dreams, and it took great effort to make it tangible for the reader to grasp. My hope is that all my readers out there experience the beauty of dreams that I experienced with this piece of work, and will continue with me as I journey further into the depths of this series.

I want to say a big thank-you to all my fans. At times, I doubt myself and what I am doing, but then I'll get an amazing email, message, or social media comment saying how much they loved the story, a certain character, the writing, or that they're just excited about a writing update, which then gives me strength and reinforcement. Without these positive words of encouragement, I think I would be in a completely different place, so thank you to all those who have done so. I also want to thank the readers who have read my book (and now books) multiple times. I never thought I would see the day, but here we are, and I am blown away that not just one person, but many people that I know, have reread my first novel.

I also want to thank my husband for all the encouragement and support that he has given me over the years. He was my first beta reader for both books, and he is just as excited and dedicated to this story and these characters as I am. He has given me valuable input when needed, all of it exceptionally reliable and sound.

A very big thank-you to Mansik Yang (Yam) for creating such beautiful imagery of my characters and world. I feel truly humbled to have him working with me on this project. Never have I experienced working with anyone who understands my art style as much as he has. I truly believe he sees my story within his mind's eye as he illustrates, and every time, the art comes out beautiful, perfect, and exactly how I imagined it.

And lastly, a huge thank-you to Crystal from Pikko's House, my line and copy editor, and Amy from Story Centric Editing, my developmental editor. My story wouldn't be what it is today without them. And one last thank-you to my proofreader, Sarah from Pikko's House, who wasn't taking on any new jobs but made an exception for my manuscript.

ABOUT THE AUTHOR

Beth Hodgson was born and raised in Minnesota. During her college years, she worked and went to school in downtown Minneapolis, the city that inspired the kingdom of Arcadia. She worked as a graphic artist and illustrator for several years, then switched industries to retail management in high fashion.

Currently, she is married and lives in Southern California. She is a full-time mom and writes in her spare time. When not writing, Beth loves to make costumes, doodle her characters, play video games, and do occasional freelance beta reading for authors. Her favorite color is violet, but she has a secret love for green. She also has a major obsession with pixel art.

CPSIA information can be obtained
at www.ICGtesting.com
Printed in the USA
LVHW070940110623
749455LV00008B/398

9 781732 713024